FORMS OF LIFE

Forms of Life

CHARACTER AND
MORAL IMAGINATION
IN THE NOVEL

MARTIN PRICE

YALE UNIVERSITY PRESS
NEW HAVEN AND LONDON

Published with the assistance of the Frederick W. Hilles
Publication Fund.

Designed by Sally Harris
and set in Garamond type.
Printed in the United States of America by
Vail-Ballou Press, Binghamton, N.Y.

Library of Congress Cataloging in Publication Data

Price, Martin, 1920–
    Forms of life.

    Includes bibliographical references and index.
    1. Fiction—History and criticism.   2. Characters and
characteristics in literature.   3. Literature and morals.
I. Title.
PN3341.P7   1983   809.3'927   82-16064
ISBN 0-300-02867-9

                    10 9 8 7 6 5 4 3 2 1

    Chapter 1 is reprinted in somewhat altered form from *Literary Theory and Struc-
ture: Essays in Honor of William K. Wimsatt,* ed. Frank Brady, John Palmer, and
Martin Price (New Haven: Yale University Press, 1973).
    Chapter 2 appeared originally in *Forms of Narration,* ed. J. Hillis Miller (New
York: Columbia University Press, 1971), and is reprinted with the permission of
the publisher.
    Chapter 3 appeared in different form in *Imagined Worlds: Essays on Some English
Novels and Novelists in Honour of John Butt,* ed. Maynard Mack and Ian Gregor
(London: Methuen, 1968), and is reprinted with the permission of the publisher.
    The first half of chapter 4 appeared in *Nineteenth Century Fiction* 30 (1975):
261–81, and is reprinted by permission of the editors.
    Chapter 12 and portions of chapter 3 appeared originally in *Critical Inquiry* 1
(March 1975): 605–22 and *Critical Inquiry* 2 (Winter 1975): 269–79; both are
reprinted by permission of the University of Chicago Press. © 1975 by The
University of Chicago.

To
Mary Price

Contents

Acknowledgments

This book has been long in the writing, and I have incurred more debts than I can readily cite. I have learned more about the novel from Paul Pickrel than from anyone else, and the approach I have taken in this book owes much to the work of Lionel Trilling. It was Maynard Mack whose patience and encouragement helped me to put down the earliest and most revised portion of the book. And I owe a great deal to those students, teachers and taught, who have taken my education in hand.

In a sense this is a Bread Loaf book. It comes in part out of my teaching at the Bread Loaf School of English and out of lectures I was permitted to give there as Robert Frost Professor and as Elizabeth Drew Lecturer. I am particularly grateful for the friendships my wife and I made there—with Beth and Paul Cubeta, Lucy and Wylie Sypher, Ethel and George Anderson, Faith and Laurence Holland, among others.

The John Simon Guggenheim Memorial Foundation awarded me a fellowship, and Yale University provided much aid, as well, for the writing of this book. I am indebted for various kinds of help and encouragement to many people: Frank Brady, Leo Braudy, Robert Caserio, A. Bartlett Giamatti, James Laney, Mary Mattern, Georges May, Gary Saul Morson, Claude J. Rawson, Meredith Skura, René Wellek, Alexander Welsh, and Margaret Wimsatt. Perhaps my greatest debt has been to the formidable presence and warm memory of William Kurtz Wimsatt.

I received help in preparing the manuscript from Sheila Huddleston, Brooke Baldwin, and—most of all—James di Loreto, whose care has been great and good will inexhaustible. Finally, it has been a pleasure to work with Ellen Graham and Lawrence Kenney of the Yale University Press.

Introduction

This is a book about ways in which character has been imagined and presented in some novels of the nineteenth and early twentieth centuries. It is not an historical survey of the idea of character but rather an exploration of how much of the spectrum of attitudes and feelings we loosely call human is used by different writers, and to what ends.

"Character, in any sense in which we can get at it," Henry James wrote in an essay on Anthony Trollope, "is action, and action is plot, and any plot which hangs together . . . plays upon our emotion, our suspense, by means of personal references. We care what happens to people only in proportion as we know what people are." [1] We recognize this most clearly at those moments when the plot turns on a recognition or hangs on a decision. We often call it a belated recognition, in the spirit of those who find it easier to live others' lives than their own.

We see this in Dorothea Brooke's review in her mind of her discovery of Rosamond and Will Ladislaw together: "Was she alone in that scene? Was it her event only?" There is in such moments a coming to reality, an "unselfing," a readiness to see one's experience from the perspective of others. This need not be an act of renunciation. For Emma Woodhouse such a moment comes in the realization that "Mr. Knightley must marry no one but herself!" This introduces in turn a rereading of her past and a confirmation of her belief that she never cared for Frank Churchill. "She saw that there had never been a time when she did not consider Mr. Knightley as infinitely the superior, or when his regard for her had not been infinitely the most dear. She saw, that in persuading herself, in fancying, in acting to the contrary, she had been entirely under a delusion, totally ignorant of her own heart. . . ." Pip's acceptance of Magwitch is another such moment: "For now my repugnance to him had all melted away, and in the hunted wounded shackled creature who held my hand in his, I only saw a man who had meant to be my benefactor, and who had felt affectionately, gratefully, and gener-

ously towards me with great constancy through a series of years. I only saw
in him a much better man than I had been to Joe."[2]

In this movement to new awareness character and plot, as James says, are
one. Increasingly, in the novels which this book discusses, the plot is internalized, so that external event seems more a vehicle than the action proper.
But external and internal are shifting terms at best. There are forms of comedy, and especially farce, where a plot happens *to* characters, its resolution
brought about not by anyone's intention but by the miraculous contrivances
of contingency. There are stories in which the discovery that nothing will
ever happen is the grim or ludicrous revelation, as in James's own "The Beast
in the Jungle." And there are those, as Lionel Trilling observed of Edith
Wharton's *Ethan Frome*, which reveal that "moral inertia, the *not* making of
moral decisions, constitutes a large part of the moral life of humanity."[3]

It is here that questions of moral imagination arise. What I mean by the
term is the depth and adequacy of the novelist's conception of experience:
the degree to which he recognizes the complexities of decision or action or
inaction and the effort or release involved in solving or ignoring or evading
problems. A moral imagination, as I would use the term, does not mistake
the evasion for the solution, but it may be able to accept one as much as the
other. It may disclose a level of motive that the characters do not suspect,
but it need not find in their innocence a failure. Henry James can again
supply a text. When *The Bostonians* appeared, a number of readers identified
the character of Miss Birdseye with Elizabeth Palmer Peabody. To one of
those readers, his brother William, James wrote with concern:

> Miss Birdseye was evolved entirely from my moral consciousness, like every
> person I have ever drawn, and originated in my desire to make a figure who
> should embody in a sympathetic, pathetic, picturesque, and at the same time
> grotesque way, the humanitary and ci-devant transcendental tendencies which
> I thought it highly probable I should be accused of treating in a contemptuous
> manner in so far as they were otherwise represented in the tale. I wished to
> make this figure a woman, because so it would be more touching and an old,
> weary, battered, and simple-minded woman because that deepened the effect.[4]

To this I add another case. In his fine book on James Joyce, C. H. Peake
points to the difference between D. H. Lawrence's "passionate and adventurous moral energy as he seeks . . . to 'lead our sympathy away in recoil from
things gone dead' " and Joyce's "greater readiness to trace what is humbly
good, in the meanest circumstances and forms of experience. . . ." As Peake
remarks, the "moral vision of an artist . . . cannot be reduced to discursive
statement, not because it is too vague, impressionistic and confused but
because it is too exact, detailed and coherent." While Joyce's "statement
that Bloom is a 'good man' does little or nothing to define Bloom's nature,"

the "image of Bloom created in *Ulysses* defines with some precision what the word 'good' meant for Joyce."[5] What Peake claims for Joyce (and I have hardly done justice to the full claim he makes) seems to me to apply as well to Henry James's account of what he has invented Miss Birdseye to mean.

Finally, I should like to explain the phrase that I have borrowed for the main title of this book. It comes from Ludwig Wittgenstein's later philosophy. Wittgenstein's emphasis on the uses of language—on meaning as use—makes him watchful for those confusions we create for ourselves by using words outside the language-game to which they belong. As Anthony Kenny puts it, "The comparison of language to a game was not meant to suggest that language was a pastime, or something trivial: on the contrary, it was meant to bring out the connection between the speaking of language and nonlinguistic activities. Indeed the speaking of language is part of a communal activity, a way of living which Wittgenstein calls a 'form of life.' "[6]

The certainty we feel in playing language-games arises from their deep roots in forms of life—"something that lies beyond being justified, as it were, . . . something animal." Or at least primitive: "Any logic good enough for a primitive means of communication needs no apology from us. Language did not emerge from ratiocination." We depend upon something more rudimentary than logical grounds: "Does a child believe that milk exists? Or does it know that milk exists? Does a cat know that a mouse exists?"[7]

Wittgenstein's conception of language-games does justice to the unsystematic nature of our minds and lives. We bring to different areas (or dimensions) of experience words that arise out of distinctive needs and interests; and the presence of the same words in several games may produce uneasiness, deadlock, confusion. But we do for the most part have the ability to move readily from one language-game to another. It is that flexibility which makes us human. The ironist can play on the presuppositions that underlie a language-game, as when Jane Austen describes an evening with an imperious hostess: "The party then gathered round the fire to hear Lady Catherine determine what weather they were to have on the morrow."[8]

Forms of life, then, are those shared activities which give us our languages. We are made conscious of these forms of life by doubts and conflicts, threats and defenses. We find ourselves running against the limit of language and become aware of the depth of its sources and the toughness of its structure. "The problems arising through a misinterpretation of our forms of language have the character of *depth*. They are deep disquietudes."[9] Such disquietudes awaken us to the activities which constitute our lives: "Giving grounds . . . comes to an end;—but the end is not certain propositions' striking us immediately as true, i.e. it is not a kind of *seeing* on our part; it is our *acting*, which lies at the bottom of the language-game." The language-game is "not reasonable (or unreasonable). It is there—like our life."[10]

That movement downward from the surface of experience to the encounter with these forms of life gives the novel its sense of depth, and the movement from the surface of the self to a deeper self which participates in these forms is the most characteristic structure of the novel. That deeper self—or *other* self, for it is a discovery more than a choice—provides the sanction for the conscious life.

Novels are, whatever else, instruments of thought. They shape, condense, clarify, intensify experience so that meaning or its absence or its ambiguity is not only more easily attained, but its attainment is the end of the experience the novel provides. I have dealt in my opening chapter with the implicit agreement or contract that must exist between reader and writer and considered some of the functions that this contract allows the novel to serve. The second chapter is concerned with the problem of structure and the relevance that we perceive, or half-perceive, as we read. It is interesting to look back from the end to see how all led us there (if in fact it did), but more interesting are the kinds of awareness that emerge as we read: the sense that each image or word is somehow either creating or resisting a pattern, resonantly repetitive or somewhat alien, pointless, not altogether assimilable, or at least not yet.

The third chapter is devoted to the nature of literary characters: how they differ from real persons and yet must refer to them and draw their force from what we know their experience to be like. As Mary Warnock puts the problem of imagination, we "see the forms in our mind's eye and we see these very forms in the world. We could not do one of these things if we could not do the other. The two abilities are joined in our ability to understand that the forms have a certain meaning, that they are always significant of other things beyond themselves. We recognize a form as a form of something, as Wittgenstein said, by its relations with other things."[11]

Chapters 4 to 8 deal with novels which give society central importance, in which individuals are defined by their adherence or opposition—and the quality of each—to social norms. Jane Austen makes close observation of manners. The range of overt action is comparatively narrow, but, as always, it provides our indirect knowledge of motives and morals. As Henry James observed, Jane Austen's heroines "give us as great an impression of 'passion'—that celebrated quality—as the ladies of G. Sand and Balzac. Their small gentility and front parlour existence doesn't suppress it, but only modifies the outward form of it."[12] The relationship between manners and passions is perhaps Jane Austen's real subject, but her sense of human limitation makes her versions comic. In Stendhal (chapter 5) the irony is more radical. The society Stendhal creates is the passionless formal world of post-Napoleonic France. Stendhal's heroes must operate within this society, their heroism turning in the process to Machiavellian astuteness, their spontaneity escaping only in unattended moments or in those crises through which the heroes find themselves. They come to a deeper self, which they have tried to suppress and as a result have never quite known.

In Dickens (chapter 6) I have stressed the way in which society exacts of individuals, whether they be the masters of society or its victims, routine and simplification. Some become brilliantly comic figures whose lives are obsessively repetitive. Others choose their limitations more knowingly, sacrificing much of their selves for the sake of power and its exercise. Finally, there are those characters who are less conspicuous because more troubled and diffident, less aggressive or flamboyant, caught up as the others are not in problems of moral choice. The concern with moral decision becomes central in George Eliot (chapter 7), for the decisions her characters make grow out of a long process of egoism or sympathy. Sympathy is for Eliot a cognitive power as well as a moral one. Our capacity to enter imaginatively into the lives of others is a process of irreversible growth. It provides us with knowledge we can never resign and must act upon.

Tolstoy's novels (chapter 8) have central figures who search restlessly for a meaning in their lives. They stumble, lurch, fall into fatuous error, but eventually come to recognize that they have been too quixotically ambitious to see what lies within themselves and all about them. In contrast are those great Tolstoyan characters who cannot fully believe in life's possibilities or who have cut themselves off from all that might provide their lives with support. More explicitly than any of the other novelists considered, Tolstoy is concerned with the forms of life.

The last five chapters deal with novels in which the moral world is largely internalized. Characters live in society and act upon it, but the novelist is particularly concerned with the confusions, terrors, and heroism that lie within consciousness. In Henry James (chapter 9) there is emphasis on what remains concealed, unexpressed, or only implied, and the narrative process is often made obscure enough to force us to infer, as best we can, the attitudes of the characters on whom it depends. The characters themselves are often victims of an all-but-willed blindness. On the other hand, recovery from blindness or self-deception may require, as for Maggie Verver, a secret and difficult campaign whose gestures are delicate and all but imperceptible to most but—for those who recognize them—intensely dramatic.

Joseph Conrad (chapter 10) insists on the dependence of all outward action upon the "idea." Conrad is constantly teased, even tormented, as James is not, by the issue of skepticism, that is, the necessary failure or perversion of the idea as one tries to live by it. Conrad finds consciousness at once essential and very costly; its cost can be the loss of purpose or the surrender of action. In D. H. Lawrence (chapter 11) consciousness is again of primary concern, and Lawrence is distrustful of those structures of service and fidelity Conrad tends to celebrate. For Lawrence is interested, as Conrad hardly is, in those depths of consciousness which seem to be indistinguishable from physical being but are in fact deeper yet. They are seen as a flow of metaphysical being which gives vitality and is in constant movement or change; the quickness that Lawrence celebrates finds only a small portion of its life in traditional forms. Its primary state of being is what Lawrence calls "transit." The chapter on E. M. Forster's *A Passage to India* deals with elements in Forster's world that are close to Lawrence's. The dark forces of Lawrence's world become somewhat mysterious and somewhat ludicrous in Forster; he hangs between a moral and rational view that can shade into a pharisaic colonial righteousness or a mystical view that risks farcical squalor and sentimentality. Most important, Forster sees no way of choosing between them.

In the final chapter I have discussed three works that contain portraits of the artist. Each of them traces the emergence of the artist and of the work of art from the circumstances of the artist's life. They differ in the degree to which they stress the transience and precariousness of artistic structures, but they share a common concern with the process by which the work emerges. As a result, these works tend to move away from moral concerns of a traditional sort and deal with the prior difficulties of wresting stability and order (of which the order of art is their principal instance) from the larger experience of process and change in which human lives take such form as they do. If they celebrate an aesthetic order rather than a moral, these novels pay tribute, nevertheless, to "the beauty of mortal conditions," for it is from these conditions that the forms of art emerge and it is from them that the work of art draws its meanings.

I can best sum up the tendency of the book as an effort to study those moments where the self seems to give way to a deeper or an other self. This may be seen as a moment of transcendence; yet it need not have a religious ground. It may, in Bernard Williams's terms, "be an appeal to something *there* in human life which has to be discovered, trusted, followed, possibly in grave ignorance of the outcome." Williams cites D. H. Lawrence's phrase, "find your deepest impulse, and follow that," and Williams goes on: "The notion that there *is* something that is one's deepest impulse, that there is a discovery to be made here, rather than a decision; and the notion that one trusts what is so discovered, although unclear where it may lead—these . . . are the point." [13]

Iris Murdoch sees art as a means of freeing us to recognize a reality usually hidden from us in "the self-centered rush of ordinary life." The greatest art, as she sees it, is "impersonal" because "it shows us the world, our world and not another one, with a clarity which startles and delights us simply because we are not used to looking at the real world at all." The forms of such art are used "to isolate, to explore, to display something which is true," and the ability to achieve such truth is a moral as well as an artistic achievement.[14]

If claiming for art the disclosure of reality seems excessive, one may turn to P. F. Strawson's cooler view of the way a novel may affect us. When "some ideal image of a form of life is given striking expression in the words or actions of some [fictional] person, its expression may evoke a response of the liveliest sympathy from those whose own patterns of life are as remote as possible from conformity to the image expressed. It is indeed impossible that one life should realize all the ideal pictures which may at one time or another attract or captivate the individual imagination."

Strawson allows that the "region of the ethical" may be "a region of diverse, certainly incompatible, and possibly practically conflicting ideal images or pictures of a human life, or of human life." But such incompatible pictures may secure our imaginative if not our practical allegiance. And this is, Strawson suggests, not merely the case but something to be desired. "Any diminution in this variety would impoverish the human scene. The multiplicity of conflicting pictures is itself the essential element in one of one's pictures of man."[15] It is that multiplicity I have tried to present.

1 ✳ The Fictional Contract

We are all of us born into a world with social and linguistic rules. We inherit both kinds of rules, and each of them shapes us even as it supplies us with the means of becoming ourselves: ourselves, but not any selves. And yet selves that can question the system they inherit. We may question the contracts that have been made for us—whether, in fact, they are contracts at all, to which we have never given assent and to which there are no alternatives. "We may as well assert," David Hume wrote, "that a man, by remaining [aboard] a vessel, freely consents to the domination of the master; though he was carried on board while asleep, and must leap into the ocean and perish, the moment he leaves her."[1] If we could change vessels rather than leap into the sea, our remaining in a given vessel might become an implicit act of assent. We should have committed ourselves, it might be thought, to accept the advantages and to incur the obligations life in that vessel presents.

The matter of language is different. We have become aware of the degree to which any language divides and arranges reality, in effect all but imposes a metaphysics, with nouns as substances and adjectives their attributes. A more sardonic view, like George Orwell's, might see a language created to prevent or at least to stultify thought and thereby to impose voluntary bondage on the minds of those who use it. But most languages allow us free exercise of thought and imagination. If we feel constrained by formal styles or class dialects, we may ease those stringencies by adapting our system of language (what Saussure called *langue*) to a personal or group idiom (*parole*) that articulates and conveys our distinctive awareness. The distinction between *langue* and *parole,* as Jonathan Culler puts it, "is essentially a distinction between institution and event, between the underlying system which makes possible various types of behavior and actual instances of such behavior."[2]

The fictional contract is less imposing and intimate than the institutions of society or language, and yet it is an institution in its own right. We read

I

fiction with an acceptance of its peculiar use of language; for, while it is literal or metaphorical in the way that all language is, it does not refer in the way that language usually does. It pretends to be making reference, and the reader accepts the pretense and cooperates with it. As John Searle puts it, "literature" is "the name of a set of attitudes we take toward a stretch of discourse. . . . Roughly speaking, whether or not a work is literature is for the readers to decide, whether or not it is fiction is for the author to decide." Fiction is made possible by conventions that allow the author "to use words with their literal meanings without undertaking the commitments that are normally required by those meanings." These conventions "break the connection between words and the world" that we expect of literal discourse; they break them intentionally, in a sense theoretically.[3] "Art," as Arthur Danto says, "is the kind of thing that depends for its existence upon theories; without theories black paint *is* just black paint and nothing more." Danto demonstrates how the same image may acquire different meanings as we bring different theories to bear upon it. Each of these theories establishes conventions of a certain kind. "The difference . . . between naturalistic novels, fairy stories, works of science fiction, and surrealistic stories is in part defined by the extent of the author's commitment to represent actual facts, either specific facts about places like London and Dublin and Russia or general facts about what it is possible for people to do and what the world is like."[4] A realistic novel places its fiction in a world that obeys familiar laws, that has either a literal location or the simulation of one, where events are caused in the way they are in actual life. These conventions may extend to the form of plot; the magical or providential resolutions of romance are not to be expected of the realistic novel. "The author will establish with the reader a set of understandings"—what I have called a fictional contract— "about how far the horizontal conventions of fiction break the vertical conventions of serious speech."[5]

The fictional contract, then, is an implicit understanding which rests, first of all, upon the idea of the fictional as opposed to the literal or to the deceptive and mendacious. Upon this initial condition may be constructed the kinds of contract that set the terms for different modes, like realism, or for genres, like pastoral or comedy. Not every contract is faithfully fulfilled, and in fact an author may wish to induce a set of expectations only in order to surprise us with a variation. This may serve to make us recognize how readily and unthinkingly we have accepted a set of conventions and how arbitrary conventions may be. But the variation, while it may induce self-consciousness or achieve a reversal of all our expectations, will presumably justify its duplicity with the reward of new insight.

The kinds of services for which these contracts provide are often treated too simply, as if novels provide us only with the pleasures of form or the satisfactions of vicarious experience. As the novel has become a major literary form, its possibilities have been extended and again and again newly realized. The novel has become an institution, and we cannot but recognize the functions it has come to serve, even if no one novel serves all and some are served by few. The amplitude of its form allows the novel to provide far more social and physical detail than other kinds of writing. The freedom with which the novelist can move between the inside and the outside of his characters allows for ironic awareness of a special kind. One can only cite other resources: the interplay of plots or actions; the slow rhythm of disclosure and the protracted reading time; the ease with which documents of all sorts can be incorporated into the text as well as the pseudodocumentary guise the novel can assume; the play between forms of discourse, lyrical and colloquial, public and private, descriptive and analytical.

So long as we read a novel with a sense of its possibilities, its institutional history, we are to some extent ready for the appearance of any of them and to an equal extent aware of their absence. Even more, we may become conscious of the ways in which different functions of the novel are simultaneously satisfied. If the plot provides suspense and awakens a cognitive interest, the same plot may direct our feelings or change them. What I propose to do in this chapter is simply to survey some of the principal functions the novel has in fact served. I shall try for adequate range, but with no hope of completeness. Once I have discussed these functions separately, I want to consider briefly the extent to which they limit or reinforce each other. How fully can the same novel satisfy a range of functions at once? If this suggests a definition in turn, I shall leave it for the reader to draw. There are three principal functions I wish to discuss: the novel as game or pure form; the novel as expressive act; and the novel as a source of knowledge, as record or model.

It is the nature of games that they are self-enclosed, creating a world that obeys fixed rules but also encompassing much that is accidental or unpredictable. The resistance may come of chance (the fall of the cards) or of competition (the strategy of an opponent). To win the game one must follow the rules in order to shape the unpredictable into a form that is prescribed; one cooperates with chance or outmaneuvers an opponent, but one can win only by observing the procedures agreed upon. A game is, moreover, an end in itself. We may play it for distraction or use it as a means of aggression; we may rage in frustration or crow with self-satisfaction at the close; but the game has a definable end, whatever else we may make of the process. We know, of course, that games like novels may provide valuable exercise in skill and even moral training; but these uses do not affect the rules that constitute the game as a game.

We may regard the process of reading a novel as a game between two players, one the reader and the other the author; or we may see it as a game like solitaire, where the reader is required to impose some kind of order on the materials that are given to him. The latter view stresses the novel as artifact, self-contained and without reference to an author. But it presents problems. To read a novel is to discover the order latent in its materials rather than simply to impose one by a set of rules. In some sense each novel suggests to the reader the order he may expect to find, in its use of convention and by its opening movement: we could not speak of suspense unless there were a limited range of expectations within which there remains crucial unpredictability. In that sense, the novel both sets the rules and provides the challenge, whether or not we become fully aware of the author's presence behind the work he has created. When we become fully aware of that presence, we may wish to speak of the rhetoric of the novel.

So long as we engage in the game, it bounds our awareness and holds our attention; if we turn away from it, we know we are leaving the area it circumscribes. This is largely because the rules of the game create a world of "institutional facts," to which our responses are regulated and even defined by a system of "constitutive rules."[6] We do not confuse the words of fiction with statements of fact or the references to fictional characters with allusions to real people. In fact, one may speak of artistic representation as itself an institution. As Richard Wollheim observes of a similar case, "it is hard to see how the resemblance that holds between a painting or a drawing and that which it is of would be apparent, or could even be pointed out, to someone who was totally ignorant of the institutions . . . of representation."[7]

We can see the gamelike aspect of the novel more clearly by considering a relatively pure case: the detective story. We read it for the exercise of the puzzle, and we hardly recall it more than any other puzzle unless its impurities give it other kinds of interest. When we read a detective story, we do not really regard murders as murders: for we are interested in the problems that the convention of a murder creates. The problems, moreover, are presented in a distinctive way. We take for granted that much of the information we are given will be ambiguous; clues may be misleading or false in emphasis. It is our task to play against the author, remaining vigilant where he most wishes to lull our suspicions, refusing what strike us as false leads, inventing surmises that go beyond the proffered evidence. Some detective stories present a series of solutions, each new one overturning and correcting the last, until by the close we reach one that takes into account every possibility that has been raised. Anyone who reads detective stories knows that there are certain moves the author should not make: he should not allow the solution to depend upon evidence that is withheld from the reader, and he should not make the criminal a character who is introduced late in the story. Such moves are regarded as cheating, as is the reader's turning to the back of the book before he earns his way to it.

The detective story is more game than novel. Its characters may be rudimentary (unless the puzzle stresses complex motives rather than the mechanics of opportunity), and its plot tends to be more ingenious than plausible. We should hardly tolerate this mode of narration if its function were not precisely to tease and test us, although we accept something close to it in Henry James or Joseph Conrad in return for a different kind of reward. (In their novels we may feel that the arbitrary form of disclosure—the evasions and suppressions—is meant to direct our attention to what we, like the characters, would readily evade.) The detective novel reduces the problems of following a story to those of making appropriate inferences and avoiding false suggestions. But upon such procedures (with less need for eluding the author's tricks) all the more complex experience of the novel is based.[8]

There are novels which insistently call attention to the rules they impose and even mock us with the strenuous efforts they demand of us. We are not allowed to lose ourselves in the game, and yet the reminder that we are playing, however strenuously, may have a liberating effect as well: we are made aware of our own contribution to the game, of the skills we are required to employ and of the pleasure we find in exercising them. The self-conscious game is a special case of the gamelike aspect of most novels, but it helps us see what is present all the time.

To treat the novel as game is to concentrate our attention upon the puzzle-solving aspect and perhaps to recognize it as more fundamental than we usually do. The puzzle shows, in a trivial and therefore all the more obsessive way, a concern with form—with imposing, discovering, at any rate achieving it. Passive participation in games of mere chance involves little more than hopeful waiting; but most games involve some skill, and therefore an active effort to bring form into being. The success of a game depends, in large measure, on its providing sufficient resistance to call forth exertions and yet not so much as to make the effort futile. There are times when the game is already won but must still be played out, the outcome no longer seriously unpredictable and the resolution almost mechanically carried through, according to set laws. One may see this as the counterpart of what has often been criticized as the schematic in the novel: a pattern is so firmly established that, once it is mastered, its application presents no new problem and becomes only passive execution. Things do not simply fall into place; they jostle one, as it were, in their readiness to get there, and one feels oneself more the instrument of a design than the discoverer, much less the creator, of one.

The impulse to achieve form and order need not detain us. It is so general and so fundamental as to need little (or infinite) explanation: we may see it as the impulse to control, to humanize, to shape the casualty of events to the order of our minds, to abolish waste and obscurity by converting disorder to design. The goal of the impulse is to convert all content to form, to trace in every element of the work some purposiveness that makes it necessary rather than accidental, to find relevance in every detail and meaning in every event. This is a grand ambition and not to be achieved; the goal simply shapes the direction of the impulse. To state it in terms of meaning is already to look beyond the merely gamelike or formalistic aspect of the novel, and, if one were cautious enough, one would use a term like *pattern* rather than *meaning*. For while the novel is composed of words with meanings that designate events which in turn have meanings, the question at stake is whether the novel as a whole is controlled by meaning. One can readily think of novels which "come out" merely as games or as rituals come out; they achieve a rounding or closing of form, a binding of loose ends, a resolution that satisfies all the expectations that the form has aroused.

Full control by form is scarcely to be attained. For the movement to that goal begins in the arbitrary and accidental, and these remain in some degree unpurged, untransformed. They embarrass and impugn any tyrannical ideal of form. The forming process rather than the achieved form tends to be the primary interest of game-player or novel-reader. The completion of the form is an acceptable resting point, a sufficient resolution, but not a total extinction of accident. What makes a resolution sufficient? In a game we know when we have won. We have attained the degree of order that the rules require, and this will vary with the nature of the materials. Loose ends remain. A checkmate does not require a swept board, and a slam will require a certain number of tricks. In the arts we do not know when we have won, and we tend to be haunted by an ideal conception of form—for example, that of organic unity—that induces despair or, worse, encourages desperate ingenuity in exacting a design. If unity were the sole end of structure, we should be able to attain it at the sacrifice of all that makes unity interesting; but, in fact, only such a degree of unity is desirable as will accommodate other functions. What unity the work achieves will suffice to give it closure, but it may include a number of unresolved contraries and ironic reservations.

Here the analogy with the game breaks down: without clear rules, the novel cannot be won or lost, it can only be more or less satisfactorily resolved. What such resolutions can mean becomes most clear where critics have discussed the question of how a given novel might have been completed (Dickens's *Mystery of Edwin Drood* or Mann's *Confessions of Felix Krull*) or whether an open novel like *Tristram Shandy* has in fact been completed.[9] But in a sense every critical dispute about the interpretation of a novel is a dispute about how it is meant to end. There is more general agreement that novels are resolved than about which of the possible resolutions one should accept. One can, if one wishes, devise innumerable "plots" (as one can draw an infinity of curves through any limited set of algebraic coordinates), each an implicit commentary upon every other. Like many theoretical possibilities, this is more interesting to contemplate than to practice.

The forming process varies with the kind and degree of form that is sought, but it underlies all kinds and degrees as something more constant than any of them, and it becomes an occasion for attention in its own right. *Michelangelesque, Mozartian,* and *Wordsworthian* are terms that have as much weight as do the titles of particular works, and they are terms invoked as readily by passages as by completed works. Yet none of these terms would have its full weight if the power it names did not include the formation of a complete work. The game provides a simple analogy again; once a game is won or lost, we may—if there is record or notation, even sharp enough memory, to permit it—wish to replay it, to trace a sequence of moves in order to enjoy once more the mastery they exhibited. There is a fine instance of the power such a passage may have in Kenneth Clark's discussion of Rembrandt's self-portraits:

> More than any of the series, the Kenwood portrait grows outward from the nose, from a splatter of red paint so shameless that it can make one laugh without lessening one's feeling of awe at the magical transformation of experience into art. By that red nose I am rebuked. I suddenly recognise the shallowness of my morality, the narrowness of my sympathies and the trivial nature of my occupations. The humility of Rembrandt's colossal genius warns the art historian to shut up.[10]

Clark is referring to more than formal mastery, but all else is grounded in that and follows from it. The critic, if not the historian, will shamelessly go on talking, trying to get behind the screen of the "magical," impatient with the silence of awe. And, anyway, critics do not laugh very easily.

Something of the sort may be seen in the criticism of the novel. The scale of most works permits one to talk with great precision only about passages. The passages presuppose the larger form and gain their import only as they refer to what precedes or follows, quite literally from their status as passages. Yet it is here, in the local situation, where ends and means are concentrated in a complex moment, engendered by the past and governed by the future, that the full value of the form is felt. One can, in the novel, speak of such moments as instances of "truthfulness," of full respect for the casualty and complexity of the actual; but they are constituted by the form and by what the form itself is constituted to admit. To put it in bizarre but emphatic terms, they are moments of institutional life. If they recall comparable moments of actual experience and seem true to them, it is in large part because we conceive actual experience in their terms.

I have discussed games of skill and chance. More important than the game is the larger sense of play, for example the kind of play that might be called mimicry or impersonation. Whether it is based on actual models or on invented selves, it becomes a release from constraint, a freeing of the power to choose one's identity or roles, a holiday from the life one has inherited or earned. This is that "power of improvisation and joy" that Roger Caillois calls *paidia,* and it can be related to those cases of self-induced vertigo or intoxication he also treats (as *ilinx*). So it can unless it acquires discipline and exemplifies, as well, something of the "taste for gratuitous difficulty" Caillois calls *ludus.* [11] One thinks of those imagined worlds that novelists not only create but rather compulsively map, codify, and particularize—down to street names, income figures, and shopping lists that will never enter into the novel itself. These have been explained by the need to imagine fully that some novelists feel; one can accept that but still ask further questions. These model worlds are not so much designed to reveal some aspect of the actual world as to create an alternative world whose rules are tighter than the actual world's and are gratuitously imposed. In effect, their very "realism" turns the actual into game. Caillois cites the theater as a form of activity that disciplines mimicry; the novel can serve more obliquely but perhaps even more elaborately—since it does not require powers of performance—to achieve the same end. Related to this, and perhaps more clearly tied to psychic needs, is the novel as ritual: constantly reenacting patterns of conflict and resolution—as in the traditional genres of light fiction, the western or romance—and providing (whatever else) the reassurance of the reconstituted form.

2

The creation of form may be an end in itself, satisfying what E. H. Gombrich calls the "sense of order." [12] But in most novels it opens into a second function: the novel engages and shapes the feelings of both author and reader. This raises questions of projection and identification, of fantasy and, in a special sense, of therapy. The institutional rules are essential to this exercise, for the fear of some of our deepest feelings—the resistance to acknowledging and expressing them—is alleviated by the formal pattern into which they can be admitted. We can start from either side of the transaction, as it were; with the feelings that require a formal structure or with the structures that admit a kind of feeling (in some sense regressive) that we usually suppress.

The first approach is closer to Freud's treatment of dreams, the second to his treatment of jokes. Both require the elaborate and highly poetic devices of condensation and displacement, but both exhibit them in a process of local or small-scale ordering. The fluidity of dreams permits rapid transitions from which one need not look back; the structure need not achieve a sustained consistency. The brevity of jokes permits a compact, if intricate, structure, often generated by a single act of verbal play. Neither can account in itself for the sustained form of the novel or provide more than a partial and suggestive analogy.

To speak of fear of our feelings need not conjure up specters of repressed sexual impulses, although they clearly have a central place. Let me cite instead two passages from Raymond Williams on the Victorian social novel:

> Like Alton Locke, Felix Holt becomes involved in a riot; like him, he is mistaken for a ringleader; like him, he is sentenced to imprisonment. This recurring pattern is not copying, in the vulgar sense. It is rather the common working of an identical fear, which was present also in Mrs. Gaskell's revision of John Barton. It is at root the fear of a sympathetic, reformist-minded member of the middle classes at being drawn into any kind of mob violence. . . .
>
> These novels, when read together, seem to illustrate clearly enough not only the common criticism of industrialism, which the tradition was establishing, but also the general structure of feeling which was equally determining. Recognition of evil was balanced by fear of becoming involved. Sympathy was transformed, not into action, but into withdrawal. We can all observe the extent to which this structure of feeling has persisted, into both the literature and the social thinking of our own time.[13]

While Williams's analysis seems just, I think he scants the uses of form. These are novels written according to certain rules, or at least certain conventional expectations, of which the resolved and "happy" ending is one of the most conspicuous. We have to acknowledge that these novelists worked within such forms and brought to them the awareness, however disabled by fear, that Williams discusses. The form of these works did not provide the vehicle for meeting the problems fully. It provided instead the vehicle for expressing feelings that yield only somewhat strained resolutions. But this use of the novel has a counterpart in work of the preceding century like Fielding's *Tom Jones*. Fielding constructed a novel in which an artlessly imprudent hero could not hope to acquit himself with success in a world of self-interest. Fielding insists upon the need for prudence, but he presents many portraits of men whose self-regard is both prudent and contemptible. In contrast, Jones's generosity of spirit makes him all but incapable of prudence, and at most a somewhat theoretical convert to it at the close. In order to extricate his hero from the consequences of imprudence, Fielding must perform the work of a wise providence; the contrivance of the plot is the perfect vehicle of the author's ambivalence, and the reconciliation is imposed by means as "magical" as in the novels Williams treats. Yet without the contrivance we could not have had the celebration of generosity.

What I have done is to reverse Williams's direction, to claim that the vehicle releases feelings rather than that it simply exhibits a fear of them. That it does both is my real argument. There is a limit to those feelings that can be acknowledged, and to the degree that they can be; if the novel expresses only some, it has at least given these a form.

In order to accomplish this end, the novel may give experience the coherence of romance, the moral clarity of melodrama, the causal inevitability of tragedy. These forms are gratifyingly schematic and, as genres, lucidly rule-bound; they contain the complexities that would otherwise be chaotic or overwhelming. As Ernst Kris puts it, the "maintenance of the aesthetic illusion . . . stimulates the rise of feelings which we might otherwise be hesitant to permit ourselves, since they lead to our own personal conflicts. It allows in addition for intensities of reaction which, without this protection, many individuals are unwilling to admit to themselves." The pleasure of such an aesthetic experience as what Aristotle calls catharsis is "a double one, both discharge and control." We destroy reality in order to construct its more tolerable and comprehensible image: "Every line or every stroke of the chisel is a simplification, a reduction of reality. The unconscious meaning of the process is control at the price of destruction. But destruction of the real is fused with construction of its image." Most of all, the process is a tribute to the power of the ego in ordering its world: "The control of the ego over the discharge of energy is pleasurable in itself." [14]

This last point brings us to the problem of identification. The experience of which we read gains immediacy; we entertain it to some degree as if it were our own. We feel with some of the characters, and we accept their situation as one in which we imagine ourselves as actors. How completely do we enter into the experience of the characters? As in a dream, our own capacities for feeling are exercised by the characters in which we invest them. ("A dream," as Freud remarked, "does not simply give expression to a thought, but represents the wish fulfilled as a hallucinatory experience.") [15] In the full sense of identification, the feelings are so completely exercised as to preclude even marginal self-awareness. Such a state is perhaps pathological if it is more than transitory, and it may be more easily sustained in adolescence than later. The common process is far more complex and interesting. We may enter into a character to a considerable degree and "perform" his feelings somewhat as a musician performs a sonata. But we tend to retain some power of disengagement: we are able to move back from or out of the character, to see him with detachment as well as sympathy.

This detachment will, in fact, be encouraged by the novelist's own presence: at the very least, the composing power of the novelist will serve to detach us from simple identification. Beyond that, we have the explicit voice of the narrator, as he recounts the story or even as he presents the character's thoughts through indirect discourse. The difference between the words in which the character himself might think and the words in which the narrator presents his thoughts creates at least a trace of dissonance or a shadow of irony.[16] And in the larger structure of the novel we are as readers constantly aware of patterns, of relevances, that the characters may exhibit without recognizing. In a novel of multiple plot, for example, like George Eliot's *Middlemarch,* any one story is embedded in a structure of relationships with other stories that have as much prominence for us but may be at the margin of a given character's awareness or totally beyond his ken. We may be Lydgates or Dorotheas, but we do not live our lives in constant juxtaposition with those other selves, as they do in the novel of multiple plot. At its most pointed, this will be dramatic irony; but in a more tenuous form it is present everywhere and affects our sense of any character or event. The very limitation of scale makes us see the relationships within the novel more steadily than we ever do in life.

Again, the words in which the novelist writes are words he will have applied to other characters in the same story; each novel is a verbal matrix, and, while the degree of ordering will vary from case to case, there is at least the likelihood that the words will bind and relate elements as the elements themselves can scarcely imagine. All of these devices serve, then, to keep us aware of the fictionality of the work and of the characters. Yet they do not rule out a large degree of sympathy; we are flexible enough to move in and out, back and forth, without totally sacrificing one aspect for the sake of others. The novel modifies the possibilities of identification but does not annihilate them.

As the form of the novel emerges, our identification shifts more and more from character to author. "We started out as part of the world which the artist created; we end as co-creators: we identify ourselves with the artist." As Kris observes, "however slight, some degree of identification with the artist, unconscious or preconscious, is part of any aesthetic reaction," and it may be awakened early in our reading by the overt play in the language of narration as well as by the narrative voice.[17] As the novel approaches resolution, however, the process is intensified. The central character, with whom we have identified, may himself undergo precisely this kind of shift, a broadening of awareness that takes in the whole pattern of which he is a part, release from the peculiar blindness or limitation that has beset him and produced the complications of the plot. If so, the shift of identification is a twofold one: both character and, with him, reader move toward and effectively reach the author's awareness. The central character who signally fails to do so, who remains essentially blind or obtuse, seems often to have too little consciousness to permit sufficient identification: it is the complaint made about Emma Bovary by readers as different as Henry James and D. H. Lawrence.[18]

This opening out of awareness becomes, often, an exemplary therapeutic moment. The central character may enact it, or the reader may come to it alone. At some point the constrictions of selfhood give way to an openness and objectivity of vision, as in Dorothea Brooke's looking through the window near the close of *Middlemarch* or Emma's recognition of her love for Knightley and of the vulnerability it suddenly discloses. Iris Murdoch has frequently written about this therapeutic power of art and made it the subject of some of her novels. Her view of our normal condition stresses the blindness of our egoism. "We are anxiety-ridden animals. Our minds are continually active, fabricating an anxious, usually self-preoccupied, often falsifying *veil* which partially conceals the world." We are cured in part as we can "take a self-forgetful pleasure in the sheer alien pointless independent existence of animals, birds, stones and trees." So art, while it can easily fall into "self-consoling fantasy," is at its best "a thing totally opposed to selfish obsession."

> Good art reveals what we are usually too selfish and too timid to recognize, the minute and absolutely random detail of the world, and reveals it together with a sense of unity and form. This form often seems to us mysterious because it resists the easy patterns of the fantasy, whereas there is nothing mysterious about the forms of bad art since they are the recognizable and familiar rat-runs of selfish daydream. Good art shows us how difficult it is to be objective by showing us how differently the world looks to an objective vision. . . .
>
> The great deaths of literature are few, but they show us with an exemplary clarity the way in which art invigorates us by a juxtaposition, almost an identification, of pointlessness and value. The death of Patroclus, the death of Cordelia, the death of Petya Rostov. All is vanity. The only thing which is of real importance is the ability to see it all clearly and respond to it justly, which is inseparable from virtue. Perhaps one of the greatest achievements of all is to join this sense of absolute mortality not to the tragic but to the comic. Shallow and Silence. Stefan Trofimovich Verhovensky.[19]

I am not so much interested in the therapeutic power of all art as in the therapeutic process that emerges within the novel. It emerges as form emerges and as our identification shifts from character to creator. And it involves as well, to recall Kris's point, the assertion of the powers of the ego. This need not be, as in Murdoch's analysis, a triumph over self-consoling fantasy; it may even be a triumph for such fantasy if our culture has imposed a distrust of self and a submissiveness to institutions that defrauds us. Stendhal's world of post-Napoleonic France and Italy is such a culture, and, while Stendhal is no uncritical proponent of instinct, his heroes gain their dignity in part by the jealous protection of their ego from culture. Philip Rieff has stated the problem very well:

> To maintain the analytic attitude, in the everyday conduct of life, becomes the most subtle of all the efforts of the ego; it is tantamount to limiting the power of the super-ego and, therewith, of culture. The analytic attitude expresses a trained capacity for entertaining tentative opinions about the inner dictates of conscience, reserving the right even to disobey the law insofar as it originates outside the individual, in the name of a gospel of a freer impulse. Not that impulse alone is to be trusted. It is merely to be respected, and a limit recognized of the ability of any culture to transform the aggressiveness of impulse, by an alchemy of commitment, into the authority of law. Freud maintained a sober vision of man in the middle, a go-between, aware of the fact that he had little strength of his own, forever mediating between culture and instinct in an effort to gain some room for maneuver between those hostile powers. Maturity, according to Freud, lay in the trained capacity to keep the negotiations from breaking down.[20]

The point I would draw from Rieff to supplement or balance Murdoch's is that the novel may favor either culture or instinct in its expressive function, or it may reach for that balance that Rieff and many literary critics as well have called maturity.

Roy Schafer has thrown light on this process by treating the psychoanalytic dialogue as a conflict or collaboration in narratives. As the patient, or analysand, presents his story, the analyst may suggest how the story might be retold. He "establishes new, though often contested and resisted, questions that amount to regulated narrative possibilities." The patient begins, from the analyst's point of view, as an "unreliable narrator," who will become in time "coauthor of the analysis as he/she becomes a more daring and reliable narrator." The point where collaboration begins may be seen as a counterpart of peripety, or reversal, in Aristotle's account of plot. The original narrative may express a sense of being wronged or victimized and accordingly present the self as passive and incapable of responsibility. This mixture of defense and projection may give way to "some kind of curative reorganization." I borrow the last phrase from Meredith Skura, who sees the moment of reversal as the "revelation not only of a specific fact but of a fact that changes everything, that makes us give up one set of values and the belief that the world conforms to them, and shows us how to find another." So it is in both the literary work and the therapeutic process: "The critical questions no longer remain, because the terms in which they have been defined are no longer relevant."[21]

Finally we must consider the expressive function of the novel that is evoked by the term *myth*. It is difficult to separate the descriptive from the evaluative force of that term, but in its modern use, drawn from the comparative study of religions and popular beliefs, it seems to mean a narrative (or set of narratives) that offers a large-scale interpretation of shared experience. It has, therefore, generalizing force as well as concreteness. Whether myth wins full credence or not need hardly arise; its effect is like that of a common sacrament, whatever dogma may underlie it. The hero is each of us, or rather all of us; and the episodes of his history become a scripture in which we can read our nature.

So at least the "myth critic" might assert, and he may, like Northrop Frye, see all literature as the vestiges of primitive myths, displaced from their original form by secularization, fragmented as one aspect or another of the hero, or of the cycle of his myths, is given prominence. Behind each literary work, for Frye, looms the original, integral cycle of myths or at least a systematic vision of all literature as its reassembled fragments. Not all myth critics share Frye's love of system, but most see some allusive element in the reenactment of a mythical pattern in a novel. The reenactment is, as a rule, unconscious and imperfect on the part of the characters. The myth is relived through necessity rather than deliberately performed. It is imperfectly embodied in modern circumstances and in limited actors (who may be heroic but scarcely heroes); and the author, if he is fully conscious of the myth he evokes, will probably be as much moved by an ironic sense of its somewhat frustrate survival as by a trust in its power to invest events with profound suggestions.

Implicit in all of this is the belief that both author and reader reach some deeper level of reality, or at least more spacious awareness, through the recognition of a mythical dimension in the novel. There is, for one thing, often an allusion to titanic figures and to those vast spaces in which their drama was once played out. This may be a recession to the prehistorical time of myth, a backward movement through the successive enactments—the numerous Prometheus figures or earth goddesses, let us say—of an archetypal pattern. Corresponding to the long recession in time there may be a sense of deep descent into the most elementary feelings of man, as recorded in those narratives which retain a recognizable archaic identity through all their later adaptations.

If this view of myth has any validity, it could explain the revelatory power the novel sometimes seems to achieve—revelatory of mysterious forces within man through myths in which they were first or most forcefully projected. Such revelation is tied to what I have called therapy. The myths seem to awaken and even to endorse primitive impulses, that is, to invite regression and to celebrate instinct. Much of the recent celebration of myth sees it as a necessary corrective to the costly repressions and featureless attenuation of identity that civilization has exacted. The feelings, critics would claim, need to recover their elemental grandeur; it is their reality that we have neglected. To restore our awareness of them may lead once more to a reality principle but on better terms.

I have presented the case for myth criticism in as neutral a way as I could, but some problems must be raised. Critics often imply that the recognition of myth in a novel confers power and complexity. This is doubtful. In contrast, the appeal to myth often makes for distention and rhetorical coercion, a vehement insistence upon more than the author's imagination can realize. One must recognize that it is an ironic and self-conscious use that is made of myth by novelists of great stature—Mann, Joyce, and Gide come at once to mind. Further problems arise when the work makes no direct allusion to myth but is credited with mythical power by enthusiastic critics. And where it does make direct allusion, is that allusion an evocation of a full myth or is it similar to many other allusions, historical or literary, that call up exemplary figures in particular aspects? Is George Eliot's evocation of Saint Teresa in the prelude to *Middlemarch* a reference to myth or history? Does not the novelist need, in some measure, to re-create the myth if he is to make full use of it?

One can recognize in certain novelists a tendency to surround their heroes with mystery and to make them loom larger in the mists of surmise. If this is accompanied by the use of a somewhat primitive setting, as in Conrad's use of Patusan in *Lord Jim,* it may have the effect of mythicizing the central character. In the case of the "Jim-myth," the process of generalizing, of making Jim a representative man and his case a universal predicament, is conducted by Marlow; one might even say that Marlow mythicizes Jim more than Conrad does. One might, but in fact Conrad shows similar tendencies elsewhere and even in the opening chapters that precede Marlow's narration in this novel. Still, to be a mythmaker is to adopt a technique which is in itself allusive, and to see a myth in the process of creation is hardly to respond to myth in the full sense that many critics propose.

3

The third function may be called cognitive: it includes all the ways in which the novel provides knowledge, informs us or gives us new insight into the world about us. In the simplest sense, the novel often provides a record of how people live. We read novels to learn about the career of a scientist, the customs of a fishing village, the manners of a bygone age. The novel may set out to be documentary or it may become a document. The kind of record it provides will vary in degree and kind of ordering. Novels may be profuse in details of the surfaces of life, acute in fixing social attitudes, sometimes quite theoretical in analyzing what they represent. In the last case the narrative moves toward illustration and example, offering an instance of general principles that may be explicitly stated or at least strongly implied. One thinks of those novels which fuse socialist realism with Marxist analysis; but more often such novels are transparently allegorical.

How committed the author himself may be to a hypothesis or how conscious of one does not matter. Any novel can provide the reader with a sense of experiment, of regarding his experience under a certain aspect, of trying out a set of values or a new archetype. I have not tried to distinguish between a new way of seeing and a new way of judging. Each tends to imply the other. The testing of values may encourage a more metaphorical or symbolic technique. One thinks of the satiric works that strip away all those elements that make conduct plausible, or that magnify latent motives by making them deliberate. One gets a brutalized world, without the confusions and pretexts of society, a world where ugly motives can for once be seen in bold clarity. Is there really anything more, the satirist may ask. Isn't this what it really amounts to? And can you bear to face it without disguise?

Whether the governing spirit is satirical or sympathetic, whether the novel's form is documentary or symbolic, the shaping of experience will move toward what might be called a model. The value of the model is that it finds a manageable scale or form. It encloses a section or isolates a dimension of reality upon which we wish to concentrate our attention, and it frees it of distracting irrelevance. In the scale model of a street, for example, we may include a typical number of cars and pedestrians moving in normal patterns, but we are interested in the pattern of traffic flow rather than the dress of the people or the make of their cars. Like the game, the model is highly conventional and operates according to a scale and to laws of its own. But its end is to study the reality it represents and perhaps to manipulate it experimentally.

Satiric models tend to exhibit the neglect of a significant value. They are dystopias, presenting as intention and as system the obliviousness or muddle of conventional societies. Utopias, or the green worlds of pastoral romance and comedy, are societies which release in turn natural powers that man rarely allows himself to enjoy in conventional society. But all novels serve in some measure as a testing of values, an exploration of what their realization costs or confers. Any novel tends to reduce the pluralism of values that the world offers and to concentrate upon a few. In the simplest fiction, the values at stake are two, and they stand in simple opposition. It creates characters who are significantly related to each other by simple contrast or likeness. In more complex novels, characters do not form simple uniform classes. What they have in common is more elusive and less easily extricated from their individuality. They embody common values, but they embody them in different ways and to different degrees. The difficulty of discovering the values of the novel is like the difficulty of following the story. In both cases, the difficulties are created by elements that are seemingly opaque or irrelevant.

To discern those principles which govern the novelist's creation of a set of asymmetrical characters requires delicacy and tact, almost as much as governed the creation in the first place. For the complexity of relationships corresponds precisely to the complexity of the principles that the novelist, however consciously, has embodied in them. One finds oneself saying, "not this, but somewhat more like that," "not quite, but almost," "in this respect but not in that." If one asks whether such models can be said truly to simplify what they present, the answer must lie in the very process of deliberation they impose. We have been given the weights and quantities, as it were, by which to calculate. That we can never reach a precise sum or balance is to be expected. That we can become aware of where such a balance might lie, that all of the structure may be imagined in relation to this balance, is itself a striking simplification. We have simplified certain elements in order to get with precision at the peculiar complexity that, in a given novel, most matters.

Models may exist on different scales within the novel that is itself a model for the outward reality. In Dickens's *Little Dorrit* the Marshalsea prison is a self-contained world with its own social structure. It proves to be the counterpart of the larger social world, the "superior sort of Marshalsea" that William Dorrit's family enters upon his release. Within the novel are other models of self-imprisonment: the Circumlocution Office, with its wholehearted dedication to the program of How Not To Do It; the tutelage in respectability under Mrs. General; Mr. Merdle's captivity by the Chief Butler. If each reinforces the next, it does so in a different key, or scale, or context; the common relationships that each of these models embodies are extended in scope but also in meaning as they are contained within the one large model that is the novel itself.

Can we call such models metaphors? The models of science, as Max Black observes, have much in common with metaphors. "They, too, bring about a wedding of disparate subjects, by a distinctive operation of transfer of the *implications* of relatively well-organized cognitive fields. And as with other weddings, their outcomes are unpredictable." The use of a model may "help us to notice what otherwise would be overlooked, to shift the relative emphasis attached to details—in short, to *see new connections*." We may wish to distinguish theoretical models that are purged of their "negative analogy" and can become fully accurate accounts of real operations rather than mere analogues. But, in fact, as Black points out, there "is no such thing as a perfectly faithful model; only by being unfaithful in *some* respect can a model represent its original." And as with all representations, "there are underlying conventions of interpretation—correct ways for 'reading' the model."

Yet this operational model—whether it is a scale model or a relational model—exists for the sake of studying what it represents. It is "designed to serve a purpose, to be a means to some end. It is to show how the ship looks, or how the machine will work, or what law governs the interplay of parts in the original; the model is intended to be enjoyed for its own sake only in the limiting case where the hobbyist indulges a harmless fetishism." [22] In novels the model may achieve the roundness of a fictional "world," with its own coherence and with a rich enough surface to allow one to enter into it imaginatively without needing to be aware of its application or its metaphorical status. We may enjoy it as vicarious experience; we may try to come to terms with it as we might play a game. To the extent that it is like reality but tellingly different from it (as a model must be), it may offer just that playlike release into a simplified order. We may enjoy the pleasure of being for a while someone of supremely demanding impulse who is securely locked into a structure, like Alice's Red Queen. While the novel may serve many of the functions Black attributes to the model, it serves others as well; and each delimits the adequacy with which others can be met.

To discuss the novel as model calls attention to its representation of the actual and to its formalization of it, but neglects the movement of narrative. To recover this we must turn, as critics have increasingly done, to the analogy with historical narrative. Perhaps the boldest analogy has been drawn by the philosopher W. B. Gallie, who analyzes the structure of histories by considering what it means to follow a story. Gallie opposes that view of history which sees its proper function as formulating laws by which actual events can be predicted and therefore explained. Such a view of history would transform it into a social science whose distinctive property would be the pastness of its subject matter; it would free history of its concern with the temporal, for the laws to be formulated would make at most incidental reference to time (as in Boyle's law of gases). Gallie, like other historical narrativists, sees history as having a radically different structure: it is a "species of the genus Story," and its narrative form is essential to its mode of explanation. The conclusion of a story is "not something that can be deduced or predicted," and the sense of following a story "is of an altogether different kind from the sense of following an argument so that we see that its conclusion *follows*."

Gallie's account of followability stresses the presence of contingencies— "through or across" which we follow the story—and the acceptability of its events rather than their necessity or causal chain. The acceptability of events will depend upon their providing "some indication of the kind of event or context which occasioned or evoked," or at least made possible, succeeding events. This "main bond of logical continuity" leads toward the conclusion, which we cannot predict but which ("often without being even vaguely foreseen") "guides our interest almost from the start." Gallie compares following a story with following a game; in both "we accept contingency after contingency as so many openings up of yet other possible routes towards the required although as yet undisclosed conclusion. In the case of a story, where there are no definite rules to help us decide what contingencies can be accepted into it, it is up to the writer to vindicate his acceptance of a given contingency in terms of the subsequent, sufficiently continuous, development of his story." [23]

Gallie's strong emphasis on the following of a story has been criticized by Louis Mink, who distinguishes sharply between following and *having followed* a story. While "experiences come to us *seriatim* in a stream of transience" they "must be capable of being held together in a single image . . . in order for us to be aware of transience at all." This "thinking together in a single act" Mink calls comprehension. "To comprehend temporal succession means to think of it in both directions at once, and then time is no longer the river which bears us along but a river in aerial view, upstream and downstream seen in a single survey." What Mink does is to transform the process of temporal succession into one of spatial comprehension; "in the understanding of a narrative the thought of temporal succession as such vanishes—or perhaps, one might say, remains like the smile of the Cheshire Cat." [24] This seems to me to surrender the narrativist position altogether. True, Mink reduces narrative to configuration rather than to the deductive application of general laws, but history becomes for him like the elaborate "spatial" pattern of images we may extract from a novel at the sacrifice of its process of unfolding. We are back to the model, but we have lost the narrative.

I do not think that a second reading is so radically different from a first. We know the actual conclusion and are not drawn on by suspense; yet, if we cannot suppress such knowledge, we can depress its force. It is too simplistic a view of the reading process to say that we must either know the end or be moved by curiosity to discover it, for we can recover the sense of surprise with which we meet each new contingency and, even more, see how it is absorbed into a more complex pattern of continuity. Relieved of the urgency of suspense, we may attend all the more to the emergence of pattern. As Gallie observes, we may at moments feel we *are* the hero, through full identification, and at other moments become the "detached inactive observer." It is "an unusually rapid movement and interplay between the two standpoints that characterises our appreciation of the story's development" (47–48).

The last phrase is telling: we are not simply following the story but appreciating its development. We have moved to some degree from identification with characters to what Kris calls identification with the author, and it is this movement I have discussed as a "therapeutic" function of the novel. Mink makes a similar point about the relation of narrative to life. "Life has no beginnings, middles or ends; there are meetings, but the start of an affair belongs to the story we tell ourselves later, and there are partings, but final partings only in the story" (p. 557). The shaping of experience frees it of immediacy as it is given form; we move from immersion to reflection, from temporal anxiety to spatial comprehension, from the attitude of an agent to the attitude of an understanding observer or creator. This process has begun within the narrative itself. As the story progresses, the options a character may take become fewer, the patterns of continuity become clearer, the conclusion seems ready to emerge. The interplay between standpoints begins to favor the more inclusive or detached one, unless in fact the hero we follow reaches that standpoint, too, and we share it with him.

But this does not exhaust the problematic relation of the novel to historical narrative. One can say of the latter that for the most part the author must designate his subject initially. Its limits may not be clear, and the themes that govern the account will emerge only gradually; but there is, in a work that is avowedly expository and tied to the factual, an explicit initial commitment, and the historian must show or argue, as he progresses, the relevance of what he includes. It is this subject that becomes the figure in his design, emerging from a ground of contingencies that do not trouble us so long as they provide the figure with definition and extension. It is only when such contingencies disturb the figure itself and create a new figure–ground relationship that they become significant contingencies and earn our full attention.

In the novel the subject remains far more open. The reader starts with the assumption that a pattern of significance will emerge; this is, so to speak, one of the terms upon which the institution of the novel rests. The material adduced is chosen by the author with this end in view; it seldom, therefore, provides the resistance of historical materials. The consequent ordering should, as a result, be fuller and more intense. As in historical narrative, there are figure–ground relationships, and the inevitable contingencies and irrelevancies that form the ground will be accepted so long as they provide occasions for the figure to maintain itself or develop. The comparatively high degree of coherence the novel promises may lend more expectation that each element—even those that normally constitute ground—will emerge as significant, and as a rule a greater proportion will, many having been created with just such a function in mind. The elements of the novel are, one might say, saturated with purposiveness as true historical materials cannot be. Accordingly, the reader is ready to accept a greater measure of apparent irrelevancy and to wait for implicit connectedness to be revealed in the process of unfolding. Because of the greater openness of subject and form and the greater coherence that emerges in the narrative, the narrative process may become more crucial than in history, less guided by expository suggestion and explicit assertion of pattern. The presentiment of the conclusion becomes, as Gallie indicates, more magnetic for being held off and for only gradually emerging.

The more the novelist tries to create the surface density and complexity of actual experience, the more he will create detail that has the resistance of historical fact. Some of the detail may be actual historical event or literal and identifiable setting; that may extend to the customs and manners of a given segment of society. These become limits within which the novelist must work, and they are all the more readily accepted as ground by the reader, for, as Gallie observes, it is "in contrast to the generally recognised realm of predictable uniformities that the unpredictable developments of a story stand out, as worth making a story of, and as worth following" (p. 26). I should prefer to alter terms somewhat; the very contingency of everyday life is predictably unpredictable and readily accepted as the ground of those significant contingencies that fully engage the figures and alter their nature. The full significance of the predictably unpredictable may be established in retrospect, as when Fielding makes clear, once we know the identity of Mrs. Waters, how adroitly he managed the casual comings and goings at Upton so as to prevent her being seen (and thus identified) by Partridge.

The novel often admits contingencies that make sense in symbolic terms. When Jacky Bast turns out, in Forster's *Howards End*, to have been Mr. Wilcox's mistress, this has a moral aptness that makes it persuasive, and the self-conscious artifice of Forster's narrative provides us with a key of expectation that makes acceptance complete. In a novel whose central phrase is "Only connect," such a connection is precisely the sort that needs to be made; and it is only Mr. Wilcox who finds it difficult to face. There are, of course, novels much more fully controlled by such symbolic relationships or "magic" causality than Forster's, and such novels encourage the comparison that Frank Kermode has drawn with theological rather than secular history— with a history that, through such correspondences as typology and through a strong teleological vision of first and last things, can overcome the resistance of historical fact and make its materials as malleable as the novelist's. The chief resistance Kermode treats is the necessary postponement of promised apocalypse, when historical fact fails the teleological pattern imposed upon it and requires that the narrative be revised so as to accommodate a new ending. In other ways, the divine historical narrative resembles the fictions of the novelist, saturated as they are with purposiveness, ready to trace surprising connectedness, and eventuating in a completed pattern such as only story (rather than history) can provide.[25]

What I have been charting might be called the "overdetermination" of the form of the novel. Freud uses the term in his analysis of dreams to show how one manifest, or surface, meaning can express several separate wishes or latent meanings. This is achieved by condensation, by the formation of composite images, like verbal puns, that accommodate several meanings. But overdetermination works no less in jokes and, in fact, in all our behavior. Whatever choices we make will represent the convergence or resultant of several forces: our rational estimate of the future, our sense of what we owe to ourselves in the way of consistency of purpose, our latent and unacknowledged impulses. Some of these forces may be overwhelmed by the urgency of others, for the forces will inevitably vary in power for each act.

When we try to explain our choice we may resort to a principle of complementarity, seeing the action as the result of one force or another; for each will serve to account for it. But this kind of explanation often proves inadequate, for each force more or less subtly dislocates or subdues the others, and the full explanation requires an awareness of all. One of the dangers of enthusiastic psychoanalytic explanation of literary works is that the action of latent impulses may be traced without sufficient regard for the structure which shapes their expression and without whose protection they might remain suppressed. On the other hand, to trace the cognitive structure of a work—its pattern of meanings—will explain the occasion for the psychological expression but may not be able to estimate its force; and it is this difficulty that, with an account of multiple functions, I have tried to meet.

4

A few more words about structure: the novel, as I conceive it, is a model of realities in the world outside it (which includes other novels but much more besides).

As the narrative moves through time, duration becomes the frame of a plot, which may be episodic or progressive, a collection of events or a concatenation. There may, of course, be all kinds of variation and departure: flashbacks, stories within stories, shifts from one narrator to another, a circular movement that in some sense denies the linear movement, a progression that is thematic rather than causal. But all of these depend on the prior conception of a linear, progressive plot, whether simple or multiplex. The onward movement of narrative carries along the agents and their circumstances, evincing parallels or contrasts between them with occasional sharpness and clarity. The plot shows an intention at work, but many novelists try to keep the intention or the thematic progression from becoming oppressively clear; they want some of the randomness and contingency that gives the feel of the improbable actual. Whatever the degree of specification, however schematic or circumstantial the narrative, it carries a certain amount of detail. Details may suggest the density of lived experience and have that "realistic" function, whatever else; but they are often captured by another intention as well, to make a thematic or symbolic point. To the extent that a detail fulfills more than one function it acquires a necessity that we recognize when we realize how much is undone by its removal.

What is more difficult to discuss is the complex kind of awareness that is required for following a story. It is hard to speak of without invoking circuitry. Clearly we encounter details with a sense (often subliminal) of their meeting or disappointing or even defying expectation. And we acquire many kinds of expectation as we move through a novel. We may follow Roland Barthes's example in *S/Z* by recognizing, as we move, "codes" or strands of meaning or, even, in Wittgenstein's terms, distinct language-games. To use the metaphor of the code makes clear that such strands may be discontinuous but still identical (as is not true of the strands that are plaited into a rope, for example). The narrative movement takes us through details that have varying kinds of linkage, for they may belong simultaneously to more than one code; at the moment we encounter them they have indeterminable relevance. We may perceive more than we can quite articulate, and that very sense of multiple implication, varying degrees of complexity, alternative thinning out and fusing of significances is one of the ways in which (with more order and implicit relevance, more visible intention than life holds for very long) the experience of a novel is analogous to the experience of life. But, of course, the experience of the novel is freer because it is more restricted. It may involve, as I have suggested, play and cognitive mastery, and it may exercise and train or correct our feelings. Those feelings are more freely bestowed and more coolly tested without the overload of consequence that life provides. "But," we should be warned, in Iris Murdoch's words, "because of the muddle of human life and the ambiguity and playfulness of aesthetic form, art can at best only explain partly, only reveal almost; and of course any complex work contains impurities and accidents which we choose to ignore." [26] Some of those impurities and accidents can be taken as incongruity or irrelevance, and it is the problem of relevance to which I turn next.

2 ✳ Relevance and the Emergence of Form

Every realistic novel gives us innumerable details: how people look, what they wear, where they live. We generally accept these details as what Henry James called "solidity of specification." [1] They give us the air of reality, the illusion of life, without which the novel can hardly survive. Yet clearly there can be no end to such specification if we allow it full range. At what point do we set limits and by what means? Can there be pure irrelevance? And, if not, what degrees of irrelevance can we admit?

When we read a novel, we adjust more or less insensibly to the kind of relevance it establishes. We may prepare for an expansive exploration of the setting, for a solid evocation of the virtual past. Or we may settle instead for a deep descent into a consciousness, only surmising from rumination and memory the world that surrounds it. Or we may adapt to an undefined locale, perhaps one with strange, gamelike rules of probability, where encounters obey laws we can only puzzle our way into grasping. The reader is apt to find the right key, to frame appropriate expectations, and to give himself up to mastering the terms of the fictional contract the author has established. To discover appropriate canons of relevance may require little effort in a conventional work; it may be a major source of interest in the experimental novel, where the experiment is performed upon the reader as well as upon the material.

In the realistic novel we expect the principal characters to have a broad range of attributes, and we assume that the more attributes they have, the less important some must be. What of the color of the heroine's hair? In archetypal romance blond hair all but commands a state of innocence, gentility, and moral earnestness, whereas dark hair promises commanding will, adroitness, and a strong instinctive life. That is, the typology of romance is such that attributes are comparatively few and are tightly coordinated. In realistic novels the color of hair need not imply moral attributes; there is a lower degree of relevance imposed, and some attributes seem to be given

24

only to create a convincingly full portrait. Yet even there we are inclined to seek significance, to expect a higher degree of relevance than the writer seems to claim. This may reflect the tendency we have in our own experience to create patterns, to relate elements, to simplify, to classify. Our first impressions are often based upon stereotypes, upon conventional categories by which we assimilate the unfamiliar or bewildering. It is only with closer knowledge and extended interest that we begin to differentiate, to specify distinctive patterns or telling peculiarities, to construct an individual.

Let us consider briefly the introduction of Mary and Henry Crawford into Jane Austen's *Mansfield Park*. Mary Crawford has lost her London home and is seeking, with some misgivings, "to hazard herself among her other relations." The first meeting is auspicious:

> Miss Crawford found a sister without preciseness or rusticity—a sister's husband who looked a gentleman, and a house commodious and well fitted up; and Mrs. Grant received in those whom she hoped to love better than ever, a young man and woman of very prepossessing appearance. Mary Crawford was remarkably pretty; Henry, though not handsome, had air and countenance; the manners of both were lively and pleasant, and Mrs. Grant immediately gave them credit for everything else.   [chap. 4]

Mr. Grant, although a parson, looks a gentleman; the only attributes of Mrs. Grant that are noted are her manners and her facilities for entertainment; and the Crawfords, too, are surveyed for their promise as diverting visitors.

In the next chapter, the Crawfords are studied more closely by Maria and Julia Bertram, the two willful and self-absorbed daughters of Sir Thomas:

> Miss Crawford's beauty did her no disservice with the Miss Bertrams. They were too handsome themselves to dislike any woman for being so too, and were almost as much charmed as their brothers, with her lively dark eye, clear brown complexion, and general prettiness. Had she been tall, full formed, and fair, it might have been more of a trial; but as it was there could be no comparison, and she was most allowably a sweet pretty girl, while they were the finest young women in the country.

We notice that Mary Crawford's "clear brown complexion" is admitted in contrast to the Miss Bertrams' fairness; but it is only one element in the image of a "sweet pretty girl," that self-comforting category under which Maria and Julia can accept her presence. To go on:

> Her brother was not handsome; no, when they first saw him, he was absolutely plain, black and plain; but still he was the gentleman, with a very pleasing address. The second meeting proved him not so very plain; he was plain, to be sure, but then he had so much countenance, and his teeth were so good, and

he was so well made, that one soon forgot he was plain; and after a third interview, after dining in company with him at the parsonage, he was no longer to be called so by anybody. He was, in fact, the most agreeable young man the sisters had ever known, and they were equally delighted with him. Miss Bertram's engagement made him in equity the property of Julia, of which Julia was fully aware, and before he had been at Mansfield a week, she was quite ready to be fallen in love with.   [chap. 5]

Jane Austen uses free indirect discourse that catches the idiom of a character but may compress his reasoning, as a speeded-up film mechanizes motion. Through it she catches the rapid, almost mechanical process of rationalization by which a marriageable gentleman is found to have extraordinary charms. Henry's somewhat undistinguished appearance is searched for graces that will accord with his manner: his teeth emerge, glistening with assimilated wit and sexual vitality. In Tolstoy's *Anna Karenina* Vronsky is another man with fine teeth, and they are part of that splendid animal, so much in love with his own body, that Vronsky even at best largely remains. They are an aspect of Vronsky's limiting, if radiant, physicality, related to his love of the regiment, of St. Petersburg society, of social as well as athletic games. For Henry Crawford the teeth are of less import; they are part of the hastily devised blazon of masculine charms the sisters require to adapt him to their narcissistic version of the future.[2]

What this encounter, like every other, reveals is the movement toward specification. E. H. Gombrich has described brilliantly, through the analogy of the hobbyhorse, the way in which a sense of relevance governs our search for attributes, in fact constitutes the forms we ascribe to things or people. The hobbyhorse begins as a broomstick that a child uses as a substitute for a horse. Having found that he can use it for riding, he may project into it other attributes of horsiness—give it a tail, ears, a mane, perhaps a saddle. The child has begun with what we might call the generalized form of a horse; he specifies it more and more as its functions are called forth in play. Is this a representation of a horse? Or rather a substitute for one? The moral of Gombrich's fable is that "substitution may precede portrayal, and creation communication."[3] We work out from needs and we use substitute objects to satisfy them; we project upon those objects the attributes that new needs require.

What does Gombrich's hobbyhorse tell us about the novel? First, it reminds us that the representation of fictional reality may grow out of conventional or archetypal forms, whether we see them as projections, as forms of play, or as models for control. They may acquire more and more differentiation as the images become actors in myths and the myths are adapted to our local anxieties or desires. Even more, Gombrich's analogy can show us that the elaborate forms of realism may be generated less by the desire to represent the actual than by the pressure of conventions reaching outward for more complex differentiation. George Eliot, in the famous seventeenth chapter of *Adam Bede,* renounces the easy fictions of romance for the more difficult truths of realism. By this she means an extension of the conventions of romance into a realm where plots are bent to absorb the actualities of historic life, where the traditional characters are bleached and thickened until they become our colorless and undistinguished neighbors. George Eliot is not offering to give us a literal picture of social reality but to "give a faithful account of men and things as they have mirrored themselves in my mind." This in fact becomes an extension of high forms to include the subliterary, even the antiliterary, details of a "monotonous homely existence." The "exact likeness" is the limiting point of the entire process whereby the generalized form is differentiated so sharply as to direct our feeling where it does not normally flow, so that it does not need to "wait for beauty" but flows with resistless force and brings beauty with it." She sacrifices proportion and the "divine beauty of form" so as to extend art, as the Dutch painters had, to "those rounded backs and stupid weather-beaten faces that have bent over the spade and done the rough work of the world." The point I would stress is the deliberate—even militant—extension of forms rather than the effort at literal representation or record.[4]

So in the encounter I have cited from Jane Austen there is a generalized image, cast in social terms, then specified in various ways by observers. How far this specification is carried will depend on the character who observes or on the governing themes of the novelist. There are certain attributes that Jane Austen requires for her conception of reality, others that would distract or confuse us in following her kind of action. As Gombrich says, "If the hobby-horse became too lifelike, it might gallop away on its own" (p. 8). To take this view of the novel is to see relevance itself expanding to require new detail, and the irrelevant detail becomes the boundary at the limit of expansion.

Frank Kermode in *The Sense of an Ending* draws a sharp distinction between the simplicity of myths and the complexity of fictions, between wishful pattern and the skeptical testing of that pattern against the contingencies of the actual. Only in such testing can myths be disconfirmed, and the result of such disconfirmation will be those reversals, or peripeties, Aristotle finds in complex plots. The need to readjust expectations creates the mature fiction that incorporates contingencies without despairing of form. The myths of which Kermode writes have often been adapted wishfully and conventionally to the more familiar situations of contemporary life, converting archetype into stereotype. It is these generalized forms with which the realistic novel always quarrels, breaking their limits by extension and insisting upon the stubbornness of the actual.

In *Anna Karenina,* Tolstoy gives an account of the artistic process that confirms this view. Mikhailov, the painter, is making a "sketch of a figure of a man in a fit of anger." The paper on which he is working is spotted with candle grease, and the grease spot suggests a new pose for the figure:

> He was drawing this new pose when he suddenly remembered the energetic face, with a jutting-out chin, of a shopkeeper from whom he bought cigars, and he gave the man he was drawing that shopkeeper's face and chin. He laughed with delight. The figure he was drawing, instead of being dead and artificial, had sprung to life and could not possibly be altered. It was alive and was clearly and unmistakably defined. The drawing could be corrected in accordance with the requirements of the figure; one could, and indeed one should, find a different position for the legs, change completely the position of the left arm, and throw back the hair. But in making these changes he did not alter the figure, but merely removed what concealed it. He merely removed, as it were, the coverings which made it impossible to see it; each new stroke revealed more and more the whole figure in all its force and vigor as it had suddenly appeared to him by the action of the grease spot.[5]

We may notice the stress first on the generalized form of an angry man, then the arbitrary suggestion in the form of the grease spot, the outward drive of an inner content or vision that seizes upon actual details of any sort to find specification, most of all the "force and vigor" of the conception that must be adequately embodied. Most interesting is the simultaneous sense of embodiment and of revelation. Once the artist finds, through contingency, a necessary outward form, that form must in turn be protected from, stripped free of, the merely habitual or trivial irrelevancy. This double aspect of the concrete detail—at once a condition of revelation and a threat of irrelevancy—is crucial.

At what point does the covering achieve full opacity? Virginia Woolf, in her famous essay "Mr. Bennett and Mrs. Brown," warns against the reliance on mere social convention. She wickedly imagines the English public speaking:

> Old women have houses. They have fathers. They have incomes. They have servants. They have hot-water bottles. That is how we know that they are old women. Mr. Wells and Mr. Bennett and Mr. Galsworthy have always taught us that this is the way to recognize them.

The Georgian novelists "have given us a house in the hope that we may be able to deduce the human beings who live there." In contrast, Mrs. Woolf defends "an old lady of unlimited capacity and infinite variety; capable of appearing in any place; wearing any dress; saying anything and doing heaven knows what."[6]

Any dress? Why then should we learn that Emma Bovary, when she first appears to Charles, wears a dress of blue merino wool with flounces?[7] Emma's dress is no more a thing than a statement, no more a covering than a revelation. The fine wool, the romantic blue of Emma's fantasies, the flounces that contrast with the farmhouse but accord with its self-indulgent luxuries—all these are intimations of Emma's nature and also, for Charles Bovary, intimations of a life of the senses such as he has never known. The details of Emma's dress are not mere social forms, although they include them. They mark the convergence of several themes, not all of them fully established as yet in the narrative. Their meaning catches at once something of Emma's temperament and Charles's, something of the economic pattern that will mark her career, something of the incongruity Flaubert will exploit so elaborately in the scenes of the agricultural fair. The details avoid the telltale simplification of the smart novelist with a so-called eye for detail, where the detail tends to make a strong and simple sociological assertion. Emma's dress is full of implication, some of it only retrospectively clear; but there is no suspension of narrative movement to permit it, as it were, to make its assertion, nor is there that discontinuity of literal narrative that marks the intervention of a symbol.

How, then, does the novelist prevent these objects, the conditions of plausible actuality, from becoming mere covering? How does he preserve the function of the actual as a language, that is, as relevance? This may be done in part by the presence of a narrator, commenting upon events as George Eliot does, generalizing their import, serving as a reminder and model of the whole process of translation of object into statement. Without such a narrator, there is the effect of ordonnance, of clear artifice of arrangement, of cumulative repetition. Of *Anna Karenina* Tolstoy wrote in a letter:

> . . . if the shortsighted critics think that I merely wanted to describe what appealed to me, such as the sort of dinner Oblonsky has or what Anna's shoulders are like, then they are mistaken. In everything . . . I wrote I was guided by the need of collecting ideas which, linked together, would be the expression of myself, though each individual idea, expressed separately in words, loses its meaning; is horribly debased when only one of the links, of which it forms a part, is taken by itself. But the interlinking of these ideas is not, I think, an intellectual process, but something else, and it is impossible to express the source of this interlinking directly in words; it can only be done indirectly by describing images, actions, and situations in words.[8]

Those linkages reveal, as fully as the most eloquent narrator, the control of the author and the bold use of pattern. We can see one instance when Levin comes to visit his old friend Stiva Oblonsky. Levin has come to propose to Kitty; Stiva and Kitty's older sister Dolly are estranged since she has discovered his affair with a French governess. Levin calls on Oblonsky at his office, where we see Oblonsky's remarkable tact and charm as a bureaucrat, and they meet again for dinner. As they enter the restaurant there is a "sort of suppressed radiance" on Oblonsky's face; he gives his order to the Tartar waiter, he jokes with the painted French woman at the cashier's desk. Levin tries to guard his own idealized vision of Kitty in this place of unclean sensuality.

They are greeted by a "particularly obsequious white-headed old Tartar [waiter] so broad across the hips that the tails of his coat did not meet." The waiter allows Oblonsky to order in Russian but repeats the name of each dish in French, hurries off, to return "with a dish of oysters, their pearly shells open, and a bottle between his fingers." Once he has poured the wine, the fat old waiter looks at Oblonsky "with a smile of undisguised pleasure." For Levin, "this continuous bustle of running about, these bronzes, mirrors, gaslights, Tartars—all this seemed an affront. . . . He was afraid of besmirching that which filled his soul." But Levin can only remark aloud on the difference from meals in the country, got over as quickly as possible so as to return to work—whereas here, in Moscow, "you and I are doing our best to make our dinner last as long as possible and for that reason have oysters." When Oblonsky replies, "That's the whole aim of civilization: to make everything a source of enjoyment," Levin's response is simply, "Well, if that is so, I'd rather be a savage."

Somewhat later they discuss Oblonsky's affair with the governess. Levin is incredulous and unsympathetic; he refuses Oblonsky the comfortable pathos of seeing love as a tragic dilemma. And Oblonsky replies coolly:

> . . . you are a thoroughly earnest and sincere man. That is your strength and your limitation. You are thoroughly earnest and sincere and you want all life to be earnest and sincere too, but it never is. You despise public service because you think its practice ought to be as singleminded as its aims, but that never happens. You want the activity of every single man always to have an aim, and love and family life always to be one and the same thing. But that doesn't happen either. All the diversity, all the charm, all the beauty of life are made up of light and shade.

Then Tolstoy gives us one of his moments of ironic omniscience: "And suddenly both felt that, though they were friends and had dined and wined together, which should have drawn them closer, each was thinking only of his own affairs and was not really concerned with the other" (I, 10). Tolstoy has made the dinner, which occurs early in the novel, the basis of many of the linkages that will run through the book—most essentially the linkages of those who, with varying degrees of awareness and self-acceptance, take an aesthetic view of life and those who, with all the strain and quixotic intensity it may involve, take an ethical view. In Oblonsky's grace and tact, his contentment in the shallow waters that are secure and comfortably warm, we see aspects of Vronsky as well. In Levin's intransigent need to commit himself totally and to exact a meaning for his life we see the heroic possiblities, so cruelly unrealized, of Anna herself. The fat and obsequious old Tartar waiter fills out the scene of such a restaurant as Oblonsky would frequent, but he is also a striking statement of the irreducible hedonism that underlies the aesthetic vision of the beauty of life made up of light and shade.

There is a border area where details are pulled between the demands of structure and the consistent texture of a plausible fictional world. Their nature is not unlike those details of our own lives that are jointly to be explained by outward circumstance and inward motive. Each of us is thrown into a world he never made, and yet each of us makes of it what he must. At some level of conscious or unconscious action we choose ourselves and our world. One of the dazzling and perhaps terrifying aspects of Freud's vision is that it seems everywhere to supplant chance by choice, to shackle accidents in the tracing of purposiveness. It does not preclude contingencies, for it cannot determine what will enter into our experience, but it can show the way we use and shape that experience.

The analogy for the novel is the measure of relevance it may confer upon the most peripheral and accidental detail. Yet to live in a state of unrelieved and intense relevance is something like paranoia, a condition of lucid and overdeterminate design. Such a vision imposes its design at every point, obsessively and repetitiously. The design is everywhere present and everywhere visible. The novel gives us instead the complex awareness of seeing the tough opacity of the actual and at the same time seeing it as a radiant construction of meaning. To get at how this is done requires that we consider for a moment the famous gestalt figure of the duck-rabbit. The same drawing accommodates either image and can be read as either, but it cannot be read simultaneously as both. It is related to those subtler ambiguities of form that we see in puzzles of figure and ground. The figure, if it is given sharp enough definition, will always seek to constitute itself against the interruption of another form; it will seem to thrust the other form back into third-dimensional space as a ground. So long as there is greater definition or familiarity in one form, it will prevail in our perception as figure. These puzzles of perception give us a hint about the structure of novels.[9]

The openings of novels serve to set the rules of the game to be played by the reader. The degree of specification in setting, the presence or absence of a persona behind the narrative voice, the verbal density of the style—its metaphorical elaboration or cultivated innocence—all these are ways of indicating the nature of the game, of educating the responses and guiding the collaboration of the reader. If a novel moves through disjunct sets of characters in successive chapters, we are teased with the problem of how they shall be connected—by the working of the plot (like Esther Summerson and Lady Dedlock) or by thematic analogy (like Clarissa Dalloway and Septimus Smith). But once the novel enters into full narrative movement, the problem of how it shall be read becomes a matter of less immediate concern or full attention. Once its premises are given, the world of the novel becomes the scene of an action, and our commitment to the narrative movement tends to absorb our attention. Narrative may be said to depress the metaphorical status of character and setting; it gives a coherence to all the elements on the level of action that deflects attention from their meaningfulness and from their position in the structure. One can see something very much like this in pictorial representation. The use of perspective makes us read each detail of a painting as it might relate in space to every other detail in a three-dimensional "virtual world." It will require a very strong linear pattern or color relationship to win our attention once more to the flat surface from which we have imaginatively departed.

The narrative movement, with its strong temporal flow and its stress upon causal sequence, may compel full attention to itself. The setting becomes the necessary ground of the action, the characters the necessary agent. But shifts from figure to ground may be instantaneous and, where both figure and ground are more complex, far less dramatic than in the didactic example of the duck-rabbit. At moments the causal sequence moves entirely within the consciousness of the principal character, and the external action becomes the ground against which character is displayed.

Let us consider a sequence of such moments in *Anna Karenina*. First there is the instance of the mowers. Levin has been troubled by the difficulty of persuading the peasants to accept his agricultural programs. He is more immediately oppressed by the skeptical condescension of his half-brother, the intellectual Koznyshev, who always had the power to shake or completely undo Levin's convictions. Levin decides to join the peasants in order to escape from thought and from the frustrations of self-consciousness.

> The longer Levin went on mowing, the oftener he experienced those moments of oblivion when it was not that his arms swung the scythe, but that the scythe itself made his whole body, full of life and conscious of itself, move after it, and as though by magic the work did itself, of its own accord and without a thought being given to it, with the utmost precision and regularity. Those were the most blessed moments.   [III, 5]

As he joins the workers at dinner time, all constraint between them vanishes, but when Levin returns home, his brother's condescension resumes. Koznyshev is filled with the well-being of having solved two chess problems, and Levin must find a pretext for escape so that he can guard his own memory of communion and of blissful self-transcendence.

These moments of oblivion recur in the novel; they accompany the death of Levin's brother and the birth of his son:

> But both that sorrow and this joy were equally beyond the ordinary conditions of life. In this ordinary life they were like openings through which something higher became visible. And what was happening now was equally hard and agonizing to bear and equally incomprehensible, and one's soul, when contemplating it, soared to a height such as one did not think possible before and where reason could not keep up with it.   [VII, 14]

It is at these moments that the events of Levin's life, his long quixotic career of experiment and debate, come to their fullest intensity. These are moments where all the action passes into the shaping of a self and the outward action gives way to internal dialectic. As it does at the very close.

> I shall still get angry with my coachman Ivan, I shall still argue and express my thoughts inopportunely; there will still be a wall between the holy of holies of my soul and other people, even my wife, and I shall still blame her for my own fears and shall regret it; I shall still be unable to understand with my reason why I am praying, and I shall continue to pray—but my life, my whole life, independently of anything that may happen to me, every moment of it, is no longer meaningless as it was before, but has an incontestable meaning of goodness, with which I have the power to invest it.   [VIII, 19]

At the close of the novel Levin at last achieves a fusion of temporal movement with the sense of meaningfulness that has marked these moments of oblivion, of temporal arrest. For it is meaningfulness more than timelessness that matters; the arrest of time is the intimation of meaning, a sudden ascent above the stream of events and the uncertainties that beset him so long as he remains immersed in that stream. For Levin these moments are a freedom from the conditioned, the determined, the horizontal flow of time.

This slipping in and out of time, from surges of doubt and perplexity to moments of arresting meaningfulness, is comparable to shifts in our process of reading the novel. We move from the temporal action to moments where character subsumes action, where ground shifts to figure. So too we move, in a more general way, from the flow of temporal succession to a pattern that might be called spatial, where the recognition of relevance leaps to the center of attention and displaces the narrative sequence or the imagined world. The very repetition of this pattern of moments of oblivion and transcendence is one way in which Tolstoy's novel calls attention to the full dimensions of Levin's being, to the elements of his character that are absent from Oblonsky's. The intensity with which Levin encounters these moments is placed in contrast with Oblonsky's equable and conscienceless hedonism. To say "placed in contrast" is perhaps to beg the question, but a spatial metaphor is hard to avoid.

As critics have often observed, to speak of temporal and spatial forms is at best to use imperfect analogies. "Temporal form" stresses the ongoing movement and irreversible direction of narrative; "spatial form," the simultaneity of presentation that a painting allows. We study the painting through time and apprehend its various relationships of line and color successively, but we can see them presented before us at once. Some have preferred the metaphor of musicalization to spatialization. It does justice to temporal movement, and it stresses, as does the spatial metaphor, a structural pattern that can be schematically represented. What is at stake, clearly, is neither space nor time but the awareness of structure that relates elements in all parts of the book. I hope I will not confuse matters by evoking a new metaphor. I derive it from Roger Fry's account of a Sung bowl, written out of no concern with literary analogy and therefore all the more useful:

> . . . we apprehend gradually the shape of the outside contour, the perfect sequence of the curves, and the subtle modifications of a certain type of curve which it shows; we also feel the relation of the concave curves of the inside to the outside contour; we realize that the precise thickness of the walls is consistent with the particular kind of matter of which it is made, its appearance of density and resistance; and finally we recognize, perhaps, how satisfactory for the display of all these plastic qualities are the color and the dull luster of the glaze. Now while we are thus occupied there comes to us, I think, a feeling of purpose; we feel that all these sensually logical conformities are the outcome of a particular feeling, or of what, for want of a better word, we call an idea; and we may even say that the pot is the expression of an idea in the artist's mind. Whether we are right or not in making this deduction, I believe it nearly always occurs in such esthetic apprehension of an object of art.[10]

Fry's bowl has its various aspects, each of them apprehended in itself and yet all related by an idea, a purposiveness that can account for the simultaneous accommodation of diverse elements and function in a single structure. We can attend to the glaze of the bowl quite apart from its form; we can see the exterior outline without relating it to the inner curve; we can see the bowl as a structure without much concern for its function. And yet we cannot quite do any of these things in isolation. Each may become momentarily the center of our attention, but there is always some latent awareness of the interrelatedness of all these aspects.

It is through this analogy that I would return to the irrelevant detail. It is not, of course, irrelevant, but it has so attenuated and complex a relevance as to confirm rather than directly to assert a meaning. Its meaningfulness, in fact, may become fully apparent only as the total structure emerges. It serves meanwhile a sufficient function in sustaining the virtual world in which the structure is embodied. One can say that its particularity is all that we are required to observe in its immediate configuration, yet only so much particularity is created as is consonant with that conceptual force the detail acquires in the large structure. The local configuration, then, has the potential lucidity of a model and the actual density of an event.

Roland Barthes tried to isolate the detail which has no conceivable relevance, which seems mere arbitrary fact or event, "neither incongruous nor significant." He takes such a detail to have as its function the very assertion (on another level) that it is the real; what it signifies is the category of the real itself. This is ingenious, but it rests upon an ambiguous and sliding use of "signification." If one imagines a family reunion where all degrees of kinship are represented and one or two people attend whose kinship cannot be clearly established at all, shall we say of the one or two that they represent the human family or the community of mankind? This is to extend the idea of kinship to a point where it becomes an equivocation, and something of the sort occurs in Barthes's treatment of the irrelevant detail. These limiting cases—of kinship or of relevance—awaken our consciousness of what it is that relates all these elements. Does the limiting case signify as other instances signify; or does it violate the rules of a language-game and make us aware of the game itself?[11]

Elsewhere, Barthes wrote that

> a narrative is made up solely of functions, for there are several kinds of correlations. . . . Even though a detail might appear univocally trivial, impervious to any function, it would nevertheless end by pointing to its own absurdity or uselessness: everything has a meaning or nothing has. To put it in a different way, Art does not acknowledge the existence of noise (in the informational sense of the word). It is a pure system: there are no wasted units, and there can never be any, however long, loose, or tenuous the thread which links them to one of the levels of the story.[12]

But details do not offer themselves as clearly relevant or irrelevant. It is only the special case where the detail insists upon its relevance or, as it may in some versions of surrealism or of the absurd, upon its irrelevance. Even if, in retrospective analysis, we see certain details as limiting cases of relevance, we can hardly separate them from that dense tissue of events out of which the structure emerges. For that emergence is always imperfect and incomplete. The full import of any detail remains a problem at best, just as does the structural form itself. We may achieve approximations in either case, but we may easily force meanings by distortion of emphasis or failure of tact. The elements of a novel shift in function, I have tried to show, as the work unfolds and as new linkages are revealed. For this reason we can never with confidence ascribe a single purpose or meaning to a detail, nor can we give an exhaustive reading of the structure.

Let me illustrate this with a final example, one drawn from Dickens's *Bleak House.* In the neighborhood of Chancery we encounter the deaths of Captain Hawdon, the lover of Lady Dedlock and the father of Esther Summerson, and of his drunken landlord, Krook. On both occasions we study the responses in Chancery Lane and especially in the nearby pub, the Sol's Arms:

> . . . where the sound of the piano through the partly-opened windows jingles out into the court, and where Little Swills, after keeping the lovers of harmony in a roar like a very Yorick, may now be heard taking the gruff line in a concerted piece, and sentimentally adjuring his friends and patrons to Listen, listen, listen, Tew the wa-ter-Fall! Mrs. Perkins and Mrs. Piper compare opinions on the subject of the young lady of professional celebrity who assists at the Harmonic Meetings, and who has a space to herself in the manuscript announcement in the window; Mrs. Perkins possessing information that she has been married a year and a half, though announced as Miss M. Melvilleson, the noted syren, and that her baby is clandestinely conveyed to the Sol's Arms every night to receive its natural nourishment during the entertainments. "Sooner than which, myself," says Mrs. Perkins, "I would get my living by selling lucifers." Mrs. Piper, as in duty bound, is of the same opinion; holding that a private station is better than public applause, and thanking Heaven for her own (and, by implication, Mrs. Perkins's) respectability. By this time, the potboy of the Sol's Arms appearing with her supperpint well frothed, Mrs. Piper accepts that tankard and retires in-doors, first giving a fair good-night to Mrs. Perkins, who has had her own pint in her hand ever since it was fetched from the same hostelry by young Perkins before he was sent to bed. [chap. 32]

Little Swills, Mrs. Perkins, Mrs. Piper, and the suspect Miss M. Melvilleson have no conceivable relation to Dickens's plot, and this alone is a distinction in a book so elaborately contrived. Yet there they are, enormously lively and entertaining, insisting on the stability of a world that may also contain the outrageous and terrible. They are there and, being there, they demand a share in the structure of the book. To call them ground is not to absolve them of meaning, for ground and figure interlock at least through significant contrast. They may be reminiscent of that rougher texture at the lower part of the statue or the building, at once an element of the design and yet a vestige of the resistant materials from which the work was fashioned. They are not to be put by entirely; if they contribute to the condition of illusion or testify to the real, they also budge somewhat the inner meaning or structure of the work. It must be extended, however slightly, to admit their presence. So long as they have this power, the meaning remains always in process, the form always emerging.

3 ✵ The Other Self:
Problems of Character

If characters exist for the sake of novels, they exist only as much as and in the way that the novel needs them. Jane Austen's world is a strikingly limited one. It is a world of visits and conversations, which usually take place in houses and gardens. We do not see people at work; we do not directly encounter violent action or violent passion. The limits of what may be said are fairly narrow. We are given, in effect, a shallow and well-lighted stage where we can see the comedy of manners played out with great attention to speech and gesture. The point of this world becomes clear as soon as we see the full import that manners can hold. The shallow stage of Jane Austen is a scene where discrimination—tact, intelligence, self-awareness—can play out its part, unconfused by darker or deeper impulses. We are permitted to concentrate upon a limited portion of the full social scale, upon a limited portion of the full emotional range of people, upon a specific kind of action which involves feeling and intelligence. The feeling is never of the depth we see in Dickens or D. H. Lawrence, the intelligence is not the kind we see in George Eliot or Dostoevsky. The characters are differentiated to the degree that the story requires, and we can certainly extend their powers to the solution of other problems; but their powers are uniquely defined in the solution of precisely these problems, for it is these problems that have called those powers into being.

Character, then, is an invention, and it is with that I wish to start. At the beginning of his study of the nude in art, Kenneth Clark asked, "What is the nude?" and offered this answer:

> It is an art invented by the Greeks in the fifth century just as opera is an art form invented in seventeenth-century Italy. The conclusion is certainly too abrupt, but it has the merit of emphasizing that the nude is not the subject of art, but a form of art.
>
> It is widely supposed that the naked human body is in itself an object upon

37

which the eye dwells with pleasure and which we are glad to see depicted. But anyone who has frequented art schools and seen the shapeless, pitiful models that the students are industriously drawing will know this is an illusion. The body is not one of those subjects which can be made into art by direct transcription. . . . [T]he various parts of the body cannot be perceived as simple units and have no clear relationship to one another. In almost every detail the body is not the shape that art has led us to believe it should be.

Not only is the nude itself an invention, Clark pointed out, but each of the great poses of antique sculpture must be seen as inventions in their own right, new instances of "how the naked body has been given memorable shapes by the wish to communicate certain ideas or states of feeling."[1]

It is through this analogy that we can enter the problem of character. The analogy holds in certain obvious ways. We have a daily and intimate acquaintance with our naked body and recognize that a sense of identity is somehow tied to it. As Merleau-Ponty has written, "The perceiving mind is an incarnated mind. . . . For contemporary psychology and psychopathology, the body is no longer mostly an object in the world, under the purview of a separated spirit. It is on the side of the subject; it is our point of view on the world, the place where the spirit takes on a certain physical and historical situation."[2]

The counterpart of this awareness of the body is the equally familiar awareness of that stream of images, feelings, ideas, and fantasies that make up mental life. Just as we live within, through, and out from the body, so we live immersed in this stream of mental processes. Nakedness, Clark observed, is not the nude; he called his book "a study in ideal form," and it is in character that we find the psychic counterpart of the nude. In tracing the emergence of the classical Apollo, Clark observed the process which E. H. Gombrich was later to treat:[3] Greek art "starts from the concept of a perfect shape in the interests of imitation" (p. 31). This is a movement outward from conceptual form toward embodiment, a movement in which the geometric order of ideal form both admits and contains "the most sensual and immediately interesting object, the human body" (p. 25). We may say that such a "concept of a perfect shape" makes the fullness of the body admissible.

There are moments when we are required to stand outside ourselves. We are suddenly forced to consider the self we have known from the inside and to consider it in terms that are not our own familiar words for our feelings and hopes. We must describe ourselves in a language that applies to others as readily as to ourselves. We are cut off from the stream of private associations and personal history, and we must articulate what we have often felt but seldom needed to recognize, much less to capture in categories that will make sense to others. How difficult this proves is an index of our self-awareness. There are some who have seen themselves largely in the terms of public language; there are others who rarely have done so. The latter will feel strangeness and inadequacy in what they can articulate.

This movement from immersion to reflection, from inside to outside, from subject to object, from I to he, becomes a problem of characterization. Boswell wrote at the head of his *London Journal:* "A man cannot know himself better than by attending to the feelings of his heart and to his external actions." The terms are striking. He is both actor and spectator, agent and observer; as we read on in the journal we see that he is experimentalist as well, creating situations in which he can surprise his feelings or test his actions. As he attends to the feelings of his heart or analyzes his actions in light of their motives, he can find a way of describing himself, and to describe himself is, for Boswell, a way of controlling himself. He is interested in making a character as well as recording one, but the two interests shift in importance. What makes Boswell remarkable is his openness, candor, and curiosity; he is as much fascinated by the problems he encounters in himself as he is by the discipline of shaping himself; and at times the interest in self-discovery supplants the concern with self-control.

Most of the inventories of self and attempts at self-characterization we undertake are directed to some purpose. Questions like "Who am I?" are demands for a specific kind of answer. If we are asked to recount our intellectual history, many episodes will remind us that our intellectual life is not autonomous but affected, even shaped, by other elements of the self. Such episodes may undo the simplifications that our purpose imposes and allow us a momentary glimpse into the wholeness of the self. Yet our intellectual life does have a measure of autonomy, and our purpose requires that we limit our attention to the matter at stake.

The self is rarely a simple, massive conception. More often we are drawing out of it those aspects that meet attention because they serve some immediate purpose. The purpose is usually a social one, set by our relations with others, directed by their claims or demands upon us. Those aspects of the self that respond to social demands have been called roles, and social psychologists, who study the self as it performs in and is shaped by society, have given careful attention to the problems of role-playing. One extreme position sees the self as nothing more than the structure of its roles:

> The learned repertoire of roles is the personality. There is nothing else. There is no "core" personality underneath the behavior and feelings; there is no "central" monolithic self which lies beneath the various external manifestations. . . . The "self" is a composite of many selves, each of them consisting of a set of self-perceptions, which are specific to one or another major role, specific to the expectations of one or another significant reference group.[4]

(Reference groups have been defined as "those groups to which the individual relates himself as a part or to which he aspires to relate himself psychologically." They serve as "major anchorings" for one's sense of identity.) A great deal of empirical study and subtle analysis has been given to the way in which a self is constructed of roles or, in a more moderate view, the way in which a self orders the roles to which it is committed. "In carrying out roles," a theorist writes, "one is involved in a continual process of validation and modifications," but it may also be claimed that one "leaves some mark, however faint, upon the cultural definition." If the self has been built out of roles, it may in turn affect the roles it assumes.[5]

George Herbert Mead traced the emergence of the sense of a self to participation in social activity. Mead uses as a model the game in which each player learns his own role through sensing the other players' expectations of him.

> A person is a personality because he belongs to a community, because he takes over the institutions of that community into his own conduct. He takes its language as a medium by which he gets his personality, and then through a process of taking the different roles that all the others furnish, he comes to get the attitude of the members of the community. Such, in a certain sense, is the structure of a man's personality. . . . The structure, then, on which the self is built is this response which is common to all, for one has to be a member of a community to be a self. Such responses are abstract attitudes, but they constitute just what we term a man's character.

"It is a structure of attitudes, then, which makes a self, as distinct from a group of habits," and one becomes a true self as he includes "as elements in the structure or constitution of his self" not only particular attitudes of other individuals toward him but those of the "generalized other," the "social group as a whole to which he belongs." We may see in the "generalized other" the system of values involved in our conception of self. It was precisely against this submission to an impersonal other that existentialism protested—this surrender of the self as an initiating and free agent to the impersonal anonymity of merely social existence, the loss of authenticity in becoming an object for others to act through or upon. The self ceases to live but is lived by the impersonal other, the public or the mass, the whole system of awarding and imposing roles. If the man we meet is going to do nothing but punch our ticket, he need not become more than an undifferentiated conductor. He remains accounted for by a simple role, and so do we for him. But as we come to know people whom we expect to see longer or know better, we want to go further toward comprehending them and toward revealing ourselves.[6]

This is true of our experience of fictional characters. It would be possible to make long lists of all the attributes of characters that are never supplied. We do not know what most characters eat. We hear about servants in Jane Austen's novels, but we rarely see them. The things revealed about Emma Bovary are the very things ignored in Henry James's heroines. Rarely does a critic speculate about Robinson Crusoe's sexual frustration during his long years on the island. What of the missing attributes? The fact is that we do not miss them. We adjust insensibly to the rules of relevance the novel establishes. We can make surmises about the attributes that are missing, but we are hardly inclined to do so unless the novel invites it.

For we do not live all of our lives among complex personalities, nor do we live all of our conscious lives *as* complex personalities. We rely on other people maintaining their roles, and we feel an obligation to do the same. This does not, of course, preclude knowing that an individual is assuming a role, that we can look behind it when we wish, that we can drop our usual roles on occasion and resume them again with little difficulty. There is, in short, a flexibility in role-playing that makes it work without sheer dehumanization. But much of our lives depends on others' maintaining their roles and requiring of us only so much of a response as the role itself demands.

"It may be argued," D. H. Lawrence wrote, "that man lives most intensely when he works. That may be, for some few men, for some few artists whose lives are otherwise empty. But for the mass, for the 99.9 per cent of mankind, work is a form of non-being, of non-existence, of submergence." With considerable irony Lawrence described his heroine Ursula Brangwen as becoming "more and more an inhabitant of the world of work, and of what is called life."[7]

In a similar vein Virginia Woolf wrote:

> Every day includes much more non-being than being. . . . A great part of every day is not lived consciously. One works, eats, sees things, deals with what has to be done; the broken vacuum cleaner; ordering dinner; writing orders to Mabel; washing; cooking dinner; book-binding. When it is a bad day the proportion of non-being is much larger. I had a slight temperature last week; almost the whole day was non-being. The real novelist can somehow convey both sorts of being. I think Jane Austen can; and Trollope; perhaps Thackeray and Dickens and Tolstoy.

One reason, I think, that these writers can convey nonbeing is that they do not regard it so categorically. For these periods of routine, of small choices and largely disengaged thought, can be seen as periods of latency and transition, periods in which those moments of being are allowed their gestation and growth. We may see our lives as continuous and at varying levels of consciousness. But to call portions of our life nonbeing is to make them discontinuous with the moments of being, a diminishment or impairment or suppression of the self by circumstance. Whether or not we draw the distinction as sharply as Virginia Woolf, we recognize the conventions beneath whose somewhat vacuous surface or bland inattention we continue to live. And, of course, Woolf takes this into account elsewhere: "life—say 4 days out of 7—becomes automatic; but on the 5th day a bead of sensation (between husband and wife) forms which is all the fuller and more sensitive because of the automatic customary unconscious days on either side." [8]

I have pursued the analogy of fictional character and our conceptions of self in order to emphasize two things. First, there is considerable artistry inherent in our normal behavior, and the intensification and direction it gains in a work of art does not obliterate a continuity, or at least an analogy, of art and life. Second, the flexibility of role-playing and the purposiveness of it, directed to and by a dramatic situation, prepare us to accept more readily the flexibility of characterization. It may range from mere sketching in of necessary roles to the most complex construction of a person revealed in the conflict or in the successive adoption of roles. But, more important, the terms in which character is conceived and the level at which it is sought are governed by the larger purposes of the novel. The novel provides the society in which the individual character finds definition.

2

The analogy between society and the novel will take us only a short way, however. A novelist with a keen sense of form, like Henry James, longs for a society that has a complex and lucid structure—like a novel. Balzac, James tells us, had the good fortune to live amid

> social phenomena the most rounded and registered, most organized and administered, and thereby most exposed to systematic observation and portrayal, that the world had seen. There are happily other interesting societies, but these are for schemes of such an order comparatively loose and incoherent, with more extent and perhaps more variety, but with less of the great enclosed and exhibited quality, less neatness and sharpness of arrangement, fewer categories, subdivisions, juxtapositions. Balzac's France was both inspiring enough for an immense prose epic and reducible enough for a report or a chart.

Balzac lived "in an earthly heaven so near perfect for his kind of vision that he could have come at no moment more conceivably blest to him," for he escaped the "fatal fusions and uniformities inflicted on our newer generations, the running together of all the differences of form and tone, the ruinous liquefying wash of the great industrial brush over the old conditions of contrast and colour."

For a novelist whose subject is the conditions of social life, for whom "man is on the whole cruelly, crushingly, deformedly conditioned," a society with complex structure may provide the forms other novelists may need to invent.[9] The novel not only claims, by virtue of offering itself as a work of art, a high degree of structure, but it is a structure which has some unifying end, some principle of composition. Without such a presumption, we have no way of considering the relevance of details or of establishing, to the extent that we can, their irrelevance. The unity of a novel is expressed most succinctly in thematic terms. This presupposes that a narrative is shaped so as to disclose meaning; to apprehend the form is to find a way of stating the meaning toward which a novel moves. Such a theme is rarely stated overtly in the work; to extricate it from the work is not to hold it up for contemplation in its own right but rather to see it as the general statement that is given intensity, precision, suggestiveness, and fullness of implication by the work itself. The theme may be the starting point of our *study* of the work, for it is the most general principle of structure we can derive from the work. By turning it back into the work, we can see a radiance in details.

If we start with theme, we can ask of each element, What is it for? The way in which an author conceives character is part of this unitary purpose. Nor should this be taken as a narrowly rhetorical view of fiction, for the energy of what is imagined may only undo the end for which it is created. We always commit ourselves—in an act of imagination—to more than we fully recognize. We are all aware of the mixed pleasure and horror an author can feel at finding his characters demanding lives of their own, shouldering aside his program, or suddenly dying of inanition. And there are many authors who count on characters' taking over the direction of the work, as it were, once they come into fictional life. We need not credit every willful surrender of the author as a real one. He may be sensitive to a deeper level of motive than he can summon at will and wait for its emergence; the internal logic of his characters may force him to do what he could not allow himself to see that he intended. But the intention I am concerned with is the intention revealed by the structure of the work; to call it intention at all is only to claim some purposiveness, at whatever level of consciousness.

We may wish to claim that the purpose of a novel's action is to reveal or examine or celebrate life under a certain aspect, to shape experience so as to make sense of a roughly formulable kind. The formulation is its theme. To achieve this the writer creates a model, a small-scale structure whose proportions and internal relationships have some analogy with the realities we know. We set the model beside those realities as a way of eliciting analogy, not of imposing it. The scale of a work of art always seems smaller than that of life if only because what it presents is more intensively ordered, more transparently significant, more readily encompassed and studied, more sharply framed and closed than a segment of actual experience. And for the same reasons, a work of art may be all the more tellingly problematic, just as an ambiguity has more form than a welter or sharp conflict more point than miasmic suspicion.

The simple tale is a naive form whose shape is its very end. We delight in the fact that it comes out. It has a kind of symmetry, clear design, an artful building of suspense, and a satisfying resolution, like the resolution of a musical form. But the novel is usually more than that. The resolution of its form is somehow consonant with the disclosure of meaning, and there are some novels whose only resolution is the disclosure of meaning. We have the expectation of meaning, and the novel which never quite fulfills the expectation still demands some effort to discover the meaning it does not freely yield. Its effect, whether the author wishes or not to achieve such an effect, is created in part by its institutional form, by the very expectation that it will disclose meaning even when it does not. But of course what interests us about the meaning is how it is earned or what defeats or defers its assertion. The statement may be, after all, somewhat familiar once we articulate it as theme, just as a theatrical role like Hedda Gabler or Iago may be all too familiar until we see a new actor invest it with remarkable meaning. The novel implies a statement, but it does not exist for the sake of its statement; rather, the novel makes a statement so that it can be a novel.

Characters may be said to exist within a novel as persons in a society, but the "society" of the novel is one of intensive and purposive structure. We read the novel immersed in its complexity, it is true, but with confidence in its resolution and its ultimate significance. (I cannot intervene too often with the point that the resolution may be a puzzle or a problem, as long as it seems to be where the work intends to get rather than where it happens to end.) This sense of total structure inevitably qualifies the attention we give to the characters; it need not diminish that interest, but it complicates it. Characters simply cannot be persons in the sense that we commonly know persons in life. It is clear enough that many characters we have read about are more vivid to us than persons we know in daily life, that in a certain sense these fictional persons are more "real" than most actual persons. But to say this conceals more problems than it clarifies. Actual persons are curiously open; they have lives yet to live, they impinge upon us in direct ways. We confront them; we can affect them. We see them as coming closer to us or receding, and if they recede we may miss them. In all these respects, and countless others, real persons have an urgency and an incompleteness that the persons of fiction cannot have.

A fictional character lives within a work of fiction. He may spill over and demand a work of his own, as Falstaff does a play of his own. We may be able to invent new experiences for him beyond the range of those the author has invented, as Pamela Hansford Johnson invented new scenes for Proust's characters. But if a character spills over from a literary work, it is not into our lives, but into another work appropriate to his nature. We may, it is true, come to see people we know in terms of fictional characters. We may even imagine ourselves in such terms, whether in daydreams or in more serious moments. But if characters are like persons, still we must recognize wherein they differ from actual persons and what makes them the peculiar kind of thing that is part of a work of fiction. We must recognize how much of their lives in a novel may be closely linked or counterposed to other lives of which they have no awareness at all, or at best an imperfect one. The action moves around characters as well as through them, and sometimes it reduces them to a pattern which they can hardly imagine.

When we read a novel, whatever we need to know about a character is revealed to us in that work. By the end of the work our awareness of the character has come to some kind of resting point. We know by then all that we need or at least all that we are meant to know. All the questions or problems that are raised by the character are resolved. If they are not, if the novel deliberately leaves the character ambiguous, the very ambiguity is a resting point. This is where we are meant to be left, the point of what we have read. It is ambiguity to be taken as ultimate, not one such as in actual life we seek to get beyond. In that sense one can say that characters exist for the sake of novels rather than novels for the sake of character.

3

Victorian critics often found character more absorbing than the structures it inhabited (somewhat as we do language) and created in turn that ultimate tribute to the mysteries and subtleties of character, the dramatic monologue.[10] But in that form alone we can see the movement through Ezra Pound and T. S. Eliot toward a symbolist mode, where character becomes at most the constellated form of image patterns, historical allusions, philosophical themes. Gerontion exhibits the burden of history and loss of belief, and he has all but dissolved into the large themes he suggests. Eliot's poem denies us the surface and texture of personality: we are deep within a self, ruminating, arguing, pleading, and we are immersed in a predicament that seems to shift from depth to depth. By any inclusive definition of the term, Gerontion is a character; yet he seems at once less and more.

The symbolist, or modernist, novel has a high degree of internal coherence. So intense is the coherence that characters tend to dissolve into the elaborate verbal structure of the work, becoming nodes, as it were, of images or motifs; or they dissolve into aspects of one central character, dialectical forces within one mind. Figure gives way to ground, or at best there is a shimmering iridescence. Is Augustus Carmichael more substantial, more central in *To the Lighthouse* than the painting of Lily Briscoe or Mr. Ramsay's quotations from Tennyson and Cowper? Are characters allowed inconsistency or complexity? Can they have histories? Do the things they possess and handle have an independent reality or are they symbolic stage properties like the skull that Mrs. Ramsay covers with her scarf, the scarf that is later to fall in the section called "Time Passes." And is the very existence of that section, where all the principal actors are off the stage, where the house itself enacts the themes of the novel, an indication of the low estate to which character has fallen?

One can trace a single instance of the movement from states of mind to something more fragmentary, less coherent. In Virginia Woolf one can take a moment when Charles Tansley feels injured by Mrs. Ramsay's carelessly asking, "Are you a good sailor, Mr. Tansley?":

> Mr. Tansley raised a hammer: swung it high in air, but realising, as it descended, that he could not smite that butterfly with such an instrument as this, said only that he had never been sick in his life. But in that one sentence lay compact, like gunpowder, that his grandfather was a fisherman; his father a chemist; that he had worked his way up entirely himself; that he was proud of it; that he was Charles Tansley—a fact that nobody there seemed to realise; but one of these days every single person would know it. He scowled ahead of him. He could almost pity these mild cultivated people, who would be blown sky high, like bales of wool and barrels of apples, one of these days by the gunpowder that was in him.[11]

In this passage we are given Tansley's answer in indirect discourse, for it is only a small part of the pattern of thought and feeling that rages through his mind. Tansley's anger has grounds, which he recalls, and it swells into contempt as it introduces his dream of vengeful power.

In a comparable passage Nathalie Sarraute catches a moment when a solicitous mother-in-law presents Alain with a dish of grated carrots: "They're especially for you, you told me you adored them. . . ."

> One day he had had the misfortune, in a moment of abandon, a moment when he had felt relaxed, satisfied, to toss that at her casually, that secret, that revelation, and like a seed that falls on fertile soil, it had sprouted and is now growing: something enormous, an enormous oleaginous plant with shiny leaves: Alain, you like grated carrots.
>
> Alain told me he liked grated carrots. She's lying in wait. Always ready to spring. She seized upon that, she holds that between her clenched teeth. She has caught it. She pulls. . . . Dish in hand, she turns upon him a pair of gleaming eyes. But with one gesture, he disengages himself—a brief, lissome gesture with his lifted hand, a movement of his head. . . . "No, thank you.

. . ." He's gone, there's no one left, it's an empty envelope, the old garment cast off by him, a piece of which she's clenching between her teeth.[12]

Sarraute uses an imagery of violence as does Woolf; but the narrative has moved closer to the processes of mind, through extended figures that capture a bizarre fury. Sarraute has said that the "character as such (his personality, his situation) does not hold any interest . . . except as the support of these movements," movements fugitive and transitory, which "take place very rapidly, somewhere on the extreme edge of consciousness." They "hide behind our gestures, beneath the words we speak," and they give meaning to those words and to our actions besides. Because these "tropisms" (turns and recoils of attraction or repulsion) are so rapid and so secret, they must be communicated by means of "equivalent images" that give the reader "analogous sensations." The movements must be broken up and spread out as in a slow-motion film, to fill "a hugely amplified present." There is often an intensely comic effect as Sarraute elevates momentary spite or terror into brilliant images that seem ludicrously disproportionate; the effect is like Sterne's tracing in precise detail the arc of a gesture or the cadence of a feeling. For Sarraute the narrative and characters alike are staging areas for these tropisms, and the surface action may be trivial or indeterminate.[13]

We are far more concerned with the infrastructure than the wholeness of persons in such a case. We have come to movements so brief and minute that they hardly sustain narrative at all. They are like a brilliant volley that makes the game itself seem only a pretext. In the past such movements were offered as the accompaniment of narrative, as a suggestion of the feelings that are only imperfectly expressed in speech. Stephen Heath presents a fine instance of George Eliot's use of such a tropism as the resonance of dialogue or, in Nathalie Sarraute's term, as the "sous-conversation" that may come to seem the genuine life of human relationships. This exchange is between the gently adoring Rex Gascoigne and Gwendolen Harleth:

> "Should you mind about my going away, Gwendolen?"
> "Of course. Everyone is of consequence in this dreary country," said Gwendolen, curtly. The perception that poor Rex wanted to be tender made her curl up and harden like a sea-anemone at the touch of a finger.
>
> [*Daniel Deronda*, I, 7]

The figure that Sarraute might use to render feeling in process is used by George Eliot as a comment on Gwendolen's response, made in terms that Gwendolen herself cannot imagine or accept.[14] It is part of the self-discovery toward which Gwendolen is moving: the frightening recognition that she is incapable of love.

The creation of character is a form of art, whatever else, and the modernist novel seems at times to have abjured this art for others, as cubism shattered the portrait and disposed its elements in new ways. The analogy is more than trivial, I think; for the redistribution of the elements of character does not totally destroy it. The effect in cubist painting is to tease one with visual ambiguity, with the "introduction of contrary clues which will resist all attempts to apply the test of consistency." As E. H. Gombrich puts it, "each hypothesis we assume will be knocked out by a contradiction elsewhere, so that our interpretation can never come to rest and our 'imitative faculty' will be kept busy as long as we join in the game." Picasso's *Portrait of Ambroise Vollard* (1909–10) provides a counterpart to the fate of character in some versions of the modernist novel: Edward Fry stresses the difficulty of coming to terms with a cubist portrait:

> The real subject . . . is not Vollard but the formal language used by the artist to create a highly structured aesthetic object. Obviously it would be incorrect to call this painting an abstraction, since it bears a specific relation to external, visual reality; indeed, the persisting fascination of this and other 'analytical' cubist paintings of the following two years is precisely the result of an almost unbearable tension experienced by the viewer. He is delighted by the intellectual and sensuous appeal of an internally consistent pictorial structure, yet he is also tantalized by the unavoidable challenge of interpreting this structure in terms of the known visual world.

Or, as Gombrich puts it, cubism marshals "all the forces of perspective, texture, and shading, not to work in harmony, but to clash in visual deadlock." It succeeds in "countering the transforming effect of an illusionist reading." Yet the tension of which Fry writes does not allow the cubist work to become abstract.[15]

The tension in the cubist portrait is perhaps a special case of the tensions we always find in art. As Edgar Wind has written, "art is an exercise of the imagination, engaging and detaching us at the same time: it makes us participate in what is present, and yet presents itself as an aesthetic fiction. . . . Art lives in this realm of ambiguity and suspense, and it is art only as long as the ambiguity is sustained."[16] I have tried to catch this ambiguity in the emergence of form, an emergence never completed in a work of art, yet never relinquished.

Another kind of tension is claimed by Leo Bersani, who fears that too much concern with form will lead the author to slight those "fragmented desires," of intense if regressive passion, which have only an episodic realization. Bersani finds this concern for coherence an "ideology of the self" that can best be met with "deconstruction of the self," an acceptance of "the discontinuous, the fragmentary, and the peripheral." Bersani would have us question the "unity of personality assumed by all humanistic psychologies."

He recognizes a double tendency in literature, and he does so in order to free its disordering from its ordering power:

> Literature . . . invites us to return to that variety of scenes of desire which is stifled by the interpretive tracing back of all desires to a single, continuous design in a supposed maturing of desire. The literary imagination reinstates the world of desiring fantasies as a world of reinvented, richly fragmented and diversified body-memoirs. But, at the same time, it also gives ample space to those processes by which we make a continuous *story* of our desires, processes which also teach us to give up the intensities of an infinitely desirable halluci-nated world for the somewhat disappointing enjoyments of fulfilled desires.[17]

This in turn leads me to a contrast that Meredith Skura has drawn between the traditional literary critic and the psychoanalytic critic (or the analyst interpreting the "text" of his patient's narrative). "The literary critic," she writes, "usually assumes that the governing conventions in the text and in his reading should coincide," whereas the analyst may act "as if he had never heard of literary conventions." He "looks for naturalistic, literal mimesis where there is none, or he takes what other readers perceive as conventions and interprets them as literal facts about the fictional world." For he is "al-ways ready to see another meaning or a pattern latent in the whole text, which conflicts with the manifest one and which the literary critic would probably ignore because it is so fragile, peripheral, and unelaborated in the ordinary way." He is "interested in the remnants of even the most primitive stages of thought. . . . No wonder the critics have mistrusted the analyst. It has taken them a long time to learn not to ask the 'wrong' questions about literature, and they are understandably wary about anyone who systemati-cally sets out to do so."[18]

The psychoanalytic or hermeneutic critic may deny that there *are* any "wrong" questions about literature (except perhaps the "right" ones). The questions one asks, at any rate, enforce one's conception of literature and determine where one finds it. What I have called the fictional contract is an acceptance of conventions and a regard for the intentions the form of the work seems to embody. Opposed to this would be what Paul Ricoeur has called "interpretation as an exercise of suspicion," often based in Nietzsche, Marx, and Freud, attempting as did these forerunners "to make their 'con-scious' modes of deciphering coincide with the 'unconscious' *work* of cipher-ing which they attributed to the will to power."[19] Finally, the hermeneutic critic may wish to study the momentum of words themselves, as the unfore-seen implications of metaphor result in verbal deadlocks that may correspond to the visual deadlocks of cubism (or even the ambivalent fantasies of surre-alism). I have no wish to question or quarrel with such criticism here, only to distinguish its aims from my own.

4

When he wrote on "the retreat from character" in the modernist novel, W. J. Harvey spoke of the "uneasiness, suspicion, embarrassment or downright contempt" with which critics responded to the praise of characters in fiction. For amused contempt, I would cite a critic trying, as he writes of Thomas Pynchon, to dispose of the misleading claims of the novel. If we were to learn what people meant by novels, he proposes, we might find that "novels are used mainly as psychological mirrors by their readers, having a function analogous to the astrological chart or the do-it-yourself psychotherapy manual."[20] For greater ferocity there is the critic who defends Shakespeare's interest in "undoing and dissolving" characters as much as in creating them. An excessive regard for character, René Girard goes on, "will systematically choose as most Shakespearean what is really least so, at least in the form in which it is chosen. It will thus provide not only our realistic stodginess but also our romantic self-righteousness with the only type of nourishment they can absorb."[21] Beside these, I would put Harvey's more skeptical proposal that we regard the novel, like Shakespeare's drama, as a mixed mode, let us say with "George Eliot at the naturalistic end of the spectrum and Kafka at the non-naturalistic."

> But between the two, fine shades and interminglings are to be expected. Where, for example, would we place a work like Camus's *La Peste?* (And, of course—I hasten to forestall objections—isn't it too simple to dismiss Kafka as simply non-naturalistic? Many of his parables are clearly rooted in social observation and their total effect is often paradoxical—a naturalism of the fantastic.)

Harvey goes on to recognize the frequent presence of a "non-realistic effect" in George Eliot, and his fine book about her novels is devoted in considerable part to a study of their conventions.[22]

There is stronger and sadder questioning of character by the philosopher Richard Rorty. Can those who live in a post-Freudian world, he asks, "still take seriously literary works of the nineteenth-century, relatively unironical sort? Can they, for example, still be moved by novels about people succumbing, or not succumbing, to traditional moral temptations?" I would hope so, although I should disallow the term "traditional," and I would want to discount Rorty's conception of literature as "the organ of secular morality." For the novelists with whom I am concerned have been critical of "traditional" moral solutions, have explored rather than transmitted moral principles, have been skeptical but not, for the most part, demoralized or cynical. (Conrad is perhaps the most problematical case, but it is not the influence of Freud that shapes his irony.) To return to Rorty:

The current struggle in American literary circles between robust, old-fashioned storytelling novelists and ironist critics is a symptom of the inability of intellectuals to take such novels seriously as moral testimonies. They mine them for ambiguity, intertextuality, and the like, because they do not really recognize *morality* as a possible form of life.[23]

I have borrowed Wittgenstein's phrase "forms of life" for the title of this book in part because I feel that morality is not only a possible form of life, but, for better or worse, a necessary one. My concern is not so much with morality itself as with the moral imagination that creates literary character and shapes it, much as it creates and shapes us as persons. I do not wish to discuss moral imagination further now, for what I have to say will become evident in later chapters. I can, however, cite the indispensable sentence from Henry James: "The essence of moral energy is to survey the whole field." What I should like to do here is to mention some of those forms of life out of which our conception of a person or of character emerges. There are many philosophical questions to be raised about such concepts as personal identity, moral responsibility, and freedom; but much of our lives involves the experience which gives rise to those questions. It is the centrality of such experience I want to make clear.

We can start with that form of life we can call blaming, judging, punishing. Here the legal philosopher is helpful, as he paradoxically claims "a right to punishment." This right "derives from a fundamental right to be treated as a person," and the denial of it implies "the denial of all moral rights and duties." Herbert Morris is opposing the logic (or, we might say, the grammar) of punishment to the logic of therapy: "In a system of punishment a person who has committed a crime may argue that what he did was right. We make him pay the price and we respect his right to retain the judgment he has made. A conception of pathology precludes this form of respect."[24] It is the common attention to and respect for intentions and choices that constitutes a society of persons. As H. L. A. Hart puts it, our law should "reflect in its judgments on human conduct distinctions which not only underlie morality, but pervade the whole of our social life. This it would fail to do if it treated men merely as alterable, predictable, curable or manipulable things." For this reason, Hart believes, "there will be a place for the principle of responsibility even when retributive and denunciatory ideas of punishment are dead."[25] (I shall return to this with an essay by P. F. Strawson in the chapter on George Eliot.)

A second form of life that may govern our thought creates the idea of personal identity through time. Some, like J. L. Mackie, would see this as an institution which is a condition of our thought rather than a consequence.[26] Others, like Richard Wollheim, distinguish between a formal unity which our lives necessarily and neutrally have and an "ideal unity" which we create and make normative. Wollheim provides a subtle account of how "mental connectedness" serves to create personal identity. He treats the pathology of memory: an earlier event may reenter the mind through memory with all its original vigor and without adaptation to the present self. This is, in effect, obsession, all of its original affective energy at work at every recurrence. Repression may provide its obverse, and a third instance of "undue influence of the past" is the transformation of memory into fantasy, which takes on "the character of another life." A person's life exhibits "pattern and wholeness," in contrast, as "the influence of the past . . . is neither excessive nor insufficient."

Wollheim takes autobiography as a literary model of this construction of personal identity. It is a "literary genre singularly dedicated to the notion of pattern in life or the ideal of wholeness," poised as it is "between the writing and the rewriting of a life." A life may be rewritten "so as to impart to that life a unity it never had—that is, malignly"—paranoia comes to mind, as in Miss Wade's "history of a self-tormentor" in Dickens's *Little Dorrit;* "or it may be rewritten benignly—that is, so as to achieve, even at a late hour, some reconciliation with the past." Wollheim sees in Freudian psychotherapy the opportunity for the memory to be "turned against" the misuse that was made of it; this is a process of "working-through." It would accord with the revised narrative of which Roy Schafer speaks, shared by therapist and patient. Wollheim sees us deriving these norms of an ideal self from "more primitive or elementary ways" of regarding feelings and desires, "coming to accept some and to reject others, to look upon some as belonging to us and others as external to us, to identify with some and to repress, to inhibit, to deny others."[27] This, as Freud recognized, can be a costly process, and Leo Bersani tries to mitigate those costs in literature. The costs, however, may not seem too high for the sense of identity and self-realization that they buy.

Finally, there is the form of life we call agency and embody in narrative action. Gombrich explains the Greeks' invention of illusionistic images by their departure from the dominance of "conceptual art" in order to meet the demands of narrative: "where the poet was given the licence to vary and embroider the myth and to dwell on the 'how' in the recital of epic events, the way was open for the visual artist to do likewise."[28] Frank Kermode has pursued this process in literary narrative. Where Gombrich observes that each narrative gives us "unintended information," Kermode writes of a parable that, "being a coherent narrative [it] says more than is strictly necessary" to make its point. Once these unnecessary details have been introduced, a resolute interpreter will try to give them relevance, to supply them with a full weight of meaning, which in turn will require a revised narrative. (I have raised this problem with a passage from *Bleak House* at the end of the previous chapter.) There follows a kind of leapfrogging pattern: "narrative begot character, and character begot new narrative. In the course of these developments, new gaps may be inevitable. This is how interpretation works in fiction." Or as Kermode puts it, as he discusses the figure of Pilate: the "story went in search of a character, and more narrative followed, to explain the character further." Kermode presents a fascinating account of the growth of Pilate from a function to a character, from a considerate judge to a "civilized debater," each stage of his growth affecting in turn the meaning of Jesus' trial.[29]

It is fair enough to say that as a character assumes several functions, the problem of making him plausibly consistent requires a further depth of representation. The complexity of novels comes not simply of their length and number of characters. It comes as much of the tension between meaning and representation, between event and idea. Even more, it comes of those tensions between resemblance and difference among characters. If characters are too symmetrically disposed about a simple principle of good and evil or life and death, they impoverish each other. If they are disposed in asymmetrical but still palpable relationships, they create questions about principle and arouse disturbances of feeling—and thereby give energy and life to events.

I should like to return briefly to the arguments of Leo Bersani. I have quoted the final words of A Future for Astyanax, where the dialectic of that book is given its fullest statement. The thrust of Bersani's argument is to release those kinds of intensity which are sacrificed to unified structures, whether of the self or of the work of fiction. He advances the possibility of "an esthetic and ethic of the fragmented self," which would enable us to "resist the appeal of that unity of personality assumed by all humanistic psychologies." I have tried to make a case for the different kinds and degrees of characterization the novel may create. But clearly Bersani is after something more, what he calls the "deconstruction of character."

This goes beyond the exploration of forces within the self and below the levels of consciousness that we can see in such novelists as D. H. Lawrence or Nathalie Sarraute. Bersani stresses the "discontinuous impulses" of "partial selves": "Desiring impulses no longer contained by conscience are perhaps even more ferocious than the vengeful desires sanctioned by conscience." In such episodic discontinuity there is "a greater movement *among* different forms of desire and of being than in a world of fixed character structures."[30]

There are two related problems in this. The first is the unity of the literary work. Unity is not a dominant concern in recent literary theory. There is a reaction against the doctrine of organic form—a romantic doctrine that was readily adapted (with frequent acknowledgment of Coleridge) to complexity of verbal processes and the precarious balance of attitudes. The value of unity, however, was precisely that it had been a prior condition from which a recognition of complexity could arise. To the extent that diverse experiences can be held together and made to comment upon each other, to shift between division and reconciliation, we have a work whose inclusiveness achieves a complex view of experience. Such a work converts experiences into an experience, diversity into complexity. It enables us to entertain at once what could hardly be brought together without the peculiar strength and clarity of artistic structures.

The second problem concerns the unity of the self. I think I can best discuss this through an instance of the work of art and its interpretation—through Richard Wollheim's account of Freud's interpretation of Michelangelo's *Moses*. We are asked by Freud to see the figure "not as being about to break out into rage, but as having checked a movement of anger. By seeing it as a study in suppressed action, that is self-mastery, we can also see it as a study in character and at the same time avoid any inconsistency with the compositional indications." As Wollheim observes, "Freud is to be seen, not simply as revealing to us the deepest layers of a particular representation, but as indicating how these layers, particularly the deepest of them, are revealed in the corresponding statue." Yet the revelation of character "cannot be unconstrained, otherwise it would cease to be of aesthetic interest. There must be some element in the work that at any rate slows down, or controls, the pace of revelation." [31]

The tension between feelings that we see in Moses' suppressed rage or checked anger would be like what Lessing regarded as a "fruitful moment," one which catches experience in the process of change or character in the strain of conflict. Clearly the "self-mastery" which Wollheim cites would be what Bersani wishes to undo. Yet we recognize a peculiar intensity in those moments of conflict and resolution which involve the whole range of our feelings, concerns, and beliefs. More than one level or dimension is elicited in such conflicts, and they often bring a complex sense of who we are and of what a self means. This is not to question Bersani's cultivation of discontinuous impulses. But it is to ask how totally discontinuous such impulses can be and how much their intensity may depend on the pressure (and the presence) of what they keep out. Great as may be the importance of recognizing and realizing (the moralist would say "indulging") the "fragmented self," can this provide an aesthetic or an ethic, as Bersani suggests? The problem is to distinguish fantasy from art, and Wollheim's remark about the need for constraints to slow down or control the pace of revelation seems to me of great cogency. Such constraints emerge in conflicts and tensions, which are perhaps the means of calling up aesthetic as well as ethical experience, whatever form they take.

5

The status of character in a novel is not unlike the status of words. Words acquire their meanings from the range of their use in our lives, and to say that words refer only to other words produces a startling effect of unreality. While words bring meanings to a text from their use outside it, they are often part as well of an intricate verbal structure. But if novels are verbal structures, they may also be structures of imagery and thematic pattern— the remarkable images of space, for example, in *Middlemarch*—which do not depend on the use of the same words from one instance to another. For we could not read at all if we could not read *through* words. They are not simply transparent, but they cannot be opaque. Transparency yields illusion and opacity play; as with words, so with characters, which become counters for play on another level. Every element in the novel, from the most abject article or expletive to the most complex character, draws its import and value from some degree of reference to or reminiscence of a world outside. The elements acquire new import and status from their use in a fictional work; but, while they do not denote as in literal assertions, their power of reference is essential to their nature.

Recent literary theory has come to prize the signifier at the expense of the signified, to dismember words so as to expose implications that lie hidden in syllables, to trace words (somewhat as the myth critic does characters) to their etymological archetypes, to discern in them the play of innumerable codes, none privileged more than others. This makes for a stress upon the autonomy of words that comes close to what Arthur Danto calls the Opaque Theory in painting, "the theory that the artwork is only the material it is made from; it is canvas and paper, ink and paint, words and noise, sounds and movements." Of a painting that "aspires to become identical with its own material counterpart," we can only speak "in a vocabulary of real discourse." But "the moment an artistic predicate is applied—such as 'has depth'—we have left the material correlate behind and are dealing with the work of art, which can no more be identified with matter than with content." [32] As Margaret Macdonald puts it, the character of Jane Austen's Emma is "not simply identical with the words by which she is created. Emma is a 'character.' As such, she can, in appropriate senses, be called charming, generous, foolish, and even 'lifelike.' No one could sensibly use these epithets of words." [33] A character is one of the institutional forms of fiction, and it is, as I have tried to show, a form that is closely related to the idea of a person—itself perhaps another institution—in life outside.

There is a shift in level of discourse as we move from the words of which characters are made to the institutional form of character itself. It is possible to produce either wit or confusion by moving between these levels. One may agree with William Gass that "literature is language, that stories and the places and the people in them are merely made of words"—but here I resist—"as chairs are made of smoothed sticks and sometimes of cloth or metal tubes." [34] It is precisely because words differ from wood and cloth that they can be used to produce stories. They have a sensory form and, having syntactical form as well, they can be used to build structures. But words also refer, and they refer at various levels of generality from image to concept. To say that "there are no descriptions in fiction, there are only constructions," is both true and misleading; it is true enough that "we do not have before us some real forest which we might feel ourselves free to render in any number of different ways" (pp. 17—18). But an imaginary forest may, like Marianne Moore's imaginary garden, contain real trees and toads. We can recognize choices the novelist has made because we have some sense of what real forests are, and, while we do not usually question the forest the novelist gives us, we can distinguish it easily enough from forests he might have given us.

"Characters in fiction," Gass observes, "are mostly empty canvas. I have known many who have passed through their stories without noses, or heads to hold them; others have lacked bodies altogether, exercised no natural functions . . . and apparently made love without the necessary organs" (p. 45). But they have not lacked bodies in the sense that we imagine them as dismembered. If the canvas is empty, that is because the image is in shadow or left indeterminate, not that the canvas has portions without paint. (Of course the painter may use bare canvas or paper as part of his structure, but that is not incompleteness or neglect.) So in life, when a conductor approaches us in the railway car, we don't look to see if he has legs. Fictional characters are only partially specified—as must be the case with anyone we consider, including ourselves. Without such limitation we could never apprehend them.

Yet character may embody what has not before quite existed because no structure has been built to contain just those features. Such a construction would puzzle us if we could not infer other features that might support them. "What is the shape of Achilles' nose? What color were his eyes? Achilles is what Achilles does; he has no secret wishes, secret dreams; he has no cautiously hidden insides" (p. 16). Odysseus can discover Achilles when he is disguised as a woman, but if he had found Achilles pregnant, we should really have "hidden insides." The character whom the novelist creates may behave as one who is concealing a secret wish. We know of it only as an inference from what he does, and we assume that what he does may have been invented by the novelist in order to lead us to make such an inference.

If the character is all verbal surface at one level, he is all implication and suggestion of human life on another.

At another point, Gass makes clear how our selective attention works in fiction as in life. "We do visualize, I suppose. Where did I leave my gloves? And then I ransack a room in my mind until I find them. But the room I ransack is abstract—a simple scheme. I leave out the drapes and the carpet, and I think of the room as a set of likely glove locations" (p. 42). If a room must provide glove locations at one point, purloined letter locations at another, evidence of affluence or vulgarity at another, its specification grows more solid with the variety of functions it serves, just as does a character's. For novels are structures in which we forge a sense of relevance as we move through them. It is not always clear which aspect of a setting or a character will be confirmed at a later moment or how many attributes will require a part in our conception of either.

This raises another issue, the one made familiar by the title of a well-known essay by L. C. Knights, "How Many Children Has Lady Macbeth?" Knights warned us against indulging in gratuitous fantasies about literary characters and imagining events in their lives that lie outside the world we are shown. The subject of Anna Jameson's work, the girlhood of Shakespeare's heroines, would be an instance of what Knights repudiates. Knights's emphasis is on the poetic structure of Shakespeare's plays, and that may suffer neglect to the extent that we treat characters as if they were simply persons.

A. D. Nuttall has written cogently on the problems raised by Knights. He restates Knights's argument as an objection to "the practice of drawing inferences from the unseen with respect to persons of the play." The ground for Knights's view, as Nuttall restates it, is close to Gass's remarks about the empty canvas:

> A real person . . . is liable to be doing things when we are not watching him. But with dramatic characters this is simply not the case. They are the true Berkeleian objects. Their *esse* is *percipi*. Their existence really does depend wholly upon their being perceived. It is illogical to ask whether Falstaff is *really* a coward since Falstaff is not *really* anything at all. Illusion is what he is made of.

To this Nuttall's reply is strong and decisive. Each moment of a drama requires that the audience make inferences, and if ever "audiences started refusing to do this, every drama ever written would grind to a halt."[35] The very fact that the dramatic representation is, by its nature, different from life requires that one infer how one is to take it, how to read its symbols and gestures. "A proper awareness of the real status of dramatic elements *presupposes* a readiness to make inferences about off-stage events." Nuttall draws

upon the work of Maurice Morgann and of John Bayley to get at the peculiar
energy of those characters that awaken our curiosity by their openness or
indeterminacy, their "special dimension of inferable identity," or what W.
J. Harvey calls "gratuitous life."

Nuttall argues that the characters which stimulate inference by making
us "feel there is more to be said" are also the characters that may seem the
most lifelike.

> By a curious irony this incompleteness, this want of finality in formulation
> achieves a greater naturalism than the most meticulous description. It is rather
> like the way in which a rough impressionist painting can bring one closer to
> the actual experience of looking at things on a sunny day than the most labo-
> riously exact Flemish painting. The truth is that one of the characteristics of
> real people as opposed to the common run of fictitious personages is that there
> is much more about them that we do not know. Shakespeare's characters fall
> into the category of real life. This is the truth behind all the figurative talk
> about Shakespeare giving us Nature herself, about the integrity and indepen-
> dence of his characters.

The incompleteness or want of finality that Nuttall cites is created not simply by the quantity of traits but by the puzzling or inconsistent nature of
those that are most conspicuous. The puzzles are like those ambiguous surfaces that force us to create a third dimension of depth in order to accommodate the elements in a new *Gestalt*. So, too, impressionist painting refracts
light into intense color but also reduces linear articulation: we seem to get
the immediacy of direct visual response without conceptual structures imposed upon it.

Nuttall's final point is that the openness of characters is one where "the
hints shade off into nothing and yet there seems to be much more of the
character to guess at. Here of course anyone's guess is as good as anyone
else's. We have strayed into the region of the utterly unverifiable." So while
"indefinite characterization certainly provokes a multitude of questions, it
simultaneously implies that those questions have no answers." Nuttall would
insist upon a point beyond which it is futile to pursue hints, where no discovery remains to be made because there is nothing more to discover. Such
pursuit can, nevertheless, "bring out vividly the way in which the original
is mysterious," and it remains valuable so long as it does not reduce the
mystery to the excessive lucidity of overreading (p. 119).

Dealing with similar issues, W. J. Harvey defended the kind of speculation and inference which show "a regard for and interest in a character, a
human being, as something more than a creation of language or a function
in the total context of the play." This is a recognition that a character, for
all the conventions of his literary life, may acquire some degree of autonomy.

Dickens or Tolstoy or Shakespeare often create a character more ample and suggestive than his functions seem to require. But that very "autonomy" may prove to be functional after all and transform an occasion from typicality to profundity. Such speculations, therefore, may, as Harvey suggests, "compose a large part of the character's reality for us" and may serve to constitute the drama that is implicit in its words.[36]

Critics have a tendency to underestimate the powers of the reader and to seek rather officiously to save him from dangers which may not be very threatening. Here the critic might be likened to the parent whose anxieties are based less upon present circumstances than upon his own memory of childhood and upon its traces of unresolved difficulties. One form of this underestimation is the fear that a reader who shows an interest in a character of any complexity must be irresistibly drawn into regarding the character as a real person. We all know innumerable cases—some I would hope our own—where the reader *has* taken a character as an alter ego or an ideal or model or possibly a scapegoat and has responded to the character without serious regard for the work which has called him forth. Something very much like this takes place in our encounters with actual people, and we can recognize a greater readiness for this kind of response at certain ages or in certain temperaments.

Fiction itself is full of instances of misreadings that lose sight of the conventional nature of fiction and take it as a form of vicarious life. The memory of such naive readings, of Emma Bovary at her convent school or Partridge at the play, seems to haunt some critics, as the memory of a debauch does a convert. Harvey is helpful in reminding us of the flexibility of awareness we can expect of readers: "We *do* lend imaginative belief in fiction, but at the same time we know it to be fiction" (p. 215).

This solicitude for the reader is a special form of a deeper and broader concern: the fear that we will take the world presented to us in fiction (or other works of art) as if it were a reliable image of reality. This is the problem of reification: man mistakes his own creations for something independent of him and submits unconsciously to the authority of fantasms of his own making. The problem has a history. Its formulation may derive ultimately from Hegel's dialectic, in which Spirit must alienate itself from itself and objectify itself in an outward form. But each objectification is penetrated by a new stage of consciousness, which in turn is the occasion for new objectification. This dialectical process by which the Spirit attains to ultimately absolute self-awareness is a historical one, and each stage of consciousness is an era.

Ludwig Feuerbach demystified Hegel's system by tracing the dialectical process as man's gradual realization that the God or Spirit who orders his world is a projection upon the universe (that is, an objectification) of his own powers. "The divine being is nothing else than the human being, or rather, the human nature purified, freed from the limits of the individual man, made objective—i.e. contemplated and revered as another, a distinct being." Feuerbach offers man a true humanism, a dispelling of mystery, and a release from the self-deceptions which have "objectified" his nature as an unapproachable deity. "To place anything in God, or to derive anything from God, is nothing more than to withdraw it from the test of reason, to institute it as indubitable, unassailable, sacred, without rendering an account *why*. Hence self-delusion, if not wicked, insidious design, is at the root of all efforts to establish morality, right, on theology." This "groundless arbitrariness" which we confer upon morality only conceals the "rational, just, human" morality which has "its ground of sacredness in itself." [37]

It is from this humanism that the early Marx departed. "Prometheus is the foremost saint and martyr in the philosophical calendar," he wrote in the preface to his doctoral dissertation. [38] In contrast to German Idealist philosophy, "which descends from heaven to earth," however, Marx chose "to ascend from earth to heaven," to "set out from real, active men" and study "the phantoms formed in the human brain" as "sublimates of their material life-process." [39] What concerned Marx was the alienation from himself that man feels in his daily work. As his products acquire a money-value or a status as commodities, man finds himself part of an impersonal system and the passive victim of economic laws beyond his understanding. Those projections that Feuerbach traced in man's religion, Marx saw at work in all of man's culture, as man loses the power "to recognize himself in a world he has himself made." An economic commodity is simply "labor congealed in an object," and with this objectification (or, as Marx later described it, the "fetishism of commodities") man becomes dehumanized. [40]

A romantic poet like Blake could call for a wakening to imaginative energy that would throw off these impositions upon its freedom. Marx had less trust in man's power to think his way out of the world of institutions and dogmas with which, in some ultimate sense, he had enslaved himself. For Marx at any rate all had to grow much worse before man could be exacerbated into the action that would free him. But it is the interim that concerns us.

As our economic life produces classes antagonistic to each other, our forms of thought become—as Marx saw it—the vehicles of interests we cannot recognize. Alienation from ourselves produces an opacity of motive, a screening of our real motives from our consciousness; we remain unaware of our ideological commitments and persuade ourselves that we are seeking truth. In a process that has been likened to the Freudian concept of rationalization, the "real motives impelling [man] remain unknown to him, [for] otherwise it would not be an ideological process at all. Hence he imagines false or apparent motives. Because it is a process of thought, he derives both its forms and its content from pure thought, either his own or that of his predecessors." Ideology becomes "pure thought": each new class is compelled to "represent its interest as the common interest of all the members of society." It "will give its ideas the form of universality, and represent them as the only rational, universally valid ones."[41]

It is here that the concerns of literary theory emerge; for recent Marxist and structuralist critics wish to free us of this ideological confusion. They try to make us see that the work of art is not a mere image or reflection or copy of nature. In trying to show wherein it may carry its own ideological import, critics have engaged in various kinds of analysis or "deconstruction." They wish to make us see the work of art as something "produced" by an author who must be partial, tendentious, ideological—without, of course, any necessary awareness that he is. Indeed, his conviction that he is rendering reality may be necessary to his art and will be perfectly sincere. It is our task to see his work as *his* and thereby to see it as the creation of a limited author, with his own commitments to one aspect of reality. As Raymond Williams observes, "real social relations are deeply embedded within the practice of writing itself, as well as in the relations within which writing is read. To write in different ways is to live in different ways. It is also to be read in different ways, in different relations, and often by different people" (p. 205). If we take into account the social constitution of the writer's self and of his symbolic universe, we may also recognize more fully the import of artistic creativity: "the capacity to embody and perform, a profound activation of what may be known but in these ways is radically known, in detail and substance; and then the rare capacity to articulate and to form, to make latencies actual and momentary insights permanent." The writer may be engaged in self-discovery or in "self-making."

What should, however, be recognized as well is that a work of fiction may well outlast its author's historical situation, and that it may lose whatever implicit alignment it once had. The ideological elements of a work of art tend to fall away in time; "the words of a dead man / Are modified in the guts of the living." The more timebound meanings prove of less interest, if in fact of any; and they must—if the work is to survive as more than an historical document—be transposed into new terms and relations, as Dante's world is transposed by a secular reader from doctrine to metaphor, from a spiritual to a moral reality.

Works of fiction, once created, have their own life. It is, of course, a life within social worlds and, so to speak, socialized minds. But the symbolic figures and conflicts, once created, have the power to stretch or complicate our awareness, to resist the limitations of our accustomed thought. Whether they have much efficacy until (as we say) their day has come and we can make clear transpositions to current issues will depend on the readers that encounter them and on the freedom those readers have to voice their response. What troubles me in much recent criticism is the readiness to embrace, and to make an assumption of, the belief that, since each of us has his unconscious alignment, the notion of "disinterestedness" is a bourgeois fiction, meant only to persuade us to accept ideological import without question or resistance. I believe that disinterestedness is a difficult virtue to attain, but I should not wish to resign the ambition of attaining it, much less deride the conception. For disinterestedness is something we seek in all the processes of the law and justice, and it is, after all, the virtue we must claim when we seek to demonstrate its absence.[42]

6

My argument may seem to have come full circle. If character is an invention, its artistic effect depends upon its reference—however abstract and formalized, celebrative or derisive—to persons as we know them in the world outside. I have earlier cited cubist paintings as one instance of the tensions we find in art; and I should like to return, through them, to the art of Cézanne. Michael Podro has written of the way Cézanne creates a sense of depth by his use of overlapping, varicolored brush strokes which induce some uncertainty as to how they should be read.

They may, for example, leave us "mentally hovering" between seeing one continuous object or two discrete ones separated in space. Effects like these "involve a constant sense of the actual painted surface of the canvas as a point of mental return":

> We are caught in immensely delicate and elusive suggestions of depth; and we
> are led back to the painted surface of the canvas partly because we are made so
> aware of our own perceptual activity, and partly because Cézanne constantly
> isolates and emphasizes planes parallel to the picture surface, and suggests con-
> tinuities between features as if they lay on such planes.

Podro sees cubism as reversing the tendencies that come to a counterpoise in Cézanne's balance "between, on the one hand, taking the picture surface for granted—assuming that looking into a picture we are to be carried into an illusion of depth—and on the other, sustained attention to the painted surface." Once the cubists have accomplished this reversal, "we are only occasionally or fragmentarily carried into an illusion and are constantly following the interlocking facets on the surface." The cubists leave behind Cézanne's concentration on the "observable world" and concentrate instead on the puzzles of perception, or as Podro puts it, "perceptual exhilaration within the technical procedures of painting."[43]

Any analogies must be imperfect and tentative, but we might see the verbal surface in fiction as the counterpart of the painted surface in Cézanne and the cubists. The verbal surface may be only the means of creating illusion, or it may claim attention and become the "point of mental return" from each movement into virtual time or space. The point I should want to draw from this analogy is that we soon become familiar with varying degrees of tension between surface and depth in painting or between formalization and representation in fiction. These may be degrees of realism, in narratives which include and require more or less of the information we would expect to receive about actual persons. (This can be made more vivid if we oppose the kinds of information we receive about epic heroes to those we receive about characters in realistic novels.) I have tried to emphasize the difference between our acquaintance with actual persons and our response to characters; but the difference is reduced as we compare *stories* about real people and works of fiction. As we read factual accounts we are often captivated by the implicit form they exhibit or the ease with which they lend themselves to fictional conventions. They are like *objets trouvés* or persons with great natural talent; they both confirm our artistic efforts with the testimony of nature and mock our labors to achieve what they so freely give. These prodigies of spontaneous form are remarkable for how much they achieve without art, but they are seldom if ever sources of great art in themselves. Still, they serve to warn us against creating an absolute distinction between fictional art and life, between characters and persons.

When Edgar Degas said that "the air of the old masters is totally unlike the air we breathe," he was insisting to the full upon the distinctive kind of coherence, of spatial sense and fall of light, in Titian or Rembrandt or in any work of art as opposed to the experience of actual life. Cézanne was, I think, as much aware of the distinction but was interested in more than epigram. He spoke of the need to develop at once both the eye, "through the outlook on nature," and the brain, "through the logic of organized sensations." When he showed his work to a visitor, "his fingers followed the limits of the various planes on the canvases. He showed exactly how far he had succeeded in suggesting the depth and [showed] where the solution had not yet been found; here the colors had remained color without becoming the expression of distance." [44]

To translate from one language to another is to come up against the imperfect match between systems which use different categories for experience and make different distinctions. Matisse wrote (in 1943) of the leaves that Claude and Poussin painted: "They have invented their own way of expressing those leaves. So cleverly that people say they have drawn in their trees leaf by leaf. It's just a manner of speaking: in fact they may have represented fifty leaves out of a total of two thousand. But the way they place the sign that represents a leaf multiplies the leaves in the spectator's mind so that he sees two thousand of them. . . . They had their personal language. Other people have learned that language since then, so that I have to find signs that are related to the quality of my own invention." Or he discusses the rendering of the body: "There are two sorts of artist . . . some who on each occasion paint the portrait of a hand, a new hand each time, Corot for instance, and the others who paint the sign-for-a-hand, like Delacroix. With signs you can compose freely and ornamentally. . . ." And finally Matisse wrote eloquently of the freedom which comes of mastery that is now second nature, so that the artifice is never in doubt but can be taken for granted: the artist places color "in accordance with a natural, unformulated, and completely concealed design that will spring directly from his feelings; that is what allowed Toulouse-Lautrec, at the end of his life, to exclaim, 'At last, I no longer know how to draw.' "[45]

I shall in the chapters which follow be talking much of the time about what characters think and feel. I shall not, I think, be confusing these characters with real persons, and I have no wish to induce that confusion in others. But these characters are, within the frame of their fictional world, no less than fictional persons. They have a clarity of definition and relationship that allows us to speak with more assurance and directness about their actions than about those of people. We could, of course, show wherein that clarity is given them by the tilt of emphasis and the coherence of structure that mark the novels wherein they live, move, and have their (virtual) being. I have chosen to talk about what novels come to mean more than about how they generate their meaning (although I hope to suggest that as well, if only by implication). I shall, to use Matisse's example, be talking about Claude's or Poussin's leaves more than about their calligraphy. But I think the two are inseparable and imply each other.

4 ✳ Austen:
Manners and Morals

Let us imagine a picture story in schematic pictures, and thus more like the narrative in a language than a series of realistic pictures. . . . Let us remember too that we don't have to translate such pictures into realistic ones in order to "understand" them, any more than we ever translate photographs or film pictures into coloured pictures, although black-and-white men or plants in reality would strike us as unspeakably strange and frightful.[1]

Jane Austen's novels present a world more schematic than we are accustomed to find in more recent fiction. The schematism arises in part from her "vocabulary of discrimination,"[2] those abstract words which classify actions in moral terms. Wittgenstein's remarks recall the adaptability of our responses, the readiness of our minds to discover how a literary work conveys its meanings and to make insensible adjustments to the forms its signs may take. Black-and-white photography can make discrminations and tonal gradations that cannot be achieved by color, just as, in another case, an engraving can define a structure through line that a painting renders with less precision in its fuller range of effects. Translation into a new medium or language sharpens our awareness of certain elements and of the functions they serve. Our initial question is to ask what Jane Austen's mode of fiction is designed to reveal.

Let us consider a passage in which Elinor and Marianne Dashwood accompany Lady Middleton to a party in London:

They arrived in due time at the place of destination, and as soon as the string of carriages before them would allow, alighted, ascended the stairs, heard their names announced from one landing-place to another in an audible voice, and entered a room splendidly lit up, quite full of company, and insufferably hot. When they had paid their tribute of politeness by curtseying to the lady of the house, they were permitted to mingle in the crowd, and take their share of the heat and inconvenience, to which their arrival must necessarily add.[3]

Much that might be shown is not. (One may think of the ball Emma Bovary
attends at Vaubyessard or the Moscow ball at which Kitty loses Vronsky to
Anna Karenina.) We trace the rituals of entry with the Dashwood sisters,
reaching the goal only to find it acutely oppressive. At this point the irony
becomes firmer and the diction more abstract ("their tribute of politeness")
as they observe the required forms, and are "permitted" to participate in the
mutual affliction that such a party too easily becomes. The pattern of the
experience, not least the ironic pattern of the final clause, takes the place of
particular detail.

Another ball is that held at the Crown in *Emma:*

> The ball proceeded pleasantly. The anxious cares, the incessant attentions of
> Mrs. Weston, were not thrown away. Every body seemed happy; and the praise
> of being a delightful ball, which is seldom bestowed till after a ball has ceased
> to be, was repeatedly given in the very beginning of the existence of this. Of
> very important, very recordable events, it was not more productive than such
> meetings usually are.   [38]

One can say of either scene that Jane Austen presents it for recognition rather
than seeks to imagine it anew. It is meant to recall a world we know or at
least know about, and there is little effort to catch its sensory qualities or
evoke it pictorially. Instead, we have, in John Bayley's words, "the negligent
authority of a world that is possessed without being contemplated."[4] It is
seen from the inside of its physical and moral structure. What Jane Austen
stresses in the first case is the tissue of ceremony and protocol that shrouds
an unpleasant reality. In the second, a scene of comparative informality where
all the guests are known to each other, we see the social machine run smoothly
and comfortably.

In a world of recognition, people are defined less by isolated features than
by their total address. We see characters in Jane Austen's novels as we see
many people in life, recognizing them as familiar but hardly able to enu-
merate their features. We may recognize a friend at a distance by stance or
gait, by the way he enters traffic or passes others on the street. The process
of recognition is composed of a series of small perceptions which, if their
combination is right, bring along a familiar total form. In some cases, a very
small number of perceptions (or, for the novelist, specifications) will serve.
Jane Austen's introduction of characters tends to stress qualities that are not
directly visible but will shape and account for the behavior that follows.

> The Musgroves, like their houses, were in a state of alteration, perhaps of
> improvement. The father and mother were in the old English style, and the
> young people in the new. Mr. and Mrs. Musgrove were a very good sort of
> people; friendly and hospitable, not much educated, and not at all elegant.

Their children had more modern minds and manners. There was a numerous family; but the only two grown up, excepting Charles, were Henrietta and Louisa, young ladies of nineteen and twenty, who had brought from a school at Exeter all the usual stock of accomplishments, and were now, like thousands of other young ladies, living to be fashionable, happy, and merry. Their dress had every advantage, their faces were rather pretty, their spirits extremely good, their manners unembarrassed and pleasant; they were of consequence at home, and favorites abroad.

Here Jane Austen provides us with representative members of a social class, its two generations exhibiting change without conflict. The Musgroves look toward modernity as warmly as Sir Walter Elliot retraces his lineage in his favorite book. The Musgroves are representative, even undistinguishable from most others of their age and class; yet happy, assured, comfortable in their world, all that Anne Elliot is not. In the sentences that follow, we have an explicit report of Anne's thoughts, but here too the author imposes her own ironic presence:

Anne always contemplated them as some of the happiest creatures of her acquaintance; but still, saved as we all are by some comfortable feeling of superiority from wishing for the possibility of exchange, she would not have given up her own more elegant and cultivated mind for all their enjoyments; and envied them nothing but that seemingly perfect good understanding and agreement together, that good-humoured mutual affection, of which she had known so little herself with either of her sisters.   [*Persuasion*, chap. 5]

We can be sure that the narrative voice supplies the characterization of Anne's mind, serving up, so to speak, the reasons for the superiority that Anne probably thinks she feels as mere difference.

We have so far considered a world given us for recognition but an action that is ingeniously directed toward a happy ending. We are never in serious doubt, as we read Jane Austen's novels, that they will take a comic form and find a bright resolution. There are countless indications of this as we read. They come from the narrative control, its brisk judgments and ironic asides, and the cool tone which in almost every case keeps us from that self-forgetful immersion in a scene that a literature of sentiment demands. There is only a small distance between a narrative voice that orders events pointedly, describing them in terms which are full of implicit judgment, and a voice that, becoming self-conscious, calls attention to the artifice of the whole narrative process.

The comic frame of these novels permits us to scrutinize the world they present with detachment and to observe its incongruities with great precision. It is in manners that Jane Austen's world exhibits greatest density, for manners are concrete, complex orderings, both personal and institutional. They are a language of gestures, for words too become gestures as they are used to sustain rapport. Such a language may become a self-sufficient system: polite questions that expect no answers, the small reciprocal courtesies of host and guest, or elder and younger; the protocol and management of deference. The code provides a way of formalizing conduct and of distancing feeling. We need not feel the less for giving our feeling an accepted form; yet of course we may, for the code of manners provides disguise as readily as expression.

The control that manners provide is made clear in *Emma*. All the company at Hartfield have been invited to spend an evening with the Westons at Randalls. John Knightley is outraged at the imposition:

> "here are we . . . setting forward voluntarily, without excuse, in defiance of the voice of nature, which tells man, in every thing given to his view or his feelings, to stay at home himself, and keep all under shelter that he can;—here are we setting forward to spend five dull hours in another man's house, with nothing to say or to hear that was not said and heard yesterday, and may not be said and heard again tomorrow." [13]

In contrast we have the effusive Mr. Elton:

> "This is quite the season indeed for friendly meetings. At Christmas every body invites their friends about them, and people think little of even the worst weather. I was snowed up at a friend's house once for a week. Nothing could be pleasanter. I went for only one night, and could not get away till that very day se'nnight."

We may shudder in behalf of Mr. Elton's friend and as much in behalf of John Knightley's hosts. But in fact both men must adjust to the social scene.

> Some change of countenance was necessary for each gentleman as they walked into Mrs. Weston's drawing-room;—Mr. Elton must compose his joyous looks, and Mr. John Knightley disperse his ill-humour. Mr. Elton must smile less, and Mr. John Knightley more, to fit them for the place.—Emma only might be as nature prompted, and shew herself just as happy as she was. To her, it was real enjoyment to be with the Westons. [14]

One could perhaps speak of John Knightley's initial attitude toward this society as "unregulated hatred," which undergoes regulation as he enters the drawing room. His charges are accurate enough so far as they go. Yet the standard of conversation upon such occasions need not be demanding; clearly the warmth of having "friends about them" (in Mr. Elton's words) is sufficient for most, and the conversation of friends may be an occasion, above all, for recognition and reaffirmation, for pleasures that are only incidentally registered in the words spoken. "The happiest conversation," Dr. Johnson once remarked, "is that of which nothing is distinctly remembered but a general effect of pleasing impression"; and elsewhere he spoke of it as "a calm quiet interchange of sentiments."[5]

While manners may be a self-sufficient code, at their most important they imply feelings and beliefs, moral attitudes which stand as their ultimate meaning and warrant. Both passion and principles are stable. When they change, the change is slow and massive. When they are in conflict, the conflict is sharp and convulsive. In the middle range, that of manners, change is frequent, less momentous, and less costly; we call it accommodation. To the extent that manners allow us to negotiate our claims with others, they become a system of behavior that restrains force and turns aggression into wit or some other gamelike form of combat.

So at least we may say of manners in the ideal sense. Yet Jane Austen's concern is not simply with good manners but with manners of all kinds, boorish, insolent, graceful, rigid, pompous, or easy. Manners have considerable suppleness and ambiguity. We may see in them a comic incongruity: the failure of behavior to realize intention, the use of the conventions of courtesy to express cold distaste or angry resentment. The novelist must always recognize the conflict between the code of a society and the code of moral principle; manners may become a code of socially acceptable immorality. David Lodge has stated the issue with admirable clarity:

> In brief, Jane Austen creates a world in which the social values which govern behaviour at Mansfield Park are highly prized . . . but only when they are informed by some moral order of value which transcends the social. . . .
>
> A code of behaviour which demands such a delicate adjustment of social and moral values is by no means easy to live up to. It demands a constant state of watchfulness and self-awareness on the part of the individual, who must not only reconcile the two scales of value in personal decisions, but, in the field of human relations, must contend with the fact that an attractive or unexceptionable social exterior can be deceptive.

Lodge provides us with two codes, one of terms that establish "an order of social or secular value" (for example, agreeable, correct, fit, harmony, peace, regularity) and another of terms that suggest "a more moral or spiritual order of value" (for example, conscience, duty, evil, principle, vice). The former code tends to assert "the submission of the individual to the group," the latter "the possibility of the individual having to go against the group." The two codes overlap; they are not "unambiguously distinguished or opposed," and their interpretation requires, therefore, considerable power of discrimination.[6]

There are, moreover, times when the moral, as much as the social, order can itself become a refuge from self-awareness. To live entirely by principle, as Mrs. Norris persuades herself she does, or as Fanny Price in a quite different way would like to do, may be almost as destructive as to remain oblivious of a moral order. What seems most important to Jane Austen is a mind that has range and stretch, an unconstricted consciousness that can make significant choices. This is not to suggest that Jane Austen's characters must engage in vice to know its import, nor is it to deny that Fanny Price, even when she is all but imprisoned in fears of doing wrong, earns our sympathy.

One of the most original and influential critics of Jane Austen was Lionel Trilling, and he was never sharper than in his discussion of the "chief offence" of *Mansfield Park* for the modern reader:

> This lies . . . in the affront it offers to an essential disposition of the modern mind, a settled and cherished habit of perception and judgment—our commitment to the dialectical mode of apprehending reality is outraged by the militant categorical certitude with which *Mansfield Park* discriminates between right and wrong. This disconcerts and discomfits us. It induces in us a species of anxiety. As how should it not? A work of art, notable for its complexity, devotes its energies, which we cannot doubt are of a very brilliant kind, to doing exactly the opposite of what we have learned to believe art ideally does and what we most love it for doing, which is to confirm the dialectical mode and mitigate the constraints of the categorical. *Mansfield Park* ruthlessly rejects the dialectical mode and seeks to impose the categorical constraints the more firmly upon us.[7]

There is often a moment, however, recognized only in retrospect, when a great "offence" becomes a new orthodoxy. We may have reached a moment—to judge by recent books on Jane Austen—when moral rigor has a renewed attraction, even a romantic appeal; and it is not to question the praise *Mansfield Park* has been given to see it as a telling symbol of what we may miss in our lives and prize all the more when we find it in a novel. The leech-gatherer of Wordsworth's poem appears on the moor just when the poet's delight has turned to despair, and the aged pedestrian has a meaning for the poet he hardly has for himself: "Such a figure, in such a place, a pious self-respecting, miserably infirm . . . Old Man telling such a tale!"[8]

If we are to disencumber Jane Austen of the role of moralist, we must distinguish between moral assertion and moral imagination. Let me present an instance from *Sense and Sensibility*. Mrs. Ferrars, who is an imperious and vain mother, fond of her least worthy children, disinherits her son Edward when he announces his intention to marry Lucy Steele. But Lucy breaks the engagement in order to marry the new heir, his brother Robert, and frees Edward in turn to marry Elinor Dashwood, whom he genuinely loves. Edward turns to his mother for forgiveness:

After a proper resistance on the part of Mrs. Ferrars, just so violent and so steady as to preserve her from that reproach which she always seemed fearful of incurring, the reproach of being too amiable, Edward was admitted to her presence, and pronounced to be again her son.

Her family had of late been exceedingly fluctuating. For many years of her life she had had two sons; but the crime and annihilation of Edward a few weeks ago, had robbed her of one; the similar annihilation of Robert had left her for a fortnight without any; and now, by the resuscitation of Edward, she had one again.

In spite of his being allowed once more to live, however, he did not feel the continuance of his existence secure, till he had revealed his present engagement; for the publication of that circumstance, he feared, might give a sudden turn to his constitution, and carry him off as rapidly as before.				[56]

In the first of these sentences we see a mock-rationale such as alone can explain Mrs. Ferrars's behavior in any terms but the true one, willfulness. In the second paragraph, the irrational vigor of that will is felt in the fluctuating fortunes of her family, as members in turn suffer "annihilation" and "resuscitation." And finally this fiction of her godlike power to crush and restore is assumed with literal mock-solemnity. The comic energy expands in the course of the passage: Mrs. Ferrars's fantasies are recognized as her reality, as well they may be, since her will is almost matched by her power; and the narrative quietly accepts her vision, by a method that is akin to free indirect discourse.

Clearly Jane Austen means us to see the tyranny and the failure of love, but these are too obvious to demand our full attention; they are the substratum upon which the fantastic edifice of will is erected, and the elaboration of that edifice commands our wonder. Or to change the metaphor, we can see the singular tenacity with which character is sustained, the formidable genius of the passions to find pretexts and saving illusions or, somehow, at any rate, to generate an idiom of respectability. We can see this even more in the brilliant second chapter of the novel, where John and Fanny Dashwood collaborate in casuistry. They pare away his obligations to his sisters ("related to him only by half blood, which she considered as no relationship at all"). They magnify the value of what they might surrender ("How could he answer it to himself to rob his child, and his only child too, of so large a sum?"). They reduce the claims of others upon them ("They will be much more able to give *you* something"). And at last they cultivate resentment to dissolve any obligation to fulfill his father's request ("Your father thought only of *them*"). The projected settlement of three thousand pounds contracts at last to officious advice and (perhaps) an occasional small gift. What is dazzling is not merely the selfishness of the Dashwoods, formidable as that is, but the brilliant efficiency and ease of their self-justification.

It is here that one sees Jane Austen's moral imagination shaping comic invention, as it so often had in Henry Fielding before her. For the progressive contraction of the Dashwoods' spirit is caught with that splendid assurance of movement we can see in Lady Booby's resolution to call back Joseph Andrews once she has dismissed him. The movement defeats all scruple with a splendid show of moral righteousness.

It is by such deftness that one can best identify comic movement. It eludes scruple just as it eludes physical obstacles; the comic decision has much in common with the comic chase in films; there is the same miraculous evasion of every blocking force, whether the strictures of reason or the traffic ahead. In the comic hero such movement becomes the deft avoidance of threatening intrigues, of blocking elders, of false rigidities and narrow conventions. In such fools as the Dashwoods or Mrs. Ferrars, the deftness lies in prompt obedience of their consciousness to their passion; and what it eludes is not a false restriction but the censorship of decency. So of Lucy Steele, the author writes that her intrigue and its success "may be held forth as a most encouraging instance of what an earnest, an unceasing attention to self-interest, however its progress may be apparently obstructed, will do in securing every advantage of fortune, with no other sacrifice than that of time and conscience" (61).

It may, of course, be said that Jane Austen uses her comic celebration of ingenious villainy as a way of insisting all the more, through ironic understatement, upon its evil. The hard egoism that makes these characters imperturbable provides a striking contrast to the vulnerability and pathos that both Elinor and Marianne at times exhibit. The moral insight which the irony evokes and reinforces lives deep in the conception of the novel and informs all its parts. Yet the insight is not what the novel seeks to create, but is rather that upon which it draws. Such comic characters as the John Dashwoods may be morally discredited, but they survive admirably. The novel rests not so much upon their satiric exposure as upon their comic performance.

We can see this most clearly in *Pride and Prejudice.* Whatever his deficiencies as a father, Mr. Bennet has a superb relish for folly; the fools, as Rachel Trickett observes, are "all funnier for his comments on them, and he thus sustains and increases the comic force." He plays Jaques, with all his "irresponsible detachment," to Elizabeth's Rosalind, and he sets off all the more Elizabeth's growth beyond detachment. "He sets the scale of criticism though he is criticized himself, and it is in the relation to him that we recognize the heroine's good sense and her real feelings."[9] We are struck with the continuity, at the close, of the comic pattern. Mrs. Bennet remains as she was at the outset, and this is "perhaps lucky for her husband, who might not have relished domestic felicity" if she were not "still occasionally nervous and invariably silly." Mr. Bennet has made his accommodation; and while he has missed the luxury of having Collins as a son-in-law, he can be content with the outrageous Wickham. The brief crisis of moral assertion and self-reproach has passed, and the Bennets are restored to the climate of comedy.

There may be an element of pathos in a comic character, as is the case with Miss Bates. Her compulsive talking awakens us to the narrow life that finds fulfillment in this kind of release. We need not keep in focus the emptiness that finds vicarious existence in gossip or the ardor for attachment that intensifies and distends each minute detail of commonplace encounters. In short, our sense of all the displaced feeling that floods into silly words does not overweigh the impression of their silliness, nor does our sense of motive distract our attention from the resourcefulness of the motive power, the alacrity with which all experience is translated into an obsessive idiom. We retain enough comic detachment for the most part to regard Miss Bates with amusement, and it is significant that our own surprise at her modest expression of pain after Emma's insult marks a shift in our awareness of Miss Bates somewhat as, through Knightley's comments, it marks an epoch in Emma's "development of self" (47).

For those who are themselves self-absorbed, such bores as Miss Bates may become very irksome. The attention they fail to give makes the attention they demand all the more troubling. Screened from others by their volubility, needing only the pretext of an audience, they yield little of what one feels is owed one; and for one with claims so large as Emma's, they represent a peculiar affront. So that we find Emma chafing under the strain, while Knightley is sufficiently his own man to be detached and liberal: he can endure the nonsense, see the pathos and warmth, and recollect above all the duties of consideration.

Miss Bates is a special case of the bores and fools we find throughout Jane Austen's novels. Some are aggressively sociable, like Sir John Middleton; others archly prying like his mother-in-law, Mrs. Jennings; some pretentious and alternately servile or smug like Collins, some oppressively rude and patronizing like Augusta Elton. What they all share is deficiency of awareness, indifference to others' feelings or privacy, obtuseness about their own motives. They tend to be great talkers, talking not so much for victory, like Dr. Johnson, as for survival; they retain their stable existence, their life of untroubled repetition, by blocking off reality with talk.

The comic limitations remain in those characters who are at once more plausible and treacherous. They seem, at first, to be of the very spirit of comedy themselves, for they are dedicated to play. And they help to remind us that Jane Austen's novels have themselves provided the materials of a game of allusions for generations of "Janeites." Games have every charm until they are used to displace broader awareness and deeper feelings. It is

this charm we see in such figures as Frank Churchill or the Crawfords. Frank
has "smooth, plausible manners," but he wins Mr. Knightley's criticism,
even before he arrives, for his failure to visit his father. Knightley's words
are like the more peremptory moral assertions that Jane Austen herself adopts
at times. Of Tom Bertram she writes, at the close of *Mansfield Park*, "He
became what he ought to be, useful to his father, steady and quiet, and not
living merely for himself" (462). So in *Emma*, she writes of Mrs. Weston:
"She was happy, she knew she was happy, and knew she ought to be happy"
(36). Knightley speaks in similar vein about Frank Churchill: " 'There is one
thing, Emma, which a man can always do, if he chuses, and this is, his duty;
not by manoeuvring and finessing, but by vigour and resolution. It is Frank
Churchill's duty to pay this attention to his father. He knows it to be so, by
his promises and messages; but if he wished to do it, it might be done' "
(18). Frank Churchill is essentially a young man who cannot resist "manoeuvring and finessing." His love of games comes out in his readiness to
foster Emma's unpleasant conjectures about Jane. Frank knows the truth and
cannot reveal it; but he gains enormous pleasure from helping Emma to
imagine scandal that permits her the comfort of superiority to Jane. Frank
in turn can enjoy his superiority to Emma: he is playing a game of his own
in which she participates unknowingly and to her ultimate shame. Even if
we credit his belief that Emma has guessed the truth, the game he thinks he
is playing with Emma and the game she, in her ignorance, thinks she is
playing with him are both of them little less shameful than the actual ones,
and we see their culmination at Box Hill. In fact, Knightley sees in Frank's
professed belief a further sign of his disingenuousness:

> "Always deceived in fact by his own wishes, and regardless of little besides his
> own convenience.—Fancying you to have fathomed his secret. Natural
> enough!—his own mind full of intrigue, that he should suspect it in others.—
> Mystery; Finesse—how they pervert the understanding! My Emma, does not
> every thing serve to prove more and more the beauty of truth and sincerity in
> all our dealings with each other?"   [51]

Emma, in her recovery, recognizes Frank's motives as all too much like her
own: "I am sure it was a source of high entertainment to you, to feel that
you were taking us all in. . . . I think there is a little likeness between us."
But what distinguishes Frank from Emma is his reluctance to give up the
game. As he dwells lovingly upon his memories of others' deception, Jane
says "in a conscious, low, but steady voice, 'How you can bear such recollec-
tions, is astonishing to me!—They *will* sometimes obtrude—but how you
can *court* them!' " (54)

Frank Churchill's games strike us as immature; they are games of exclusion and superiority. Henry Crawford's games are a more radical part of his

nature and far more painful in their consequences. As he is first introduced in *Mansfield Park* we learn of his lighthearted intention to make the Bertram sisters like him. "He did not want them to die of love; but with sense and temper which ought to have made him judge and feel better, he allowed himself great latitude on such points" (5). The Bertram sisters are "an amusement to his sated mind," but one feels that the satiation is as much with himself as with familiar pleasures. Henry's love of role-playing seems a search for distraction, from a self he indulges but hardly respects. The accounts that William gives of naval service fire Henry's fancy: the "glory of heroism, of usefulness, of exertion, of endurance, made his own habits of selfish indulgence appear in shameful contrast" (24). And later with Edmund he imagines himself a clergyman preaching, only to recognize shrewdly enough his need even in such a fancy to exercise power over an audience and to coerce an eager response. But it is significant that Henry reveals his unsteadiness and does so with no cynical pleasure. Fanny, once he has planned to win her heart, awakens in him a deeper purpose.

Henry has "moral taste enough" to respond to her sensibility and her capacity for feeling. His decision to make her his wife is in some sense what Shaftesbury saw in the awakening of taste, the beginning of an ascent from the aesthetic to the moral, from gallantry to a love of the Good.[10] These are large terms to bring to this text, but it seems clear that Henry Crawford would wish to be saved from a self that wearies him and to find a new order of life in marriage to Fanny. He had, we are told, "too much sense not to feel the worth of good principles in a wife, though he was too little accustomed to serious reflection to know them by their proper name"; and so, in his praise of her firmness of character, he has unknowingly "expressed what was inspired by the knowledge of her being well principled and religious" (294). There is considerable subtlety in this identification of an attraction that Henry Crawford feels but cannot recognize. His relapse is a failure not of consciousness but of will: "the temptation of immediate pleasure was too strong for a mind unused to make any sacrifice to right." Henry acts as he does with no love for Maria, and "without the smallest inconstancy of mind" toward Fanny, the one woman "whom he had rationally, as well as passionately loved" (48).

Henry Crawford's relapse is more interesting and moving than his sister's self-betrayal. Throughout the novel, Mary carries herself with great style, if not always with delicacy. She accepts her own outrageousness disarmingly: "Selfishness must always be forgiven, you know, because there is no hope of a cure," or, "Nothing ever fatigues me, but doing what I do not like." In a world where the worst are hypocritical and the best inhibited, this seems fresh and natural—except of course that it also seems calculated to gain its end. Mary is insincere only in assuming that sincerity alone—and it is often courageous—should acquit her. Her sincerity loses its spontaneity. As we hear it too often, it seems calculated. And it vanishes altogether in the painful exposure of that last "saucy playful smile" which seems held by the text as in a frozen film sequence, its futility turning to grimace.

There is a troubling moment at the close of *Mansfield Park*. Edmund has seen Mary's limitations and avowedly rejected her, but Fanny can see that the choice is not yet a firm resolve. At that moment, as if to administer a dose of truth that will cure or kill, Fanny tells him that the prospect of his brother's death and of his own inheritance may have restored him to eligibility in Mary's eyes (47). It is a cruel revelation but perhaps a necessary one. Edmund is seldom seen without irony during the last part of the book; and it is appropriate that by demanding Fanny as a confidante of his grief, he find himself in love with her. "She was of course only too good for him; but as nobody minds having what is too good for them, he was very steadily earnest in pursuit of the blessing." As for Fanny herself, she "must have been a happy creature in spite of all that she felt or thought she felt, for the distress of those around her" (48).

The larger irony that informs all of Jane Austen's comic art is a sense of human limitation. This is not a cynical vision; it may be affectionate enough, even a tribute to those feelings we value warmly. In *Sense and Sensibility* Elinor and Edward wait impatiently for the parsonage to be refurbished in time for their marriage: "after experiencing, as usual, a thousand disappointments and delays, from the unaccountable dilatoriness of the workmen, Elinor, as usual, broke through the first positive resolution of not marrying till every thing was ready" (50). The use of "as usual" catches the typicality both of their situation and of Elinor's decision. That they sense their situation as unique is equally clear; they are understandably self-absorbed and impatient with workmen who seem, through some strange indifference, "unaccountably" dilatory. There is gentle amusement with the irrationality, so little typical of Elinor but so generally typical of brides. One is reminded of Gibbon's account of his parents' marriage: "Such is the beginning of a love tale at Babylon or at Putney," or even more of his account of his own coming to an awareness of love: "it less properly belongs to the memoirs of an individual than to the natural history of the species."

Jane Austen constantly insists upon the limitations of our feelings. Does Henry Tilney love Catherine Morland? Yes, but the narrator "must confess that his affection originated in nothing better than gratitude; or, in other words, that a persuasion of her partiality for him had been the only cause of giving her a serious thought. It is a new circumstance in romance . . . and dreadfully derogatory of an heroine's dignity" (30). Is Willoughby a rake? No, he genuinely loves Marianne. "But that he was for ever inconsolable, that he fled from society, or contracted an habitual gloom of temper, or died of a broken heart, must not be depended on—for he did neither. He lived to exert, and frequently to enjoy himself" (50). So, too, Henry Crawford might well have won Fanny Price's love, for "her influence over him had already given him some influence over her" (48). And Colonel Brandon wins all of Marianne's love in time, for Marianne "could never love by halves" (50). The endings of the novels insist upon the capacity for self-repair and recovery; they provide the consolation of the finite for those who are easily deluded. Mrs. Grant's words to Mary Crawford on marriage are apt: " 'You see the evil, but you do not see the consolation. There will be little rubs and disappointments every where, and we are all apt to expect too much; but then, if one scheme of happiness fails, human nature turns to another; if the first calculation is wrong, we make a second better; we find comfort some-where' " (5).

"I purposely abstain from dates," we read at the close of *Mansfield Park,* "that every one may be at liberty to fix their own, aware that the cure of unconquerable passions, and the transfer of unchanging attachments, must vary much as to time in different people.—I only intreat every body to believe that exactly at the time when it was quite natural that it should be so, and not a week earlier, Edmund did cease to care about Miss Crawford, and became as anxious to marry Fanny, as Fanny herself could desire" (48).

This pleasure in human absurdity gives us, in Charles Lamb's words, "all that neutral ground of character, which stood between vice and virtue; or which in fact was indifferent to neither, where neither properly was called in question; that happy breathing-place from the burthen of a perpetual moral questioning"; it allows us to "take an airing beyond the diocese of the strict conscience." [11] It is one thing to see men and women as fallible, another to insist that they are corrigible. If nature can be trusted to correct what men cannot, if man is never quite so good or evil as he intends or imagines, we are freed of the stringency of the moral passions, which, as Lionel Trilling has remarked, can be "even more willful and imperious and impatient than the self-seeking passions." Our moral judgments are at once necessary and dangerous; they exercise our deepest passions, but they terminate our free awareness. The commitment they require brings an end to exploration and openness. In that sense, among others, the moral passions are "not only liberating, but also restrictive," and the subtlest task of "moral realism" is "the perception of the dangers of the moral life itself." It is the sense of the problematic that we must preserve, a sense of the difficulty of such judg-ments, of their cost and of the dubious gratification they often provide. [12]

The comic sense is compatible with moral imagination if not moral pas-sion; its awareness of limitation need not provide a surrender of all judg-ment, and in fact the idea of limitation is itself a judgment. Yet it is also a recognition that the moral passions cannot trespass beyond certain limits.

The effort to sustain moral consciousness at the same level of intensity in all our experience becomes a form of destructive anxiety. We may sense the consequences of the imperceptible choice and insist upon the fact of choice; yet we cannot always be bringing scruple and moral vigilance to each gesture of our lives or even, easier though it may prove, of the lives of others. There is at last a residual innocence we must grant to experience, a power to absorb us, to awaken curiosity, to claim our attention and affections with simple immediacy. We can see this best in the detached and free observation an otherwise busy mind like Emma's can achieve on the village street:

> Harriet, tempted by every thing and swayed by half a word, was always very long at a purchase; and while she was still hanging over muslins and changing her mind, Emma went to the door for amusement.—Much could not be hoped from the traffic of even the busiest part of Highbury;—Mr. Perry walking hastily by, Mr. William Cox letting himself in at the office door, Mr. Cole's carriage horses returning from exercise, or a stray letter-boy on an obstinate mule, were the liveliest objects she could presume to expect; and when her eyes fell only on the butcher with his tray, a tidy old woman travelling homewards from shop with her full basket, two curs quarrelling over a dirty bone, and a string of dawdling children round the baker's little bow-window eyeing the gingerbread, she knew she had no reason to complain, and was amused enough; quite enough still to stand at the door. A mind lively and at ease, can do with seeing nothing, and can see nothing that does not answer.   [27]

It is not often, however, that we find Emma's mind both "lively" and "at ease." Its liveliness is usually a form of "eagerness" or self-assertion, such as we find in different ways in Marianne Dashwood or in Mary Crawford, to whom Edmund Bertram would grant the "rights of a lively mind." This "eagerness" betrays impatience with the limits of the actual: it may take the form of a wishful shaping of reality with self-gratifying fantasy or (in the case of Mary) more deliberate cultivation of outrageous assertions as much for their effect as for their partial truth. Those who are fully "at ease" may achieve something of what Wordsworth celebrated as a "wise passiveness," that is, an openness to experience that restrains the shaping will and allows oneself to be confronted by whatever is unpredictably there. We may see this receptiveness as opposed to both the moral passions and the self-seeking passions, for in both we find a closing of the mind to the variety of experience, an assumption of superiority, whether in the name of principle or in the name of wit. Marianne's impatience with the vulgarity of Mrs. Jennings, Mary Crawford's impatience with the dull conventionalities of the pious, and Emma's impatience with Miss Bates have this much in common.

Once Emma has been reproached by Mr. Knightley for being so "unfeel-ing" and "insolent" in her wit, she begins to be freed of the force of self-seeking passions and to undergo a true "development of self." By the time she is ready to receive Knightley's proposal, she has achieved something like the receptiveness Wordsworth celebrated: "Never had the exquisite sight, smell, sensation of nature, tranquil, warm, and brilliant after a storm, been more attractive to her. She longed for the serenity they might gradually introduce" (49). Not the least significant word in that passage is "gradually." We think of Anne Elliot's walk to Winthrop: "where the ploughs at work, and the fresh-made path spoke the farmer, counteracting the sweets of poetical despondence, and meaning to have spring again" (10).

The Recessive Heroines

It is frequently the fate of Jane Austen's heroines to come to a moment of self-understanding which is also the recognition of their mistreatment of others. Some of her heroines, however, require no alteration. What happens to them, instead, is that they are finally acknowledged by others to have deep feelings of their own. The turning point for these heroines is one of justification rather than exposure and correction. It is a movement from virtual invisibility to the esteem and affection of others. Elinor Dashwood and Fanny Price are two of the heroines who emerge only slowly into the awareness of others (Anne Elliot would be a third), and it is to their role in the novels that I should like to return.

One may approach *Sense and Sensibility* through the antitheses of Pope. In the *Essay on Criticism,* Pope tries to hold together the traditionally opposed faculties of Wit and Judgment. The two faculties, therefore, must work together, the one animating, the other deliberate; the one productive, the other selective; the one ready to generate luxuriant growth, the other seeking to shape and govern.

> For Wit and Judgment often are at strife,
> Tho' meant each other's Aid, like Man and Wife.

Again, we may see this union as a proper weighting of the two elements, so that one does not tyrannize over the other:

> As Shades more sweetly recommend the Light,
> So modest Plainness sets off sprightly Wit:
> For Works may have more Wit than does 'em good,
> As Bodies perish through Excess of Blood.

Pope is concerned with the tension of contraries and the surprising ways in which opposites may be reconciled. In a couplet he later discarded, he wrote of the need for art even in disorder:

But Care in Poetry must still be had,
It asks Discretion ev'n in running Mad.[13]

It is upon some such union of powers that Jane Austen seems to base *Sense and Sensibility.* To Elinor are given strong feelings and the will to govern them, cool judgment that consults the common advantage, objectivity and prudence that arise in part from her affection for those who have all but relinquished responsibility for themselves. To Mrs. Dashwood and Marianne are given "eagerness of mind" that can become exquisite self-torment. The mother is the more limited and naive; the daughter the more capable and willful. And mother and daughter together produce a cycle of sentimental indulgence: they will their grief, foster it, revive it anew when the occasion has begun to fade. In contrast to the luxury of sensibility is the effort of exertion; in contrast to the withdrawal into self-enclosed feeling is the movement outward to meet and perhaps master the world.

The contrast is a typical one in Jane Austen's novels: the sentimental imagination projects a world of feeling which the self may then passively enjoy. All it encounters must submit to the forms of that world. Marianne can love Willoughby because he adroitly echoes her sentiments and gives her back the sensibility she esteems in herself. Mrs. Dashwood favors herself in the daughter who resembles her, and she imposes upon Elinor the burden of exertion for all of them. With the burden comes the stigma of being fit for the practical efforts of the unimpassioned. In this novel Jane Austen has split apart in the two sisters those aspects of the self she more often combines in a single heroine, and the novel has a dialectical clarity that is less schematic in her later books.

If Elinor seems excessively self-effacing, we must remember how little she is encouraged to be anything else and how great is the burden of prudence that is foisted upon her by others. Only when Marianne achieves a stable and self-sustaining balance within herself is Elinor freed from the exertion that must always subdue the expression of her private feelings. This exertion also saves Elinor from the destructive power of undivided feeling; unlike Marianne she can lose herself in the problems or needs of others. This pattern of contrast anticipates what happens in *Emma.* Only with the surrender of self-pleasing fantasies is the other self allowed to come into its own; when Emma can relinquish the world of sentimental imagination, the actual world is given back to her in all its vitality and sufficiency. In contrast to the development of Marianne Dashwood or Emma Woodhouse is the contrary movement we see in Elinor Dashwood or later in Anne Elliot: "She had been forced into prudence in her youth, she learned romance as she grew older: the natural sequel of an unnatural beginning" (4).

Through much of the novel Marianne is a heroine of authenticity. Restraint appears to her "not merely an unnecessary effort but a disgraceful subjection of reason to commonplace and mistaken notions." What for Elinor are the costly but necessary "forms of worldly propriety"—those manners in which principles find expression—become for Marianne merely the "commonplace notion of decorum," the imposition of mediocre minds and stultified feelings. If there had been "any real impropriety in what I did," she exclaims, "I should have been sensible of it at the time, for we always know when we are acting wrong" (13). She is not the first to throw back criticism as if it were a counsel of hypocrisy: "I have often been open and sincere where I ought to have been reserved, spiritless, dull, and deceitful" (10).

If Marianne is the heroine of authenticity, Elinor is the victim. When Willoughby leaves without explanation, Elinor thinks "with the tenderest compassion of that violent sorrow which Marianne was in all probability not merely giving way to as a relief but feeding and encouraging as a duty." The compassion and the shrewd judgment are compatible enough, but for Elinor to raise even a question about Willoughby's intentions wins her mother's immediate reproach: "You, Elinor, who love to doubt where you can—it will not satisfy you, I know." Or again: "Oh! Elinor, how incomprehensible are your feelings! You had rather take evil upon credit than good. You had rather look out for misery for Marianne and guilt for poor Willoughby than for an apology for the latter" (15).

Stuart Tave has argued persuasively that Elinor is the true heroine of the novel, that it is her story more than Marianne's, and that her feelings are deeper and stronger.[14] We are frequently told, but with deliberately understated emphasis, that Elinor's sufferings are almost as great as Marianne's; and one of the strongest tributes to Elinor's feeling is the account of the joy she feels at the signs of her sister's recovery: "Marianne restored to life, health, friends, and to her doting mother was an idea to fill her heart with sensations of exquisite comfort and expand it with fervent gratitude; but it led to no outward demonstrations of joy, no words, no smiles. All within Elinor's breast was satisfaction, silent and strong" (43). And so she continues at Marianne's bedside, "calming every fear, satisfying every inquiry of her enfeebled spirits, supplying every succour, and watching almost every look and breath." Within her family, her powers of control and clear intelligence only bring the demand for further exertions on behalf of others. In her love of Edward Ferrars, she is thrust into the position of having to receive without apparent emotion Lucy Steele's malicious confidences about her engagement to Edward. Elinor never doubts Edward Ferrars's love for herself; she is realistic enough to trust her feelings. "His affection was all her own. She could not be deceived in that." But she can pity him for his entrapment by someone "illiterate, artful, and selfish." And she can recognize that his bond is not for him to break. She faces, therefore, "the extinction of all her dearest hopes," but she cannot confide her grief to her mother or her sister or endure the uncontrolled emotions with which they would receive her news (23).

In all aspects of her life Elinor is called upon for exertions of a heroic order; she must sustain the lives of others without allowing her efforts to become visible. In fact, one can almost say that Elinor is herself scarcely visible to others except as they require her support and service; what they cannot see is the depth of feeling she possesses. This neglect of Elinor's claim to be a real and independent person is very much like the neglect we see by the egotists of the daily goodness of life, of that round of duties and affections that finds its reward in the fulfillment it brings. When Edward Ferrars discusses with Marianne the claims of the picturesque, he teases her by opposing to the aesthetic pleasures of irregularity the moral claim of the quotidian and homely: "I do not like ruined, tattered cottages. . . . I have more pleasure in a snug farmhouse than a watch-tower, and a troop of tidy, happy villagers please me better than the finest banditti in the world." Such views might seem complacent and philistine if they were not mockingly asserted in defiance of fashion and of that assumption of superiority that fashion supports. Marianne "looked with amazement at Edward, with compassion at her sister. Elinor only laughed" (18). But what Edward is espousing on a small scale is what Pemberley or Donwell Abbey might stand for in opposition to the improvements of Sotherton. Or one may take the contrast from Sir Walter Scott's article on Jane Austen: "Upon the whole, the turn of this author's novels bears the same relation to that of the sentimental and romantic cast, that cornfields and cottages and meadows bear to the highly adorned grounds of a show mansion, or the rugged sublimities of a mountain landscape."[15]

Perhaps the most remarkable scene in *Sense and Sensibility* is that in which Willoughby tells his story to Elinor. When Willoughby comes, hoping to save Marianne's life by his confession, Marianne is already out of danger. Elinor can hear him out, then, without the anxiety and anger she would have felt earlier. But Elinor hears him with reluctance. She sees in him now not merely the man who has driven Marianne to a dangerous extreme of grief, but also the seducer of Eliza Williams, Colonel Brandon's ward. Willoughby, as Brandon says, has "done that which no man who *can* feel for another would"; but even Brandon could believe at one time that Marianne's influence "might yet reclaim him." To an extent it has: Willoughby can plausibly claim that the vanity which he first exercised in trying to win Marianne's love has come to be replaced by sincere devotion. As sincere as Willoughby can have. It is only after he has achieved the security of a wealthy marriage that he allows himself to look back with full remorse. The anguish he felt in deceiving Marianne is by now a source of comfort to him, an assurance that he was capable of genuine love. He has come to give that message to Marianne: that he *was* capable of genuine love and felt it deeply.

But he also seeks absolving pity from Elinor: "Am I—be it only one degree—am I less guilty in your opinion than I was before?" And of course he is, for his motives have been more muddled and shabby than could have been supposed, although he could hardly have inflicted more suffering with a worse heart (44). And for Elinor, in turn, when the occasion for judgment has passed and she can hardly reproach Willoughby more than he has himself, there is a reflux of pity. She can see him as spoiled by an early independence, a man with a considerable talent for destruction, with himself a principal victim. She knows that it is irrational to revive such feelings now, but they are a tribute to the charm he can still exercise: "by that person of uncommon attraction, that open, affectionate, and lively manner which it was no merit to possess, and by that still ardent love for Marianne, which it was not even innocent to indulge" (45). This mixture of sentiments is the furthest that Elinor moves toward sharing Marianne's sensibility.

Lionel Trilling saw "no more momentous scene in English fiction than that in which Marianne Dashwood's alienated spirit, her hope of making a wild dedication of herself to unpathed waters, undreamed shores, is justified by the sudden sympathy and even admiration which her dutiful sister Elinor gives to the distraught consciousness of Marianne's lover, the faithless and destructive Willoughby." For, Trilling observed, "the archaic ethos" in Jane Austen's novels is typically "in love with the consciousness that seeks to subvert it."[16] Mr. Knightley and Emma Woodhouse are a telling instance of that love, of the wedding, in Pope's terms, of "fixed principles" with "fancy ever new."

I am inclined to stress as much the new freedom of feeling which Elinor can enjoy once she has been relieved of her task as guardian. She can now entertain a fuller sense of what Marianne must have felt than she could allow herself to feel at the time. There is something theatrical and shallow about Willoughby that she overlooks under the stress of his remorse and the emergence of his sincerity. Elinor "now realizes that she would not but have heard his vindication for the world, and now blamed, now acquitted herself for having judged him so harshly before." Later, in the presence of others, Elinor can allow herself a more imaginative and persuasive vision of what might have come of his marriage to Marianne. Would they have been happy? "He would then have suffered under the pecuniary distresses which, because they are removed, he now reckons as nothing" (47).[17]

The author is somewhat more dry and reserved before the novel ends. There is no reason to doubt Willoughby's sincerity, but there may be some reason to doubt the depth of his self-awareness. "His wife was not always out of humour, nor his home always uncomfortable; and in his breed of horses and dogs, and in sporting of every kind, he found no inconsiderable degree of domestic felicity" (5). And perhaps the same may be said of Marianne, who with "no sentiment superior to strong esteem and lively principles" becomes Colonel Brandon's wife. She must surrender the flattering image of becoming a "sacrifice to an irresistible passion" and even of devoting herself to "retirement and study." She descends from a "heroine" to a wife, and in the process, we may feel, comes to maturity of feeling. For Jane Austen, as for Wordsworth's stoic, "the Gods approve / The depth, and not the tumult of the soul."

The peculiar solitude of Fanny Price lies not simply in the neglect by others of her feelings and needs. It lies as well in her inability to acknowledge her feelings openly. We see this in her early homesickness, which she fears is ungrateful; in her reluctance to ask Sir Thomas questions about his travels lest she seem to preempt the place of his daughters; in her difficulty in criticizing Mary Crawford lest she indulge (and betray) her jealousy; in the central fact that she can never speak of her love for Edmund, even when she is courted by Henry Crawford. Confirmed and encouraged in moral principles by Edmund, she must try to maintain them alone while he accommodates them to his love for Mary Crawford. Fanny is left the solitary rigorist, insisting awkwardly and gracelessly upon principles that others compromise and, what is almost worse, continue to profess in their pursuit of self-indulgence. Edmund, Sir Thomas, and Mrs. Norris are the other spokesmen of principle—Edmund blinded to his own negligence, Sir Thomas all too often persuaded that his interest must accord with principle, Mrs. Norris the *reductio ad absurdum* of low-minded greed and high-toned viciousness. In such company, Fanny's protestations have a ring, not of hypocrisy— for she is sincere enough—but of naive and inflexible solemnity.

When Sir Thomas returns during the theatricals, he is hurt by the behavior of his children; but he imposes once more an atmosphere "all sameness and gloom." Fanny points out in his defense, there "was never much laughing in his presence." If their evenings had never been merry, that is the fate, she suggests, of all young people "when those they look up to are at home" (21). While Edmund accepts this observation, we need not. After the ball at which she comes out, radiantly happy, Fanny begins to be struck by the lack of animation at Mansfield Park: "Last night it had been hope and smiles, bustle and motion, noise and brilliance in the drawing-room, and every where. Now it was languor, and all but solitude" (29). Mansfield Park is not an image of ideal social order; it is not the Pemberley that Elizabeth and Darcy will create, nor the Donwell Abbey of Emma and Knightley. By the close of the novel the "timid, anxious, and doubting" Fanny has been replaced by Susan, whose "more fearless disposition and happier nerves made everything easy to her there.—With quickness in understanding the tempers of those she had to deal with, and no natural timidity to restrain any consequent wishes, she was soon welcome, and useful to all" (48).

Jane Austen's creation of a heroine so fearful and self-distrustful as Fanny should not, I think, be taken as a celebration of those traits. Fanny, like Elinor or Anne Elliot, embodies the daily, simple goodness that the witty and ingenious tend to overlook but may, as is the case with Henry Crawford, come to find strangely affecting. Fanny embodies it in a form that is both touching and amusing. She can never become conscious of anger or jealousy without a guilty effort at once to control and suppress it. She clings rather desperately to principles that Edmund has helped to inculcate, principles which he in turn seems to set aside or to apply with greater laxity as he comes under the influence of Mary Crawford. Much of the novel presents Fanny maintaining principles she has learned from Edmund, but hesitating to invoke what he neglects, "lest it should appear like ill-nature."

Fanny is often rigid in holding to principles, reluctant to admit the value of mixed motives. When Mary Crawford suggests that Edmund's clerical vocation may have been affected by the knowledge that there was a "very good living" kept for him, he responds with amusement, "which you suppose has biassed me." Fanny at once cries, "But *that* I am sure it has not." Edmund, in part out of affection for Mary, is more circumspect and more ready to admit the possibility: "The knowing that there was such a provision for me, probably did bias me." It is not wrong, he concludes, so long as he has not chosen for interest against his inclination (11).

Fanny's expostulations on the wonders of nature and of man do credit to her earnestness and her observation, but they are familiar to a degree that only one so unpracticed as Fanny would fail to realize.[18] Mary Crawford may be no more original (although she clearly means to be and thinks that she is), but her mind can play with more boldness. She does not achieve the elevation of Fanny's sentiment, for she has no taste for an experience at once so humbling and transcendent as the sublime. If she often seeks to shock or amuse, she sounds at any rate like herself. One feels that Fanny always tries to feel as she thinks she "ought" (of Henry Crawford she exclaims, "No, he can feel nothing as he ought") whereas Mary enjoys the liberties of the unpretentious, the downright, even the cynical—most of all, the spontaneous. Mary expects her confessions to be discounted as wit or accepted as charm; Fanny, who is always sincere, seems afraid of what she finds in herself, always on the watch for a passion to correct.

We tend to feel that Mary is better than she claims, and that in contrast Fanny is rather morbidly self-distrustful. When Fanny faces up to the presumption she has shown in nursing her love for Edmund, she is hard upon herself:

Why did such an idea occur to her even enough to be reprobated and forbidden? It ought not to have touched on the confines of her imagination. She would endeavor to be rational, and to deserve the right of judging of Miss Crawford's character and the privilege of true solicitude for him by a sound intellect and an honest heart.

What seems unfortunate in this passage of free indirect discourse is that Fanny seems to wish to earn the right to judge Mary, as if that were somehow a reward or at least a consolation for virtue. That is not, surely, what she thinks she means. And the author draws back into a longer comic vision to mitigate Fanny's severity with herself:

> She had all the heroism of principle, and was determined to do her duty; but having also many of the feelings of youth and nature, let her not be much wondered at if, after making all these good resolutions on the side of self-government, she seized the scrap of paper on which Edmund had begun writing to her, as a treasure beyond all her hopes. . . . There was a felicity in the flow of the first four words, in the arrangement of "My very dear Fanny," which she could have looked at for ever.
>
> Having regulated her thoughts and comforted her feelings by this happy mixture of reason and weakness, she was able, in due time, to go down and resume her usual employments. . . .   [27]

"This happy mixture of reason and weakness" is a more generous judgment than Fanny can allow herself, and it is at the very center of Jane Austen's comic vision. The "heroism of principle" is a genuine aspiration; it only requires more of Fanny than even she can attain, and she is touching as well as naive in her dedication. The "happy mixture" of motives saves us from ourselves, grants our humanity its less-than-heroic complexity, and allows us the grace of inattention or innocence by which to sustain this mixture.

So later Fanny recalls that Edmund and Mary Crawford have had differences: "They had talked—and they had been silent—he had reasoned—she had ridiculed—and they had parted at last with mutual vexation. Fanny, not able to refrain entirely from observing them, had seen enough to be tolerably satisfied." But surely this last is not Fanny's view of herself; the author has reverted to her own view, from outside the frame. But has she? Who is entertaining the thoughts of the next two sentences? "It was barbarous to be happy when Edmund was suffering. Yet some happiness must and would arise, from the very conviction that he did suffer" (28). The author moves in and out of Fanny's mind and idiom. There is not enough space, one might say, in Fanny's heroic but narrow morality, and the author must include it in the larger, more generous, vision of comedy. Comedy, not satire: the mockery is not turned upon Fanny's morality but upon the tense, vigilant heroism which might crack and shatter if it were not for the mitigation of unacknowledged pleasures.

The irony becomes more delicate in a later passage, where Fanny receives the news of the sinful flight of Maria Rushworth with Henry Crawford. Fanny is in a state of sleepless misery, "shudderings of horror," and fits of fever and chills. Here the free indirect discourse catches her view of the action, and we feel in her idiom a stretching to do justice to the moral shock she feels:

> A woman married only six months ago, a man professing himself devoted, even *engaged*, to another—that other her near relation—the whole family, both families connected as they were by tie upon tie, all friends, all intimate together!—it was too horrible a confusion of guilt, too gross a complication of evil, for human nature, not in a state of utter barbarism, to be capable of!—yet her judgment told her it was so.

One may recognize Fanny's attempt to separate out the infamy of the act from its injury to herself—"that other"—and to see it as a test of all we mean by "human nature." There is nothing to mock here, but there may be some degree of suggestion that Fanny's terms of unexampled horror are such as could accommodate more terrible events. So, too, when she imagines the effect of this upon the Bertrams, her language swells:

> Sir Thomas's parental solicitude, and high sense of honour and decorum, Edmund's upright principles, unsuspicious temper, and genuine strength of feeling, made her think it scarcely possible for them to support life and reason under such disgrace; and it appeared to her, that as far as this world alone was concerned, the greatest blessing to every one of kindred with Mrs. Rushworth would be instant annihilation.   [46]

It is part of Jane Austen's purpose that Fanny's intense response should be phrased in terms one cannot take altogether at face value. The excess (like her expostulations on sublimity) has a touch of innocence and naivety in it, and we are surely meant to feel that. So on the next page, when Fanny learns that Edmund is coming to take her back from Portsmouth to Mansfield, she is troubled by incompatible feelings as only someone might be who has tried with all her powers for propriety or integrity of feeling: "Tomorrow! to leave Portsmouth to-morrow! She was, she felt she was, in the greatest danger of being exquisitely happy, while so many were miserable. The evil which brought such good to her! She dreaded lest she should learn to be insensible of it." She has learned in Edmund's letter of a new calamity, though a lesser one, Julia Bertram's elopement to Scotland with Yates; and Fanny is troubled by her inability to sustain the moral vision she means wholly to accept:

> Julia's elopement could affect her comparatively but little; she was amazed and shocked; but it could not occupy her, could not dwell on her mind. She was obliged to call herself to think of it, and to acknowledge it to be terrible and grievous, or it was escaping her, in the midst of all the agitating, pressing, joyful cares attending this summons to herself. [46]

Running through Fanny's moral shock and grief for others is the incongruous note of potential happiness: she is free of Henry Crawford's attentions, to which she had begun to succumb against her judgment, and Edmund is probably separated by the events from Henry's sister. There is some comedy in Edmund's error. As he finds Fanny, wan with the enforced months at Portsmouth and its tormenting discomforts, he attributes "an undue share of the change," if not all of it, to Henry's desertion of her. He commiserates with her more than she quite deserves, and when he compares her loss with his own, he provides a new source of pleasure for Fanny: "No wonder," he exclaims, "you must feel it—you must suffer. How a man who had once loved, could desert you! But *your's*—your regard was new compared with—Fanny, think of *me!*" As of course she does. Later, when he speaks of his disenchantment with Mary, he fears he may awaken Fanny's pain over the betrayal by Henry Crawford. "You do not wish me to be silent?—if you do, give me but a look, a word, and I have done." The next paragraph consists of a short sentence: "No look or word was given" (47).

In those six bald words are implied all of Fanny's eagerness and incipient hope. It is that mixture of feeling that Jane Austen catches so beautifully in these sentences to which all of the foregoing has been leading: "She must have been a happy creature in spite of all that she felt *or thought she felt,* for the distress of those around her. She had sources of delight that must force their way" (48; italics added).

Fanny, like most of Jane Austen's heroines, has imperfect self-knowledge, but she acquires new strength of feeling and will at Portsmouth. She assumes for the first time an office of authority in her concern for Susan, and she comes to the gradual recognition that in Henry Crawford she is loved by a man who is "altogether improved" by that love. She is "quite persuaded of Henry's being astonishingly more gentle, and regardful of others, than formerly," of his being, in effect, more like herself. Fanny draws from this recognition only the small hope that Henry will cease to persevere in his suit; yet, as she wishes eagerly that Susan can be offered a new home, she recognizes that Henry, "had it been possible for her to return" his regard, would freely have supported the idea. "She thought he was really good-tempered, and could fancy her entering into a plan of that sort, most pleasantly" (41). Fanny is not prepared in the least to forsake Edmund for Henry; but it seems clear enough that she would turn to him if Edmund were to marry Mary. "Her influence over him had already given him some influence over her" (48).

Lionel Trilling, in a passage I cited earlier, argued that "the judgments of *Mansfield Park* are not dialectical," but rather, as in no other of Jane Austen's novels, "uncompromisingly categorical." For what in the Crawfords appears as a new freedom is shown to be "not an effect of liberation but an acquiescence in bondage, a cynical commitment to the way of the world." *Mansfield Park* offers in this "militant certitude" an "affront" to an "essential disposition of the modern mind, a settled and cherished habit of perception and judgment." [19] This is so bold and forceful a reading that one is hard put to dissent without offering one that is bolder. I can only venture the view that *Mansfield Park* is a work of more radical irony than Jane Austen's other novels—radical in that it exempts no characters from criticism. [20] We may be amused by the naivety of Catherine Morland almost to the very end of *Northanger Abbey,* but her naivety is part of a natural freshness and spontaneity of feeling that sets her apart from Isabella Thorpe and wins Henry Tilney's affection. In Fanny Price's naivety there is less value, or at least more pain and genuine disability. The conversations in which Fanny and Edmund sift the motives and faults of Mary Crawford are (when they are not used to show Edmund's self-deception) instances of two people with little belief in their own power to charm trying through mutual support to withstand the charm of the Crawfords. (It is, in turn, this absence of confident grace and verbal freedom that gives them a deeper charm for the Crawfords.)

Fanny's morality has little ease; except with William, she seems tensely and anxiously good. This, Jane Austen makes clear, is a contingent fact, not of the essence of goodness. Fanny is like Elinor Dashwood in seeming all but invisible to those about her; she is accepted so long as she is reliable, noticed only when she is not. Both heroines suppress most of their feelings, Elinor in order to be serviceable to others, Fanny through self-distrust as well. Each is denied the kind of presence which easy manners supply, but there is an unobserved intensity, an undemonstrative delicacy, that is at work in them; and Jane Austen presents this depth of character as too often silent or unregarded, whether it be found in a muted heroine or in that deeper self which underlies the surface of manners and waits to be acknowledged.

5 ✳ Stendhal:
Irony and Freedom

An Age of Reaction

Stendhal's irony is more radical than Jane Austen's. His characters tend to be unstable compounds, and they demand a shifting and flexible response from the reader. That response is enacted for us by the narrator, who regards his hero from constantly varying distances and directions. Stendhal's rhetoric recalls, in its shifts and dodges, the example of Byron's *Don Juan*. That poem, like Stendhal's novels, is a work of an age of reaction and political repression, of institutionalized banality. Behind both lie the French Revolution and the remarkable career of Napoleon. The vitality of the revolution and of the young Napoleon is brilliantly caught at the opening of *The Charterhouse of Parma*. But the horizon has closed like a heavy lid: as Mosca says to Fabrice, the "essential quality in a young man of the present day, that is to say for the next fifty years perhaps . . . is not to be liable to enthusiasm and not to show any spirit." [1]

The turn to reaction began with Napoleon himself. If only, Stendhal could write in 1821, "Napoleon possessed the *unspoiled* qualities of greatness which he displayed in 1796, if the habit of despotism had not made him prefer talentless sycophants to men of energy and tact. . . ." But "in 1804, Napoleon brought prudery into fashion and by his influence established her on the throne of morality." He found it "to be in his own interests as the despotic founder of a new dynasty." [2] The most painful moment of all for Stendhal was the ceremony at which Napoleon, having induced the pope to come to Paris to crown him, seized the crown in his hands and placed it on his head himself. Stendhal noted the occasion in his diary: "I reflected all day long on this open alliance of all the charlatans. Religion coming to sanctify tyranny, and all that in the name of the happiness of mankind. I rinsed out my mouth by reading a little of Alfieri's prose." [3]

More appalling for Stendhal, perhaps, than the betrayal of political free-

90

dom was France's reversion to all those discredited forms of hypocritical morality that the revolution overthrew. France became like the England Stendhal deplored: "Everything is pervaded by the most loathsome *cant*. Anything which is not a description of wild and energetic feeling is stifled by it; it is quite impossible to write a light-hearted page in English." [4] What the lighthearted means to Stendhal is suggested in some remarks on Ariosto: "It is only *after a comic passage* that my feelings can be deeply moved. . . . Only in *opera buffa* can I be moved to tears. *Opera seria,* by deliberately setting out to arouse emotion, promptly prevents me from feeling any. . . . Hence my complete aversion to tragedy, and my aversion, amounting to *irony,* to tragedy in verse." [5]

Stendhal wrote in 1824 that for "twenty years or more, a film of the filthiest hypocrisy has been spreading like a loathsome leprosy over the life and manners of the two most civilized peoples in the world." In France every man in office "sneers at the pious-cynical posturing of his superiors while feeling called upon to wear a similar mask of episcopal righteousness for the benefit of his subordinates." As for England, Stendhal quotes the closing lines of Byron's preface to cantos VI–VIII of *Don Juan:* "The cant which is the crying sin of this double-dealing and false-speaking time of selfish spoilers. . . ." [6] "The truth is," Byron wrote to his publisher Murray, "that in these days the grand *primum mobile* of England is *cant,* cant political, cant poetical, cant religious, cant moral; but always *cant,* multiplied through all the varieties of life." [7]

Byron's *Don Juan* is a poem whose tone is of the greatest importance. Stendhal, in fact, remarks on how little Byron sought to achieve "negative capability": "Like Rousseau, he was constantly preoccupied with himself and with the effect he produced on others. Hence his marked hatred for Shakespeare; I believe furthermore that he even despised him for having been able to transform himself into Shylock, a vile Venetian Jew, or Jack Cade, a contemptible demagogue." Nor does the ironical humor of *Don Juan* ever become a sufficient screen: "This humor does not bear too close an examination; instead of gaiety and light-heartedness, hatred and unhappiness lie beneath. Lord Byron has only been able to depict one man: himself." But in another sentence, Stendhal can see Byron trying to undermine British seriousness: "in *Don Juan,* he is gay, witty, sublime and pathetic." [8]

It is that interplay and constant shifting of posture and tone which gives *Don Juan* its strength. The older poet mocks the illusions of his young hero but envies the power by which the illusion is sustained. For, without the illusion (or, more properly, the power of the imagination) the world becomes an arbitrary and purposeless succession of fantasies, which we only make the more painful by our conviction of sin.

Julien Sorel

In *De l'amour* (1822) Stendhal describes the kind of man he was later to
create in Julien Sorel: "Cold, brave, calculating, mistrustful, argumentative,
always in fear of being stimulated by someone who might secretly be laughing at them, a little jealous of those who had witnessed great things under
Napoleon, such were the young people of this period, more to be respected
than to be liked." [9] If this were all one could say about Julien Sorel, *The Red
and the Black* would not be a very interesting novel. Julien is a provincial of
peasant ancestry, but he exhibits a natural aristocracy once the opportunity
is given him. He is a man of talent—perhaps of genius—divided between
generous youthful passion and the more solemn duty he feels he owes his
honor—or his pride, or (Stendhal implies) his vanity. Schooled in the sensibility of Rousseau (especially the thin-skinned resentments of *The Confessions*)
and in the military address of Napoleon, he is displaced in the provincial
bourgeois world. He feels at once below it by birth and above it by nature—
peasant or aristocrat, but at least not a grasping bourgeois hypocrite like
M. Valenod or the mayor, M. de Rênal.

Stendhal contemplates Julien Sorel somewhat as Byron does Don Juan.
The digressions from the narrative are less extensive in Stendhal, but they
are still tellingly frequent, deliberately unsettling, and unpredictable. The
narrator assumes shifting roles.[10] There is the fastidious Parisian who finds
"the tyranny of public opinion" in these provincial towns of France unsup-
portable. In the next chapter, the narrator assures the reader of his consideration: "although I mean to speak to you of provincial life for two hundred
pages, I shall not be so barbarous as to inflict upon you the tedium and all
the *clever turns* of a provincial dialogue" (I, 2). Perhaps the most telling of
the early contrasts of Paris and the provinces is in our view of Mme de Rênal:
"in the eyes of a Parisian, that artless grace, full of innocence and vivacity,
might even have suggested ideas of a mildly passionate nature. Had she had
wind of this kind of success, Mme de Rênal would have been thoroughly
ashamed of it. No trace either of coquetry or affectation had ever appeared
in her nature" (I, 3). The epigraph to the second part of the novel, which is
largely set in Paris, is the brief sentence from Sainte-Beuve: "She is not
pretty; she wears no rouge." What Stendhal sets forth in Mme de Rênal, as
Byron does in Haidée, is the natural woman of acute feeling, without self-
consciousness. For the Parisian emotions not only involve self-consciousness; they are so implicated in vanity as to become sentiments that one feels
one owes one's role, emotions one enjoys to the discomfiture—at least to the
rapt and jealous attention—of others. The impurity of such feelings comes
of the fact that one loves not another but oneself loving another, beheld with

admiration by still others.[11] Mme de Rênal's feelings are neither so complicated nor corrupt, but we see M. de Rênal's nervous wish, in hiring Julien
as his children's tutor, to win distinction by that act and to assume superiority to his townsmen. The need to outdo others makes M. de Rênal subject
to Julien's power to confer his services upon such a rival as M. Valenod, and
the farce of master-servant relationship, at once tyrannical and obsequious,
is a large element in the sardonic comedy of the novel.

If the narrator repudiates the stodgy conformism of the provinces, he can
turn upon himself to celebrate the possibilities for spontaneity the provinces
allow:

> In Paris, Julien's position with regard to Madame de Rênal would very soon
> have been simplified; but in Paris love is the child of the novels. The young
> tutor and his timid mistress would have found in three or four novels . . . a
> clear statement of their situation. The novels would have outlined for them the
> part to be played, shown them the model to copy; and this model, sooner or
> later, albeit without the slightest pleasure, and perhaps with reluctance, vanity
> would have compelled Julien to follow. . . . Beneath our more sombre skies,
> a penniless young man, who is ambitious only because the refinement of his
> nature puts him in need of some of those pleasures which money provides, is
> in daily contact with a woman of thirty who is sincerely virtuous, occupied
> with her children, and never looks to novels for examples of conduct. Every-
> thing goes slowly, everything happens by degrees in the provinces: life is more
> natural.   [I, 7]

But, if we allow ourselves to relax our vigilance and accept these contrasts,
we are shortly pulled up by the narrator's urbane regard for technical mastery:

> We need not augur ill for Julien's future; he hit upon the correct form of words
> of a cunning and prudent hypocrisy. That is not bad at his age. As for his tone
> and gestures, he lived among country folk; he had been debarred from seeing
> the great models. In the sequel, no sooner had he been permitted to mix with
> these gentlemen than he became admirable as well in gesture as in speech.
>   [I, 8]

And, further on, there is a recognition of the strength of provincial naivety
in fostering the energies of unimpaired confidence: "Even if we allow him
Julien's imagination, a young man brought up among the melancholy truths
of Paris would have been aroused at this stage in his romance by the cold
touch of irony. . . . The young peasant saw no obstacle between himself
and the most heroic actions, save want of opportunity" (I, 12).

The shifting grounds of the narrator's amusement or admiration involve
both a scorn for the ignorance of the provinces and a greater scorn for the
sophistication of Paris. At times he writes as a practiced lover amused by

Julien's clumsiness; at times he looks back from his own jaded assurance with envy of the intensity and hopefulness of the young barbarian. The irony resembles Byron's. In both cases there is a contrast between intensity and duration, between the brilliance of the moment and the long stultified life of empty forms. The latter Stendhal identified with Paris. He was later to write of his novel that its "treatment of Parisian love is absolutely new. . . . It is love in the head compared with love in the heart." [12]

Within Julien himself Stendhal draws a similar contrast: spontaneity and tenderness, on the one hand; guile and willfulness, on the other. In their very first encounter, Julien and Mme de Rênal are both disarmed; he by his relief in finding her warm, gracious, youthful; she by her relief in finding that her children's tutor is neither "an unwashed and ill-dressed priest" nor a potential martinet. Julien's relief allows him to forget his shyness or his aggressive defenses; Mme de Rênal is able to laugh "with all the wild hilarity of a girl." Julien's youth and almost feminine beauty are reassuring to Mme de Rênal; and, while she can hardly help nettling Julien at moments ("Do you really know Latin?" she asks in the pleasure of her relief), he is easily mollified. But, as he feels more comfortable in Mme de Rênal's presence, he summons up that self-confirming will that belongs to his ambition: "The bold idea at once occurred to him of kissing her hand. Next, this idea frightened him; a moment later he said to himself: It would be cowardly on my part not to carry out an action which may be of use to me, and diminish the scorn which this fine lady probably feels for a poor workman only just taken from the saw-bench" (I, 6). Inaudible trumpets summon him to the battlefield (it frequently offers itself as class warfare, a new revolution of the downtrodden and insulted). Julien takes hold of her hand and kisses it. Mme de Rênal is too surprised to respond, too slow in feeling indignation to voice it at once. But this first scene presents the dialectic that works throughout their relationship: the tenderness gives way before an imagined perception of a slight to his pride. With the slight is awakened the reassertion of will, the insistence upon his duty to himself and the need to see her as an enemy to defeat.

For long stretches Julien can surrender to the wonderful ease of accepting the pleasures that are given to him:

> Julien, meanwhile, had been living the life of a child since he had come to the country, as happy to be running after butterflies as were his pupils. After so much constraint and skilful diplomacy, alone, unobserved by his fellow-men, and, instinctively, feeling not in the least afraid of Madame de Rênal, he gave himself up to the pleasure of being alive, so keen at his age, and in the midst of the fairest mountains in the world.   [I, 8]

But chance permits him to touch Mme de Rênal's hand as he gesticulates. They are not alone; but Julien feels at once the duty to recapture the withdrawn hand and to hold it like a captured fortress. "The idea of a duty to be performed, and of making himself ridiculous or rather being left with a sense of inferiority if he did not succeed in performing it, at once took all the pleasure from his heart" (I, 7). When at last, in the company of her friend Madame Derville, he seizes Mme de Rênal's hand, and holds it until it ceases to resist him, he experiences tremendous happiness; but it is the triumph of will, and he hardly has feeling to spare for Mme de Rênal. He has performed his duty and achieved heroism.

When Julien achieves a new victory in winning better terms of employment from M. de Rênal, he withdraws for a day or two to the mountains above Verrières. The height and isolation represent for him "the position to which he was burning to attain in the moral sphere. The pure air of these lofty mountains breathed serenity and even joy into his soul" (I, 10). Standing there on a high rock, he can see a hawk in flight and think himself Napoleon. Stendhal keeps in play our sympathy with the young man's asserting his rights in an unequal world, our amusement at Julien's self-absorption and desperate need to empty life of all but tests and occasions for triumph, our concern for someone so generous and innocent as Mme de Rênal as she falls more and more in love with a young man who sees her somewhat as Oedipus saw the Sphinx. There is brilliant comic disproportion in Julien's melodramatic view of his career, but there is also a genuine heroism for all the fatuity (and cruelty) with which it seeks occasions for self-assertion. His greatest fear is that he may be tempted by his friend Fouqué's offer of a secure but unremarkable life. "Like Hercules, he found himself called upon to choose not between vice and virtue, but between mediocrity ending in an assured comfort and all the heroic dreams of his youth" (I, 12).

Julien's will seems always to send him forward to accomplish more than he dares hope he can; to meet danger gives him the sense of being fully alive. Stendhal describes with brilliant detail Julien's desperate coercion of himself to visit Mme de Rênal's room at two o'clock in the morning. So demanding is the effort to get there that he loses all his will at the moment he arrives:

> Seeing him enter, Madame de Rênal sprang quickly out of bed. "Wretch!" she cried. There was some confusion. Julien forgot his futile plans and returned to his own natural character. Not to please so charming a woman seemed to him the greatest disaster possible. His only answer to her reproaches was to fling himself at her feet, clasping her round the knees. As she spoke to him with extreme harshness, he burst into tears.   [I, 15]

But whatever the success his spontaneity achieves, Julien constantly reasserts his duty to himself and insists upon playing the part of a man accustomed to subduing women to his will. The immediate joy must always be sacrificed to the next attainment, and the natural self suppressed by his ambition and his fear of ridicule. There are moments, as Julien gains confidence as a lover, when he can surrender the pleasures of gratified vanity, the triumphs of hypocrisy and strategy, for the deeper pleasure of sincere devotion.

It has been said that Julien is "completely unhypocritical towards himself about the role he is playing." [13] For Julien persuades himself that he is governed by rational plans and realistic goals, or at least that he is dedicated to the heroic vision that exacts dutiful efforts. What he cannot see in himself is suggested by Stendhal in various ways. During what Julien takes to be his last visit to Mme de Rênal's room, she is filled with grief and tortured with the remorse she will feel all the more when he has gone. She is "like a barely animated corpse," and for a moment Julien is stung with the thought that she has ceased to love him. But finally Julien is moved by the lack of warmth in her embraces: "he could think of nothing else for some leagues. His spirit was crushed, and before crossing the pass, so long as he was able to see the steeple of Verrières church, he turned round often" (I, 23). The passage has its own understatement, and it seems to suggest what Julien has no clear way of identifying and accepting. The steeple becomes more than the highest structure in Verrières; it fuses with the love of Mme de Rênal to imply, however obliquely, a sanctity by which Julien is moved but cannot acknowledge.

The scenes in Paris are dominated by the figure of Mathilde de la Mole, for her pride and her exercise of will set the keynote of that world. Mathilde nourishes the vision of heroism enacted by her sixteenth-century ancestor Boniface de la Mole. By the touchstone of that imagined grandeur everything about her seems stale and flat, not least the adulation paid her. If she suffers from the conviction that nothing in her world has the authenticity of past heroism, she is all the more contemptuous of those who do not share her contempt for herself. "I can see nothing but a sentence of death that distinguishes a man. . . . [I]t is the only thing that is not bought" (II, 8). Mathilde disheartens Julien by despising what he is only coming to enjoy; but it is a flash of contempt in his eyes that shocks her and wins her esteem. Like many who are cynical, Mathilde lives in a high romantic fantasy, a fantasy so exacting that it devalues reality. She wants the risk and intensity of a grand passion, but she is terrified that it will turn out to be squalid and banal. Julien seems the only man she knows who is unmoved by the "fear of bad form" (II, 12).

Julien in turn is repelled by Mathilde's self-consciousness, so much like his own. Her eyes show, deep down, a "cold, malevolent scrutiny. Is it possible that this is love? How different from the look in Madame de Rênal's eyes" (II, 12). Paris is the scene of will and mastery. Nothing is so troubling as the fear of a hoax or of ridicule. Nothing is so effective as a cool, contemptuous deception, such as, with the help of Korasoff, Julien plays upon Madame de Fervaques, and through her upon Mathilde. Love itself becomes a form of politics in the world of Paris, an instrument of power; when Mathilde surrenders her will to Julien's, there is something forced and unspontaneous about their passion. "Passionate love was far more a model which they were imitating than a reality with them" (II, 16). Each of them is fulfilling a duty to the imagined self, but in the process each yields power to the other. This provides relief but also introduces new anxiety. They are unaware of the hatred in their love. There is even a kind of competitive pride in their daring, as when Mathilde cuts off one side of her hair. And Mathilde hugs Julien so tightly that she almost suffocates him, all the while protesting that he is her master, she his slave. The farce is the more brilliant for the tortured solemnity of the passions. It is to be seen again in the cabals of right-wing statesmen and clergy; it appears as well in Julien's adoption, with a new name, of a new father. "Can it indeed be possible . . . that I am the natural son of some great nobleman banished among our mountains by the terrible Napoleon? Every moment this idea seemed to him less improbable. . . . My hatred for my father would be a proof . . . I should no longer be a monster!" (II, 35)

This unreal world is distended to the point of collapse, and Julien's shooting of Mme de Rênal frees him of it. She has, he thinks, written a letter denouncing him as a hypocrite who has seduced Mathilde de la Mole in order to make his fortune. The shooting is one of those events that reveals a dimension of Julien Sorel which has been unknown even to him. His rage seems uncharacteristic; the letter is hardly couched in Mme de Rênal's words, and he might easily discredit it. But it is more as if he were moving back out of this world that has become too much and too little at once. One can only speculate about the motives, Stendhal means to imply. One recognizes Julien's sense of the peculiar betrayal by Mme de Rênal of his deepest feelings, feelings he was hardly able to recognize, much less acknowledge, when they arose, feelings which have gained in authenticity by contrast with all the success that has followed. And once he has committed this somewhat insane revenge, Julien is freed of all his ambition and released into the deeper self that has been covered over by strategem and fantasy.

His final days are a stripping away of belief he can no longer sustain, of ambitions that have come to seem trivial. There are strains and difficulties. The visit of Father Chélan is almost a vision of the death of the spirit. The old priest wears "a settled look of apathy" which impugns all visions of courage and nobility. Julien sinks into self-pity, senses the power of death and the weakness of any willed Roman grandeur of defiance. But Fouqué's generosity restores a sense of the sublime; and at this point the narrator contemplates what Julien might have become: "age would have given him an easy access to emotion, he would have been cured of an insane distrust. . . . But what good is there in these vain predictions?" (II, 37)

The speculation, of course, like the narrative itself, is a fiction. Nor does

Stendhal gain plausibility by discussing his hero as if Julien were a real person rather than his own invention. What does he gain? Every novelist creates something more or less than he may have intended, if, in fact, his intentions have ever been consciously formulated. An invention acquires its autonomous imaginative force. To speculate about Julien Sorel's possibilities is to question the nature of this invention and its power. Julien is not made more real as a person, but he becomes more distinct as an act of Stendhal's imagination. These final chapters give us a new awareness of Julien, now in repose in a high tower which frees him of worldly involvement and allows him to see Mathilde—and himself as her former counterpart—with generosity, even pity. This movement out of the repertory of now-discarded roles into the deeper self raises problems. Might there possibly be a self deeper than any commitment it has chosen to live by? We see these problems raised in Julien's view of Mathilde: "How could he fail to see in this manner of speech and action a noble, disinterested sentiment, far above anything that a petty, vulgar spirit would have dared? He imagined once again that he was in love with a queen, and after a few moments it was with rare nobility of speech and thought that he spoke to her" (II, 38). His thoughts are perhaps too noble to meet hers. Mathilde feels elevation in his presence; but it is in large part because he reactivates that half-mad vision of her noble ancestor, Boniface de la Mole, whose head Marguerite of Navarre recovered and carried away. Mathilde clings tenaciously to this pride he has restored to her. So at the end of the novel, because Julien has aspired to rest in the cave high on the mountain, Mathilde buries his head there when the others have left. But she adorns the natural cave with "marbles sculptured at great cost in Italy." She is locked in her own vision, and she profanes the natural cave with the absurd grandeur she applies to it.

Julien, well before his death, is weary of her exertions and "tired of her heroism": "It would have required a simple, artless, almost timid affection to appeal to him, whereas on the contrary Mathilde's proud spirit must always entertain the idea of a public . . ." (II, 39). It is to Mme de Rênal that he returns at last and to his earliest self. He addresses the court as a "peasant" who had "the audacity to mingle with what the pride of such men calls society" (II, 41). And as he endures Mathilde's feverish rage and adoration, he concentrates his inner vision upon the bedroom in Verrières. "He saw the *Gazette de Besançon* lying on the counterpane of orange taffeta. He saw that snowy hand clutching it with a convulsive movement; he saw Madame de Rênal weep. . . . He followed the course of each tear over that charming face" (II, 42). When he finally has Mme de Rênal with him, their passion, intense and "free from all pretence," creates for both of them a state of indifference to the world, of "mild gaiety." Julien's new and quiet self-acceptance is set off, after his death, by Mme de Rênal's helpless and fatal grief and by Mathilde de la Mole's insane adoration of the man whose head she has made her own.

The Emergence of the Hero

In *The Red and the Black* the countercurrent to ambition and to the assumption of a limiting role proves at last to be not the mature worldliness of a Marquis de la Mole but the simplicity and selflessness of Mme de Rênal—and of Julien Sorel in his last days. In *The Charterhouse of Parma* Stendhal presents a far stronger and more appealing image (in Gina Sanseverina and Mosca) of worldly wisdom, of the generous and humorous pursuit of happiness; and he subjects it to questions through a series of reversals. His hero, Fabrice del Dongo, is presented in the first half of the novel as a young man hardly at home in the world of either intellect or wit, curiously gullible, and with little personal involvement in politics or religion. Except for his personal charm there is little in Fabrice to claim attention; but Stendhal so manages his story that what seem Fabrice's deficiencies turn out at last to be the index of a deeper (and therefore invisible) commitment which transcends all forms of worldliness. Fabrice, throughout the novel, lives in an order of experience that is at odds with hedonism. His devotion thrives on difficulty and discipline. His love for Clélia shows an authenticity which is almost ascetic in its indifference to all that Gina and Mosca live for and brilliantly embody.[14] We see its counterpart in the passages from Salviati's diary under which Stendhal retraces his own feelings in his work on love:

> I was a mere child at Napoleon's court and in Moscow. I did my duty, but I was unaware of the heroic simplicity which comes from entire and whole-hearted self-sacrifice. For instance, it is only within the last year that I have come to understand the simplicity of Livy's Romans. Previously I found them dull by comparison with our own most dashing colonels. What they did for their Rome, I find in my heart for Leonore.[15]

But cutting across both drabness and deviousness is a moment of direct and open pleasure:

> *Don Quixote* made me die of laughter. Please be good enough to remember that since the death of my poor mother I had never laughed. I was the victim of an unremitting aristocratic and religious education. . . . Imagine the effect of *Don Quixote* in the midst of such horrible gloom! The discovery of this book . . . was perhaps the greatest moment of my life.

Later, Henry Brulard calls it "the only book that did not inspire me with distrust."[16]

Perhaps such a revival of freedom as Italy enjoyed must always be a brief

one. The Directory soon began "to show mortal hatred of everything that
was not commonplace"; and as a result the Austrian empire succeeded in
reimposing the authority of the old, the bigoted, and the morose until Napoleon's new victory at Marengo. But, as we have seen, Napoleon himself,
as he grew in age and authority, created a new imperialism and a new respectability. The freedom and vitality of the early days survive only in those
few who can sustain their memory and live by their ideals. What makes the
opening of the novel so important is that its insistence upon intensity as
opposed to endurance can suggest two alternatives: a life of pleasure or of
almost religious commitment—of vigorous passion or of an almost inhu-
manly perfect devotion.

Warmth and generosity are best seen in the figure of Gina. Her older
brother, Fabrice's father, the Marchese del Dongo, has arranged for Gina's
marriage to a "personage of great wealth and the very highest birth"—

> but he powdered his hair; in virtue of which, Gina received him with shouts of
> laughter, and presently took the rash step of marrying the Conte Petranera. He
> was, it is true, a very fine gentleman, of the most personable appearance, but
> ruined for generations past in estate, and to complete the disgrace of the match,
> a fervent supporter of the new ideas.   [1]

When her husband is murdered, Gina does not seek resignation. Rather she
laments "the courage of a fool who allows himself to be hanged without a
word of protest." Gina is untroubled by poverty. In Milan it "does not
present itself to trembling souls as the worst of evils," and she prefers it to
the wealth of contemptible suitors. When she accepts her brother's invitation
to stay at his castle of Grianta on Lake Como, she is moved by the sublimity
of the landscape—the wooded hills "which the hand of man has never yet
spoiled and forced to *yield a return*," a scene that evokes Tasso and Ariosto
and speaks of love. Beyond the hills lie the more remote snow-covered Alps,
whereas in the foreground are the massive structures, at once self-assertion
and self-defense, of the marchese. Boating on the lake with her nephew,
Gina braves a sudden storm with all the boldness her brother lacks. She
and Fabrice almost drown, "but the spirit of boredom, taken by surprise,
was banished from the feudal castle" (2). Boredom is the essential curse of a
world that has conspired to crush freedom and to exact conformity, to defend
itself against the unexpected and the exceptional. Byron presented this boredom in the English cantos of *Don Juan;* Stendhal found it in Restoration
France and especially Paris.

In the *Life of Henry Brulard,* Stendhal set his boredom against *espagnolisme,*
the fierceness of temper he associated with his Spanish (or Italian) ancestors.
"My aunt Elisabeth," he wrote, "had a Spanish soul. Her character was the
quintessence of honour. She completely transmitted to me this way of feel-

ing, whence arose a ridiculous series of follies committed through over-scru-
pulousness and nobility of soul" (12). These Spanish feelings kept him up in
the clouds: "I thought of nothing but honour and heroism. I had not the
least trace of smooth-tongued (or Jesuitical) hypocrisy." If he shows pride in
his integrity, Stendhal insists upon his ineptitude as well: this *espagnolisme*
"makes me even now, at my age"—he is writing at fifty-three—" appear an
inexperienced child, a madman *increasingly incapable of any serious business* in
the eyes of that authentic bourgeois, my cousin Colomb (whose exact words
these are)" (21). Childlike, mad, quixotic—these terms apply in some measure to Gina but even more to her nephew Fabrice.

The young Fabrice adores the Priore Blanès, the parish priest of Grianta,
a man with almost no Latin and with an insane devotion to astrology. Fabrice
does not trust the Priore's predictions, but he acquires a faith in the infalli-
bility of his own omens and forebodings. We are told later, of the more
mature Fabrice, that "his half-belief in omens was for him a religion, a
profound impression received at his entering upon life. To think of this belief
was to feel; it was a happiness." Fabrice tries to justify this belief with rational argument; but in fact he remains a stubborn worshipper in a pagan
creed—"and he would have felt an invincible repugnance for the person who
denied the value of omens, especially if in doing so he had had recourse to
irony" (8). The superstitions of childhood, upon which the deepest sense of
self may rest, resent the cool appraisals of irony most of all. Gina, in turn,
as she finds excitement in the storm, also cultivates enthusiasm for the primitive in Priore Blanès's astrology; she spends evenings, like Fabrice, in one
of the Gothic towers of the castle.

Omens are what lead Fabrice to join Napoleon's forces. Or so it would
seem. Such mind as he has shown has "taken seriously all the religious teaching" instilled into him by the Jesuits, and his "fanaticism" has made his
mother shudder. But when he is hunting or boating, he feels close to the
irreverent Francophile coachmen and grooms. What leads him to support
Napoleon is not clear. The omens free Fabrice of the need to examine his
motives; and they release his least conscious, most imperious, feelings. One
suspects that his resentment of his father and older brother—the preposterous, reactionary Marchese del Dongo and his young Ascanio—play a part in
Fabrice's coming to his decision; but he is most explicit about Napoleon's
having been a good friend to Gina's husband: "He wished to give us a country, and he loved my uncle." Whether Fabrice suspects that his father was
one of Napoleon's officers is much less certain. But all these motives—if that
is what they are—are precipitated into action by the omen of an eagle, the
bird of Napoleon, flying "majestically past" on its way to Paris. Later, Gina
explains Fabrice's schooling in the Napoleon myth: "When he was five years
old, my poor husband used to explain these battles to him; we put my

husband's helmet on his head, the boy strutted about trailing his big sabre. Very well, one fine day he learns that my husband's god, the Emperor, has returned to France" (5).

When Fabrice accepts this idea "from above" and resolves to go to Paris to join Napoleon's forces, he feels tremendous relief: "All the sorrows that . . . have been poisoning my life, especially on Sundays, seemed to be swept away by a breath from heaven." There is another, more personal omen that confirms the first. Fabrice thinks of the chestnut tree that his mother planted with her own hands in the winter of his birth. If it is in leaf, he too must emerge from the torpor in which he feels himself languishing in the "cold and dreary castle." And of course the tree has leaves, which Fabrice kisses as he reverently turns the soil around the trunk. The tree seems a totemic symbol of his deepest self—unconscious, mysterious, and sacred to him. Through it he almost attains the stable self-sufficiency of a natural thing; his religion is primitive but deep, the more powerful for being embodied in omens at once natural and mute (2).

The adventures of Fabrice in France and at Waterloo are in part the comedy of the naive idealist—robbed, suspected, even imprisoned for a month as a spy. His pitifully inept disguise seems an insult to the French police, who can only wonder what deeper reality it seeks to hide. It is really Fabrice's appeal to motherly women—most notably the *vivandière* of the battlefield canteen—that permits him to survive. This version of Waterloo seen from the underside by a stranger who neither knows what to expect nor has any acquaintance with the participants, who most of all has neither a place nor a function there, is one of ludicrous disorder, surprise, inconsequence. He does not know he has seen Napoleon, much less his own father.

Fabrice revels in the presence of distinguished generals, guides his horse with anguish around the bodies of the wounded, and attains satisfaction in finding himself at last under fire, a "real soldier." There is something in these scenes of the comedy of Julien Sorel's over-planned campaign against Mme de Rênal. In the midst of a terrible world with whose reality others are fully engaged, Fabrice is single-mindedly testing himself, asking himself whether he has the stuff of heroism. At every point he encounters the unsettling muddle of contingency; if there are real suffering and the possibility of greatness, there is nothing of the heroic composition that allowed a General Wolfe, for one, to die with glory in Benjamin West's painting.

Instead of the camaraderie of the heroes of Ariosto and Tasso there are petty vanity, unscrupulous cheating, sheer desperation. Instead of heroic contest there is the ugly actuality of a sickening corpse: "what struck him most of all was the dirtiness of the feet of this corpse which had already been stripped of its shoes and left with nothing but an old pair of trousers all clotted with blood. . . . A bullet, entering on one side of the nose, had gone out at the opposite temple, and disfigured the corpse in a hideous fashion. It lay with one eye still open. . . ." (3).

It is hard to "retain one's enthusiasm surrounded by a pack of vile scoundrels," and there are the simple, less than heroic urgencies of hunger and fatigue. A measure of heroism is allowed Fabrice as he is wounded defending a bridge; but the blood he loses liberates him "from all the romantic element in his character." Symptomatically, when Fabrice learns that his brother has reported him to the Milanese police, he takes out his rage by picking a quarrel with a phlegmatic Genevan. In the process, Fabrice forgets all the laws of honor; instead of proposing a duel, he draws his dagger and reverts to "instinct, or, more properly speaking, to the memories of his earliest childhood." Fabrice, one feels, is never securely beyond this regression. He remains as much at home in his "archaic" feelings as he does in the primitive religion of omens (5).

In the public world, Fabrice has no clear ambition, and he accepts the instructions of Mosca and Gina. They are caught up in the world of Parma, whose political intrigue they despise but enjoy as a fascinating game. And it is Mosca, the superbly political man, who has the clearest view of what is open to Fabrice. The "essential qualities" of a young man in the period in which they happen to live are "not to be liable to enthusiasm and not to show any spirit." Fabrice's early enthusiasm for Napoleon has disqualified him for a military career, for he can no longer be sufficiently trusted. (Mosca himself has fought with Napoleon's forces in Spain, but long ago.) Yet, Mosca suggests, there is the church, where Fabrice can, with Mosca's help, become an archbishop like his ancestors. Gina is repelled at the prospect; but Mosca persuades her that there is no alternative in this age made for "barristers" rather than gentlemen. Fabrice can remain a "great gentleman," and he can, if he chooses, remain "perfectly ignorant" while becoming an archbishop.

Fabrice, like Gina, is at first repelled by the prospect. He rejects altogether a life of genteel idleness and "vulgar happiness." He has a lofty sense of what he may become, and he would prefer a military career, even as a soldier in the American republic; but he comes to accept Mosca's realism. Not without reluctance, for he has not before "taken into account this horror of enthusiasm and spirit" with which he must learn to live among absolute monarchs. He enters the seminary with melancholy detachment. He feels all too strongly his inability to fall in love (except of course with his aunt, Gina, and that is impossible). He cannot give himself fully to the women he successfully courts, nor is there any serious question of religious devotion. He goes to Naples to begin his education in that "complicated science," theol-

ogy. He accepts without comment the advice that he blindly believe all he
is taught and that he resist every temptation to shine through wit and critical
intelligence.

Four years later, Fabrice is no closer to having found commitment. He has
been a diligent student; and he has acquired a keen interest in archeology.
He finds himself plunged into politics during his first interview with the
Prince of Parma. Ernesto tries to trap Fabrice into revealing dangerous enthusiasms, but Fabrice is a model of prudence and sententious rectitude.
"The Prince felt himself almost defied by such correctness of manner and
such unassailable rejoinders coming from a youth fresh from college." Fabrice's remarks are so correct as to seem consummate tact or hypocrisy. He
seems to be playing a "thrilling game" with the prince, intimating a defiance
with which he cannot quite be charged. But, in fact, as we are told—and
we must be told, for we can hardly enter a consciousness that seems not yet
to exist in Fabrice, that reveals itself so contradictorily and enigmatically—
the prince is mistakenly oversubtle and misses the open countenance in his
effort to detect the mask. For Fabrice "believed practically everything that
we have heard him say; it is true that he did not think twice in a month of
these great principles. He had keen appetites, he had brains, but he had
faith" (7).

Once more we find a peculiar innocence in Fabrice. He seems to be able
to sustain discordant feelings and dissonant attitudes—a taste for liberal
newspapers and the most irreproachably reactionary sentiments, an enthusiasm for Napoleon's heroism and a complete acceptance of the legitimacy of
absolute monarchs. Deep beneath the somewhat bored, smooth detachment
of his public manner lies the intensity of childlike feeling. Afraid of his love
for his aunt, unable to lose himself in the distractions of a new affair, he
returns to Grianta to recover the feelings of his earlier days. It is an escape
from difficulty into the sublime landscape of Lake Como, where he can make
heroic resolutions and fully expect to execute them. He regrets his privileges:
"the fine enthusiasm for virtue which had just been making his heart beat
high changed into the vile pleasure of having a good share in the spoils of a
robbery." He reasserts his belief in omens, and he can, not without the
narrator's irony, transcend a reality that "still seemed to him flat and muddy"
(8). The tower itself, where he hides and looks out, restores memories of
childhood; and he can leave behind "the complicated interests of that nasty
little court." This day which he spends imprisoned in a belfry is "perhaps
one of the happiest days of his life" (9).

The quality of the experience is comparable to one of his own which Stendhal records:

> I think it was at Rolle, where we arrived early, that, drunk with happiness
> from reading *La Nouvelle Héloïse* and from the thought of visiting Vevey, pos-

sibly mistaking Rolle for Vevey, I suddenly heard a full peal of majestic bells
ring out from a church standing on the hillside a quarter of a league above
Rolle or Nyon, and I climbed up to it. I saw the beautiful lake spread out
before my eyes, the sound of the bells was an enchanting music which accompanied my ideas and made them seem sublime.

I believe this was my nearest approach to *perfect happiness*.[17]

Fabrice pays another visit to his tree, finds a withered branch, and cuts it off
"reverently"; the tree has grown superbly, almost doubling its height in five
years. Nor does the broken branch seem to matter; the tree will "grow all
the better" for its spread beginning "higher from the ground."

The visit to Grianta ends with an episode that is significant for the difference it reveals between Fabrice and Mosca. When he is more than a mile
from the border, still liable to capture and long imprisonment, Fabrice encounters a footman, "very neatly dressed in the English style," riding one
horse and leading another, singing beautifully as he rides along the road. "If
I reasoned like Count Mosca," Fabrice thinks as he waits in hiding, "when
he assures me that the risks a man runs are always the measure of his rights
over his neighbors, I should blow out this servant's brains with a pistol
shot." This would allow him a safe escape, and he could later send money to
the man's family—"but it would be a horrible thing to do!" (9) Instead,
Fabrice holds up the man, improvises a story to explain his theft, and rides
off with the horse. Later, as he tells about the adventure and his plans to
repay the footman, Mosca points to the risks that Fabrice has overlooked and
explains, moreover, that such practical measures as a suitable forged passport
might have forestalled the risks in the first place. Mosca stands for all the
wisdom of accommodation, and he is keenly aware of what Fabrice's capture
might have meant to his aunt. He mocks the "romance" Fabrice has enacted—Fabrice is "truly *primitive*," he remarks to Gina. They are surrounded, Mosca reminds them, "by tragic events"; they are "not in France,
where everything ends in song."

When Fabrice recalls a stunning romantic adventure of an ancestor, Mosca
insists that they now live in an unromantic age:

> In all ages, the base Sancho Panza triumphs, you will find, in the long run,
> over the sublime Don Quixote. If you are willing to agree to do nothing ex-
> traordinary, I have no doubt you will be a highly respected, if not respectable
> Bishop. . . . Your Excellency acted with great levity in the affair of the horse;
> he was within a finger's breadth of perpetual imprisonment.   [10]

We are left with these alternative visions. Mosca is willing to incur the cost
of murder where the risks are so great; but he is neither cynical nor bloodthirsty and would prefer to avoid the risks as well as the murder. Fabrice
ascribes to him a kind of calculation that is hardly just to Mosca's decency

or to his concern for Gina's feelings. On the other hand, while Fabrice cannot kill the footman, he does not claim a principle: "That footman looked so nice in his English jacket! it would have been such a pity to kill him!" Or, again, as he broods over the decision he has made and sees its folly, "still his heart could not accustom itself to the bleeding image of the handsome young man, falling from his horse, all disfigured." Mosca's expediency may be more humane than a conscience which is enforced by images and so easily crossed with impulse.

This contrast is essential to the novel. Mosca has all the worldliness that Fabrice lacks and has no wish to acquire. Mosca is a shrewd player in the farce that encloses him, preserving independence and integrity within that inmost enclosure, the private realm. Mosca must wear powder in his hair; at forty-five he has outlived the era of glory and imagination. But he is completely without self-importance and averse to gravity; he first succeeded with Gina because he had "the courage to be shy" in her presence. He is beyond pretence except for what an actor must use upon the stage; and he finds in Gina's vitality an escape from the boredom of the role that is all too easy to play, and play well, in Parma. He is "almost sincere" in offering to resign his post, and so is Gina in turn when she assures Mosca that he is the man she likes best. They are both adroit performers in a world where hypocrisy is essential, and they are free of that self-deception which would be worse.

Mosca recognizes that the public policy of Parma "for the next twenty years is going to consist in fear of the Jacobins," and everything "that can in any way reduce this fear" will be accepted as "supremely moral." Parma is a model of tyranny, so small that it seems like a lucid model of greater structures, a game whose clear rules and small board allow for concentrated skill. As part of the game, Mosca can arrange Gina's marriage to the aged Duca Sanseverina, who will instantly leave Parma in return for a long-coveted honor. At the center of the game is the prince himself, trying to live in the style of Louis XIV, terrified of assassins, and constantly seeing himself, as it were, through the eyes of greater rulers. Mosca supports the prince's dignity and covers his fears while finding ways to control his will.

Is this immoral? It is true, the author notes, that such things are no longer done in France, where the only passion to survive is that for money. But Mosca hardly seems less moral than those he must manipulate. When Archbishop Ladriani, a man "born on his knees before the nobility," calls upon him, Mosca always puts on a uniform to receive him. Mosca is a man of displaced virtue; he has "one of those rare spirits which make an everlasting remorse out of a generous action which they might have done and did not do" (8). If Mosca cannot dedicate himself to a cause, as he once did, if he must devote himself to managing a foolish monarch with excessive power, he at last finds enough to interest him in the game that it has become. Gina plays the game differently. She has enormous charm and boldness; her impatience makes for risks—in this she is closer to Fabrice—but makes at times for triumphs that a shrewder politician would never have imagined possible. She is, Mosca recognizes, "a woman who acts always on the first impulse; her conduct is incalculable, even by herself; if she tries to plan out a course in advance, she goes all wrong; invariably, when it is time for action, a new idea comes into her head which she follows rapturously . . . and upsets everything." It is perhaps too distrustful a view of Gina; she has more control than this suggests, although her outward control is often achieved only through inward obsession. But her spontaneity and brilliant recklessness, her love of risk and danger, are qualities that Mosca enjoys as much as he distrusts. She allows him to live at another depth, to find a self he has supposed himself no longer to possess.

Unlike Mosca, Fabrice is intense but narrow. If his self is divided, what is visible to others is only a kind of restlessness that propels him into more and more hectic misadventures. His life is episodic. He is almost always seen in an ironic light, for he tends to slight the actual, only to be caught up by it. When he enters the church of San Petronio in Bologna, simply because he does not dare show himself elsewhere without a passport, he is transported with religious devotion. "He threw himself on his knees and thanked God effusively for the evident protection with which he had been surrounded." But as Fabrice repeats the Seven Penitential Psalms from memory, it does not occur to him to question Mosca's plan to make him an archbishop. "It had never entered his thoughts that his conscience might be concerned. . . . This is a remarkable characteristic of the religion which he owed to the instruction given him by the Jesuits of Milan." They have warned against self-scrutiny as "a step towards Protestantism." Stendhal's irony doubles upon itself. "A Frenchman, brought up . . . in the prevailing irony of Paris, might, without being deliberately unfair, have accused Fabrice of hypocrisy at the very moment when our hero was opening his soul to God with the utmost sincerity and the most profound emotion." As Fabrice leaves the church, he buys candles to be burned before Cimabue's Madonna. But in the piazza outside he finds himself surrounded by insistent beggars. "Fabrice had great difficulty in escaping from the rabble; the scene brought his imagination back to earth. 'I have got only what I deserve,' he said to himself; 'I have rubbed shoulders with the mob' " (12).

When Fabrice is imprisoned in the Farnese Tower and falls in love with Clélia, a similar irony clings to him; but it begins to turn to wonder. Whereas Fabrice has been foolishly unworldly before (as well as frenetically devoted to play), he begins at last to emerge as a man who has only been waiting to find whole-hearted devotion. In this case, his love for Clélia takes on many of the qualities of the courtly love of twelfth-century Provence (about which

Stendhal had written in his book on love). The conditions of the Farnese Tower itself, and of Fabrice's escape-proof room, demand an elaboration of ingenious devices for communication that is reminiscent of the codes and ceremonies of an earlier kind of clandestine and reverent love. When Fabrice ascends the tower, his view of Parma is cut off, but he can see with distinctness the peaks of the Alps. The exaltation of the view is readily associated with his vision of Clélia: "So it is in this exquisite world that Clélia Conti dwells; with her pensive and serious nature, she must enjoy this view more than any one; here it is like being alone in the mountains a hundred leagues from Parma." As Fabrice, aloof from the pettiness of the world below, falls deeply in love without yet knowing it, he begins to feel the stirrings of heroism within himself: "Can I be one of those stout hearts of which antiquity has furnished the world with several examples?" He is impressed with his own cheerful acceptance of prison: "perhaps I have a great character." As he becomes aware of his love, he realizes that it is not merely "greatness of heart" that accounts for his acceptance of the prison. Stoic virtue gives way to romantic dedication (18).

Just as the love becomes most intensely idealized, the obstructive physicality of the surroundings asserts itself. Fabrice bores a hole in his wooden shutters with the cross of a rosary; he devises an alphabet to hold up so that messages can be spelled out. Each small victory over the material obstructions that hold the lovers apart becomes a splendid achievement; life is filled for both of them with plans for circumvention and moments of communion. Fabrice achieves a new delicacy of address, and he revels in the paradoxical freedom of this escape from the world. Beyond, in the old kind of freedom he now scorns, lie all of Gina's desperate efforts to save his life and arrange for his escape. But Fabrice has forgotten Gina in his sublime love for Clélia.

Clélia, in turn, whose appearance is "instinct with nobility" and whose manner shows "profound indifference to everything . . . vulgar" finds herself hating Gina without knowing why. "She understood nothing of the profound melancholy which had taken hold of her character, she felt out of temper with herself" (15). She believes she feels pity, thinking how happy Gina would be "if for a moment only she could see him as I see him now." But she finds herself alluding, when she writes a note to Fabrice, to the "fresh amours with which popular malice credited" Gina; and Clélia is then shocked by the baseness she finds in herself. Clélia must come to terms with all kinds of feelings she has never known before; they alienate her from her father and turn her against the thought of the marriage he has arranged (18).

Fabrice shows the doubleness of love—terror before his beloved, prostrate reverence; but also a calculated attempt to involve her in correspondence. He becomes a cunning strategist. Even as Fabrice worships Clélia, he has designs on her freedom and is capable of employing ruses. His devotion is sincere enough; he is properly convinced that he has never loved anyone before, that Clélia has erased all his past life. And yet both lovers are capable of more than they can recognize—more jealousy and possessiveness, more cunning, and more selfish obliviousness of others. Stendhal's irony both pays tribute to their intensity and mocks their self-deception. The self-deception can, of course, in its way be a tribute to intensity; for it takes much to overcome the scruples of people so virtuous and idealistic. Yet the innocence is drawn into complicity, as it is used by the passions to disarm all suspicions of their nature.

Gina Sanseverina begins to change as Fabrice does and in large part because Fabrice does. She has never been more splendid than in her bold contempt for the prince and her threat to leave Parma; she sets the terms for her staying, and only Mosca's courtierlike, or perhaps professional, concern for the prince's dignity makes him remove the phrases that would have ensured Gina's triumph. The imprisonment of Fabrice, which Mosca's omission has made possible, allows the prince to torture Gina with fears for Fabrice's life. These fears drive her to more and more desperate efforts, and their desperation is only the more ludicrously revealed by Fabrice's reluctance to be saved. All the histrionic pleasure Gina took in managing the stratagems of the court gives way to bitterness. The court becomes a "foul sewer." The game has ended, Mosca has proved only an assiduous courtier, the "souls of mud" are in power (16).

The desperation of Gina is clearest when she turns from Mosca and Fabrice to Ferrante Palla; his violence replaces Mosca's diplomacy, his devotion provides all she has hoped from Fabrice. "There goes the one man who has understood me. . . . [T]hat is how Fabrice would have acted, if he could have understood me." Balzac was enchanted by the figure of Ferrante Palla— a brilliant poet, a political radical, a Robin Hood, a St. John in the wilderness, a "savage fascinated by an angelic beauty." Gina thinks him "slightly mad," but with "a good and ardent soul." He has been secretly devoted to her for nearly two years and is ready to serve her in any task. When she engages him to poison the prince, a "sort of gaiety" returns; it is a recovery of power. "Once her revenge was settled, she felt her strength, every step that her mind took gave her happiness." And the narrator adds: "I am inclined to think that the immoral happiness which the Italians find in revenge is due to the strength of their imagination; the people of other countries do not properly speaking forgive; they forget." But if this comment is a tribute, a short while later we find another kind: "One sees that the Duchessa's mind had become really unbalanced since she had begun to think seriously of Fabrice's escape. The peril of this beloved creature was too much for her heart, and besides was lasting too long." She allows herself "to take a step that was not only horrible from the moral point of view, but also fatal to the tranquillity of the rest of her life" (21). She arranges for a splendid celebration on her estate and for the streets of Parma to be flooded by the water in the reservoir of her palace. There is a splendid release of energy; but it is, all of it, a show of senseless violence as well; and Gina's fixed and terrible stare makes others think of madness. She suffers the tortures of Fabrice's indifference, or rather of his devotion to Clélia; and when the news of the prince's poisoning finally comes, the futility of that ugly act—done, as she now persuades herself, for Fabrice—causes her to faint with grief and anger (23).

The violence released by the duchess becomes an abortive popular revolt under Ferrante Palla. "But for me," Mosca explains to Gina, "Parma would have been a Republic for two months, with the poet Ferrante Palla as Dictator." As he adds later, "it would take a hundred years in this country for the Republic to be anything more than an absurdity." Ferrante's own words in his printed letter to Gina seem as apt as any: "how is one to create a Republic without Republicans?" In any case, Ferrante's enthusiasms and untidy life are of a piece. His wife and five children suffer poverty while he proudly declines gifts for them. The rebellion he leads hardly seems a political act; at least there is no clear account of the cause Ferrante has adopted. Irving Howe has a generous account of Ferrante, although much of it is given to the splendid absurdity created by Stendhal's "political wit." To call Ferrante "the man who remains in principled opposition no matter how absurd it makes him seem" may suggest stronger principles than Ferrante ever reveals and an absurdity that is heroically defiant rather than largely oblivious of reality. I can agree with the view that "he is the only man whose recklessness matches that of Sanseverina"; but I should argue that they become closely comparable at a time when Gina has lost confidence, when her recklessness is more desperation than boldness.[18]

The apparent deficiencies and blank areas of Fabrice's character have been translated by Stendhal into a process of unconscious waiting for an occasion when his kind of powers and his capacity for devotion can find their objects. The "false" life he must lead until then is a passive acceptance of whatever policies or doctrines are pressed upon him and a frantic parody of the pursuit of happiness, which combines restless activity with somnambulism or, if one prefers, with profound alienation. As Fabrice begins to emerge and to dedicate himself, with considerable awkwardness and ludicrous industry, to an intense love, the self-sufficient urbanity and poise of his aunt—and to some degree of Mosca—begin to give way. Mosca finds himself uncontrollably jealous of Fabrice; Gina devotes herself more and more to gaining Fabrice's freedom and, perhaps unconsciously, expects his gratitude to take a form like love. (She simply cannot face the matter of incest, neither clearly accepting it as a final obstacle nor rejecting its force.) When she realizes that she has lost him to Clélia, that he has left the tower most reluctantly, the strain is great, and she ages rapidly.

The political operations in which Gina and Mosca become engaged because of Fabrice's jeopardy separate them increasingly. Gina finds herself covering the violent measures she has taken with Ferrante Palla's help by seeking to seduce the young prince. She must make him fall in love, as Mosca warns; but she is not prepared for the wretched kind of force a cowardly young prince will impose. For once her boldness has no real claim upon the prince, and she must accept his terms: "If I see Fabrice again not poisoned, if he is alive in a week from now . . . my honour, my womanly dignity, everything shall be trampled under foot, and I will give myself to His Highness" (25). It is a promise which poisons her life and which she hopes to escape. But a new threat to leave Parma does not suffice. The prince is obstinate, like all pusillanimous creatures who finally reach a decision; and he is all the more insistent because Gina has refused his offer of marriage. She submits to him and immediately leaves Parma, to see Fabrice no more; she becomes Mosca's wife, but she dies a very short time after Fabrice's death. That Gina has no role to play in the last chapters may be in part the difficulty of Stendhal's need to compress his work into two volumes. But the implications are clear, I think. She has ceased to be part of Stendhal's novel; she has used up the life that has relevance to Fabrice. In one of the last encounters of which we learn, she is jealously tormenting him with details of the splendid life into which Clélia has married. Mosca's case is different; for, while his life has gained its color and warmth from Gina, his worldliness is more profound and stable.

The final stages of Fabrice's life are no less farcical than the earlier. Clélia has compromised her vow never to see him again by meeting him in the darkness; but her father's illness (it was for his survival that she made the vow earlier) leads her to renew its strict observance. Comedy follows:

> Fabrice, who was developing a character closely resembling that of his mistress, went into retreat in the convent of Velleja, situated in the mountains, ten leagues from Parma. Clélia wrote him a letter of ten pages: she had sworn to him, before, that she would never marry the Marchese without his consent: now she asked this of him, and Fabrice granted it from his retreat at Velleja, in a letter full of the purest friendship.
>
> On receiving this letter, the friendliness of which, it must be admitted, irritated her, Clélia herself fixed the day of her wedding. . . .   [26]

Nor is it Clélia alone who is nettled by Fabrice's piety; his old friend the archbishop becomes jealous of Fabrice's new reputation for sanctity, which raises invidious comparisons. But the new piety is only a willed response to Clélia's marriage, and it easily gives way to explosions of rage, until at last the lovers can arrange once more to meet.

Stendhal makes the swings and changes more violent at the close, as their lives seem more frantic, less susceptible to either control or resolution. Clélia suffers remorse and uses her pregnancy to hide from Fabrice. In order to draw her out, Fabrice becomes a more and more powerful and popular preacher, winning great crowds by his burning imagery and passionate delivery (beneath which he maintains an unblinking watchfulness for Clélia's appearance). It is Clélia's jealousy of Fabrice's devoted followers that finally leads her to hear him. But a new reconciliation gives way in turn before Fabrice's demand that his son live with him. In the process of bringing this about through preposterous subterfuges, Fabrice loses first his son's life, then Clélia's. His own entry, for his last year, into the Carthusian monastery becomes the ultimate emptying of life of worldliness. What more it contains we never see. The devotion to Clélia, and the kind of masquerade it generates, suggest the capacity for faith that Fabrice may have. But all of that is beyond the scope of the book. Stendhal remains resolutely in the world, and he does not look beyond it.

Stendhal's characters have a sense of style. Style is perhaps the only form of integrity one can sustain in their world. We can see it in the advice Gina transmits from Mosca to Fabrice as he is about to enter the seminary. It is advice which takes for granted the squalor of mind Julien Sorel finds in his seminary and which refuses as a result to take seriously the claims of any institution, including the Church itself. *

> Believe or not, as you choose, what they teach you, *but never raise any objection.* Imagine that they are teaching you the rules of the game of whist; would you raise any objection to the rules of whist? I have told the Conte that you do believe, and he is delighted to hear it; it is useful in this world and in the next. But, if you believe, do not fall into the vulgar habit of speaking with horror of Voltaire, Diderot, [and] Raynal. . . . Believe blindly everything that they tell you at the Academy. Bear in mind that there are people who will make a careful note of your slightest objections. . . .   [6]

What creates this sense of style is the recognition that all institutions are used to maintain repressive power and that the powerful are too insecure to act honorably. The only freedom lies in cool indifference to the appeals institutions make, a readiness to turn them to one's own will, and a clarity of mind that comes of never thinking in their terms. All of this describes Mosca and Gina, and it describes the effect Fabrice sometimes produces but hardly what he thinks.

While any comparisons must start by acknowledging tremendous differences, the roles of Mosca and Gina in Stendhal's novel may recall the roles of Henry and Mary Crawford in *Mansfield Park;* the roles of Fanny and Edmund, in turn, are played here by Clélia and Fabrice. There is something ultimately self-defeating in the style that Mosca and Gina assume. For Gina it is clearly not enough to withstand or control her love for Fabrice; and her impatience and frustration make her play less deft and more destructive—destructive of herself as much as of others. If Mosca can sustain his role to the last, one must remember that it is Gina who has first awakened him from boredom; there is tedium in the dexterous self-sufficiency he achieves. The game is only interesting when the stakes—the cost of losing, the dangers one must elude—are sufficiently high. And perhaps all games must pall if they are played too long.

Fabrice, on the other hand, has no serious interest in the game as such, nor does he find pleasure in the exercise of the faculties it demands. He remains outside the game, playing at times with unconscious success, with an indifference to the outcome that makes him seem like a superb tactician. But his life lies elsewhere, and it is released by his imprisonment. Julien Sorel's freedom comes late in *The Red and the Black,* as a recovery of the innocence he has put behind him. Fabrice achieves that freedom in a form that, for Gina and Mosca, can only seem the denial of life. Stendhal has deferred the emergence of Fabrice's authentic vitality, letting us see him as deficient, hollow, restless, unmotivated. Once the reversal has been made, the novel has enough space left for its consequences to be explored, in the torment of Gina and the clumsy contrivances that are the nearest approach to worldliness Fabrice and Clélia can achieve. Stendhal, it need hardly be said, does not subject Gina and Mosca to the kind of moral judgment that Jane Austen makes of Mary and Henry Crawford. But one is teased by his statements that he wrote this novel with a clear anticipation of the death of Sandrino, the child of Fabrice and Clélia, who dies in large part as a result of Fabrice's effort to abduct him. Stendhal even claimed, in the manuscript of *Lamiel,* that the death of Sandrino alone had made him undertake the novel. At any rate, his publisher Dupont frustrated that intention by refusing Stendhal the space to realize it.[19] One thinks of two later novels in which the death of a child is a culminating event: Dostoevsky's *The Brothers Karamazov* and André Gide's *The Counterfeiters.*

Henry James saw in Stendhal the belief that *"passion,* the power to surrender oneself sincerely and consistently to the feeling of the hour, was the finest thing in the world"; thus "naïveté of sentiment in any direction, combined with great energy, was considered absolutely its own justification." In *The Charterhouse,* he feels, "there is so little attempt to offer any other, that through the magnificently sustained pauses of the narrative we feel at last the influence of the writer's cynicism, regard it as amiable, and enjoy serenely his clear vision of the mechanism of character, unclouded by the mists of prejudice. Among writers called immoral there is no doubt that he best deserves the charge; the others, beside him, are spotlessly innocent." Elsewhere James wrote of a "painful tension of feeling under the disguise of the coolest and easiest style."[20] I think that the strongest tension lies between the worldliness of Gina and Mosca and the curiously ascetic devotion of Fabrice that ends in the monastery. This is not to reinstate any simple morality but only to recognize the full play of the romantic spirit in Stendhal as in Byron. Of the young lovers in *Don Juan,* Byron wrote: "Love was born *with* them, *in* them, so intense, / It was their very Spirit—not a sense."[21] What matters is intensity of spirit rather than pleasure or happiness. It is, after all, a severe discipline.

6 ✳ Dickens:
Selves and Systems

System and Form

Dickens's novels circle around the theme of dehumanization. The social system is large in scale and impersonal, hardened into institutions inherited from the past, manageable only by those who have a clear view of their interest. The system is a fusion of aristocratic privilege and middle-class commercialism, supported by a legal structure that can be used to preserve or extend power. Its scale is so great that no one need feel personal responsibility; the system perpetuates itself, and it buries in oblivion both victims and rebels. But it survives only through the passive assent of those it exploits, and it wins that assent by dazzling them with the promise of respectability, by distributing almost everywhere some version of success or superiority to console the actual emptiness.[1] To understand this assent, one must look inside the individual and see what ambitions are realized and which fantasies are cultivated by the system. The system is an index to individual character, just as the composite pattern of individual temperaments explains the power of the system.

The most striking feature of the system Dickens presents is the penalty it places upon generous feeling. Those who succeed are oblivious of others, superbly efficient operators but deficient persons. Most efficient of all are the lawyers and financiers, such as Tulkinghorn or Merdle, men who work in a limited field, where they can control the machinery of institutions. The cost of success is the suppression of "irrelevant" feelings, where feeling is strong enough to survive at all. Roles are not simply imposed by the system; the system could not exist if men did not welcome this kind of reduction. The long tradition of comic and picturesque characterization, of the dynamics of humors and ruling passions, serves Dickens in his conception of both self and society. For each person is potentially a system within, and we can see the sacrifice of fullness and balance to dominant passions and prepossessions.

A single passion may direct all the others and reduce the person to the repetitive performance of a single role. The role is repetitive, but the performance may be unpredictably resourceful, finding new gestures, extending
its range, assimilating more and more of experience to its one purpose. This
effect of repetitive assertion making new and unforeseeable conquests is much
like the effect of wit: the personality operates like a constantly extended
metaphor. The vehicle of the metaphor, in this case, is the role the person
maintains and, in effect, becomes.[2]

There can be great comic force in this extension of roles. The characters
who enact them are relieved of the complexity of choice, and the release they
enjoy seems an enviable escape from the common difficulties of judgment.
When these roles are harmless and sustaining, they seem almost to be a
blessing; but when they encroach on the claims of others and become impe-
riously demanding we feel their lack of flexibility, their impoverished awareness, their restriction of feeling. The pleasures of irresponsibility are often
assumed as privilege, and there is a tendency for these roles, however humble
their players, to resemble those of an indifferent aristocracy. A figure like
Old Turveydrop in *Bleak House* models himself on the Prince Regent and
takes for granted the exertions of his son and daughter-in-law in sustaining
his comforts. In a more savage form, Blandois in *Little Dorrit* is persuaded
that he is a gentleman (although he is a transparent scoundrel) and will
readily murder or defraud to maintain the delusory role.

At what point does the comic shade into something ugly? At what point
does its irresponsibility seem painful or cruel? When does resourceful efficiency cease to seem a triumph of style and become an obsession? It is here
that Dickens achieves distinctive power. His elaborate structures hold these
characters, amusing or deplorable, helpless or scheming, in a pattern where
each comments on others, defines by analogy common traits that several
share, yet gives us a sense of the differences within likenesses. Old Turveydrop, with all his squalid aristocratic pretensions, affects our view of Sir
Leicester Dedlock and makes us see their dependence upon forms as in some
sense comparable. Responsibility may be embodied in a central, rather colorless, figure, and the anarchic impulses that resist and immobilize it in others
far more vivid. Jarndyce's earnestness in *Bleak House* is set against Harold
Skimpole's winsome pseudoinnocence as one such impulse and Boythorn's
more innocent rage as another.[3]

Dickens's characters are aspects of a common predicament, each caught
up in the enactment of his own version. We see the various dimensions of
desperate hope in the claimants upon Chancery. The intensity of belief, caught
with brilliant clarity in Gridley or Miss Flite, contributes to the meaning of
Richard Carstone's gradual submission to an insane dream. Each, moreover,
supplies the details of performance that make of the whole a dense reality, as

full and seemingly solid as the real world, yet more clearly ordered and aticulated. The characters differ from each other in effect—some absurd and mechanical, others thoughtful; pathetic or ludicrous, tortured or insensible. The differences are as accidental as those that life can furnish, but beneath them is a meaningfulness that circulates through the whole fictional world and within each character.

How baffled are we at the convergence of worlds and levels in miracle plays? How many are disturbed by the double awareness of a great actor's use of a familiar voice and gestures and of the role in which he gives them a new value? There may be paradoxes in responding to a play with involvement and yet knowing it is a play, in shuddering with horror at a tale and yet enjoying the security of knowing it to be a tale, in feeling intense sympathy with another person and yet reserving a sense of identity. But these paradoxes arise only as we separate out the contrary processes and set them in sharp opposition; our awareness is at once more rapid and sensitive, more flexible and supple, than the ways in which we talk about it. If Dickens gives us different modes within one novel, with characters who are perceived at different levels of awareness, we accept them more readily than we can later justify having done so. In the same way, we can respond to the voice of the teller and still lose ourselves to some degree in his tale. To some degree: for we are free to respond to aspects of it more fully through the very freedom that knowing it is a tale permits.

Dickens's novels have the confident artifice of a writer who trusts his readers to make an appropriate response. He seems unembarrassed by the recurrent demand for formal coherence that gave literature at different times the three unities, the proscenium stage, or canons of realism in the novel. The coherence of Dickens's later novels is one of theme, analogy, and plot. If the parts threaten to become independent centers of interest, the circulatory movement of theme and analogy hold them together. The artifices of elaborately contrived plot involve all the elements with each other, bringing them overtly and inescapably together as the novel moves toward resolution. Could these events really have happened? Are they probable? The questions miss their point. What, rather, do these events assume? For the plot has the inevitability of thematic progression more than the probability of a causal sequence. Dickens's plots involve too many characters and too many hidden relationships to permit the rigor of a single action working out the consequences of a mistaken choice, as in classical tragedy. They are closer to romance plots with surprising disclosures and satisfying resolutions. We count on resolution; it is by that expectation that our attention is directed; and, given the sense of direction which narrative provides, we can absorb a great range of experience that narrative gathers and orders along the way.

Looked at in detachment, outside the institutional structure of the novel, these resolutions may seem ironic commentaries on the brute contingency of our lives. Another way of considering the closure of these novels is suggested by Robert Caserio: "Dickens's sense of plot relies upon a notion that small groups of separate characters or persons are somehow all the same character or person." Caserio takes further than I have the analogies of character and theme that run through the books. One character may realize or complete another character's life: if "the Dickens characters feel the need to resolve conflicts within themselves, they discover—as the reader discovers—that the conflicts are not imponderable and inexpressible but defined in others who are outward personifications of the conflicts they feel within." This pattern is not unlike our use of surrogates—children to achieve what we have failed to do or exemplary sacrificial figures to pay the cost of our common failings. Caserio sees Lady Dedlock helping Rosa to overcome those class distinctions that once victimized her. While Richard Carstone and George Bagnet "duplicate the self-dislike and indolence of Hawdon in his last years," we are made to feel that something of both Hawdon and Carstone "is saved in the rescue of George by Mrs. Bagnet."[4]

Self and Society

Great Expectations has a simpler structure than the greatest of the later novels, and in it one can see most clearly the interplay of self and society. For the story of Pip is a study of how a boy is first led into entering the world of social forms, then at last into discovering its deadness and falseness. The title is, or course, crucial to the meaning of the book; for it refers not only to Pip's expectations but to the expectations that certain characters entertain and impose upon others to act out for them, notably Magwitch's dream of creating a gentleman in Pip and Miss Havisham's vengeful dream of raising Estella to break men's hearts. Miss Havisham is the clearer case and perhaps the more important, for we see her long, wasted life of festering outrage; and we see her schooling Estella in the ways of scornful seductiveness. F. H. Bradley put her case in one of his bitter apothegms: "We all cling to our wrongs, for they keep us for ever in mind of our rights, and we hug our hatreds, since without them how little would be left to some of us."[5] Miss Havisham has been cruelly wronged, although the event was in part created by her own will; more to the point is what she has made of her suffering. She stops time so as to live in a constant state of betrayal; she enjoys her wounds too much to let them heal. Moreover, she converts Estella into her instrument for repeating the wrong again and again at the expense of others' feelings. She has turned her suffering into the cycle of one wrong avenging another; and it never enters her imagination that Estella can feel anything but gratification as she sustains the cycle. As she finally repents, Pip asks himself:

And could I look upon her without compassion, seeing her punishment in the ruin she was, in her profound unfitness for this earth on which she was placed, in the vanity of sorrow which had become a master mania, like the vanity of penitence, the vanity of remorse, the vanity of unworthiness, and other monstrous vanities that have been curses in this world? [49]

Pip finally reverses the process of Miss Havisham's vanity; he breaks the cycle of wrongs by his compassion for Magwitch. Even more, he helps to place her vanity among others that we see in this novel and in others of Dickens, among those natural feelings that become perverse and destructive. One of these is the vanity of unworthiness, and it is there we find a clue to Pip's own feelings. For Pip, as we see him in childhood, is given every reason to feel his own unworthiness. His sister fills him with terror and guilt: he is born to be a criminal. He is a terrible burden to her, she makes clear, recounting "a fearful catalogue of all the illnesses I had been guilty of, and all the acts of sleeplessness I had committed" (4). It is small wonder that at Christmas dinner Pip should be pronounced "naturally wicious." Pip, he tells us, was always treated as if he had "insisted on being born in opposition to the dictates of reason, religion, and morality" (4).

Pip's shame is filtered through the voice of the mature Pip, who has grown into self-acceptance, who can feel the child's terror but present it with detachment, amused by Mrs. Joe's vehement pretensions and the logic of her inverted Christmas feast. That detachment controls the terrifying episode of the first chapter. Pip's encounter with the escaped convict, Magwitch, is filled with confusion and terror, but it also permits Pip's eyes to see more than the heart can yet know: as the convict goes away, "he looked in my young eyes as if he were eluding the hands of the dead people, stretching up cautiously out of their graves, to get a twist upon his ankle and pull him in." In a chapter full of suggestions, this seems one that might be heeded, like the "beacon by which the sailors steered . . . an ugly thing when you were near it" and the gibbet that stands out beside it, still dangling a dead pirate's chains. For a moment Pip thinks the convict might be the pirate come back to life, "going back to hook himself up again." The clutching hands of the dead, the dead pirate returning to his gibbet, the linking of beacon and gibbet, all suggest a cyclic pattern such as we see in Miss Havisham's sorrow: old wrongs keeping alive by creating new (1).

This pattern of self-perpetuation runs through the later novels, in the form of legal precedent, of inheritance, of cultivated grievance. In the case of Pip, the pressure of shame prepares him for snobbery. The escape from Mrs. Joe's disapproval is an escape into a world where Estella will scorn him no less, but scorn him for his coarseness and commonness, which are at least more specific and more easily put off than total unworthiness. One can, in fact, say that Pip wants her scorn. To overcome it he can accept the doubtful gentility of Satis House and adopt the point of view that makes him see Joe as what he himself has been and knew no better than to be, coarse and common. Estella's scorn is the obverse of Pip's golden dream; his vision of her as unattainable, aloof and cruel, is the counterpart of his goal of redemptive gentility, a demanding discipline that constantly judges him and judges those whom he has loved. He seeks Estella's scorn, and he scorns in turn: the verb is too strong and simple, but it is perhaps better than a more precise one.

Pip's relation to Estella is, in itself, a reenactment of traditional versions of courtly love: the "cruel fair" remains elusive and sets impossible tests. This kind of romanticism is shown as perverse, a turning away from solid reality, a life of self-imposed fantasy and of self-impoverishment, as spurious as the social warmth of the Finches of the Grove. Dickens associates it with the ruined garden of Satis House, with the monstrous death-in-life of Miss Havisham's "romantic" obsession, with the vacuous idleness of Pip and Herbert Pocket. Running through the novel is another kind of romanticism, one that we may associate with Wordsworth and with George Eliot's *Adam Bede* (which had appeared the year before Dickens undertook this novel): the dignity of the natural rural life. It is a dignity that builds upon harshness as well as fertility (Adam Bede's mother as well as the Poysers, Mrs. Joe and Orlick as well as Biddy), that accepts the narrowness or stupidity of such a life as the cost of its depth and directness of feeling. This kind of romanticism uncovers reality that others overlook or despise. One may stress its visionary aspect, but the vision is conferred by elemental feeling turned upon unlikely objects rather than the projection of fantasies of self into exotic or glamorous prospects.

The sharpest moment of confrontation between these kinds of romanticism comes near the close of the novel, when Pip returns to the Marshes, ready to accept what he can no longer have:

> The June weather was delicious. The sky was blue, the larks were soaring high over the green corn, I thought all that countryside more beautiful and peaceful by far than I had ever known it to be yet. Many pleasant pictures of the life that I would lead there, and of the change for the better that would come over my character when I had a guiding spirit at my side whose simple faith and clear home-wisdom I had proved, beguiled my way. They awakened a tender emotion in me; for, my heart was softened by my return, and such a change had come to pass, that I felt like one who was toiling home barefoot from distant travel, and whose wanderings had lasted many years.   [58]

The irony is clear and forceful: the place of return is now a self-contained world where Biddy is for once too preoccupied to imagine Pip's feelings except as part of her own: "it's my wedding day," she cries out, "and I am married to Joe!" (58) Pip's yearning, trimmed now from the extravagance of great expectations but still self-absorbed, has no place in this world. There must be a long interval of solid work before the "poor dream," in all its aspects, can be relinquished and Pip can encounter Estella again. When they meet at last, each is a fantasist who has grown into maturity, each is a fantasy that has dwindled into humanity. They are smaller, more humane, aware of the impoverishment the dreams have imposed, capable of respect for each other's reality.

The case of Estella is as compelling as Pip's. We can catch glimpses throughout the book of her sense of playing a role that has been imposed upon her by others out of their own needs, by Pip no less than Miss Havisham. For Pip "it was impossible to dissociate her presence from all those wretched hankerings after money and gentility that had disturbed my boyhood—from all those ill-regulated aspirations that had first made me ashamed of home and Joe. . . . In a word, it was impossible for me to separate her, in the past or in the present, from the innermost life of my life" (29). So, too, when Miss Havisham sees Estella again, "there was something positively dreadful in the energy of her looks and embrace . . . as though she were devouring the beautiful creature she had reared" (38). What is Estella's response? She sees herself as controlled, directed, used. "We have no choice, you and I," she tells Pip, "but to obey our instructions. We are not free to follow our own devices, you and I." Even more she is frighteningly dissociated from any sense of self, and Pip remarks, acutely, "You speak of yourself as if you were someone else." When she regards herself, it is as part of the cycle Miss Havisham perpetuates through her, in parrying with her jealous and demanding relatives:

> "It is not easy for even you," said Estella, "to know what satisfaction it gives me to see those people thwarted, or what an enjoyable sense of the ridiculous I have when they are made ridiculous. For you were not brought up in that strange house from a mere baby.—I was. . . .
>
> It was no laughing matter with Estella now, nor was she summoning these remembrances from any shallow place. I would not have been the cause of that look of hers, for all my expectations in a heap.   [33]

But the intensity of feeling she betrays at this moment fades away again, and she reverts to detachment: "as if our association," Pip notes, "were forced upon us and we were mere puppets."

Estella's detachment becomes her way of punishing Miss Havisham. "Her graceful figure and her beautiful face expressed a self-possessed indifference to the wild heat of the other, that was almost cruel" (38). And she enacts the cyclical movement in a way Miss Havisham cannot have foreseen, for all her coldness is now turned upon her teacher: "I have never been unfaithful to you or your schooling. I have never shown any weakness that I can charge myself with." The cold logic of this scarcely conceals the vindictiveness; the detachment and dissociation are used as a means of expressing her hatred of the role imposed upon her and her sense of what she has been denied. Yet it is also an unremitting rejection of responsibility, a responsibility she has not been taught to imagine or accept: "I am what you have made me."

Dickens presents Estella speaking in "calm wonder" as if she were discovering a process, and in some sense she may be, but we can sense more at work than mere cognition. There is a triumphant demonstration that she cannot have any feeling for the woman who now so hungrily wants it, and of whose hunger Estella is acutely aware:

> "If you had brought up your adopted daughter wholly in the dark confinement of these rooms, and had never let her know that there was such a thing as the daylight by which she has never once seen your face—if you had done that, and then, for a purpose had wanted her to understand the daylight and know all about it, you would have been disappointed and angry?"
>
> Miss Havisham, with her head in her hands, sat making a low moaning, and swaying herself on her chair, but gave no answer.
>
> "Or," said Estella, "—which is a nearer case—if you had taught her, from the dawn of her intelligence, with your utmost energy and might, that there was such a thing as daylight, but that it was made to be her enemy and destroyer, and she must always turn against it, for it had blighted you and would else blight her;—if you had done this, and then, for a purpose, had wanted her to take naturally to the daylight and she could not do it, you would have been disappointed and angry?"   [38]

And then finally there is the cool Q.E.D.: "So . . . I must be taken as I have been made. The success is not mine, the failure is not mine, but the two together make me." Whatever she is, then, is not hers. She has no self, only a role.

There is one last scene in which Estella, determined to marry Bentley Drummle, performs her role. First, there is the half-mocking, half-defensive depersonalization:

> "It seems," said Estella, very calmly, "that there are sentiments, fancies—I don't know how to call them—which I am not able to comprehend. When you say you love me [she is speaking to Pip in Miss Havisham's presence], I know what you mean, as a form of words; but nothing more. You address nothing in my breast, you touch nothing there. I don't care for what you say at all. I have tried to warn you of this; now, have I not?"   [44]

When Pip protests the insanity of marrying a brute like Drummle, Estella sustains her role; she might have been touched "if she could have rendered me at all intelligible to her own mind." And when Pip continues to protest, it becomes clear that Estella's incomprehension is something more than it seems: "On whom should I fling myself away? . . . Should I fling myself away upon the man who would soonest feel (if people do feel such things) that I took nothing to him?" When Pip repeats that Drummle is a stupid brute, Estella replies, "Don't be afraid of my being a blessing to him. . . . I shall not be that." What comes through unmistakably is her feeling, deep enough for all her performance, that she is incapable of genuine love, that she is a fit wife for only such a brute as Drummle, that her coldness or cruelty will not matter in such a marriage. And beneath this level is the other: she cannot change because Miss Havisham has made her this way, or she will not change lest she gratify Miss Havisham. Her feeling for Pip seems genuine enough so far as she can acknowledge it, but she cannot trust it or herself.

Eventually, in both the endings of the novel, suffering has been strong enough at Drummle's hands to teach her understanding, or at least to free her from the cycle which she had, in her willful and "disobedient" obedience, accepted as inevitable.

In her depersonalization, Estella resembles Lady Dedlock; in her self-distrust and self-hatred, Fanny Dorrit and Bella Wilfer. It is important to see in all these figures of Dickens's later novels women who are moved by deep and often conflicting feelings, solaced by grievance in most cases, tempted by roles that hide their feelings and offer a carapace of social success which is also the prison they seem to feel they deserve. It is in cases like these that we can see very clearly how an inauthentic social system reflects the disorder within the self and how each tends to support the other, as the system offers roles by which the self escapes the pain of full awareness.

One of the most striking features of *Great Expectations* is the way in which many characters are caught inextricably in the cycle of grievance or wrong. Magwitch, sympathetic as he is, imposes his fantasy of revenge on Pip by making him a gentleman, a gentleman that Magwitch can flaunt, at least in his mind's eye, as his own creation and his reply to a society that has abused and scorned him. But still more telling is Magwitch's compulsive pursuit of Compeyson, even at the expense of his own freedom and survival. Pip can accept Magwitch, at the end, forgive him for the cruel temptation by which he has unknowingly seduced his young beneficiary, and even sustain Magwitch's dream by telling him that his daughter has become a lady. Magwitch achieves far less self-awareness, for all his warmth. Of Molly we expect even less; she remains Jaggers's housekeeper, under his constant vigilance and restraint.

Wemmick, as many have observed, remains the divided man, cultivating warmth and love in his toy suburban fortress, seeking "portable property" with ruthlessness in the City, where he is a manipulator of people and institutions, a part of the system. His employer, Jaggers, is more complex if less picturesque; for his other self is thoroughly concealed by the roles he adopts. It appears at moments, perhaps, in the hand-washing with scented soap (although that could be part of his contemptuous role as much as some deeper compulsion of guilt), most acutely when Pip penetrates his secrecy. In response to Pip's confession of love for Estella and his despair of realizing those "poor dreams," Jaggers acknowledges "poor dreams" of his own—or at least he guardedly acknowledges that "poor dreams" have "at one time or another, been in the heads of more men than you think likely." Jaggers also reveals the depth of compassionate feeling he keeps hidden:

> "Put the case that he lived in an atmosphere of evil, and that all he saw of children, was, their being generated in great numbers for certain destruction. Put the case that he often saw children solemnly tried at a criminal bar, where they were held up to be seen; put the case that he habitually knew of their being imprisoned, whipped, transported, neglected, cast out, qualified in all ways for the hangman, and growing up to be hanged. Put the case that pretty nigh all the children he saw in his daily business life, he had reason to look upon as so much spawn, to develop into fish that were to come to his net—to be prosecuted, defended, forsworn, made orphans, bedevilled somehow. . . . Put the case, Pip, that here was one pretty little child out of the heap who could be saved. . . ."   [51]

More typical of Jaggers is the role he performs, treating his dinner guests as if they were witnesses in court, unbending to offer his professional appreciation, almost an aesthetic response (like Mr. Bennet's in *Pride and Prejudice*), to Bentley Drummle's criminal potentialities: "I like the fellow, Pip; he is one of the true sort" (26). We see Jaggers immersed in the system of legalism, buying witnesses but maintaining the fiction of ignorance, constantly assuming a posture that bullies men into servility or into truth, neither improving nor debasing the existing order, except for the isolated instances of Estella and her mother. Even there, he places Estella with a woman who can offer wealth and gentility but only at the expense of humanity, and of this Jaggers seems oblivious. He is legalism itself, one is tempted to say, not even driven by such perverse forces as Tulkinghorn in *Bleak House*; a decent, disappointed man who can see through but not beyond the system.

Finally, there is the figure of Orlick. He is like Rigaud in *Little Dorrit*, less a principal agent than a limiting case, a reduction to the most obvious and violent form of what others embody in more acceptable measure, with more claims upon our sympathy, or with more respectable disguise. When he savagely beats Mrs. Joe, he turns his mistress into a fawning slave. The relationship is best described, as it happens, by Miss Havisham's confused idea of real love: "It is blind devotion, unquestioning self-humiliation, utter submission, trust and belief against yourself and against the whole world, giving up your whole heart and soul to the smiter" (29). This in turn is the relationship Miss Havisham seeks successfully to produce between Pip and Estella; the slave of Estella must prove himself worthy by scorning Joe.

Orlick has been likened to Pip or seen as his alter ego, a surrogate for Pip's darker impulses, and in a limited sense this is true.[6] But in a more important sense it is not. Orlick is all grievance; and Pip differs in his working through to a sense of individual responsibility: "I could have done you no harm, if you had done yourself none." Orlick insists upon his simpler version: "You done it; now you pays for it" (53). He remains in the cycle of the smiter and the smitten.

The "vanity of unworthiness" may induce Pip to accuse Biddy of malice when she offers truth or to snub Joe and recoil from Magwitch; but Dickens makes more of Pip's tendency to cringe before the judgment of those who are distinctly "other." When Joe proposes to visit him in London, Pip fears especially that Joe will be seen by Bentley Drummle. "I had little objection to his being seen by Herbert or his father, for both of whom I had a respect; but I had the sharpest sensitiveness as to his being seen by Drummle, whom I held in contempt. So, throughout life, our worst weaknesses and meannesses are usually committed for the sake of the people whom we most despise" (27). (Or, one might add, "fear," as Pip fears and adores Estella.) It is the impossibility of being accepted by them as he is that confers their power. Drummle, who "either beats, or cringes" (48), has the same kind of power over Pip that Mrs. Joe did in his childhood or that Orlick wins over Mrs. Joe, the power to make him condemn himself and frantically seek a role in which he can appease the severe judge. Pip has internalized the pattern that others play out, as Dickens's heroes generally do, but that pattern is also to be seen in the action of others and in the larger action of the social system.

The World of Little Dorrit

The longer novels create a field within which a system is amply realized. These novels are themselves societies or systems within which characters are bound together by ties of various kinds—kinship, shared motives, imitation, opposition. I shall deal first with the system that is Little Dorrit and move out to aspects of other late novels. We must look at the society to which Little Dorrit alludes in order to see what kind of society it is and to what end it is created. We must in this case consider the circumstances in which the novel was written and first read.

The Crimean War evoked Dickens's bitterest accounts of the state of Britain. The "absorption of the English mind in the war" enraged Dickens. Now "every miserable red-tapist flourishes war over the head of every protester against his humbug. . . ." But Dickens felt as well the profound "alienation of the people from their public affairs": "until the people can be got up from the lethargy which is an awful symptom of the advanced state of their disease, I know of nothing that can be done beyond keeping their wrongs continually before them." The "English gentilities and subserviences render a people unfit" for representative government.[7]

The Church was hardly a liberating force, tied up as it was in its own engrossing disputes (aroused in this case by the *Essays and Reviews* of 1860):

> all in one forever quarrelling body—the *Master of the New Testament* put out of sight, and the rage and fury always turning on the letter of obscure parts of the Old Testament, which itself has been the subject of accommodation, adaptation, varying interpretation without end—these things cannot last. The Church that is to have a part in the coming time must be a more Christian one, with less arbitrary pretensions and a stronger hold on the mantle of our Saviour, as He walked and talked upon this earth.[8]

A year before his death Dickens, at the close of his will, exhorted his children "humbly to try to guide themselves by the teaching of the New Testament in its broad spirit, and to put no faith in any man's narrow construction of its letter here or there."[9]

All of these feelings seem to meet in a letter Dickens wrote as he was in the process of creating the Circumlocution Office, that splendid bureaucracy staffed by nepotism and devoted only to its self-perpetuation:

> What with teaching people to "keep in their stations"; what with bringing in the soul and body of the land to be a good child, or to go to the beer-shop, or to go a-poaching and go to the devil; what with having no such thing as a middle class (for though we are perpetually bragging of it as our safety, it is nothing but a poor fringe in the mantle of the upper); what with flunkeyism, toadyism, letting the most contemptible lords come in for all manner of places, reading The Court Circular for the New Testament, I do reluctantly believe that the English people are habitually consenting parties to the miserable imbecility into which we have fallen, and *never will help themselves out of it*. Who is to do it, if anybody is, God knows. But at present we are on the down-hill road to being conquered, and the people *will* be content to bear it, sing "Rule Britannia" and *will not* be saved.
>
> In No. 3 of my new book I have been blowing off a little indignant steam which would otherwise blow me up, and with God's leave I shall walk in the same ways all the days of my life; but I have no present political faith or hope— not a grain.[10]

The Circumlocution Office is devoted to halting change, to miscarrying ideas, to burying in scorn or indifference the least sign of independence, originality, or public concern. Dickens presents it with a mixture of outrage and delight. His "indignant steam" becomes at last a tribute to the cool enormity of the bureaucratic performance. Only one of the Barnacles is fully conscious of what they are all up to, or frank enough, at any rate, to acknowledge it. He is cheerfully cynical, as if the absurdity of seeking redress is a joke to be shared with an intelligent petitioner like Arthur Clennam and as if the attempt to elicit information were a game which the petitioner can never win but may develop great skill in playing: "Try the thing and see how you like it. It will be in your power to give it up at any time, if you don't like it. You had better take a lot of forms away with you. Give him a lot of forms!" This is said by young Ferdinand Barnacle, who understands that the office is a "politico-diplomatic hocus pocus piece of machinery for the assistance of the nobs in keeping off the snobs." Such clearheaded awareness is enough to make him a statesman. Near the end of the novel, Arthur Clennam, now in the Marshalsea, is visited by Ferdinand Barnacle, who speaks openly of the function of his office:

> "It is there with the express intention that everything shall be left alone. That is what it means. That is what it's for. No doubt there's a certain form to be kept up that it's for something else, but it's only a form. Why, good Heaven, we are nothing but forms! Think what a lot of forms you have gone through. . . . It's like a limited game of cricket. A field of outsiders are always going in to bowl at the Public Service, and we block the balls."

Ferdinand Barnacle offers the final justification of the Circumlocution Office; it provides the mystification that the people want: "our place is not a wicked Giant to be charged at full tilt; but only a windmill showing you, as it grinds immense quantities of chaff, which way the country wind blows. . . . We must have humbug, we all like humbug. We couldn't get on without humbug. A little humbug, and a groove, and everything goes on admirably, if you leave it alone" (II, 28).

From the Circumlocution Office exfoliate all kinds of pretension and humbug. During his rounds of the office, Clennam is sent to call on Mr. Tite Barnacle of Mews Street, Grosvenor Square. Mews Street is itself a hanger-on, "not absolutely Grosvenor Square, but . . . very near it," and enormously expensive because of its "fashionable situation"—"a hideous little street of dead wall, stables, and dunghills." In the damp, ill-smelling, "squeezed" little house, Tite Barnacle sits, afflicted with gout, "altogether splendid, massive, overpowering, and impracticable. He seemed to have been sitting for his portrait to Sir Thomas Lawrence all the days of his life" (I, 10). Dickens lavishes detail here upon the tawdriness of pretension as he does later upon the transparent shifts with which the aristocratic hangers-on maintain their status in their very limited (but free) quarters at Hampton Court. All the genteel arrangements—"many objects of various forms, feigning to have no connection with their guilty secret, a bed"—require a conspiracy of silence and blindness. "Callers looked steadily into the eyes of their receivers, pretended not to smell cooking three feet off." Dickens traces the costly ritual, the painstaking elaboration of trivial evasions and feeble props by which status is maintained. Much of the novel is devoted to the fictions by which people live, persuaded like Mr. Tite Barnacle or the "civilized gypsies" of Hampton Court that they impose their dignity upon others, scarcely able to imagine that the fictions are also a prison which they can never leave (I, 26). Or, more strictly, the fictions become a prison for those who still possess a sense of reality; for the rest the fictions are reality enough.

The captivity is strikingly presented in the financier Merdle's fears of his Chief Butler. A system may have its idol, but he tends to be in turn dependent on those priests who maintain its traditions and rituals. Merdle does not seem to gain any sense of power or any pleasure even from fraud. Rather he clasps his wrists "as if he were taking himself into custody" (I, 33). He wanders through his splendid house dreading encounters with his Chief Butler; the sight of this "splendid retainer always finished him." After all the sustaining flattery he receives from distinguished men as "a being of might," he returns home and, "being instantly put out again in his own hall, like a rushlight, by the Chief Butler," he goes "sighing to bed." When the bankrupt Merdle commits suicide, his Chief Butler provides society's epitaph: "Sir, Mr. Merdle never was the gentleman, and no ungentlemanly act on Mr. Merdle's part would surprise me" (II, 25).

Mrs. Merdle assumes the power her husband's wealth confers with no hesitation or self-doubt. She has an "extensive bosom, which required so much room to be unfeeling enough in. . . . It was not a bosom to repose upon, but it was a capital bosom to hang jewels upon, and he bought it for the purpose." Mrs. Merdle is the high priestess of Society, but she demurely claims to be its victim, while her parrot shrieks with derisive laughter. "We know," she tells Fanny and Amy Dorrit, that Society is "hollow and conventional and worldly and very shocking, but unless we are Savages in the Tropical Seas (I should have been charmed to be one myself—most delightful life and perfect climate, I am told), we must consult it." Or later she laments, "Society suppresses us and dominates us—Bird, be quiet!" (I, 20)

The transparence of the forms and the efforts that sustain them are most evident when Mrs. Gowan goes to seek Mrs. Merdle's approval of her son's wedding to Pet Meagles. Henry needs the Meagles's money, and Mrs. Merdle, as expert in the "matrimonial market" as her husband is in the financial, decrees that Pet is a "sufficiently good catch":

Knowing, however, what was expected of her, and perceiving the exact nature of the fiction to be nursed, she took it delicately in her arms, and put her required contribution of gloss upon it. . . . And Mrs. Gowan, who of course saw through her own threadbare blind perfectly, and who knew that Society would see through it perfectly, came out of this form, notwithstanding, as she had gone into it, with immense complacency and gravity.   [I, 33]

"Society, the Circumlocution Office, and Gowan are of course three parts of the one idea and design," Dickens wrote to John Forster.[11] Henry Gowan presents a pattern of motives more complex than bureaucracy or Society can offer. The institutions are seen as machines, their operators freed of any conflicts of feeling or any restraint by a reality principle. They are, as a result, brilliant metaphors for those patterns of collective insanity that Dickens describes as "gentilities and subserviences." Dickens presents, with an exhilaration of excess, patterns of humbug, commercialism, and pretension.

In Henry Gowan we see the process by which a man of intelligence is enfranchised in viciousness. As he comments on others, a patronizing contempt speaks through Gowan's words. By condoning everyone's failings, he manages to reveal them. His purpose is to persuade the world that "there is much less difference than you are inclined to suppose between an honest man and a scoundrel." Gowan "has sauntered into the Arts at a leisurely Pall-Mall pace," Doyce observes, "and I doubt they care to be taken quite so coolly." It is typical of Henry Gowan that he has chosen to become a painter both because it comes easily to him and because it allows him to "grieve the souls of the Barnacles-in-chief who had not provided for him." When they try to make his work fashionable, the public resists. Gowan's disappointment at having offered himself for sale only to find no buyers has left him with a grievance which he exercises as if it were an awkward honesty. "I am not a great impostor," he tells Clennam. "Buy one of my pictures and I assure you, in confidence, it will not be worth the money. Buy one of another man's—any great professor who beats me hollow—and the chances are that the more you give him, the more he'll impose on you. They all do it." All success is an "imposition" in a world that is ruled by fraudulence. "What a jolly, excellent, lovable world it is!"

Gowan adopts the tone of a disappointed man so as better to insist upon how much he deserves, and he disparages the Barnacles "lest it should be forgotten that he belonged to the family" (II, 6). He makes much, with airy laughter, of his family's feelings that he has married beneath him, for he bitterly resents his dependence on Mr. Meagles's allowance. Later, Gowan befriends Blandois and keeps him on display as a ridiculously transparent instance of universal fraudulence: "There he stands, you see. A bravo waiting for his prey, a distinguished noble waiting to save his country, the common enemy waiting to do somebody a bad turn, an angelic messenger waiting to do somebody a good turn—whatever you think he looks most like!" Struck by Gowan's lack of earnestness or stability, Little Dorrit wonders "whether it could be that he has no belief in anybody else, because he has no belief in himself?" (II, 11) Gowan is a brilliantly conceived and executed character, densely imagined, and an important dimension of the design of the whole book. Besides, he is, as Dickens felt, a kind of character that had "never been done."

The other character of comparable complexity and fullness is Fanny Dorrit, whom we can observe completing the process of self-imprisonment in the fictions of Society. Bribed, threatened, and scorned by Mrs. Merdle, she devotes her life to winning her revenge. Although she despises Mrs. Merdle's son, Sparkler, she cannot resist marrying him: "I shall make him fetch and carry, my dear, and I shall make him subject to me. And if I don't make his mother subject to me, too, it shall not be my fault" (II, 6). Is it worthwhile? Fanny hesitates for a long while; "she was ashamed of him, undetermined whether to get rid of him or more decidedly encourage him, distracted with apprehensions that she was every day becoming more and more enmeshed in her uncertainties, and tortured by misgivings that Mrs. Merdle triumphed in her distress."

When her sister protests the futility of living an unhappy life for the sake of tormenting Mrs. Merdle, Fanny replies in a "desolate tone": "It wouldn't be an unhappy life, Amy. It would be the life I am fitted for." Yet once she has decided to accept Sparkler, Fanny responds to Amy's tears with her own. "It was the last time Fanny ever showed that there was any hidden, suppressed, or conquered feeling in her on the matter. From that hour the way she had chosen lay before her, and she trod it with her own imperious step" (II, 14). We see her shortly after, "completely arrayed for her new part . . . no longer feeling that want of a defined place and character which had caused her so much trouble" (II, 15). At the close of the book, after the collapse of Merdle's empire, we find Fanny and Mrs. Merdle in as fashionable a house as they can afford, "inhabiting different floors of the genteel little temple of inconvenience to which the smell of the day before yesterday's soup and coach-horse was as constant as death to man." Fanny is "proud, fitful, whimsical . . . resolved always to want comfort, resolved not to be comforted, resolved to be deeply wronged, and resolved that nobody should have the audacity to think her so" (I, 33). Little Dorrit cares for Fanny's neglected children as she once cared for Fanny herself.

It is important to see how these more complex characters lend substance to—and gain import from—the extravagance and mindless self-assertion of others. There is no problem of congruity in Fanny's scenes with Mrs. Merdle, for in those scenes Fanny is seen as vindictive and single-minded, almost as uncomplicated as the Bosom herself. But in the scenes with her sister all the suppressed shame and regret are released, and they make Fanny's progress toward her imprisonment a moving study of dehumanization.

Little Dorrit exhibits, as do all of Dickens's major novels, a pattern of family resemblances which relates characters to each other in varying ways, with alliances or parallels in one aspect cutting across differences in another. Clearly William Dorrit cadging from visitors as the Father of Marshalsea, unable to face the coppers poor Plornish gives him or any other affront to his precarious dignity, is somewhat like the great Merdle cowering before his Chief Butler. But William Dorrit's dining in state, on the food Amy has saved from her own meal, resembles Mrs. Clennam's spare but elegant meals, particularly the handsome dish of oysters she sends back in self-punishment. And Mrs. Clennam's "grim luxuriousness" in her airless room may be recalled as Mrs. Merdle "composes herself voluptuously, in a nest of crimson and gold" (I, 20). Mrs. Clennam's boast that she knows "nothing of summer and winter, shut up here" (I, 3) may be recalled in Christopher Casby's "sober, silent, air-tight house," where there is a "grave clock, ticking somewhere up the staircase; and . . . a songless bird in the same direction, pecking at his cage, as if he were ticking too" (I, 13). Or to bring social extremes together, we can relate Mrs. Merdle's game of primitivism ("my dear, I am pastoral to a degree, by nature" [II, 33]) to the Plornishes' "little fiction," an interior wall "painted to represent the exterior of a thatched cottage" ("To come out of the shop after it was shut, and hear her father sing a song inside this cottage, was a perfect Pastoral to Mrs. Plornish, the Golden Age revived" [II, 13]).

These resemblances are not the most important ones; they will not strike everyone who reads the book, and they need not. But they indicate the kind of analogy that Dickens's structure makes possible and the great range of possibilities that the system, "the one idea and design," accommodates. Any account of *Little Dorrit* as a novel must consider the various forms of imprisonment that run through the novel. They take the form of senility and mental retardation, of dogmatic religion and the worship of wealth, of self-distrust and of paranoid rage. The temptation of the prison as delusory freedom, as escape from difficulty and responsibility, is treated early in the account of William Dorrit: "If he had been a man of strength of purpose to face those troubles and fight them, he might have broken the net that held him, or broken his heart; but being what he was, he languidly slipped into this smooth descent, and never more took one step upward" (I, 6). The debtors' prison is one form of surrender, but, as we see in the use of such phrases as "genteel fiction" or "genteel mystification," the higher world has its own kinds of captivity. H. M. Daleski makes the important point that arrest of movement, of action, of mind appears throughout the novel, whether in the denial of time by Mrs. Clennam or in the circular motion that creates the perfection of How Not To Do It. One may contrast the deadly "stare" of the sun in the opening chapter with the changes and seasons seen in the vitality of a healthy autumn day. The fields are ploughed, fruit has ripened, leaves fall, the ocean in "its whole breadth" is "in joyful animation" (II, 34). A principal contrast with "arrest" is the growth toward fulfillment. So energetic is the vitality of normal growth that the arrest must become a strenuous pressure, a violence committed upon oneself or upon others. We see this most sharply, perhaps, in the self-torment of Miss Wade, who has learned to interpret all experience as a grievance, or in the self-punishment of Mrs. Clennam, who has created a "monstrous idol" of her "vindictive pride and rage." Both women cling to their wrongs, Mrs. Clennam in severe self-punishment, Miss Wade in bitter retaliation. Neither can relinquish her torment; once Mrs. Clennam does so, her house falls as if it had been the edifice of her will, and she survives it only in three years of paralysis and "rigid silence."

Beside these characters, Flora Finching provides a brilliant comic transposition of the theme. She was Arthur Clennam's love of twenty years before; but she has become "diffuse and silly." "Is not Papa precisely what he was when you went away?" she asks, hoping that time has not served her worse. But for Clennam she is the girl "whom he had left a lily" and who has now "become a peony" (I, 13). She is a large woman, a little given to drink, locked up in a coy and breathless monologue. Within its protection she can believe what she says, as in her account to Amy Dorrit of Clennam's feelings and her own: " 'We were all in all to one another it was bliss it was frenzy it was everything else of that sort in the highest degree, when rent asunder we turned to stone in which capacity Arthur went to China and I became the statue bride of the late Mr. F' " (I, 24). She has moments of shrewdness which she cannot sustain and perhaps conceals from herself. She buries them in a torrent of girlish and "literary" talk, constantly testing her power to charm but—with a flash of that shrewdness—careful not to test it too far. There is an element of pathos in all this, but the repetitive comic pattern is dominant, and it is intensified by the coupling of Flora with the heritage which has been left to her widowhood, Mr. F's Aunt. That little old woman, "with a face like a staring wooden doll too cheap for expression" shows even in repose "extreme severity and grim taciturnity" (I, 13). She emerges from her own dark fantasies only to hurl out her cryptic abuse, "breathing bitterness and scorn, and staring leagues away" (I, 23). She displays "implacable hostility" to Arthur Clennam (such as he half-expects of the world), raging as she does so with more overt insanity than Miss Wade or Blandois. She has the wonderful comic force—accompanied as it is with Flora's bland tolerance—of a fierce hostility without basis or meaning, a rage that is terrible and ludicrous and yet harmless, like the frightening grimaces monkeys enact inside their cages. She cuts the blandness of Flora's chatter; and she at least raises the question of whether most malignity is not after all "motiveless," however many grievances it may have collected in its brief.

The central characters, Little Dorrit and Arthur Clennam, have a peculiar mixture of weakness and strength. Clennam, returning after twenty years in China to a mother who has never loved him, has no force of assertion, "no will," as he says (I, 2). But if his nature has been "disappointed from the dawn of its perceptions," it has "not quite given up all its hopeful yearnings yet" (I, 3). He rejects the "whimpering weakness and cruel selfishness" of the embittered; he has "a mind too firm and healthy" to nourish grievance or self-pity (I, 13). But he thinks of himself as too old and too much a failure to court Pet Meagles, and he permits himself to see Little Dorrit only as "his delicate child." She, in turn, is used to a life of self-effacement and exertion, never embarrassing her family with any hint of their dependence on her, needed but unloved. She is an "invisible" figure (I, 4), as Elinor Dashwood is in *Sense and Sensibility*. More than that, she not only seems a child to others, but often sees herself as a child. Only for Maggy, the large woman whose mind stopped in a fever at the age of ten, is Amy a "little mother." By the end of the novel they have learned to see themselves through each other's eyes; Arthur becomes younger and Amy Dorrit older, and both have grown out of their damaged unassertive selves into a capacity for more confident love.

Does Dickens offer us Little Dorrit as an "angel in the house"? She does, of course, recall to Mrs. Clennam the "patient Master who shed tears of compassion for our infirmities" and in whose life there is "no vengeance and no infliction of suffering" (II, 31). Yet I think Dickens is as much aware, and means us to be aware, of Little Dorrit's deficiencies as Jane Austen was of Fanny Price's. Lionel Trilling saw these deficiencies as leading us to see in her "not only the child of the Marshalsea, as she is called, but also the Child of the Parable, the negation of the social will." I would not question that this may be suggested, and Alexander Welsh gives that suggestion a context in the heroines of other Victorian writers as well.[12] But I should also stress the degree of psychological reality Dickens achieves. Arthur Clennam, when he is a prisoner himself in the Marshalsea, sees Little Dorrit in a new light. He wonders at her wearing her "old, worn dress" (II, 29). She has thought, as she tells him, that "you would like me better in this dress than any other. . . . I have always kept it by me, to remind me: though I wanted no reminding." By remaining faithful in memory to the past, and thereby to reality, both Amy Dorrit and Clennam have earned the right (and the freedom) to grow and move forward. With his recovery from illness and Doyce's assurance that their partnership stands, Arthur fully overcomes his reserve and self-mistrust; and Little Dorrit, though insisting on that name, finally puts off the wistful timidity she has shown wherever her own happiness is concerned. It is Daniel Doyce who has set the note for this muted triumph: "You hold your life on the condition that to the last you struggle hard for it" (I, 15). Doyce embodies "a calm knowledge that what was true must remain true . . . and would be just the truth, and neither more or less." It is that "calm knowledge," really a new depth and stability of self, that we see in the last sentence of the book: "They went quietly down into the roaring streets, inseparable and blessed; and as they passed along in sunshine and shade, the noisy and the eager, and the arrogant and the froward and the vain, fretted and chafed, and made their usual uproar" (II, 34).

The Energies of the Self

The characters who seem most typically and resplendently Dickensian are those who are at once most free and most compulsive. Pecksniff, in *Martin Chuzzlewit,* is infinitely resourceful in "finding the most unexpected ways of being himself," as Mary McCarthy has described the comic character.[13] He seems like a tireless student of rhetorical feints and rhapsodies, his moral instrument always in tune and ready for performance; and one can admire him as a brilliantly cunning hypocrite or as a superbly efficient machine. In fact, he is somewhere between the two, for he depends upon "sounds and forms," using "any word that occurred to him as having a good sound and rounding a sentence well, without much care for its meaning" (2). Pecksniff's performance is almost musical, but it is also handsomely syntactical; he creates the effect of thought without the burden of meaning. He is so rapid and effortless in generating cant that he can hardly be said to have devised hypocritical utterance. He does not suffer pangs of conscience or the strain of effort, and he seems, as a result, free in a way that responsible, just, or painstaking men never can be. He catches that tendency all of us have to lapse into roles that relieve us of the strain of thought and decision. We go on playing, and after a while overplaying, the fixed and familiar self that others expect, but we do this through weariness or neglect or inattention. A character like Pecksniff, however, is never jaded; and we never know how much thought goes on within him. He is so prompt with his characteristic speech or gesture that we are tempted to wonder whether he has an interior at all. This is the very obverse of the deviousness we associate with hypocrisy; Pecksniff's ease and flamboyance seem to lend him an air of spontaneity, even of innocence.

Pecksniff's irrepressible sanctimoniousness seems at moments to contain an assertion of will and a measure of malice; but then nothing quite means anything, and one risks vertigo in trying to separate out the feelings it might, in another, express. This becomes more elaborate when Mrs. Lupin tells Pecksniff about old Martin Chuzzlewit's condition:

"He is better, and quite tranquil," answered Mrs. Lupin.

"He is better and quite tranquil," said Mr. Pecksniff. "Very well! ve-ry well!"

Here again, though the statement was Mrs. Lupin's and not Mr. Pecksniff's, Mr. Pecksniff made it his own and consoled her with it. It was not much when Mrs. Lupin said it but it was a whole book when Mr. Pecksniff said it. "I observe," he seemed to say, "and through me, morality in general remarks that he is better and quite tranquil." [3]

This embodiment of morality is to be seen in the least gesture. Just as the silver-haired Patriarch of *Little Dorrit,* Christopher Casby, "disposed of an immense quantity of solid food with the benignity of a good soul who was feeding someone else" (I, 13), so Pecksniff is seen "warming his back . . . as if it were a widow's back, or an orphan's back, or an enemy's back, or a back that any less excellent man would have suffered to be cold" (3).

In *Little Dorrit,* after Merdle is dead, he turns out to have been a "heavily-made man, with an obtuse head, and coarse, mean, common features" (II, 25), and Casby, when shorn by Pancks of his silver hair, is a "bare-polled, goggle-eyed, big-headed lumbering personage" (II, 32). So Pecksniff dwindles when he is alone. Just after he has pressed his courtship on Mary Graham and has in effect threatened her with blackmail, he is alone for a moment:

He seemed to be shrunk and reduced, to be trying to hide himself within himself, and to be wretched at not having the power to do it. His shoes looked too large, his sleeve looked too long, his hair looked too limp, his features looked too mean. . . . For a minute or two, in fact, he was hot, and pale, and mean, and shy, and slinking, and consequently not at all Pecksniffian. [30]

Pecksniff, in fact, does not exist except in performance any more than Merdle exists without his money or Casby without his hair.

Dickens, in this novel full of rhetoric, often adopts the idiom of his characters, and he does so most brilliantly in the fussy and fantasticated execution of transition. Chapter 20 closes with a loud knocking at Pecksniff's door, and chapter 21 begins in America:

The knocking at Mr. Pecksniff's door, though loud enough, bore no resemblance whatever to the noise of an American railway train at full speed. It may be well to begin the present chapter with this frank admission, lest the reader should imagine that the sounds now deafening this history's ears have any connexion with the knocks on Mr. Pecksniff's door. . . .

Pecksniff's kind of rhetoric becomes a way of life in America; a people brutish in manners are hypnotized by abstractions and preposterously lofty in

sentiment. In England, the counterpart of Pecksniff's rhetoric is Tigg's magnificent Anglo-Bengalee Disinterested Loan and Life Assurance Company.
That fraudulent business is born fully grown, a large brass plate on its door
to stare down skepticism, the offices sumptuous and solid enough to confer
financial stability. And the very heart of the Anglo-Bengalee is the "vast red
waistcoat" that Bullamy, the porter, wears. More properly the waistcoat
wears and acts through Bullamy. "Being charged to show Jonas out, it went
before, and the voice within it cried as usual, 'By your leave there, by your
leave!' " (27)

Pecksniff's power of imposition finds its necessary victim in a credulous
Tom Pinch, who needs to believe in Pecksniff and is almost shattered when
he comes at last to see through his master's fictions. Tom is suddenly robbed
of all stability: "There was no Pecksniff; there had never been a Pecksniff;
and all his other griefs were swallowed up in that." So much reality makes
all of his previous life seem suddenly unreal. It is too much at first for Tom
to bear, and he has to retreat: "it was as much as Tom could do to say his
prayers without him. But he felt happier afterwards, and went to sleep, and
dreamed about him as he Never Was" (31).

Tom Pinch raises troubling questions. His credulity, in a sense, creates
Pecksniff, somewhat as Little Dorrit's constant service sustains the Father of
the Marshalsea. Such belief is a power of selfless devotion that can be given
only by a virtuous, even angelic, soul; yet as a social force it can seem merely
that need for humbug with which the airiest of Barnacles consoled Arthur
Clennam. Little Dorrit may wish not to see the vanity of her childish and
dependent father, or try not to acknowledge it, even though she must know
his humbug well in order to protect it. Pinch's devotion has less justification
than Little Dorrit's, and it borders on the naive admiration the tenants of
the Bleeding Heart Yard show to the silver-haired Patriarch. Dickens has
some of Jeremy Bentham's scorn for the fictions by which men enslave themselves, but he has sympathy for the needs, whether real or imaginary, which
they fulfill.

Dickens's great and monstrous talkers produce splendid verbal structures;
these are self-enclosing and cannot be abandoned except at the cost of existence. Pecksniff can wilt for a solitary moment or two, but he must resume
his fiction; and he exists only to the degree that he has occasion to produce
it anew.[14] An artist like Dickens, in contrast, is master of his fictions. They
are for him the exercise of freedom. There are moments when Pecksniff *almost*
seems to be looking around the corner of his own idiom, laughing behind a
straight face, inviting us to share the joke and help him keep it up. "My
feelings, Mrs. Todgers, will not consent to be entirely smothered, like the
young children in the Tower. They are grown up and the more I press the
bolster on them, the more they look around the corner of it" (9).

Such moments never arise for Sairey Gamp. She has a rudimentary sense of what is decorous and of how to create a favorable impression. It is her enthusiastic elaborations that take a turn toward the bizarre and achieve splendid comic effect: " 'Ah!' repeated Mrs. Gamp; for it was always a safe sentiment in cases of mourning. 'Ah dear! When Gamp was summoned to his long home, and I see him a-lying in Guy's Hospital with a penny-piece on each eye, and his wooden leg under his left arm, I thought I should have fainted away. But I bore up' " (19). Mrs. Gamp's self-interest outruns whatever small talent she has for hypocrisy. We see her with a "leer of mingled sweetness and slyness; with one eye on the future, one on the bride, and an arch expression in her face, partly spiritual, partly spiritous, and wholly professional and peculiar to her art" (26). She declares, it is true, "I feels the sufferins of other people more than I feels my own"; but within a few pages she and Mrs. Prig work over their helpless patient with righteous disregard of his feelings and a strong sense of duty to their own comfort (29). " 'Bite a person's thumbs or turn their fingers the wrong way,' said Mrs. Gamp, smiling with the consciousness of at once imparting pleasure and instruction to her auditors, 'and they comes to, wonderful, Lord bless you!' " (46)

Sairey Gamp's crisis occurs when Betsy Prig challenges the authority and finally the existence of the often-cited Mrs. Harris. Under the strain of Mrs. Prig's doubts, Mrs. Gamp calls up her image of Mrs. Harris with great particularity; but she cannot quite recover her customary assurance (or is it by now belief?), and to speak again of Mrs. Harris requires extraordinary effort. Mrs. Harris has been the supply of sanction and praise for all Sairey Gamp wished to do. She is only more ludicrously fictitious than those props that most people need, and she takes her place in the spectrum of fictions that the characters of *Martin Chuzzlewit* live by—the innocent fictions by which Mark Tapley or Tom Pinch accommodate themselves to the egotists, the more elaborate fictional worlds invented and sustained by hypocrite and swindler, the windy idealism of American rhetoric that accompanies sharp practices, the macabre terrors of a fearful victim and his guilty murderer.

Frustration and Aggression

Dickens catches the enormous energies of self-assertion in the structures those energies create and inhabit. In Pecksniff and Mrs. Gamp the assertion creates an idiom—virtually *is* an idiom—that seems generated without much intervention of thought. The words come from a deeper source than thought, and they push back all question or resistance. But these energies of the self are no less powerful in their suppression. Carker sees this in Edith Dombey. He recognizes the strife within her even as "haughty languor and indifference come over it, and hide it like a cloud." Edith sees herself as once "taught to scheme and plot when children play," now "hawked and vended" by her mother, until, as she says, "the last grain of self-respect is dead within me, and I loathe myself." It is "her energy of shame and strong pride" that require a high manner of haughtiness to conceal them (27). Like Estella, she feels an emptiness in herself, or worse; for she is terrified of her power to corrupt or destroy others. She warns Florence not to learn from her: "That I should teach you how to love, or be loved, Heaven forbid!" (35) It is her feeling for Florence that becomes the one element of her nature she can trust, and Dombey's jealousy of it is most painful of all to Edith: "You have made me sacrifice . . . the only gentle feeling and interest of my life" (47). She becomes aware of Carker's observation of her true feelings and tries to wear a mask before him, as Lady Dedlock does before Tulkinghorn, but with as little success. Edith expresses her scorn as she motions that Carker be seated: "No action could be colder, haughtier, more insolent in its air of supremacy and disrespect, but she had struggled against that concession ineffectually, and it was wrested from her" (37). The slight gesture and the enormous tension of which it is the issue—these are surpassed later when Carker kisses her hand. Alone in her room, "she struck it on the marble chimney-shelf so that, at one blow, it was bruised and bled" (42).

As Barbara Hardy says, Edith's initial weariness is a "very real fatigue caused by the hard work of constant unnatural performance and advertisement." The "mask of world-weariness" is, in fact, "a mask for moral energy," which can only be spent in frustration and rage, in bitter pride and guilt. In rejecting Carker as a lover, however, Edith "uses him humiliatingly, giving him the name of a seducer in order to ruin Dombey and herself, but in the process executing a spirited and subtle sexual revenge on the man who has seen through her reserve." Barbara Hardy's account restores the complexity that critics have too often denied Edith, and it catches the mixture of motives in her actions—their moral outrage, vindictiveness, and assertion of pride.[15]

The sources of Lady Dedlock's guilt are different, but she, too, wears a mask of weariness. Even in Paris, "my lady Dedlock has been bored to death. Concert, assembly, opera, theatre, drive, nothing is new to my Lady, under the worn-out heavens" (2). Her "exhausted composure" shows the strain of performing a role which is false to what has most deeply moved her; she believes her lover and her child both to be dead. It is her unaccustomed animation that betrays her to Tulkinghorn when she happens to recognize her lover's handwriting in the copy of a legal paper. This is the opening which will allow Tulkinghorn to discover her secret, and it begins the action which leads eventually to her death at her lover's grave.

The world of Lady Dedlock's boredom is the life of aristocratic ceremony which preempts feeling: "There are ladies and gentlemen . . . not so new but very elegant, who have agreed to put a smooth glaze on the world, and to keep down all realities. For whom everything must be languid and pretty. Who have found out the perpetual stoppage. Who are to rejoice at nothing and be sorry for nothing. Who are not to be disturbed by ideas" (12). Here, in *Bleak House,* Dickens anticipates the "stoppage" of thought in the Circumlocution Office and the "gloss" which Society applies to its fictions in *Little Dorrit.* Here also are the frozen gravity and vulnerable rigidity of Sir Leicester, devoted to his wife and altogether incapable of imagining Tulkinghorn's motives. Her secret exerts enormous pressure upon her, and Tulkinghorn, as counterpressure, demands that she remain silent and stay at Chesney Wold. When she can run away at last after Tulkinghorn's death, she leaves without knowing how her husband feels: that it is "she, who, at the core of all the constrained formalities and conventionalities of his life, had been a stock of living tenderness and love" (54). The dignities which Tulkinghorn has so jealously upheld are only a surface, after all, for Sir Leicester as well as his wife, but a surface which all but smothers the life within. When Sir Leicester stipulates that he will "revoke no disposition" he has made in his wife's favor, his "formal array of words might have at any other time, as it has often had, something ludicrous in it; but at this time it is serious and affecting" (58).

Edith Dombey and Lady Dedlock have assumed roles which are the denial of their deepest feelings, and the performance of the role is exacted at the moment it becomes most painfully unreal and oppressive. In both cases, there is at last a bursting out into flight and disgrace, an escape that achieves release from intolerable constriction. A third such case, Mrs. Clennam's departure from her "cell of years," has the fierce intensity of paralysis overcome by a commanding purpose. Although the paralysis has been in some sense self-imposed, it has become a way of life. Nor is it fully overcome. "This is not recovery; it is not strength; I don't know what it is," Mrs. Clennam says to Little Dorrit. Once she has exerted this last energy of will and self-assertion, the paralysis returns completely and finally.

In each of these cases the energy consumed in preserving stability and surface is a measure of the power of the feelings that are suppressed. When Arthur Clennam recalls the "legions of Sundays" he has endured, "all days of unserviceable bitterness and mortification," he thinks of the "resentful Sunday . . . when he sat down glowering and glooming through the tardy length of the day, with a sullen sense of injury in his heart" (I, 3). And the retreat of the Casbys is a "sober, silent, air-tight house—one might have fancied it to have been stifled by Mutes in the Eastern manner" (I, 13). In each case the refuge is absurdly and expensively propped up, like the Clennam house, and as likely to collapse.

Perhaps the most complex treatment of this suppression in Dickens's he-

roes is Eugene Wrayburn in *Our Mutual Friend*. He exhibits displacement of
feeling: what leads him to take refuge in the contemptible triviality of the
Veneerings is the resentment of M. R. F., "my respected father," who has
forced him to become a barrister. We see Wrayburn's feelings emerge when
his friend and counterpart, Mortimer Lightwood, first recounts the story of
the Harmons to the guests at the Veneerings' table. While Lightwood tells
it with a certain amount of languid irony, he reveals some of the feeling the
story awakens in him. "It is hidden with great pains, but it is in him. The
gloomy Eugene, too, is not without some kindred touch." When others
laugh, Wrayburn "trifles quite ferociously with his dessert-knife." (I, 2).
But these feelings are usually suppressed under the guise of indolence. "If
there is a word in the dictionary under any letter from A to Z that I abomi-
nate," Eugene declares, "it is energy. It is such a conventional superstition.
Such parrot gabble!" Mortimer agrees and adds, with little risk, "show me
something really worth being energetic about, and *I*'ll show you energy." A
less than admiring narrator adds: "And it is likely enough that ten thousand
other young men, within the limits of the London post-office town-delivery,
made the same hopeful remark in the course of the same evening" (I, 3).

Wrayburn and Lightwood cultivate their sense of boredom, almost luxu-
riate in the futility of their profession; for in that at least they are undoing
their fathers' prearrangements. But Wrayburn has been moved by Lizzie
Hexam: "That lonely girl with the dark hair runs in my head." He begins
to feel dishonest as they pursue evidence to support Rogue Riderhood's accusation of her father. But this moral conflict adopts the outward form of a
"ridiculous humour," and "intensification of all that was wildest and most
negligent and reckless" in him, "something new and strained" (I, 13). When
he visits Lizzie after her father's death and offers to pay for her schooling, he
is self-deprecating but genuinely uncertain about his motives. "I confess
myself a man to be doubted," he says, and adds, "I am a bad idle dog."
When Jenny Wren asks why he doesn't reform "and be a good dog," he falls
back on that passivity which is also a demand: "Because . . . there's nobody
who makes it worth my while." When Lizzie demurs at accepting his help,
he goes on, still rather airily, "I propose to be of some use to somebody—
which I never was in this world, and never shall be on any other occasion."
As he tries to argue Lizzie out of "false pride," he reveals more of himself
than he supposes: the "passing appearance of earnestness, complete conviction, injured resentment of suspicion, generous and unselfish interest."

Eugene keeps protesting his avoidance of cant: "I might have got myself
up, morally, as Sir Eugene Bountiful. But upon my soul, I can't make such
flourishes, and I would rather be disappointed than try." Yet his protective
cynicism begins to give way. He may distrust moral postures, but he must
begin to recognize and insist upon certain virtues, even in himself: "I hate

to claim to mean well, but I really did mean honestly and simply well, and I want you to know it." He cannot sustain this very long. When Lizzie accepts his help he reverts to his old manner: "I am thinking of setting up a doll, Miss Jenny." And Jenny's reply is acute: "You had better not. . . . You are sure to break it. All you children do" (II, 2).

Later, under Lightwood's questioning of his motives, Wrayburn maintains his old indolence: " 'You know what I am, my dear Mortimer. You know how deadfully susceptible I am to boredom. You know that when I became enough of a man to find myself an embodied conundrum, I bored myself to the last degree by trying to find out what I meant. You know that at length I gave it up, and declined to guess any more.' " Lightwood feels more and more fear of what Wrayburn intends in his relations with Lizzie. Wrayburn seems to defy the prejudices of social class which would keep him from wishing to marry her: "There is no better among my people at home; no better among your people." But his answer is an evasion, and Lightwood persists in questioning Eugene's design: "What is to come of it? What are you doing? Where are you going?" Wrayburn's passivity becomes by now a dangerous self-indulgence. He declares himself "incapable of designs," too bored or weary to carry one out. To Lightwood's questions he can only reply with the "troublesome conundrum" that he remains to himself. Can he solve it? Can he control his actions or choose his motives? Can he become responsible for his actions? No, he can't. "I give it up!" (II, 6)

Wrayburn is almost ready to believe himself capable of love. He is struck by his own energy. "Did you ever see me take so much trouble about any thing, as about this disappearance of hers?" he asks Lightwood. "I ask, for information." Wrayburn's alienation from himself is sincere enough so far as it goes; but it precludes the assumption of responsibility. When he asks, "What do I mean?" he speaks "with a perplexed and inquisitive face, as if he actually did not know what to make of himself" (III, 10). He can only throw himself wholeheartedly into the immediate effort to find Lizzie; but he must leave unexamined and uncommitted what will follow. His finding of Lizzie makes him face those questions he had deferred. "He looked at her with a real sentiment of remorseful tenderness and pity. It was not strong enough to impel him to sacrifice himself and spare her, but it was a strong emotion." Lizzie cannot help but reveal the abjectness of her love; Eugene recognizes her purity, her remoteness, even her transcendence of all his troubled feelings. "He held her, almost as if she were sanctified to him by death, and kissed her, once, almost as he might have kissed the dead" (IV, 6).

When Lizzie has left him, Wrayburn engages in soliloquy, astonished by the tears he has shed, at the same time aware of his power over her. As he thinks of marrying her, he summons up the views of M. R. F.: "You wouldn't marry for some money and some station, because you were frightfully likely to become bored. Are you less frightfully likely to become bored, marrying for no money and no station? Are you sure of yourself?" And Wrayburn concludes: *"Not* sure of myself." He rejects the "profligate and worthless" manner of "levity," however, and seeks earnestness in his thoughts of her. But as soon as he defiantly asserts his true devotion, he slips away from it into his knowledge of his power over Lizzie. "To try no more to go away, and to try her again" is the "reckless conclusion" he comes to. As he does so, he hears another introjected voice, Mortimer Lightwood's, saying, "Eugene, Eugene, Eugene, this is a bad business!" It is while he is in that state of irresolution ("Out of the question to marry her . . . and out of the question to leave her") that Wrayburn is attacked and all but killed by Bradley Headstone (IV, 6).

The schoolmaster Headstone is earnest in all the ways that Wrayburn is not; he is a slow, ambitious, and passionate man. His earnestness has worked hard "to get what it had won, and . . . to hold it now that it was gotten" (II, 1). Whereas Wrayburn affects languor and idleness in the hope of somehow being restored by a sense of purpose, Headstone is in command of a purpose he can hardly restrain. Headstone is a structure of precarious controls, as much energy required for suppression as for achievement. He blusters about his moral superiority ("a better man than you with better reasons for being proud"), but he seems hard put to believe in it (II, 6). Why does he want to marry Lizzie? This tightly "decent" man seems stirred by passion he has heretofore held in control, and there is only additional stimulation in Wrayburn's rivalry. At any rate, the sight of Lizzie and Wrayburn together is explosive: "It seemed to him as if all that he could suppress in himself he had suppressed, as if all that he could restrain in himself he had restrained, and the time had come—in a rush, in a moment—when the power of self-command had departed from him" (II, 11).

When Headstone proposes marriage, Lizzie is shocked by his intensity. "The wild energy of the man, now quite let loose, was absolutely terrible." Hardly less terrible is his fierce effort to exercise control; he grasps a stone in the wall and wrenches at it. As he concludes his proposal, declaring, "I am in thorough earnest, dreadful earnest," the mortar that holds the stone begins to crumble and fall. When she refuses him, he brings his "clenched hand down upon the stone with a force that laid the knuckles raw and bleeding," and he exclaims, "Then I hope I may never kill him!" By this point Headstone wants as much to win Lizzie away from Wrayburn as to have her for himself. His self-respect, he now asserts, "lies under that fellow's feet, and he treads upon it and exults above it." That, as he says with the legalism of paranoia, is "how the case stands, so far" (II, 15).

Wrayburn recognizes the malicious pleasure he takes in goading Bradley Headstone to madness. "The amiable occupation has been the solace of my life, since I was baulked [by Lizzie's departure]. . . . I have derived inex-

pressible comfort from it." It is as if all the confusion and frustration Wrayburn feels within himself were released in this torture of Headstone, and
possibly in the danger this creates for himself (III, 10). Headstone, in turn,
feels himself becoming murderous and takes a grim pleasure in it: "Under
his daily restraint, it was his compensation, not his trouble, to give a glance
towards his state at night, and to the freedom of its being indulged" (III,
11). Here Dickens is concerned with the movement toward crime: the struggles of murderers are *toward* murder. Headstone knows that he will gain
nothing by finding Lizzie Hexam through following Wrayburn; but the sight
of them together may suffice to drive him into the violent action he seems
to have come to desire most of all.

In both these men Dickens presents enormous force of feeling that finds
no issue but a destructive one. Wrayburn is frustrated by his own division;
he can scarcely admit to himself his design of seducing Lizzie, he can face
even less the bolder and more difficult choice of marrying her. The boredom
of which he complains and which he professes to fear in marriage seems,
finally, the strain of evasion. It is the kind of evasion and resentment he has
so far shown in his submission to his father's will. He has become a barrister
for all his hatred of the career, he hates it the more because it has been
imposed upon him, and he perhaps hates himself most for allowing this to
happen. Somewhat like Henry Gowan, he cultivates transparent fools—his
Blandois is Lady Tippins. But such diversion hardly fills the "emptiness"
Lizzie sees in him. Wrayburn falls back on class superiority and torments
Headstone as a release for his own feelings. Headstone's frustration demands
the release of murder; all his decency and tight respectability have gradually
become more a source of rage than a defense of achievement. Wrayburn's
action is not more admirable for being less directly destructive. And one can
see in both his torment of Headstone and his design upon Lizzie the old
mixture of insolence and indolence.

The recovery of Wrayburn from the near-death he suffers is the most important of the many instances of rebirth the novel provides, sometimes per-
versely or ironically, sometimes quite genuinely. We see it in John Harmon's
near-death and the new role he sustains. We see it in the dustheaps being
combed for treasure, in Mr. Venus's taxidermy, in Charley Hexam's success,
in Betty Higden's escape. We see it in both Bella's growth into a capacity
for love and in the new life she creates for her father. We see it in its most
rudimentary form with the resuscitation of Rogue Riderhood. So long as it
is life itself the watchers wait for, all are full of awe and hope. Once life
resumes the form of Rogue Riderhood, feelings cool and hearts harden. "The
spark of life was deeply interesting while it was in abeyance, but now . . .
there appears to be a general desire that circumstances had admitted of its
being developed in anybody else, rather than that gentleman" (III, 3).

Dickens plays here as throughout the book on the pain of life and the difficulty of rebirth: "And yet—like us all, when we swoon—like us all, every day of our lives when we wake—he is instinctively unwilling to be restored to the consciousness of this existence, and would be left dormant if he could" (III, 3). The chapter which presents Betty Higden's death, at the end of her foolish and touching flight, catches this final note in the "tender river whispering . . . 'Come to me, come to me!' " (III, 8) This theme reaches to its fullest expression in the figure of Jenny Wren, and it is her presence which is summoned to preside over the rebirth of Wrayburn. A crippled girl—with a crooked back and a small, twisted frame—she has had precocity forced upon her by a drunken, irresponsible father. She must help earn their living and keep him out of trouble, and she assumes the role of a shrewish parent, as if concern, however harsh, is what she most misses in her father's insensibility. Jenny's life is shot through with pain, and she often finds the vent it requires in anger. She is full of dislike for those children who taunt her—"calling names in through a person's key hole, and imitating a person's back and legs." She can summon up visionary punishments for them: "There's doors under the church in the Square—black doors, leading into black vaults." She would cram them in and lock the door, blow pepper in through the key hole and then taunt them once they were sneezing (II, 1). There is no need to stress the compensatory nature of such a fantasy or of her more generous visions, so reminiscent of Blake's Songs of Innocence. As she sits at work she smells "miles of flowers," the "white and pink May in the hedges, and all sorts of flowers that I never was among." As she describes such visions, her manner is "for the moment quite inspired and beautiful." And the vision expands to those children she saw—"not chilled, anxious, ragged or beaten" but rather descending in long bright slanting rows, saying "Who is this in pain?" " 'When I told them who it was, they answered, "Come and play with us!" When I said, "I never play! I can't play!" they swept about me and took me up, and made me light' " (II, 2). The visions of release seem, if anything, sadder than those of rancor and retaliation, if only because escape seems sadder and more hopeless than aggression.

In her role of dolls' dressmaker Jenny Wren pretends to create and control the lives of others, and, even more, she sees herself exacting service from the fashionable people whose costumes provide her with models. These are fantasies of power. But the most brilliant of fantasies are those she evokes on the city rooftop where her friend, the Jew Riah, has spread a carpet like a garden in a desert. She explains the appeal of this place to the mean-spirited Fledgeby:

> "But it's so high. And you see the clouds rushing on above the narrow streets, not minding them, and you see the golden arrows pointing at the mountains in the sky from which the wind comes, and you feel as if you were dead. . . .

Oh, so peaceful and so thankful! And you hear the people who are alive, crying, and working, and calling to one another down in the close dark streets, and you seem to pity them so! And such a chain has fallen from you, and such a strange good sorrowful happiness comes upon you!"

And then almost with surprise she turns to Fledgeby: "But you are not dead, you know. . . . Get down to life!" As Riah accompanies Fledgeby she calls after him, "Come back and be dead!" And when Riah returns, he sees "the face of the little creature looking down out of a Glory of her long bright radiant hair, and musically repeating to him, like a vision, 'Come up and be dead! Come up and be dead!'" (II, 5) Jenny's irony is like Blake's; her vision is wrested out of pain and can only be imagined as a condition that utterly transcends the life she knows by experience. She needs such vision to sustain a difficult life, and no more is claimed for it than the strength or solace that imagination brings.

Dickens himself plays, as Samuel Palmer might have done, with the visionary aspect a natural scene may take:

So, in the rosy evening, one might watch the ever-widening beauty of the landscape—beyond the newly-released workers wending home—beyond the silver river—beyond the deep green fields of corn, so prospering, that the loiterers in their narrow threads of pathway seemed to float immersed breast-high—beyond the hedgerows and the clumps of trees—beyond the windmills on the ridge—away to where the sky appeared to meet the earth, as if there were no immensity of space between mankind and Heaven. [IV, 6]

The "as if" insists upon the distance that we seem in vision to surmount. One recalls Lizzie Hexam with the body of Betty Higden, who has escaped her sufferings in death. Lizzie "very softly raised the weather-stained grey head, and lifted her as high as Heaven" (III, 8).

It is appropriate, almost necessary, that Eugene Wrayburn send for Jenny Wren as he lies in pain and near death. Dickens rehearsed this in his Memorandum Book: "As to the question whether I, Eugene, lying ill and sick even unto death, may be consoled by the representation that coming through this illness, I shall begin a new life, and have energy and purpose and all I have yet wanted: *I hope* I should, but *I know* I shouldn't. Let me die, my dear." When Eugene asks Jenny "if she has seen the children" and "smelt the flowers," her reply is, "I never see them now, but I am hardly ever in pain now." Eugene asks her, nevertheless, "to have the fancy here, before I die." All of Eugene's practical concern at this point is with stopping police inquiries so that Lizzie's reputation will not be injured by the story of Headstone's murderous jealousy. He has come out of himself and is able to feel responsibility for Lizzie's plight.

Jenny Wren nurses Wrayburn with a "natural lightness and delicacy of touch" learned in her needlework, but even more with a percipience that makes her "an interpreter between this sentient world and the insensible man." It is Jenny who saves Eugene by giving him a purpose: to make Lizzie his wife (IV, 10). And it is Lizzie who foresees his having "a mine of purpose and energy" once he recovers (IV, 11). Eugene has chosen, so to speak, between Lizzie and Lady Tippins. And in his wake, Twemlow, the extra leaf of the Veneerings' table, cultivated by the social climbers for his link to landed aristocracy, the readily awed and accommodating little man—Twemlow too is reborn and insists, against Lady Tippins and Podsnap and all the other voices of society, that Lizzie Hexam is a lady.

7 ✻ Eliot:
The Nature of Decision

The Moral Subject

"The notion that peasants are joyous, that the typical moment to represent a man in a smock-frock is when he is cracking a joke and showing a row of sound teeth, that cottage matrons are usually buxom, and village children necessarily rosy and merry, are prejudices difficult to dislodge from the artistic mind, which looks for its subjects into literature instead of life." George Eliot evokes, as one alternative, the "slow gaze, in which no sense of beauty beams, no humour twinkles—the slow utterance, and the heavy slouching walk." She scorns sentimental idealization. "The selfish instincts are not subdued by the sight of buttercups, nor is integrity in the least established by that classic rural occupation, sheep-watching. To make men moral, something more is requisite than to turn them out to grass."[1]

Of all English novelists, George Eliot was the most deeply concerned with moral experience, and it is from that concern that her realism emerged. To speak of moral experience is to speak of failure as much as success, of the difficulties of attaining moral freedom as much as of its exercise. When she praised Goethe, it was for his "mixed and erring" characters, "saved from corruption by the salt of some noble impulse." And she praised Goethe for a method that was "really moral" in its influence. "It is without exaggeration; he is in no haste to alarm readers into virtue by melodramatic consequences; he quietly follows the stream of fact and of life; and waits patiently for the moral processes of nature as we all do for her material processes." It is his "large tolerance" that makes for his moral superiority. "We all begin life," she added drily, "by associating our passions with our moral prepossessions, by mistaking indignation for virtue, and many go through life without awaking from this illusion." But a few learn from "their own falls and their own struggles, by their experience of sympathy . . . that the line between the virtuous and the vicious, so far from being a necessary safeguard to morality, is itself an immoral fiction." She observed elsewhere that "he who hates vices too much hates men, or is in danger of it, and may have no blame to spare for himself."[2]

George Eliot attempted work of great subtlety, the study of how a man's virtues are implicated in and in some measure promote his errors. We can see this most sharply in the scene where Lydgate wins—or is entrapped by— Rosamond Vincy. When Lydgate seeks her out at home, she is surprised into naturalness; the usual "perfect management of self-contented grace" that she has learned at Miss Lemon's school gives way to "a certain helpless quivering." "That moment of naturalness was the crystallising feather-touch: it shook flirtation into love." When Lydgate shows concern, he elicits only tears; and her dependence brings in response an "outburst of tenderness"— because as a doctor, he is "used to being gentle with the weak and suffering." And so he leaves the house "an engaged man, whose soul was not his own, but the woman's to whom he had bound himself." The event is produced by the vulnerability and generosity of the two characters rather than by any calculation. Yet the ironic shift from the intimate rendering of mixed motives to the long-term entrapment in consequences is sharp. Even this brief scene makes clear that Eliot is concerned with the medium in which morality lives: the ways in which our choice may be limited by circumstances or even made for us—as if without our conscious consent or assertion of will—by the structure of the situation in which we find ourselves. Or we may see the converse: a decision made peremptorily by the intervention of some force we recognize as our deepest self.[3]

Much of this vision of moral complexity arises from George Eliot's insistence upon inevitable cost. She has no patience with the teaching of her fellow-novelist Miss Jewsbury ("Constance Herbert"), that nothing we "renounce for the sake of a higher triumph, will prove to have been worth the keeping." Such "copy-book morality" is a denial of the real; "if it *were* the fact, renunciation would cease to be moral heroism, and would simply be a calculation of prudence." The notion that Duty has both a stern face and a "hand full of sugar-plums" undermines morality. It offers "somthing extrinsic as a motive to action, instead of the immediate impulse of love or justice, which alone makes an action truly moral."[4] To see man as able to evade the cost and consequences of his act is to reduce him to moral insignificance. And yet there is a danger also in devoting oneself too fully to the very complexity of man's moral life, in tracing the necessary determinants of our seemingly free acts. We risk "the gradual extinction of motive—the poisoning of feeling by inference."[5]

For responsibility carries with it the sense of our free acceptance of duties and our free recognition of obligation. The moment of decision is one in which we reveal most clearly the complexity of our nature. We can study a man's moral awareness externally and see the slow accretion of those principles and habits which gain repeated confirmation in his choices and his expectation of others. When we consider moral experience of our own internally, however, taking our point of vantage within the institutions of morality and their various offices—obligations, promises, choices—all those shaping forces drop away. We must accept as an ultimate "given," as a commanding motive, the sense of duty or obligation with which we have been inculcated. We have shifted from a study of how our moral attitudes are formed to the decision we must make in exercising them.

P. F. Strawson has written very well about the contrast between those attitudes in which we express praise, resentment, or forgiveness and those detached objective attitudes in which we see another person "as an object of social policy; as a subject for what, in a wide range of sense, might be called treatment; as something . . . to be managed, or handled or cured or trained; perhaps simply to be avoided. . . . If your attitude towards someone is wholly objective, then though you may fight him, you cannot quarrel with him, and though you may talk to him, even negotiate with him, you cannot reason with him."

Those attitudes, in which we make demands upon others (and expect their demands upon us, and finally come to make comparable moral demands upon ourselves) Strawson, for obvious reasons, calls participant attitudes. They may, as he notes, be inhibited by another's abnormality or immaturity, by the deficiency of another's moral sense. But such inhibition leads us to see the other as "posing problems simply of intellectual understanding, management, treatment, and control." We can, at times, adopt such "objective" attitudes toward those whom we have come to believe normal or mature. "We *have* this resource," Strawson says, "and can sometimes use it: as a refuge, say, from the strains of involvement; or as an aid to policy; or simply out of intellectual curiosity. Being human, we cannot, in the normal case, do this for long, or altogether." Too painful an involvement may lead us to seek more certain relief in avoidance. "But what is above all interesting is the tension there is, in us, between the participant attitude and the objective attitude. One is tempted to say: between our humanity and our intelligence. But to say this would be to distort both notions."

Strawson is interested in how our belief in determinism would affect these attitudes. If an objective attitude were the appropriate accompaniment to such a belief, it would in effect dehumanize us. We may adopt the objective attitude when, for one reason or another, the participant attitudes cannot be sustained; but, Strawson suggests, we do not adopt it on theoretical grounds as believers in determinism. "Quite apart from the issue of determinism, might it not be said that we should be nearer to being purely rational creatures in proportion as our relation to others was in fact dominated by the objective attitude? I think this might be said; only it would have to be added, once more, that if such a choice were possible, it would not necessarily be rational to choose to be more purely rational than we are." [6]

This contrast between objective and participant attitudes is not unlike one that has been used by Jerome Schneewind in tracing the difference between Utilitarian and Intuitionist ethics in Victorian England. The Utilitarians stressed the importance of consequences, the Intuitionists of intentions. The Utilitarians were deterministic, the Intuitionists libertarian. "In a variety of ways Utilitarianism presents a morality which is . . . appropriate to the life of the large society or city and to the relations between strangers, while Intuitionism speaks more clearly for a personal morality, drawn from the life of the small group or family, from the relations between old acquaintances or close friends." The Intuitionists stressed the moral function of exemplary persons, whose character is more complex than are any of the principles it exemplifies. An exemplary person, such as Daniel Deronda is for Gwendolen Harleth (or Mordecai in turn for Deronda), is known as he knows others, through sympathy and intuition; and his personal example is more immediate and more subtle than any moral rules can be. Schneewind sees in George Eliot the "conceptual tension between an Intuitionist attitude toward morality and a determinist attitude toward the universe." *Daniel Deronda* embodies the principle that "one finds one's duty when one finds one's identity . . . and one is free insofar as one is able to love one's duty and live for its sake." [7]

The conceptual tension of which Schneewind writes was felt by George Eliot in her reflections on the problem of moral freedom. She is aware of the claims of determinism, but she also recognizes that "to occupy the mind in contemplating human action as a chain of necessary sequences must neutralize practice."

> We are active beings because we are capable—and in proportion as we are capable—of receiving impressions and reacting in movement. But to be considering whether impressions could have existed but for an illimitable series of antecedents, and to be regarding whatever is to be a series of necessary effects in the abstract, is to lock up the nature in a dark closet away from the impressions without which character must become a shrivelled unripe fruit.

Eliot likens this debilitation of our moral life to the "dulling, paralyzing reflection" by which a painter displaces his immediate impressions with a "dim imperfectly imagined series" of traditional images.

"Life and action are prior to theorizing, and have a prior logic in the conditions necessary to maintain them." [8] Eliot insists upon the fact that much of our best conduct is due to "sympathetic impulses" rather than to theory. Why have people devoted themselves to caring for others? "Not because they were contemplating the greatest happiness of the greatest number of mankind—or their own achievement of utmost possible excellence [these phrases take care, in turn, of both Utilitarian and Intuitionist]—or their own happiness here or hereafter." She does not, however, see these "sympathetic impulses" merely as spontaneous feelings. They are the outcome of our lives, of our moral histories; the impulse is the stronger for the actions we have learned to perform and to accept in ourselves.[9]

What we in turn recognize as readers is the need—if we are to read with sense at all—to feel ourselves into the moral imagination of the characters. We may shift back and forth, from inside to outside, as with Bulstrode; but we cannot begin to understand the experience the novel presents without some participation in the moral realities within which its characters live. "For there is no art which is not dependent for its characterizations either on its deep connections with life or on its want of such connections: at one extreme we have dramatic poetry, at the other pierced porcelain."[10] The full depth of the connections with life can be seen in those sequences of perception and association out of which we create our "moral tradition." The "satisfaction or suffering" that accompany these sequences and determine our response are "deeply organic, dependent on the primary vital movements, the first seeds of dread and desire, which in some cases grow to a convulsive force, and are ready to fasten their companionship on ideas and acts which are usually regarded as impersonal and indifferent." We can see the "first seeds of dread and desire" most clearly in *The Mill on the Floss,* where the shaping power of childhood experience is presented with brilliant precision.[11] There is, finally, no better account of the convulsive force of feeling in conflict with our sense of reality than the treatment of Lydgate's youthful proposal to the French actress:

> He knew that this was like the sudden impulse of a madman—incongruous even with his habitual foibles. No matter! It was the one thing which he was resolved to do. He had two selves within him apparently, and they must learn to accommodate each other and bear reciprocal impediments. Strange, that some of us, with quick alternate vision, see beyond our infatuations, and even while we rave on the heights, behold the wide plain where our persistent self pauses and awaits us. [15]

That "persistent self" is the kind of reality we are at last forced to acknowledge, a necessity we can neither circumvent nor transcend. A man is most free in Spinoza's view (as Stuart Hampshire presents it), "and also feels himself to be most free, when he cannot help drawing a certain conclusion" because of the "evidently compelling reasons" in favor of it. "Then he cannot hesitate. The issue is decided for him without any exercise of his will in decision." In contrast Hampshire describes the man who is not free, "not entirely active and self-determining but, at least in part, unknowing and passive in his motivation, since that which moved him to action was below the level of conscious thought. He was not altogether free in his decision, and he knows and feels that he was not, because he did not himself recognize its necessity." There is a peculiar fusion of logical and moral necessity in Spinoza, of the kind that George Eliot, herself a translator of Spinoza, finds in the submission to "undeviating law." [12]

Any artist, Iris Murdoch argues, would "appreciate the notion of will as obedience to reality, an obedience which ideally reaches a position where there is no choice. . . . So that aesthetic situations are not so much analogies of morals as cases of morals." She regards the realism of the artist or the moral agent as a "moral achievement," an overcoming of the absorption in self and a turning outward from the false unity the self imposes upon the world in fantasy toward the "great surprising variety" of that world. She provides a kind of parable of this process:

> I am looking out of my window in an anxious and resentful state of mind, oblivious of my surroundings, brooding perhaps on some damage done to my prestige. Then suddenly I observe a hovering kestrel. In a moment everything is altered. The brooding self with its hurt vanity has disappeared. There is nothing now but kestrel. And when I return to thinking of the other matter it seems less important. And of course this is something which we may do deliberately: give attention to nature in order to clear our minds of selfish care. . . .
> A self-directed enjoyment of nature seems to me to be something forced. More naturally, as well as more properly, we take a self-forgetful pleasure in the sheer alien pointless independent existence of animals, birds, stones and trees. "Not how the world is, but that it is, is the mystical." [13]

Spinoza's rationalism derives its moral decisions from the nature of things; they are acts of "obedience to reality." There are other ways of giving this sense of "necessity" to decisions; most of the efforts to bridge the gap between "is" and "ought" are efforts to push back the decision from a moment of apparently free choice among real alternatives to an earlier process of becoming implicitly committed to a decision that will, when we come to choose, seem already made for us. John Searle moves back from the "ought" to those "institutional facts" which imply a commitment in their very existence. Within the institution of promising, to say what we will do is not to make a prediction but to make what J. L. Austin called a "performative utterance." We are speaking inside the institution, and we enter, so to speak, into the contractual relations which sustain it and are implied in turn in its language. [14]

Iris Murdoch moves back from the decision to the vision created by a slow process of attention: "a refined and honest perception of what is really the case, a patient and just discernment" which is the result of "moral imagination and moral effort." Such attention involves "unselfing," becoming free of the fantasies the self so often requires; and it attains a vision not so much of new facts as of previously unrecognized configurations of experience. These configurations carry with them moral import. "If I attend properly I will have no choices, and this is the ultimate condition to be aimed at." By the time "the moment of choice has arrived the quality of attention has probably determined the nature of the act."[15] This slow work of attention, with so little immediate issue in outward act, can best be rendered as a narrative process. The narrative may have philosophic interest as well as literary: the "portrayal of moral reflection and moral change . . . is the most important part of any system of ethics." As Hilary Putnam puts it, "Novels and plays do not set moral knowledge before us. . . . But they do . . . something for us that must be done if we are to gain any moral knowledge."[16]

In a recent book, Alisdair MacIntyre tries to meet the difficulties of moral disagreement by recovering the narrative structures in which choices were traditionally imagined and made. MacIntyre believes that "modern moral utterance and practise can only be understood as a series of fragmented survivals from an older past"; therefore "to adopt a stance on the virtues will be to adopt a stance on the narrative character of human life." So for Homeric characters, "it is only within their framework of rules and precepts"—we might say their institutions—"that they are able to frame purposes at all. . . . All questions of choice arise within the framework; the framework itself therefore cannot be chosen." When we come to understand a "segment of behavior," therefore, we describe the action as part of one or another narrative history. The narrative histories in turn must be placed in settings—institutions, practices, communities—which have histories of their own. Each agent is in some degree author of his actions, but "we are never more (and sometimes less) than the co-author of our own narratives. Only in fantasy do we live what story we please." For we enter into society "with one or more imputed characters—roles into which we have been drafted"; one could say, following G. H. Mead, that our characters are given to us by the expectations of our "generalized other." And we are accountable to others as they are to us. The "narrative of any one life is part of an interlocking set of narratives"; and "this asking for and giving of accounts itself plays an important part in constituting narratives."[17]

In setting forth some of the ways in which MacIntyre embeds moral decisions or acts in narrative structures I have not done justice to his account, nor do I know whether his account will accomplish what he hopes. But it is an interesting way of working back from an "ought" to that reticulation of historical conditions, of institutional frameworks, and of accountability to others which can make up the novelist's world. While MacIntyre discusses Jane Austen, his scheme would seem to me to apply more aptly to the large constructions of George Eliot's world, with their interlocking narratives, their interplay of public and private selves, their sense of the force of institutions—whether legal, professional, or economic. In *Middlemarch* even the quality of the dyes used in the ribbon factory of the Plymdales has something to do with the hypocrisy or self-deception of Bulstrode as well.

Moral Decision

One day Mr. Farebrother, the Vicar of St. Botolph's, says to Lydgate, "The world has been too strong for *me,* I know. . . . But then I am not a mighty man—I shall never be a man of renown. The choice of Hercules is a pretty fable; but Prodicus makes it easy work for the hero, as if the first resolves were enough. Another story says that he came to hold the distaff, and at last wore the Nessus shirt. I suppose one good resolve might keep a man right if everybody else's resolve helped him."

The Choice of Hercules is one of the great themes of moral literature and painting. In works of Annibale Carracci, of Nicolas Poussin, of Benjamin West we see the hero standing between an austere figure of virtue who points toward a rugged upward slope and a reclining figure of Pleasure whose enticements he has just foresworn or is about to foreswear. But Mr. Farebrother recalls Hercules' terrible death as well. Mortally wounded by Hercules, the dying centaur Nessus sought revenge by telling Deianira that his blood would have the power to make Hercules faithful to her. When Deianira comes to fear losing Hercules, she dips his shirt in the blood she has preserved. Its poison (perhaps the fatal poison of Hercules' own arrow) produces Hercules' terrible death: in the torture of fiery pain he tries to rip off his shirt and in his violence rips his flesh from his bones. Hercules' fate is the consequence in part of his impetuous slaying of Nessus, in part of his inducing the jealous suspicion of Deianira, in part of her yielding to the treacherous advice of Nessus. What happens is the convergence of mistaken intentions, spite, ignorance, and love: one cannot point to any single choice or act of will as the sufficient cause of Hercules' torture and death. If we blame his arrogance or impetuosity or sensuality, none of these—nor all together—demands the fate he suffers. There is something terrifyingly disproportionate in those consequences which arise out of a constellation of separate wills. The death of Hercules is the very denial of the power of choice.

"The Vicar's talk was not always inspiriting: he had escaped being a Pharisee, but he had not escaped that low estimate of possibilities which we rather hastily arrive at as an inference from our own failure. Lydgate thought that there was a pitiable infirmity of will in Farebrother." Lydgate is right to a degree he has not the means of understanding. And, even as he is right about Farebrother, whom success will make a stronger as well as happier man, he rather scornfully dismisses a condition into which he will himself descend in time.

The whole eighteenth chapter of *Middlemarch,* whose conclusion I have just cited, provides a striking instance of George Eliot's method and themes. It is a chapter about decision. Bulstrode is about to support the building of a new addition to the hospital which will give Lydgate scope for what he thinks to be proper medical practice, and Bulstrode means to have the salaried chaplaincy of the new hospital go to the evangelical Mr. Tyke instead of Farebrother, who has been performing a chaplain's duties as part of his parish duties. Lydgate is troubled because he has come to value Farebrother's fine intelligence and moral delicacy; but he is troubled as well by the mixed nature of Farebrother's character. Lydgate regards Farebrother's character somewhat as the moral north regards those "southern landscapes which seem divided between natural grandeur and social slovenliness." For Lydgate is troubled by Farebrother's way of playing cards for money and by his candid acknowledgment that the chaplaincy would be a welcome source of income. Lydgate has never suffered any lack of money, and his "ideal of life"—which we are made to see him achieve in his intransigency and boldness in medical matters—leads him to revulsion from Farebrother's "subservience of conduct to the gaining of small sums." Without imagining the need that prompts Farebrother, Lydgate cannot help feeling contempt for such measures.

It is not that Lydgate neglects Farebrother's virtues and his lack of pretense; but Lydgate is uncomfortable with something less than moral consistency. He cannot in good conscience cast his vote for Farebrother, whom he has so much reason to favor, nor for Tyke, whose only claim is that he is Bulstrode's candidate. Even worse is the implication that to vote for Tyke would be to serve his own interest in pleasing Bulstrode. If Lydgate is uneasy in judging Farebrother, he is the more uneasy with a decision which has no simple right choice. Lydgate wants to be free to do his work, and he wants to dismiss all those small concerns that arise from the impurity of choices: he resents "the hampering threadlike pressure of small social conditions and their frustrating complexity." And he meets the problem by refusing to meet it. He does not make his choice and arm himself, as he should, with the reasons which can support it. Instead, he leaves his decision to be made when it must; and he goes to the meeting with his judgment suspended. As the lawyer Frank Hawley declares in the meeting, "Any man who wants to do justice does not wait till the last minute to hear both sides of the question." Hawley's remark is angry and illiberal; it neglects the value of disinterested discussion. But it points to the danger that Lydgate courts in waiting for something external, whatever it may be, to help him decide. When it is left for him to cast the decisive vote, Bulstrode's opponents are short of temper: "We all know how Mr. Lydgate will vote." Aware that he is expected to vote with Bulstrode, Lydgate angrily and defiantly does so; and one feels that the true reasons for the decision have been swept away in the pride with which he meets insinuations of his subservience.

Lydgate realizes later that "if he had been quite free from indirect bias he should have voted for Mr. Farebrother." He blames the "petty medium" of Middlemarch: "How could a man be satisfied with a decision between such alternatives and under such circumstances?" What Lydgate cannot allow himself to see is that he has permitted the choice to be made by circumstances rather than by the autonomy of judgment he might have reached beforehand. It is with Farebrother's continued friendliness, and even his readiness to offer others excuses for "thinking slightly of him," that the narrative turns to his self-deprecating remarks on the choice of Hercules. And Lydgate, who has failed to make a true choice, can pity Farebrother's weakness and persuade himself of his own greater moral demand upon life.

It is the difficulty of mixed or impure motives, of complex and inconsistent natures, that disturbs Lydgate, frays his temper, and disables him for responsible judgment. Such difficulties confront us at every turn, and George Eliot gives more attention than most novelists (one thinks of Richardson and of James as in some degree her counterparts) to the conditions within which our decisions are made. The conditions may be such as to deter or prevent true choice. Mr. Vincy, as he questions Lydgate's fitness as a husband for his daughter, provides a fine comic example of the avoidance of choice:" the force of circumstances was easily too much for him . . . and the circumstance called Rosamond was particularly forcible by means of that mild persistence which, as we know, enables a white soft living substance to make its way in spite of opposing rock. Papa was not a rock. . . ."

The last shift from Mr. Vincy to Papa shows us the man at his most manipulable, under the force of Rosamond's persistence, which operates with Mrs. Vincy's submissive encouragement. Mr. Vincy cannot bring himself to inquire directly into Lydgate's means, for Lydgate's proud bearing daunts him. But the pride of Lydgate is only the assured courage of a man of superior status, and all the complexities of circumstance of a middle-class provincial become relevant:

> Mr. Vincy was a little in awe of him, a little vain that he wanted to marry Rosamond, a little indisposed to raise the question of money in which his own position was not advantageous, a little afraid of being worsted in dialogue with a man better educated and more highly bred than himself, and a little afraid of doing what his daughter would not like. The part Mr. Vincy preferred was that of the generous host whom nobody criticises. In the earlier half of the day

there was business to hinder any formal communication of an adverse resolve; in the later there was a dinner, wine, whist, and general satisfaction. And in the meanwhile the hours were each leaving their little deposit and gradually forming the final reason for inaction, namely, that action was too late.

Mr. Vincy provides a comic instance of the avoidance of choice. But the difficulties of even the most active choice can take a compelling form. Here, in "Janet's Repentance," the latest of the *Scenes of Clerical Life,* is Eliot's treatment of the clergyman, Mr. Tryan. In "convenient formula he might be seen as a man who rejoices in opposition," which "may become sweet to a man when he has christened it persecution." But in fact he is a man easily hurt by the hatred and ridicule he provokes, yet who persists in his cause. His behavior raises larger questions of Evangelicalism as a creed. "The movement was good," the author states, "though it had that admixture of folly and evil which often makes what is good an offense to feeble and fastidious minds. . . . The blessed work of helping the world forward, happily does not wait to be done by perfect men."

> The real heroes, of God's making, are quite different. . . . Their insight is blended with mere opinion; their sympathy is perhaps confined in narrow conduits of doctrine, instead of flowing forth with the freedom of a stream that blesses every weed in its course; obstinacy or self-assertion will often interfuse itself with their grandest impulses; and their very deeds of self-sacrifice are sometimes only the rebound of a passionate egoism. . . . So it was with Mr. Tryan.   [8]

For the supercilious critic he might provide the text for a "wise discourse on the characteristics of the Evangelical school in his day." But the author rejects "the bird's-eye glance of a critic": "I am not poised on that lofty height. I am on the level and in the press with him, as he struggles his way along the stony road, through the crowd of unloving fellow-men." There can hardly be a stronger assertion of a participant's view, an internal view of the clergyman's aspirations and effort. This internal view is extended to a principle of sympathy:

> surely the only true knowledge of our fellow-man is that which enables us to feel with him—which gives us a fine ear for the heart-pulses that are beating under the mere clothes of circumstance and opinion. Our subtlest analysis of schools and sects must miss the essential truth, unless it be lit up by the love that sees in all forms of human thought and work, the life and death struggles of separate human beings.   [10]

We can see here George Eliot's desire to stress the importance of feeling in our observations, the cognitive power of sympathy. ("Feeling is a sort of knowledge.")[18] She mocks "the serene air of pure intellect in which it is evident that individuals really exist for no other purpose than that abstractions may be drawn from them—abstractions that may rise from heaps of ruined loves like the sweet savour of a sacrifice in the nostrils of philosophers, and of a philosophic Deity" (22). She moves from the doctrine to the human being who maintains and realizes it, from mind and principle to the deepest and most elemental feelings, whose energy informs our beliefs.

George Eliot, as we know from F. W. H. Myers's famous anecdote, found no divine or metaphysical sanction for the claims of moral obligation. She, "taking as her text the three words . . . *God, Immortality, Duty*—pronounced, with terrible earnestness, how inconceivable was the *first,* how unbelievable the *second,* and yet how peremptory and absolute the *third.* Never, perhaps have sterner accents affirmed the sovereignty of impersonal and unrecompensing law."[19] She argued persuasively enough that we can lead a moral life without such sanctions. Upon what authority can morality rest, and how can it be freed of both obtuse complacency and disabling doubt? Clearly, for Eliot, our moral awareness finds its surest ground in sympathetic feeling. "The growth of higher feeling within us is like the growth of faculty, bringing with it a sense of added strength: we can no more wish to return to a narrower sympathy, than a painter or musician can wish to return to his cruder manner, or a philosopher to his less complete formula." Such growth produces in us a "sense of enlarged being."[20]

This sense of the irreversible, which makes a narrative of our moral life, is clearly set forth in *Romola.* When Tito encounters his adoptive father Baldassarre, now a prisoner in Florence, he denies their acquaintance: "Some madman, surely." "He hardly knew how the words had come to his lips: There are moments when our passions speak and decide for us, and we seem to stand by and wonder. They carry in them an inspiration of crime, that in one instant does the work of long premeditation" (22). Yet if the action is spontaneous, it has, nevertheless, had a long rehearsal. "Tito was experiencing that inexorable law of human souls, that we prepare ourselves for sudden deeds by the reiterated choice of good or evil that gradually determines character." So, later, when he is tempted by deceit, "all the motives which might have made Tito shrink" from it have already "been slowly strangled in him by the successive falsities of his life."

> Our lives make a moral tradition for our individual selves, as the life of mankind at large makes a moral tradition for the race; and to have once acted greatly seems a reason why we should always be noble. But Tito was feeling the effect of an opposite tradition: he had won no memories of self-conquest and perfect faithfulness from which he could have a sense of falling.   [39]

In place of a life steeped in feeling Tito's becomes one "shut up in the narrowness that hedges in all merely clever, unimpassioned men" (22), and life takes on for him "the aspect of a game in which there was an agreeable mingling of skill and chance" (35). When at last Tito betrays Savonarola, there is "no malignity" in his satisfaction: "it was the mild self-gratulation of a man who has won a game that has employed hypothetic skill, not a game that has stirred the muscles and heated the blood" (67). In contrast, Romola's feelings are those of the participant; when she becomes disenchanted with Savonarola and hears "only the ring of egoism" in his words, her faith in herself is also involved: "With the sinking of high human trust, the dignity of life sinks too; we cease to believe in our own better self, since that also is part of the common nature which is degraded in our thought; and all the finer impulses of the soul are dulled" (61).

The Beautiful and the Sublime

Of George Eliot's later novels, *Felix Holt the Radical* is the simplest in design, and it helps to make clear the central importance of decision in her work. The novel has two principal plots, each involving a character of great force and intensity. In the case of Mrs. Transome and her son Harold, the fierce hopes of compensation and deliverance that Mrs. Transome entertains are disappointed by her practical, unimpassioned son. In the case of Esther Lyon and Felix Holt, the beauty and rather self-conscious charm of Esther are eclipsed by the higher demands upon the self that Felix Holt represents.

As we first see Mrs. Transome she is a "tall, proud-looking woman" with a "somewhat eagle-like yet not unfeminine face"; she has endured life with an increasingly imbecilic husband, one of her children a wastrel and the other incommunicative abroad. All of her claims upon life evident in her style, in her "high-born imperious air," her artistic pretensions—all the claims of a "hungry much-exacting self" are denied fulfillment. She must find "the opiate of her discontent in the exertion of her will about smaller things," seizing as she can "every little sign of power" her life allows. Few except her maid Denner can imagine the anxiety and fear that are "hidden under that outward life—a woman's keen sensibility and dread, which lay screened behind all her petty habits and narrow notions, as some quivering thing with eyes and throbbing heart may lie crouching behind withered rubbish" (1).

That is a moving image, but it is not one to accommodate a tragic heroine. Here, as in the treatment of Casaubon later, we find "the pathos of a lot where everything is below the level of tragedy except the passionate egoism of the sufferer."[21] Mrs. Transome is a woman of imperious will but of limited mind. Once she was "a handsome girl, who sat supremely well on horseback, sang and played a little, painted small figures in water-colours, had a naughty sparkle in her eyes when she made a daring quotation, and an air of serious dignity when she recited something from her store of correct opinions." We see her later, her talk running on genealogies, with "no ultimate analysis of things that went beyond blood and family." By then she lives "in the midst of desecrated sanctities, and of honours that looked tarnished in the light of monotonous and weary suns." It is thus that Esther comes to regard Mrs. Transome in her "lofty large-roomed house, where it seemed quite ridiculous to be anything so small as a human being" (40).

Mrs. Transome is shocked to find her son Harold totally indifferent to all she values. He will stand not as a Tory but as a Radical candidate. He scorns the traditional regimen of the house. He seems completely insensitive to Mrs. Transome's authority or to her feelings. Instead, he is a cool, somewhat complacent man with a strong will of his own: "fond of mastery, and good-natured enough to wish that everyone about him should like his mastery" (2). He is annoyed with the lawyer Jermyn, who has turned the management of the estate to his own profit. Harold does not wish to cast off Jermyn's services so long as they can include management of his election. But he is offended by Jermyn's pretension, his rather affected dress and "general sleekness," and—with a special amusement—"his white, fat, but beautifully shaped hands, which he was in the habit of rubbing gently on his entrance into a room." Harold is hardly aware of how much his own hands, and even his corpulence, resemble Jermyn's; for he is not in the least prepared to think that this "covetous upstart" is his father. Mrs. Transome can see her son and her former lover with the painful knowledge that she is now "of little consequence to either of them" (2).

Esther Lyon, as we first see her, might be a younger version of Mrs. Transome; she has "tendencies towards luxury, fastidiousness, and scorn of mock gentility." She finds herself, in her father's house, "surrounded with ignoble, uninteresting conditions, for which there was no issue" (6). Like Harold, she is to learn her true parentage, and in her case it confirms her aristocratic style rather than affronts it. Esther is somewhat vain, somewhat given to dreams of romance nourished by Byron's poetry. She irritates Felix Holt by her triviality, but even more by a charm that he cannot altogether argue away. She has the silvery voice that will be one of Rosamond Vincy's features, but she has imaginative power of which Rosamond is incapable. For what Esther responds to in Felix Holt is a powerful devotion to truth, a fierce sense of reality—nothing less, as it turns out, than the claim of the sublime.

Felix Holt is, like D. H. Lawrence's Birkin, a somewhat confused messiah—confused as to the strength and nature of his feelings, confused perhaps by the force of his own eloquence. He has repudiated taking a living from the quack medicines that his father sold while he was alive. He refuses gentility: "Why should I want to get into the middle class because I have some learning?" He is scornful of Byron as a "misanthropic debaucher." He disdains those "niceties of speech" that "dress up swindling till it looks as well as honesty" (5). He dismisses romantic idealism: "Your dunce who can't do his sums always has a taste for the infinite." Felix is bracing: he makes moral demands upon Esther that she finds almost terrifying. He wants her, as he says, to change, to accept the solemnity of life and the need to make genuine choices. "For the first time in her life Esther felt herself seriously shaken in her self-contentment. She knew that there was a mind to which she appeared trivial, narrow, selfish." She tries to share a vision wider than her own, to imagine what Felix Holt finds in life "to make it seem valuable in the absence of all elegance, luxury, gaiety, or romance" (10). For she sees a greatness in Felix. Life with him would be a "sort of difficult blessedness, such as one may imagine in beings who are conscious of painfully growing into the possession of higher powers" (22).

Felix, in turn, is fighting against his attraction to Esther. He longs for a woman with a mind as noble as her face is beautiful—who might make a "man's passion for her rush in one current with all the great aims of his life." Felix is trying to avoid succumbing to Esther until he can make her that woman; he wants her, as he says, "to have such a vision of the future that you may never lose your best self" (27).

Esther wishes "to be worthy" of Felix; but she cannot face "wandering through the future weak and forsaken"; she feels "no trust that she could ever be good without him." Felix is resolute in renunciation. "He felt that they must not marry—that they would ruin each other's lives." He wished Esther "to know that her love was dear to him as the beloved dead were dear" (32). Here comedy intrudes. One can look beyond the characters' immediate vision to recognize that they have not left each other as they were: Felix is speaking to an Esther that no longer exists, and he is renouncing a love he is no longer able to surrender.

Once Harold Transome has lost the election and Felix Holt awaits trial in jail, Esther is given a new set of choices. She is shown to be the legitimate heiress of Transome Court. Harold Transome refuses to engage in dishonest ways of concealing or contesting her claims; rather he persuades his mother to invite Esther, and Mrs. Transome finds in her a "sweet young deference" that is very gratifying. Esther in turn is pleased with the outward forms of gentility, with "Mrs. Transome's accent, the high-bred quietness of her speech, the delicate odour of her drapery." The beautiful is assuming a strong appeal after difficulty and privation, an appeal that may outweigh the more difficult sublime that Felix represents. She is open to pleasure, uneasy at the sense of dispossession that haunts Mrs. Transome, free to imagine herself as her own novelist: "her life was a book which she seemed herself to be constructing—trying to make character clear before her, and looking into the ways of destiny" (40).

As Harold pays court to Esther, she finds him agreeable, flattering—"vulgar compared with Felix," but practical and clever. He has "an air of moral mediocrity," and the life of Transome Court, while comfortable, is deadening in its "absence of high demand" (43). Harold underestimates the claims of sublimity upon Esther. He feels no concern about Felix as rival: "Esther was too clever and tasteful a woman to make a ballad heroine of herself, by bestowing her beauty and her lands on this lowly lover. 'I am conscious,' he says with some complacency to Esther, 'of not having those severe virtues that you have been praising.' "

> "That is true, You are quite in another genre."
>
> "A woman would not find me a tragic hero."
>
> "Oh no! She must dress for graceful comedy . . . where the most thrilling event is the drawing of a handsome cheque."
>
> "You are a naughty fairy. . . . Confess that you are disgusted with my want of romance."
>
> "I shall not confess to being disgusted. I shall ask you to confess that you are not a romantic figure."
>
> "I am a little too stout."
>
> "For romance—yes. . . ."
>
> "And I don't look languishing enough?"
>
> "Oh yes—rather too much so—at a fine cigar."

To relieve Esther's concern about "his quality of widower," Harold casually explains that his first wife "had been a slave—was bought, in fact." The effect on Esther is tremendous. "Hitherto Esther's acquaintance with Oriental love was derived chiefly from Byronic poems, and this had not sufficed to adjust her mind to a new story, where the Giaour concerned was giving her his arm" (43). The unreal, now outgrown, world of romance; the fat insensibility of Harold's hedonism ("I never longed much for anything out of my reach"); and the "padded yoke" prepared for anyone who depends on Harold Transome—all these create a moment of revulsion. Esther comes to feel a contrast between the "high mountain air" she has known and the "life of middling delights, overhung with the languorous haziness of motiveless ease, where poetry was only literature." She has come to the moment when the conditions of choice are final. "It is only in the freshness of our time that the choice is possible which gives unity to life, and makes the memory a temple where all relics and all votive offerings, all worship and all grateful joy, are an unbroken history sanctified by one religion" (44).

Before Esther can complete her decision, however, George Eliot arranges that Harold Transome be seen at his best. He learns with shame that he is Jermyn's son and tells Esther that his name is now sullied and that he expects to leave England. He also assures her that strong efforts are at work to win Felix Holt's release. Esther is moved by Harold's vulnerability; she feels greater reluctance than ever before to refuse his suit. The choice becomes fully weighted: on "each side there was renunciation."

She drew up her blinds, liking to see the grey sky, where there were some veiled glimmerings of moonlight, and the lines of the for-ever running river, and the bending movement of the black trees. She wanted the largeness of the world to help her thought. . . .

A supreme love, a motive that gives a sublime rhythm to a woman's life . . . is not to be had where and how she wills: to know that high initiation she must often tread, and to feel the chill air, and to watch through darkness. It is not true that love makes all things easy: it makes us choose what is difficult. [49]

What Esther fears most is the possibility of having to bear the hardship alone, without Felix Holt, with "no better self to make a place for trust and joy." His love was "only a quivering hope—not a certainty."

At this last moment of choice, Esther is joined by Mrs. Transome. That embittered woman has already been outraged by Jermyn's refusal to keep her secret, by his asking her, in effect, to call off Harold's charges of swindling by telling him that Jermyn is his father. Jermyn rationalizes his self-exculpation, but he is, as always, unaware of others' real feelings:

There is heroism enough even in the circles of hell for fellow-sinners who cling to each other in the fiery whirlwind and never recriminate. But these things, which are easy to discern when they are painted for us on the large canvas of poetic story, become confused and obscure even for well-read gentlemen when their affection for themselves is alarmed by pressing details of actual experiences. [42]

Mrs. Transome is bitter with self-pity. How can Harold not pity her? "She was not penitent. She had borne too hard a punishment. . . . She, too, looked out into the dim night; but the black boundary of trees and the long line of the river seemed only part of the loneliness and monotony of her life."

Mrs. Transome does not want "the largeness of the world"; her desire is not for the impersonality of truth or breadth of vision. As she comes to Esther for "caressing pity," she makes clear the "dreary waste of years empty of sweet trust and affection" (50). George Eliot understands the terrible pain of suffering that does not ennoble. Esther resigns her inheritance the next morning and leaves Transome Court and Harold behind. Mrs. Transome's misery is at the last pathetic: a nemesis has overtaken her at the very moment when she dreamed of renewal. But there is little genuine insight into her own nature or the justness of her demands on life. She does not achieve resignation, nor is she dignified or transfigured by suffering as a tragic heroine might be.

Eliot makes this subtragic plot, with the blind suffering and relentless will of its heroine, a contrast to the strength that Esther achieves in her decision. Perhaps in none of Eliot's novels are the conditions of a moral choice so carefully established by the narrative, and this instance helps to make clear what a better novel like *Middlemarch* may obscure by its very richness. There is progressive refinement of circumstance in this novel: Felix Holt's distrust of domesticity, Harold Transome's pain and honesty, Esther's discovery of the amenities and the costs of wealth, Esther's coming to see herself not merely acted upon by Felix but shaping her independent vision in his absence and without the assurance of his guidance. As telling as any element in this dialectical shaping of decision is the sense of the continuity and autonomy of the self. We are given a glimpse of that self in Esther's testimony at Felix Holt's trial. She has as a woman a distinctive power in breaking through "formulas too rigorously urged on men by daily practical needs": "she is the added impulse that shatters the stiffening crust of cautious experience. Her inspired ignorance gives a sublimity to actions so incongruously simple, that otherwise they would make men smile." At this moment all of Esther's feelings converge, making "one danger, one terror, one irresistible impulse for her heart. Her feelings were growing into a necessity for action, rather than a resolve to act." Esther rises superior to all her earlier dread of ridicule: but what emerges now is "the depth below" that was then sleeping. Each moral decision is an act of self-discovery and self-realization (46).

The Emergence of the Self

In her last novel, George Eliot studied the emergence of a moral life in Gwendolen Harleth and the descent upon Daniel Deronda of an idea which can give the energy of duty to undirected moral aspiration. Eliot opens the novel with the first meeting of these two. The opening chapters of *Daniel Deronda* are intense and mysterious, mysterious because we have no knowledge of the conditions from which these events arise. "Was she beautiful or not beautiful? and what was the secret of form or expression which gave the dynamic quality of her glance? Was the good or evil genius dominant in those beams?" We see Gwendolen Harleth as Daniel Deronda first sees her; she is gambling in the casino of a German watering place, and her manner conveys "unrest," strange agitation. Her double aspect—both the physical beauty and the tortured spirit—compel Deronda's attention, but compel it against his will. "Why was his wish to look again felt as coercion and not as a longing with which the whole being consents?" Much later—some eight hundred pages later—we shall look back at the "mission of Deronda to Gwendolen" which "had begun with what she had felt to be his judgment of her at the gaming-table" (64).

This opening scene is presented externally, with the swaggering mockery of Dickens. The casino is a resort "which the enlightenment of ages has prepared . . . at a heavy cost of gilt mouldings, dark-toned colour and chubby nudities, all correspondingly heavy—forming a suitable condenser for human breath belonging, in great part, to the highest fashion. . . . It was near four o'clock on a September day, so that the atmosphere was well brewed to a visible haze." This haze has the disturbing concreteness, and the gamblers are picked out with the contemptuous precision, that Dickens often uses:

> the white bejewelled fingers of an English countess were very near touching a bony, yellow, crab-like hand stretching a bared wrist to clutch a heap of coin— a hand easy to sort with the square, gaunt face, deep-set eyes, grizzled eyebrows, and ill-combed scanty hair which seemed a slight metamorphosis of the vulture.

Among the attitudes the gamblers reveal are the rankling "sweetness of winning much and seeing others lose" and the "fierce yet tottering impulsiveness" of the man who plays by an insane system, like a "scene of dull, gas-poisoned absorption." Later Deronda will reveal his view of gambling: "There is something revolting to me in raking a heap of money together, and internally chuckling over it, when others are feeling the loss" (29).

Gwendolen plays willfully, restlessly, exulting as she wins, but suddenly arrested to find herself under Deronda's gaze. She has a momentary sense that he is "measuring her and looking down on her as an inferior, . . . examining her as a species of a lower order." Her resentment prolongs her stare in turn, until she looks away as if with "inward defiance." Gwendolen has begun to imagine herself a "goddess of luck." But that fantasy is crossed by her uneasy awareness of Deronda's gaze—it seems to express a scorn that, at a deeper level, she suspects she deserves, and therefore resents all the more. Under its influence, her luck changes. She defies Deronda, still feeling his eyes upon her although she cannot turn to face him. If she cannot win, she will at least lose "strikingly" (1).

This evening marks an epoch for Gwendolen (and to a degree for Deronda). She has fled England rather than undertake a marriage she has seen to be degrading. Now she discovers, upon her return to her hotel, that her family has lost all its money. When she pawns a necklace with the thought that she may recover her magical luck, she is outraged and shamed that Deronda observes what she has done, redeems the necklace, and sends it back to her. She has begun to find in him a judgment of herself which she guiltily supposes to be superior and ironic. His judgment will in time become, once she recognizes its genuine concern and affection, her conscience. At last she will have internalized that judgment and made it her protection against herself. As she says to Deronda, "it shall be better with me because I have known you" (36, 70).

Gwendolen Harleth is the culmination of a movement in Eliot's fiction.

In the story of Lydgate that is perhaps the best part of *Middlemarch,* there are troubling questions left by Rosamond. Eliot is brilliantly observant in her rendering of Rosamond's behavior, but Rosamond's constricted mind—"there was not room enough for luxuries to look small in"—remains to a considerable degree opaque. Perhaps that is necessary in order to win sympathy for Lydgate. We hardly question the careless superiority with which he treats her until we see in her response a condescension of another kind. In her quiet assertion of will, there is no effort to explain or justify her behavior—as if to argue its rightness would only be to yield the terms of Lydgate, whose force of mind and eloquence would carry the issue. Rosamond does not choose to meet him there. She does not feel, finally, that his arguments merit respect any more than his tactless handling of patients and colleagues. In both there is an absence of worldly wisdom. There are small but adamantine certainties in Rosamond that allow no compromise. Yet there is also opacity; her conventional beliefs are served by a massive deficiency of imagination and an equally massive concentration of will. Her education at Miss Lemon's school and her socially ambitious parents hardly account for her formidable strength. Her selfishness is not the callow thoughtlessness of her brother, Fred, but quite another kind of power.

In Gwendolen Harleth, George Eliot returns to a character like Rosamond, but of a higher style and greater opportunity. Unlike Rosamond, Gwendolen is capable of growth into a moral life, and that growth is her story. In some ways it is the most complex single story that George Eliot wrote, and it needs close attention.

Gwendolen Harleth fluctuates between a strong assertion of will and a terror at the possibilities that assertion raises. She has imperfect control of a manner that exhibits superiority too nakedly and reveals ironic amusement when it means to profess naivety. She does not know how to subdue herself in a role that requires her to imagine others' feelings. And there are moments when she is startled into spontaneity. When Klesmer criticizes her singing, he takes for granted standards that Gwendolen has never known. Of the music she has chosen he remarks; "It is a form of melody which expresses a puerile state of culture . . . the passion and thought of a people without any breadth of horizon . . . no cries of deep, mysterious passion— no conflict—no sense of the universal. It makes men small as they listen to it" (5). Gwendolen's heart sinks at the space which suddenly opens around her confident drawing-room accomplishment. For, while Gwendolen has behaved "as if she had been sustained by the boldest speculations," her aspirations have been conventional enough and have made no great demands upon her. She has been living in a world not unlike Rosamond Vincy's. Her "horizon was that of the genteel romance where the heroine's soul poured out in her journal is full of vague power, originality, and general rebellion, while her life moves strictly in the sphere of fashion" (16).

Her assertion of will is imperious in tone, but it has no high object. "My plan," she says, "is to do what pleases me." But the freedom she claims only exposes her to the terrors of the limitless. The sublime does not stir her to strength or to a sense of her own power; it fills her instead with terror. "Solitude in any wide scene impressed her with an undefined feeling of immeasurable existence aloof from her, in the midst of which she was helplessly incapable of asserting herself." At such moments she needs the presence of another person to help her recover her "indifference to the vastness in which she seemed an exile," to restore "her usual world in which her will was some avail." One may recall the imperious gestures which screen Mrs. Transome's terror of forces beyond her control (6).

The thought of marriage awakens no pleasure in Gwendolen: "the dramas in which she imagined herself a heroine were not wrought up to that close." She resists submission to another's closeness and independent will. She intends, instead, to "strike others with admiration and get in that reflected way a more ardent sense of living." Yet she is startled by her own fierce revulsion at the mild Rex Gascoigne's proposal. She weeps later in her mother's embrace, exclaiming, "I can't love people. I hate them." And other kinds of limitation frighten her: "Gwendolen dreaded the unpleasant sense of compunction towards her mother, which was the nearest approach to self-condemnation and self-distrust that she had known" (9).

S. L. Goldberg has written acutely on the problem of Gwendolen's will and on the nature of George Eliot's morality.[22] He fears the confusion of two kinds of morality—what he calls "conduct-morality" and "life-morality." The former regulates our conscious choices; its claim is "impersonal," and it presents itself in universalized rules. In contrast, life-morality seeks to "guide the *whole* self in realizing all the finest possibilities of its human nature." It is "concerned with nothing less than the whole range of a person's active existence . . . the entire mode of its life." This includes the moral will but much more, and it considers the moral will as part of a conception of character "much wider, more complex, more holistic, and more problematical than that of conduct-morality." It would not, I think, be misleading to see these kinds of morality as Kantian and Aristotelian.

Goldberg sees in George Eliot a tendency to admire uncritically a conduct-morality that identifies the "best self" with "the practice of humility and self-abnegation." In the typical plot of conduct-morality false choices find their nemesis in "appropriate condemnation and retribution" and their issue in a "redemptory 'self knowledge' (i.e., *self*-judgment)." The plot of life-morality, in contrast, leads to "the achievement of a certain self-fulfilment, reaching a deeper and richer kind of life" or "reaching the uttermost limits of the individual's particular being as it lives itself out to the very point of death." Goldberg wants us to do justice to those qualities of Gwendolen which—somewhat like those Lionel Trilling praised in Jane Austen's Emma—have the power to charm us—they are a "force of independent life."

Beside this I would set George Eliot's words on "that idea of duty, that recognition of something to be lived for beyond the mere satisfaction of self, which is to the moral life what the addition of a great central ganglion is to animal life. No man can begin to mould himself on a faith or an idea without rising to a higher order of experience: a principle of subordination, of self-mastery, has been introduced into his nature; he is no longer a mere bundle of impressions, desires, and impulses." [23] This conception of a moral life also stresses inclusiveness. One may see a life as shallow and incoherent for all its breadth of realization if it loses that depth of commitment (or of feeling) that gives it a new dimension and an active unity. There is no easy way of choosing between these two conceptions of morality—the emphasis upon the fullness of the self, within which morality has a limited place, and the emphasis upon moral maturity as a necessary attainment. There is a peculiar pathos in that moment when Dorothea offers Lydgate help. He smiles at her eagerness, much as men smile at Esther Lyon when she takes the stand. The smile is somewhat superior, somewhat rueful, a condescension toward and wonder at Dorothea's "childlike grave-eyed earnestness . . . blent into an adorable whole with her ready understanding of high experience. (Of lower experience such as plays a great part in the world, poor Mrs. Casaubon had a very blurred shortsighted knowledge, little helped by her imagination.)" There is reason to smile at her ignorance and to envy it; but she possesses a moral intensity that men like Lydgate, if they ever had it, have lost to the exigencies of "lower experience." [24]

What is striking in Gwendolen is the restless assertion and its underside of fear. She attracts Grandcourt by the force of her will and the style of her self-assertion; he is, in fact, the nemesis her nature calls up by its very lack of any object beyond herself. And she has not imagination enough to allow him a will like her own, let alone one far more practiced and exacting. When Grandcourt pays court, Gwendolen holds him off, uncertain what she will do. "This subjection to a possible self, a self not to be absolutely predicted about, caused her some astonishment and terror: her favourite key of life—doing as she liked—seemed to fail her, and she could not foresee what at a given moment she might like to do." Yet Grandcourt is "adorably quiet and free from absurdities," she tells herself; she feels sure she can manage him to suit her purposes. And yet she wonders. "She began to be afraid of herself, and to find out a certain difficulty in doing as she liked." Her uncle, Mr. Gascoigne, is a clergyman with a great respect for worldly status. He encourages the acceptance of Grandcourt and even comfortably translates it into an obligation: Grandcourt's fortune, he tells her, "almost takes the question out of the range of mere personal feeling, and makes your acceptance of it a duty." Mr. Gascoigne warns against trifling with Grandcourt lest she alienate him, and he dismisses from his own mind the rumors of Grandcourt's earlier profligacy. But Gwendolen feels in response that her uncle is "pressing upon her the motives of dread which she had already felt," that he is "making her more conscious of the risks that lay within herself." When she receives a warning letter from Grandcourt's former mistress (and the mother of his children), Lydia Glasher, she finds herself thinking. "It has come in time" (13).

But Gwendolen, once her family has lost its money, must consider means of support. When she turns to Klesmer for advice, she does it with the dread that recognizes him as part of "that unmanageable world which was independent of her wishes." There is desperation in her dream that she can become, on her own terms, a successful actress; and Klesmer reminds her of all that she has not the character to attain: "inward vocation and hard-won achievement." Gwendolen cannot begin to imagine that she must "unlearn" all she mistakenly admires in herself and undergo "unbroken discipline." But when she protests against Klesmer's judgment, he becomes crushingly explicit. After her "education in doing things slackly for one-and-twenty years," she can expect only mortification in her pursuit. "You would have to bear what I may call a glaring insignificance. . . . You would have to keep your place in a crowd, and after all it is likely you would lose it and get out of sight." There seems no room in such a world for a gambler's luck. Gwendolen tries to rise "above the stifling layers of egoistic disappointment and irritation" as she is forced to accept "a vision of herself on the common level" (23). Whatever vindictive pleasure we might have been led as readers to take in Gwendolen's discomfiture is checked by the author's demand for sympathy. Gwendolen is not much different from all of us in projecting her disappointment as a "world-nausea." "Surely a young creature is pitiable who has the labyrinth of her life before her and no clue—to whom distrust in herself and her good fortune has come as a sudden shock, like a rent across the path that she was treading carelessly" (24).

The renewal of Grandcourt's proposal—he has been stirred the more by her flight—presents Gwendolen with a new occasion for choice. It comes when she is in despair, and its coming brings terror as much as triumph. The terror is once again a fear of what she may find herself capable of doing. She consents to receive Grandcourt: "Why should she not let him come? It bound her to nothing. . . . She could reject him. Why was she to deny herself the freedom of doing this—which she would like to do." When her mother observes that there is in fact some measure of commitment in receiving him, Gwendolen swings back to the "pleasure of refusing him" (26). But it is only the pleasure one can take in a fantasy of power at the moment one senses one's real powerlessness. For the constant shifts of balance have brought Gwendolen to a "state in which no conclusion could look fixed to her":

> She did not mean to accept Grandcourt; from the first moment of receiving his letter she had meant to refuse him; still, that could not but prompt her to look the unwelcome reasons full in the face until she had a little less awe of them, could not hinder imagination from filling out her knowledge in various ways, some of which seemed to change the aspect of what she knew. By dint of looking at a dubious object with a constructive imagination, one can give it twenty different shapes.

All of Gwendolen's hesitation is tied to her memory of her encounter with Lydia Glasher. That event aroused an impulse that swept all before it—an impulse that arose from "her dread of wrong-doing." From "the dim region of what was called disgraceful, wrong, guilty, she shrank with mingled pride and terror." But now she examines that fear of guilt. Might she not help rather than injure Mrs. Glasher and her children if she were to marry Grandcourt? But what of the "indignation and loathing" she herself has felt, or might have felt, for a man with such a past? They once more support her resolution to refuse him, and that resolution compensates for the sense of powerlessness in which Klesmer's advice has left her. The renewed sense of power is the keynote of her meeting with Grandcourt. She remains largely silent, demanding of Grandcourt that he advance without encouragement. He in turn offers to withdraw if there is not hope, and Gwendolen is suddenly aware of how much more she dreads a return to the hopelessness she has escaped by his presence. She avoids a direct reply by telling him of her family's plight.

Grandcourt has learned of the meeting between Gwendolen and Lydia Glasher, and he finds malicious pleasure in the prospect of Gwendolen's accepting him in spite of her knowledge. She, in turn, needs somehow to believe in her own power; in "this man's homage to her" lies the "rescue from helpless subjection to an oppressive lot." As he offers to remove the danger of poverty for her mother and sisters, she is stirred by this almost miraculous ascent beyond all that has threatened, into a realm of freedom and self-command. When she hesitates, even so, to accept him, Grandcourt becomes all the more fascinated by the game they are playing. "Do you command me to go?" he asks, and she at once replies, "No." "She could not let him go: that negative was a clutch. She seemed to herself to be, after all, only drifted towards the tremendous decision:—but drifting depends on something besides the current, when the sails have been set beforehand."

When at last she accepts him, the word comes from her "as if she had been answering to her name in a court of justice." His tactful, undemonstrative response reinforces for the moment her sense of freedom, and she recovers her spirits. By the time Grandcourt leaves, Gwendolen has persuaded herself that he is "likely to be the least disagreeable of husbands" (27).

And yet this decision, which she is relieved to have made, is "dogged by the shadow" of her earlier decision to reject him, "which had at first come as the undoubting movement of her whole being." She has never found a question of right or wrong awaken so much terror in her. This seems "a moment when something like a new consciousness was awakened." She is at the point of accepting the belief that it no longer matters what she does, that she has "only to amuse herself" as best she can. But "that lawlessness, that casting away of all care for justification, suddenly frightened her." All she has chosen, all that will accomplish her "deliverance from the dull insignificance of her girlhood" seems now "like food with the taint of sacrilege upon it, which she must snatch with terror." She can repress that terror in the sense of daring she recovers on horseback, in the somewhat hectically high spirits with which she plays at "reigning."

Grandcourt is, of course, the obverse of all that Gwendolen distrusts in herself. He takes pleasure in ruling her, in bringing her to accept him in spite of aversion. "He meant to be master of a woman who would have liked to master him, and who perhaps would have been capable of mastering another man" (28). Grandcourt disdains open brutality; his pleasure is in knowing her frustration and blocked will, in conquering her "dumb repugnance" or observing her "rage of dumbness" (48).

George Eliot presents Gwendolen's decision with all the frightening intensity that it acquires for a young woman who has never known the check of discipline, whose will has outrun some deeper moral sense, and who has subsisted so far on the brilliant effects her beauty and her manners have won. The desolation of her marriage makes her yearn for some revival of spirit, "excitement that would carry her through life, as a hard gallop carried her through some of the morning hours." Perhaps, she thinks, "if she began to gamble again, the passion might awake." "If only she could feel a keen appetite for those pleasures—could only believe in pleasure as she used to do! . . . Her confidence in herself and her destiny had turned into remorse and dread; she trusted neither herself nor her future." She turns in imagination to Deronda: "Had he some way of looking at things which might be a new footing for her—an inward safeguard against possible events which she dreaded as stored-up retribution?" Her desire to win Deronda's concern—she hardly seeks admiration now—is perhaps the chief vestige of regard for herself. She makes him into a "priest" and ascribes to him all the wisdom she needs to guide her. Her sense of his influence upon her acts in turn as an influence upon him. "Those who trust us educate us. And perhaps in that ideal consecration of Gwendolen's, some education was being prepared for Deronda" (35).

It is that concatenation that gives the novel its strength, and, however one might wish to be rid of the solemnities and sentimentalities that surround the Meyricks and Mirah, the linkage cannot be broken. Gwendolen is pathetic in the blindness of her self-assertion, but Deronda's difficulty lies in his lack of trust in a self. He has discovered, as he thinks, that he is Sir Hugo Mallinger's illegitimate son, and he is somewhat terrified by the history that suggests: the disappearance of his mother, perhaps her disgrace, and the apparent insensitivity of Sir Hugo in such a matter, generous and affectionate as he has been to Daniel. Sir Hugo's failure to discuss what Deronda does not feel free to open stirs some resentment; but for the most part Deronda achieves submission in self-effacement. He has been on one occasion strongly troubled by Sir Hugo's casual suggestion (as it seems) that he train his voice for the concert stage; for this might be taken to deny his claim to be a gentleman, and he is reassured when Sir Hugo dismisses the idea. But Deronda withdraws from competition and the pursuit of any career. He devotes himself instead to helping Hans Meyrick win his scholarship; and, for motives he only partly recognizes, he spoils his own luck. He is full of uncertainty about what he can become, disabled as he feels he is by his origins, and he waits passively for the emergence of some purpose.

The image Deronda has, rowing on the Thames, of Mirah's "helpless sorrow" blends with "the strong array of reasons why he should shrink from getting into that routine of the world which makes men apologise for all its wrong-doing . . . why he should not draw strongly at any thread in the hopelessly entangled scheme of things." He lies in his boat, looking up at the brilliant sky. "He was forgetting everything else in a half-speculative, half-involuntary identification of himself with the objects he was looking at, thinking how far it might be possible habitually to shift his centre till his own personality would be no less outside him than the landscape . . ." (17). This moment of self-dissolution immediately precedes his rescue of Mirah and his assumption of concern, responsibility, eventually of love for her.

It is clear, once we have come to know his history, that the Deronda of the opening scene is neither so aloof nor so contemptuous as Gwendolen has imagined him. Rather, he sees her distress, her "fevered worldliness," as somehow related to the distress mingled with his own birth. Deronda, as his friend Hans Meyrick recognizes, is attracted to people by the "possibility of his defending them, rescuing them, telling upon their lives with some sort of redeeming influence." As Deronda's feelings become less diffused and more closely involved with Mirah, he finds himself more impatient for a disclosure of his origin. It might, as he knows, bring pain; but it may help him "to make his life a sequence which would take the form of duty." He wants "to escape standing as a critic outside the activities of men, stiffened into the ridiculous attitude of self-assigned superiority" (37).

It is to this yearning of Deronda's that Mordecai's words seem so directly to apply: " 'Shall man, whose soul is set in the royalty of discernment and resolve, deny his rank and say, I am an onlooker, ask no choice or purpose of me? That is the blasphemy of this time. The divine principle of our race is action, choice, resolved memory' " (42). Deronda begins to recognize the weakness in his "dislike to appear exceptional or to risk an ineffective insistence on his own opinion" (43). Once he has discovered that he is a Jew and can begin to realize that he loves Mirah, he achieves "a new state of decision," "a release of all the energy which had long been spent in self-checking and suppression." His judgment is "no longer wandering in the mazes of impartial sympathy, but choosing, with the noble partiality which is man's best strength, the close fellowship that makes sympathy practical." He has lost "the bird's eye reasonableness which soars to avoid preference"; he gains "the generous reasonableness of drawing shoulder to shoulder with men of like inheritance" (63).

It is as a reflex of that discovery of powers in himself that he can urge Gwendolen to take on any clear duty. Other duties will arise from it, and she may then look at her life "as a debt." Nor should that be feared; what we must fear is "the want of motive." With the unfolding of duties and of new demands upon her from day to day, she will find her life "growing like a plant" (65).

Grandcourt's death by drowning is at once Gwendolen's deliverance and her deepest source of terror: "I saw my wish outside me." Did she fail to throw the rope in time? What matters most is that the death is one she had wished for and dreamed of, and it summons up all the other forms of guilt. In her marriage, she wronged Lydia Glasher. "I wanted to make my gain out of another's loss . . . [I]t was like roulette—and the money burnt into me" (56).

In the same city Deronda has finally met his mother—not a guilty or wronged creature, but a magnificently proud and accomplished woman. As she says, "I did not want affection. I have been stifled with it. I wanted to live out the life that was in me." She has had a great career as singer and actress. "I was living a myriad lives in one. I did not want a child." Although she has lived for something far more serious and exacting than the pleasure of doing as one likes, she shares with Gwendolen a fierce exercise of will. She is, moreover, irredeemably the actress: "experience immediately passed into drama, and she acted her own emotions." She has been humbled by a painful and fatal disease, and she can regard her father's disapproval in a new light. The defiant and vengeful daughter can now see beyond the limits of her will. In her pain, she tells Daniel, "it is as if all the life I have chosen to live, all thoughts, all will, forsook me and left me alone in spots of memory, and I can't get away: my pain seems to keep me there." She is now ready to surrender her son to his grandfather, to yield in her struggle against a father whose death has made him invulnerable (51).

Deronda's mother is a fine conception—stern, willful, theatrical—not another Mirah but a mature and formidable counterpart of Gwendolen. She stands out against any simple celebration of morality; she has been brought down by pain and the prospect of death, but she fights the claims of her father to the last, even in the appeasement she offers by restoring Daniel's identity. Her toughness of mind is a much greater force than Gwendolen's self-assertion, and it gives a new dignity to such assertion at the moment when Gwendolen finally surrenders hers. Henry James described the story of Gwendolen as the "universe forcing itself with a slow, inexorable pressure into a narrow, complacent, and yet after all extremely sensitive mind, and making it ache with pain of the process."[25] Gwendolen "is punished for being narrow, and she is not allowed a chance to expand." This is too harsh. It is true that Gwendolen seems to offer fatuous consolation to Deronda: "*You* are just the same as if you were not a Jew." And she has a "dreadful presentiment of mountainous travel for her mind before it could reach Deronda's." She is, at the last, surrounded by the large spaces and "wide-stretching purposes" in a world which reduces her "to a mere speck." She has been "dislodged from her supremacy in her own world," and, after a long period of hysteria, she wakes to feel concern for her mother, who has been sitting up with her. "I shall live. I shall be better" (69). As we have seen in a number of such characters, for example Estella in *Great Expectations* and Marianne Dashwood in *Sense and Sensibility,* there is a loss of scale as one dwindles to a moral being; yet it is also the emergence of a self from the welter of assertion and impulse that has often provided an impressive substitute.

George Eliot makes moral experience a subject of great power, and her ultimate commitment is to the ways the world is, to the difficult, often heroically demanding recognition of both "what is unmodifiable and is the object of resignation" and what is "modifiable by hopeful activity—by new conceptions and new deeds."[26] This moral realism is related, of course, to literary realism. Realism in the novel is often the embodiment in low or commonplace persons and events of the actions traditionally embodied in heroic, saintly, or demonic forms. It is a transposition of modes. Eliot praises Houdon's bust of the composer Gluck as a "striking specimen of the *real* in art. The sculptor has given every scar made by the smallpox; he has left the nose as pug and insignificant, and the mouth as common, as Nature made them; but then he has done what, doubtless, Nature also did—he has made one feel in those coarsely-cut features the presence of the genius *qui divinise la laideur*."[27] The last phrase, about sanctified ugliness, catches intimations of the sublime; and it is there—in the sublimity of moral energy, whatever its conventional goodness—that George Eliot's subject lies.

8 ✳ Tolstoy
and the Forms of Life

Tolstoy and Wittgenstein

It is difficult to account for the remarkable sense of depth as well as breadth we feel in reading Tolstoy. Sir Isaiah Berlin, in describing that sense, has come closer than anyone else to explaining it. Tolstoy's heroes achieve a kind of serenity through coming to accept "the permanent relationships of things and the universal texture of human life." Through them we become aware of an order underlying and perhaps girding the world of our experience. It is an order which " 'contains' and determines the structure of experience, the framework on which it—that is, we and all we experience—must be conceived as being set":

> we are immersed and submerged in a medium that, precisely to the degree to which we inevitably take it for granted as part of ourselves, we do not and cannot observe as if from the outside; cannot identify, measure and seek to manipulate; cannot even be wholly aware of, inasmuch as it enters too intimately into all our experience, is itself too closely interwoven with all that we are and do to be lifted out of the flow (it *is* the flow) and observed with scientific detachment, as an object. It—the medium in which we are—determines our most permanent categories, our standards of truth and falsehood, of reality and appearance, of the good and the bad, of the central and peripheral, the subjective and the objective, of the beautiful and the ugly, of movement and rest, of past, present and future, of one and many; hence neither these, nor any other explicitly conceived categories or concepts can be applied to it—for it is itself but a vague name for the totality that includes these categories, these concepts, the ultimate framework, the basic presuppositions wherewith we function.

Those characters who, like Pierre in *War and Peace* and Levin in *Anna Karenina,* gain a measure of wisdom have learned no new facts about their world. They have come to accept the limits the world sets: "It is 'there'—

the framework, the foundation of everything—and the wise man alone has a sense of it; Pierre gropes for it; Kutuzov feels it in his bones; Karataev is at one with it. All Tolstoy's heroes attain to at least intermittent glimpses of it." [1] This is caught concisely in the account of Platon Karataev, who appears at a time when Pierre has lost faith in the meaning of-his-life. Karataev was always to remain in Pierre's memory "the personification of everything Russian, kindly, and round." When he spoke "he seemed not to know how he would conclude":

> He did not, and could not, understand the meaning of words apart from their context. Every word and action of his was the manifestation of an activity unknown to him, which was his life. But his life, as he regarded it, had no meaning as a separate thing. It had meaning only as part of the whole of which he was always conscious. His words and actions flowed from him as evenly, inevitably, and spontaneously as fragrance exhales from a flower. He could not understand the value or significance of any word or deed taken separately. [2]

Karataev lives without self-consciousness in a world whose unity admits no abstraction. He embodies God for Pierre better than the Freemasons' Architect of the Universe. He helps Pierre recover the simplicity of direct feeling. Pierre feels at last "like a man who after straining his eyes to see into the far distance finds what he sought at his very feet." (WP XV,5). Beside this spontaneous and unreflecting assurance of Karataev one can set Levin's despair near the close of *Anna Karenina:* "When Levin thought about what he was and what he was living for, he could find no answer and was driven to despair; but when he stopped asking himself about it, he seemed to know both what he was and what he was living for, because he acted and lived in a positive and determined way. . . . ." In the midst of many duties that must be performed, Levin has tried to avoid thinking about larger questions, but he is not a man to rest with comfort in evasions: "So he lived, not knowing and not seeing any possibility of knowing what he was and why he lived in the world, and worried so much by this ignorance that he was afraid he might commit suicide and yet at the same time he resolutely carved out his own individual and definite way in life." [3]

Tolstoy strikes a comic note in Levin's case as he does in Pierre's. It comes of the disparity between anxious, strenuous reflection and effortless intuition. Levin, like Pierre, finds himself returning to certitudes of childhood: "I have discovered nothing. I have merely found out what I knew. . . . . I have rid myself of deception." Levin recognizes the certainty that he has lived by whenever he has not allowed reflection to unsettle him. As he looks up at the sky, he knows that he "cannot see it except as round and finite" although he knows that "space is infinite." Could the astronomers have charted the heavens if they had not taken the earth as fixed? Could they have measured all they did if they had not made their observations in relation to one meridian and one horizon? Is not man's moral awareness such a fixed point? (*AK* VIII, 13)

There is a striking resemblance between Levin's argument and that which governs Ludwig Wittgenstein's late work, *On Certainty*. One of Wittgenstein's problems is to set the limits of skepticism. "Doubt itself rests only on what is beyond doubt." "A doubt without an end is not even a doubt." Wittgenstein treats the question of a framework that is raised by Berlin: "I do not explicitly learn the propositions that stand fast [*feststehen*] for me. I can *discover* them subsequently like the axis around which a body rotates. This axis is not fixed in the sense that anything holds it fast, but the movement around it determines its immobility."[4] But, Wittgenstein goes on, what I hold fast to is "not one proposition but a nest of propositions" (225). These propositions provide the structure upon which all our empirical knowledge must rest or into which all our experience, including the experience of uncertainty, must be fitted. "That is to say, the *questions* that we raise and our *doubts* depend on the fact that some propositions are exempt from doubt, are as it were the hinges on which those turn" (341). We must begin with such fixities: "If I want the door to turn, the hinges must stay put" (343). For doubts, like all our uses of language, arise from "forms of life." "My *life* consists in my being content to accept many things" (344).

Wittgenstein admired Tolstoy. He is said to have carried Tolstoy's brief version of the Gospels with him during the First World War, and he provided his friend, Norman Malcolm, when he in turn was a soldier, with a copy of Tolstoy's last major work of fiction, *Hadji Murad*. "I hope you get a lot out of it," he wrote Malcolm, "because there is a lot *in* it." Of Tolstoy himself, he wrote: "There's a *real* man, who has a *right* to write." He particularly admired the moral parables of Tolstoy's *Twenty-Three Tales*, perhaps out of the same desire for a morality at once clear and profound that made him enjoy Dr. Johnson's prayers and his life of Pope. We see this moral concern in his remarks on G. E. Moore, whose absence of vanity and innocence of nature Malcolm praised:

> There is . . . a *certain* innocence about Moore; he is, e.g., completely unvain. But as to its being to his *credit* to be childlike,—I can't understand that; unless it's also to a *child's* credit. For you aren't talking of the innocence a man has fought for, but of an innocence which comes from a natural absence of temptation.—I believe that all you wanted to say was that you *liked,* or even *loved,* Moore's childlikeness. And that I can *understand.*[5]

Wittgenstein was, in effect, recalling the rules for the use of praise or credit; he was telling Malcolm that in neglecting the element of moral effort or self-mastery he had used a word outside the language-game that was its home.

The conception of language-games recognizes that we have many overlapping structures of language, each somewhat arbitrary and conventional, each resting upon a distinctive kind of activity that it serves. These patterns of activity Wittgenstein called forms of life, and he used that phrase to refer to small-scale activities as well as to others that include a large portion of our existence. "Only in the stream of thought and life do words have meaning." [6] As he says, "We remain unconscious of the prodigious diversity of all the everyday language games because the clothing of our language makes everything alike." [7]

Wittgenstein felt that "the problems arising through a misinterpretation of our forms of language have the character of *depth*. They are deep disquietudes; their roots are as deep in us as the forms of our language, and their significance is as great as the importance of our language" (*PI,* par. 111).

Wittgenstein wrote *On Certainty* to meet the questions raised when G. E. Moore claimed to know the truth of such propositions as "Here is one hand, and here is another" or "The earth existed for a long time before my birth." Wittgenstein tries to show how empirical propositions, as they become part of the structure of beliefs or of the picture we inherit and take as our ground for doubts, serve a new function as well.

> The propositions describing this world-picture might be part of a kind of mythology. And their role is like that of rules of a game; and the game can be learned purely practically, without learning any explicit rules.
>
> It might be imagined that some propositions, of the form of empirical propositions, were hardened and functioned as channels for such empirical propositions as were not hardened but fluid; and that this relation altered with time, in that fluid propositions hardened, and hard ones became fluid.
>
> The mythology may change back into a state of flux, the river-bed of thoughts may shift. But I distinguish between the movement of the waters on the river-bed and the shift of the bed itself; though there is not a sharp division of the one from the other.
>
> But if someone were to say "So logic too is an empirical science" he would be wrong. Yet he is right: the same proposition may get treated at one time as something to test by experience, at another as a rule of testing. [paras. 95–98]

The consequences of Wittgenstein's position is a world without "sufficient reason," without absolutes or permanent grounds. "The difficulty is to realize the groundlessness of our believing" (*OC,* 166): "Giving grounds, however, justifying the evidence, comes to an end;—but the end is not certain propositions' striking us immediately as true, i.e., it is not a kind of *seeing* on our part; it is our *acting* which lies at the bottom of the language-game" (*OC,* 204). And Wittgenstein introduces a splendid architectural paradox: "I have arrived at the rock bottom of my convictions. And one might almost say that these foundation-walls are carried by the whole house" (*OC,* 248).

Anthony Flew has drawn interesting parallels between passages in Tolstoy's *A Confession* (written shortly after *Anna Karenina*) and passages near the close of Wittgenstein's *Tractatus*. Running through Tolstoy's review of his religious life was his recognition of the misdirected effort to find in empirical science the kind of meaning that Wittgenstein makes clear it could not reveal. As Tolstoy put it, his mistake lay in that his "reasoning was not in accord with the question" he had put; for his question ("Why should I live? . . . [W]hat meaning has my finite existence in this infinite world?") "included a demand for an explanation of the finite in terms of the infinite, and vice versa." "I asked: 'What is the meaning of my life, beyond time, cause, and space?' And I replied to quite another question: 'What is the meaning of my life within time, cause, and space?' With the result that, after long efforts of thought, the answer I reached was: 'None.' "

In response to such questions Wittgenstein wrote:

> We feel that even when all possible scientific questions have been answered, the problems of life remain completely untouched. Of course there are then no questions left, and this itself is the answer.
>
> The solution of the problem of life is seen in the vanishing of the problem.
>
> (Is not this the reason why those who have found after a long period of doubt that the sense of life became clear to them have then been unable to say what constituted that sense?)
>
> There are, indeed, things that cannot be put into words. They *make themselves manifest*. They are what is mystical.[8]

One is inclined to see in Pierre and Levin the truth of what Bertrand Russell wrote in 1919 about Wittgenstein: "He has penetrated deep into mystical ways of thought and feeling, but I think (though he wouldn't agree) that what he likes best in mysticism is its power to make him stop thinking."[9] We may want to find a term other than *mysticism,* and we might want to alter "likes best" to "needs most," for the thinking of Pierre and Levin is intense, exacting, and—so long as it pursues the questions it sets—endlessly frustrating.

Inside and Outside

> [W]hen we intend, we are surrounded by our intention's *pictures,* and we are inside them. But when we step outside intention, they are as mere patches on a canvas, without life and of no interest to us. When we intend, we exist in the space of intention, among the pictures (shadows) of intention, as well as with real things. Let us imagine we are sitting in a darkened cinema and entering into the film. Now the lights are turned on, though the film continues on the screen. But suddenly we are outside it and see it as movements of light and dark patches on a screen.[10]

Wittgenstein's discussion of our being inside or outside intention's pictures is comparable to H. L. A. Hart's treatment of the difference between an internal and external view of rules.

The internal view is enclosed, one might say, within the authority of the rules, accepts their claim, and acts in conscious awareness of them. "But whatever the rules are, whether they are those of games, or moral or legal rules, we can, if we choose, occupy the position of an observer who does not even refer . . . to the internal point of view of the group. Such an observer is content merely to record the regularities of observable behavior in which conformity with the rules partly consists. . . ." He may be able to predict the behavior of a group without recognizing the power the rules have for it. "What the external point of view, which limits itself to the observable regularities of behavior, cannot reproduce is the way in which the rules function as rules in the lives of those who normally are the majority of society."[11]

One may speak of the game or the social structure as an institution, and of the normative claims of rules as institutional facts. The detached observer, who does not participate in the life of the institution, may so describe action as to make it seem ludicrous or outrageous, and this is frequently the way in which the satirist works. He strips from complex behavior those implicit norms (or intentions) that help to explain it and renders instead the external gestures which the norms induce. The effect may be one of moral horror, as when Lemuel Gulliver describes a soldier as "a Yahoo hired to kill in cold blood as many of his own species, who have never offended him, as possibly he can." So Tolstoy describes the beginning of war:

> On the twelfth of June 1812, the forces of western Europe crossed the Russian frontier and war began, that is, an event took place opposed to human reason and to human nature. Millions of men perpetrated against one another such innumerable crimes, frauds, treacheries, thefts, forgeries, issues of false money, burglaries, incendiarisms, and murder as in whole centuries are not recorded in the annals of all the law courts of the world, but which those who committed them did not at the time regard as being crimes.   [*WP*, IX, 1]

But the rules need not be the terrible claims of patriotism and so-called just war. They may be those of artistic convention. In *War and Peace,* Natasha Rostov attends the opera in a state of mind that prevents her from making an appropriate response: "She saw only the painted cardboard and the queerly dressed men and women who moved, spoke, and sang so strangely in that brilliant light. She knew what it was all meant to represent, but it was so pretentiously false and unnatural that she first felt ashamed for the actors and then amused at them." And Tolstoy offers the deadpan vision of the alienated or uncomprehending spectator:

many people appeared from right and left wearing black cloaks and holding things like daggers in their hands. They began waving their arms. Then some other people ran in and began dragging away the maiden who had been in white and was now in light blue. They did not drag her away at once, but sang with her for a long time and then at last dragged her off, and behind the scenes something metallic was struck three times and everyone knelt down and sang a prayer. All these things were repeatedly interrupted by the enthusiastic shouts of the audience.   [VIII, 9]

With this, one may compare Flaubert's method in *Madame Bovary*. Here the novelist presents a mocking, external view of the opera (a performance of *Lucia di Lammermoor*) while showing Emma's fervent response. Her response is not simply an internal one; it is an internal view used as the occasion for fantasy. Her response is more than appropriate; she identifies Lucy's fictive life with her own, and the intensity of her response is all the more ludicrous for the external view Flaubert has given of the performance. The celebrated tenor Lagardy is performing, and we are given a brief account of his private life, for it is to the "sentimental fame" of Lagardy that Emma responds as much as to the role he performs.

A skilled ham actor, he never forgot to have a phrase on his seductiveness and his sensitive soul inserted in the accounts about him. He had a fine voice, colossal aplomb, more temperament than intelligence, more pathos than lyric feeling; all this made for an admirable charlatan type, in which there was something of the hairdresser as well as of the bull-fighter.

From the first scene he brought down the house. He pressed Lucy in his arms, he left her, he came back, he seemed desperate; he had outbursts of rage, then elegiac gurgling of infinite sweetness. . . . Emma bent forward to see him, scratching the velvet of the box with her nails. Her heart filled with these melodious lamentations. . . . [T]he voice of the prima donna seemed to echo her own conscience, and the whole fictional story seemed to capture something of her own life. But no one on earth had loved her with such love.[12]

If Natasha remains at too great a psychic distance from the opera's fictions, Emma leaves too little distance. Flaubert insists upon the physical presence of the theater. The velvet of the box is made the more real by the very obliviousness with which Emma scratches it. Flaubert's field of vision includes details that are incongruously solid. They resist and mock the fantasies of his heroine.

Tolstoy is profoundly concerned with the moments when we move from an internal to an external view. Probably the best known instance in *Anna Karenina* occurs as Anna returns from Moscow after her encounter there with Vronsky:

As soon as the train stopped at Petersburg and she got out, the first person to attract her attention was her husband. "Goodness, why are his ears like that?" she thought, looking at his cold, distinguished figure and especially at the cartilages of his ears, pressing up against the rim of his round hat. Catching sight of her, he walked toward her, pursing his lips in his usual sarcastic smile, and looking straight at her with his large, tired eyes. As she met his fixed and tired gaze, her heart contracted painfully with a sort of unpleasant sensation, as though she expected to find him looking different. She was particularly struck by the feeling of discontent with herself which she experienced when she met him. It was that old familiar feeling indistinguishable from hypocrisy which she experienced in her relations with her husband; but she had not been conscious of it before, while now she was clearly and painfully aware of it.

[I, 30]

The ludicrous sight of Karenin's ears seems to precipitate a new way of looking at him. He ceases to be a familiar presence, someone seen as all but part of herself. Instead, he has become a distinct figure, seen from a distance and very much from the outside. The observation of his ears is not, of course, the cause of what follows; it is simply the first detail registered by a new analytic view made possible through the withdrawal or absence of the usual feelings. Because it is a mere physical detail of no great consequence, it serves all the better to trigger a new way of looking at Karenin and, by the end of the paragraph, of seeing in retrospect and being able at last to identify a feeling that always shadowed their relationship. Anna has moved from the inside to the outside of her marriage. A few pages later she tries to disavow this change, and now the ears become an impediment: " 'All the same, he's a good man; upright, kind, and remarkable in his own sphere,' Anna said to herself when she had returned to her room, as though defending him against someone who has accusing him and maintaining that one could not love him. 'But why do his ears stick out so oddly? Has he had a haircut?' " (I, 33) In this instance, we have seen Anna moving from an internal to an external view of her marriage. But we can see another movement as well, toward the inside of a new relationship with Vronsky. At their first meeting, Anna expresses her concern for the widow of the railway guard killed at the station. Vronsky hurries off to make a large donation. There is no reason to think that he means Anna to learn of it; but she does, and it troubles her. "She felt there was something in this incident that had to do with her, something that should not have been." Her power over Vronsky dismays her, for his gift to the widow is the creation of a new relationship, and the action becomes, to a small degree, a claim upon her. If she were entirely indifferent to Vronsky, she might not feel so keenly that they now share a bond she should repudiate—if that were not to make too much of it. Later, in Petersburg, Anna assumes the power that Vronsky has been urging upon her. When he speaks of love during their meeting at the Princess Betsy's Anna stops him: " 'Please remember that I've forbidden you to utter that word, that odious word,' said Anna with a shudder; but at once she felt that by that very word 'forbidden,' she had shown she admitted that she had certain rights over him, and by this very fact was encouraging him to speak of love." Later, as she leaves, she returns to this: " 'Love,' she repeated slowly, speaking inwardly to herself, and suddenly . . . she added: 'The reason why I dislike the word is because it means too much to me, much more than you can understand,' and she glanced into his face' (II, 7).

Tolstoy's characters move in and out of such frames, from participation to detachment and back again, slipping out of a structure or watching it dissolve about them. Beneath or within these institutional structures—families, regiments, provincial councils, theological systems—lie those activities, those forms of life, that are the scene and source of vitality. Tolstoy, whatever his moral concerns or perhaps most of all *in* his moral concerns, was a vitalist. We have the phrases that Pierre speaks or hears or imagines in *War and Peace:* "Life is God. Everything changes and moves and that movement is God" (XIV, 3). We can see this vitalism in the fierce, often clumsy, energy of Levin's search for meaning in his life. We can see it, too, in Anna. In the moments after the first consummation of their love, she is appalled to hear Vronsky speak of their happiness. The word is too trivial for what she feels. "She felt at that moment she could not express in words the feeling of joy, shame, and horror at this entry into a new life, and she did not want to talk about it, to profane this feeling by inexact words" (II, 11).

Forms of Life and Death: War and Peace

Nicholas Rostov moves from the inside of one form of life to the inside of another when, after informing his father of his enormous gambling debt, he returns to the regiment. There, "bound in one narrow, unchanging frame, he experienced the same sense of peace, of moral support, and the same sense of being at home here in his own place, as he had felt under the parental roof. But here was none of all that turmoil of the world at large" (*WPV*, 13). He is free of difficult choices and awkward explanations; one had only to do "what was clearly, distinctly, and definitely ordered." (This is very much the appeal of military life for Vronsky as well.)

It is not, however, so simple as Nicholas might wish. He is troubled when the emperor fails to grant his petition in Denisov's behalf. Nicholas is even more profoundly troubled by the mutual esteem the emperor and Napoleon display at the Peace of Tilsit. Nicholas doesn't know quite what disturbs him, and the disturbance takes the form of vivid memories rather than reflection, memories he has repressed in his state of hopefulness:

> Terrible doubts arose in his soul. Now he remembered Denisov with his changed
> expression . . . and the whole hospital, with arms and legs torn off and its
> dirt and disease. So vividly did he recall that hospital stench of dead flesh that
> he looked around to see where the smell came from. Next he thought of that
> self-satisfied Bonaparte, with his small white hand, who was now an Emperor,
> liked and respected by Alexander. Then why those severed arms and legs and
> those dead men? . . . He caught himself harboring such strange thoughts that
> he was frightened.   [V, 18]

Rather than allow himself to acknowledge such thoughts, Nicholas drinks
heavily and rebukes a fellow officer who expresses the thoughts that trouble
Nicholas himself. The officer provides him with an occasion to fight down
his doubts. How can you judge the Emperor's actions! While the fellow
officer protests that he has never criticized the emperor, Nicholas continues:
"If once we begin judging and arguing about everything, nothing sacred
will be left! That way we shall be saying there is no God—nothing!" Nicholas comes in from the frontiers of disbelief; he has been made all too much
aware of the medium, of the assumptions and presuppositions he is terrified
of losing; and he regains assurance with a mixture of wine and rationalization
(V, 18).

Nicholas's mother, the Countess Rostov, provides us with a good instance
of someone who has moved outside the life she has always lived. She has lost
her young son Petya and her husband:

> She ate, drank, slept, or kept awake, but did not *live*. Life gave her no new
> impressions. She wanted nothing from life but tranquillity, and that tranquill-
> ity only death could give her. But until death came she had to go on living.
> . . . She talked only because she physically needed to exercise her tongue and
> lungs. . . . What for people in their full vigor is an aim was for her . . .
> merely a pretext.   [First Epilogue, 3]

One of the most consistent ways in which Tolstoy treats these forms of
life we take for granted is in his account of military command. The tenor of
his argument throughout is that the plans of commanders have little relevance to what occurs. There are too many imponderables, there is too vast a
field to encompass. Those like Kutuzov who recognize the nature of this vast
play of forces can at least learn to work with them. When Kutuzov listened
to battle reports, he attended not to the words spoken or the facts reported,
but to "the expression of face and of voice of those who were reporting." He
knew how few sane choices could be made by a commander and how much
depended on "that intangible force called the spirit of the army." Kutuzov,
therefore, listens and watches with a "concentrated quiet attention," for he
recognizes the true framework which it is not customary to acknowledge.
He knows military operations from the inside (X, 35).

A commander in chief, Tolstoy observes, "is never dealing with the beginning of any event." He is "always in the midst of a series of shifting events and so he never can at any moment consider the whole import of an event that is occurring. Moment by moment the event is imperceptibly shaping itself, and at every moment . . . the commander in chief is in the midst of a most complex play of intrigues, worries, contingencies," etc. (X1, 2). The general may give orders so as to make whatever must happen seem to have been brought about by his will, but, Tolstoy insists, the sense of freedom which we have and must act upon should not delude us into thinking we have greater powers than we do. "Only unconscious action bears fruit, and he who plays a part in an historic event never understands its significance. If he tries to realize it his efforts are fruitless" (XII, 2). Most events represent the convergence of wills unknown to each other, of circumstances which are never sufficiently recognized. It is only when an event is past that we can see it completely. Just as Kutuzov listens for what the voice rather than the words reveals, so again when he addresses the troops, they do not hear his words, but they understand his "feeling of majestic triumph combined with pity for the foe and consciousness of the justice" of the Russian cause (XV, 3).

We see Kutuzov, then, improvising a series of tactical retreats, allowing the French forces to occupy Moscow, watching them founder in their ill-conceived retreat. He does not play the game of dazzling strategy and glorious victory; only he, in fact, knows that the Battle of Borodino was a victory for the Russians and the turning point in Napoleon's expedition. Kutuzov has his own game, if that is the word for it; he is like the patient defendant who keeps prudently deferring a trial until the plaintiff litigates himself into insolvency. For his game is not winning a lawsuit but defeating the plaintiff; and sapping the plaintiff's will or his fortune is less costly and risky than confronting him in court. This is perhaps an unattractive account of Kutuzov's method, but one must think of him as a defendant who believes so completely in the justness of his cause that he does not need to declare it or defend it in a court.

Kutuzov is a man who exhibits little distinction of manner; he is corpulent and untidy, in some ways resembling both Pierre and Karataev. What he shares with them is an unheroic, even antiheroic, manner. Tolstoy is full of sympathy for the soldier's patriotic feeling, but he tends to celebrate the greatness that is thrust upon men, stability to endure and wit to improvise. There is no better instance than Prince Andrew's snatching up the fallen standard at Austerlitz as Napoleon had done at the Bridge of Arcola, and leading an improbable charge against the French. "Forward, lads! he shouted in a voice as piercing as a child's." The final simile is telling; there is a wonderful naivety about his action, and yet he is followed by a battalion in the face of the cannon which the French have captured and are about to turn around. As Andrew lies wounded on the battlefield, even the standard missing, he hears Napoleon remark of him, "That's a fine death!" (III, 13)

Prince Andrew is the antithesis of such unheroic figures as Pierre and Kutuzov. And, like all the Bolkonskis in the novel, he has turned away from life. We first encounter him at Anna Schérer's soirée, where the deadliest sin is to be natural and where Andrew gives the impression of having found everyone, but most of all his wife, "so tiresome that it wearied him to look at or listen to them." Later in private conversation Pierre sees a new aspect of Andrew, a passion of nervous excitement and morbid criticism. Andrew feels himself trapped by marriage, consigned to the role of a court lackey, caught in a narrow circle of gossip, ceremony, and triviality. He is about to go to war as a means of escape.

Throughout the novel we see Andrew looking for something to believe in with heroic devotion and abandon, but always prepared, at the least threat to the perfection of that faith, to withdraw into sardonic disenchantment. There is some part of him that is drawn to the glories of power; he enjoys helping other young men to win the success which his pride cannot accept for himself. He is ready to admire a court official like Speranski, but equally ready to be disenchanted. There is about Prince Andrew something of the Byronic hero who yearns for a greatness he can trust, but who is always afraid of being taken in and ready to meet every occasion with irony. This is a pride that seems superior, but proves, as the novel unfolds, less robust, less intelligent, than Pierre's often clumsy and childish tenacity. As he lies on the battlefield, Andrew concentrates upon the "lofty sky, not clear yet still immeasurably lofty." Yes, he thinks, "all is vanity, all falsehood, except that infinite sky." This is the peace of abstention, the repose of a mind that cannot be deceived because it has chosen emptiness (or one might call it purity). So, when Napoleon stops over him to admire what he takes to be a hero's corpse, he seems to Andrew "a small, insignificant creature compared with what was passing now between himself and that lofty, infinite sky with the clouds flying over it." It is once again "the lofty, equitable and kindly sky" that makes Napoleon's joy in victory seem nothing but "paltry vanity," a "short-sighted delight at the misery of others." The loss of blood and the apparent nearness of death make Andrew think of "the insignificance of greatness, the unimportance of life . . . and the still greater unimportance of death. . . ." How good it would be, he thinks, if "everything were as clear and simple" as it seems to his devout sister, but he cannot pray either to an "incomprehensible God," the "Great All or Nothing," or "to that God who has been sewn into this amulet by Mary." All that is great is incomprehensible, all he can comprehend is unimportant (III, 13).

I think we can see a pattern here—an intense idealism that demands more certainty than life can afford, a readiness to turn at the least threat of uncertainty to a cynical disdain. Both are forms of withdrawal from the actual, whether impatience to redeem and transfigure it or scorn for its inadequacy and betrayal. We see only the sense of betrayal in his treatment of his wife, and her reproachful face on her deathbed leaves him feeling guilty for having failed to love her. (We do not know why he married her or how he saw or imagined her then.) He can say to Pierre that there are only two evils in life: remorse and illness. "The only good is the absence of those evils." Pierre is not persuaded. "To live only so as not to do evil and not to have to repent is not enough. I lived like that, I lived for myself and ruined my life" (V, 9). His phrase "lived for myself" is a commentary on Andrew's defensiveness, and Andrew accepts it. He has, he says, tried to live for others, in the search for glory; but he has become calmer now that he lives only for himself or for those few people who are, so to speak, extensions of himself, his family.

Pierre is not discouraged by Andrew's mixture of realism and cynicism, and Andrew comes to respond to Pierre's insistent faith with a "radiant, childlike, tender look," as if he could see once more in the "high, everlasting sky" what he had seen as he lay wounded at Austerlitz. It awakens in turn something slumbering in himself, "something that was best within him." He is prepared for a new ideal form of life, which he is about to find in Natasha (V, 10).

Before he comes to that, he encounters once more the ancient oak on his estate which seems to tell him of the changelessness and futility of life: a "stupid, meaningless, constantly repeated fraud! . . . There is no spring, no sun, no happiness!" And Andrew withdraws from life again into a restful, mournfully pleasant, rather sentimental "hopelessness." It is always at such a moment that a Tolstoyan hero encounters a force of renewed life. When he sees Natasha he wonders, "What is she so glad about? . . . Why is she so happy?" The delight Natasha finds in her life is mysterious to him, and once he overhears her intense response to the beauty of the night, the ancient oak is transfigured. In his own seizure of an "unreasoning springtime feeling of joy and renewal" he is at last ready to give up living for himself alone (VI, 1).

There is a significant intertwining of two series of events, Andrew's attachment to Natasha and his regard for Speranski. He has found in Speranski the ideal of a perfectly rational and virtuous man, and he feels for him an admiration like that he had once felt for Napoleon. But just after the ball at which Natasha dances so radiantly, and where Andrew begins to love her, he finds himself seeing through Speranski's artifices and condescension. All of his hard work on the Legal Code now seems useless and foolish. He turns all the more eagerly to a world of personal feeling. As Natasha sings, Andrew finds himself choked with tears. For what? he wonders, and concludes: "The chief reason was a sudden, vivid sense of the terrible contrast between something infinitely great and illimitable within him" (one thinks of the illimitable, overarching sky) and "that limited and material something that he, and even she, was. This contrast weighed on and yet cheered him while she sang." This reconciliation of the infinite and the immediate becomes an opening up of freedom and responsibility; he believes at last in "the possibility of happiness" (VI, 11).

When Andrew learns of Natasha's relation with Anatole and has accepted the breaking of their engagement, we find him defending Speranski, who has fallen from power, against the charges of others. He finds relief from his other grief and anger in argument, and when he learns from Pierre of Natasha's illness, he voices his regret and smiles very much like his father, "coldly, maliciously, and unpleasantly." He has once again withdrawn into a defensive pride and, so to speak, seceded from life (VIII, 21).

Prince Andrew, like Nicholas Rostov, loses himself in his regiment; his hatred for his past emerges whenever he meets a former acquaintance. Then he grows "spiteful, ironical, and contemptuous." As he returns to the estate at Bald Hills, he encounters two small peasant girls who have carried plums from the hothouse in their skirts and hide when they see Andrew. He tries to spare their feelings, and for a while they involve him in a shared life: "A new sensation of comfort and relief came over him when, seeing these girls, he realized the existence of other human interests entirely aloof from his own. . . . ." It is too much to sustain. When he sees the soldiers bathing nearby in a pond, splashing happily and laughing, he feels a sudden disgust with their naked bodies and his own. It is a feeling he does not understand, and it contravenes that moment of involvement he felt in the girls' pleasure. It seems like a withdrawal from everything alive in others and himself, a cruel asceticism which is a sentence upon his own life (X, 5).

We see that again in the cold white light which seems to descend over all reality upon the eve of the Battle of Borodino. It is a fierce light "without shadow, without perspective, and without distinction of outline." He welcomes it as clear daylight and truth as opposed to the lantern-slide images that have deceived him all his life. (He is outside the forms of life he once accepted, and the figure is close to Wittgenstein's.) All that has claimed him for life now seems "simple, pale, and crude in the cold white light of this morning. . . . ." He thinks with special bitterness, which is also an unacknowledged yearning, of his romantic belief in Natasha. It is hard to extirpate altogether the sense of himself: he looks at the sunlit row of birches and thinks, "That all this should still be, but no me." And in the process the trees and all the scene about him become "terrible and menacing" (X, 24).

In retrospect one sees Prince Andrew's fluctuations between life and some form of externality—aloofness or detachment or defensiveness—some form, that is, of death. His trust in life is insufficient, in part because he brings to it tyrannical ideals; but even those may be a means of assaying its impossibility so that he may justify his retreat. Some of course of Andrew's attitudes are such as Tolstoy held, or had held, or would hold; they were always a part of him and they are given their life here in opposition to the attitudes of Pierre and Natasha, which were no less his own.

If Andrew fluctuates between two forms of life—between withdrawal into asceticism and expansion into incautious love—his father tries to impose the pattern of the life now denied him, in exerting his command upon his plain, unloved, and pious daughter. And Mary, in turn, tries to shape her life after the example of Jesus, in a constant putting of others before her. Some part of Mary fights this continual self-abasement; there is enough force of life in her to demand some fulfillment, however frighteningly the demands present themselves.

Pierre, in contrast to the Bolkonskis, tries ceaselessly to bring himself within the frame of life, enduring humiliation, accepting entrapment. "All this had to be and could not be otherwise," he reflects when the proposal he has not yet quite made is accepted by Hélène's father. "It is good because it's definite and one is rid of the old tormenting doubts" (III, 1). Pierre is often a comic figure, in part because he behaves repetitiously, in part because he is without pride, a man wholly open to what he finds in himself, somewhat like Boswell or Tolstoy himself in his curiosity about his feelings and his powers. He engages in a succession of self-deceptions. He feels, as an initiate into Freemasonry, "that he had been vicious only because he had somehow forgotten how good it is to be virtuous" (V, 1). He soars into visions of his future benevolence, persuaded by his warm feeling that he has already attained moral perfection. Later, his steward stages performances by grateful serfs who shower Pierre with gratitude.

But increasingly, even as he falls repeatedly into illusion, Pierre finds forms of active goodness, as in his reassurance of Natasha at the time of her disgrace, his delicacy in speaking with her during his illness, his participation in the battery's activities at Borodino, his rescue of a child. Even his demented plan to assassinate Napoleon is conceived as rescue and service for his fellow Russians. Natasha accepts his kindness without gratitude: "it seemed so natural for him to be kind to everyone that there was no merit in his kindness."

As a prisoner Pierre sheds the qualities that have made him seem foolish; the experience of captivity is one he assumes, so to speak, for the other characters in the novel. For while Andrew and Natasha undergo great change, Pierre's is the change which most fully combines thought and feeling, and which seems to arise from the deepest engagement with reality. He is freed of tormenting doubts; he has lost that freedom which once made the choice of occupation indissolubly difficult. He is reduced to a life where the very qualities that had made him seem clumsy in society now become appropriate and all but make him seem a hero.

His response to the landscape and the sky about him shows his difference from Prince Andrew. He sees the sun rising, making everything "sparkle in the glad light"—the cupolas and crosses of the convent, the hoarfrost on the grass, the distant hills and the river. Pierre feels "a new joy and strength in life such as he had never known before." It is at night in the brilliance of a full moon that Tolstoy presents one of those sacramental moments that are so essential to his sense of life. Pierre achieves a transcendence which is not a separation or withdrawal like Andrew's but a moment of ecstatic inclusiveness—the bivouacs and campfires, the forests and fields visible in the distance. "And further still, beyond those forests and fields, the bright oscillating limitless distance that lured one to its depths. Pierre glanced up at the sky and the twinkling stars in its faraway depths. 'And all that is me, all that is within me, and it is all I.' " He smiles at the effort men have made to imprison his soul, and then he lies down to sleep "beside his companions" (XIII, 3).

As Pierre finds freedom in imprisonment and learns what can be endured, he realizes "the full strength of life in man," he gains the power to control his attention and direct his thought. When Karataev is executed Pierre can concentrate his attention upon the French soldiers who have shot him. In another moment of defamiliarization, he recognizes one of them as the man who had burned his shirt while drying it two days before and had aroused laughter among them. At each moment that his mind turns in grief to Karataev, a consoling memory from the past deflects his attention. The inability of the mind to close in upon its suffering seems in one view helpless passivity before its associations, in another a genius for survival (XIV, 3).

"Inexorable Law"

Tolstoy's intensity is not simply the effect of brilliant gesture or image. In fact, Proust dismisses observation altogether:

This is not the work of an observing eye but of a thinking mind. Every so-called stroke of observation is simply the clothing, the proof, the instance, of a law, a law of reason or of unreason, which the novelist has laid bare. And our impression of the breadth and life is due precisely to the fact that none of this is the fruit of observation, but that every deed, every action, being no other than an expression of law, one feels oneself moving amid a throng of laws— why, since the truth of these laws is established for Tolstoi by the inward authority they have exercised over his thinking, there are some which we are still baffled by.[13]

One can see what Proust means in those mordant ironies through which Tolstoy looks beyond his characters' vision and instantiates laws in epigram. We see Anna "calling to mind Karenin with every detail of his figure, his way of speaking, and his character, and making him responsible for everything bad she could find in him, forgiving him nothing because of the terrible thing she had done to him" (II, 23). Much later, there is a terrible parallel when she has had her last quarrel with Vronsky: "All the cruelest things a coarse man could say she imagined him to have said to her, and she did not forgive him for them just as if he had really said them" (VII, 26).

Or we have Anna telling Vronsky of her pregnancy. He has been troubled by all the subterfuges both of them, not without shame, have had to practice; and he has begun to feel "revulsion against something: against Karenin, against himself, against the whole world—he was not sure which." Anna's son Seryozha, in his own uncertainties, has made Vronsky feel ill at ease and aroused in him once more "that strange feeling of blind revulsion which he had experienced of late." And with Anna's news, Vronsky turns pale and lowers his head,—Anna thinks with gratitude that he understands the full significance of the event. "But," Tolstoy proceeds, "she was wrong in thinking that he understood the significance . . . as she, a woman, understood it. At this news he felt the onrush of that strange feeling of revulsion for someone; but at the same time he realized that the crisis he had wished for had now come" (II, 22). One must suspect that some of Vronsky's revulsion is for Anna and for the power she has over him; that is a possibility she cannot allow herself to entertain until later. Again, at the steeplechase before Vronsky's fall, Anna is outraged by Karenin's protracted conversation with an important colleague. "All he cares about is lies and keeping up appearances," she thinks, without considering "what exactly she wanted of her husband or what she would have liked him to be. Nor did she realize that Karenin's peculiar loquaciousness that day . . . was merely an expression of his inner anxiety and uneasiness" (II, 28). In each of these cases there is a false estimation or an irrational judgment; Anna is too guilty or eager or bitter to see what the author discloses. In each case there is cause enough for Anna's misapprehension, but Tolstoy's immediate ironic rectification has the effect of invoking what Proust calls his laws of reason and unreason.

As soon as characters seem to obey laws of which they are unaware, the implications become ambiguous. Are they too much obsessed to see what is really there? Or are they too deeply committed to make a cool canvass of fact? Is Anna's obliviousness a form of self-absorption and fantasy, or is it the integrity of a woman who "must live her feelings right through"?[14] Against her intensity we can set those compromises and dissonances that mark most lives. The novel opens with the dissolution of a family structure. It is a temporary dissolution, but the restoration will never be complete.

Stiva Oblonsky awakens at eight o'clock as always; but, as he stretches out his feet for his slippers and his hand for his dressing gown, he realizes that he has slept on the sofa: for his wife Dolly has learned of his affair with the former governess; and when she expressed her horror, Oblonsky's face quite involuntarily "smiled its usual kind and, for that reason, rather foolish smile." It is the smile that Stiva regrets rather than the adultery, for the smile had the force of a blow for his wife. She responded with bitter words and has refused to see him.

Stiva is pained at his wife's grief. He has persuaded himself that she has pretended not to know of his infidelities, and in fact that is the attitude Dolly will assume thereafter, "letting herself be deceived, despising him, and most of all herself, for that weakness." On the occasion of this first discovery, she is divided between the need to take strong action and the pull of habit and convention. She feels outrage at the sight of his pity because it is so visibly less than love; but she is more troubled by the fear of estrangement. Stiva recognizes the "usual answer life gives to the most complicated and insoluble questions": to live from day to day and to lose oneself in the "dream of life" (I, 2).

While the Oblonskys' marriage is not a very happy one and will never get better, it is, at any rate, a structure of habits and responsibilities which, however imperfectly realized, is still a refuge from the intolerable. But it *is* imperfectly realized. We see this in Stiva's treatment of his children. When his daughter embraces him, he holds her and strokes her neck as he asks after her mother. Stiva knows that he does not care so much for his son, and he always tries therefore to treat both children in the same way. But his son senses the effort and responds to it rather than its pretense. When Stiva asks if her mother is cheerful, his daughter knows that there has been a quarrel and that her father is fully aware of her mother's disturbance but pretends that he is not. She blushes for him. He perceives that and blushes in turn.

We see the persistence of Stiva's neglect when Dolly takes the children to their country cottage in order to save expenses. Stiva has gone to Petersburg to further his career, and he has taken almost all the money in the house. He was asked by Dolly to have the cottage put in comfortable shape. He looked to the externals but neglected essential repairs. Nor was this the lack of the will to be a "solicitous father and husband." He has meant well, or at least has meant to mean well; but the roof still leaks, the cattle have been loose in the garden, there are no pots and pans, there are not enough milk and butter and eggs. The bailiff whom Stiva chose for "his handsome and respectful appearance" is of no help at all. Dolly is in despair until her old servant Matryona sets everything right, and gradually Dolly recovers her spirits and recaptures her great pride in her children (III, 7).

On a fine spring day after much preparation of their clothes, Dolly takes

her children to communion. The occasion requires that Dolly dress beautifully so as "not to spoil the general effect" and she is pleased with the admiration that she and her six children elicit from the peasants in church.
And the children behave beautifully. The smallest, Lily, takes the sacrament
and delightfully repeats, in English, Oliver Twist's words, "I want some
more, please." It is a day of all but unclouded joy. Dolly feels both love and
confidence. Near the river where they have all gone bathing, she falls into
conversation with the peasant women. Dolly finds it hard to leave these
women, "so absolutely identical were their interests." All the world about
her seems for once to belong to Dolly, to reflect her own feelings and to
embrace her with affection and admiration (III, 8).

The rapture cannot be sustained. As they return to the cottage, Levin is
waiting. He has come at Stiva's urging, but he does not want Dolly to feel
that Stiva has foisted responsibility on him. Dolly not only perceives that,
but she is touched by the "fine perception and delicacy" with which Levin
tries to spare her the shame of her husband's neglect. Here as with the exchange of blushes between Stiva and his daughter, there is a second-order
response, a response to a response. Tolstoy uses it characteristically to emphasize the implicit meanings that are shared within a form of life, but
perhaps become more oblique and difficult as the form is compromised (III,
9).

Dolly wants Levin to know that Kitty is coming to visit her. She has
suspected that he proposed and was rejected, and now, as she senses his
anger, she tries to meet it with an account of Kitty's suffering. The more
precisely Levin recalls that rejection, the more uncharitable he becomes and
the more determined not to see Kitty. Dolly tells him he is absurd, but she
says it with tenderness. She creates a distraction by addressing her daughter
in French and requiring that Tanya answer in French. This, as now everything about the family, strikes Levin as disagreeable. "Teach French and
unteach sincerity," he thinks to himself, not imagining that Dolly considered that danger for a long while before deciding it was worth the cost of
some sincerity for her children to learn French. Levin, disenchanted, prepares
to leave. The disenchantment spreads like a cloud. The children have begun
to fight, and for Dolly a "great shadow seems to have fallen over her life."
She "realized that these children of hers . . . were not only quite ordinary,
but even bad, ill-bred children, with coarse, brutal propensities, wicked
children in fact." She voices all her sorrow to Levin, and he reassures her that
all children fight. But he is no longer sincere. He thinks as he leaves, "No,
I won't try to show off and talk French with my children" (III, 10).

Both Dolly and Levin have feelings that are spontaneous, deep, and pervasive. Their world must, in Wittgenstein's phrase, "wax or wane as a whole.
As if by accession or loss of meaning." Wittgenstein's point is that our will

cannot alter the facts of the world, only its limits or boundaries; it can affect our world only by making it wholly different.[15] Tolstoy gives some of his characters an intensity of feeling that wholly alters their world. The process is faintly ludicrous even as it is touching, as in this case.

These instances may be seen as acute observation of motive and manners, as the necessary consequences of laws Tolstoy traces and confirms, as the meeting point of thematic concerns and their convergence in events of depth and resonance. Proust chooses to stress the second, to see particulars as "simply the clothing, the proof, the instance, of a law." This is in part a tribute to the sense of necessity Tolstoy gives his world; his "apparently inexhaustible fund of creation," as Proust calls it, does not need to spend itself in merely clever observations. The necessity which Proust ascribes to laws in Tolstoy he accounts for in other ways that are no less apt in his discussion of George Eliot:

> Another striking thing is the sense of gravity attached to an evil intention or to a failure of resolution, which because of the interdependence of mankind spreads its fatal repercussions in every direction; and another, the sense of the mysterious greatness of human life and the life of nature, the solemn mysteries in which we play a part while knowing no more about them than does the growing flower. . . .[16]

This concatenation of lives in fatal repercussions resembles what George Eliot calls "undeviating law," "invariability of sequence," or the "inexorable law of consequences"—patterns of order which we can recognize and to which we must submit.

The capacity for submission, for what George Eliot calls "patient watching of external fact" and "silencing of preconceived notions," is a readiness to allow possibilities their emergence, a reluctance to delimit experience to what is governable and explicable. This may be a withdrawal from visible but not from conceivable relevance, and it risks the acceptance of details, events, "observations" which may threaten as well as exemplify laws. George Eliot found the "highest form" in the "highest organism, that is to say, the most varied group of relations bound together in a wholeness which again has the most varied relations with all other phenomena."[17] We tend, today, to want to demystify a term like *organism,* which by definition represents an incalculable unity. We may recognize that the novelist often uses a few bold inconsistencies which are suggestive enough to demand of him and of us a new and more arduous effort to explain and unify. Tolstoy's boldness is so nicely judged that we are persuaded of the implicit lawfulness and consequently look for it in greater depth. I want to consider two instances.

Kitty Shcherbatsky, like Levin and Anna and even more than her sister Dolly, cannot live a half-life or dismiss her grief over Vronsky's betrayal.

We see her falling into illness that has no physical cause. She is examined by a specialist whose self-importance may be measured by his indifference to his patient's embarrassment. Kitty's mother, the Princess Shcherbatsky, feels guilty about Vronsky, and she means to be abject before the doctors. They in turn consult with each other to decide which treatment of Kitty will best satisfy her imperious mother. Dolly, who is present, asks their mother if Kitty's shame and grief are due in part to her regret that she has refused Levin, but the old princess is appalled at the thought that she is to blame for having encouraged Vronsky, and she grows angry with Dolly. Nor is she alone in her response. Kitty throws off her sister Dolly's pity with anger and cruelty: "I've enough pride," she cries, "never to let myself love a man who does not love me." And when Dolly ignores the thrust and talks directly about Levin, Kitty is all the more furious: "I shall never, *never* do what you're doing—go back to a man who has been unfaithful to you, who falls in love with another woman." Dolly is crushed by her sister's cruelty, and Kitty at last breaks down in tears. Each understands the other's feelings, and Kitty knows that she has been forgiven.

She can speak then of her changed world, so much like the one Anna will create as the climate of suicide: "everything has become odious, disgusting, and coarse to me, myself most of all. You can't imagine what disgusting thoughts I have about everything" (II, 3). Later, at the German watering place Kitty tries to achieve entire selflessness and idealism, only coming at last to realize that she has misjudged and injured others in order to sustain her aspiration. She finally dismisses her role of ministering angel as a sham. "Let me be bad, but at least not a liar, not a humbug," she cries, and she realizes that she has been "deceiving herself in imagining that she could be what she wished to be." She returns to Russia cured, "calm and serene." Kitty's pride leads to difficulties both before her marriage and after; but it is a principle of vitality. Her independence and resistance to Levin's will is a far greater thing than Dolly's bitter resignation.

Vronsky is a character who shows so much growth in the early parts of the novel that we are not quite prepared, in spite of sufficient warning, for his limitations in what follows. We first see him as an immature libertine, a brilliant and wealthy officer charmed by the innocence and adoration of a young girl of high society (all of his love affairs have been outside it). "He could not possibly believe that what gave such genuine pleasure to him, and above all to her, could be wrong." But he has no affection for the conventions of family life, and the role of husband seems "alien, hostile, and above all, ridiculous." His initial shallowness is to be seen in his "pleasant feeling of purity and freshness" at the Shcherbatskys', "partly due to the fact that he had not smoked all evening, and with it a new feeling of tenderness at her love for him" (I, 16). Even when Vronsky has become a great deal more serious, his sense of well-being finds its immediate expression in a consciousness of his body. "It gave him pleasure to feel the slight pain in his strong leg, it was pleasant to feel the muscular sensation of movement in his chest as he breathed." And Tolstoy enforces an incongruity: "the same bright and cold August day which made Anna feel so hopeless seemed exhilarating and invigorating to him and refreshed his face and neck, which were still glowing after the drenching he had given them under the tap." Somehow the face and neck seem awkwardly specific and trivial, just as the pride he feels after his first meetings with Anna seems touching but naive: "He looked at people as if they were things. A nervous young man . . . sitting opposite began to detest him for that look."

Vronsky's love for Anna makes him a far more serious and courageous man. He tends, it is true, to return easily to his old world of habit, and the first part of the novel ends on a somewhat ominous note, as habit recaptures the Vronsky we have so far seen in Moscow or on the train: "As always when in Petersburg, he left the house not to return till late at night." Unlike Anna, he has a role both in his regiment and in the society he frequents that gives him a secure sense of rightness; the role of a man pursuing a married woman had "something grand and beautiful about it and could never be ridiculous." He has not yet had to leave the world he has known in order to enter this new world that their love creates. The first real test of Vronsky is the steeple chase. He has, as we have seen, been troubled by the deceptions he has had to practice and has felt a sudden revulsion at the news of Anna's pregnancy. In the race a moment of doubt disables his customary, assured command of his horse, and through a terrible error he breaks the back of Frou-Frou, the nervous mare he is riding. Worst of all perhaps is the rage to which his remorse and frustration lead: he kicks the dying horse in the belly before he realizes fully what he has done. Much later, when Anna rejects his warning and insists upon going to the opera, where she will surely be snubbed, Vronsky is left behind in outrage. "And why does she put me in such a position?" he exclaims, and he upsets the table that holds soda and brandy. He tries to steady the table but only overturns it, and, finally, in his vexation, he kicks it over.

Between these two events Vronsky has attempted suicide. As a man who has always needed a clear code of rules, who had an essential role in the regiment that is his only family, he finds himself suddenly humbled by Karenin's forgiveness. The forgiveness leaves Vronsky feeling "ashamed, humiliated, guilty . . . kicked out of the normal way of life. . . . Everything that had seemed so firmly established, all the rules and habits of his life, suddenly turned out to be false and inapplicable." Vronsky finds himself, as it were, outside the forms of life, without purchase or balance, awed and disgraced by the generosity and dignity of Karenin. "They had suddenly exchanged roles. Vronsky felt Karenin's greatness and his own humiliation." He has lost the grandeur of the lover, and he has lost Anna; and in that moment the love that had begun to wane altogether revives. His attempt to kill himself fails, and he has prepared instead to undertake a "flattering and dangerous mission to Tashkent" when Anna recovers and returns to him. He must resign not only the new post but his commission as well; he sets about shaping new forms of life with Anna. The new forms remain unreal; they have no rooted existence, they make no earnest demand, they carry no necessity.

Endings

One way to speak of the contrast between the story of Levin and that of Anna is the expansion of Levin's life to include more and the painful contraction of Anna's life as she is excluded from those forms which have formerly sustained her. She and Vronsky have made in Italy one halfhearted attempt to create new forms, and in the sixth part of the novel that attempt is renewed in more plausible but more radically flawed forms. The sixth part of *Anna Karenina* is the most elegant in design. We move between two estates with Dolly, from Levin's to Vronsky's; and the final section brings both landlords to the provincial elections. There is, moreover, the ludicrous dandy Veslovsky, who appears at both estates. Dolly and her children are staying with Levin and Kitty. Her own country house is now, through Oblonsky's neglect, "completely dilapidated"; and Oblonsky is happy to send his family off to the country, where he can pay them occasional short visits.

With Kitty and Dolly is their mother, the princess, and the three women make raspberry jam together. Kitty feels a new relationship with her mother, something closer to equality, as they talk—three married women—about the likelihood of Varenka's receiving a proposal from Levin's brother, Koznyshev. Dolly thinks back to Stiva's courtship. Kitty asks her mother how her own marriage was settled, in what gestures or words agreement was reached. "And," Tolstoy goes on, "the three women thought about one and the same thing." It is one of those moments that Tolstoy manages with distinctive power. There is not the dissolution of membranes between people so that they become, as in Virginia Woolf, for a moment one stream of feeling. In Tolstoy, people, often locked in their own memories, participate in a common form of life.

So with a possible marriage. Koznyshev remarked with regret at Levin's wedding that he was "past all that." Varenka is a mature and selfless woman who might comfort that rather complacent intellectual. To his younger brother Levin, Koznyshev seems to lead only a spiritual existence. He is "too pure and high-minded a man" to come to terms with reality. And Kitty in turn insists that Varenka is "all spirit." There isn't, she says, "so much of this reality in her as there is in me." But the proposal fails because neither person quite wants it, and all the trivia that somehow rush to Varenka's lips have behind them her resistance to the exposure and risk of a new relationship. Koznyshev has pressed beyond his comfortable rationalization—his fidelity to the long-dead Marie. He is at the point of proposing but ready to withdraw, all too easily thrown off. And so they go on talking about mushrooms. The ludicrous, Chekhovian banalities become their defenses. "And the moment those words were uttered, both he and she understood that it was all over, that what should have been said would never be said, and their agitation, having reached its climax, began to subside."

Each of them represents a kind of half life in the novel. Varenka's conventionality and denial of life once seemed to Kitty saintliness. Koznyshev's intellectuality and condescension have had the power to shake Levin's confidence. But, in fact, each of these characters helps to define the vitality of the central figures, who risk everything because they cannot endure something less than life. Later, as the children have their tea, everyone avoids talking of what might have happened. Koznyshev and Varenka feel "like children who have failed their examinations and have to stay behind in the same class or who have been expelled from school for good" (VI, 6).[18]

Levin finds the Shcherbatsky element—Kitty's family—gaining domination on his estate, and he is annoyed that Stiva brings with him an unknown guest, Veslovsky. Levin's displeasure begins to spread. It is, on a very small and comic scale, like Kitty's sense of defilement after Vronsky's desertion or Anna's final vision of corruption before her suicide. The deep, pervasive feelings of these characters shape and color their world. The process can be ludicrous when it is not awesome; and Levin rather preposterously sees falsehood everywhere. Dolly doesn't really believe in Stiva's love even if she looks pleased that he's there; Koznyshev only pretends to like Oblonsky. Varenka is a plaster saint with her eye on a marriage partner. And Kitty is clearly flirting with Veslovsky. The last is more than Levin can endure, and he speaks to Kitty of the "horror and the comic absurdity" of his situation. Unlike Vronsky, she is "glad of the force of love for her which found expression in his jealousy." With her reassurance Levin takes Stiva and Veslovsky on a shooting party, where Levin finds his recovered spirits lowered again by their frivolity and by Veslovsky's clumsiness. Nothing goes right until finally Levin goes off by himself and brings down his birds. But Levin can have no peace until he sends Veslovsky packing.

The principal contrast of the sixth part hinges on Dolly's visit to Anna and Vronsky. Her sudden release, the children left behind, from responsibilities and concerns leaves her, during the ride, free to think about her life, to enjoy a measure of self-pity and then to daydream about a life like Anna's:

"She wants to live. God has put that need into our hearts. Quite possibly I should have done the same." A "mischievous smile wrinkled her lips, chiefly because while thinking of Anna's love affair, she conjured up parallel with it an almost identical love affair with an imaginary composite man who was in love with her. Like Anna, she confessed everything to her husband. And Oblonsky's astonishment and embarrassment at the news of her unfaithfulness made her smile." For a moment Dolly, of all people, brings Emma Bovary before us. "As is quite often the case," Toltoy observes, "with women of unimpeachable moral conduct who are rather tired of the monotony of a virtuous life, she not only condoned from afar an illicit love affair but even envied it." In Dolly's case, the effect upon Stiva must count for much.

But while Dolly finds Anna more beautiful than ever, she comes to see Anna's unhappiness as well, her inability to love her daughter, her use of contraception (a new and shocking idea for Dolly, who dreads another pregnancy), and her dependence on morphine. Vronsky has made his family estate into a little court where he is surrounded by a respectful cabinet and where he plays at life again (as he has in Italy with painting), now building a hospital. Dolly is disenchanted. The room she is given reminds her in its luxury "of the best hotels abroad." Everything in it is new and expensive, not least the "smart lady's maid" before whom Dolly is ashamed to display her "patched dressing jacket," proud as she has been of the "patches and darns" at home. She is surprised to find everyone busily at play, "grown-up people carrying on a children's game in the absence of children." Dolly feels as if she is "taking part in a theatrical performance with better actors than herself" and as if her own performance is spoiling the show. Anna is an assiduous hostess, creating unity among her guests, putting up with Veslovsky's flirtation. But Anna regrets Dolly's leaving; for the feelings that Dolly has raised, however painful, Anna recognizes as "the best part of her inner self" and a part that is being "rapidly smothered by the life she [is] leading."

Among the topics discussed at Vronsky's table is the value of rural councils and magistrates. Dolly cites Levin's scorn for these public institutions, and Vronsky replies with a vigor meant to defend his own interest in them as well. Anna observes that Vronsky has already become, in the six months they have spent on his estate, a member of five or six such institutions. "And I fear," she adds, "that with such a multiplicity of official duties, the whole thing will become a mere form." There is asperity in her tone; clearly she resents Vronsky's frequent absences to attend these meeetings, just as he feels the need to assert his freedom by going. Tolstoy treats the electoral meetings at Kashin as an ugly farce, which Levin loathes but Vronsky greatly enjoys. Vronsky, in fact, resolves to stand himself in three years if he and Anna are married by then, "just as when winning a prize at the races he felt like taking the jockey's place himself next time." The meetings at Kashin present a world of rhetoric and political manipulation. Vronsky is pleased by the "charming good form" he finds in the provinces. Only "the crazy fellow who was married to Kitty Shcherbatsky" had talked a lot of nonsense "with rabid animosity." Perhaps the typical figure at such an occasion is the amiable Sviazhsky, who stands for so much of the world Tolstoy is presenting in the novel: "Sviazhsky was one of those people who always amazed Levin because their extremely logical, though never original, ideas were kept in a water-tight compartment and had no influence whatever on their extremely definite and stable lives, which went on quite independently and almost always dia-metrically opposed to them. . . ." Whenever Levin presses Sviazhsky on a point that reveals an inconsistency, he sees a "momentary expression of alarm in Sviazhsky's eyes which he had noticed before whenever he had tried to penetrate beyond the reception rooms of Sviazhsky's mind." When Levin is troubled by his own insincerity or his failure to face the truth in matters of religion, it is with the feeling that there is "something vague and unclean in his soul." He sees himself in the position "for which he found fault with his friend Sviazhsky."

When Levin finally meets Anna in Moscow, he is altogether charmed by her seriousness, her beauty, and her intelligence. After a day of largely sense-less talk, he is moved by her naturalness and lack of self-consciousness. Levin is moved to make a witticism about French art, which has had so far to go in its return to realism: "They saw poetry in the very fact that they did not lie." Anna's face lights up with pleasure. What gives the episode its sadness is not Kitty's jealousy afterwards, but the disclosure that Anna has "done all she could . . . to arouse in Levin a feeling of love." Seductiveness is perhaps the only behavior she allows herself any more with Vronsky, and with other men as a matter of course. The obvious contrast is with Natasha at the close of *War and Peace:*

> She took no pains with her manners or with delicacy of speech, or with her toilet. . . . She felt that the allurements instinct had formerly taught her to use would now be merely ridiculous in the eyes of her husband. . . . She felt that her unity with her husband was not maintained by the poetic feelings that had attracted him to her, but by something else—indefinite but firm as the bond between her own body and soul.   [First Epilogue]

At the end we see Anna surrendering to powers of destruction, in her savage torture of herself and Vronsky, in her sad effort to stir the pitying Kitty to jealousy. Her world fills with hatred and disgust; everyone she sees is vicious or filthy. The breakdown of mind creates a stream of consciousness, and the rage of her last hours is the form her vitality takes. Unlike her husband, who finds consolation in fashionable superstition, she finds herself outside all forms of life.

In the last part of the novel, at first suppressed, Tolstoy shows the mind-less rush of Slavic patriotism and war hysteria. We enter that stream with Koznyshev when his book wins ridicule and early oblivion. He turns to the Slav question and the Serbo-Turkish war. He sees the excitement as "frivo-lous and ridiculous," but he admires its power. "The soul of the nation," as he puts it, has "become articulate." And so the intellectual devotes himself to a "great cause and forgot to think about things in his book" (VIII, 1). Vronsky has volunteered to fight for Serbia, taking a whole squadron at his own expense and evidently looking for death. Oblonsky has come into his long-sought post and is giving a farewell party for another volunteer, the unspeakable Veslovsky. Only Levin stands outside this new whirl of mind-lessness, hoping to solve his own problems, insisting that war in itself is evil. "It's not only a question of sacrificing oneself," he observes to his brother, "but of killing Turks." In reply Koznyshev glibly cites, "I came not to send peace but a sword," quoting "the passage from the Gospels that had always perplexed Levin more than any other, just as if it were the most comprehen-sible thing in the world" (VIII, 16).

Tolstoy seems to reverse George Eliot's movement, as we see it in Doro-thea Brooke's coming to awareness, moving outward from the self to include the multifarious and independent world. For Tolstoy the hero must recover the immediate. To borrow Wittgenstein's terms again, "The aspects of things that are most important for us are hidden because of their simplicity and familiarity." What Tolstoy's heroes must uncover, in short, is the framework itself of which Isaiah Berlin has written; they must dissolve false problems and find their way back to what they have always known. The emphasis must rest then upon the forms of life which we overlook or distort or deny, and those forms may be as far back as we can or should go. The language-game rests in the end upon our activities: "it is not based on grounds. It is not reasonable (or unreasonable). It is there—like our life." "What has to be accepted, the given, is—so one could say—*forms of life*." [19]

Characters like Anna are tragic figures because, for reasons that are admi-rable, they cannot live divided lives or survive through repression. We can see throughout the last part of the novel how profoundly Anna feels the need to hold Vronsky's love since theirs is not a life given shape by institutional forms—it has no necessities but their happiness, and there are no forms within which to make their love a sanctity. There seems no clear line at last between Anna's wish to believe in Vronsky's love and her readiness to believe that it no longer exists. The torture she inflicts is a reflex of self-pity she begins to suffer, and there are moments when she seems irrationally to wish to be proved right by Vronsky's rejection of her love. We sense this in her despair. Yet before she throws herself under the train, Anna crosses herself.

And the familiar gesture, one of the forms of her early life, arouses a series of memories of her childhood and girlhood until "the darkness that enveloped everything for her was torn apart, and for an instant life presented itself to her with all its bright past joys" (VII, 31).

9 James: The Logic of Intensity

Lucidity and Bewilderment

In his later novels, Henry James leaves some crucial portion of his action, and of his characters, indeterminate. He does this, in part, by giving us characters' conscious responses—at a somewhat shallow level of awareness—without accounting for their deeper motives or even, in some cases, indicating whether the surface awareness is consistent with what lies below. By a shallow level I mean only that the principal action of his novels takes place close enough to the surface of consciousness to alert us to meanings that are almost evident and therefore the more frustrating for their elusiveness. We are never given a fully determinate account of Vanderbank's feelings about Nanda, or of Lambert Strether's decision to leave Paris and Maria Gostrey behind him, or of Milly Theale's motives for leaving the money to Densher, or even of Densher's final feelings about Kate Croy. In *The Golden Bowl* we are largely kept outside the minds of Adam Verver and, to a lesser degree, of Charlotte Stant. How deeply inside Maggie and the Prince we are taken is less of a question, but even there we find some attitudes given only by implication and open to surmise.

This indeterminacy is, to a degree, a willed vagueness on the part of the characters, the "merciful muddle" or "bewilderment" they cannot do without. But the indeterminacy arises, too, from James's artistic design; the design is, of course, essential to the kind of suspense and intensity he wants to give to the experience of reading these novels and of puzzling out the motives and meanings of his characters' words. It is not a trivial suspense; it has all the depth of the search for truth where truth is almost impossibly hard, and yet urgent, to recognize.

"Lucid and ironic, she knew no merciful muddle." So James presents Kate Croy in *The Wings of the Dove,* free both of illusion and of cant. When Merton Densher demands, as the encouragement of his deception of Milly Theale,

that Kate come to his rooms, she takes "no refuge in showing herself shocked."
As he sees her "stand there for him in all the light of the day and of his
admirable, merciless meaning," he feels in some sense already "possessed of
what he wanted"—possessed at least "of the fact that she hadn't thrown over
his lucidity the horrid shadow of cheap reprobation. Of this he had had so
sore a fear that its being dispelled was in itself of the nature of bliss" (27).[1]
Later, near the close of the novel, when Densher believes that they have lost
their "dreadful game," Kate can perceive his "horror, almost, of her lucidity" (34).

That lucidity returns in the last scene, when Densher has received his
inheritance from Milly Theale, the inheritance that will finally allow him
and Kate the freedom to marry. Kate asks Densher if he is not now in love
with Milly's memory. Nor does she allow him to dismiss the possibility. She
would have been so in his place, she claims, and she recognizes his feelings:
"Your memory's your love. You *want* no other." When he meets this by
offering to marry her at once, she asks, "As we were?" But she turns away
from his assent with a final shake of her head. She is beyond the illusions he
tries to sustain, and she speaks the moving last sentence of the novel: "We
shall never be again as we were!" (38)

Earlier in the novel, Kate Croy's lucidity has taken on "a kind of heroic
ring, a note of character that belittled" Densher's "own capacity for action."
And he sees in it "the greatness of knowing so well what one wanted" (28).
Kate has been setting forth a plan for Densher and Milly, but she demands
his complicity in its formulation. "Don't think . . . I'll do *all* the work for
you. If you want things named, you must name them."

> He had quite, within the minute, been turning names over; and there was only
> one, which at last stared at him there dreadful, that properly fitted. "Since
> she's to die I'm to marry her?"
>
>   It struck him even at the moment as fine in [Kate] that she met it with no
> wincing nor mincing. She might, for the grace of silence, for favour to their
> conditions, have only answered him with her eyes. But her lips bravely moved.
> "To marry her."

Kate has undergone a long strain of "impatience for all he had to be taught."
Now he learns it or at least he emerges from the "merciful muddle" which
has allowed him to come so far. "It was before him enough now, and he had
nothing more to ask; he had only to turn, on the spot, considerably cold
with the thought that all along—to his stupidity, his timidity—it had been,
it had been only what she meant." And, while Densher feels the shock of
unmitigated clarity, she goes on: "You'll in the natural course have money.
We shall in the natural course be free." Kate use of "the natural course" is
ironic enough; but if it underlines the unnatural use they will make of Milly,

it is also a recognition that they will not induce her early death but rather console her for it. As for their use of Milly, it can only prosper: Densher will have "a free hand, a clear field, a chance—well, quite ideal." Densher is shocked again by her use of "ideal," by her single-minded concentration upon the efficacy of the plan. He doesn't raise the moral issue that so clearly distresses him. Instead he asks how Kate, if she cares for him, can "like" this procedure. And again her lucidity cuts across his questions with a "heroic ring," almost a stoical severity or a categorical imperative: "I don't like it, but I'm a person, thank goodness, who can do what I don't like" (28).

Densher accepts her instructions, persuading himself that he is merely "seeing what she would say" and that she will "somewhere break down." But she does not break down, and he finds himself continuing. The prospect is daunting: to propose marriage to a dying girl whom he does not love. But Kate has imagination enough to see the full case: "She isn't for you as if she's dying." Densher recognizes the truth of this. As they look across the room, Milly sends back to them, as if in response, "all the candour of her smile, the lustre of her pearls, the value of her life, the essence of her wealth." How explicit in Kate's or Densher's mind is that interweaving of "candour" and "lustre," of "life" and "wealth," we are not told; but they are made "grave" by "the reality she put into the plan" (28).

We can see Densher's "merciful muddle" at an earlier stage—a stage where he resembles George Eliot's characters as they find themselves not making, but having made, a decision. Densher is already acting on Kate's instructions but is troubled as to whether Kate "really meant him to succeed quite so much." He is also in frequent danger of giving himself away. When he urges Milly to return to London after her travels, he says, "Try us, at any rate . . . once more" (21). When she in turn asks whom he means by "us," he is pulled up short and quickly dispels the sense of "an allusion to himself as conjoined with Kate." So a moment later, when Milly speaks of her indebtedness to Mrs. Lowder and to Kate, she concludes, "I'd do anything . . . for Kate." Has she laid a trap for him?

> "Oh, I know what one would do for Kate!"—it had hung for him by a hair to break out with that, which he felt he had really been kept from by an element in his consciousness stronger still. The proof of the truth in question was precisely in his silence; resisting the impulse to break out was what he *was* doing for Kate.

As he avoids that danger he moves on to others, the dialogue becoming more and more intense with his sense of risk. He avoids displaying too full an acquaintance with Kate's ways; he can remark "with a good intention that had the further merit of representing a truth: 'I don't feel as if I knew her—really to call know.' "

The passage which follows is a brilliant treatment of the flickering of conflict which underlies the few spoken words; it looks forward to such passages as I have cited from Virginia Woolf and Nathalie Sarraute, a notable instance of *sous-conversation:*

> During a silence that ensued for a minute he had time to recognize that his own [words] contained, after all, no element of falsity. Strange enough therefore was it that he could go too far—if it *was* too far—without being false. His observation was one he would perfectly have made to Kate herself. And before he again spoke, and before Milly did, he took time for more still—for feeling that just here it was that he must break short off if his mind was really made up not to go further. It was as if he had been at a corner—and fairly put there by his last speech; so that it depended on him whether or no to turn it. The silence if prolonged but an instant might even have given him a sense of her waiting to see what he would do. [21]

They are interrupted by the arrival below of Milly's carriage. Densher can recognize his attraction for her as she first denies that she was going out and then proposes that he ride with her.

> Densher's happy response, however, had as yet hung fire, the process we have described in him operating by this time with extreme intensity. The system of not pulling up, not breaking off, had already brought him headlong, he seemed to feel, to where they had actually stood; and just now it was, with a vengeance, that he must do either one thing or the other. He had been waiting for some moments, which probably seemed to him longer than they were; this was because he was anxiously watching himself wait. He couldn't keep that up for ever; and since one thing or the other was what he must do, it was for the other that he presently became conscious of having decided. If he had been drifting it settled itself in the manner of a bump, of considerable violence, against a firm object in the stream. "Oh yes; I'll go with you with pleasure. It's a charming idea."

Densher is touched by "her wishing to oblige him," and, as he waits for Milly to get ready, he recognizes that "she had made him simply wish, in civil acknowledgment, to oblige *her;* which he had not fully done, by turning his corner. He was quite round it, his corner." He has, in effect, begun to deceive Milly under the comforting sense of kindness.

"It seems probable," James wrote in the preface to *The Princess Casamassima,* "that if we were never bewildered there would never be a story to tell about us." The novelist must avoid making his characters "too *interpretative* of the muddle of fate . . . too divinely, too priggishly clever." The "wary reader" urges, " 'Give us plenty of bewilderment . . . so long as there is plenty of slashing out in the bewilderment too.' " For too much intelligence precludes "the very slashing, the subject-matter of any self-respecting story." To represent bewilderment, as we have seen in the case of Densher, requires an exploration of characters' feelings with a measure of detachment, an "appreciation," on the part of the novelist. The "doing" of such characters is, "immensely, their feeling." Any "intimacy with a man's specific behaviour, with his given case, is desperately certain to make us see it as a whole. . . . What a man thinks and what he feels are the history and the character of what he does; on all of which things the logic of intensity rests."

The *"quality* of bewilderment" will depend on the nature of the consciousness invented and engaged, and it will range from "vague and crepuscular to sharpest and most critical." Each story requires its fools, who embody "the coarser and less fruitful forms and degrees of moral reaction;" but the leading interest requires a consciousness "subject to fine intensification and wide enlargement." Such a consciousness will expose the deficiencies of the fools; but the problem is to keep it from soaring too high, to "keep it connected, connected intimately, with the general human exposure, and thereby bedimmed and befooled and bewildered, anxious, restless, fallible"—and yet not with such bewilderment as will make the situation and the story "unintelligible." These persons are "intense *perceivers"*—James cites among others Isabel Archer, Lambert Strether, and Merton Densher—"even . . . the divided Vanderbank of *The Awkward Age,* the extreme pinch of whose romance is the vivacity in him, to his positive sorrow and loss, of the state of being aware."[2]

It is to the last of these cases I wish to turn, for Vanderbank displays a consciousness which can embrace two quite different conceptions of life but which cannot finally choose between them; or at least, since inaction is itself a choice, cannot choose actively or with full lucidity. There is a sense in which the very intensity of his perception is disabling, making him not a spectator but a failed participant.

The Awkward Age was an experiment in a new form: "a form all dramatic and scenic," as James wrote to a bewildered friend, "of presented episodes, architecturally combined and each making a piece of the building; with no going behind, no *telling about* the figures save by their own appearance and action and with explanations reduced to the explanation of everything by all the other things *in* the picture." And, for all that indirectness, James feels special pleasure in his central characters. "I think Mrs. Brook the best thing I've ever done—and Nanda much *done."*[3] Mrs. Brookenham and her daughter Nanda are both in love with Vanderbank, who, in his mid-thirties, is younger than Mrs. Brookenham and older than her daughter. Nanda quite frankly and simply loves Vanderbank. Her mother, whose lover he seems to be, and might as well be, but perhaps is not (if we accept the evidence of a not very generous friend), counts on Van as a member of her circle. He is, as James said, "divided," attracted by the decencies and sincerity of another kind of life, but unable to separate himself from Mrs. Brook and the bold, free talk of her circle.

The novel opens with a dramatic presentation of Van's self-division. He has just met at Mrs. Brook's a charming old man, Mr. Longdon, who has known both Mrs. Brook's mother and Van's mother as well. Mr. Longdon once courted each lady, but with no success. Van now finds himself looking at Mrs. Brook's circle through the eyes of Mr. Longdon. They provide him with the occasion—for the feelings are clearly not new—to voice his uneasy dissatisfaction with the circle, with London, with modernity and his own part in it. How deeply Van feels this and how much he merely plays at self-castigation is hard to determine and, as I have suggested earlier, is meant to be indeterminate. But there seems to be something more than amusement or complacency in his attempt to grasp and appropriate Mr. Longdon's attitude.

The older man has lived outside London for years, and Van, whose imagination "liked to place an object, even to the point of losing sight of it in its conditions," conceives what a "nice old nook it must have taken to keep a man of intelligence so fresh while suffering him to remain so fine" (1). Van can only suppose that the free talk at Mrs. Brook's must have struck Mr. Longdon as "odd." If Van shows "elation" in producing his surmise, it is not, I think, the pleasure of being shocking but the delight of his accuracy in placing Mr. Longdon and in imagining his response. Van is, moreover, almost eager to be caught out in vulgarity: when he speaks of Mrs. Brookenham as Fernanda, he at once accepts Mr. Longdon's "scruple" and admits that he does not use that name in her presence. Van cannot resist a light and rather cheap remark (too often the level of the circle's wit) when he explains how seldom his own Christian name, Gustavus, is used by Mrs. Brook. "Any implication that she consciously avoided it might make you see deeper depths." To this Mr. Longdon replies with pain: "Oh, I'm not so bad as that!" (1) When they speak of Nanda's age, which is almost nineteen but which her mother vaguely sets at sixteen, Van is amused by Mrs. Brook's vanity. "She has done so, I think, for the last year or two" (since, in fact, she has turned forty). But Van's amusement must now, because of Mr. Longdon's presence, be turned upon himself as he recognizes what he has done: "It was nasty doing that? I see, I see. Yes, yes: I rather gave her away, and you're struck by it—as is most delightful *you* should be—because you're, in every way, of a better tradition." No friendship, Van concludes, of the kind Mr. Longdon has cherished, can survive in "great towns and great crowds." London society must seem to an outsider "an elbowing, pushing, perspiring, chattering mob." But Mr. Longdon sees acutely enough that Van is too quick and glib in mocking self-deprecation. "That shows you really don't care," he says; and he adds, "You ought to, you ought to" (2).

Mr. Longdon is struck by the resemblance he finds between photographs

of Nanda and those of her grandmother, Lady Julia. Van can see an "originality" in his preferring Nanda's beauty to Mrs. Brook's. "London doesn't
love the latent or lurking," he explains, and there have been some fears about
Nanda's chance for an early marriage (2). Mr. Longdon cannot yet imagine
that Nanda is unwelcome in her mother's drawing room. She has reached the
"awkward age" at which she can no longer be hidden in the nursery but is
still too young to enter the free talk of her mother's circle. To prevent Nanda's damping the wit of their "temple of analysis," Mrs. Brook allows Nanda
great freedom to visit friends, including the unhappily married Tishy Grendon. This is no gesture of trust by Mrs. Brook: it is the laxity of indifference
and the pursuit of her own convenience. Nanda becomes in the process exposed to all the scandalous secrets that animate London conversation. She
does not regard the scandals with primness or with prurience. She does not
take pleasure in others' disadvantage. Her "lucidity" accepts truth with candor and genuine concern.

In contrast to Mrs. Brook, her friend the duchess—the title is Italian, but
Jane is English—raises her niece Aggie in protected innocence. She wants
Aggie to read only proper books, history "that leaves the horrors out." As a
"little rounded and tinted innocence had been aimed at," Mr. Longdon reflects, "the fruit had been grown to the perfection of a peach on a sheltered
wall." Little Aggie has been "deliberately prepared for consumption." Nanda,
in contrast, is a "northern savage," all the elements of her nature overt and
unforced.

> Both the girls struck him as lambs with the great shambles of life in their
> future; but while one, with its neck in a pink ribbon, had no consciousness but
> that of being fed from the hand with the sweet biscuit of unobjectionable
> knowledge, the other struggled with instincts and forebodings, with the sus-
> picion of its doom and the far-borne scent, in the flowery fields, of blood. [18]

This final contrast reveals Mr. Longdon's changing consciousness. He has
come to recognize in Nanda, for all her modernity of manners and precocious
awareness, a more radical innocence than Aggie possesses. Aggie remains
ostentatiously virginal—the ostentation is not hers but her aunt's—until she
marries. Then she breaks free with a smash, capturing her aunt's lover (who
is also her husband's friend) for herself.

Mr. Longdon comes to see how impossible it would be—for all their physical resemblance—to recreate Lady Julia in Nanda. He has lived through
that past from which his manners and his values come, and he relinquishes
any thought of preserving it at the cost of doing justice to Nanda's distinctive beauty. Vanderbank, in contrast, is less realistic. He projects into the
generation of Mr. Longdon and Lady Julia the beauty by which he measures
all he finds ugly in his own age and in himself. It is a more romantic, more

fragile, more external, perhaps more inhuman vision of the past. It arises from the division within himself, and it must be protected all the more jealously for the consolation it provides. Vanderbank cannot accept the element of modernity in Nanda, for all its candor. He sees it as defilement.

The division within Vanderbank is central to the novel. I think we must grant him a sincere enough dream of innocence, just as we must recognize the genuine appeal he has for Mr. Longdon as well as for Nanda. Mitchett says of Van at one point that he is "thoroughly straight," at another that he is "formed for a distinctly higher sphere" and that "on our level"—that of Mrs. Brook's circle—he is "positively wasted" (10). Vanderbank *is* different from Mrs. Brook and most of her circle; it may be the very division within him which accounts for the "sacred terror" others feel in him. If we take him as a man intrinsically flawed with indecisiveness—a Jamesian hollow man, like John Marcher in "The Beast in the Jungle"—we rob the book of much of its intensity. For its dramatic action arises from Mrs. Brook's effort to prevent his marrying Nanda.

One can see the quality of Mrs. Brook's world most succinctly by considering her son Harold. Harold is not made a contrast to his mother as Nanda is. He reduces to a series of comic turns the selfishness that his mother, for the most part, covers with style or wit. His mother encourages Harold to secure invitations to country houses, where, we learn, he cheats at cards. As his mother lightly says, "however Harold plays, he has a way of winning" (6). At home he pilfers any money that is not locked up, and he duns the men who visit his mother, particularly the amiable Mitchy. Harold's parents feel that they should ask Mitchy if he has been dunned; but, as Mr. Brookenham remarks, it "will be such a beastly bore if he admits it." Brookenham can't easily and doesn't want to pay his son's debts; and, somewhat like the John Dashwoods in *Sense and Sensibility,* the Brookenhams rationalize their comfortable obliviousness: "they ought to tell us, and when they don't it serves them right." (When the question of Vanderbank arises, Mr. Brookenham's reply to his wife is, "I think, Van, you know, is your affair.") Mrs. Brook offers, with no great expectation of being believed, the danger of her husband's outrage as a reason for Mitchy to conceal Harold's guilt. Thereupon she promptly adopts a contrary-to-fact construction: "if you *had* let Harold borrow," she says to Mitchy, "you would have another manner." By the end of the novel, Harold has come far out, savagely impertinent and very much, Van tells us, "the rage." He has become the lover of Lord Petherton's sister and Mr. Cashmore's wife, Lady Fanny, and thus keeps her from running off with a Captain Dent-Douglas—like Anna Karenina, as Mrs. Brook observes, to "one of the smaller Italian towns" (21). Mrs. Brook remarks of her son, "His success is true. . . . I hold my breath. But I'm bound to say I rather admire."

Mrs. Brook herself is "charmingly pretty," with "lovely, silly eyes" and a "natural, quavering tone" of voice that work together, "like a "trick that had never yet been exposed," to give her always "the pure light of youth" (4). Beneath that charm is an unblinking sense of her advantage, a powerful will, and awesome shrewdness. She is of the strain of Becky Sharp and Trollope's Lizzie Eustace. She sees Mr. Longdon as a possible benefactor because of his devotion to the memory of her mother. "The thing is," she softly wails, "that I don't see how he *can* like Harold." She looks coolly at the facts: "And I don't think he really likes *me*. . . . I mean not utterly *really*. He has to try to." But that, she concludes, won't matter. " 'He'll be just the same.' She saw it steadily and saw it whole. 'On account of mamma.' " The derisive tag from Matthew Arnold[4] helps to fix by contrast the closeness with which Mrs. Brook's vision operates as she chooses her strategy: "He *must* like Nanda" (6).

Mr. Longdon's wealth, Mrs. Brook thinks, must be immense. "I can see it growing while he sits there," she remarks to Van. "I should really like not to lose him." As she contemplates Mr. Longdon's uses, she asks Van in turn, "What can we make him do for you?" Van's blank, embarrassed response requires a stronger assertion. "How can any one love you . . . without wanting to show it in some way? You know all the ways, dear Van, . . . in which *I* want to show it." His reply returns them to the business at hand: "That, for instance, is the tone not to take with him" (14). Mrs. Brook is conscious of what attracts Van in Mr. Longdon and gives Van influence in turn. It is an image of goodness that she finds at best boring. And Mrs. Brook clearly sees the danger in Van's divided mind: "It will be him you'll help. If you're to make sacrifices to keep on good terms with him, the first sacrifice will be of me."

There are two measures Mrs. Brook uses to keep Van. One is to insist again and again on how much that is improper Nanda knows, how much she is pursued by Mr. Cashmore (who has tired of his mistress, Tishy Grendon's sister), how free she is at Tishy's to keep her own hours. The other is to insist, with the force of a willed prophecy, that he will not act. We see both of these measures at work in the remarkable twenty-first chapter. Mrs. Brook complains to Van of the cost of Nanda's presence—the reduction of their talk to the "stupid, flat, fourth-rate." She speculates on what Mr. Longdon may do for Nanda, and at last asks Van directly, "Has he given *you* anything?" Mrs. Brook still captivates Van by "the childlike innocence with which her voice could invest the hardest teachings of life." Then "with the air of a man who had suddenly determined on a great blind leap," Van reveals what Mr. Longdon asked him to keep a secret, the offer of a large sum of money to make Van's marriage to Nanda possible. Van has been reluctant to tell Mrs. Brook of this, but he is even more reluctant not to do so. Is it an effort to make her release him or an appeal for her to hold him? She is bold enough in reply: "Do you imagine I want you myself?" She refuses to plead with him and insists upon the chance of success: "Of course you know . . . that she'd jump at you." Van is still locked in uncertainty and tries to read his own motives: "Isn't there rather something in my having thus thought it my duty to warn you that I'm definitely his candidate?" And once more Mrs. Brook takes a high hand: "What kind of monster are you trying to make me out?" And then she introduces the other measure:

> Holding him a minute as with the soft, low voice of his fate, she sadly but firmly shook her head. "You won't do it."
> "Oh!" he almost too loudly protested.
> "You won't do it," she went on.
> "I *say*"—he made a joke of it.
> "You won't do it," she repeated.
> It was as if he could not at last but show himself really struck; yet what he exclaimed on was what might in truth most have impressed him. "You *are* magnificent, really!" [21]

Mrs. Brookenham's great stroke is to expose Nanda's sophistication—through a sordid French novel Nanda has read and passed on to Tishy Grendon (one, ironically, belonging to Vanderbank, whose name Nanda has inscribed in it). Mrs. Brook does this in such a way as to shock Van, and at the same time she "calls in" Nanda from Mr. Longdon's care. Her purpose is to force upon Mr. Longdon the ugliness of Nanda's life so as to make him save her by adoption and a financial settlement. When Mrs. Brook demands Nanda's return, her husband wanders into the conversation and maladroitly exclaims, "We wouldn't *take* her" (29). Mrs. Brook's resourcefulness is great. She brilliantly meets the duchess's observation that Brookenham has spoken without his cue:

> "We dressed today in a hurry and hadn't time for our usual rehearsal. Edward, when we dine out, generally brings three pocket-handkerchiefs and six jokes. I leave the management of the handkerchiefs to his own taste, but we mostly try together, in advance, to arrange a career for the other things. It's some charming light thing of my own that's supposed to give him the sign." [30]

For all her resourcefulness, Mrs. Brook's plan brings no immediate success. Vanderbank, in spite of Mr. Longdon's support, delays for months. Nanda has earlier sensed his revulsion from her modernity, as if to say to him, "I can't help it any more than you can, can I?"

> So she appeared to put it to him, with something in her lucidity that would have been infinitely touching; a strange, grave calm consciousness of their com-

mon doom. . . . [Vanderbank sprang up] as if he had been infinitely touched
. . . and there was in fact on Vanderbank's part quite the look of the man—
though it lasted but just while we seize it—in suspense about himself.   [23]

The last book of *The Awkward Age,* the one named for Nanda, is made up
in large part of Nanda's visits from three men: Vanderbank, Mitchy, and
Mr. Longdon. Vanderbank is painfully flustered and uneasy, but Nanda's
purpose is to spare him all she can. She is like Maggie Verver in the second
part of *The Golden Bowl:* "To force upon him an awkwardness was like forcing
a disfigurement or a hurt, so that at the end of a minute . . . she arrived at
the appearance of having changed places with him and of their being together precisely in order that he—not she—should be let down easily" (35).
That is a good brief account of Maggie's treatment of Charlotte Stant and,
to a degree, of the prince. Nanda not only does not reproach Vanderbank,
but she urges him not to desert her mother. "I verily believe she's in love
with you. Not, for that matter, that father would mind—he wouldn't mind,
as he says, a twopenny rap. (36)." And she adds, with unashamed maturity:
"She's so fearfully young." As she tries to reconcile them, Nanda can say,
with an implicit sense of her own life as a daughter, "You *can't* know how
much you are to her. You're more to her, I verily believe, than any one *ever*
was." Van is touched because he is also relieved: "no one who ever *has* liked
her can afford ever again, for any long period, to do without her. . . . She's
a fixed star." Nanda helps him rise to more and more celebration, almost as
if she were reviving his feelings for Mrs. Brook by making him voice them.
At the last, he reverts to an indirect apology, cast as a message to Mr.
Longdon: "Look after my good name. . . . I've odiously neglected him—
by a complication of accidents. There are things I ought to have done that I
haven't. . . . I've been a brute, and I didn't mean it, and I couldn't help
it" (36).
    When Nanda relays his message, Mr. Longdon is struck by her pride.
"Pride's all right," he says, "when it helps one to bear things." But Nanda
will not have it that way. When one wants to take most, rather than least,
from things, she says, "one . . . must rather grovel." When Mr. Longdon
wishes she didn't "so wonderfully love" Van, she bursts into tears. She sees
herself as "the horrible impossible," who *is* what Van thinks her. "We can't
help it. It isn't really our fault. . . . Everything's different from what it
used to be." She turns to Mr. Longdon, who has come so far. "Oh, he's more
old-fashioned than you." But he tried—"he did his best. But he couldn't"
(37).
    The "extreme pinch" of Vanderbank's "romance is the vivacity in him, to
his positive sorrow and loss, of the state of being aware." Van's awareness

only creates division rather than spreads to cover and to embrace. It seems, as Robert Caserio has written, that Van, rather than Longdon, is "puritanical and nostalgic, even sentimental, about the past." This is, I have tried to suggest, a reflex of his dissatisfaction with himself, the expression of that part of him which distrusts and even rebels against Mrs. Brookenham, for all his devotion to and need for her. Is it true (to pursue Caserio's account) that he has "a kind of detached, lucid endurance of the age, a lucidity that is modern because it is inactive"?[5] I should prefer, for reasons I've indicated, to stress Vanderbank's ultimate bewilderment in contrast with Nanda's hard-earned lucidity. He remains bewildered because he can never reconcile the opposed impulses within himself; he seems doomed to a joyless (if not un-pleasant) life in Mrs. Brookenham's circle. "What are parties given for in London," the duchess remarks, "but that enemies may meet?" (8)

If Vanderbank's inaction remains the crux of the plot, the culmination is the heroic generosity of Nanda in giving him "that refined satisfaction with himself which would proceed from his having dealt with a difficult hour in a gallant and delicate way" (35). It is for Nanda, in fact, to do so in order to leave Vanderbank with the sense that he has done so. In his preface to *The Spoils of Poynton* James writes of the "free spirit"—in that novel Fleda Vetch, as it is Nanda in this—"always much tormented, and by no means always triumphant . . . heroic, ironic, pathetic . . . 'successful' only through hav-ing remained free." That freedom may be earned, in Joseph Conrad's phrase, through "the supreme energy of an act of renunciation."[6] Milly Theale re-nounces any grievance in leaving the money to Densher; Densher renounces the money for himself. In this novel Nanda Brookenham renounces any claim on Vanderbank's conscience or upon his self-regard. Like Maggie Verver, later, she preserves those who have failed or wronged her, both Van and her mother. Conrad goes on to observe that a "solution by rejection must always present a certain lack of finality, especially startling when contrasted with the usual methods of solution by rewards and punishments." One can con-nect Conrad's observations with James's words in "The Art of Fiction" (1884): the "essence of moral energy is to survey the whole field." James wishes to reject an external, rule-bound conception of morality, and in the process he often celebrates the consciousness which can see around all others and enfold them in its understanding. So with the author: the "moral" sense of a work of art depends on "the amount of felt life concerned in producing it." The artist's sensibility should be a soil in which "any vision of life" can grow "with due freshness and straightness" (Preface to *The Portrait of a Lady*).[7]

James is always ready to put deeper virtues in the balance with conven-tions and rules. When he writes W. D. Howells about the French novelists he knows, he strikes such a balance: "They do the only kind of work, today, that I respect; and in spite of their ferocious pessimism and their handling of unclean things, they are at least serious and honest." There is a telling contrast drawn between Thackeray and Balzac:

> Balzac loved his Valérie then as Thackeray did not love his Becky, or his Blanche Amory in *Pendennis*. But his prompting was not to expose her; it could only be, on the contrary . . . to cover her up and protect her, in the interest of her special genius and freedom. All his impulse was to *la faire valoir,* to give her all her value, just as Thackeray's attitude was the opposite one, a desire positively to expose and desecrate poor Becky—to follow her up, catch her in the act, and bring her to shame: though with a mitigation, an admiration, an inconsequence, now and then wrested from him by an instinct finer, in his mind, than the so-called "moral" eagerness. The English writer wants to make sure, first of all, of your moral judgment; the French is willing, while it waits a little, to risk, for the sake of his subject and its interest, your spiritual salvation.[8]

Clearly James is distrustful of any moral restrictions set upon the field of consciousness. But he distrusts other restrictions no less. In his early essay on Baudelaire he writes, "to count out the moral element in one's appreciation of an artistic total is exactly as sane as it would be (if the total were a poem) to eliminate all the words in three syllables." Morality "is in reality simply a part of the essential richness of inspiration—it has nothing to do with the artistic process and it has everything to do with the artistic effect. The more a work of art feels it at its source, the richer it is; the less it feels it, the poorer it is."[9] The kind of moral imagination James brings to the case of Vanderbank, or of Densher, is to be seen in a remark he made in an early letter: "We know when we lie, when we kill, when we steal, when we deceive or violate others; but it is hard to know when we deceive or violate ourselves."[10]

"Almost Socratic"

As James presents one of Mrs. Brookenham's questions, he calls her "almost Socratic." It is an interesting observation because one feels at times a remote influence upon James of the Platonic dialogues. I have no wish to fix that influence but only to consider the kind of midwifery of ideas, like that which Socrates claims, we can find in some of James's dialogue. One of the forms of intensity James achieves is the dramatization of a process wherein a man's accepted ideas are gradually brought into question and replaced. A good instance is the evening Lambert Strether spends in London with Maria Gostrey, at dinner and at the theater. It is also a good instance of that principle of which James wrote to H. G. Wells: "It is art that *makes* life, makes interest, makes importance." [11]

In this chapter, the first of book II, Strether is learning "to find names" for many matters, and on no evening of his life has he tried to supply so many. Maria Gostrey is the "mistress of a hundred cases or categories," and Strether soon feels that she "knew even intimate things about him that he hadn't yet told her and perhaps never would." She is eliciting from him the names or categories by which he has organized experience all of his life in America, and the very process by which she elicits them requires Strether to bring them to full consciousness, and then withdraw from, circumambulate, and question attitudes he has so far taken as natural and necessary. He has not told her these things about himself because he has not known that he knew them. They emerge in consciousness through the art of her questions.

Everything about Strether's evening defines itself in opposition to the world he has known; when he has gone to the theater with his American patron, Mrs. Newsome, he has enjoyed no "little confronted dinner, no pink lights, no whiff of vague sweetness." Nor has Mrs. Newsome ever worn a dress cut so low. Strether finds himself given over to "uncontrolled perception," to a freedom of awareness that Mrs. Newsome's black dress and white ruff have never encouraged. The red velvet band around Maria's throat becomes a "starting-point for fresh backward, fresh forward, fresh lateral flights." If Mrs. Newsome's ruff suggested Queen Elizabeth, Maria Gostrey's band evokes Mary Stuart. Strether finds in himself a "candor of fancy" that takes pleasure in such an antithesis. The texture of all he sees becomes more complex; the English "types" both on the stage and in the audience will prove more varied and distinct than Woollett allowed.

As Maria Gostrey draws Strether out on the subject of his mission, she requires him to attend to those terms he has never before questioned. She often echoes a response, holding a note he has sounded until it becomes the object of their joint perception. And to see with her eyes is to begin to free himself from the limits in which he has unconsciously acquiesced. She has also a tendency to abet his most treasonous thoughts. He begins, at the theater, to feel "kindness" for the young man on the stage who wears perpetual evening dress and weakly succumbs to "a bad woman in a yellow frock." Would Chad Newsome (whom he has come to rescue) wear evening dress, too? Would Strether have to do so himself to meet Chad at a proper level?

As his own thoughts warily approach such questions, Maria Gostrey puts them so directly before him that he can hardly evade them. "You've accepted the mission of separating him from the wicked woman. Are you quite sure she's very bad for him?" Strether is startled by the question: "Of course we are. Wouldn't *you* be?" Maria refuses the comfort of easy judgment. "One can only judge the facts." Might, after all, the woman be charming? Again, Strether is startled:

> "Charming?"—Strether stared before him. "She's base, venal—out of the streets."
> "I see. And *he*—?"
> "Chad, wretched boy?"
> "Of what type and temper is he?" she went on as Strether had lapsed.

We aren't told why he has "lapsed," but presumably he is forced to ask himself whether Chad is merely a virtuous American lad seduced.

> "Well—the obstinate." It was as if for a moment he had been going to say more and had then controlled himself.
> That was scarce what she wanted. "Do you like him?"
> This time he was prompt. "No. How *can* I?"

Once Strether has acknowledged his dislike of Chad Newsome, he wishes to attribute it to the son's treatment of his mother. Mrs. Newsome inspires a rather exalted idiom: "He has darkened her admirable life." Then, as if to bring it down to earth, Strether makes the point less stuffily: "He has worried her half to death." Maria, for reasons of her own, picks up the first and, as it were, the "official" version: "Is her life very admirable?" To this Strether replies with a solemn, perhaps reverent, "Extraordinarily." James indicates the timing of these remarks: "There was so much in the tone that Miss Gostrey had to devote another pause to the appreciation of it." She proceeds to deflate Strether's dictum and perhaps also to uncover the strong managerial role of Mrs. Newsome: "And he has only *her?* I don't mean the bad woman in Paris . . . for I assure you I shouldn't even at the best be disposed to allow him more than one. But has he only his mother?"

Strether mentions Chad's sister, Sarah Pocock, and he can imply of her, as he could not of her mother, that she is not universally beloved. Maria calls up Strether's earlier "admirable": "But *you* admire her?" And this releases Strether's critical awareness: "I'm perhaps a little afraid of her." What Maria is trying to uncover is the kind of will that governs the ladies and Strether as their ambassador. When he exclaims that they would do "anything in the world for him," Maria turns that conventional tribute inside out: "And you'd do anything in the world for them?" Strether is uncomfortable; she "had made it perhaps just a shade too affirmative for his nerves: 'Oh I don't know.' " Their generosity begins to turn, under Maria's cool queries, into something like officiousness. "The 'anything' they'd do is represented by their *making* you do it."

A comic view of Mrs. Newsome begins to emerge. "She puts so much of herself into everything—." And Maria nicely picks up the absurdity: "that she has nothing left for anything else?" Strether begins to let go his admiration. Maria supposes that "if your friend *had* come she would take great views, and the great views, to put it simply, would be too much for her." Strether by now is no longer defensive; he is "amused at" Maria's "notion of the simple," but accepts her terms: "Everything's too much for her."

James catches the conflict of exaltation and vulgarity in the unmentionable thing whose manufacture is the source of Mrs. Newsome's wealth: "a small, trivial, rather ridiculous object of the commonest domestic use," Strether lamely describes it; "it's rather wanting in—what shall I say? Well, dignity, or the least approach to distinction." James looks ahead to Maria's many attempts to have him name it; with their failure she can treat "the little nameless object as indeed unnameable—she could make their abstention enormously definite." And behind this suppressed object there are sources of money even more questionable, not simply vulgar but dishonest. We begin to see Mrs. Newsome covering these wrongs with a high manner, as a "moral swell," the patron of the review that Strether edits and that few read. "It's her tribute to the ideal," Strether explains. Maria puts it otherwise: "You assist her to expiate—which is rather hard when you've yourself not sinned."

Perhaps the saddest and most significant exchange concerns the plans for Chad:

> "He stands . . . if you succeed with him, to gain—"
> "Oh a lot of advantages." Strether had them clearly at his fingers' ends.
> "By which you mean of course a lot of money."
> "Well, not only. I'm acting with a sense for him of other things too. Consideration and comfort and security—the general safety of being anchored by a strong chain. He wants, as I see him, to be protected. Protected I mean from life."
> "Ah *voilà!*"—her thought fitted with a click. "From life. What you *really* want to get him home for is to marry him."

There is something pitiable in this distrust of "life." Strether has been, as he now would have Chad be, "anchored by a strong chain." To question this prepares, of course, for his speech in Gloriani's garden, the rueful "Live all you can!"

Maria Gostrey has come to recognize the range of awareness that Strether can, with release, attain. He has modesty, simplicity, good will, conscience—beneath the conventional attitudes he has come abroad to represent are generosity and imagination. Later, Little Bilham will say to him, "you're not a person to whom it's easy to tell things you don't want to know. Though it *is* easy, I admit—it's quite beautiful . . . when you do want to" (V, 1). When Maria first asks Strether what, if he should fail, he stands to lose, he

exclaims, "Nothing!" As she leaves him, she asks once more, "What do you
stand to lose?"

> Why the question now affected him as other he couldn't have said; he could
> only this time meet it otherwise. "Everything."   [II, 1]

Has he come at last to reject the old language-game he has brought from
Woollett, to reverse the meanings of "succeed" and "fail"? Later, in Paris
with his dogged fellow American Waymarsh, the question of when he will
see Chad comes up.

> "Well," said Strether almost gaily, "I guess I don't know anything!" His gaiety
> might have been a tribute to the fact that the state he had been reduced to did
> for him again what had been done by his talk of the matter with Miss Gostrey
> at the London theatre. It was somehow enlarging.. . .   [III, 1]

The enlargement will take Strether to a vision of Chad and Mme de Vionnet, and of Paris itself, so large as to reverse all of his original judgments.
When Strether learns that the "virtuous attachment" he has imagined is not
what he thought, when he discovers that Mme de Vionnet is in fact Chad's
mistress, he has come too far to revert to his earlier moral categories. He has
already seen Mrs. Newsome's lack of imagination and force of will. He has
not been able to budge her from her preconceptions, and all that is left is
"morally and intellectually to get rid of her." He sees her "fine cold thought"
as a "particularly large iceberg in a cool blue northern sea." And Maria
complements his thought with her own: "There's nothing so magnificent—
for making others feel you—as to have no imagination" (XI, 1).

At Strether's final meeting with Mme de Vionnet in her apartment, the
aristocratic setting promises support: the "things from far back—tyrannies
of history, facts of type, values, as the painters said, of expression—all working for her and giving her the supreme chance, the chance . . . on a great
occasion, to be natural and simple." Her lie and Chad's now seem to him
"an inevitable tribute to good taste," even as he winces "at the amount of
comedy involved" in his own misunderstanding (XII, 1) But what Strether
learns is how helpless her passion for Chad has been. As she has put it
obliquely, "The wretched self is always there, always making one somehow
a fresh anxiety." And while she asserts that the "only safe thing is to give,"
she seems, after all, in her fear that Chad will leave her, "exploited." She
has made Chad better; "but it came to our friend with supreme queerness
that he was none the less only Chad." Strether finally exclaims to Mme de
Vionnet, "You're afraid for your life!" (XII, 2) Her aristocratic nature will
not save her. Strether recalls the fate of Madame Roland, the "smell of revolution, the smell of the public temper—or perhaps simply, the smell of
blood" (XII, 1). He sees Mme de Vionnet at once as "the finest and subtlest
creature" caught in a passion "mature, abysmal, pitiful."

After two reversals, then, Strether finds himself once more voicing a moral view. To Chad, who shows signs of being ready for Woollett and the "art" of advertising, who seems somewhat tired of Mme de Vionnet and perhaps unfaithful to her, Strether appeals "by all you hold sacred" to remain in Paris (XII, 4). Strether finally sees beneath the charm of his new manners Chad's limited consciousness; Chad has spoken of being tired of Mme de Vionnet "as he might have spoken of being tired of roast mutton for dinner." And Strether calls Chad to moral responsibility as intensely as he might once have done, but the moral vision comes now out of a breadth of consciousness that would have been unimaginable in his early talk with Maria Gostrey. "You owe her everything," he tells Chad, "very much more than she can ever owe you. You've in other words duties to her, of the most positive sort; and I don't see what other duties . . . can be held to go before them" (XII, 4).

As Strether later recounts the meeting to Maria Gostrey, he recognizes the "portentous solemnity" of his moral view, but, he concludes, "I was made so." And he must leave Maria and Paris so as not to get anything for himself: "To be right." Just as the early moral attitudes had to give way to the more inclusive awareness that aesthetic ordering permitted, so now the scope of the aesthetic is in turn enlarged—but in a far different way and with much more at stake—by the concern with conduct. Mme de Vionnet is more and less than she was, Chad's change seems less complete, and even Maria and her "hundred cases and categories" must be surrendered to a final view that is sterner. "It was awkward, it was almost stupid, not to seem to prize" the beauty and knowledge in Maria's life and in her offer of love (XII, 5). But, as James put it in the "project" for the novel, Strether "has come so far through his little experience that he has come out on the other side—on the other side even of a union with Miss Gostrey. He must go back as he came—or rather, really, so quite other that, in comparison, marrying Miss Gostrey would be almost of the same order."[12] The sternness comes of an acceptance of consciousness, with all its privileges and pains, at the expense of all else.

The Prince and Charlotte Stant

As *The Golden Bowl* begins, Prince Amerigo is about to take the American heiress Maggie Verver as his bride. Her father, Adam Verver, is a man of tremendous wealth who has become a collector of works of art, which he plans to house in a museum in American City. London, where the novel is mostly set, is the successor to Rome, as American City may be its successor in turn. The Prince is oppressed by history, by the long record of greed and arrogance his ancestors have attained. He is ready to escape from history through the help of American innocence. Adam Verver he regards as "simply the best man I've ever seen in my life." "I'm like a chicken, at best," the Prince explains, "chopped up and smothered in sauce; cooked down as a *crème de volaille,* with half the parts left out. Your father's the natural fowl running about the *bassecour.* His feathers, movements, his sounds—those are the parts that, with me, are left out." For all his amusement with such natural inno-cence, the Prince is serious enough: "You do believe I'm not a hypocrite? You recognize that I don't lie or dissemble or deceive?" His intensity trou-bles Maggie, for, as he perceives, "any *serious* discussion of veracity, of loy-alty, or rather of the want of them, practically took her unprepared, as if it were quite new to her" (1).

As a last gesture for himself, the Prince goes to visit his American friends, the Assinghams. They have, as it were, been his sponsors, and Fanny As-singham has introduced him to the Ververs. He asks Fanny's help in keeping him right, saving him from being wrong without knowing it. He has, he explains, no "moral sense," at least as Americans understand it.

> "I've of course something that in our poor dear backward old Rome sufficiently passes for it. But it's no more like yours that the tortuous stone stair case— half-ruined into the bargain!—in some castle of our *quattrocento* is like the 'light-ning elevator' in one of Mr. Verver's fifteen-story buildings. Your moral sense works by steam—it sends you up like a rocket. Ours is slow and steep and unlighted, with so many of the steps missing that—well, that it's as short, in almost any case, to turn round and come down again." [2]

The Prince's buoyant hopefulness is given a small shock by the arrival at the Assignhams' of Charlotte Stant. She is Maggie Verver's good friend, but she has also been, unknown to Maggie and before the Prince was known to the Ververs, the Prince's mistress. She has returned for the wedding, and she has no intention of revealing her earlier knowledge of the Prince. But she exacts from him one obligation, to go shopping with her for a present for Maggie.

It is in spite of Fanny Assingham's anxiety that Charlotte insists upon the Prince's help. He assents with some internal reservations; his anxiety is not the same as Fanny's, for he is more concerned with how this expedition might be seen by others than he is with Charlotte's renewed appeal. To accompany Charlotte without subterfuge seems the right style to maintain: "for what so much as publicity put their relation on the right footing?" Fanny gives the expedition her reluctant approval, "as representing friendly judgment, public opinion, the moral law, the margin allowed a husband about to be, or whatever." With Fanny's authorization, the Prince knows where he is. "He was where he could stay" (3).

The first words Charlotte speaks in the fifth chapter, as they have reached Hyde Park on their expedition, are a little ominous in their suggestion of duplicity. "Well, now I must tell you," she says, "for I want to be absolutely

honest. . . . I came back for this. Not really for anything else. For this."
And as the Prince seems puzzled, she adds, "To have one hour alone with
you." The very rain-washed freshness of the day seems to bless the occasion:
"It was as if it had been waiting for her, as if she knew it, placed it, loved
it, as if it were in fact a part of what she had come back for." And seems to
conspire to Charlotte's end. But what *is* her end? To reassert her love for the
Prince? To insist upon a final intimacy before his marriage—a secret expedition? To exact from him a gesture of loyalty to herself between his proposal
and his marriage to Maggie? And what is the Prince's attitude? He scorns
the ridiculous posture of showing fear, of seeming prim. And yet he seems
to have avoided Charlotte during her recent visits to Maggie. The Prince has
tried to discourage the shopping for a gift on the score of needless expense,
but Charlotte exploits her position to hold him. "Because you think I must
have so little? I've enough, at any rate—enough for us to take our hour.
. . . Mine is to be the offering of the poor—something, precisely, that no
rich person *could* ever give her, and that, being herself too rich ever to buy
it, she would therefore never have" (5).

There is about this, of course, some intimation of the Prince becoming
Charlotte's gift, but a gift she cannot really make until she has repossessed
him. There is intimation but no insistence. The gift, after all, is to be "funny"
rather than "fine," an amusing bargain. The Prince, too, is engaged "in the
policy of not magnifying." He must not allow Charlotte to seem to beg him
for his participation lest his reservations imply that this participation is a
serious matter. He agrees, therefore, to maintain the secrecy, which troubles
him, not least because it is of such importance, "of the essence," for Charlotte. He hesitates at this "making of mystery." It resembles all too much
the earlier occasions when they were lovers. "This was like beginning something over, which was the last thing he wanted." What he has sought in his
marriage—the "strength, the beauty of his actual position"—was a "fresh
start," "new altogether." Charlotte has detected his hesitation and has
mockingly challenged him to dismiss it (5).

The Prince recognizes the generosity of Charlotte's surrendering him, and
he chooses to take her demand as a trifle. How much it means to Maggie
when, years later, she learns of it depends on the adulterous relationship that
the Prince and Charlotte have since come to maintain. As Maggie says to the
Prince on that later occasion: "The idea of your finding something for me—
charming as that would have been—was what had least to do with your
taking a morning together at that moment. What had really to do with it
. . . was that you *had* to; you couldn't not, from the moment you were
again face to face. And the reason of that was there had been so much between you before—*I* came between you at all" (34).

For what Maggie can recognize after a long interval of time is that to have paid this secret tribute to their past relationship just before his marriage was for the Prince and Charlotte to keep it alive; if not to resume it, then at least to protect it from those events that might seem to end it. And it is for that reason that the Prince, who wants to be "straight," resists Charlotte as much as his pride and his pity allow. He persuades himself that his assent, in exchange for all she has given up, is "verily a trifle"; and under that persuasion he lets himself "be guided" and allows the occasion to take "the stamp of her preference." And she in turn reveals her true intention: "To see you once and be with you, to be as we are now and as we used to be, for one small hour—or say for two—that's what I have had for weeks in my head. . . . What I want is that it shall always be with you—so that you'll never be able quite to get rid of it—that I *did*" (5). It is "the moment of his life" when the Prince has "least to say." He is unwilling to resume their relationship and reluctant to be brutal; and he does, of course, find her enormously attractive. There is partial complicity in his passiveness, and there is "merciful muddle."

Charlotte reveals so remarkably full a knowledge of London that the Prince, who prides himself on his own, is "just a shade humiliated" and all but "annoyed." Charlotte reveals the same readiness and control that she will exhibit later at Matcham, where with somewhat daunting forehandedness she knows the "very train" to Gloucester before the Prince has thought to propose one.

Again and again the remarks the Prince and Charlotte exchange have overtones of deeper issues. She can buy, as she says, a "pincushion from the Baker Street Bazaar," so innocent and generous is Maggie. But that is why she must not. "We mustn't take advantage of her character," Charlotte observes. "One mustn't if not for *her,* at least for one's self. She saves one such trouble." And the recognition of Maggie's innocence grows before them. "She's not selfish enough." "It makes too easy terms for one." "And nobody . . . is decent enough, good enough, to stand it." Or at least, "not good enough not rather to feel the strain." But the Prince demurs: "May not one's affection for her do something more for one's decency, as you call it, than her own generosity . . . has the unfortunate virtue to undo?" (5)

When Charlotte exclaims how "terrible" innocence is, how it makes one pity those who have it, the Prince insists, in turn, on the possibility of helping rather than pitying them. But to help means "absolutely refusing to be spoiled," Charlotte observes, with a strong sense of its difficulty. And the Prince replies that decency finally "comes back to that." There is a pause as Charlotte walks beside him. " 'It's just what *I* meant,' she then reasonably said" (5). The irony is left to resound at the end of the chapter—Charlotte must live for the moment with all the decency she has invoked. The Prince has showed no readiness to shift its sense to one of accommodation. But the effect changes. Charlotte is pleased by the dealer's caring for his things and for them, as "right people." His taste has been "struck"; he has ideas about them, she thinks, and he will remember them. As of course he will, for the dealer perceives the drama going on between them.

When the Prince offers to make Charlotte a gift, a small remembrance, she refuses it. "It has no reference," she remarks. "You don't refer. *I* refer." In effect, he may no longer have such love for her as requires remembrance, whereas she does for him. She wishes to give him a present, therefore, but he refuses it as "impossible." She draws out the implication. A gift would become something to hide because of the occasion of its purchase: this "ramble that we shall have had together and that we're not to speak of." By now the secrecy has grown; and the "ramble" has all but become a symbolic reenactment of their earlier love. A gift for her will be a token of a love that could not be explained. "So you don't insist," she explains, and he replies— "a little wearily at last—even a little impatiently"—"I don't insist." (6)

One feels that the Prince is far less involved, far more ready to have done with what has been. He moves to the door, ready to end the episode, when the dealer speaks aloud in the "suddenest, sharpest Italian." He has understood all they have been saying. He has grasped "her possible, her impossible, title" as the Prince's former mistress. And at that point the dealer brings forth the golden bowl, a crystal pedestaled cup that is plated—more than plated, but the process is unknown—with gold. Charlotte is charmed with the cup, but the Prince leaves impatiently to wait outside. Charlotte knows that there must be something wrong with the bowl, but the dealer parries her question—it need not matter if she can't detect it and does not pay too much. "Does one make a present," she asks, "of an object that contains . . . a flaw?" One has only to mention that there is a flaw to show one's good faith and leave the recipient to find it. And he wouldn't find it, the dealer insists. Not even if it should be smashed, upon a marble floor? (As, of course, it will be by Fanny Assingham.) Crystal, the dealer explains, splits; it does not shatter. It splits in "lines and by laws of its own" (6).

Charlotte cannot afford the fifteen pounds the bowl costs, although she lies to the Prince, to whom she wishes to give it, by naming its price as five. He is shocked by the offer, for he has seen the flaw and cannot believe that Charlotte has not. It was because of what he saw that he left the shop. Nor is the Prince mollified by its very low cost. "I saw the object itself. It told its story. No wonder it's cheap." He will not accept it, however exquisite it looks, or even *because* it is so deceptively exquisite. There is an omen in the crack: for his safety, for his marriage, for his happiness. They have come to recognize by now that the search is over. Charlotte is rueful: "if we may perish by cracks in things that we don't know—!" It is as if such fastidiousness were futile and destructive. "Ah, but one does know," the Prince replies, "*I* do, at least—and by instinct. I don't fail. That will always protect me."

Charlotte despairs: "We can never then give each other anything." But the Prince assures her that anything he will ever give her will be "perfect." He seems to be claiming new moral purpose and freedom from the ties of the past, and that seems the point of his statement: "Yet I shall want some day to give you something. . . . The day you marry. For you *will* marry. You *must*— seriously—marry." She recognizes his meaning and resents it: "To make you feel better?" What neither can foresee—he in his wish to deflect her love, she in her refusal to renounce him—is that the marriage will be precisely the one to undo this resolve. At the moment, however, she accepts her dismissal with a taunt: "Well, I would marry, I think, to have something from you in all freedom" (6). She can only allow herself to believe him concerned for their safety; the possibility of his being in love with Maggie or of his taking a solemn view of marriage is more than she can credit or acknowledge.

Maggie and Adam Verver

The later events of *The Golden Bowl* are a realization of what is latent in the scenes of the shopping. Adam Verver comes to feel that his daughter Maggie, in spite of having now a husband and son, is still too much concerned with her father. It is with the intention of freeing her to be a true wife to the Prince that he marries Charlotte Stant. But Maggie only feels the greater need to show him that she did not find his demands on her too great; and she devotes herself all the more to him once he and Charlotte return to London. The consequence is, inevitably, to throw the Prince and Charlotte together; and they assume the role of "doing the worldly" for the retiring Maggie and her father. They most brilliantly and boldly assume a public role together at the beginning of part III. Their presence at a "great official party" causes Fanny Assingham alarm. They have stayed on when Maggie has, through uneasiness, gone back to her slightly invalid father. Fanny is terrified by the boldness and openness—the heroic lucidity—they show, but neither of them is troubled by her fears. Fanny senses the "presence of still deeper things than she had yet dared to fear" (14), and when she speaks to the Prince, she feels that "something as yet unnameable came out for her in his look . . . something strange and subtle and at variance with his words, something that *gave them away,* glimmered deep down, as an appeal . . . to her finer comprehension." It was, in fact, "fairly like a quintessential wink" (15). Fanny tries to bury the awareness she has gained, for it casts an ugly light on her own complicity in the two marriages. "The sense of seeing was strong in her, but she clutched at the comfort of not being sure of what she saw" (16).

When, finally, Charlotte calls on the Prince while Maggie is elsewhere with her father, she says "straight out," once they are alone together, "What else, my dear, what in the world else can we do?" (17) And, as they talk of their spouses, so obliviously devoted to each other, Charlotte exclaims, "What do they really suppose . . . becomes of one?" (18) She resolves to be direct, to accept their innocent notions and live without disturbing them. She will explain her time with the Prince as keeping him company in his solitude. "How can we understand anything . . . without really seeing that this is what they must like to think I do for you?—just as, quite as comfortably, you do it for me. The thing is for us to learn to take them as they are." Charlotte advances with sincerity a high view of their role, and the Prince yields to hers his more cautious and earnest ideas. He has been torn and bewildered, but now he follows Charlotte. He feels that his own dignity requires a conception that will allow him to rise to his opportunity, and "the luminous idea" Charlotte has expressed simply anticipates his own thoughts. "A large response, as he looked at her, came into his face, a light of excited perception all his own, in the glory of which . . . what he gave her back had the value of what she had given him." They agree that they wish to hurt no one, that they "must trust each other." And as they gravely attest to their commitment, the Prince at last declares: "It's sacred."

> "It's sacred," she breathed back to him. They vowed it, gave it out and took it in, drawn, by their intensity, more closely together. Then of a sudden, through this tightened circle, as at the issue of a narrow strait into the sea beyond, everything broke up, broke down, gave way, melted and mingled. Their lips sought their lips, their pressure their response and their response their pressure; with a violence that had sighed itself the next moment to the longest and deepest of stillnesses they passionately sealed their pledge. [18]

The passionate undercurrent that sweeps them together turns their abstentions to endearments. There is a comic necessity in the violence of their kiss, and it has—somewhat as in Stendhal—the effect of giving energy to their passion at the expense of their consciousness.

Yet it is a pride in lucid consciousness that sanctions the lovers in their stay at Matcham. They have, with intuitive sureness, made similar plans to stay on after the Assinghams' departure, to serve as the cover for Lady Castledean's affair with Rupert Blint—never has romance been harder put than to assimilate a lover named Blint. Matcham is a house which offers "high conditions" and "almost inspiring allowances."

> Every voice in the great bright house was a call to the ingenuities and impunities of pleasure; every echo was a defiance of difficulty, doubt, or danger; every aspect of the picture, a glowing plea for the immediate. . . . Courage and good-humour therefore were the breath of the day . . . [and the prince] com-

pared the lucid result with the extraordinary substitute for perception that
presided, in the bosom of his wife, at so contented a view of his conduct and
course. . . .

Maggie's placid trust, like Adam's, stirs the Prince's resentment and contemptuous pity: "They knew . . . absolutely nothing on earth worth speaking of—whether beautifully or cynically." They were "good children"; they
had no need for knowledge, and "They were in fact constitutionally inacces-
sible to it." The very simplicity with which he is thrust into Charlotte's
company seems to "publish" him as "idiotic or incapable," to humiliate
anyone who sees himself—as the Prince must—as a *galantuomo* (20).

Yet, while the Prince expands in the atmosphere of "English equivocation" and "wonderful spirit of compromise," as the exquisite day blooms
"like a large fragrant flower he has only to gather," there are a few false
notes. His relation with Charlotte seems "sweetened with rightness," but
there is a "slightly hard ring" as she speaks with some scorn of the silence
they will win from Fanny's own "fear for herself."

There is an admirable, commanding boldness in Charlotte's offering "no
explanation, no touch for plausibility" in her words to the Assinghams (21).
And yet she does not notice that the Prince winces at her naming their
situation as "safe." When he likens the day to a "great gold cup we must
somehow drain together," Charlotte recalls his refusal to accept the gilded
crystal bowl. "Don't you think too much of 'cracks,' and aren't you too afraid
of them?" And Charlotte, as it turns out, knows the train they can take to
Gloucester and, later, to Paddington. She has already looked it up; she knows
the name of the inn; she remembers the tomb they will have claimed to visit.
"How shall I ever keep anything," the Prince asks with amusement—"some
day when I wish to?" And Charlotte replies prophetically enough, "Ah, for
things I mayn't want to know, I promise you shall find me stupid" (22).

For the Prince will at last call her "stupid" (41). He may underestimate
what she knows by the close of the novel; but in two important scenes Charlotte accepts Maggie's humiliation with a satisfaction—even a greed—that
suggests how much she may not want to know the truth. Charlotte, by the
end, has allowed a "silken noose" to be slipped around her neck by Adam;
it is the price of her preserving to the last the appearance of freedom and self-
command. One has a rather terrible sense of what Charlotte might be like if
she were not confirmed in her pride. Maggie recognizes both the anguish
and the heroic pride that make for Charlotte's final posture.

In the three principal conversations between Maggie and her father, we
find an ambiguity which is not in the least destructive of intensity. We
hardly know for certain whether Maggie is protecting her father from knowledge or confirming him in it without for a moment acknowledging that she
does so; or asking her father for a costly sacrifice, and asking it without ever

wanting to test whether he remains innocent of all that she knows or—as is possible—that he knows all and more.

Maggie takes selfishness upon herself, selfishness for Amerigo: "he's my motive—in everything." She makes a point of denying that she is jealous without any mention of what might make her so. And her account of her devotion to the Prince is very close to Nanda's account to Mr. Longdon of her helpless love for Vanderbank:

> "My idea is this, that when you only love a little you're naturally not jealous— or are only jealous also a little, so that it doesn't matter. But when you love in a deeper and intenser way, then you are, in the same proportion, jealous; your jealousy has intensity and, no doubt, ferocity. When, however, you love in the most abysmal and unutterable way of all,—why then you're beyond every- thing, and nothing can pull you down."   [37]

James gives her preparation all the minute attention it deserves, for her deepest feelings hang upon what she says. She is, as we are told elsewhere, like a circus performer, her life at stake on the high wire. She must somehow make her demand upon her father without naming Charlotte as the reason, without alluding to the affair between his wife and her husband. The need to leave that unmentioned arises in part from her uncertainty as to how much he knows, but as much from the wish to leave unspoken words that can never be retracted.

> At this it hung before her that she should have had as never yet her opportunity to say, and it held her for a minute as in a vise, her impression of his now, with his strained smile, which touched her to the deepest depths, sounding her in his secret unrest. This was the moment, in the whole process of their mutual vigilance, in which it decidedly *most* hung by the hair that their thin wall might be pierced by the lightest wrong touch. It shook between them, this transparency, with their very breath; it was an exquisite tissue, but stretched on a frame, and would give way the next instant if either so much as breathed too hard. She held her breath, for she knew by his eyes, the light at the heart of which he couldn't blind, that he was, by his intention, making sure—sure whether or no her certainty was like his.   [37]

Maggie feels herself "perched up before him on her vertiginous point," bal- ancing, almost rocking, embodying in herself the "very form of the equilib- rium they were, in their different ways, trying to save. And they were saving it—yes, they were, or at least she was." She is keeping her balance, her head; she "had kept it by the warning of his eyes." She imagines what Adam may be thinking:

> He had said to himself "She'll break down and name Amerigo; she'll say it's to him she's sacrificing me; and it's by what that will give me—with so many other things too—that my suspicion will be clinched." . . . She had presently

. . . so recovered herself that she seemed to know she could more easily have
made him name his wife than he have made her name her husband. It was there
before her that if she should so much as force him just *not* consciously to avoid
saying "Charlotte, Charlotte" he would have given himself away.

She realizes then that her father is "practically *offering* himself, pressing himself upon her, as a sacrifice" and that she, in fact, has begun to depend upon
her acceptance of his offer as the cost of preserving her marriage. She acts to
the hilt her performance of selfishness, although she knows well enough that
he sees through it. Has the situation his marriage has provided not been
"exactly what he wanted"? She accepts it as serving her ends completely; she
has, by agreement, refused to consider what "may have *really* become" of
him. What could be more convenient? And so she comes to the question:
"You don't claim, I suppose, that my natural course, once you had set up
for yourself, would have been to ship you back to American City?" She has
finally made her demand, and she senses in him "something that had been
behind, deeply in the shade, coming cautiously to the front and just feeling
its way before presenting itself. 'When you go on as you do—' " But he has
"to hold himself to say it"—"you make me quite want to ship back myself.
You make me quite feel as if American City would be the best place for us."
For *us?* "For me and Charlotte" (37).

     In this moment of rather desolate triumph, Maggie sees the cost to Char-
lotte, "removed, transported, doomed." But it is her father who has named
Charlotte, not she; "she had made him do it *all* for her, and had lighted the
way to it without naming her husband." As Adam derides the idea of sacrifice, she thinks of all his invisible power. "His very quietness was part of it
now, as always part of everything, of his success, his originality, his modesty, his exquisite public perversity, his inscrutable, incalculable energy;"
and this quality "placed him in her eyes as no precious work of art probably
had ever been placed in his own." For a moment she is the "charmed gazer,
in the still museum, before the named and dated object . . . that time has
polished and consecrated." (It is important to recognize that the Ververs see
themselves as well as others as works of art, and that the Prince at moments
sees Charlotte as one. James does not make this aesthetic sense an inhuman
one.) His strength and sureness—as much in his moral as in his aesthetic
"sense"—make her conscious that "he was simply a great and deep and high
little man, and that to love him with tenderness was not to be distinguished,
a whit, from loving him with pride." She recognizes that here again, in his
sacrifice of himself, as in his marriage, he isn't a "failure." His own strength
and pride raise her too, and she can say with all conviction, "I believe in you
more than any one." As she considers all the statement means, she reaffirms
it. "And that's the way, I think, you believe in me." His answer is charm-

ingly easy: "About the way—yes." And the scene ends with his drawing her to him. "He held her hand and kept her long, and she let herself go; but it was an embrace that, august and almost stern, produced, for all its intimacy, no revulsion and broke into no inconsequence of tears" (37).

"August and almost stern"—to that phrase I would oppose the high style and accomplished grace of the Prince and Charlotte. In a speech that Charlotte does not make but that Maggie imagines for her, she says, with disdain for Maggie and her father, "Ours was everything a relation could be, filled to the brim with the wine of consciousness" (40). The lovers acquire something like the urbanity and assurance Stendhal celebrates in Mosca and Gina Sanseverina, and the scene at Matcham (which has its false notes, too) has an aesthetic appeal ("every aspect of the picture, a glowing plea for the immediate") which restores the Prince's sense of a "higher and braver propriety" than that of the Ververs (20). In contrast, Maggie, once she is awakened from her innocence, begins to recognize something threatening in that high style. She feels herself "being beautifully treated" by both Charlotte and Amerigo. Charlotte overwhelms her with "excesses of civility," "sudden little formalisms," that have the effect of "throwing over their intercourse a kind of silver tissue of decorum." Such attentions isolate her rather than comfort her, and the "worked-out scheme for their not wounding her, for their behaving to her quite nobly," comes to feel like a conspiracy. "They had built her in with their purpose—which was why, above her, a vault seemed more heavily to arch; so that she sat there, in the solid chamber of her helplessness, as in a bath of benevolence artfully prepared for her." There is a shift from benevolence to control, from generosity to coercion. "They had got her into the bath and, for consistency with themselves —which was with each other—must keep her there." The high style has become quite sinister (26).

It is a large element in Maggie's loss of innocence that she must plot against others in turn and eventually control them. But, most of all, she comes at last to do what she most dreaded, to sacrifice her father. Earlier, she had had a vision of him urging her to sacrifice him, "bleating it at her, all conscious and all accommodating, like some precious, spotless, exceptionally intelligent lamb." But "the lucidity of his intention" made such an act, even if it were otherwise thinkable, impossible. "The only way to sacrifice him would be to do so without his dreaming what it might be for" (28). As we have seen, they must both come much further before she can act; she must explore the "accumulation of the unanswered," the "confused objects" kept locked up and out of the way—buried, repressed, unacknowledged (25). It is only under the pressure of great suffering that she must finally ask her father for the sacrifice she does.

"August and almost stern"—does the phrase characterize "people whose

newfound greatness comes from making deals in which they do not lose?"
All through the book—I cite Stuart Hampshire—"the imagery of glitter and
superficial brilliance is attached to the Europeans, of watchfulness and dim
tenacity to the Americans. Thinking they are betraying the others, the Europeans betray themselves in their disunion and they are defeated. . . . The
tables have been turned, and the dry, Puritan innocence has come to seem a
kind of corruption, and the light corruption of the Europeans, which is only
amatory license and casual greed, has come to seem a kind of innocence."
This is a view that many have held, although few have stated it so well. In
the sentence I have so far omitted, Hampshire makes the ironic turn of the
novel even sharper: "Held by a silken cord, Charlotte is taken into captivity,
and the sullen power of money has prevailed over the infinitely desirable
freedom and self-indulgence, which only money can make secure."[13] This is
the kind of reading which Jane Austen's *Mansfield Park* has often received,
with Fanny Price and Edmund Bertram (as well as Sir Thomas) enacting the
"dry, Puritan innocence" (ascribed there to Evangelicalism). The "light corruption" of Henry Crawford is to elope with a vain woman who despises her
husband (who may be rightly despised, but perhaps not by such a wife—the
complexities are, as always, something of a strain), and the "light corruption" of his sister Mary is to take her brother's corruption as light.

In *The Golden Bowl* we may be struck by the genuine tenderness Maggie
and Adam feel for each other, their delicacy of address and tactful silences.
They do not, it is true, engage in the open candor that our own manners
encourage, but it seems to me at the last clear that they have come well
beyond a "puritanic innocence," that they have imposed nothing on the
Prince and on Charlotte that those "victims" do not accept. The disunion of
the lovers arises from the Prince's remorse. He can assert, as he talks to
Maggie of the golden bowl they failed to purchase and left for her to find,
"You've never been more sacred to me than you were at that hour—unless
perhaps you've become so at this one." They are not words of insincere consolation. Maggie feels "as if something cold and momentarily unimaginable
breathed upon her, from afar off, out of his strange consistency" (34). In the
moment that follows, the Prince cuts himself off from Charlotte and resolves
to give her no account of what Maggie knows. Maggie has spared the Prince;
she has wanted to say (but could not), "arrange yourself so as to suffer least,
or to be, at any rate, least distorted or disfigured." She has a "glimpse of the
precious truth that by her helping him, helping him to help himself, as it
were, she should help him to help *her*." She gets into the "labyrinth" with
him; and, as he prepares to commit himself to her, there "occurred between
them a kind of unprecedented moral exchange over which her superior lucidity presided." She is no longer controlled, and she refuses to control the
others in turn by the mode of exploitation they have used. Her lucidity is
not Kate Croy's; it is awareness of more than one's interest and its necessities.

Charlotte's role in the novel is the most destructive and the most pitiable, and she raises most clearly the question of consciousness. Charlotte Stant is of the company of Madame Merle and Kate Croy; she is as courageous and perhaps as ruthless as Mrs. Brookenham; she has led a difficult and lonely life with great resourcefulness and a certain splendor. She is most impressive at the Foreign Office reception with which part III opens. Everything goes to make "her personal scheme a success, the *proved* private theory that materials to work with had been all she required and that there were none too precious for her to understand and use." She senses a crisis in her remaining alone with the Prince at the reception, and the ease with which she accepts a crisis helps her "to the right view of her opportunity for happiness" (14). She meets Fanny Assingham's criticism with "good humour, candour, clearness and, obviously, the *real* truth." But the directness, like "her fine and slightly hard radiance," seems always to exceed necessity, to edge toward self-assertion and at least a hint of aggression. A somewhat edgy pride, a somewhat imperceptive scorn make her massively "stupid." She can bring no moral imagination to her great encounters with Maggie. In each case she exacts humiliation and is disarmed by her own sense of power. When Adam, in effect, holds her in a "silken noose," ready to go with him to America, Maggie hears Charlotte's voice—"high and clear and little hard"—as she exhibits the Verver collection to visitors. Maggie hears in the "high coerced quaver"—and the Prince does too—"the shriek of a soul in pain."

But what Maggie can hear is what Charlotte cannot hear in others and cannot believe that others hear in her. Charlotte must believe that she can carry off her role, and Maggie helps Charlotte hide humiliation by allowing her "the sense of highly choosing." Pride becomes "the mantle caught up for protection and perversity." Charlotte "flung it round her as a denial of any loss of her freedom." She cannot confess to a sense of doom because she cannot admit that she has incurred one, that she has been false. And so Maggie offers the support of a new abjection. She draws down Charlotte's rage and accusations—which Charlotte seems utterly to believe for the present: "How I see that you loathed our marriage!" And when Charlotte demands, "You haven't worked against me?" Maggie takes the question as if it were a "captured fluttering bird" she held to her breast. "What does it matter—if I've failed?" (39) As Ruth Yeazell has written, Charlotte's "sudden declaration of love for Adam and American City may be a simple lie, yet it may also represent a glorious self-delusion—a delusion so deeply willed that it has become, in a manner of speaking, the truth."[14] James wrote of belief in an essay on immortality; and there, too, he treats the value of a saving belief (perhaps a "merciful muddle"):

If one acts from desire quite as one would from belief, it signifies little what name one gives one's motive. By which term action I mean action of mind, mean that I can encourage my consciousness to acquire that interest, to live in that elasticity and that affluence, which affect me as symptomatic and auspicious. I can't do less if I desire, but I shouldn't be able to do more if I believed.

What matters most, I think, is that we recognize a failure in Charlotte of the moral imagination we find in Maggie. In its place is the rather fierce will to believe that mitigates an otherwise intolerable sense of loss. May Charlotte yet make a life for herself in American City? Adam implies as much, and Maggie rises in imagination to the "vision of all he might mean." She hears in her father the "note of possession and control," and it promises that Charlotte "wasn't to be wasted." Adam has the "ability to rest upon high values." Maggie and Adam look once more at the "early Florentine sacred subject" he gave her on her marriage. "The tenderness represented to her by his sacrifice of such a treasure had become, to her sense, a part of the whole infusion"; the "beauty of his sentiment looked out at her, always from the beauty of the rest, as if the frame made positively a window for his spiritual face." That is as far as James comes toward allegory, and it is not very far at all. What he is bringing into focus is the similarity of such acts of sacrifice to the works of spiritual intensity of Florentine artists. He wants us also to see the pain they may cost, and we are left with the Prince holding Maggie, saying, "See? I see nothing but you." But "the truth of it had so strangely lighted his eyes that, as for pity and dread of them, she buried her own in his breast." The pity and dread are not for a repining captive; they are for the pain and vulnerability of the kind of love which she has felt and which he now shares. It is a moment of supreme lucidity and of the frightening fullness of consciousness.

10 ✻ Conrad:
The Limits of Irony

In *The Fable of the Bees* Bernard Mandeville created a dazzling paradox: private vices are public benefits. The more self-indulgent a nation, the more trade it generates: the more people it must employ in the manufacture and transport of luxuries, the more services it will require and reward. On the contrary, an abstemious people are content with little, live on their own productions, remain a self-subsistent nation with little need for commerce or expansion and of little note in the world. Clearly such a paradox seems to undermine morality; and it was designed, in fact, to reveal the confusions of moral idealism. What Mandeville does is to name as vice any action or appetite which is self-regarding or self-interested. How much self-interest leads to vice? There is Mandeville's hook: the least trace of self-interest or of incidental pleasure, even if it should coexist with far more significant service to others, will convict an action of being a form of vice. Public benefits, on the other hand, are the bustling energy and prosperity of a society—its richness, complexity, amplitude—rather than its culture, justice, or morality. Mandeville has made his definitions so restrictive as to allow him a double standard; in private actions, there is little room left for virtue; in public actions, little room for vice.[1]

Something like this occurs in Conrad. Conrad is fascinated by the nature of belief: the degree to which it commands loyalty and is shared by men, the extent to which it outruns actuality and becomes "idea," the precariousness it shows when one man's skepticism undermines the conviction of others. Much of the time, struck by the lack of apodictic certainty in these beliefs or the lack of sufficient reason for holding them, Conrad calls them illusions. We hold these beliefs regardless of their truth because they serve our human purposes or social needs. But what if our beliefs *are* true? That hardly matters. If any belief, true or not, can be construed as also offering us confidence or pleasure, as offering us in short anything more or other than truth, it may be considered illusion. There are few beliefs on which humans act which cannot, on these terms, be categorized as illusions; for the limits of truth are made so narrow as to seem all but evanescent.

On the other hand, it is only by the power to give oneself wholly to a belief, to act upon it without doubt or question, as if it were absolute, that man can achieve the heroism or idealism he most admires. But the devotion is not enough in itself. To be heroic is to live consciously behond one's means, to surpass that so-called realism which reduces life to fit the limited powers of the general run of mankind. Heroism becomes an intensity of belief that may be either grand or terrible; its sublimity elevates it above conventional standards of morality. In *Lord Jim* Marlow speaks of the Dutch pepper traders of the seventeenth century:

> Where wouldn't they go for pepper? For a bag of pepper they would cut each other's throats without hesitation, and would forswear their souls of which they were so careful otherwise: the bizarre obstinacy of that desire made them defy death in a thousand shapes. . . . . It made them great! By heavens! it made them heroic. . . . They left their bones to lie bleaching on distant shores, so that wealth might flow to the living at home. To us, their less tried successors, they appear magnified, not as agents of trade but as instruments of a recorded destiny, pushing out into the unknown in obedience to an inward voice, to an impulse beating in the blood, to a dream of the future. They were wonderful; and it must be owned they were ready for the wonderful. . . .

In this passage commercial greed and fierce competition are transformed, sublimated by their excess into a heroism we admire for its boldness and tenacity. Conrad later remarked that "mere love of adventure is no saving grace. It is no grace at all. It lays a man under no obligations of faithfulness to an idea and even to his own self. . . . There is no sort of loyalty to bind him in honour to consistent conduct." And Conrad insists upon the importance of work; the English did not go out for the sake of adventure, they "went out to toil in adventurous conditions."[2]

Like Mandeville's merchants, the pepper traders turn private vices into public benefits. It is significantly in traders that Conrad sees heroic achievement. It is their neglect of ideal purpose—their "bizarre obstinacy"—that makes them able to transcend themselves, to act as if they were moved by a "dream of the future." But sublimity carries its terrors as well: the idea, whatever its grandeur, may become an insane refusal to acknowledge the actual. The sublime may tumble into the ludicrous, where what thinks itself transcendence is mere insufficiency, where intensity of commitment is blind self-assertion. Our illusions are testimony to the outrageously exalted conception we entertain of our nature. Conrad constantly juxtaposes the magnificence of a commanding idea with the impoverishment or denial of life that it may require. Is man redeemed by such an idea or enslaved by it? Conrad can turn his argument either way: disdain for the man who does not participate in the idea or mockery of the man who sacrifices the actual good for the specter of the ideal.

A point of special concern for Conrad is the strain of self-consciousness, which may arise from isolation or from doubt. His epigraph from Novalis for *Lord Jim* suggest this. "It is certain my conviction gains infinitely, the moment another soul will believe." The abverb "infinitely" reveals how tortured solitary belief may be. But a shared belief depends upon the mutual support of its participants. They may be likened to a shipwrecked crew who keep each other afloat by locking arms. If the circle is broken, everyone is threatened at once. Or to change the figure, it is the straggler from the ranks, like Jim, who makes the rest of the marchers aware of their own weariness and of the effort they must sustain. It is here that we sense most clearly the pain of self-consciousness, that most disabling of afflictions in heroic endeavor.

Typically, Conrad lavished his rage upon self-consciousness. "You know how bad it is," he wrote to Edward Garnett, "when one *feels* one's liver, or lungs. Well, I feel my brain. I am distinctly conscious of the contents of my head. My story is there in a fluid—in an evading shape. I can't get hold of it." In the same key of morose frivolity, he writes of his son Borys: "I would like to make a bargeman of him: strong, knowing his business, and thinking of nothing. That is *the* life, my dear fellow! Thinking of nothing! O bliss!" And a few months later he wrote to another friend in a similar vein: "I am like a tight-rope dancer who, in the midst of his performance, should suddenly discover that he knows nothing about tight-rope dancing. He may appear ridiculous to the spectators, but a broken neck is the result of such untimely wisdom." [3] Conrad used a similar figure in *The Secret Agent* for a police inspector's troubled interview with his superior: "He felt at the moment like a tight-rope artist . . . if suddenly in the middle of the performance, the manager of the Music Hall were to rush out of the proper managerial seclusion and begin to shake the rope." Significantly, there is an *indignant* "sense of moral insecurity engendered by such a *treacherous* proceeding joined to the immediate apprehension of a broken neck. . . . And there should be also some scandalized concern for his art, too, since a man must identify himself with something more tangible than his own personality." There is even a special blow to pride in that "the rope was not (so much) shaken for the purpose of breaking his neck, as by an exhibition of impudence." [4] Conrad has brought together various ways in which we face this sudden awakening to the processes we are usually allowed to take for granted: fear, anger, insult or shame, the sense of being ridiculous or absurd. Such coming to consciousness is so painfully unsettling that few can wish for it. As Conrad puts it in writing of himself, "the tragic part of the business is *my being aware of it.* . . . Which proves the saving power of illusions." [5]

Yet, however painful self-consciousness may be, the unthinking surrender to illusion seems in turn like a form of self-mutilation. Here, again, Conrad can turn his paradox in either direction. When his socialist friend Cunninghame Graham wrote of the value that Singleton, the stalwart seaman in *The Nigger of the Narcissus,* might have acquired with an education, Conrad replied: "Would you seriously . . . cultivate in that unconscious man the power to think. Then he would become conscious—and much smaller—and very unhappy. Now he is simple and great like an elemental force. Nothing can touch him but the curse of decay. . . . Nothing else can touch him— he does not think."[6] But in *Typhoon,* where he created another simple, inarticulate man, Captain MacWhirr, Conrad describes him as one who has sailed over the oceans "as some men go skimming over the years of existence to sink gently into a placid grave, ignorant of life to the last, without ever having been made to see all that it may contain of perfidy, of violence, and of terror. There are on the sea and land such men thus fortunate—or thus disdained by destiny or by the sea." The absence of imagination gives MacWhirr the stability under stress that Lord Jim notably lacks: MacWhirr is not the victim of too vivid an imagination of disaster: "If the ship had to go after all, then, at least, she wouldn't be going to the bottom with a lot of people in her fighting teeth and claw. That would have been odious. And in that feeling there was a humane intention and a vague sense of the fitness of things."[7] But must one, in order to effectuate this "humane intention," be "ignorant of life," like an "elemental force"? Clearly Conrad can find a middle ground. As C. T. Watts points out, "instinct and intellect may sometimes be curbed and blended . . . by the school of tradition, necessity and authority. . . . When Singleton steers with care, he acts instinctively only in so far as his instincts have been chastened by training, and intellectually only within a narrow range of simple decisions which have become almost instinctive."[8]

The question is not whether Conrad could escape paradox but why he tried so often to achieve it. Why did he force together words which he had subjected to such restrictive or expansive redefinition? Why did he like to insist that all beliefs are illusions, that all innocence is ignorance, that all consciousness is pain or conflict, that fidelity to a cause is lapse of thought, that wholeheartedness is blindness? In part, it seems to satisfy his need to see through our shifts and pretexts, as when he compares living actors unfavorably with marionettes, As he describes the living actors, they gradually turn from make-believe to insincerity, from art to deception: "There is a taint of subtle corruption in their blank voices, in their blinking eyes, in the grimacing faces, in the false light, in the false passion, in the words that have been learned by heart."

But I love a marionette show. . . . Their impassibility in love, in crime, in mirth, in sorrow,—is heroic, superhuman, fascinating. Their rigid violence when they fall upon one another to embrace or to fight is simply a joy to behold. I never listen to the text mouthed somewhere out of sight by invisible men who are here to day and rotten to morrow. I love the marionettes that are without life, that come so near to being immortal![9]

The marionettes have the clarity and rigidity of the ideal. Their lifelessness enjoys the immortality of the inorganic as opposed to the corruptibility of the human. Just short of this rigidity is the obsessed idealist. Of Don Quixote, Conrad wrote: "He rides forth, his head encircled by a halo—the patron saint of all lives spoiled or saved by the irresistible force of imagination. But he was not a good citizen."[10] The pairing of "spoiled or saved" permits Conrad to move in either direction. What he often chooses is to move in both directions, like the Dutch printmaker Escher, to produce a deadlock for ironic contemplation.

Conrad enjoys presenting an impossible choice, as in an early letter to Marguerita Poradowska:

> But you are afraid of yourself; of the inseparable being forever at your side—master and slave, victim and executioner—who suffers and causes suffering. That's how it is! One must drag the ball and chain of one's selfhood to the end. It is the [price] one pays for the devilish and divine privilege of thought; so that in this life it is only the elect who are convicts—a glorious band which comprehends and groans but which treads the earth amidst a multitude of phantoms with maniacal gestures, with idiotic grimaces. Which would you be, idiot or convict?[11]

This grim pleasure in seeing through conventional and acceptable contrasts to a more radical distinction which offers no easy choice is evident in many of Conrad's letters to Cunninghame Graham:

> I envy you. Alas! What you want to reform are not institutions—it is human nature. Your faith will never move that mountain. Not that I think mankind intrinsically bad. It is only silly and cowardly. Now *You* know that in cowardice is every evil—especially that cruelty so characteristic of our civilisation. But without it mankind would vanish. No great matter truly. But will you persuade humanity to throw away sword and shield? Can you persuade even me—Who write these words in the fulness of an irresistible conviction? No. I belong to the wretched gang. We all belong to it. We are born initiated, and succeeding generations clutch the inheritance of fear and brutality without a thought, without a doubt, without compunction—in the name of God.[12]

This has the strength of taking a full view of the worst, but it is also reductive and fatalistic. A few of the wretched gang are somehow able to see through the thoughtless brutality of others. Is it finally the supreme disenchantment to see through those few too, not excluding oneself? Conrad cannot resist the pleasures of disenchantment; mistaking it, I should say, for detachment, perhaps for wisdom. It is an attitude he often treats with scorn in others, but the scorn itself is elevated to another level in the process and wins a new exemption.

In 1908, Conrad wrote to protest Arthur Symons's suggestion that he gloated over scenes of cruelty and was obsessed by visions of spilt blood:

> One thing that I am certain of is that I have approached the object of my task, things human, in a spirit of piety. The earth is a temple where there is going on a mystery play, childish and poignant, ridiculous and awful enough, in all conscience. Once in I've tried to behave decently . . . I've tried to write with dignity, not out of regard for myself, but for the sake of the spectacle, the play with an obscure beginning and an unfathomable *dénouement*.
>
> I don't think that this has been noticed . . . Thus I've been called a heartless wretch, a man without ideals and a *poseur* of brutality. But I will confess to you under seal of secrecy that *I don't believe* I am such as I appear to mediocre minds.[13]

Presumably, it is not at Symons himself that the last phrase is flicked, but it is a note of condescension into which Conrad often falls.

The best statement of Conrad's readiness to see through man's typical errors and self-deception lies in his tribute to Anatole France: "He is a great analyst of illusions. He searches and probes their innermost recesses as if they were realities made of an eternal substance." Thus far Conrad is praising his French contemporary for the intention he himself avows in a letter to Sir Sidney Colvin: "all my concern has been with the 'ideal' value of things, events, and people. That and nothing else." It is the "ideal" value that interests Anatole France:

> He feels that men, born in ignorance as in the house of an enemy, and condemned to struggle with error and passions through endless centuries, should be spared the supreme cruelty of a hope for ever deferred. He knows that our best hopes are unrealisable; that it is the almost incredible misfortune of mankind, but also its highest privilege, to aspire towards the impossible; that men have never failed to defeat their highest aims by the very strength of their humanity, which can conceive the most gigantic tasks but leaves them disarmed before their irremediable littleness. He knows this well because he is an artist and a master; but he knows, too, that only in the continuity of effort there is a refuge from despair for minds less clear-seeing and philosophic than his own. Therefore he wishes us to believe and to hope, preserving in our activity the consoling illusion of power and intelligent purpose. He is a good and politic prince.[14]

What should be noted, I think, is that Conrad esteems hopes to the degree that they surpass the feasible, that he admires the aspiration that outruns realization and should leave us, if we were to become fully aware of our nature, to despair of its attainment. That some can live with that awareness, Conrad indicates in his words on Henry James:

> [The] usual methods of solution by rewards and punishments, by crowned love, by fortune, by a broken leg or a sudden death . . . are legitimate inasmuch as they satisfy the desire for finality, for which our hearts yearn with a longing greater than the longing for the loaves and fishes of this earth. Perhaps the only true desire of mankind, coming thus to light in its hours of leisure, is to be set at rest. One is never set at rest by Mr. Henry James's novels. . . . You remain with the sense of the life still going on. . . . It is eminently satisfying, but it is not final. Mr. Henry James, great artist and faithful historian, never attempts the impossible.[15]

Even Anatole France in turn may forget those hard truths that are the basis of his "profound and unalterable compassion." To become an active socialist, he must be able "to discard his philosophy; to forget that the evils are many and the remedies are few . . . that fatality is invincible, that there is an implacable menace of death in the triumph of the humanitarian ideal. He may forget all that because love is stronger than truth." Such love encourages us to action, as truth may not, for the reasons that Conrad set forth in *Nostromo*: "Action is consolatory. It is the enemy of thought and the friend of flattering illusions. Only in the conduct of our action can we find the sense of mastery over the Fates." But that "consoling illusion of power and intelligent purpose," indulged too freely, may only induce the "supreme cruelty of a hope for ever deferred." Conrad was moved by his reading of Tolstoy to speak of Christianity as "the only religion which with its impossible standards, has brought an infinity of anguish to innumerable souls—on this earth."[16]

Again Conrad warns, in writing of Alphonse Daudet, there may be a "considerable want of candour" in the "august view of life." The "blind agitation" hardly deserves the "artistic fuss made over it." The august view and the artistic fuss may be "consoling'"; but "it is scarcely honest to shout at those who struggle drowning in an insignificant pool: You are indeed admirable and great to be the victim of such a profound, of such a terrible ocean!" Daudet does not fall into such portentousness; nor "does he sit on a pedestal in the hierarchic and imbecile pose of some cheap god whose greatness consists in being too stupid to care." His characters are "seen," and "the man who is not an artist is seen also, commiserating, indignant, joyous, human and alive in their very midst. Inevitably they *marchent à la mort*—and they are very near the truth of our common destiny; their fate is poignant, it is intensely interesting, and of not the slightest consequence." [17]

That last phrase, like so many in Conrad, makes one ask what kind of consequence is to be expected, what kind of meaning and how much of it should one hope to find in life. Marlow states the problem in *Lord Jim*: "Are not our lives too short for that full utterance which through all our stammerings is of course our only and abiding intention? I have given up expecting those last words, whose ring, if they could only be pronounced, would shake both heaven and earth" (21). Marlow speaks with disappointment of our need to surrender the hope; but is the hope a sensible one to begin with? Does life have a meaning? Is there an ultimate wisdom? The questions need only to be asked to make us wonder whether they do not provide Conrad with a rhetoric of nostalgia. George Eliot sees no source of meaning in our lives but what we give them, nor does she insist upon a radical disjunction between what we must believe and what we can do. She makes do without opiates, but she credits man's capacity for generosity and aspiration, and she sees in this a sufficient realism. Conrad can take a similar view at times. He speaks of the artist's need for hope and for "all the piety of effort and renunciation" that hope implies. "To be hopeful in an artistic sense it is not necessary to think that the world is good. It is enough to believe that there is no impossibility of its being made so." [18]

Conrad can also allow himself to see the "idea" being mysteriously born in common actions—in this case of men at sea:

> Who can tell how a tradition comes into the world? We are children of the earth. It may be that the noblest tradition is but the offspring of material conditions, of the hard necessities besetting man's precarious lives. But once it has been born it becomes a spirit. Nothing can extinguish its force then. Clouds of greedy selfishness, the subtle dialectics of revolt or fear, may obscure it for a time, but in very truth it remains an immortal ruler invested with power of honour and shame.

This recognition of the emergence of spirit from its material conditions counteracts the arrogance of pessimism (as Conrad describes it), that "elated sense of his own superiority" with which an author takes a "proud and unholy joy" in the discovery of evil. Such arrogance robs him of that "absolute loyalty towards his feelings and sensations an author should keep hold of in his most exalted moments of creation." [19] There seems to be at least some measure of implicit reproach, or at least of warning, to himself in these remarks. They serve in Conrad's discursive prose the function that characters like Decoud perform; they permit Conrad to recognize and perhaps exorcise aspects of himself.

Something of this is at work in a well-known passage of *A Personal Record*.

There Conrad rejects the "ethical view of the universe," much as he had Christianity, for the cruel hopes and absurd disappointments it creates. He would rather believe that the function of the universe was "purely spectacular" and "in this view—and in this view alone—never for despair!" When we resign the expectation of an ethical meaning, we can give "unwearied self-forgetful attention" to the "living universe reflected in our consciousness." The only task left is "to bear true testimony to the visible wonder, the haunting terror, the infinite passion and illimitable serenity; to the supreme law and abiding mystery of the sublime spectacle." Yet the experience of the spectacle is the inverse of a religious or ethical view; it is constituted by the absence of meaning, the nostalgia for which it holds off with a romantic defiance. To see the universe as spectacle is to adopt a stance outside of life, our powers to affect it no longer in question, our concern replaced by ironic wonder, our faith converted into a perhaps resentful bravado.[20] But seen under a less ironic view, in the famous preface to *The Nigger of the Narcissus,* the artist speaks not only to "our capacity for delight and wonder," but "to the latent feeling of a fellowship with all creation—and to the subtle but invincible conviction of solidarity." That sense of solidarity unites us in feeling, in common aspirations and illusions; it "binds together all humanity—the dead to the living and the living to the unborn."[21] We come round, then, to the beliefs which we must live by as either convicts or idiots, with full awareness or with none. At its most romantic the conscience can glory in its indomitable power—a power of unaccountable commitment and despotic illusion. But the obverse side of that assertion is the inevitable threat to all belief. What Bertrand Russell saw in Conrad himself we can often see in his fiction: "he thought of civilized and morally tolerable human life as a dangerous walk on a thin crust of barely cooled lava which at any moment might break and let the unwary sink into fiery depths."[22]

We find Conrad's characters divided between those who have accepted illusion as the cost (or reward) of action and those who can recognize—not without pathos—the fragility of man's illusions. To the extent that we are idiots, we take the illusion as truth and act unquestioningly in its name, tyrants and slaves at once of the idea. To the extent that we are convicts, we recognize the illusion for what it is and see beyond it to the ironic indifference of the "sublime spectacle." We may live by our traditional moral beliefs without needing to claim some illusory authority for them; but the very reflection which makes us recognize these beliefs as the "illusions" they are may disqualify us in turn for action. Conrad speaks of detachment as a faculty born of a "sense of infinite littleness" and "yet the only faculty that seems to assimilate man to the immortal gods." It is to the wisdom but not the power of the gods that man is assimilated. Those characters who can live with truth live alone and are ineffectual, and here we return to the aesthetic spectacle.

How can "romantic feeling of reality" subsist with the knowledge of the truth? "It only tries to make the best of it, hard as it may be; and in this hardness discovers a certain aspect of beauty." [23]

Lord Jim

Conrad's *Lord Jim* is a work that explores and profoundly questions romanticism, and it takes the form of a meditation on the romantic hero. To Jim falls the burden of action and to Marlow that of reflection. Marlow can fully exercise his powers of thought because, within the novel, nothing else is required of him. There is no action for his consciousness to block or disable. And while in a real sense Marlow's own fate—or his conception of himself— is tied to his reflections on Jim, still we recognize in Marlow a power to subsist without certitudes. Marlow is not "romantic" to the same degree as Jim; but the memory of having been romantic has great importance for him. He is in that respect not unlike the narrator of Byron's *Don Juan,* disabused and critical of youthful folly but at the same time envious of its capacity for passion and of the grandeur of its illusions. Marlow has, one can say, unfinished business with romantic dreams. We know little about what has intervened between the time of such dreams and the moment of his meeting Jim, but it is clear that the enormity of Jim's failure and the tortured incomprehension with which Jim tries to evade his guilt have the power to unsettle Marlow like a painful memory of his own. He must hold unremittingly to what he knows is reality lest Jim's imagination somehow contaminate his own.

Jim has come out of a peaceful life where no issues were raised, much less met; his father, a parson, "possessed such certain knowledge of the unknowable as made for the righteousness of people in cottages without disturbing the ease of mind of those whom an unerring Providence enables to live in mansions" (1). Like his father, Jim can overlook difficulties: if he is immobilized by danger, he can believe that his superior courage disdains the vanity of display. As a young officer, Jim makes his choice without awareness that he has done so. He sails as chief mate on the *Patna*—having chosen to remain in the East—and we see its remarkable cargo of eight hundred passengers, Moslems from all kinds of life, joined together by "the call of an idea," as "pilgrims of an exacting faith" (2).

In the transition from the close of the second chapter to the third Conrad gives two pictures of the *Patna* traversing Eastern waters. In the first, we see it from the outside in its fragility under the eye of the merciless sun, the identical hot days "falling into an abyss forever open in the wake of the ship." The ship holds on "her steadfast way black and smouldering in a luminous immensity, as if scorched by a flame flicked at her from a heaven without pity." But in the calm amidships, where the five white officers live, there is only the "assurance of everlasting security." Jim, as he stands a watch on the bridge, feels "the great certitude of unbounded safety and peace that could be read on the silent aspect of nature, like the certitude of fostering love upon the placid tenderness of a mother's face." In his undemanding tasks Jim is free to entertain dreams of "valorous deeds." They have "a gorgeous virility" and "the charm of vagueness," and he imagines there is "nothing he cannot face" (3).

Conrad gives us only the shallow surface of dreams that Jim indulges; their imagery, based in part on "light holiday literature," is not drawn from the private world and local scenes Jim inhabits. The very generality is appropriate enough, for it represents at once withdrawal from the actual, the indefinite solitude of a gentle narcissism, and the triteness of a conventional mind. Jim has not yet begun to live. He is sufficiently defined for himself by his contrast with the passengers and the rest of the officers. The latter are grotesquely ugly, particularly the captain, who looks "like a clumsy effigy of a man cut out of a block of fat." But their grossness and obscenity only confirm Jim's belief in his privileged world: "They could not touch him; he shared the air they breathed, but he was different . . ."(3).

The novel begins in medias res with Jim as a ship-chandler, a customer's man, persuading ships' captains to trade with the dealer whose profits he promotes. But, apart from that brief glimpse of Jim, we come to know him most clearly at the official hearings after the *Patna* disaster, where he alone of his ship's officers presents himself, and in his dinner and conversation with Marlow. The note of all that is to follow is given in the painful exposure Jim makes of his self-contempt. When he hears someone say "Look at that wretched cur," he takes for granted that the words have been directed at him. He spins about, ready to fight Marlow or whoever else may have spoken. For a moment Jim has the opportunity to attribute the feelings he has about himself to someone else and to fight them in some external and immediate way. But even that sad consolation is denied him by the sight of an actual dog. All that remains is Jim's open avowal, a new source of shame, of his expectation that he will be thought a cur. When Marlow overtakes him and taxes him with running away, Jim is instantly defiant and proud: "From no man—from not a single man on earth." But there is, of course, one man he doesn't consider; it is from himself that he is running away (6).

The long scene in the dining room and on the verandah of the hotel is a fine study of Jim's desperate evasion of the painful truth of his role on board the *Patna*. Here, for the first time, he has a history with which he is concerned and we are involved, and he begins to acquire identity. We learn in this scene what has not been established earlier, that the *Patna* has survived the officers' desertion and has been towed to port by a French vessel. The

crime, therefore, has become a pure instance of the failure to observe the
code of duty. It has unrelieved ugliness rather than any of the spurious grandeur it might have acquired from horror. And Marlow finds Jim's manner
confusing at first: "He talked soberly, with a sort of composed unreserve,
and with a quiet bearing that might have been the outcome of manly self-
control, of impudence, of callousness, of a colossal unconsciousness, of a
gigantic deception. Who can tell! From our tone we might have been discussing a third person, a football match, last year's weather." The unreality
of the talk persists; for Jim seems to exhibit "some conviction of innate
blamelessness," and he exhibits it, contradictorily, in the severe judgments
he makes of his action. He achieves simultaneously a specious honesty of
self-accusation and a specious severity of judgment. The judge and the defendant are mingled in one man, the judge gaining the sympathy the defendant exacts, the defendant gaining the honor due to the judge.

Marlow sees through this spectacle of Jim's self-deception: "I didn't know
how much of it he believed himself. I didn't know what he was playing up
to—if he was playing up to anything at all—and I suspect he did not know
either; for it is my belief no man ever understands quite his own artful dodge
to escape from the grim shadow of self-knowledge." At moments the delusion becomes so outrageous that Marlow must respond with an irony that is
a mixture of the therapeutic and the vindictive. For every fall into painful
self-awareness Jim finds a "fresh foothold" on self-justification. He is most
painfully transparent as he thinks with incredulity of the fact that the threatened bulkhead held. He is soon well beyond that fact into a vision of the
ship sinking ("My god! what a chance missed!") and seems lost in a "fanciful
realm of recklessly heroic aspirations." As Jim becomes absorbed in a vision
of the heroism he might have achieved, his face betrays "a strange look of
beatitude." Marlow's reply is an angry defense of the actual: "If you had
stuck to this ship, you mean!" And Jim is shocked into awareness, "as though
he had tumbled down from a star" (7).

Jim's sophistry converts a moral sanction, which must be absolute for the
man who acknowledges a duty, into the calculus of probability. He thinks
back to the thin bulkhead, which should, by all expectation, have given.
"There was not the thickness of a sheet of paper between the right and wrong
of this affair." To that Marlow can reply only with the grim irony of one
who insists upon those necessary distinctions that constitute our moral life:
"How much more did you want?" Jim goes on obliviously lamenting the
unfairness of his plight: "Not the breadth of a hair between this and that,"
and Marlow responds with vicious point, "It is difficult to see a hair at
midnight." Marlow's feelings are important here: "I was aggrieved against
him as though he had cheated me—me!—of a splendid opportunity to keep
up the illusion of my beginnings, as though he had robbed our common life

of the last spark of its glamour." "And so," he adds savagely, "you cleared out—at once" (11).

Jim's imagination is quite different from the subtle awareness which Marlow displays. His imagination has no room for sympathetic regard for others' feelings; it is too busy with fantasies, whether wishful or defensive. When he speaks of his peculiar unreadiness to act, it is as if he were still in the midst of irrevocable disaster; his fancy overleaps the actual and plunges him into the horror that seems once more to be ahead. In retrospect Jim's panic and hysteria have disguised from him the fears he did have and lead him to swear that it was not death he feared. Not death perhaps, Marlow reflects, but "he was afraid of the emergency. . . . He wanted to die without added terrors, quietly, in a sort of peaceful trance." And one is led to think back to those moments of easy languor aboard the untroubled *Patna,* when nothing could seem véry threatening, and at worst one would die a glorious hero, even watching with an indulgent but superior glance the posthumous ceremonies that honored one's achievement.

Marlow sees from the outside what must be Jim's fierce internal conflict, his struggle "with an invisible personality, an antagonistic and inseparable partner of his existence—another possessor of his soul." Marlow feels a kind of vertigo in watching the process: this experience of Jim's "subtle unsoundness" opens into a deeper sense of what all of us share with Jim, and Jim's desperate efforts recall the occasions when the truth is so intolerable that we can survive only by transforming it into some saving illusion. Jim's own helpless surrender to what he needs to believe is at once "fabulously innocent" and "enormous." He can ignore the Malay helmsmen who remained unquestioningly fast at their post in the face of calamity; "there had been no order," one of them testified, "he could not remember an order; why should he leave the helm?" (8)

The bestiality of the other officers and the gross farce of their clumsiness seem an affront to any conception of human dignity. Jim can only feel "an element of burlesque in his ordeal." It is robbed of whatever grandeur danger and resistance might have attained; his disdain loses its import in the muddle of chance events and of traduced intentions. Jim can only see himself as wronged, maligned, mocked: "as though he . . . had suffered himself to be handled by the infernal powers who had selected him for the victim of their practical joke."[24] He cannot bring himself to take responsibility for either his action or his inaction. He can only remember himself as the well-meaning victim of cruel disgrace. "The infernal joke was being crammed devilishly down his throat, but—look you—he was not going to admit of any sort of swallowing motion in his gullet." And so Jim crosses the impossible gap between his intention and his act: "I had jumped . . . it seems" (9).

Conrad so manipulates the narrative that it introduces a series of counter-

parts and contrasts to Jim. The most striking is Brierly, a captain who is one
of the board of inquiry. Brierly is a man of proven courage and confident
superiority, a man who has risen to command without indecision or self-
doubt. But the case of Jim—whose family is known to Brierly's—has not
aroused Brierly's usual contempt and impatience. It has suddenly, by its
disclosure of Jim's "subtle unsoundness," awakened Brierly to whatever in
himself has remained unexamined or hidden from his consciousness. Brierly
tries to persuade Jim to run out; he is even willing to pay Jim to escape this
needless public disgrace, a disgrace which (for reasons we cannot know)
threatens Brierly's own vision of himself. Finally, making careful arrangements for his first mate to succeed him, weighting his body with belaying
pins, a week after Jim's inquiry has ended, Brierly suddenly jumps overboard. Marlow describes his suicide as "the posthumous revenge of fate for
that belief in his own splendour which had almost cheated his life of its
legitimate terrors." Or does not that belief triumph after all? "Who can tell
what flattering view he had induced himself to take of his own suicide?" (6).

The case of Brierly is one of several to which Jim's is related. There is the
French lieutenant who remained aboard the *Patna* for thirty hours while a
gunboat towed it into port. There is the case of little Bob Stanton, "the
shortest chief mate in the merchant service," who died trying to rescue a
large woman who had fallen overboard. As one spectator remarks, "It was
for all the world, sir, like a naughty youngster fighting with his mother."
Both the lieutenant and Bob Stanton are figures without any superficial show
of heroic dignity; they provide a sharp contrast with Jim's promising and
deceptive appearance (13).

These counterparts or alternatives might be seen, in Peter Ure's phrase, as
"enemies of the story, enemies of the imagination." [25] It may be also apt to
call them enemies of the romantic. For they accommodate the claims of the
imagination in different ways, but they do not inhabit a dream with the
tenacity and wholeness of faith that Jim—for want, perhaps, of greater wisdom—does. In one sense, Jim's persistence is the result of weakness. As the
center of this novel, Jim's imagination is all the better for its innocence.
What Conrad once said of himself applies as well to his treatment of Jim. It
is "not my depth," he wrote to Edward Garnett, "but my shallowness that
makes me so inscrutable." [26] Jim's inability to understand himself—his failure even to guess what forces are at work within him—frees his power to act
out his beliefs, and the puzzle he presents through his very simplicity is
what a sophisticated witness like Marlow needs. Our interest in Jim derives
from Marlow's meditation upon him.

Stein is the full romantic of the novel, a man who has lived freely and
dangerously, who has loved deeply, and who has become a scholar and at last
a collector of beetles and butterflies. Marlow sees in him a peculiar power,
like that of the artist:

I respected the intense, almost passionate, absorption with which he looked at a butterfly, as though on the bronze sheen of these frail wings, in the white tracings, in the gorgeous markings, he could see other things, an image of something as perishable and defying destruction as these delicate and lifeless tissues displaying a splendour unmarred by death.

Stein seems to preserve in imperishable form what comes into being through the perishable; the lifeless creatures in his collection embody "beauty, accuracy, harmony, the balance of Nature's colossal forces, the perfect equilibrium of the mighty Kosmos" (19).

The most striking instance of this process occurred on the remarkable day when Stein shot himself out of an ambush and found, as he looked for signs of life in one of the three bodies, the shadow of a rare and beautiful butterfly, one he had always dreamed of catching. There is some implicit connection between his deep love for his family, his brave and shrewd facing of his enemies, and this rare prize, the butterfly "sitting on a small heap of dirt." What Stein achieves is an abstraction of form from living matter; and, when he turns his attention to Jim he is, inevitably, interested in Jim as a problem. For one can say that man's form exists less in his physical structure than in his dream, his guiding motive and vision. Stein is fully aware of the precariousness of all life; he has lost his wife and daughter and begun a new career after their death. Man, unlike the butterfly, "will never on his heap of mud keep still." He is, instead, consumed by conflicting dreams: "He wants to be a saint, and he wants to be a devil—and every time he shuts his eyes he sees himself as a very fine fellow—so fine as he can never be."

As Stein contemplates the problem, he too seems to lose substance and to hover "noiselessly over invisible things," to dissolve into a world of idea. And he comes to his well-known statement:

A man that is born falls into a dream like the man who falls into the sea. If he tries to climb out into the air as inexperienced people endeavor to do, he drowns—*nicht war?* . . . No, I tell you! The way is to the destructive element submit yourself, and with the exertions of your hands and feet in the water make the deep, deep sea keep you up.

Man, as Stein has remarked, comes "where he is not wanted, where there is no place for him"; the sea is the destructive element because it is not the element to which man is naturally adapted, and yet it is the only one in which he can live. Or one can take the sea as the realm of idea—always evanescent, always exacting—in which alone man can live; the realm of "fact," the world of land and air, will kill more surely than the other. But to keep alive in the water is to commit oneself to unceasing effort and ambition: "To follow the dream, and again to follow the dream—and so—*ewig—usque ad finem.* . . ." Marlow imagines before him "a vast and uncertain expanse, as of a crepuscular horizon on a plain at dawn—or was it, perchance, the coming of the night." He recognizes Stein's own obduracy and boldness, following his dream "without faltering, and therefore without shame and without regret" (20).

Marlow has earlier described Stein's courage as "like a natural function of the body—say, good digestion, for instance—completely unconscious of itself." Marlow cannot attain the unconscious rightness that is given only in action. He has come to mistrust the crepuscular light as less charming than deceptive and to see the expanse as a desolate plain, its bright edge indicating only "an abyss full of flames." The vision of Stein turns under Marlow's eyes from benign to terrible.

Stein himself recognizes the problem as he speaks of Jim: "He is romantic—romantic. . . . And that is very bad—very bad. . . . Very good, too." To Marlow's doubts he replies with a full sense of the terror and the value of consciousness: "What is it by that inward pain makes him know himself? What is it that for you and me makes him—exist?" Stein becomes for Marlow a man who has achieved "all the exalted elements of romance." And Jim's "imperishable reality" (rather than the actual man) gains "irresistible force" in a realm where "absolute Truth . . . floats elusive, obscure, half submerged, in the still silent waters of mystery" (20).

Conrad leaves Marlow in a half-mesmerized state, his mind excited by mystery and hope, the world of idea curiously close, even visible in the seemingly disembodied forms of Stein's half-darkened rooms. Marlow is haunted, moreover, by the intensity of life that is achieved through following the dream; intensity—or one may call it authenticity, since it makes all other moments seem so unreal as to become betrayals of our proper nature. Marlow can speak with raillery to his listeners, but he is trying to convey the power of what they may not sense:

> I could be eloquent were I not afraid you fellows had starved your imaginations to feed your bodies. I do not mean to be offensive; it is respectable to have no illusions—and safe—and profitable—and dull. Yet you, too, in your time must have known the intensity of life, that light of glamour created in the shock of trifles, as amazing as the glow of sparks struck from a cold stone—and as short-lived, alas!

This evocation of a life that achieves intensity, that commands the self in the name of an idea and wrests from torpor or mediocrity the momentary illusion, is clearly a romantic conception of experience, where brief intensity so thoroughly transcends the cool, dull succession of the quotidian as to become a higher reality. And yet, granted the power of such moments, is all life to be found in them? Perhaps only for those who are "imaginative" in the full and ambiguous sense of that term. Marlow professes to have no imagination, and we take that to mean that he is neither the victim nor the master of imagination, not so much the fantasist or the hero as the man of acute perception (21).

Marlow presents our world as a tissue of imagined relationships. From our travels, as he says, we return to "our superiors, our kindred, our friends," and those who have no person waiting for them "have to meet the spirit that dwells within the land, under its sky, in its air, in its valleys . . .—a mute friend, judge, and inspirer. Say what you like, to get its joy, to breathe its peace, to face its truth one must return with a clear consciousness." The spirit of the place is made up of the feelings, affections, loyalties we have known there, and we can find renewed communion with it only if we have not betrayed those sentiments that have become grounded in the remembered or imagined place itself. Those who return, Marlow says (speaking, one assumes, for himself), "not to a dwelling but to the land itself, to meet its disembodied, external, and unchangeable spirit—it is those who understand best its severity, its saving power, the grace of its secular right to our fidelity, to our obedience." Each of us is "rooted to the land from which he draws his faith together with his life." And Marlow is sure that Jim felt "the demand of some such truth or some such illusion—I don't care how you call it, there is so little difference, and the difference means so little"; and "those who do not feel do not count" (21).

But it is only a small step from this conception of a land as the source and locus of our sentiment— of men tied to each other by the countless ligatures of kinship, loyalty, faith, and love—to the more oppressive image of those ranks in which we march together: "Woe to the stragglers! We exist only in so far as we hang together. He had straggled in a way, he had not hung on; but he was aware of it with an intensity that made him touching, just as a man's more intense life makes his death more touching than the death of a tree" (21). Jim remains, then, "a straggler yearning inconsolably for his humble place in the ranks." Much later, when Marlow has seen Jim's apparent regeneration in Patusan, he all but scorns his own place in the ranks: "I felt a gratitude, an affection for that straggler whose eyes had singled me out, keeping my place in the ranks of an insignificant multitude. How little that was to boast of, after all!" (35). Jim's intensity has elicited from Marlow an intensity of a different kind, a somewhat frightening sense of how much that we take as the ground of our existence is a convention we have created for ourselves. And all such creations, if they have no other ground in reality, must of necessity be arbitrary, illusory, a necessity only of our imagination rather than of nature itself. Those ranks we keep become a somewhat humiliating image of our jealously preserved interdependence, and our fear of those who may awaken us to the rigid artifice of our cadence and our files.

In the views ascribed to the "privileged man" who receives Marlow's let-

ter, all the narrow and rigid assertions of class, color, and race are assumed
as if they were necessary structures:

> "We want its strength at our backs," you had said. "We want a belief in its
> necessity and its justice to make a worthy and conscious sacrifice of our lives.
> Without it the sacrifice is only forgetfulness, the way of offering is no better
> than the way to perdition." In other words, you maintained that we must fight
> in the ranks or our lives don't count.

This final phrase evokes a debasing conformity, especially if the ranks are
formed by those who share "a firm conviction in the truth of ideas racially
our own, in which name are established the order, the morality of an ethical
progress." We do not need to know much about Conrad's criticism of Kip-
ling or his views of the Spanish-American or Boer wars to recognize the
dangers implicit in the mind of the "privileged man," a counterpart of the
American banker Holroyd in *Nostromo* (36).

The problems that are awakened here cannot be easily put by. There
is a confidence we gain from knowing that our beliefs are shared, there *is* a
peculiar strength that men gain from a common faith and from the deep
sentiments that tie them to their land. All of these are important bonds, and
they may be essential—or almost so—to man's imaginative existence. He
gains a moral existence from accepting these claims upon him, from a
sense of duty or obligation and from the recognition that these are claims
upon others and recognized as such. And yet, as we contemplate our lives,
the demands we make upon ourselves often seem factitious and corrupt: a
mixture of coercion and dependence, a nightmare of unrealizable hopes and
impoverishing ideals. Conrad uses Jim himself as the crux of such problems;
we may admire his moral redemption in bringing order and light to Patusan,
we may pity the intolerable and unassuageable shame he feels at any thought
of the *Patna,* but we must be troubled by the extravagant expectations he
uses to test himself.

The portion of the novel that deals with Patusan is different in form but,
I think, a necessary realization of the earlier part. There Jim struggled against
truth, trying to retreat into his dream. In the second part Jim follows his
dream *usque ad finem,* as Stein proposed. He gains tremendously in self-con-
fidence, and he earns that confidence by unequivocal actions. And yet, he
remains to the last "a straggler yearning inconsolably for his humble place
in the ranks." Jim's feelings are divided even at the time of his greatest
triumph. "You have had your opportunity," Marlow says, but Jim is less
certain:

> "Had I? . . . Well yes. I suppose so. Yes. I have got back my confidence in
> myself—a good name—yet sometimes I wish . . . No! I shall hold what I've

got. Can't expect anything more." He flung his arm toward the sea. "Not out there anyhow." He stamped his foot upon the sand. "This is my limit, because nothing less will do."

This last phrase conveys the imperious egoism, the demand for respect that is only the obverse of his profound self-distrust (35).

Conrad surrounds the scene of Patusan with a sense of the imaginative force that has carried the pepper traders into the Eastern seas, their "blind persistence in endeavor and sacrifice." In contrast to their fierce endeavor is the miserable Rajah Allang, who nominally rules the territory: a "dirty, little, used-up old man with evil eyes and a weak mouth, who swallowed an opium pill every two hours." We see Jim in the Rajah's compound, self-possessed, diplomatic, but austerely reserved: "his stalwart figure in white apparel, the gleaming clusters of his fair hair, seemed to catch all the sunshine that trickled" into the Rajah's dim hall. Jim "appeared like a creature not only of another kind but of another essence." This is an evocation of those simple contrasts we might expect of boys' stories, the romances which Conrad is often deliberately reinterpreting and undercutting. Patusan is a "totally new set of conditions" for Jim's "imaginative faculty to work upon." It is in effect the scene of romance. But this triumph can happen only because, like Jim himself, Patusan is beneath notice, a country "not judged ripe for interference" by European or Asian powers (22).

All the internal conflicts of Patusan have revolved about "trade"; the Rajah Allang has claimed a monopoly, "but his idea of trading was indistinguishable from the commonest forms of robbery." In contrast, a more legitimate power is exercised among the Malayans by Doramin and his son, Dain Waris—almost figures of heroic legend. As an introduction to Doramin, Stein has given Jim a ring that is a token of an old friendship. "It's like something you read of in books," Jim remarks in the midst of his boyish "elated rattle" (23). It is at the top of the hill he first captured from the Rajah's forces that Jim is seen by Marlow:

> He dominated the forest, the secular gloom, the old mankind. He was like a figure set up on a pedestal, to represent in his persistent youth the power, and perhaps the virtue, of races that never grow old, that have emerged from the gloom. I don't know why he should always have appeared to me symbolic. Perhaps this is the real cause of my interest in his fate.   [27]

Marlow's concern has been with providing a refuge, and he is offended by Jim's easy romantic dream of it as a great chance. Offended but understanding: "Youth's insolent; it is its right—its necessity; it has got to assert itself, and all assertion in this world of doubts is a defiance, is an insolence." Jim's insolent hopes are simply the bright side of his unforgiving memory of his

disgrace. "It is not I or the world who remember," Marlow shouts at him.
"It is you—you, who remember." But, as Jim observes, Marlow does too
(23).

Yet there follows once more the boyish defiance of reality: "Don't you
worry, by Jove! I feel as if nothing could touch me. Why! This is luck from
the word Go. I wouldn't spoil such a magnificent chance!" It is no wonder
that Marlow concludes, "I am fated never to see him clearly" (23).

The adventures on Patusan during the two years before Marlow's visit
establish Jim as the arbiter and source of order in Patusan. They win him
the friendship of Dain Waris and the love of Jewel, the daughter of the
Portuguese trader Cornelius. In an episode which resembles Stein's own story,
Jim is warned by Jewel of an ambush and shoots his way out, killing a man
in the process. In that act, Jim's imagination serves his courage as it had his
cowardice earlier. He holds his shot deliberately:

> He held it for the tenth part of a second, for three strides of the man—an
> unconscionable time. He held it for the pleasure of saying to himself, that's a
> bad man! He was absolutely positive and certain. He let him come on because
> it did not matter. A dead man, anyhow. He noticed the dilated nostrils, the
> wide eyes, the intent, the eager stillness of the face, and then he fired.   [31]

Afterward, Jim "found himself calm, appeased, without rancour, without
uneasiness, as if the death of that man had atoned for everything." And,
once he has brought peace to Patusan and gained command of the imagination of its people, he can speak to Marlow with "dignity" if not eloquence,
with "a high seriousness in his stammerings," even a solemn "certitude of
rehabilitation." "That is why," Marlow concludes, "he seemed to love the
land and the people with a fierce egoism, with a contemptuous tenderness."
It is almost as if Jim cannot yet so fully believe in that rehabilitation as to
be free of the egoism which it should appease. For clearly that egoism is a
strenuous defiance of doubt. And Jim seems unable to respect, even while he
loves, the people of Patusan for the trust they show him.

Marlow is teased and teases himself at every point; there can be no repose
in his view of Jim. The precariousness of Jim's achievement is caught in
what is perhaps the strongest passage in the novel. Jewel is afraid that Jim
will leave her. She recalls the sadness of her mother's life. "I don't want to
die weeping," she says to Marlow, and her remark summons up all the "secular gloom" that Jim has seemed to dispel from Patusan. She presents a
vision of "passive unremediable horror," and Marlow records its force:

> It had the power to drive me out of my conception of existence, out of that
> shelter each of us makes for himself to creep under in moments of danger, as a
> tortoise withdraws within its shell. For a moment I had a view of a world that

seemed to wear a vast and dismal aspect of disorder, while, in truth, thanks to our unwearied efforts, it is as sunny an arrangement of small conveniences as the mind of man can conceive. But still—it was only a moment: I went back into my shell directly. One *must*—don't you know—though I seemed to have lost all my words in the chaos of dark thoughts I had contemplated for a second or two beyond the pale. These came back, too, very soon, for words also belong to the sheltering conception of light and order which is our refuge.   [33].

And it is as part of that sheltering conception that Marlow last sees Jim. That final view is the romantic ending the novel seems to earn:

> For me that white figure in the stillness of the coast and sea seemed to stand at the heart of a vast enigma. The twilight was ebbing fast from the sky above his head, the strip of sand had sunk already under his feet, he himself appeared no bigger than a child—then only a speck, a tiny white speck, that seemed to catch all the light left in a darkened world. . . .   [35]

Everything in the image is open to symbolism: gathering darkness that frames Jim's figure—childlike as it seems, standing on no visible firmness but on sheer groundlessness, surrounded by the infinity of sky and sea—and, concentrating within itself all our faith, the illusory light that one does not dare surrender.

But, of course, Conrad's novel does not end there. For immediately upon this follows the account of Gentleman Brown, the last of Jim's counterparts. Brown, who has turned his own act of desertion into a career of terror, almost a didactic "demonstration of some obscure and awful attribute of our nature" (44), has had his rifleman kill a man from a great distance; and by that action—arbitrary, absurd, terrifying—he has threatened to destroy the fabric of order Jim has created.

When Jim returns, Brown offers to negotiate; but he is enraged by all that Jim seems to stand for, in effect all that Brown has devoted his life to rejecting with a peculiar hatred. Brown angrily tries to cut Jim down to his own size, to shock him out of his cool superiority. "I came here for food. . . . And what did *you* come for?" Brown thinks the answer is wealth, but he has found his way into Jim's own terrors; Brown has a "satanic gift for finding out the best and weakest spot in his victims." And so he plays upon their common guilt: "I am here because I was afraid once in my life. Want to know what of? Of a prison. That scares me, and you may know it—if it's any good to you. I won't ask you what scared you into this infernal hole, where you seem to have found pretty pickings" (41). There runs through Brown's talk ("as if a demon had been whispering advice in his ear") a "vein of subtle reference to their common blood, an assumption of common experience; a sickening suggestion of common guilt, of secret knowledge that was like a bond of their minds and of their hearts" (42).

The effect, clearly, is to disable Jim, to make him unready to take the measures that judgment might propose. Jim does not try to disarm Brown; he allows him "a clear road or else a clear fight." Jim's servant, Tamb' Itam, can only feel in this response a "saddened acceptance of a mysterious failure." Jim offers to answer with his life to the people of Patusan for any harm that should come to them "if the white men with beards were allowed to retire." He knows that Jewel and Tamb' Itam would have killed Brown and his crew just as he, with neither doubt nor regret, killed the man who held him in ambush (or as Stein had before him). He is unable to take any effective action because of the compromising sense of being no better than, no different from, Brown. As he says of Brown (and clearly of himself) to Jewel, "Men act badly sometimes without being much worse than others."

The outer world has entered Patusan, offered its reminder of his failure, reduced him once more to self-doubt and hesitation; and, by reaction, to exalted pride. "He was inflexible, and with the growing loneliness of his obstinacy his spirit seemed to rise above the ruins of his existence." Jewel can scarcely believe in his failure to act, and when the consequences of that failure cost the life of Dain Waris, she pleads with Jim to save himself by escaping. But he refuses. "I should not be worth having," he tells her. " 'For the last time,' she cried menacingly, 'will you defend yourself?' " " 'Nothing can touch me,' he said in a last flicker or superb egoism." And as he leaves, asking her forgiveness, she calls back "Never! Never!" Jim offers himself to Doramin, accepting full responsibility for his son's death, and the old man shoots him. "They say that the white man sent right and left at all those proud faces a proud and unflinching glance. Then with his hand over his lips he fell forward, dead" (45).

The true ending splits apart those forces that for a moment find balance in Stein's butterfly. Jim passes away "under a cloud, inscrutable at heart, forgotten, unforgiven, and excessively romantic." Two themes are brought to the surface here—one is the proud, contemptuous, and desperate defiance Jim has expressed so often: "Nothing can touch me." The other is his infidelity not only to Jewel but to life as he pursues the sublime opportunity "which like an Eastern bride had come veiled to his side."

We see him "tearing himself out of the arms of a jealous love at the sign, at the call of his exalted egoism. He goes away from a living woman to celebrate his pitiless wedding with a shadowy ideal of conduct. Is he satisfied—quite, now, I wonder? We ought to know. He is one of us. . . ."

We have a last view of Jewel leading a "soundless inert life" in Stein's house. And as for the romantic collector—he has aged, and waves his hand sadly at his butterflies (45).

Conrad has forced apart the heroic and the authentic; the shadowy ideal becomes the successful rival of the living woman. The heroic is made a proud assertion of the ego, but of a self-distrustful ego which gains spurious strength from acts of unsparing self-judgment. The heroic, finally, seems childish and wistful, the bluster of the straggler who wants nothing more than to be taken into the ranks. And on the other hand, the ranks themselves are scorned by Marlow, who is fully aware of the narrowness and rigidity of the principles that hold them together. Conrad remains both romantic and skeptic, each opposing the other, but neither quite controlled or limited. It is a book without balance or repose, and it seems to me Conrad's greatest work because of the generosity with which each alternative is imagined.

Nostromo

In *Nostromo* Conrad's irony becomes more inclusive, enfolding the political history of a nation as well as the motives of individuals. The central irony is that of "material interests." They alone seem to possess the power to bring order to Costaguana. They require stability for their profitable operation, and they bring peace through their great financial power, through bribery or an improved standard of living. The danger of "material interests," in turn, lies in their use of the power they acquire, making men instruments of an institution and sacrificing them when they fail to be useful.

The story of the Gould concession opens in Italy, where Charles and Emilia meet. She is staying with an old aunt, the widow of an Italian nobleman who gave his life in Garibaldi's cause. The *marchesa* now leads "a still, whispering existence" in a part of "an ancient and ruinous palace, whose big empty halls downstairs sheltered under their painted ceilings the harvests, the fowls, and even the cattle, together with the whole family of the tenant farmer." It is there that Charles brings the news of his father's death. The death has been caused by the torment of the unworked silver mine, whose ownership Mr. Gould has not been allowed to relinquish and for which he has been forced to pay a stiff annual fee. It has been a grotesque but fatal farce. Charles and Emilia meet "in the hall of the ruined *palazzo*, a room magnificent and naked, with here and there a long strip of damask, black with damp and age, hanging down on a bare panel of the wall. It was furnished with exactly one gilt armchair, with a broken back, and an octagon columnar stand bearing a heavy marble vase ornamented with sculptured masks and garlands of flowers, and cracked from top to bottom." Charles stares at the urn as he speaks and kisses her hand. Emilia weeps in sympathy, "very small in her simple, white frock, almost like a lost child crying in the degraded grandeur of the noble hall, while he stood by her, again perfectly motionless in the contemplation of the marble urn" (I, 6).

Conrad uses the setting of the palazzo to suggest the world the Goulds will enter, the "degraded grandeur" comprehending both the original idealism with which their silver mine will be worked and the long history of corruptibility to which Gould's service to material interests will add another chapter. One can both recognize the Goulds' new hope as they stand in the decayed palazzo and read, in the painted ceiling above them, the grandeur of an older generation which has had to yield to fowls and cattle its uselessly large and formal spaces. Conrad does not insist upon allegorical meanings, but he exacts from his scene a high degree of initial suggestion and of ultimate relevance. Some of it is perhaps apparent at once to Charles, who stares at the cracked urn "as though he had resolved to fix its shape forever in his memory." But it is not clear what he sees. The scene, garrulous with suggestion for us, like the sounding church bell "thin and alert" in the valley below, is something of which the Goulds are perhaps touchingly, even pathetically, oblivious. They are excited now by a future "in which there was an air of adventure, of combat—a subtle thought of redress and conquest." It is a prospect which earns for Charles Gould an ironic comment which he does not hear and could hardly imagine: "Action is consolatory. It is the enemy of thought and the friend of flattering illusions. Only in the conduct of our action can we find the sense of mastery over the Fates" (I, 6).

The enthusiasm with which Emilia later speaks of the mine, deprecating her genuine idealism with a "slight flavor of irony," charms visitors to the Casa Gould; but it does not lead them to imagine any higher end than the acquisition of wealth. The betrayal of Emilia's idealism and its faint pathos are suggested by the niche in the steps of their house where a Madonna stands "with the crowned child sitting on her arm." More visible and audible is the "big green parrot, brilliant like an emerald in a cage that flashed like gold." Like the player piano in *The Secret Agent* or its ancestor, Mrs. Merdle's derisive parrot in *Little Dorrit,* the parrot performs at irregular intervals; it sometimes screams out "Viva Costaguana", or calls the servant "mellifluously . . . in imitation of Mrs. Gould's voice", or as suddenly takes "refuge in immobility and silence."

The Goulds feel "morally bound to make good their vigourous view of life against the unnatural error of weariness and despair." In order to accomplish this, Charles Gould needs the financial support of Holroyd, an American millionaire with "the temperament of a puritan and an insatiable imagination of conquest." Holroyd wants to conquer the world for the "purer forms of Christianity" and for American business; the two goals are fused in the cant of a ruthless idealism. It is not the only idealism Charles Gould encounters outside his own. Another version is the republican eloquence and vision of freedom of Antonia's father, Don José Avellanos. Emilia Gould thinks Charles muddleheaded for equating the two forms of idealism, but Charles has the confidence of a man convinced of his own realism. Others may declaim, he says, "but I pin my faith to material interests." He has, he thinks, no illusions; he is "prepared to stoop for his weapons" (I, 6).

During the years of her travel in Costaguana with her husband, Emilia Gould has come to know the land beyond the coastal settlements, "a great land of plain and mountain and people, suffering and mute, waiting for the future in a pathetic immobility of patience." Everywhere she finds "a weary desire for peace, the dread of officialdom with its nightmarish parody administration without law, without security, and without justice" (I, 7). The history of Costaguana has been a grotesque succession of forms of power, some barbarous, some virtuous but weak, none stable for long; it is a history of contingency, of upset and overturn, with only the misery of the people a constant presence beneath the various forms that oppression may take. Charles Gould puts up with idiocy and venality; he lives within a fortress of polite silence. The land has changed as the mine has grown; the original waterfall of San Tomé survives only as a memory in Emilia Gould's watercolor sketch. Emilia keeps alive the idealism she has shared with Charles: "she endowed that lump of metal"—the first silver ingot produced by the mine—"with a justificative conception, as though it were not a mere fact, but something far-reaching and unpalpable, like the true expression of an emotion or the emergence of a principle" (I, 8). But Emilia becomes at last an ineffectual and lonely spectator, dismayed by the weight of power that the mine carries in the new political state of its own creation, Sulaco.

Dr. Monygham, who shares her vision, is another bitter spectator. He has learned, he thinks, to live without illusions; his self-respect had been destroyed under torture when he found himself betraying others to the dictator, Guzman Bento. Like Lord Jim, he is "the slave of a ghost," haunted by his failure. He has created "an ideal conception of his disgrace," not a false reading of the past but "a rule of conduct resting mainly on severe rejections." Dr. Monygham's "eminently loyal nature" can trust only someone so innocent and helpless as Emilia Gould. For her husband's efforts he has only scorn:

> The administrador had acted as if the immense and powerful prosperity of the mine had been founded on methods of probity, on the sense of usefulness. And it was nothing of the kind. The method followed had been the only one possible. The Gould Concession had ransomed its way through all those years. It was a nauseous process. He quite understood that Charles Gould had got sick of it and had left the old path to back up that hopeless attempt at reform. The doctor did not believe in the reform of Costaguana. . . . What made him uneasy was that Charles Gould seemed to him to have weakened at the decisive moment when a frank return to the old methods was the only chance. Listening to Decoud's wild scheme had been a weakness.   [III, 4]

This passage is interesting as much for the moral confusion it embodies as for that which it attacks. Charles Gould is blamed for pretending to high purpose while using base means. Could he have exercised it more fully by some other means? No, his method was "the only one possible," but we must recognize it for what it is. Charles Gould has in fact tried to free himself of the base methods; his very eagerness to do so led to his support of so weak a reformer as Ribiera. Would it have been better both to practice base means and renounce a high purpose? This would seem to Dr. Monygham more sensible since the high purpose of reform was, in his eyes, foredoomed. And now Dr. Monygham is troubled because Gould turns to Decoud's plan for an independent Sulaco instead of using his silver, as he has before, to buy off the latest would-be Caesars, the Montero brothers. As we see, Gould is more realistic in this than Dr. Monygham.

One is left with a morality that scorns bribery but scolds Gould for repudiating it, that questions Gould's success but fears his failure; it is a morality that can question any action since its grounds for judgment shift between an exacting idealism and a cynical despair. Any form of success must be unthinkable for Dr. Monygham, and any apparent success must reveal itself to be a new and more insidious form of failure. Only the commitment to personal loyalty survives the larger pattern of Dr. Monygham's fatalism. The doctor is loyal to the mine because it "presented itself . . . in the shape of a little woman, . . . the delicate preciousness of her inner worth, partaking of a gem and a flower, revealed in every attitude of her person." In the presence of danger "this illusion acquired force, permanency, and authority. It claimed him at last!" Dr. Monygham's loyalty to Mrs. Gould is as ruthless as any of the illusions we see in the novel: it steels him "against remorse and pity" (III, 8). As he undertakes deception in her cause, he feels that he is "the only one fit for that dirty work." Like Lord Jim, Dr. Monygham feels disabled by his failure; he "believed that he had forfeited the right to be indignant with any one—for anything." It is only the "exaltation of self-sacrifice" that can support him.[27]

Martin Decoud, different as he is from Dr. Monygham, shares his distrust of Charles Gould's unstable mixture of moral idealism and material interests. The distrust comes in each case, I would argue, from a deeper idealism that each tries to disguise as (or reduce to) a personal loyalty. Decoud does not have Monygham's shame of betrayal (or, in Dickens's phrase, his "vanity of unworthiness"). Decoud seems, as we first encounter him, a supercilious young expatriate, a smatterer in satiric journalism, a man who prefers the boulevards of Paris to the barbarism of his own country. He is torn between a despair of ever bringing order to Costaguana and the infamy of serving interests whose motives or whose realism he can easily impugn.

Decoud suffers from a kind of spoiled idealism; he cannot admit impurity of motive without feeling betrayed and controlled by it. Antonia, who does not suffer from the same fastidiousness, rejects his cynicism: "Men must be used as they are. I suppose nobody is really disinterested, unless, perhaps, you, Don Martin." For whenever Decoud puts aside an idealistic goal (which he nevertheless uses as a touchstone of others' actions), he reverts to a cynicism which seems to take people at their worst. "You read all the correspondence, you write all the papers," he says to Antonia, "all those state papers that are inspired here, in this room, in blind deference to a theory of political purity." But Gould's company and his mine are the "practical demonstrations" of what is possible. "Do you think he succeeded by his fidelity to a theory of virtue?" And yet, for all the guilt he may have incurred, Gould has been too weak to carry bribery far enough to buy off the Monteros (I, 5).

Decoud professes himself unmoved by the claims of patriotism; such "narrowness" of belief must be "odious" to "cultured minds." But at a deeper level, Decoud seems bitterly disappointed in his country, where patriotism has too often been "the cry of dark barbarism, the cloak of lawlessness, of crime, of rapacity, or simple thieving." Even as he denounces Costaguana, Decoud is "surprised at the warmth" of his own words. Antonia picks up that point: "The word you despise has stood also for courage, for constancy, for suffering." Decoud cannot accede to Antonia's faith: for him a conviction remains only a "particular view of personal advantage either practical or emotional." He rejects patriotic illusions. He claims "only the supreme illusion of a lover." This is Decoud's form of authenticity. He can accept none of the hypocrisy, the self-deception, or fanaticism he sees in Costaguanan patriotism; he holds to a principle he can acknowledge as quixotic but also as personal and sincere.

In political affairs Decoud has cultivated detachment: he "imagined himself to derive an artistic pleasure from watching the picturesque extreme of wrongheadedness into which an honest, almost sacred, conviction may drive a man." It seems to Decoud that every conviction, to the extent that it is effective, becomes delusion or madness; the man who has come to accept a belief is no longer in command of it or himself. But while he regards himself as a connoisseur of madness, enjoying the colorful virulence of others' obsessions, he tries to preserve decency in skepticism. He deposits in his skeptical better self the full awareness he must relinquish as a propagandist. His better self preserves its integrity, and he wishes it to remain an asylum, an eventual place of return for the activist, the ideologist and propagandist, he finds himself becoming (I, 5).

Decoud can participate in action only by scorning the limitations—he would say dishonesty—that action imposes. Yet some of his best feelings, concealed from his ironic consciousness as they must be to survive, are at work in his political action. Emilia Gould sees a "tremendous excitement under its cloak of studied carelessness," betrayed in "his audacious and watchful stare, in the curve, half-reckless, half contemptuous, of his lips." Nevertheless, he mocks his own enthusiasm as he proposes that Sulaco secede and become a new state. His devotion to the new cause is born, he insists, of love for Antonia rather than any idealism of Charles Gould's kind. Gould, he insists to Emilia, "cannot act or exist without idealizing every simple feeling, desire, or achievement" (II, 6).

Decoud wants no such sublimation. He ascribes it to Antonia, and it clearly has some part in her appeal for him; but he thinks he undertakes the cause he has devised only to be able to remain with her (since, he adds mockingly, she refuses to run away). While Decoud scorns Gould's "sentimental basis for action," he appeals nevertheless to Emilia Gould's concern for the victims she has protected: "Are you not responsible to your conscience for all these people? Is it not worthwhile to make another effort, which is not at all so desperate as it looks?" Yet, having said this, Decoud must separate himself from her husband's idealism. "I cannot endow my personal desires with a shining robe of silk and jewels," he boasts. "Life is not for me a moral romance derived from the tradition of a pretty fairy tale." With the supremely ironic blindness of the self-styled realist, Decoud asserts, "I am not afraid of my motives."

At the mention by Mrs. Gould of the banker Holroyd, Decoud comes to a second plan—not only to create an independent state of Sulaco but to save the next shipment of silver from capture by the Monteros. In effect, he accepts the material interests in the simplest sense of that phrase: "This silver must be kept flowing north to return in the form of financial backing from the great house of Holroyd." For the task of saving the silver Decoud thinks of Nostromo. He trusts Nostromo's self-interest; Nostromo came to Costaguana, by his own account, to seek his fortune. Emilia puts her trust in Nostromo's integrity; old Viola has called him "the incorruptible." "I prefer," she says to Decoud, "to think him disinterested, and therefore trustworthy." Neither of them can quite imagine Nostromo's vanity and his dependence upon others' regard (II, 6).

Nostromo is neither mercenary nor idealistic in the ways that they imagine. As Teresa Viola recognizes, he is under the spell of his reputation, eager to gain distinction by being "invaluable" to people like Captain Mitchell. He is precisely opposed to old Giorgio Viola, in whom the "spirit of self-forgetfulness, the simple devotion to a vast humanitarian idea" has bred "an austere contempt for all personal advantage." Viola cries out fiercely in behalf of Garibaldi's followers:"We wanted nothing, we suffered for the love of all humanity!" (I, 4) Nostromo has little of this thoughtful idealism; he is the captive of an image rather than of an idea. It is a handsome image. We see it best in the swaggering performance with which he turns off the anger of a pretty *morenita* and allows her to cut the silver buttons from his coat.

Whereas Charles Gould is a captive of an idea and an institution, Nostromo becomes the captive of the literal silver. Doomed to possess it, daring to spend it only very slowly, unable to return it because of the missing bars with which Decoud weighted his body, he becomes "the slave of a treasure with full self-knowledge" (II, 12). He must live by stealth and suffer a disabling sense of falseness, and he feels at the last that the silver has killed him. As she comforts Giselle Viola, who loved Nostromo, Emilia Gould has the "first and only moment of bitterness in her life," and speaks in terms worthy of Dr. Monygham himself: "Console yourself, child. Very soon he would have forgotten you for his treasure." (III, 13). In effect, as Emilia Gould recognizes, Nostromo transposes the pattern of Charles Gould to another key. Nostromo turns out to be a far less interesting, far less complex character than he promises to be at first, and that is true of Gould as well. This has been explained by H. M. Daleski as the "thwarting of the conventional expectations" awakened by the characters and the mine itself. Just as the idealism is replaced by impoverishing obsession, so these characters have less and less life.[28]

With studied irony, Conrad allows Captain Mitchell to introduce us to the new state of Sulaco. His naive pride in the new republic is the means by which we learn how the events initiated by the doctor and Nostromo have concluded. He provides a requiem for the heroic dead and an altogether uncritical account of how heroism and dedication have been absorbed into new institutional structures. Father Corbelán is now a cardinal-archbishop. Hernandez, who was once a kind of Robin Hood, a glorious outlaw, is now minister of war. Even Dr. Monygham has an institutional role as inspector of state hospitals. The war to free Sulaco has been ended by an "international naval demonstration" in the harbor; a United States cruiser was the first to give official recognition to the new state. Once more Conrad has forced together the heroism in which the state is conceived with the bureaucratic structure and scene of imperialist enterprise it becomes.

The next stage of Sulaco's history is suggested in the doctor's conversation with Antonia Avellanos and Father Corbelán. They are now involved in promoting a campaign to annex the rest of Costaguana to the new power of Sulaco. For Antonia this would be a means of using the wealth of the new state to relieve the oppression of fellow countrymen. Dr. Monygham ridicules this hope: "Yes, but the material interests will not let you jeopardize their development for a mere idea of pity and justice." He characteristically adds: "And it is just as well perhaps." The true support for Antonia's hope has been found in "the secret societies amongst immigrants and natives, where Nostromo . . . is the great man." Such a movement, Dr. Monygham adds, may simply exploit the appeal of "the wealth for the people." With all his cynicism about both forces, Dr. Monygham expects violence:

"There is no place and no rest in the development of material interests. They have their law, and their justice. But it is founded on expediency, and is inhuman; it is without rectitude, without the continuity and the force that can

be found only in a moral principle. Mrs. Gould, the time approaches when all
that the Gould Concession stands for shall weigh as heavily upon the people as
the barbarism, cruelty, and misrule of a few years back."

It will "provoke resentment, bloodshed, and vengeance, because the men
have grown different." Does this mean simply that men will become disaf-
fected with the mine or does it imply that they have now acquired higher
expectations of their worth and rights? (III, 11).

What are we to make of Dr. Monygham and Emilia Gould? They lack the
"polished callousness" or even the simple worldliness that might make for
tolerance of the mixed motive or belief in its usefulness. He is a man of deep
feeling, whose vulnerability creates "his sardonic turn of mind and his biting
speeches." He shares Emilia's "still and sad immobility." Both accept the
fatality of forces that have been released and can no longer be recalled. Mrs.
Gould's nightmare vision is of an "immense desolation" in which she survives alone "the degradation of her young ideal of life, of love, of work—all
alone in the Treasure House of the World." Both have the moral intensity
of quietism. Emilia Gould thinks: "There was something inherent in the
necessities of successful action which carried with it the moral degradation
of the idea" (III, 11). The alternatives to the process are either unsuccessful
action or none at all. There may be a grandeur of despair in such an assertion
that compensates for the inability to act. Not to act is at least to commit no
error and do no wrong. It leaves the realm of politics to one or another
pattern of fanaticism or cynicism. In Nostromo there are intimations of a new
radical, perhaps revolutionary, movement, emerging under the cover of Nostromo's leadership but under the real direction of "an indigent, sickly, somewhat hunchbacked little photographer, with a white face and a magnanimous soul dyed crimson by a bloodthirsty hate of all capitalists, oppressors
of the two hemispheres" (III, 12). Rarely has a magnanimous soul been so
poorly housed and so passively governed by rage.

I have tried to get at the way in which Conrad's tendency to reduce experience to the outrage of an impossible choice requires characters of a special
kind. In Lord Jim the puzzle surrounds the hero. He is generously conceived,
neither shown as master of his fate nor made a moral bankrupt. Marlow in
turn is a figure of fuller consciousness, deeply concerned with the questions
which Jim exemplifies but which Marlow alone can formulate. Marlow fails
to save Jim; he can only observe the destiny Jim achieves once he goes to
Patusan. And the initial hope gives way to something darker and enigmatic.
In Nostromo Conrad has created characters who are victims of an idea. We see
that theme announced early: the "cool purity" of the white peak of Higuer-
ota—a "colossal embodiment of silence"—seems to fade into (Conrad is very
cinematic) the white hair of the anachronistic old Garibaldino Giorgio Viola.

Charles Gould pursues an idea which requires means that threaten to subvert its end; his failure lies in his uncritical commitment to "material interests," and that is in turn reflected in the dehumanization imposed upon him by the idea. His "subtle conjugal infidelity" to Emilia is like Jim's to Jewel—each man turns to an idea as to "an Eastern bride" who has come "veiled to his side." In Jim's case it is "a pitiless wedding with a shadowy ideal of conduct"; in Gould's with a sense of "redress and conquest." Conrad stresses the futility of Gould's achievement: the peace of the Sulaco we come to under the guidance of Captain Mitchell is made, like that of Geneva in *Under Western Eyes,* to seem complacent and indifferent to the claims of any idea. It is at most a superficial peace, for the promise of new violence is inherent in the dialectic of material interests.

What I miss is some intimation of men being moved by mixed motives without inevitably succumbing to the lowest. There seems at moments something rigged in Conrad's demonstration of futility, of the impossibility of Costaguana's ever achieving a government both tolerable and stable. It is not hard to be realistic if one rules out hope, and it is not hard to be ironic—it is in fact hard not to be—if all forms of political activity lead to the same inevitable futility. Unlimited irony can easily turn into fatalism.

Decoud, we are told by the author, "died from solitude and want of faith in himself and others." Solitude creates "a state of soul in which the affectations of irony and scepticism have no place." Decoud can no longer set himself against the world but is absorbed into it at the cost of his identity. "In our activity alone do we find the sustaining illusion of an independent existence as against the whole scheme of things of which we form a helpless part" (III, 10) The fatalism of "form a helpless part" and the skepticism of "sustaining illusion" make one wonder whether a novelist who writes these words would succumb, or fear that he might succumb, as Decoud does. One recalls Conrad's words about writing *Lord Jim*: "Everything is there: descriptions, dialogue, reflexion—everything—everything but the belief, the conviction, the only thing needed to make me put pen to paper." [29]

Many have felt that Conrad is trying to exorcise something by forcing himself to imagine his way into Decoud—just as there were moments in the writing of *The Secret Agent* when he was, as he tells us, an "extreme revolutionist." If Decoud is a "victim of the disillusioned weariness which is the retribution meted out to intellectual audacity," he seems a thinner character in his death than in his life. One may feel that he is not so much "swallowed up in the immense indifference of things" as sentenced and executed by his author. I wonder why so few are ready to question the propriety of Decoud's suicide, to ask, that is, whether it seems an action that follows from his nature rather than a somewhat superstitious reprisal against the irony and skepticism that the author otherwise overindulges. [30]

But the problem of Decoud is only part of what seems to me troublesome in the novel. As I have indicated, the central characters are captivated by "illusion," with little capacity to recognize or resist it; or, if they are without illusion, they are without power or hope as well. The book achieves some tragic force. It does not achieve that force by demonstrating the inevitable corruption and the implicit blindness of all action, at least of all action that professes a purpose or an ideal. For Conrad's feelings are truer than his thought. There is more complexity in his presentation of characters than there is in his analysis; and, if we see more in what they do than Conrad's ironic handling allows for, it is because they have won their claims upon our minds and feelings in those unattended moments when Conrad's oversight allows them some freedom.

11 ✳ Lawrence:

Levels of Consciousness

The New Vision of Character

He sat still like an Egyptian Pharaoh, driving the car. He felt as if he were seated in immemorial potency, like the great carven statues of real Egypt, as real and as fulfilled with subtle strength, as these are, with a vague inscrutable smile on the lips. He knew what it was to have the strange and magical current of force in his back and loins, and down his legs, force so perfect that it stayed him immobile, and left his face subtly, mindlessly smiling. He knew what it was to be awake and potent in that other basic mind, the deepest physical mind. And from this source he had a pure and magic control, magical, mystical, a force in darkness, like electricity.

It was very difficult to speak, it was so perfect to sit in this pure living silence, subtle, full of unthinkable knowledge and unthinkable force, upheld immemorially in timeless force, like the immobile, supremely potent Egyptians, seated forever in their living subtle silence. . . . .

They ran on in silence. But with a sort of second consciousness he steered the car towards a destination. For he had the free intelligence to direct his own ends. His arms and his breast and his head were rounded and living like those of the Greek, he had not the unawakened straight arms of the Egyptian, nor the sealed, slumbering head. A lambent intelligence played secondarily above his pure Egyptian concentration in darkness.[1]

I have chosen these passages from *Women in Love* to open a discussion of D. H. Lawrence because they present so clearly the difference of levels of consciousness with which Lawrence is always concerned. The first image, of the throned Egyptian statue, is mysterious and remote. The "inscrutable smile," like the archaic smile of early Greek sculpture, is "vague" because it expresses a force beneath consciousness, or at least of consciousness at its very limits, "the deepest physical mind." What consciousness there is seems turned upon itself, an enjoyment of poise and power that leaves the face "subtly, mindlessly smiling." The remoteness suggests dimensions that exceed all conventional measure of scale or time: the figure is "upheld immemorially in timeless force." It is a sublime image whose "living, subtle silence" is a denial of the life we know in our "second consciousness."

The second consciousness is a play of "free intelligence," and it finds embodiment in the rounded arms and torso, the human head, alert with "lambent intelligence." It moves in a human space and can manage the world. One feels, perhaps, that this second consciousness is capable of mocking its rigid Egyptian self, capable at least of ironic challenge like Montaigne's:

> We seek other conditions because we do not understand the use of our own, and go outside of ourselves because we do not know what it is like inside. Yet there is no use our mounting on stilts, for with our stilts we must still walk on our own legs. And on the loftiest throne in the world we are still sitting only on our own rump.[2]

Earlier in the novel the "sealed, slumbering head" of a pharaoh has been used as an image of specious solemnity. It occurs as Birkin feels revulsion from the others at Hermione Roddice's country house.

> He was so much used to this house, to this room, to this atmosphere, through years of intimacy, and now he felt in complete opposition to it all, it had nothing to do with him. How well he knew Hermione as she sat there, erect and silent and somewhat bemused, and yet so potent, so powerful! He knew her statically, so finally, that it was almost like a madness. It was difficult to believe one was not mad, that one was not a figure in the hall of kings in some Egyptian tomb, where the dead sat all immemorial and tremendous.   [8]

Birkin sees the other guests as chess figures deployed about their queen. "But the game is known, its going on is like a madness, it is so exhausted." Hermione recognizes the anger with which Birkin rises and goes out, but she remains fixed in place: "her indomitable will remained static and mechanical, she sat at the table making her musing, stray remarks."

Lawrence's thought is, typically, dialectical. It proceeds through oppositions in which each term may claim full adequacy but where each must be limited by another: "Anything that *triumphs,* perishes. The consummation comes from perfect relatedness." Counterpoise and synthesis are the ultimate good: "The true God is *created* every time a pure relationship, or a consummation out of twoness into oneness takes place." If a man achieves such a "pure relation" within himself, a "sheer gleam of oneness out of manyness, then this man is God created where before God was uncreated. He is the Holy Ghost in tissue of flame and flesh, whereas before, the Holy Ghost was but Ghost." Such a moment of creation transcends time and place. And it is wrong to hope to fix this relatedness, "to tie a knot in Time. . . ." It cannot rest very long in fixed categories. For, while the "consummation is timeless," we nevertheless "belong to time, in our process of living." "Only perpetuation is a sin."[3] "Life, the ever-present, knows no finality, no finished crystallization. The perfect rose is only a running flame, emerging and flowing off, and never in any sense at rest, static, finished. Herein lies its transcendent loveliness."[4]

Lawrence sometimes speaks of consummation or relatedness as if it were a reduction of all differences to unity; but for the most part, he insists, as he does most strikingly in *Women in Love,* on a state where the individual "submits to the yoke and leash, but never forfeits its own proud singleness, even while it loves and yields." Birkin's words perhaps claim too much for singleness in their effort to overcome the traditional meaning of oneness in love. The balance is hard to attain, and the contexts in which assertions are made become essential to their meaning.

Whether or not we call it vitalism (as I think we should), this is a system of belief wherein the enemies of life are the static, the bounded, the protracted, the deliberately controlled. Lawrence found the clue to Whitman's (and to much of his own) poetry in "the sheer appreciation of the instant moment": "Eternity is only an abstraction from the actual present. Infinity is only a reservoir of aspiration: man-made. The quivering nimble hour of the present, this is the quick of Time."[5] Or, as Lawrence wrote in *The Crown,* "We can no more stay in this heaven than the flower can stay on its stem. We come and go." We cannot sustain ourselves with "stale memory of a revelation," for it will only become captivity. "It is no good living on memory. When the flower opens, see him, don't remember him." For "the next time will come. And then again we shall *see* God, and once more, it will be different. It is always different."[6]

This pattern resembles a religious impulse that scorns and seeks to shatter any faith that hardens into dogma. The essence of a true faith is that it be a relatedness rather than an institution, a communion rather than a church. "What is alive, and open, and active is good. All that makes for inertia, lifelessness, dreariness, is bad. This is the essence of morality."[7] Clearly, morality becomes a form of vitality, an active and ongoing process, like a vigilant and demanding protestantism that questions both belief and believer. Carried to its furthest extreme, such a morality rejects any belief as soon as it can be formulated, any believer as soon as he thinks himself saved. "No ideal on earth is anything more than an obstruction, in the end, to the creative issue of the spontaneous soul. Away with all ideals." (This is Lawrence drawing out of Leo Shestov what he felt Shestov could not bring himself to acknowledge.) In his discussion of Whitman's democracy Lawrence makes the same point: "The great lesson is to learn to break all the fixed ideals, to allow the soul's own deep desires to come direct, spontaneous into consciousness. But it is a lesson which will take many aeons to learn."[8]

Lawrence, paradoxically, sees spontaneity as a discipline. Birkin asserts to Gerald Crich, "It's the hardest thing in the world to act spontaneously on one's impulses" (2). Like the Romantics, and particularly Blake, Lawrence finds the true identity of the self in the assertion of creative power. "Every single living creature is a single creative unit, a unique, uncommutable self. Primarily, in its own spontaneous reality, it knows no law. It is a law unto itself." In its material being, the self may be passive or determined from outside; it must submit to "all the laws of the material universe. But the primal, spontaneous self in any creature has ascendance, truly, over the material laws of the universe; it uses these laws and converts them in the mystery of creation."[9]

Freedom, then, becomes a new kind of obligation, a moral achievement. Lawrence saw in the American Indian "all the repulsive dignity of a static, indomitable will." The Indian might be granted "all the noble . . . beauty of arrestedness," but he was "benumbed against all life." He "failed in the great crisis of life" by not having "the courage to yield himself to the unknown that should make him new and vivid." This failure Lawrence tends to ascribe to the arts of primitive culture, such as the black statuette in Halliday's rooms. Lawrence's point is that they are not so much primitive as arrested in a state of consciousness and knowledge which can no longer yield to contraries. The primitive is the oldest of forms; its survival is easily seen as a long dying, an unbroken protraction of a single force. The primitive's failure is potentially the failure of all of us: "We *must* choose life, for life never compels us. . . . Unless we submit our will to the flooding of life, there is no life in us." The will clings to the known, to the achieved; it hopes to create a stable ego within which we dwell as in a walled city or as in a circle of light.[10]

As Ursula Brangwen reviews her life, she sees it as a confusing history: "In every phase she was so different. Yet she was always Ursula Brangwen. But what did it mean, Ursula Brangwen? She did not know what she was. Only she was full of rejection, of refusal. . . . That which she was, positively, was dark and unrevealed, it would not come forth." She begins to recognize the limitations of the familiar world, an area "lit up by man's completest consciousness" that she took for "all the world." She is aware of the surrounding darkness, but unable to comprehend it or the "points of light, like the eyes of wild beasts," gleaming within it. Now, suddenly, the familiar circle of light wherein trains and factories and science exist seems reduced to a street lamp where children play in the security of a blinding light, "not even knowing there was any darkness." She can no longer accept that denial of the darkness, and, while she sees in its whirling motion "shadow-shapes of wild beasts," she sees also the shadow-shapes of angels. Those who have gained freedom have come to see, as Blake would have us see in *The Marriage of Heaven and Hell,* that what seemed to be the "gleam in the eyes of the wolf and hyena" is in fact the "flash of the sword of angels, flashing at the door to come in." The "angels in the darkness" are "lordly and terrible and not to be denied, like the flash of fangs" (15). The monsters and wild beasts are creatures of our own imagining, the projections of fears that only conceal from us the sanctities and deepest urgencies of life. But the angels are terrible precisely in their urgency and their demand.

Like the Romantics before him, Lawrence wants to claim the freedom to shape and even to create our world with imaginative power; he wants no less to claim for that power an authority that transcends the individual and his psychology. It must be shown to be the life-force itself acting through the self: "We are only the actors, we are never wholly the authors of our own deeds or works. IT is the author, the unknown inside us or outside us. The best we can do is to try to hold ourselves in unison with the deeps which are inside us."[11] Lawrence's deepest self shades into the unconscious; but we may not feel freedom in obeying its promptings unless we feel it to *be* our self, and not mere compulsion. Lawrence stresses the difficulty of defining and identifying this self. It appears to us often as an inhuman force or will that threatens our conscious life; and yet, as with the beasts which become angels, this threatening force is the deeper self we cannot deny. Man's "deepest desire" is "to be himself, to be this quivering bud of growing tissue which he is."[12]

To acknowledge the depth of the self is, implicitly, a repudiation of self-consciousness and of the exercise of will. "The mind itself is one of life's later-developed habits." The ego is "a sort of second self," a "body of accepted consciousness . . . inherited ready-made." This, in turn, generates the "ideal self," that is, the self born of ideas, "the self-conscious ego, the entity of fixed ideas and ideals, prancing and displaying itself like an actor. And this is personality." We may try to create "downwards from the mind" as in Blake's imagery of Newton or Urizen as Pantocrator: "God, the Anima Mundi, the Oversoul, drawing with a pair of compasses and making everything to scale, even emotions and self-conscious effusions." The alternative and true source of creation is from the "forever inscrutable quicks of living beings, men, women, animals, plants."[13]

The deepest self then is inscrutable, inhuman, amoral; yet the only true morality is to act from that self. In an amusing poem called "Moral Clothing" Lawrence begins, "When I am clothed I am a moral man, / and unclothed, the word has no meaning for me." To have pockets requires moral earnestness about theft, and even a shirt is a garment of moral responsibility. Only when he is stripped naked is man "without morals and without immorality":

> And if stark naked I approach a fellow-man or
>   fellow woman
> they must be naked too,
> and none of us must expect morality of each other:
> I am that I am, take it or leave it.
> Offer me nothing but that which you are, stark and
>   strange.
> Let there be no accommodation at this issue.[14]

There is a more intense and brilliant statement by Birkin in *Women in Love:*

> There is . . . a final me which is stark and impersonal and beyond responsibility. So there is a final you. And it is there I would want to meet you—not in the emotional, loving plane—but there beyond, where there is no speech and no terms of agreement. There we are two stark, unknown beings, two utterly strange creatures, I would want to approach you, and you me. And there could be no obligation, because there is no standard for action there, because no understanding has been reaped from that plane. It is quite inhuman,—so there can be no calling to book, in any form whatsoever—because one is outside the pale of all that is accepted, and nothing known applies.

When Ursula feels this as a demand that she surrender her will to his, and protests that it is "purely selfish," Birkin insists that it is not. "I deliver *myself* over to the unknown." They must pledge to "cast off everything, cast off ourselves even, and cease to be, so that that which is perfectly ourselves can take place in us" (13). It is a remarkable pledge, one that surrenders self for the perfecting of self, and for a perfecting that is not felt to be our own achievement except that we choose it. A passage from the essay "Life" is relevant: "There is an arrival in us from the unknown, from the primal unknown whence all creation issues. . . . This is the first and greatest truth of our being and of our existence. How do we come to pass? We do not come to pass of ourselves."[15] But once he has stressed a timeless force always at work in us and finding expression through us, Lawrence must stress in turn the constant newness of this creation. It is never the execution of a preexisting design:

> Even an artist knows that his work was never in his mind,
> he could never have thought it before it happened.
> A strange ache possessed him, and he entered the struggle,
> and out of the struggle with his material, in the spell of the urge
> his work took place, it came to pass. . . .

And Lawrence closes with a fine irony. God looks at his creation with wonder: "Let me think about it! Let me form an idea." The divine fiat becomes only an acknowledgment of the mystery of its own creation.[16]

Lawrence felt that his friend Edward Garnett had resisted the newness of his work and had been impatient with its experiments: "All the time, underneath, there is something deep evolving itself out in me. And it is *hard* to express a new theory, in sincerity." Lawrence resented Garnett's calling his work "common" (that is, vulgar). He protested that he was a "passionately religious man." He could not write except from the depths of his experience, and it was "only when the deep feeling doesn't find its way out" that his "Cockneyism and Commonness" emerged, and "sentimentality and purplism."

In a famous letter to Garnett Lawrence tried to explain what is new in his work. What is "non-human, in humanity, is more interesting to me than the old-fashioned human element—which causes one to conceive a character in a certain moral scheme and make him consistent." It is the "inhuman will" that interests Lawrence:

> I don't so much care about what the woman *feels*—in the ordinary usage of the word. That presumes an *ego* to feel with. I only care about what the woman *is.*
> . . . You mustn't look in my novel for the old stable *ego*—of the character. There is another *ego,* according to whose action the individual is unrecognizable, and passes through, as it were, allotropic states which it needs a deeper sense than any we've been used to exercise to discover are states of the same single radically unchanged element. (Like as diamond and coal are the same pure single element of carbon. The ordinary novel would trace the history of the diamond—but I say, "Diamond, what! This is carbon." And my diamond might be coal or soot, and my theme is carbon.)[17]

This text has been interpreted in various ways. Clearly it is parallel to Birkin's words about the impersonal self, and Mark Schorer has aptly cited the sentence of Birkin's that best sums them up: "I want to find you, where you don't know your own existence, the you that your common self denies utterly."[18] Lawrence's vitalism requires a new vision of character, with less coherence on a single level ("the old stable *ego*") and with constant movement among levels (or allotropic states). Birkin and Ursula move down below the ego, through the deeper self to the dark impersonal powers which are the center of its being, which are Being itself. The surface gives way to reveal depth, then begins to reform anew with a consciousness of all that lies below it. The terms in which the self is conceived give way to new terms. The apparent self gives way to the other self, which it may obstruct or disguise or protect, whose energy it may pervert or direct. For the characters themselves cannot remain too long, nor we as readers, in that dark realm of silent reality; we must reascend from Being to time and space and the lambent intelligence of the rounded and living Greek self.

The Structure of the Novel

"Because a novel is a microcosm," Lawrence wrote in his study of Thomas Hardy, "and because man in viewing the universe must view it in the light of a theory, therefore every novel must have the background or the structural skeleton of some theory of being, some metaphysic. But the metaphysic must always subserve the artistic purpose beyond the artist's conscious aim. Otherwise the novel becomes a treatise." [19] The artist's proper task is not to force experience into the pattern of a theory but to achieve and reveal a new relation. Van Gogh's image of sunflowers is "neither man-in-the-mirror nor flowers-in-the-mirror" (neither a conventional expressive or mimetic image), "neither is it above or below or across anything." That seems to take care of idealization, abstraction, and transcendence. But not quite. "It is between everything, in the fourth dimension." "And this perfected relation between man and his circumambient universe is life itself, for mankind. It has the fourth-dimensional quality of eternity and perfection. Yet it is momentaneous." [20]

The attainment of this relatedness is what matters, however we describe it. "The novel is the highest example of subtle inter-relatedness that man has discovered" (528). With relatedness morality returns. As we have seen before, Lawrence is impatient with traditional morality, with formal codes and dead precepts. Yet he makes our openness to life a moral choice. "And morality is that delicate, for ever trembling and changing *balance* between me and my circumambient universe, which precedes and accompanies a true relatedness" (528). This inclusive awareness and precise feel for balance is for Lawrence moral imagination. The novelist becomes immoral by "putting his thumb in the scale, to pull down the balance to his own predilection," and— here we see the theologian again—it is the "helpless, unconscious predilection" that is the worst (529). For such an unconscious act is the work of a soul not sufficiently cleansed or free. To repeat Henry James's words, the "essence of moral energy is to survey the whole field."

Yet the novelist must also achieve sufficient respect for the way the world is. He must remain sensitive to all the emotions ("including love and hate, and rage and tenderness") that "go to the adjusting of the oscillating, unestablished balance between two people who amount to anything." If something new is to emerge we must be made aware of the process of its emergence. "A new relation, a new relatedness hurts somewhat in the attaining; and will always hurt. So life will always hurt. Because real voluptuousness lies in re-enacting old relationships, and at the best, getting an alcoholic sort of pleasure out of it, slightly depraving." (530). Works of art have this power too. "Cézanne's apple hurts. It made people shout with pain. And it was not until his followers had turned his art into an abstraction that he was ever accepted." [21] Cézanne' new relation is "a real attempt to let the apple exist in its own separate entity, without transfusing it with personal emotion." Cezanne's great effort was "to shove the apple away from him, and let it live of itself" (567). In refusing to show matter as "only a form of spirit," he freed matter from the "tyranny of mind," the "sky-blue prison." It hurts to have matter before us "without the winding-sheet of abstraction" (568). The "touch of anything solid hurts us" (570).

The mind is full of "all sorts of memory, visual, tactile, emotional." The cliché is a "worn-out memory that has no more emotional or intuitional root, and has become a habit." But what we often welcome as novelty is just a "new grouping of clichés." It is easily accepted; "it gives the little shock or thrill or surprise," and it does not hurt (576). Cézanne, in his desire to be "true to life," tried to replace our conventional mode of "mental-visual consciousness" with one that is "predominantly intuitive, the awareness of touch" (578). "The eye sees only fronts, and the mind, on the whole, is satisfied with fronts. But intuition needs all-aroundness, and instinct needs insideness. The true imagination is for ever curving round to the other side, to the back of the presented appearance" (579). It is not, I think, by a very strained analogy that one can see this as an account as well of Lawrence's novels and the characters within them. Lawrence's conception of character includes disjunctions between moods or attitudes, seeming inconsistencies, sudden and unmotivated gestures. It is the apparent illogicality to which we respond in Lawrence's new kind of character, somewhat as we do to the ambiguities we find in a two-dimensional representation of a three-dimensional world. We surmise some deeper motivation, some implicit consistency or "inner logic" that will sustain the incongruities of the surface. One can say that the surface of Lawrence's novels with its gaps and discontinuities requires that we move to a deeper level of character and motive, to an insideness rather than a readable surface or "front."

Lawrence has similar ways of getting at the "whole consciousness" at work in the novel. The novel is "the highest form of human expression ever attained. Why? Because it is so incapable of the absolute." [22] The final loyalty of the novel is to quickness, to the vividness and energy of life. The principal character "must have a quick relatedness to all the other things in the novel: snow, bed-bugs, sunshine, the phallus," etc. (420). All absolutes are damnable. "Man handing out absolutes to man, as if we were all books of geometry with axioms, postulates, and definitions in front. God with a pair of compasses! Moses with a set square!" (421). The novel shows instead that "everything is true in its own relationship, and no further" (422).

Out of this comes a new metaphor for character: "It is the flame of a man, which burns brighter or dimmer, bluer or yellower or redder, rising or sinking or flaring according to the draughts of circumstance and the changing air of life, changing itself continually, yet remaining one single, separate flame, flickering in a strange world. . ." (423). But the flame is not precisely the character as we know it; it is a principle of life or reality that is felt through the visible character. "In the great novel the felt but unknown flame stands behind all the characters, and in their works and gestures there is a flicker of its presence. If you are *too personal, too human,* the flicker fades out, leaving you with something lifelike, and as lifeless as most people are" (419). Lawrence urges the novel as a form of therapy upon those who must learn again to feel. "If we can't hear the cries far down in our own forests of dark veins, we can look in the real novels and there listen-in. Not listen to the didactic statements of the author, but to the low, calling cries of the characters, as they wander in the dark woods of their destiny." [23]

Stages of Consciousness: The Rainbow

The Rainbow is a novel about three generations, but it is, even more, a novel about stages or states of consciousness. From the initial "drowse of blood-intimacy," the "heated, blind intercourse of farm life" we follow Tom Brangwen to his all-but-wordless courtship of Lydia Lensky, and at last to the freedom she gives him from himself. The second stage recounts the wedding of Lydia's daughter Anna to her cousin Will Brangwen; it has greater complexity and conflict, and it concludes with a division in their lives between a secret sensual intensity and a conventional, unachieved existence in the world outside. Finally, their daughter Ursula reveals the strain of the "modern," its loss of traditional beliefs and refusal of traditional roles, both its yearning and its arrogance. Like Conrad, Lawrence is aware of the painfulness of consciousness. He trusts it more, I think, because he has a stronger sense of the other dimensions of self.

At each of these stages Lawrence makes us aware of "the felt but unknown flame" that "stands behind all the characters." This is sometimes achieved by rhetorical intensity, in large part a method of repetition and parataxis, which is the author's own "struggle for verbal consciousness," the "passionate struggle into conscious being" that Lawrence speaks of in his foreword to *Women in Love.* This emergence into consciousness is at once painful and strange; it keeps experience from seeming "too personal, too human." While the "flame" is felt in the energy of language, it is more fundamentally the energy of metaphysical thought which finds expression in the rhetoric. This is not to say that experience is used simply to demonstrate principles or cosmic truths. The concrete experience, dragged into living speech, coming to expression through the "pulsing, frictional to-and-fro" of words, is at once instance and archetype.[24] Its metaphysical dimension is not caught in conceptual categories but rather in the revelation it affords—in its clarity and energy—of an awareness until now indescribable because unrecognized. There are occasions when, through biblical diction or religious allusion, Lawrence brings to that experience suggestions of traditional mystery and overtones of sanctity. But these do not commit Lawrence to an ultimate system or to "higher" meanings. His metaphysics shifts too often in idiom and image— accommodated to one realm or another, biological, theological, moral, whatever—to provide any finality. Lawrence has no interest in substance, but only in process.

The sense of process is nicely caught in Tom Brangwen's vision at the time of his daughter's wedding:

> He felt himself tiny, a little upright figure on a plain circled round with the immense, roaring sky; he and his wife . . . walking across the plain, whilst the heavens shimmered and roared about them. . . . There was no end, no finish, only this roaring vast space. . . . What was sure but the endless sky? But that was so sure, so boundless. [5]

The title of the book suggests the relations between generations, each providing a doorway or an opening for the next. We see this in Anna as she lapses "into vague content": "If she were not the wayfarer to the unknown, if she were arrived now, settled in her builded house, a rich woman, still her doors opened under the arch of the rainbow, her threshold reflecting the passing of the sun and moon, the great travellers, her house was full of the echo of journeying." (6). The flame behind the characters is suggested at other times by an idiom which hovers between traditional metaphor and the language—the jargon, one might call it—of "doctrine." As Tom falls in love with Lydia Lensky, it is as if he has "another centre of consciousness," as if somewhere in his body a strong light were burning. Tom goes about without seeing what he does, "drifting, quiescent," in a "state of metamorphosis." At a deeper level he is "letting go his will, suffering the loss of himself, dormant always on the brink of ecstasy, like a creature evolving to a new birth." And that theme is given complex statement through landscape images which enact the endless movement, the harsh discontinuities of loss and death, and the brilliant uncovering of new depths of reality:

> He could not bear to be near her, and know the utter foreignness between them, know how entirely they were strangers to each other. He went out into the wind. Big holes were blown into the sky, the moonlight blew about. Sometimes a high moon, liquid-brilliant, scudded across a hollow space and took cover under electric, brown-iridescent cloud-edges. Then there was a blot of

cloud, and shadow. Then somewhere in the night a radiance again, like a vapour. And all the sky was teeming and tearing along, a vast disorder of flying shapes and darkness and ragged fumes of light and a great brown circling halo, then the terror of a moon running liquid-brilliant into the open for a moment, hurting the eyes before she plunged under cover of cloud again.   [1]

In the next generation, Anna and Will are more conscious, more free to accept experience. We see them in their marriage-bed like the lovers of John Donne's "The Good-Morrow." Their room is a "core of living eternity": "Here was a poised, unflawed stillness that was beyond time, because it remained the same, inexhaustible, unchanging, unexhausted" (6). But they must waken into the world of time, where it is already midday; and Will begins to feel "furtive and guilty," drawing up the blind "so people should know they were not in bed any later." Will's "orderly, conventional mind" is where he lives in the ordinary daylight. But in church as in marriage he wants "a dark, nameless emotion, the emotion of all the great mysteries of passion." He attaches no "vital importance" to his everyday world nor does he "care about himself as a human being." His only reality lies in "his dark emotional experience of the Infinite, of the Absolute." For Anna, in contrast, the "thought of her soul" is "intimately mixed up with"—perhaps simply identical with—"the thought of her own self." She envies Will's "dark freedom and jubilation of the soul," but she hates it too (6). She rebuffs the claim of all mystery and mysticism; she mocks the symbols he adores until, under the pressure of her will, he becomes ashamed of his religious ecstasy.

Will and Anna do battle in defense of themselves, she of her conscious self and powerful will, he of his dark subterranean self. In their visit to Lincoln Cathedral, Will enters as if he were "to pass within to the perfect womb." The interior becomes a dark scene of ecstasy for him: "the perfect, swooning consummation, the timeless ecstasy. There his soul remained, at the apex of the arch, clenched in the timeless ecstasy, consummated." Anna is stirred by his rapture but adamantly defiant. She thinks of the open sky above the cathedral, and she cannot see it as a blue vault—not as a closed architectural form—but as "a space where stars were wheeling in freedom, with freedom above them, always higher." She spurns the sanctity of the altar and claims "the right to freedom above her, higher than the roof." As she frees herself of the enclosing unity of the cathedral, she insists upon the diversity and contrariness it includes—the grotesques, "little imps that retorted on man's own illusion." They "winked and leered" and denied that the Gothic structure was absolute; they offered "separate wills, separate motions, separate powers." And so she succeeds in divesting the cathedral of its power over herself and over Will. For Will, too, it now seems "too narrow" to contain life, and he thinks of the "whole blue rotunda of the day." He comes to see that "a temple was never perfectly a temple, till it was ruined and mixed up with the winds and the sky and the herbs." So that, at last, while he still loves the Church, it is only as a symbol; and for that very reason it exacts all the more devotion. "He was like a lover who knows he is betrayed, but who still loves, whose love is only the more intense. The church was false, but he served it the more intensely" (7). And this is a dead end, a cessation of growth: "Something undeveloped in him limited him, there was a darkness which he could not unfold, which would never unfold in him" (8). So, too, in place of the "great adventure in consciousness," Anna has accepted "the rich drowse of physical heat," an absolute of sensuality. She is content with the "heat and swelter of fecundity," but her daughter Ursula, in passionate opposition, craves for "some spirituality and stateliness" (10).

Lawrence makes the story of Ursula essentially her attempt to become herself. By the close of the novel, her adventure in consciousness is hardly complete, but she has eluded the nets that might bind her movement. Unlike her mother, who will have "nothing extra-human," Ursula is "all for the ultimate." The church seems to her "a shell that still spoke the language of creation." She sees herself as one of the daughters of men to whom the sons of God will descend—"one of the unhistoried, unaccountable Sons of God." She rejects the natural and merely human, demanding some union with the mysterious and inexplicable "Absolute World." She learns to dissociate the spiritual from the ascetic. "The Resurrection is to life, not to death" (10). Yet, while she comes more and more to accept the everyday world, there is still "some puzzling, tormenting residue of the Sunday world within her, some persistent Sunday self, which insisted upon a relationship with the now shed-away vision world" (11). Her religious sense survives outworn doctrine and requires its new observances and its new sanctities; that remains a central part of the problem of how to become herself.

The inevitable interpenetration of spirit and sense, of visionary thought and physical desire, leads into Ursula's first attachment to Anton Skrebensky. He seems to her a worldly embodiment of spiritual energy, perhaps one of the Sons of God. He represents for Ursula all the freedom she wants for herself: an aristocratic scorn for convention, bold irreverence, the achievement of one's "maximum self." It is in fact her own maximum self that Ursula seeks in what she thinks is her love for him. As they make love, the moon becomes a symbol of that maximum self gaining freedom: "Oh, for the cold liberty to be herself, to do entirely as she liked." If one hears echoes of Gwendolen Harleth, they are not inappropriate, even to the fear of the self she seeks to realize. Skrebensky serves her will but hardly seems otherwise to exist, and the "burning, corrosive self" she has become now terrifies her.

Before Ursula encounters Skrebensky again, she has tried several paths that prove to be culs-de-sac. The first is her love for her teacher, Winifred Inger. Lawrence presents something of what he will more fully realize in Gerald Crich and Gudrun later. Winifred Inger and young Tom Brangwen, Ursula's homosexual uncle, become lovers and at last are married, to live in the hideous Yorkshire colliery town where Tom's managerial career allows him to escape his self-hatred by serving the great machine. Winifred, too, finds an escape from "the degradation of human feeling" in the "impure abstraction, the mechanisms of matter." It is an escape from the self that is tempting to Ursula. She must make "a great, passionate effort of will" before she rejects the industrial machine as "meaningless." She is "miserable and desolate," but she will never give way to serving "such a Moloch as this" (12).

A second false path comes in teaching school, where she becomes part of a machine of another sort, a "hard, malevolent system," unexamined, un-questioned, demanding of the teachers that they suppress their humanity. Ursula must lend herself to the "unclean system of authority," where power alone matters, and which can work only if one resorts to force. When she finds herself caning a pupil, Ursula feels that she is "in the hands of some bigger, stronger, coarser will." Lawrence is, I think, quite explicitly seeing in this "will" of the system a parody of that inhuman will that for him is an authentic depth of self. Ursula feels herself brutalized rather than caught up in vital impulse (13).

The third false path is an offer of marriage from Anthony Schofield, the brother of a fellow teacher. He is the chief gardener of a country house, and he lives in a beautiful park. Ursula feels guilty in refusing him but fright-ened at how close she has come to acceptance. "Her soul was an infant crying in the night. He had no soul. Oh, and why had she? He was the cleaner." He lacks a "soul" precisely in being so much one with the land he works, and it is her standing apart and seeing that beauty from the outside that has "separated them infinitely." He lacks the kind of consciousness with which she is burdened; he is a pastoral figure. "The true self is not aware that it is a self. A bird as it sings, sings itself. But not according to a picture. It has no idea of itself." Yet this nostalgia for simplicity, like the Tolstoyan hero's yearning for the reality of the peasants, cannot suffice. She is "a traveller on the face of the earth" and he "an isolated creature living in the fulfillment of his senses." Ursula's history is like a pilgrimage made up of encounters with those who fall along the way or seek to detain her in their own accommoda-tions with life (14).

Ursula must learn again upon Skrebensky's return that she cannot achieve fullness of self through someone who has not enough self of his own. The limits of Skrebensky are his conventional desire to be an unthinking part of a system, "just a brick in the whole great social fabric" (11). Time and military service in Africa have not changed his nullity. When he escapes from his social self, it can only be as a holiday, since he believes utterly in that self. Ursula, on the other hand, is becoming more and more sure of her "permanent self," and she is ready to let her social self survive as it can. The world exists only in a secondary sense, but "she existed supremely." For an interval "he and she stood together, dark, fluid, infinitely potent, giving the living lie to the dead whole which contained them." They feel assured, once again like Donne's lovers: "They were perfect. Therefore nothing else existed." They feel "absolute and beyond all limitations," the only ones to inhabit "the world of reality" (15).

It is too much to sustain, for it is only a temporary escape from that other reality they try to persuade themselves they have annulled. She cannot supply him with the being he lacks. She must throw off his heavy need for her, for he feels like a corpse—one of "those spectral, unliving beings which we call people in our dead language." At last he becomes an incubus, weeping at the thought of losing her, pressing his need upon her "like a fate she did not want." He seems to her "added up, finished. She knew him all round, not on any side did he lead into the unknown." They make love for the last time on the shore under a fiercely bright moon. "The moon was incandescent as a round furnace door, out of which came the high blast of moonlight." In this scorching brilliance Ursula speaks in "a ringing, metallic voice," kisses him with "a hard, rending, ever-increasing kiss." Their struggle for consummation becomes an ordeal and agonizing failure for him.

Later, Ursula recognizes that "Skrebensky had never become finally real." She had "created him for the time being, but in the end he had failed and broken down." She remembers him with liking, "as she liked a memory, some bygone self." He was perhaps too much a projection of her own desire and need, readily destroyed under the cold brilliance of desire become will. Ursula's destructive self-assertion has been savage in part because it was defensive. She has found herself about to marry Anton "out of fear of herself," unable to "rouse herself to deny" what he and everyone else has taken for granted. She veers between contempt for him and humiliating self-reproach as she considers a "bondaged sort of peace" in which she will become his wife and bear his child (15).

Ursula needs at last to be free of her history, to become "unhistoried, unaccountable" like the Sons of God. "The kernel was the only reality: the rest was cast off into oblivion." Like the religion which refuses enclosure by a cathedral roof, the self must refuse the limits of a personality, a "stable ego," a social role. It is the madness induced by self-betrayal that drives Ursula out into the rain. She feels threatened by the tree-trunks in the storm; they "might turn and shut her in as she went through . . . their grave, booming ranks" (16). Finally, she encounters a wheeling herd of wild horses that block her way. They are "maddened like her, their breasts clenched . . . in a hold that never relaxed . . . running against the walls of time, and never bursting free." Their frustrate and tortured motion, eddying and uncontrolled, so much like the motions of her thought, threatens to crush her. Instead, it induces a last frantic effort that saves her life and loses the child she is bearing. Her final vision of the rainbow, like a covenant of new life, sees the "horny covering of disintegration" (the image is insectile) cast off so that "new, clean, naked bodies," like kernels free of their husk, "would issue to a new germination" (16).

The Accession into Being: Women in Love

The feelings of the characters in *Women in Love* find symbolic occasions for their expression. That Anna and Will conduct their conflict in Lincoln Cathedral is plausible enough and powerfully imagined. But in *Women in Love,* we might say, the characters are almost always in Lincoln Cathedral. From the first chapter the imagery of glistening northern whiteness is associated with Gerald Crich, and it recurs as a metaphor in different matrices or contexts, only to emerge as the literal setting of the final chapters. So, too, in a reverse pattern, the vast industrial system Gerald Crich creates is by the end encapsulated in the granite factory frieze Loerke has designed. The "glamour of blackness" that Gudrun finds, with an unstable mixture of attraction and repulsion, in the colliery landscape and the mines themselves is comparable to the disturbing power of Halliday's African sculpture. These movements in and out of narrative surface, with their curious fusions and reversals of figure and ground, have a part in generalizing event and character, of drawing connections between private feelings and social structures, between the state of one's mind and the state of a culture.

The industrialist Thomas Crich makes clear the problems of consciousness that reach new intensity in *Women in Love.* He has caged his wife in his unrelenting kindness. "With unbroken will he had stood by this position with regard to her, he had substituted pity for all his hostility, pity had been his shield and his safeguard, and his infallible weapon. And still, in his consciousness, he was sorry for her, her nature was so violent and so impatient." Even as he dreads her scorn he thinks of her—or he wills himself to think of her—as a "white flower of snow." Crich brings the same enabling self-deception to his career as a mine-owner, profiting from the use of his workers while he seeks their love, "trapped between two half-truths and broken":

He wanted to be a pure Christian, one and equal with all men. He even wanted to give away all he had, to the poor. Yet he was a great promoter of industry, and he knew perfectly that he must keep his goods and keep his authority. This was as divine a necessity in him, as the need to give away all he possessed— more divine even, since this was the necessity he acted upon. Yet because he did *not* act on the other ideal, it dominated him, he was dying of chagrin because he must forfeit it. He wanted to be a father of loving kindness and sacrificial benevolence. The colliers shouted to him about his thousands a year. They would not be deceived.   [17]

Since the characters in *Women in Love* tend to be more self-aware than those in *The Rainbow,* they must find more devious and complex ways of eluding that awareness. We can call this repression, as when Lawrence describes Gudrun's cheek as "flushed with repressed emotion." Lawrence does not, I think, mean by the term all that Freud does, but his sense of "repression" goes well beyond deliberate suppression. Gerald and Gudrun show the strain of denying feelings that sometimes escape them and are then seen with a somewhat prurient intensity or furtive self-distrust. They veer rather violently between rigid ordering and a sense of blind self-abandon.

The chapter called "Rabbit" is the most brilliant instance of this release from repression. There is preparation for the release in small, limited gestures whose import is all the greater for their obliquity. As Gudrun walks in the garden with Gerald, "her reverential, almost ecstatic admiration of the flowers caressed his nerves. She stooped down, and touched the trumpets, with infinitely fine and delicate-touching finger-tips." But when Gudrun tries to hold the rabbit Bismarck, it lashes out and scores her wrists with its claws. A "heavy cruelty" wells up in Gudrun, and Gerald observes it "with subtle recognition." As the rabbit eludes him, his own rage is excited, and he brings his hand down "like a hawk" on the neck of the rabbit. It screams with terror and submits. As he looks at Gudrun, she seems "almost unearthly": the scream of the rabbit has "torn the veil of her consciousness." The complex feelings they betray and recognize in each other are brilliantly caught:

Gudrun looked at Gerald with strange, darkened eyes, strained with under-world knowledge, almost supplicating, like those of a creature which is at his mercy, yet which is his ultimate victor. He did not know what to say to her. He felt the mutual recognition. And he felt he ought to say something, to cover it. He had the power of lightning in his nerves, she seemed like a soft recipient of his magical, hideous white fire. He was unconfident, he had qualms of fear.   [18]

She adopts a note of "vindictive mockery" to cover her shame, but the shame is evident enough. There was a "league between them, abhorrent to them both. They were implicated in abhorrent mysteries." Later they exchange smiles of "obscene recognition" as fellow initiates (18). They share the desire both for cruel domination and for painful surrender, and they are drawn together by their fascination with power. One of the sources of power—power to use against Gerald—that Gudrun eventually finds is her verbal play with Loerke; with him Gudrun can bring to consciousness what Gerald cannot face. "From their verbal and physical nuances they got the highest satisfaction in the nerves, from a queer interchange of half-suggested ideas, looks, expressions, and gestures, which were quite intolerable, though incomprehensible to Gerald. He had no terms in which to think of their commerce, his terms were much too gross" (30).

Gerald's nerves are caressed by Gudrun; Gudrun and Loerke later achieve satisfaction in the nerves. The nerves are channels of feeling, clearly; but they are also the source of consciousness and thought. As we have seen, Lawrence stresses the levels of self. At the upper reaches of consciousness are intellectual activity and the play of ideas; and, with a saturation of feeling, often aggressive, the play of wit and irony. Perhaps above, perhaps below, but closely related is the assertion of will. Further below is the play of sensation, of color, taste, touch. Further yet is the more fully sensual or sexual life. And as one descends below consciousness, beyond the ego and its defenses, one moves toward the loss or dissolution of self that becomes an experience of the timeless or immortal. One can speak of that experience as an intensity so great as to obliterate all awareness of limits, whether of self or time or place. It is timelessness in that intensity displaces duration. (Lawrence wrote of the Russian writer Rozanov that he was "the first to see that immortality is in the vividness of life, not the loss of life.")[25] As we see in the chapter "Excurse" this intensity is not only the "marvellous fullness of immediate gratification, overwhelming, out-flooding from the deepest source," but, at the same time, "the most intolerable accession into being." One can speak of a descent into the undifferentiated stream of Being, the river of life itself; it must be followed in turn by a resumption of the self (perhaps on new terms) and a return to the limits of singleness and consciousness. This descent and return is, clearly, a sacramental occasion in Lawrence's religion, and it has its mystery; "the immemorial magnificence of mystic, palpable, real otherness." The adjectives are not otiose: "real" is defined by the conjunction of the "mystic" and the "palpable."

In contrast to this full experience of otherness is the partial descent, stopping short of the pain of a new reality, finding only a satisfaction of the nerves in its failure to be free of self, like Ursula's tortured encounters with Anton Skrebensky under the brilliant moon in *The Rainbow*. As Lawrence wrote in a letter to Catherine Carswell (16 July 1916): "So that act of love which is a pure thrill, is a kind of friction between opposites, interdestructive, an act of death. There is an extreme *self-realization, self-sensation* in this friction against the really hostile opposite."[26] Sensuality itself can be a premature destination, as we see in the African statuette. With the "dark involuntary being" denied or unrealized, the frustrated energies ascend into will, seemingly conscious and in the control of mind. Birkin charges Hermione Roddice with this. Her passion is a lie. "It isn't passion at all, it is your *will*. It's your bullying will" (3). When Hermione boasts of her power of will, Ursula is struck by the "strangely tense voice," and responds with a "curious thrill," only in part of repulsion, to the "strange, dark, convulsive power" Hermione reveals. Birkin's response is less equivocal: "Such a will is an obscenity" (12). We see the same will in Gerald Crich's relations with Minette: "her inchoate look of a violated slave, whose fulfillment lies in her further and further violation, made his nerves quiver with acutely desirable sensation. After all, his was the only will, she was the passive substance of his will. He tingled with the subtle, biting sensation." (7).

Hermione Roddice is perhaps the clearest instance of radical fluctuation between the pleasure in receiving pain and the satisfaction in causing it. We first see her, extravagantly dressed, moving "as if scarcely conscious," walking with "a peculiar fixity of the hips, a strange unwilling motion"—seeming "almost drugged, as if a strange mass of thought coiled in the darkness within her, and she was never allowed to escape." She is "full of intellectuality," and "nerve-worn with consciousness." She seems to assert invulnerability through her rank and wealth and power, but under the show of pride she feels "exposed to wounds and to mockery and to despite." For she lacks a "robust self." Instead, she is at home with all that is "highest" in thought or art; she trusts in her "higher" knowledge, she wants to believe that Birkin will see "how she was, for him the 'highest,' " his "highest fate" (1).

When Hermione visits Ursula's classroom, she praises Gudrun's little sculptures: "The little things seem more subtle to her." But Ursula resists the love of subtlety: "A mouse isn't any more subtle than a lion, is it?" Hermione goes on to fear that the children may learn too much: "Hadn't they better be animals, simple animals, crude, violent, *anything* rather than this self-consciousness, this incapacity to be spontaneous?" It is an important issue, placed early in the novel to distinguish between willed oblivion and true spontaneity. Hermione is, in fact, giving voice to her own torture, at the same time taunting Birkin with the withering effect of consciousness. The young, she says, may be "really dead before they have a chance to live." Birkin cuts across this: "Not because they have too much mind, but too little." And Birkin goes on to strip away Hermione's self-deception: "You don't want to be an animal, you want to observe your own animal functions, to get a mental thrill out of them. . . . Passion and the instincts—you want them hard enough, but through your head, in your consciousness" (3). It is a cruel and humiliating charge, and it expresses, whatever more, Birkin's desire to escape her and, with her, some part of himself. When the break finally comes, her mind is a chaos and she struggles "to gain control with her will, as a swimmer struggles with the swirling water." Hermione's will gives way in an act of convulsive release, "unconscious in ecstasy" when she brings a ball of lapis lazuli down on Birkin's head—or seeks to, for he throws up an arm to save himself. Hermione, once she has lost Birkin, is a "priestess without belief," her "desecrated sanctities" leaving "only devastating cynicism" where the beliefs had been (8).

Gerald Crich and Gudrun Brangwen carry the contradictions we see in Hermione much further. Both of them are curiously guarded and vigilant. Birkin observes of Gudrun's sculpture that "she must never be too serious, she feels she might give herself away. And she won't give herself away— she's always on the defensive" (8). So, too, Gerald, when he talks with Birkin, "would never openly admit what he felt" (16). This finally bores Birkin: "Gerald could never fly away from himself in real indifferent gaiety." Instead, he has a passion for talk and especially for metaphysical discussion. But he does not take it very seriously. It is words he loves. For all his geniality and seeming strength, Gerald seems "always to be at bay against everybody." Especially, one can say, against himself. We learn early in the novel that he shot and killed his brother when as children they played with a gun. Was it a pure accident? Can there be a pure accident? Ursula can't believe that there was not an "unconscious will" behind it, but Gudrun is outraged by the suggestion. Birkin earlier has spoken about a crime's needing both a murderer and a murderee. A murderee is "a man who in a profound if hidden lust desires to be murdered." Gerald, in a sense, is both; he expects violence because he both dreads and wants it so much (2).

Halliday's African statues, and particularly one of a woman in childbirth, disturb Gerald, for they suggest "the extreme of physical sensation, beyond the limits of mental consciousness." Anything which represents a loss of control seems to him obscene (6). The next day he asks Birkin about the statue; he has spent the night with Minette, and the statue's face makes him think of hers. He hates the explicitness of its barbarity, but Birkin sees in the statue a "complete truth," the work of a culture that has carried pure physical sensation to its utmost. "It is so sensual as to be final, supreme." Like all art, it hurts. Gerald wants, however, "to keep certain illusions," just as he wants to leave money for Minette so as to separate that experience from the rest of his life (7).

Gudrun has a bolder mind than Gerald, and she allows herself to move freely and provocatively among the miners. She finds the "glamourous thickness of labour and maleness" exciting, both "potent and half-repulsive":

> This was the world of powerful, underworld men who spent most of their time in the darkness. In their voices she could hear the voluptuous resonance of

darkness, the strong, dangerous underworld, mindless, inhuman. They sounded also like strange machines, heavy, oiled. The voluptuousness was like that of machinery, cold and iron.

Sometimes Gudrun feels this "hideous and sickeningly mindless." Sometimes she imagines herself pursued like a "new Daphne, turning not into a tree but a machine." The miners arouse in her "a strange, nostalgic ache of desire, something almost demoniacal, never to be fulfilled." The nostalgic ache is clearly not a yearning for the past but for a reduction to a simpler level of being, less conscious, a retreat from the difficulties of being fully human. It is the organism yearning to be reduced to mechanism or the mental to the more purely instinctive (9).

Gerald is first awakened to Gudrun's capacities by her cold, cutting indifference to Hermione's malicious dropping of her sketchbook in the water.

Gerald watched Gudrun closely, whilst she repulsed Hermione. There was a body of cold power in her. . . . He saw her a dangerous, hostile spirit. . . . In her tone she made the understanding clear—they were of the same kind, he and she, a sort of diabolic freemasonry subsisted between them. Henceforward, she knew she had her power over him. [10]

We see her flaunting of power when she dances provocatively before the castle at Shortlands. She ignores Gerald's warning of danger, and, when she sees a "faint domineering smile on his face," she strikes it. She feels "unconquerable desire for deep violence against him." But her will controls this. "She shut off the fear and discovery that filled her conscious mind. . . . She was not going to be afraid." When Gerald says, "You have struck the first blow," she replies, "I shall strike the last." A few minutes he tells her he loves her and grasps her arm "as if his hand were iron." She is afraid, and she responds "as if drugged, her voice crooning and witch-like" (14).

Lawrence provides Gerald Crich with a history, and he defended his deployment of it in the book. Of the chapter to be called "The Industrial Magnate," Lawrence wrote to Catherine Carswell: "I want it to come where it does: you meet a man, you get an impression of him, you find out *afterwards* what he has done. If you have, in your arrogance, writ him down a nobody, then there is a slap in the eye for you when you find he has done more than you have done."[27] But Lawrence provides no such surprises; instead, we are interested in the ways in which his symbols expand to contain more and more of experience, unpredictably relating distinct realms to each other within the structure of a single temperament. Gerald, we learn, has "feared and despised his father," and the father, characteristically, has disliked his son without allowing himself to know it. Thomas Crich's long illness and slow death are torture for Gerald. With "something of the terror of a destructive child," he sees himself "on the point of inheriting his own destruction." He has in his youth refused to see or believe in the colliery; after Oxford he traveled in savage regions. But finally comes his chance to control the Crich industrial power. All that he ignored now becomes "subjugate to his will," and he rejects the specious humanitarianism his father tried halfheartedly to live by. Gerald sees the industry as a great machine obeying the will and mind of a single man. He introduces a brisk and heartless efficiency, planned by experts, reducing the workers to "mere mechanical instruments." At first the miners hate him; but they come to discover that participation in a "great and perfect system" is the kind of freedom they really want. It is, again, freedom from consciousness, the reduction of the organic to the mechanical, of work to something self-sufficient and depersonalized. Gerald finds himself reduced by the machine he has created; he tries to escape a feeling of emptiness that leads to near-madness. (17).

The torture of watching his father's refusal to accept death and of seeing the slow extinction of a stubborn will (Gudrun admires the self-possession and control of the dying man) leads Gerald to the "subterranean desire to let go." When the death finally comes, he goes to the Brangwen house and slips up to Gudrun's room. She accepts his love; he gains strength from her and sinks to sleep on her breast like a child. It is the "sleep of complete exhaustion and restoration." But Gudrun has been "destroyed into perfect consciousness." She feels the "awful, inhuman distance which would always be interposed between her and the other being." She lies in an "exhausting super consciousness" until Gerald leaves in the morning; she is resentful of his power over her, her inability to withstand it, her submission to an "ecstasy of subjection" (24).

This scene is matched by a later one in the Alps. As Gudrun stands at night brushing her hair, she sees Gerald's face in the mirror as he stands behind her. She feels the pressure of his stare, "not consciously seeing her, and yet watching, with fine-pupilled eyes that *seemed* to smile, and which were not really smiling." She tries to bring him back with a question, but fails. There ensues a "strange battle between her ordinary consciousness and his uncanny, black-art consciousness." She is terrified by the force of his presence: "she felt she could not bear it any more, in a few minutes she would fall down at his feet, grovelling at his feet, and letting him destroy her." At last she finds a solution. She asks him to look in her bag for a small box. As he does so, she knows she has broken the spell, distracted him, freed herself of vulnerability. He has not perceived her panic, and now she has control again. Lawrence does not make the states of mind very determinate. She seems to fear something unconscious and murderous in him. And her escape from him is one instance of the seesaw of power that marks the last stages of their life together. Once more she lies awake as he sleeps, and she thinks about his power to organize industry. He is a splendid instrument: he could become a "Napoleon of peace, or a Bismarck." As she allows herself this dream of power, something snaps, and a "terrible cynicism" overcomes her. "Everything turned to irony with her. . . . When she felt her pang of undeniable reality, this was when she knew the hard irony of hopes and ideas." He seems a "superhuman instrument" ready to be used. But then the irony returns: "What for?"

As Gudrun lies awake thinking of all that might be achieved, each goal is stripped of promise: "one outside show instead of another." There is nothing to wish for. "Everything was intrinsically a piece of irony to her." At least there could be isolated, discrete "perfect moments." She awakens Gerald, thinking, "Oh, convince me, I need it." He reflects her "mocking, enigmatic smile" with his own. After they have made love, Gudrun hears a song from outside: "Gudrun knew that that song would sound through her eternity, sung in a manly, reckless, mocking voice. It marked one of her supreme moments, the supreme pangs of her nervous gratification. There it was, fixed in eternity for her" (29).

I have dealt with the scene at some length because it marks both Gudrun's ascendancy and the cynicism which leaves her without purpose or belief. She turns increasingly to the small, sardonic Loerke. He is an artist, and he intrigues her by his "old man's look" and "uncanny singleness"—a kind of stability and self-subsistency that Gerald lacks and that Gudrun, who lacks them, too, thinks the mark of an artist. Loerke has a photograph of a granite frieze he made for a "great granite factory in Cologne": "It was a representation of a fair, with peasants and artisans in an orgy of enjoyment, drunk and absurd in their modern dress, whirling ridiculously in roundabouts, gaping at shows, kissing and staggering and rolling in knots, swinging in swing-boats, and firing down shooting-galleries, a frenzy of chaotic motion." For Gudrun, Loerke represents the "rock bottom of all life." He has dispensed with all illusions; he is a "pure, unconnected will," the "very stuff of the underworld." Birkin sees him as a "little obscene monster of the darkness," who "hates the ideal utterly." A "gnawing little negation," he appeals to all who "hate the ideal also in themselves" (29).

Ursula resists Loerke's appeal. She is outraged by the photograph of his statuette of a massive, rigid stallion on whose back sits sideways a naked girl "as if in shame and grief." Gudrun admires the work with "a certain dark homage," but Ursula blasts it with the kind of direct attack on its moral assumptions that Lawrence often makes in his criticism. Loerke condescendingly tells Ursula that the work of art is autonomous and has "no relation with the everyday world." They are, he says, "two different and distinct planes of existence, and to translate one into the other is worse than foolish." Gudrun joins him: "*I* and my art," she exclaims, "they have *nothing* to do

with each other." Lawrence has, of course, shown us otherwise. Ursula will
have none of this, and she is dealing as well with the repression we have seen
throughout:

> "As for your world of art and your world of reality . . . you have to separate
> them because you can't bear to know what you are. You can't bear to realise
> what a stock, still, hide-bound brutality you are really, so you say 'it's the
> world of art.' The world of art is only the truth about the real world, that's
> all—but you are too far gone to see it."   [29]

Ursula has been accurate enough in supposing the girl to be one whom
Loerke treated brutally. She has caught the perversity in Loerke's conception
of the girl and of the horse in relation to her. If Ursula makes the method of
moral criticism too easy, she is at any rate taking Loerke's work more seriously than the others. And she is making a claim for consciousness against
the narcosis of aestheticism. However philistine she seems, she stands for the
awareness which Gudrun and Gerald cannot endure. What makes Loerke
appeal to Gudrun most of all is his ability to make her cynicism explicit and
unashamed. He provides a form of play in which the intolerable can be made
amusing.

Gudrun and Loerke play a game of "infinite suggestivity, strange and
leering, as if they had some esoteric understanding of life . . . that the
world dared not know" (30). It is a game of "subtle inter-suggestivity," a
"satisfaction in the nerves," a cultivation of the "inner mysteries of sensation." One can see the point in Lawrence's remarks on Poe: "For him the
vital world is the sensational world. He is not sensual, he is sensational. The
difference between the two is the difference between growth and decay." [28]
In Gudrun and Loerke there is a displacement of the sensual into the sen-
suous; it is eroticism without passion, "the subtle thrills of extreme sensation
in reduction." At a deeper level Gudrun sees through this; she is not, at
moments, so abandoned to cynicism as Loerke. She knows, however, that
there is "no escape." She must "always see and know and never escape." She
must always be "watching the fingers twitch across the eternal, mechanical,
monotonous clock-face of time." More than Gerald, she cannot escape consciousness, barren and despairing as hers is; she can no longer achieve the
sleep that is freedom from self.

In the final conflict of Gerald and Gudrun, each gains power in turn, "one
destroyed that the other might exist, one ratified because the other was nulled"
(30). Gerald cannot bear to "stand by himself, in sheer nothingness." When
he finally tries to strangle her, he is persuaded that her struggling is "her
reciprocal lustful passion in this embrace." Roused to consciousness by
Loerke's intervention, he feels only disgust and goes off into the snow, believing himself doomed to be murdered, and at last stumbling into the sleep
of death.

Loerke has provided only a catalyst in the relation of Gerald and Gudrun. In providing Gudrun with an absolute of sensation, he is a counterpart of Halliday's African statuette, especially as Birkin describes it. The statue embodies thousands of years of onward movement into pure sensuality, long after the desire for creation has lapsed and all the other powers of the self have atrophied. It represents a "knowledge arrested and ending in the senses, mystic knowledge in disintegration and dissolution." But if this is the African process, its parallel and counterpart in the north is "the vast abstraction of ice and snow," "ice-destructive knowledge, snow-abstract annihilation" (19). In Loerke we find a northern version of dissolution, full of sensual ideas but playing with them within the ego, turning them to knowledge. Each of the extremities is a false end; each is a stage of consciousness that has become an absolute, a stopping place, arresting the movement into the unknown and toward new creation. Gudrun voices this sense of entrapment in a cul-de-sac, the belief in endless repetitive continuity rather than the discontinuity of a new life. To Ursula, who wants to free herself entirely of the old world, Gudrun asks, "But isn't it really an illusion to think you can get out of it?" Gudrun is skeptical about getting beyond love to something, as Ursula puts it, that "isn't so merely *human*." And Ursula thinks, "Because you never *have* loved, you can't get beyond it" (29).

Birkin's is the fullest consciousness in the novel. Lawrence achieves a nicer precision in his novels than in his other prose; and he achieves it in part by a mockery of Birkin's limitations. Birkin is an instance of the "last man," the prophet of a new order who must still live in the old, making his ascent of Pisgah but with no expectation of knowing directly the world he wishes to bring into being. There are dangerous temptations for such a figure, as we see in Shaw's hero in *Man and Superman:* self-pity and self-dramatization, particularly in the role of a prophet or Salvator Mundi. Related to this is the danger of allowing the negations one must insist upon to become an end in themselves, to become so absorbed in the process of dissolution as to lose a sense of its transitional function.

In the discarded "Prologue to *Women in Love*," Birkin reacts vindictively and jeeringly against Hermione's adoration of him and her cultivation of an "ecstasy of beauty." Interestingly, Birkin's attitude toward her recalls Paul's toward Miriam in *Sons and Lovers* ("He hated her, for her incapacity for love, for her lack of desire for him. . . . Her desire was all spiritual, all in the consciousness").[29] It recalls to a degree Ursula with Skrebensky ("all the soul was caught up in the universal chill-blazing bonfire of the moonlit night . . . the silver-cold night of death, lovely and perfect"). And it shows radical "vibration between two poles," between Hermione, "the centre of social virtue," and a "prostitute, anti-social, almost criminal" (102). Birkin's homosexual impulse, strong, perhaps shared unconsciously by Gerald Crich, remains a secret kept by Birkin "to himself" and even "from himself." He "knew what he felt, but he always kept the knowledge at bay"—perhaps the closest we get to Lawrence's conception of repression (167). "It was in the other world of the subconsciousness that the interplay took place . . . the relieving of physical and spiritual poverty, without any intrinsic change of state in either man" (96). In all of this we sense the frustration most of all:

> Never to be able to love spontaneously, never to be moved by a power greater than oneself, but always to be within one's own control, deliberate, having the choice, this was horrifying, more deadly than death. Yet how was one to escape? How could a man escape from being deliberate and unloving, except a greater power, an impersonal, imperative love should take hold of him?   [97]

Birkin is enduring the winter, but he is skeptical of the spring. There can at present be "only submission to death of this nature" and—if one can attain it—a "cherishing of the unknown that is unknown for many a day yet, buds that may not open till a far off season comes, when the season of death has passed away (98).

Colin Clarke has written eloquently about Lawrence's use of the Romantic theme of dissolution as necessary to rebirth, the paradox of finding birth through death, a paradox that can be expanded into the phases of a cycle.[30] But Lawrence stresses most of all the temptation to rest in death, to lose oneself in those absolutes of spirit or sense that relinquish movement for stability. Both Birkin and Ursula are tempted by such surrender, but each exposes the fallacies of the other; and in a sense they exacerbate themselves into passion and life. The effect is often somewhat comic, and the book gains power from that ironic stretch of consciousness in Lawrence. Ursula finds Birkin's despair "too picturesque and final," implicitly insincere or self-indulgent. She wants him as a lover, but he seems in love with his role; it is a disease he doesn't "want to be cured of." She admires his vitality and despises this "ridiculous, mean effacement" into a prig and a preacher. As she says later, "I don't trust you when you drag in the stars. . . . If you were quite true, it wouldn't be necessary to be so far-fetched." And she goes deeper: "You don't fully believe yourself what you are saying." He has set a goal, of a "pure balance of two single beings" as "the stars balance each other." If no actual experience can be expected to attain it, it may be only a cynical way of avoiding actual love. She makes him call her "my love" at last and accept the limited and immediate (13).

While Ursula seems to deny the flame that stands behind the person, she is insisting upon the need to give oneself to another rather than avoiding life with interminable theory. When Birkin speaks of the dark river of dissolution, the long process of death that we mistake for life, Ursula is enraged again. Birkin insists upon discontinuity; the new beginning doesn't come "out of the end" but "after it." There will be a new cycle of creation, but not for them. Ursula is bitter: "You are a devil, you know, really. . . . You *want* us to be deathly." He gives in to love and scorns his "other self" as a "word-bag," but "still somewhere far off and small, the other hovered." Birkin wants something more than love, but he accepts the love that is offered him, whimpering to himself, "Not this, not this" (14).

Ursula, however, has her own times of loving death. They come when she despairs of Birkin's love; she neither expects nor wants a new birth. In the chapter called "Moony" she has her own "profound grudge against the human being." (It is characteristic of Ursula to have a grudge rather than a theory.) What seems her "marvellous radiance of intrinsic vitality" is in fact a "luminousness of supreme repudiation"; and she sits in shadows watching her counterpart in the "white and deathly smile" of the moon. When Birkin comes cursing Cybele, the pagan goddess whose priests were unmanned, casting stones into the water to smash the floating image, he is clearly attacking with ferocity what he imagines Ursula (and, earlier, Hermione) to stand for, an image of the threatening female will. But of course the image reforms, the flakes of light regathered, like a rose calling back its scattered petals.[31]

Birkin asks Ursula for the "golden light" in her, and he turns off her suspicion of his wish to dominate by asking her in turn to drop her "assertive *will*," her "frightened apprehensive self-insistence." And he in turn acknowledges that he loves her. But he tries to distinguish the sensual fulfillment they will have from the "profound yearning" for something more. He thinks of the African statuette and its remarkable progression along a path of sensual understanding, but he thinks also of Gerald Crich and the "white demons of the north," of the alternative dissolution into whiteness and snow. And he comes at last to a third way, a "way of freedom":

> The individual soul taking precedence over love and desire for union . . . a lovely state of free proud singleness, which accepted the obligation of the permanent connection with others, and with the other, submits to the yoke and leash of love, but never forfeits its own proud individual singleness, even while it loves and yields.[32]   [19]

Once Birkin and Ursula achieve the resolution of their love, they decide to resign from the "world of work" (the world in which Gerald finds so much of his fulfillment). They are going away, but to nowhere in particular. "It isn't really a locality," Birkin says. "It's a perfected relation." It is in fact "transit."

They can no longer endure the "tyranny of a fixed milieu." They must be rid of the past and of possessions. They believe that they must, like a statue of Rodin or Michelangelo, "leave a piece of raw rock unfinished to your figure. You must leave your surroundings sketchy, unfinished, so that you are never contained, never confined, never dominated from the outside." (For Gerald life is "artificially held *together* by the social mechanism" [5].) They give away a handsome old chair they have bought. (Gudrun in contrast thinks of the "wonderful stability of marriage," a "rosy room, with herself in a beautiful gown, and a handsome man in evening dress who . . . kissed her.") As they cross the channel to Ostend, Birkin feels "overcome by the trajectory," the "wonder of transit," the "utter and absolute peace . . . in this final transit out of life." But Ursula is filled with a sense of "the unrealized world ahead," the "unknown paradise," a "sweetness of habitation, a delight of living quite unknown, but hers infallibly." She leaves behind her old identity, that "creature of history" who is "not really herself" (29). She belongs now only "to the oneness with Birkin, a oneness that struck deeper notes, sounding into the heart of the universe, the heart of reality, where she had never existed before."

It is a movement without destination, and Lawrence deliberately ends with Birkin's reluctance to be content in this one relationship. "You are enough for me, as far as a woman is concerned. . . . But I wanted a man friend, as eternal as you and I are eternal." Ursula rejects the idea; it's "an obstinacy, a theory, a perversity" (31). But Birkin remains unpersuaded. It is not an ominous close but a calculated anticlimax. Nothing ends, nothing stops. There is not the ironic juxtaposition of Conrad's versions of Jim, nor Linda Viola's cry of unrequited passion as it fills the dark gulf with the voice of illusion and pronounces for Dr. Monygham the enviable and sinister triumph of Nostromo. Lawrence's ending does not preclude difficulty and difference, but the openness of the debate, the freedom of quarrel and banter, seems to presume a confidence in process and becoming that Conrad neither has nor wants to have.

12 ✻ Forster:
Inclusion and Exclusion

One may as well begin with Miss Bartlett's words to Lucy Honeychurch. The scene is Florence, the Pension Bertolini. The ladies have been given rooms that overlook an interior court. Mr. Emerson and his son offer their own rooms in exchange: rooms with a view. Miss Bartlett is offended by the indelicacy of the proposal, but Lucy is less certain how to take it: " 'No, he is not tactful; yet have you noticed that there are people who do things which are most indelicate, and yet at the same time—beautiful?' " " 'Beautiful?' said Miss Bartlett, puzzled at the word. 'Are not beauty and delicacy the same?' " [1]

Miss Bartlett's delicacy is the tiresome self-assertion of a threadbare ego. She uses gratitude as reproach, self-denial as accusation. That she does this unconsciously makes her invulnerable to criticism; that she thinks she acts for the sake of others forces the others to preserve guilty and resentful silence. Miss Bartlett is a fine portrait of the tyranny of the underdog; she has only to allude with delicacy to her dependence on others' wealth to free herself of any reproach of selfishness.

We find Miss Bartlett taking her inevitable place in that crucial scene where, walking out on a natural terrace to admire a magnificent view, Lucy Honeychurch comes unexpectedly upon George Emerson. "For a moment he contemplated her as one who had fallen out of heaven. He saw radiant joy in her face, he saw the flowers beat against her dress in blue waves. The bushes above them closed. He stepped quickly forward and kissed her.

"Before she could speak, almost before she could feel, a voice called: 'Lucy! Lucy! Lucy!' The silence of life had been broken by Miss Bartlett, who stood brown against the view" (6).

Such a discovery releases all of Miss Bartlett's powers. She works "like a great artist," presenting to Lucy "the complete picture of a cheerless, loveless world in which the young rush to destruction until they learn better." In contrast, George's father, Mr. Emerson, is the celebrant of the open, the naked, and the sincere. "The Garden of Eden," he declares in the manner of

Blake, "which you place in the past, is really yet to come. We shall enter it when we no longer despise our bodies." His wardrobe bears the inscription, "Mistrust all enterprises that require new clothes." But when three young men bathe in a pond, their clothes lie in bundles on the bank and proclaim in a voice like Miss Bartlett's, "We are what matters. Without us shall no enterprise begin. To us shall all flesh turn in the end." Miss Bartlett, one might say, seems a creature composed entirely of scarves and buttons (12).

And yet at the close of the novel, when George Emerson and Lucy are married and have returned to Florence, they brood over Miss Bartlett's role. It was she who arranged for Lucy to meet George's father, to be shaken by him out of cant, waste, and muddle. For Mr. Emerson "robbed the body of its taint, the world's taunts of their sting" and taught Lucy "the holiness of direct desire." Could Miss Bartlett have meant this to happen? George offers his surmise:

> That from the very first moment we met, she hoped, far down in her mind, that we should be like this—of course, very far down. That she fought us on the surface, and yet she hoped. I can't explain her any other way . . . she is not frozen, Lucy, she is not withered up all through. She tore us apart twice, but . . . that evening she was given one more chance to make us happy. We can never make friends with her or thank her. But I do believe that, far down in her heart, far below all speech and behaviour, she is glad.   [20]

What are we to make of Miss Bartlett? Is she one character or two? Is the final revelation too ingenious, too surprising, too romancelike? Has a flat character suddenly become round at the wave of the novelist's wand? The final treatment of Miss Bartlett is a stroke of wit, much like the gratuitous confirmation of a truth otherwise demonstrated, as when a sacred pun confirms the plain truths of revelation.

For *A Room with a View* is a novel about repression, muddle, and bad faith; to allow Miss Bartlett her view at some level of unconscious passion— "far down in her heart"—is to celebrate the holiness of the heart's affections and to permit those affections to perform one of their miracles, acting beneath Miss Bartlett's consciousness but making her their instrument. A neat resolution, even a brilliant one, but one that tends to undermine Forster's own categories of flat and round characters.[2]

I should prefer to define those categories in different terms. The repetitive character, in Forster as much as in Dickens, is often powerfully obsessive. He has found a way of meeting all situations, and it may require outrageous energy to preserve this response as well as to shut out all the complexities it avoids. One may see this monotonous and costly expense of energy at work or one may see the vestige of that energy in the husk of a person, a self withered into a type, emotions trivialized into rigid manners, a character who is—in Forster's terms—all clothes. As the sociologist Peter Berger has put it: "Society gives us names to shield us from nothingness. It builds a world for us to live in and thus protects us from the chaos which surrounds us on all sides. It provides us with a language and with meanings that make this world believeable. And it supplies a steady chorus of voices that confirm our belief and still our dormant doubts. . . . [Society] is a conspiracy to bring about inauthentic existence. . . ."[3]

The central theme in Forster's earlier novels is the eruption of reality, its bursting through structures that have been built to disguise or conceal it. In *Aspects of the Novel* Forster writes of the tension between the vision of "life in time" and that of "life by values" (2). The violence that runs through his novels—he spoke of the scene in Marabar Caves as "a good substitute for violence"[4]—is a way of dramatizing the insufficiency of life in time, without which of course there can be no life by values either. Sequentiality and logic must be shattered by coincidence or inconsequence, by sudden deaths and improbable meetings. At such moments life in time gives way to romance. In *Howards End* Forster writes about the common "tragedy of preparedness," the sad waste of "staggering through life fully armed." "Life, " he goes on, "is indeed dangerous, but not in the way morality would have us believe. It is indeed unmanageable, but the essence of it is not a battle. It is unmanageable because it is a romance, and its essence is romantic beauty" (12). *Romantic beauty* sounds soft and Edwardian. What Forster's romance serves to admit, however, is nothing less than reality. In contrast to it is the specious order of life in time: "Actual life is full of false clues and sign-posts that lead nowhere. With infinite effort we nerve ourselves for a crisis that never comes" (WW 33). There is no better way of describing the overpreparedness of the flat characters, always ready for an imaginary crisis in the armature of a rigid posture.

Reality is, of course, a slippery term. Our ontology is a commitment to what we have chosen to regard as real and what as derivative. Forster's emphasis upon sincerity, self-awareness, and personal relationships becomes a way of dismissing those long stretches of life when we feel little or feel what we are told to feel or, worst of all, try to feel what we have persuaded ourselves we should feel. The unreal has almost inevitably a social setting, for, while Forster is no rebel against the idea of society, he remains a connoisseur of its inauthenticity. He learned from Jane Austen, he tells us, "the possibilities of domestic humour," but he adds, "I was more ambitious than she was, of course; I tried to hitch it on to other things" (WW 34). The chief of those other things, I would propose, is the idea of reality.

In his comments on a fragmentary novel, *Arctic Summer*, Forster draws a distinction between the heroic man who is at home in reality and the more commonplace one who belongs to society:

I think I know about March. He is first and foremost heroic, no thought of self when the blood is up, he can pounce and act rightly, he is generous, idealistic, loyal. When his blood is not up, when conditions are unfavourable, he is apt to be dazed, trite and sour—the hero straying into the modern world which does not want him and which he does not understand. . . .

How should such a character be presented? Impressionistically—that is to say he should come and go, and not be documented, in contrast to the Whitbys and Borlases [other characters in the novel], who can't be documented too much. . . . The only way to present this hero was to root him as little as possible in society, and to let him come and go unexplained. T. E. Lawrence, whom I did not then know, offers a hint.[5]

Related to this contrast is the one Forster draws in his essay, "Anonymity: An Inquiry":

Just as words have two functions—information and creation—so each human mind has two personalities, one on the surface, one deeper down. The upper personality has a name. It is called S. T. Coleridge, or William Shakespeare, or Mrs. Humphry Ward. It is conscious and alert, it does things like dining out, answering letters, etc., and it differs vividly and amusingly from other personalities. The lower personality is a very queer affair. In many ways it is a perfect fool, but without it there is no literature, because unless a man dips a bucket down into it occasionally he cannot produce first-class work. There is something general about it. Although it is inside S. T. Coleridge, it cannot be labelled with his name. It has something in common with all other deeper personalities, and the mystic will assert that the common quality is God, and that here, in the obscure recesses of our being, we near the gates of the Divine.[6]

Forster's contrast between the time-bound and social, on the one hand, and the heroic and impersonal, on the other, is one way of separating the less real from the more, and it governs both the structure of the novels and the conception of character. For the characters are, so to speak, people of the book: whatever their source in Forster's experience, "the original material," as he tells us, "soon disappears, and a character who belongs to the book and nowhere else emerges." The novelist can make his characters more fully "explicable" than actual people—"we get from this a reality of kind we never get in daily life"—but he also exercises the "right to intermittent knowledge": he may enter characters' minds at will but refuse to enter as well, he may show us limited aspects of his characters and even different aspects of each (WW 33). Forster's conception of character is flexible. One may say that his characters are only people enough to be characters. They are created by a system of notation and reference which permits varying degrees of closeness and varying levels of consciousness, and everywhere we find the filter of free indirect discourse, of characters' thoughts reported in the novelist's words and inevitably shaped in the process, sometimes dryly undercut or gently dislocated from inherent plausibility toward ironic incongruity.

In *A Passage to India* we enter frequently into Fielding's mind, more occasionally but significantly into Mrs. Moore's, only once into Professor Godbole's and then at a moment when he is meditating. We never see into Godbole's upper personality, in short, and it is the dehumanizing force of Mrs. Moore's vision more than her normal sensibility that concerns us. Each character is real in a somewhat different dimension of its being.

Critics have often remarked that there is no dominant character in this novel, and there is certainly none untouched by weakness or ineffectuality. The slightness of the characters is due not to their imprecision but to the powerful design which contains them. The presence of India is both ground and theme. It serves to provide setting but it embodies, in its own brilliant metaphors, the central themes that shape the characters as well. They are not figures *in* a landscape but figures *of* a landscape. Forster was afraid at one point that "the characters are not sufficiently interesting for the atmosphere. This tempts me to emphasize the atmosphere, and so to produce a meditation rather than a drama."[7]

D. J. Enright speaks of India—"too big, too diverse, too elusive, to possess what we call 'character' "—as a "vast amorphous Anti-Character," against which human characters "dwindle in the direction of types or even caricatures."[8] I should not see India as a rival force, an Anti-Character, but as a common predicament. There "is scarcely anything in that tormented land," Forster wrote in 1922, "which fills up the gulf between the illimitable and the inane, and society suffers in consequence. What isn't piety is apt to be indecency; what isn't metaphysics is intrigue."[9] The common predicament of Forster's characters is the problem of interpretation. "How can the mind take hold of such a country?" India is in part a country of the mind, or rather a country that creates anxiety by its resistance to the mind's utmost efforts. "Perhaps life is a mystery, not a muddle; they could not tell. Perhaps the hundred Indias which fuss and squabble so tiresomely are one, and the universe they mirror is one. They had not the apparatus for judging."[10] And each kind of apparatus creates its own version of reality. What gives this novel its peculiar form is that the enigmatic resistance India offers to interpretation is stated and restated at each level. As in earlier novels a few phrases gain resonance through repetition, but here their effect is different. If "panic and emptiness" or "telegrams and anger" are clear Wilcox leitmotifs in *Howards End,* the effect of such repetition in *A Passage to India* is less to clarify and consolidate than to unsettle and perplex. Chandrapore, we are told at the outset, is "edged rather than washed by the Ganges," and "the Ganges happens not to be holy here." Later, when Godbole sings to Krishna,

"Come, come, come," he explains that in the song the god refuses to come; then he insensibly alters that to "neglects to come" (7). Such terms as "happens" and "neglects" catch the note of contingency—the formless and seemingly accidental nature of experience. So later "the countryside was too vast to admit of excellence. In vain did each item in it call out, 'Come, come.' There was not enough god to go round" (8). Here the "Come, come" is no longer Godbole's; it is a universal cry, and it is disappointed again, not by refusal, not by intention, but simply by insufficiency. There is too much body for spirit to inhabit, too much matter for form to shape.

So too there is just enough suggestion of intention to make India's illegibility the more telling. "The sky settles everything—not only climates and seasons but when the earth shall be beautiful. By herself she can do little—only feeble outbursts of flowers. But when the sky chooses, glory can rain into the Chandrapore bazaars or a benediction pass from horizon to horizon. The sky can do this because it is so strong and so enormous" (1). We have the sense of power but of uncertain purpose, of the arbitrary made all the more striking by its irresistible force. So, Godbole's song invites but resists comprehension. "At times there seemed rhythm, at times there was the illusion of a Western melody. But the ear, baffled repeatedly, soon lost any clue, and wandered in a maze of noises, none harsh or unpleasant, none intelligible. . . . The sounds continued and ceased after a few moments as casually as they had begun—apparently half through a bar, and upon the subdominant." The song, one might say, does not end; it straggles into silence (7).

India is full of sounds, but there is not enough meaning to make them a language. Where everything is ambiguous—assertion or expletive? message or noise?—there is no determining what has meaning, much less what the meaning may be. Or, in contrast, the very assumption that there should be meaning may lead one to project it with paranoid intensity. The novel is full of phrases that undergo misadventure, whose intention is lost in their reception. This is inevitable in a climate of political domination, of deference and condescension. Everywhere suspicion and distrust force men into confirming their identity by herding in clubs or compounds. And each group inevitably creates its own language, by whose distinctive grammar it seeks to construe what others say. The consequence is that blurring of words into dissonance, the surrender of sense to sheer echo. Words return with new and mocking meanings, with too many, or with none at all. When Mrs. Moore utters her benediction on the wasp, her voice floated out, we are told, "to swell the night's uneasiness" (3).

We are frequently guided in the process of interpretation, learning how to read remarks before we can misread them or they are misread by others. When Hamidullah's servants shout that dinner is ready, they "meant that

they wished it was ready and were so understood, for no one moved." When
Aziz visits Hamidullah's wife in purdah, it is "difficult to get away, because
until they [that is, the men] had their dinner she would not begin hers, and
consequently prolonged her remarks in case they should suppose she was
impatient." When Aziz recites poetry, no one demands meaning but only
mood; they take "the public view of poetry," "never stopping to analyze,"
never bored by "words, words" (2). But while we are taught to interpret
some messages, we are left to encounter other remarks or events that remain
puzzles. Is a thing really a sign or a sound a message, or is it like the snake
that seems really to be a mere tree? We are often left uncertain; the novel
has its own impassivity.

Perhaps the most fundamental metaphor for this problem is that of incarnation, with its inevitable puzzles as to how spirit and flesh may join, as to
how much flesh the spirit can sustain or how little it can inhabit, as to why
the spirit requires a spot of filth to make it "cohere" (at the moment of the
Despised and Rejected). These questions are like the problem of why the
spirit required or chose a stable and manger in an obscure province for the
Christian nativity. India as always carries its puzzles beyond Christianity's
"acceptable hints of infinity." As Aziz and Fielding take their final ride, "the
scenery, though it smiled, fell like a pavestone on any human hope. They
cantered past a temple to Hanuman—God so loved the world that he took
monkey's flesh upon him—and past a Saivite temple, which invited to lust,
but under the semblance of eternity, its obscenities bearing no relation to
those of our flesh and blood" (37). The Marabar Caves are the ultimate instance of matter refusing spirit—"They are older than anything in the world
. . . flesh of the sun's flesh. . . . Nothing attaches to them." They, too,
give the illusion of meaning, in the invitation of the polished surface of their
circular chambers. But their form, for all its apparent design, proves the
very denial of meaning. There are caves with "nothing inside them: if mankind grew curious and excavated, nothing, nothing would be added to the
sum of good or evil" (12).

Within this common predicament of the need to interpret and of its constant frustration, Forster creates characters who bring different kinds of apparatus for judging. Each of them seems a deliberate selection from the whole
range of human motives and perceptions. They embody different kinds of
reality, and we are constantly teased with the question that is more clearly
answered in the earlier novels, whether they embody different degrees of
reality, whether one is to be preferred to or exalted above others.

Aziz is the most fully realized character in the book. He provides the
narrative matrix, he undergoes the most varied and intense experience, and
he includes the greatest range of feeling. We see him as host and guest, as
friend and father, in his scientific skill and his erotic fantasies. He occupies

that most awkward and anxious place in the structure of Indian society—somewhere between the ancient mysteries of Hinduism and the administrative modernity of the English. As a Moslem he is more a rationalist in his religion than the Hindu, perhaps even more than a Christian like Mrs. Moore. He is warm, generous, eager to be loved and to show regard; and also prickly, resentful, easily depressed and frightened. Still, in the author's words, "he possessed a soul that could suffer but not stifle, and led a steady life beneath his mutability" (6).

Of all the characters in the novel Aziz is most steadily consumed by anxiety, aware of how he is regarded by others, needing confirmation in his own identity, finding it only momentarily and in part through shutting out what he cannot bear to see. In the party at Fielding's he is made comfortable by his host's casual good will, and he fortunately finds no provocation in the women. "Beauty would have troubled him, for it entails rules of its own, but Mrs. Moore was so old and Miss Quested so plain that he was spared this anxiety." He can at first be "entirely straightforward." But, as the ladies lament the failure of their Indian host to fetch them, he soon swings to identification with the English. "Slack Hindus," he exclaims. "It was as well you did not go to their house, for it would give you a wrong idea of India. Nothing sanitary. I think for my own part they grew ashamed of their house and that is why they did not send." And carried along by his fantasy of identification, in spite of the fact that he has just been describing his own home, he invites everyone to his bungalow. When the literal-minded Miss Quested eagerly asks the address, he is filled with horror and changes the subject. In another moment, he is carried away into a glorious nostalgic dream of Mogul justice. He is sentimental and irresponsible, exhibiting the "tenderness of one incapable of administration."

When Ronny Heaslop comes and, with the obtuseness of an assured administrator, ignores the Indians, Aziz cannot give up the "secure and intimate note of the past hour" and becomes "offensively friendly" and provocative. "He did not mean"—how often that phrase must occur in the novel—"to be impertinent to Mr. Heaslop. . . . He did not mean to be greasily confidential to Miss Quested . . . nor to be loud and jolly towards Professor Godbole." Aziz loses all taste and control.

The unpleasantness Aziz attains is only a symptom of his anxiety. "He isn't a bounder," Fielding protests. "His nerves are on edge, that's all." What makes the scene fascinating is not only the dramatic tension Forster gives it, but the way in which it catches, at a level that is far deeper and more momentous than the merely aesthetic, the lack of proportion and of taste that characterize India. It is not just that Aziz would have spoiled a room that Fielding has the good taste to leave unadorned. More delicate and more moving is the difficulty Aziz has in sustaining an identity, in knowing on what terms he can meet the English. Behind his anxiety lie the social and political enigmas of India; its metaphysical puzzles never trouble him and hardly enter his awareness. Hinduism scarcely provokes his curiosity. And so, in cheerful ignorance, he can lead the others to the Marabar Caves (7).

For Aziz the deepest religious experience is his communion with Mrs. Moore. It survives and governs his life, a moment somehow taken out of time—purified of its irritation at Mrs. Callendar's snub and its aggressive beginnings—preserved as a vision of disinterested union, a moment of release from a politicized world. Forster said of Mrs. Wilcox that he was "interested in the imaginative effect of someone alive, but in a different way from other characters—living in other lives" (WW 30). This is the case with Mrs. Moore. Not only does she become the goddess Esmiss Esmoor, but she presides over Aziz's generous forgiveness of damage payments from Adela.

In the final section, when her uncanny son Ralph comes to Mau, Aziz is once more shaken by her survival. Aziz has retreated to a native state and removed all the sources of strain he felt in Anglo-India; this has meant giving up the serious practice of medicine as well. The false note is that Aziz has built his new life on the belief that he has been betrayed by Fielding. He is unsettled to learn that Fielding has married Stella Moore rather than Adela Quested. In his treatment of Ralph he adopts some of the cruelty Callendar had shown to the Nawab's grandson. When Ralph exclaims, "Your hands are unkind," Aziz protests that he is causing no pain. Ralph quietly agrees. "But there is cruelty." Ralph's candor is a revival of Mrs. Moore's directness. "You should not treat us like this," Ralph says. "Dr. Aziz, we have done you no harm." At this moment a prisoner is released from the jail nearby as part of the annual Hindu festival. "Mixed and confused, the rumours of salvation entered the Guest House." Aziz is released from his anger, his hands become kind, and he acknowledges Ralph Moore's intuitive power: "Then you are an Oriental." As he says it, Aziz shudders. "Those words— he had said them to Mrs. Moore in the mosque in the beginning of the cycle, from which, after so much suffering, she had got free. Never be friends with the English! Mosque, caves, mosque, caves. And here he was starting again."

At this moment Forster makes Aziz himself acknowledge and accept the pattern of nonlogical repetition, of "life by values" as opposed to "life in time." More than that, Aziz repeats the titles of the two parts of the novel itself, "mosque, caves," and makes their structure the pattern of his own memory. It is a moment at which Aziz seems almost to dissolve into thematic form; it is appropriately at the close of the novel that the principal character comes to an awareness closest to the author's. The shudder is a token of an action whose impulses lie below consciousness; yet Aziz makes the action his own, avows and intends it, and becomes free in the process (36).

Adela Quested and Cyril Fielding are, in contrast with Aziz, trapped within the limits of liberal, rational intelligence. They are well-meaning, tolerant, open. Adela is high-minded, theoretical, and unconsciously patronizing; but she has courage and conscience. Her crisis is one induced by insincerity. Adela and Ronny are brought together in the ride with the Nawab and Miss Derek by their difference from the others—"to the animal thrill there was now added a coincidence of opinion" (8). It is hardly enough for marriage, as Adela comes to recognize; and her revulsion from the insincerity to which she is committed affects her at the caves. Instead of the vertigo of meaninglessness and the horror of total unity that Mrs. Moore feels, Adela's less imaginative mind demands a literal cause and, in its breakdown, invents one. The worst of her later suffering is the recognition of this self-betrayal. To Fielding, she becomes—under the stress of her suffering—a real person. But for Hamidullah, she does not. Her behavior "rested on cold justice and honesty; she had felt, while she recanted, no passion of love for those she had wronged." Her sacrifice "did not include the heart." But the point of Adela's charge is that her mind—honest and admirable—is out of touch with her feelings, does not know her heart (26).

Fielding in a comparable way suffers an excess of detachment, an inability to escape his intelligence and to lose himself in feeling. About Aziz he thinks, " 'I shall not really be intimate with this fellow,' " and then, " 'nor with anyone.' And he had to confess that he really didn't mind." He is content to help people, but he travels light: "Clarity prevented him from experiencing something else" (11). When he talks with Indians, his line of thought does not trouble them, but his words are "too definite and bleak" (9). The most expansive vision of Fielding's humanism is the interlude at the close of the second part of the novel, the assertion of Mediterranean order and form which just precedes the formlessness of the Hindu festival. Venice provides escape from anxiety into assurance. It offers the "harmony between the works of man and the earth that upholds them, the civilization that has escaped muddle, the spirit in a reasonable form, with flesh and blood subsisting" (32).[11] This vision of Italy is different from the overrefined ones of Philip Herriton or Cecil Vyse, but it is different too from the sacramental violence in the Piazza della Signoria or in Monteriano.[12] It becomes, in this novel, an image of ideal incarnation. In the earlier, fragmentary work, *Arctic Summer,* Forster gave a vision of Italy to the unheroic man, Whitby:

> The train ran downward into a beauty that admits romance but is independent of it. Youth demands colour and blue sky, but Martin, turned thirty, longed for Form. Perhaps it is a cold desire, but it can save a man from cynicism; it is a worker's religion, and Italy is one of its shrines. . . . She, like himself, had abandoned sentiment; she existed apart from associations by the virtues of mass

and line: her austere beauty was an image of the millennium towards which all
good citizens are cooperating.[13]

That is a somewhat chilling version of the religion of Form, but it serves to
suggest the limitations that are at least implicit in Fielding's too. For if these
images, like the characters of Adela and Fielding, have human centrality,
they also have an austerity that seems more pinched than august, a clarity
that may even seem like a defense against reality. The characters sense this
themselves: "As though they had seen their own gestures from an immense
height—dwarfs talking, shaking hands and assuring each other that they
stood on the same footing of insight." There is a "wistfulness," a suspicion
of being cut off from a reality their rational clarity cannot quite admit exists
(29).

Mrs. Moore and Professor Godbole are the characters whose status is most
equivocal. They lack the human centrality that we associate with rational
awareness, with moral responsibility, with form on a limited scale. They are
less fully human than the others, and we are teased with the question of
whether they are something more.

Mrs. Moore's age sets her apart from most of the characters in the novel.
It is presumably not greater than Mrs. Turton's. What matters again is that
it creates anxiety: the strain of fatigue and depression induced by a world
suddenly grown incomprehensible and a god who has lost much of his cred-
ibility. "She found [God] increasingly difficult to avoid as she grew older,
and he had been constantly in her thoughts since she entered India, though
oddly enough he satisfied her less. She must needs pronounce his name frequently, as the greatest she knew, yet she had never found it less efficacious.
Outside the arch there seemed always an arch, beyond the remotest echo a
silence" (5).

Mrs. Moore appears to us in only a few aspects. She has no elaborately
documented history; large areas of concern do not touch her. We see her first
in the mosque with Aziz; her generosity and candor dissolve his anger and
free his deeper self. As she recalls the episode later, she realizes how easily
"it could be worked into quite an unpleasant scene. The doctor had begun
by bullying her, he had said Mrs. Callendar was nice, and then—finding the
ground safe—had changed; he had alternately whined over his grievances
and patronized her, had run a dozen ways in a single sentence, had been
unreliable, inquisitive, vain. Yes, it was all true, but how false as a summary
of the man; the essential life of him had been slain" (3). This ability to see
reality without confusion and outside merely social categories is the most
impressive of Mrs. Moore's qualities. We see her first in gestures of inclusion, openness, and extension: ready to accept invitations, to be accepted in
turn as a Moslem. None of her later meetings with Aziz is so satisfactory as

the meeting in the mosque, but each of them builds upon and confirms that meeting. In fact, most of the feeling one might hope to see in her personal relationships is displaced into the curiously limited and intense relationship with Aziz. And one may see even in that relationship something of a withdrawal from the personal to the impersonal, a turning from the limited and timebound to the cosmic and illimitable. As she herself senses, God enters prematurely into her discussion of most matters, such as imperial policy. "God has put us on the earth in order to be pleasant to each other. God . . . is . . . love." Her son attributes this religious strain to "bad health," and among the ironies is the fact that in some measure he is right (5).

The scene in the cave presents the dark, ironic side of pantheism; a God without personality, a God who includes wasps as well as men, crocodiles as well as moonlight, is wonderful and terrible like the Ganges, but ultimately impassive, indifferent, a formless smother. "Pathos, piety, courage—they exist, but are identical, and so is filth. Everything exists, nothing has value." Unlike Adela Quested, Mrs. Moore cannot project her sense of violation upon another person. She must live with the metaphysical vision itself. She realizes that she doesn't want to communicate with anyone, "not even with God." She bristles thereafter with resentment and irritation; she refuses to testify at the trial of Aziz, although she has no doubt of his innocence. Gradually the sense of outrage takes the form of self-hatred, a sense of her own evil as well as the evil of others ("Good, happy small people. They do not exist, they were a dream") (14, 22). We may be reminded of two comparable experiences: one is the sense of universal vileness Anna Karenina feels as she moves toward her suicide, the other is the spectacle of a vast disorder that Marlow finds opened by the grief of Jewel in *Lord Jim*.

It is only at the moment of her departure from India that Forster gives us something like a social history of Mrs. Moore's beliefs. As she withdraws, turned petty and peevish, unable to entertain any "large thought," we are made to see the rather naive expectations that were the conscious surface of a deeper disquietude. She was attracted by a goal that seemed beautiful and easy—"To be one with the universe! So dignified and simple." Now she senses that the abyss may offer not profundity but pettiness, that the serpent of eternity may be made of maggots. She shelters herself in intense self-pity, and she rejects all consolation lest she lose that shelter. Even so, as she leaves India, its variety and particularity reassert themselves. Asirgarh offers noble bastions and a mosque; they disappear and then return, without meaning, without connection ("What could she connect it with except its own name?") but with stubborn and indestructible life. The universe is dissolving into a number of things, each existing in its own right, none enhanced or eclipsed by absorption into unity, none simply legible as a sign (23).

Mrs. Moore's beliefs have a history, but Professor Godbole's do not. Of all the principal characters, he remains the most opaque. We are allowed to enter his mind only during the ritual, and the consciousness we then explore is devoted to the exercise of meditation. Earlier, Godbole is always presented as out of phase with the social world about him, abrupt, unpredictable, and impassive as India itself. When we first see him at Fielding's, his discussion of the Marabar Caves seems a thrilling game to Aziz. "On [Aziz] chattered, defeated at every move by an opponent who would not even admit that a move had been made, and further than ever from discovering what, if anything, was extraordinary about the Marabar Caves." But Godbole is so inscrutable that one cannot with confidence ascribe intention to him. Is Aziz justified in believing him an opponent? Are the countermoves merely imaginary? (7).

It is Godbole's prayer that causes him and Fielding to miss the train for the Marabar Caves. When Fielding sees him again, after the arrest of Aziz, Godbole politely hopes that "the expedition was a successful one." Does he not know of its consequences? "Oh, yes. That is all around the College." And he proceeds to question Fielding, who is sick with concern about Aziz, on the matter of an appropriate name for a new school to be founded in Mau. It is too much for Fielding, and he puts the question to Godbole inescapably: "Is Aziz innocent or guilty?" No, not inescapably, for Godbole dances away: " 'Dr. Aziz is a most worthy young man. I have a great regard for him; but I think you are asking me whether the individual can commit good actions or evil actions, and that is rather difficult for us.' He spoke without emotion and in short tripping syllables." The inhuman effect of the voice contributes to the stupefying vision of unity: "Because nothing can be performed in isolation. All perform a good action, when one is performed, and when an evil action is performed, all perform it." Godbole illustrates:

> "I am informed that an evil action was performed in the Marabar Hills, and that a highly esteemed English lady is now seriously ill in consequence. My answer to that is this: that action was performed by Dr. Aziz." He stopped and sucked in his thin cheeks. "It was performed by you." Now he had an air of daring and of coyness. "It was performed by me." He looked shyly down the sleeve of his own coat. "And by my students. It was even performed by the lady herself. When evil occurs, it expresses the whole of the universe. Similarly when good occurs."

That final anticlimax, the all but simpering gestures, the single-minded reductionism—all of these become near-farcical attributes of the proponent of unity. To borrow words Forster used on an earlier occasion (1921), Godbole exhibits "the same mixture of fatuity and philosophy that ran through the whole festival." He seems to deny the reality of suffering, and at the very least he reduces responsibility to something so diffuse as to become trivial.

If one substitutes for the attempted rape of Adela Quested almost any public crime—whether it be assassination, forced labor camps, or something so comparatively pardonable as high crimes and misdemeanors, this doctrine of responsibility becomes appalling. Fielding protests: "You're preaching that evil and good are the same." Godbole's reply must be given in full:

> "Oh no, excuse me once again. Good and evil are different, as their names imply. But, in my own humble opinion, they are both of them aspects of my Lord. He is present in the one, absent in the other, and the difference between presence and absence is great, as great as my feeble mind can grasp. Yet absence implies presence, absence is not non-existence, and we are therefore entitled to repeat, 'Come, come, come, come.' " And in the same breath, as if to cancel any beauty his words might have contained, he added, "But did you have the time to visit any of the interesting Marabar antiquities?"   [19]

This passage deserves attention. If "absence is not non-existence," we might seem to approach the idea of intention, of a God who refuses rather than neglects to act. And we might in turn approach the moral vision of worshipping God because he is good rather than because he is God. But, if any of this is hinted, it is immediately lost in ludicrous inconsequence. In his guide to *Alexandria,* Forster presents comparable mysteries of Neoplatonism with as much lucidity as mystery permits: "We are all parts of God, even the stones, though we cannot realise it; and man's goal is to become actually, as he is potentially, divine. . . . The Christian promise is that man shall see God, the Neo-Platonic—like the Indian—that he shall be God." [14] But here we are left with the muddle of religious paradox, moral insensibility, and social nicety. The muddle will be redeemed in the Temple festival, but, while one can see its eventual place in the dialectic of the novel, one must hold on to the element of fatuity in Professor Godbole's vision of unity. For Godbole remains serene amid all the muddles that so demoralized Mrs. Moore. His mind stretches to embrace all of Krishna's guises, whereas her mind recoiled and her heart congealed with the terror of the undifferentiated and formless. Both have moved beyond moral involvement, Mrs. Moore in her refusal to testify, Godbole in his sudden disappearance.

One may feel that Professor Godbole's elasticity comes from a deficiency of awareness rather than from a mysterious depth. For Mrs. Moore's recoil is far more readily understandable. Dr. Johnson wrote a sentence that has its relevance:

> To love all men is our duty, so far as it includes a general principle of benevolence, and readiness of occasional kindness; but to love all equally is impossible; at least impossible without the extinction of those passions which now produce all our pains and all our pleasures; without the disuse, if not the abolition, of

some faculties, and the suppression of all our hopes and fears in apathy and indifference. [*The Rambler,* no. 99]

Forster had drawn an important contrast in "The Gods of India," a book review that appeared in 1914:

Religion, in Protestant England, is mainly concerned with conduct. It is an ethical code—a code with a divine sanction, it is true, but applicable to daily life. We are to love our brother, whom we see. We are to hurt no one, by word or deed. We are to be pitiful, pure minded, honest in our business, reliable, tolerant, brave. . . .

The code is so spiritual and lofty, and contains such frequent references to the Unseen, that few of its adherents realize it only expresses half of the religious idea. The other half is expressed in the creed of the Hindus. The Hindu is concerned not with conduct, but with vision. To realize what God is seems more important than to do what God wants. He has a constant sense of the unseen . . . and he feels that this tangible world, with its chatter of right and wrong, subserves the intangible. . . . Hinduism can pull itself to supply the human demand for morality just as Protestantism at a pinch can meet the human desire for the infinite and the incomprehensible, but the effort is in neither case congenial. Left to itself each lapses—the one into mysticism, the other into ethics.[15]

This passage helps to make clear the polarity in Forster's conception of character in *A Passage to India.* It is caught at one extreme in the Anglo-Indians and at the other by Godbole—the one a social and moral uniformity that denies personal vision or undisciplined feeling, the other an openness to all possibilities so complete as to exclude nothing; the one all inauthentic order, the other all transcendence and obliviousness of humanistic claims. The former is the ideology of the efficient administrator, the latter the mystical faith of those who cannot be trammeled or troubled by consistency and order. Aziz can participate to an extent in both of these extremes, but he is at home in neither. India itself I have called their common predicament. Its landscape suggests the threat it offers to those who expect meaning; its political and social life represent that threat in visible, limited, but still insoluble form. The predicament India embodies is not restricted to one time or place.

Mrs. Moore and Godbole are more receptive than others to a world of apparent contingency; but they differ from each other. Mrs. Moore finds her faith stretched to the point of collapse and savage disenchantment, whereas Godbole is never seen (except perhaps at the final moments of the Temple ritual) as in the least troubled by any cost his faith exacts. To the skeptic, the adept may seem like a dupe, and Forster never quite allows us to lose all of our skepticism. Forster writes the novel in the style of a lucid, ironic, liberal intelligence, and the style presses its limits in order to indicate its insufficiency. The ineffable is intimated through incidents that may be symbolic but need not be. They are part of such a welter of farcical incongruity that we can only tentatively accredit their meaningfulness. Nor can we altogether disallow it. They create the vertigo of the uninterpretable.

Godbole, of course, is to provide Aziz with a new post in Mau, and he is to summon up the vision of Mrs. Moore, to love her as God, and to summon God on her behalf. There is no question of his benignity and of the sincerity of his doctrine; but he contributes his "highbrow incoherence" (I borrow the phrase from Natwar Singh)[16] to the total pattern of mystery and muddle, of spirit and flesh, of meaning and misinterpretation. The festival will introduce the grossness of the melting butter running down the forehead, the tatty indecorum of the music and decorations, the jolly disorder of practical jokes, the untidiness of accident—all dimensions of this disparity between matter and spirit. Godbole contributes to that pattern the comic immediacy of a man enmeshed in the matter he aspires to ignore—his pince-nez is caught in his garlands, just as his reaching behind him for his food makes it all the more grotesquely conspicuous. Like Mrs. Moore he is less a person than the other principal characters, and, even more than she, he seems to expose directly, almost without mediation, that deeper self that is at once a perfect fool and the nearest approach to the gates of the Divine.

One might close with a brief glimpse of two minor characters who catch supremely well the puzzles of incarnation which lie at the center of the book. The first is the punkah wallah, the man who pulls the fan in the courtroom. "He had the strength and beauty that sometimes come to flower in Indians of low birth. When that strange race reaches the dust and is condemned as untouchable, then nature remembers the physical perfection that she accomplished elsewhere, and throws out a god." He seems "apart from human destinies, a male fate, a winnower of souls," but in fact he scarcely "knew that he existed and didn't even know that he worked a fan, though he thought he pulled a rope." When the trial has been dismissed and the court abandoned, he remains alone, "the beautiful naked god," still "unaware that anything unusual had occurred" (24).

Near the close of the novel, a model of the village of Gokul—the Hindu Bethlehem as it were—is pushed into the waters by a splendid servitor, "naked, broad-shouldered, thin-waisted—the Indian body again triumphant." As the boats containing Aziz and the English visitors collide, they drift forward "helplessly against the servitor. Who awaited them, his beautiful dark face expressionless." Again, we have the impassivity, the resistance to meaning, as the ritual peters out in mud, straggling crowds, "ragged edges of religion . . . unsatisfactory and undramatic tangles." The theme of the festival, earlier voiced by Mrs. Moore, has been characteristically misspelled—"God is love"—untidy, resisting meaning, but also suggesting obliquely an "if" for an "is." God if love. We create God through our love. Love creates meaning. Two cheers for morality (36).

The subtlety of the novel lies in its unrelieved tension of flesh and spirit, exclusion and invitation, the social self and the deeper impersonal self. At one extreme are the caricatures caught in the social grid—the Turtons and Burtons. At the other are the characters who slip out of the meshes of social responsibility through despair or obliviousness. We move from the elaborate rituals of Anglo-India to Mau, where the only aspects of life we are shown are ecstasy and negligence. Where does the mind rest? The difficulty with looking at reality directly is that reality will tend to dissolve: "not now, not here, not to be apprehended except when it is unattainable." Transcendence dehumanizes, the deeper self is a source rather than a habitation, we cannot see the unseen. We only glimpse it through paradox, violence, or farce; and each of these contributes something to Forster's conception of character.

13 ✳ The Beauty of Mortal Conditions: Joyce, Woolf, Mann

"Sceptically, cynically, mystically, he had sought for an absolute satisfaction and now little by little he began to be conscious of the beauty of mortal conditions."

The sentence is from the sketch which was Joyce's earliest version of his portrait of the artist.[1] It reveals some of the difficulty of that process by which the work of art emerges from the conditions of its creation and the artist from the natural man. Artistic creation may be one of the ways of most fully realizing the self, but it is achieved only as the artist is freed of impediments within the self and of exigencies outside. And yet the problem of liberation is a subtle one; for the artist may too easily be delivered of much that makes him human and gives his experience depth.

Joyce provides us with an amusing illustration of that danger. Stephen Dedalus, having attained a state of spiritual exaltation, finds in himself a serene transcendence:

> The world for all its solid substance and complexity no longer existed for his soul save as a theorem of divine power and love and universality. So entire and unquestionable was this sense of the divine meaning in all nature granted to his soul that he could scarcely understand why it was in any way necessary that he should continue to live. [4]

This pitch of spirituality cannot be sustained very long. It is an episode in the longer process that Joyce traces from the earliest sensory and associative images to the full powers of mind as they are shown in the creation of a poem and the enunciation of an aesthetic. Even those achievements are stages in the process that culminates (to use Richard Ellmann's phrase) in "the gestation of a soul," in the emergence of the artist from—or better, in—the young man. This final state is achieved by a fuller consciousness; and by its very nature it is joined to the world.

It is with that process that I shall be concerned in this chapter. It is a process in which form emerges from the conditions which have given rise to it, that is, either created the form or called it forth. The form cannot free itself too completely from those conditions lest it lose the very point of its existence. One of the appeals of literary realism, in which it shows a resemblance to history, is its recognition of a stubborn and resistant world of fact, from which events or patterns cannot be easily exacted. For this resistance must be more than dialectical; it cannot be dissolved by an act of the mind. After we have come to recognize the categories which our thought must impose and the work of interpretation that is implicit in our experience (as opposed to innocent eyes and brute facts) there is still an unaccommodating otherness with which the artist must negotiate or struggle if his art is to be brought to power. The work of art embodies some memory of or allusion to the conditions that attend on and perhaps all but prevent its existence.

These conditions, once they have ceased to be a threat to the pure idea and have been assumed into the work of art, may yield up their beauty in unforeseen ways. We have seen something of this occur in many of the novelists I have discussed. I should like to cite one more analogy from painting. It is drawn from a discussion of Cézanne's landscapes by Meyer Schapiro. Instead of imposing an "ideal schema," Cézanne achieves a "more complex relationship emerging slowly in the course of the work. The form is in constant making and contributes an aspect of the encountered and random to the full appearance of the scene. inviting us to endless exploration." The "encountered and random," or as Schapiro puts it a page or two earlier, "the aspect of chance in the appearance of directly encountered things," suggests the unassimilable world of fact, with all its contingency and indifference to idea. It is a theme of Iris Murdoch's writing, too: "The great artists reveal the detail of the world." We can almost say that the value of form is less the order it creates than the way it heightens those details which resist it. "The pointlessness of art is not the pointlessness of a game; it is the pointlessness of human life itself, and form in art is properly the simulation of the self-contained aimlessness of the universe."[2] What this emphasis brings to our awareness is the peculiar intensity that the novel can lend a detail, a gesture, an event—not by loading it with symbolic import but by giving us the sense of what it is to see such detail when it is rich with the possibility of meanings, no one of which has yet been precipitated or asserted.

The first chapter of the *Portrait* concludes with Stephen's first act of self-assertion. It is an act of heroism if not defiance, a firm insistence upon justice against the Jesuit headmaster's casual dismissal of Father Dolan's cruelty. And while Stephen is later to learn of the "hearty laugh" his elders had over his protest, at the moment he can feel only triumph in his return down the lonely corridor to be chaired by his fellow students. But if a self has begun to be defined, it is still to be tested in Stephen's battle "against the squalor

of his life and spirit" and "the riot of his mind." The instability of Dedalus
family life, the "changes in what he had deemed unchangeable," deflect
Stephen from the world about him to one of daydream, of an imagined
meeting with "the unsubstantial image . . . his soul so constantly beheld."
The meeting is to be release and transfiguration: "Weakness and timidity
and inexperience would fall from him in that magic moment." But, in fact,
the passivity of expectation afflicts him with a kind of paralysis.

At school, Stephen shows a mixture of defiant assertion and humiliating
compliance, of heretical beliefs and "habits of quiet obedience." The deadlock creates a riot of brutal passion in his imagination, consequent guilt and
horror with himself, and withdrawal from others. "By his monstrous way of
life he seemed to have put himself beyond the limits of reality. Nothing
moved him or spoke to him from the real world unless he heard in it an echo
of the infuriated cries within him" (2).

Joyce treats Stephen with little irony during this season of torment. The
release is not yet transfiguration. There is no holy encounter with a romantic
heroine, but instead the surrender to a prostitute whose tongue he feels upon
his own as "an unknown and timid pressure, darker than the swoon of sin,
softer than sound or odour." Self-destruction seems inextricably tied to necessary self-assertion: "It was his own soul going forth to experience, unfolding itself sin by sin, spreading abroad the balefire of its burning stars and
folding back upon itself, fading slowly, quenching its own lights and fires"
(3).

Throughout the second and third chapters Joyce creates an undertone of
comic disproportion between Stephen's view of his sins and the appearance
they present to us. There are wonderfully subtle doubts Stephen can pro-
pound through curious and ingenious questions. There are fantasies in which
he has submitted Emma to "his brutelike lust . . . and trampled upon her
innocence." There are indecent pictures he has drawn and obscene letters he
has inscribed and scattered to be found by passersby. The intensity of self-
excoriation these actions induce finds its relief in a sentimental fantasy of
forgiveness and reward. He dares not approach God or even Mary directly,
but he draws Emma beside him (involving her in more complicity than is in
fact her due) in a "wide land under a tender lucid evening sky." Mary becomes the all-forgiving mother of "children that had erred" and confers
Emma's heart upon him in the process: "Take hands, Stephen and Emma. It
is a beautiful evening now in heaven. You have erred but you are always my
children. It is one heart that loves another heart. Take hands together, my
dear children, and you will be happy together and your hearts will love each
other" (3).

If the sentimental forgiveness is one extreme, the Bosch-like fantasies of
fiends mocking with terrifying gibberish or of goatish monsters encircling

him in a filthy field are the other. The disproportion between fantasy and
actuality creates an ironic space around Stephen's anguish. When at last he
makes confession in a strange church, the priest's formulaic questions are too
general and inclusive for the uniquely terrible sin that Stephen feels he has
committed:

—I . . . committed sins of impurity, father.
The priest did not turn his head.
—With yourself, my child?
—And . . . with others.
—With women, my child?
—Yes, father.
—Were they married women, my child?
He did not know. His sins trickled from his lips, one by one, trickled in
shameful drops from his soul festering and oozing like a sore, a squalid stream
of vice.   [3]

Again, after his purgation, Stephen's religious devotion becomes brilliantly
callow, and he anticipates Samuel Beckett's heroes in a number of ways.

By means of ejaculations and prayers he stored up ungrudgingly for souls in
purgatory centuries of days and quarantines and years; yet the spiritual triumph
which he felt in achieving with ease so many fabulous ages of canonical penances
did not wholly reward his goal of prayer since he could never learn how much
temporal punishment he had remitted by way of suffrage for the agonising
souls. . . .

That note of arithmetical literalness is splendidly deflating, as is the embarrassment of flesh that cannot easily be mortified: "To mortify his smell was
more difficult as he found in himself no instinctive repugnance to bad odours,
whether they were the odours of the outdoor world such as those of dung
and tar or the odours of his own person among which he had made many
curious comparisons and experiments" (4). But, of course, protracted selflessness somehow gives rise to irritability and anger; the new assurance of
grace begets the anxiety that he may have "really fallen unawares."
    The irony that surrounds Stephen's religious dedication prepares for the
scene in which he rejects a priestly vocation. The inauthenticity and suppressions that have marked his own devotions reappear for him in the imagined
Jesuit's face, "shot with pink tinges of suffocated anger." The scene turns on
a resurgence of self. Stephen accepts his "destiny to be elusive of social or
religious orders," to "learn his own wisdom apart from others." The fall he
dreaded earlier now seems inevitable; and he commits himself to the natural
world, "the misrule and confusion of his father's house and the stagnation of
vegetable life." At home he hears a sad choir of family voices, singing as

they await still another move for a cheaper rent. Stephen listens "to the overtone of weariness behind their frail fresh innocent voices," and the voices open into "an endless reverberation of the choirs of endless generations of children," giving utterance (in Newman's words) to "pain and weariness yet hope for better things."

It is on the shore that Stephen's vocation is made clear: "the artist forging out of the sluggish matter of the earth a new soaring impalpable imperishable being." He imagines himself soaring upward, "delivered of incertitude and made radiant and commingled with the element of the spirit." As he walks alone on the shore, he has overcome passivity and emerged from the "house of squalor and subterfuge." It is then that he sees the girl who carries in her form all the suggestion of romantic heroines, of Emma, of the Virgin, and, most of all, of "the beauty of mortal conditions" (4).

In the final chapter of the novel, Joyce sets forth the claims upon Stephen of both church and nation and meets them with the vocation of the artist. Ireland has become a constellation of demands and affronts, and Stephen sees its debasement in the statute of Tom Moore, the "national poet": "He looked at it without anger: for, though sloth of the body and of the soul crept over it like unseen vermin, over the shuffling feet and up the folds of the cloak and around the servile head, it seemed humbly unconscious of its indignity." Stephen is reminded of Davin, "the peasant student," "one of the tame geese," regarding Ireland with the same uncritical acceptance he shows for the Roman Catholic religion, "the attitude of a dullwitted loyal serf." Davin in turn evokes the Irish peasant woman who invited him to her bed, a "type of her race and his own, a bat-like soul waking to the consciousness of itself in darkness and secrecy and loneliness." At every point Stephen opposes the Irish scene with associations that come from elsewhere—Newman, Cavalcanti, Ibsen, Jonson. "Try to be one of us," Davin asks. "In your heart you are an Irishman but your pride is too powerful." But Stephen must see Ireland's claims as captivity: "When the soul of a man is born in this country there are nets flung at it to hold it back from flight. You talk to me of nationality, language, religion. I shall try to fly by those nets." He parries the claims that his friend Cranly advances in Ireland's behalf, the most compelling of them Stephen's mother's wish that he remain in the faith. "Whatever she feels, it, at least, must be real," Cranly insists. "It must be. What are our ideas or ambitions? Play. Ideas!" Cranly asserts that Stephen has more religious faith than he knows, that his doubts are only an expression of that faith. And it is through his replies to Cranly that Stephen extricates himself from all the claims made upon him: "I will not serve that in which I no longer believe whether it call itself my home, my fatherland or my church: and I will try to express myself in some mode of life or art as freely as I can and as wholly as I can, using for my defence the only arms I allow myself to use—silence, exile, and cunning."

The aesthetic Stephen formulates is a culmination of this movement toward freedom. It is not an assertion of the purity of art but of its autonomy. Out of the natural feelings there emerges a peculiar "aesthetic emotion," not so much a distinct kind as a distinct form of emotion. The feelings of practical life—kinetic, concerned with possession or avoidance but in either case with motion—undergo an "arrest."

It is in such moments of arrest that we enter a "mental world." We are beyond the "purely reflex action of the nervous system" and reach a realm of free contemplation, an "esthetic stasis" in which we feel no excitation to action, but rather "an ideal pity or an ideal terror." This stasis is experience framed, discontinuous with the stream of ordinary feelings; the framing is achieved by aesthetic form—"the rhythm of beauty." Stephen states the freedom of the aesthetic response with mock-solemnity: we "try slowly and humbly and constantly to express, to press out again, from the gross earth or what it brings forth [Lynch has amiably protested, "please remember, though I did eat a cake of cowdung once, that I admire only beauty"], from sound and shape and colour which are the prison gates of our soul, an image of the beauty we have come to understand—that is art." Stephen (and certainly Joyce) is too much the Aristotelian to speak of the objects of the senses as the "prison gates of our soul" except with a certain ironic exaggeration. He is perhaps stirred by Lynch's grossness to insist upon the cognitive, upon an intellectual beauty that contrasts with sensory impressions. But as he speaks, the novelist insists in turn upon the concreteness of the physical world: "They had reached the canal bridge and, turning from their course, went on by the trees. A crude grey light, mirrored in the sluggish water, and a smell of wet branches over their heads seemed to war against the course of Stephen's thought."

Stephen's definition of art includes the senses as much as the intellect: it is "the human disposition of sensible or intelligible matter for an esthetic end." What matters is that both are liberated from the practical, the moral, the kinetic; if the immediate object of beauty is pleasure, it remains indifferent to judgments of good and evil. Stephen is freeing the work of art as he is freeing himself from the claims that are being pressed upon both—duty to church and to country. The aesthetic becomes a privileged experience: it has autonomy within its own province, and it has the duty to itself, as it were, of becoming a work of art, just as Stephen owes himself the initial duty of becoming an artist.

While Stephen adamantly asserts the autonomy of art and the transfiguration of natural experience into the work of imagination ("Life purified in and reprojected from the human imagination"), he does not expound a doctrine of Art for Art's Sake. He is dedicated to freeing art of its captivity by typical "natural pieties—social limitations, inherited apathy of race, an adoring mother, the Christian fable." Joyce himself had no esteem for the Celtic

revival, for hermeticism and magic, for "the union of faith and fatherland."
As he wrote in "Drama and Life," the first paper he read aloud at a college
society, "Art is marred by . . . mistaken insistence on its religious, its
moral, its beautiful, its idealizing tendencies. A single Rembrandt is worth
a gallery full of Van Dycks." Idealism and romance are to be avoided. "Life
we must accept as we see it before our eyes, men and women as we meet
them in the real world, not as we apprehend them in the world of faery."[3]

One finds in the young Joyce as in Stephen the wish to use art as a means
of restoring nobility to Ireland. "I am an enemy of the ignobleness and
slavishness of people but not of you," Joyce wrote to Nora (29 August 1904).[4]
At about the same time in his earliest version of the *Portrait,* Joyce described
his character (or himself) as "at the difficult age, dispossessed and necessi-
tous, sensible of all that was ignoble in such manners [of his contemporaries]
who, in revery at least, had been acquainted with nobility." So Ireland's one
belief is "in the incurable ignobility of the forces that have overcome her."
One thinks of the "breakwater of order and elegance" the young Stephen
tries to build, the "squalor and subterfuge" he wants to put behind him. By
the end of the novel, he has come to a vision of what his art may achieve.
This emerges from the bitterness with which he regards the "sleek lives of
the patricians of Ireland," squandering their authority in acquisitiveness and
triviality:

> How could he hit their conscience or how cast his shadow over the imaginations
> of their daughters, before their squires begat upon them, that they might breed
> a race less ignoble than their own? And under the deepened dusk he felt the
> thoughts and desires of the race to which he belonged flitting like bats, across
> the dark country lanes, under trees by the edges of streams and near the pool-
> mottled bogs.

But to achieve such a purpose, he must first of all become an artist.

The composition of a poem turns this process so theoretically expounded
into fallible actuality. The villanelle emerges from inchoate feeling. The
"morning knowledge" to which Stephen awakens is a state of purity; and
only gradually, under the stress of recall, Stephen moves from seraphic ecstasy to erotic fantasy, from the sense of himself as passionless spirit to the
role of Gabriel as the seraph of annunciation, from white flame to rose and
ardent light, from the seraphim breathing upon him to the choirs of the
seraphim falling from heaven, he among them. The willful heart of the actual virgin—Emma Clery—becomes the lure of a temptress worshipped as
the Virgin might be, smoke of praise like "incense ascending from the altar
of the world." The feelings have so far moved through a stream of associations, and now they are suddenly blocked: "Smoke went up from the whole

earth, from the vapoury oceans, smoke of her praise. The earth was like a swinging swaying censer, a ball of incense, an ellipsoidal ball. The rhythm died out at once; the cry of his heart was broken." Broken by the full recollection of the whinnying, centaurlike laughter of Moynihan in the lecture room: "What price ellipsoidal balls! chase me, ladies, I'm in the cavalry." We may recall with pleasure the "sabbath of misrule" of Moynihan's "rude humour"; but Stephen is incapable of absorbing so affronting an aspect of reality. He must free himself of the threat of incongruity; if, as Walter Shandy remarked, "there is no passion so serious as lust," there is no poetry so solemn as its sublimation.

As he writes out the stanzas of the villanelle, Stephen summons up more and more concretely the image of Emma. The "lumps of knotted flesh" in his "lumpy pillow" recall the "lumps of knotted horsehair in the sofa of her parlour on which he used to sit." All his distrust of her is reawakened with her attraction. She is timid, orthodox, given to flirting with the priests, who make her feel safe. Moved to anger by his memories, Stephen summons up girls he has casually encountered, girls whom he has glanced at. Emma becomes, in the process, representative, an embodiment of the secret of her race (like the peasant woman Davin encountered). And, as she is magnified and made more innocently devious, Stephen's competitive sense awakens him to self-assertion against the "priested peasant" she favors. "To him she would unveil her soul's shy nakedness, to one who was but schooled in the discharging of a formal rite rather than to him, a priest of eternal imagination, transmitting the daily bread of experience into the radiant body of everlasting life." The triumphant vision of himself as priest of imagination makes his poem a "eucharistic hymn," and the transubstantiation of feeling into art has been accomplished. Almost. For, moved by the renewal of his poetry, of his capacity to honor her in verses again, he comes to a more generous vision of her innocence, to a more hopeful dream of her responsiveness. And finally the associations move to their inevitable culmination: a fantasy of erotic fulfillment. "Her nakedness yielded to him, radiant, warm, odorous, and lavishlimbed," and the poem comes to its completion: "like a cloud of vapour or like waters circumfluent in space the liquid letters of speech, symbols of the element of mystery, flowed forth over his brain."

The villanelle is of less interest than the process of composition itself. That a poem emerges we are sufficiently persuaded; and the form of the villanelle insists upon its artfulness. That the poem is in large measure traceable to erotic fantasy and yet freed of Stephen's experience as it stands on the page is the point of the process. A finer poem might leave the associations of feeling further behind, especially if it were achieved by subtler and tighter thought than this poem has demanded. This transfiguration is, in short, not so complete as to transcend its sources; it can be seen in process and recapitulates the aesthetic argument that has preceded it. But that is Joyce's purpose, which a better poem might not serve so well.[5]

The book ends with Stephen freed—not without doubts, second thoughts, regrets—to leave Ireland and to embrace "the loveliness which has not yet come into the world." He turns away from what might seem aestheticism, for his conception of art is more strenuous and severe. "I go to encounter for the millionth time and to forge in the smithy of my soul the uncreated conscience of my race." As the artist has emerged from the young man, so the conscience of Ireland may emerge from the artist. It is a high calling, no mean or middle flight.

2

Art in the *Portrait* is the transfiguration of reality and of self, the emergence of the vocation and the artist. While it is generated by feeling and rooted in social circumstance, and while it may in turn aspire to give Ireland a new sense of her dignity, still it achieves what it does only as art. Its integrity requires the freedom of the artist, freedom from being made the instrument of his nation or his church. In *To the Lighthouse* we are no less concerned with genesis and transfiguration. Art becomes the attempt to order experience, to achieve stability, to fix the transitory in a pattern that seems to transcend time. The difficulty of creation lies in the resistance of materials and in the self-doubt of the artist. Art demands strenuous efforts, but their success often comes in a sudden moment of ecstatic assurance and power. The novel celebrates those moments of creative power, but it claims little for their material achievement. There are moments of vision, created by the artistry of Mrs. Ramsay and kept alive in the memories of her friends and children; there are works like Lily Briscoe's, which seem of little consequence except as they embody the process of creation itself. A comic futility is often implicit in the anticlimax of what the process yields; and this takes two forms—the diminishing of the achievement or, as in the following passage, the mock-heroic inflation of the effort:

> Who then could blame the leader of that forlorn party which after all has climbed high enough to see the waste of the years and the perishing of stars, if before death stiffens his limbs beyond the power of movement he does a little consciously raise his numbed fingers to his brow, and square his shoulders, so that when the search party comes they will find him dead at his post, the fine figure of a soldier? Mr. Ramsay squared his shoulders and stood very upright by the urn.[6]

In Joyce's portrait we trace the unfolding of sensibility from childhood to maturity, the forming of that sensibility in the search for freedom, and the moral vision of what Ireland may become. In *To the Lighthouse* there is radical alternation between self-doubt and self-assertion, between withdrawal and expansion. The freedom sought is freedom from internal doubt rather than from institutions; it is the momentary power to hold and shape experience in an act of imagination.

The heroic artist of Woolf's novel is divided between the commanding charm of Mrs. Ramsay and the shy, self-distrustful effort of Lilly Briscoe. One can easily see, if one chooses, two aspects of the author herself. We have ample testimony to her power to charm, not least from the viewpoint of the child, as Quentin Bell and Nigel Nicolson have indicated; and one senses Woolf's own awareness and occasional distrust of that power.[7] But there is also the aspect of herself that she embodies in Lily Briscoe. Near the time she was completing *To the Lighthouse* Virginia Woolf described herself in her diary as an "elderly dowdy fussy ugly incompetent woman; vain, chattering and futile."[8] In *To the Lighthouse* Lily undertakes the serious business of the artist with risk and labor, constant fear and frequent sense of futility, intense dedication and a small measure of triumph. But all of these elements enter into Mrs. Ramsay's life as well; she is an artist in materials that have no permanence, but she is no less the creator of "significant form."

I have borrowed the phrase first coined by Clive Bell and used to better purpose by Roger Fry. "He wanted art to be art," Virginia Woolf wrote of Fry, "literature to be literature, and life to be life. He was an undaunted enemy of the sloppiness, the vagueness, the sentimentality which has filled so many academies with anecdotes of dogs and duchesses. He detested the storytelling spirit which has clouded our painting and confused our criticism."[9] Fry tried to distinguish between the emotions aroused by the subject represented in a picture and the emotions resulting from the contemplation of its form. The latter seemed to him "more profound and more significant spiritually than any of the emotions which had to do with life."[10] The work of art frees us of moral and practical attitudes towards the objects it presents. "As a result, we *see* the [object] much more clearly; see a number of quite interesting but irrelevant things, which in real life could not struggle into our consciousness, bent, as it would be, entirely upon the problem of our appropriate reaction." If the detachment of an aesthetic response frees us alike from moral urgencies and associative fantasies, the dissolution of the object may carry this further. Such dissolution occurs when the formal relationships within the picture cut across the boundaries of the objects represented; that is, when "the coherence of the separate patches of tone and colour within each object is no longer stronger than the coherence with every other tone and colour throughout the field."[11]

While Fry's doctrine might encourage abstraction, it need not. What it encourages more fundamentally is the full exercise of our aesthetic emotions in creating or responding to formal patterns. "Rembrandt expressed his profoundest feelings just as well when he painted a carcass hanging up in a butcher's shop as when he painted the Crucifixion or his mistress." But the formalism is less rigorous in an interesting essay published by the Hogarth Press in 1924, *The Artist and Psycho-Analysis*. Fry distinguishes between art as wish fulfillment and art as formal design, but he illustrates the distinction with works of fiction:

> The novels that have endured do not represent wish-fulfilment to any considerable extent. They depend on the contrary for their effect, upon a peculiar detachment from the instinctive life. Instead of manipulating reality so as to conform to the libido, they note the inexorable sequence in life of cause and effect, they mark the total indifference of fate to all human desires, and they endeavour to derive from that inexorability of fate an altogether different kind of pleasure—the pleasure which consists in the recognition of inevitable sequences. . . . [N]o one who hoped to get an ideal wish-fulfiment would go to *Mme Bovary* or *Anna Karenina* or even *Vanity Fair*.

This sounds very much like the inevitability that Aristotle stresses in tragic plots; but it could as well suggest the inexorable movement of time, as seen in the waves and the lighthouse beams of *To the Lighthouse*. Fry tries to account for our "pleasure in the recognition of order, of inevitability in relations":

> I sometimes wonder if it . . . does not get its force from arousing some very deep, very vague, and immensely generalized reminiscences. It looks as though art had got access to the substratum of all the emotional colours of life, to something which underlies all the particular and special emotions of actual life. It seems to derive an emotional energy from the very conditions of our existence by its revelation of an emotional significance in time and space. Or it may be that art really calls up, as it were, the residual traces left on the spirit by the different emotions of life, without however actually recalling the actual experiences.[12]

Fry suggests the conflict between the two kinds of emotion in a manner not so very different from Joyce's account of the "arrest" which marks the tension (or the equilibrium) between opposed emotions. The conflict of wish fulfillment with a sense of inevitable sequence (as, in Joyce's terms, pity unites us with the "human sufferer," fear with the "secret cause") may invoke experience of depth on either side. Such a conflict (or fusion) is suggested by the counterpoint of Clarissa Dalloway with Septimus Smith—of an "insane instinct for life" and the "impulse towards death," of "the effort to create order and meaning" and "the urge to despair in isolation."[13] Fry also translated an essay by Charles Mauron which spoke of "psychological volumes."

"As the painter creates a spatial being, the writer creates a psychological being." The "idea that the writer's end is solely to model a spiritual volume, would relegate sternly to the background the documentary value of a work of literature." Thus Mauron's emphasis reinforced that made by Virginia Woolf in her attack upon the novel of social reality and social causation, the more journalistic novel of Bennett, Wells, and Galsworthy; but it also suggests Lily Briscoe's abstract painting.[14]

In *To the Lighthouse* the constant threat of futility and meaninglessness takes the form of time passing, of the welter of change and impermanence, the erosion of purpose, and the contraction of vision. Time has the sound of the waves; and Mrs. Ramsay hears it when, for a moment, other sounds cease, and there is an intermitted moment of quiet. The sound of the waves, like the stroke of the lighthouse beam, has a double aspect; it may comfort or chill, as it marks one's participation in life and absorption in prospects and intentions or as it marks one's isolation and sense of vertiginous loss and separation. So the waves seem at times to "beat a measured and soothing tattoo to her thoughts" and murmur like an old cradle song, "I am guarding you—I am your support." But there are other times when "like a ghostly roll of drums" they made "one think of the destruction of the island and its engulfment in the sea, and warned her whose day had slipped past in one quick doing after another that it was all ephemeral as a rainbow—this sound which had been obscured and concealed under the other sounds suddenly thundered hollow in her ears and made her look up with an impulse of terror" (I, iii).

There is the same sense of the intermitted moment—the stilling of human action and the naked utterance of time's passing—in the second section of the novel. "Nothing, it seemed, could survive the flood" (II, ii). Darkness creeps in, slips past defenses, swallows up hard detail, dissolves outlines, and obliterates objects. Duration itself is denied all meaning; "it seems impossible that . . . we should ever compose from their fragments a perfect whole to read in the littlest pieces the clear words of truth" (II, iii). We attend to things, the spaces that once held life, the vestiges and artifacts, as they run down to decay; and, bracketed as the most fortuitous of casualties, we learn of the death of Mrs. Ramsay, of her daughter in childbirth, of her son in battle. The tone of the section becomes bitterly ironic, as all evidence of benignity and bounty, of order and hope, is turned upon itself. The sea carries the "purplish stain" of a sunken ship, the victim of a mine or torpedo. The waves disport themselves "like the amorphous hulks of leviathans whose brows are pierced by no light of reason, and mounted one on top of another, and lunged and plunged . . . in idiot games, until it seemed as if the universe were battling and tumbling in brute confusion and wanton lust aimlessly by itself" (II, vi, vii).

Without instructions, prompted by the memory of Mrs. Ramsay, the aged Mrs. McNab still tries to keep up the house; but she is no longer capable of doing all that is needed. "It was beyond the strength of one woman, she said. They never sent. They never wrote." The lighthouse beam stares wth equanimity as the house teeters at the edge of destruction. It is ready to fall. "But there was a force working; something not highly conscious; something that leered, something that lurched; something not inspired to go about its work with dignified ritual or solemn chanting." When one of the Ramsay girls writes, Mrs. McNab and Mrs. Bast set about laboriously to restore the house to use. The sounds of life return—barks, bleats, hums, squeaks, "always on the verge of harmonising" but never fully harmonized; as the Ramsays return and with them Lily Briscoe, the voice of the waves seems to resume its consoling tone. "Through the open window the voice of the beauty of the world came murmuring, too softly to hear exactly what was said—but what mattered if the meaning were plain?" (II, ix, x).

Cosmic indifference, with its counterpart of human instability, provides the ground for most of the action of the novel; only in the second section does it move forward to become the figure as the human actions that resist it recede to become ground. The leering, lurching insensibility of Mrs. McNab is human survival at its most rudimentary—another anticipation of Samuel Beckett's world, sheer protoplasmic endurance, "persistency itself" (II, v). The play of chance, the blindness of fertility—of growth without form, of change without purpose—the constant running down of whatever order has been established—all of this is what the characters confront at their moments of isolated awareness.

The only response to this confusion lies in the effort to create order, to assert a human power. Yet even Mrs. Ramsay can feel relief in contraction and the withdrawal from effort. "All the being and doing, expansive, glittering, vocal, evaporated; and she shrunk, with a sense of solemnity to being oneself, a wedge-shaped core of darkness, something invisible to others." She sinks below the daylight world of personal relationships. "Beneath it is all dark, it is all spreading, it is unfathomably deep. . . . Losing personality, one lost the fret, the hurry, the stir; and there rose to her lips always some exclamation of triumph over life when things came together in this peace, this rest, this eternity." This seems withdrawal into essential being, a featureless reality where she finds freedom, peace, stability, and where she seems to become one with the long steady stroke of the lighthouse. (There are resemblances to the deeper self as it is imagined by Lawrence and Forster.) In a state that has intimations of metaphysical depth and yet the mindlessness of trance, she hears herself exclaiming, "We are in the hands of the Lord." And, having said it, Mrs. Ramsay at once rejects it—as a consoling lie, an insincerity. And as she returns to full wakefulness, she regards the light with "some irony in her interrogation." She looks at "the steady light, the pitiless, the remorseless, which was so much her, yet so little her." The light serves now to fuse two kinds of awareness. The first is her sense of a world where there is no reason, order, justice, where no happiness lasts, a world no Lord could have made. The other is the sense of exquisite and intense happiness which can be won, however briefly: "and the ecstasy burst in her eyes and waves of pure delight raced over the floor of her mind and she felt, It is enough! It is enough!" (I, xi) In a letter to Gerald Brenan in 1922, Woolf wrote of such an event:

> we live, all of us who feel and reflect, with recurring cataclysms of horror: starting up in the night in agony. Every ten years brings, I suppose, one of those private orientations which match the vast one which is, to my mind, general now in the race. I mean, life has to be sloughed: has to be faced: to be rejected: then accepted on new terms with rapture.[15]

In Lily Briscoe we can see the effort of art in the strictest sense. Lily is a painter in a postimpressionist manner; her work is at once a severe discipline, an almost overpowering challenge, and a refuge from the dangers of human relationship. Lily's painting is something which seems almost to lose reality as she steps back from it; her trust in her art is so tenuous that it can hardly survive a moment's detachment. But if she cannot bear to have Mr. Ramsay see her work, she can trust the gentler William Bankes and even talk to him about her intentions. For it is only of her intentions that she can speak with confidence. The "passage from conception to work" is "as dreadful as any down a dark passage for a child"; it is only "some miserable remnant of her vision" which her canvas holds (I, iv).

As Lily explains to Bankes, her art is a work of construction. She is not after a likeness, nor does she wish to evoke the pleasant associations that William Bankes draws from the subject matter of his favorite painting. She is constructing a tribute to her subject—to the extent that Mrs. Ramsay and James are a "subject"—in the very ordering of color and space, "the question being one of the relations of masses, of lights and shadows." A light here requires a shadow there. "Mother and child then—objects of universal veneration, and in this case the mother was famous for her beauty—might be reduced, he pondered, to a purple shadow without irreverence" (I, ix). Lily cannot articulate her subject except in visual forms. "Her pictures do not betray her. Their reticence is inviolable. . . . [T]hey yield their full meaning only to those who can tunnel their way behind the canvas into masses and passages and relations and values of which we know nothing." Or, to borrow further from Virginia Woolf's account of Vanessa Bell's work: "No stories are told; no insinuations are made. The hill side is bare; the group of women is silent; the little boy stands in the sea saying nothing. If portraits there are, they are pictures of flesh which happens from its texture or its modelling to be aesthetically on an equality with the China pot or the chrysanthemum." [16]

But Lily's triangular purple shadow is something more abstract than this; and each element of her work is part of a rigorous design. "She saw the colour burning in a framework of steel; the light of a butterfly's wing lying upon the arches of a cathedral." Or, as Lily thinks of it later: "Beautiful and bright it should be on the surface, feathery and evanescent, one colour melting into another like the colours on a butterfly's wing; but beneath the fabric must be clamped together with bolts of iron" (I, ix; III, v).

The work itself becomes impersonal—and in the process of creating it the artist herself seems to lose personality—"Subduing all her impressions as a woman to something much more general; becoming once more under the power of that vision which she had seen clearly once and must now grope for among hedges and houses and mothers and children—her picture" (I, ix). And yet for all its impersonality the work of art requires intense emotion, "the determination not to be put off, not to be bamboozled. One must hold the scene—so—in a vise and let nothing come in and spoil it." One wants to "be on a level with ordinary experience, to feel simply that's a chair, that's a table, and yet at the same time, It's a miracle, it's an ecstasy. The problem might be solved after all." For a moment, a flounce moves inside the window and seems to mark the reappearance of Mrs. Ramsay. Lily feels all "the old horror come back—to want and want—and not to have. Could she inflict that still? And then, quietly, as if she refrained, that too became part of ordinary experience, was on a level with the chair, with the table. Mrs. Ramsay—it was part of her perfect goodness—sat there quite simply, in the chair" and "cast her shadow on the step" (III, xi). If the painting brings back Mrs. Ramsay, Mrs. Ramsay becomes part of the composition; she becomes "part of ordinary experience" and provides her triangular shadow. The picture is neither an act of representation nor a direct expression of feeling; it is a structure which controls the feelings it admits, which builds forms out of the feelings it has evoked.

Lily's painting is, moreover, a sustained act of attention. As Roger Fry was to write in 1933, "Most men live through one experience after another without, as it were, stopping the current of life to enquire further about them—with the artist certain experiences have the power to arrest his attention so much that he turns aside from the current of life and waits until he has fixed that experience fully in his consciousness and extracted its full savour." This is a process that lies deeper than conscious plan or calculation: "His reaction is coloured by all sorts of subconscious associations and feelings, of which he is naturally unaware, but which affect profoundly the form taken by the work of art and which have the power to stir up corresponding subconscious feelings in the spectator." Art seems to have "magic power" over us "because the effect on our feelings often far transcends what we can explain by our conscious experience."[17]

We can at most surmise the features of Lily Briscoe's painting. But it embodies feelings in Lily of which we are made more fully aware than she. She is too deeply caught up in the process of feeling to see its pattern, and she is—for us—one of a group of characters undergoing comparable experi- ences. So at the close, Mr. Ramsay has reached the lighthouse with James and Cam. Mr. Carmichael stands up "as if he were spreading his hands over all the weakness and suffering of mankind." Lily thought "he was surveying, tolerantly and compassionately, their final destiny." For a moment the struc- ture of events is such as to give Mr. Carmichael the crowning role; the intensity of Lily's feeling gives him the posture of an ultimate meaning, a hidden God who rouses himself from lethargy (or opium dreams) to pro- nounce the world good—"as if she had seen him let fall from his great height a wreath of violets and asphodels which, fluttering slowly, lay at length upon the earth" (III, xiii). It is almost a parody of the blessing of closure. At that moment James admires his father, who "rose and stood in the bow of the boat, very straight and tall, as if he were saying, 'There is no God.' " And Cam, too, sees her father "as if he were leaping into space." They follow him as he springs, "lightly like a young man . . . on to the rock." And at that moment Lily's composition is completed: "she drew a line there, in the centre. It was done; it was finished. Yes, she thought, laying down her brush in extreme fatigue, I have had my vision" (III, xii, xiii). "I meant *nothing* by the lighthouse," Virginia Woolf wrote Roger Fry. "One has to have a central line down the middle of the book to hold the design together."[18]

The emphasis in Lily Briscoe is upon the construction by the artist, the hard work, the firm control; and the painting itself suggests an autonomy of art in that it uses its structure of forms to contain the force of the actual. The painting achieves an order that makes no reference to time; it makes life stand still.

The chief work of art in *To the Lighthouse* is not, however, Lily's painting but Mrs. Ramsay's dinner. Even more than the painting, the dinner is an ephemeral structure, existing only to create a form that will survive at most as memory. Mrs. Ramsay approaches it with the same discouragement and sense of futility we have seen in Lily: she sees before her "an infinitely long table and plates and knives"—and she is beyond caring for anyone or any- thing. "She had a sense of being past everything, through everything, out of everything . . . as if there was an eddy—there—and one could be in it, or one could be out of it, and she was out of it. It's all come to an end, she thought. . . ." This experience of being isolated, on the outside of life, excluded or detached from a common human venture, is characteristic of a despair that seems, in more benign moments, a stern acceptance of bitter truth. Mrs. Ramsay, as she ladles soup, feels "more and more strongly, outside that eddy; or as if a shade had fallen, and, robbed of colour, she saw things truly. The room (she looked round it) was very shabby. There was no beauty anywhere. . . . Nothing seemed to have merged. They all sat separate. And the whole effort of merging and flowing and creating rested on her."

And so the effort starts, weakly, with weary reluctance, like the sailor's who "thinks how, had the ship sunk, he would have whirled round and round and found rest on the floor of the sea." Lily sees Mrs. Ramsay as if she were "drifting into that strange no-man's land" where one cannot follow, which creates a chill as we watch the departure. "How old she looks, how worn she looks, Lily thought, and how remote." But even as Lily perceives the initial isolation and the weary discouragement of Mrs. Ramsay, she sees that a change has begun to take place. For Mrs. Ramsay has committed herself to William Bankes, as if her pity for his loneliness has given her reason to live. "He is not in the least pitiable," Lily thinks in protest. "He has his work. . . ." And at once Lily thinks of her own work and of a way to compose her picture (as ten years later she will succeed in doing).

But Lily is not free to lose herself in her work. While William Bankes is being drawn into the dinner party by Mrs. Ramsay, Lily is still distracted by the presence of Charles Tansley opposite her. He is ferociously defensive, determined not to be drawn into the "sort of rot" that people speak at the dinner table—all of it "silly, superficial, flimsy." Just as Mrs. Ramsay seems to pity men for their sterility, Tansley resents women for their shallow "charm." And so aggressively (he feels awkward, too, about not having dinner clothes), he asserts himself once more: "No going to the lighthouse tomorrow, Mrs. Ramsay." It is the malice of realism, as it were; a vindictiveness of truth opposed to desire, dream, or aspiration. And his aggressiveness is taken by Lily as a discrediting of herself: "Women can't write, women can't paint. . . ." She knows why he is saying what he does, but she cannot altogether withstand the blow without some parry; and so she asserts herself by mocking him: "Oh, Mr. Tansley . . . do take me to the lighthouse with you. I should so love it." She succeeds in unsettling him; he feels her scorn, he feels the inadequacy of his clothes and manners; he feels despised by all the women at the table. He must fight back and says, "all in a jerk, very rudely, it would be too rough for her tomorrow. She would be sick." But by now Tansley has escaped into a fantasy of self-pity. He wants, as Lily does, to withdraw to his work, where he can feel successful, in control, at ease. But he has been radically unsettled. and he must dredge up his financial independence ("he had never cost his father a penny since he was fifteen. . . . [H]e was educated by his sister") to support his image of his own competence, if only to cover the embarrassment he now feels at the childish assertiveness of his last remark. He recalls his affection for Mrs. Ramsay and his desire to prove to her that he is "not just a dry prig." But she can't be reached; she is talking to William Bankes about people he does not know.

Those people are the Mannings, from whom Mr. Bankes has had a letter. Mrs. Ramsay recalls Herbert and Carrie, whom she has not seen for twenty years. She hovers over the scenes in which she last saw them, moments preserved in a remembered space through which she can now move "like a ghost." But, in fact, they have gone on living and changing as she has, and the Mannings may have thought of her no more than she has of them. This sense of an independent life from which she is excluded is "strange and distasteful," like the idea of death. And now even Mr. Bankes asserts himself, if gently. "People soon drift apart," he remarks, feeling pleasure in having remained part of both these worlds. As he prepares his own defenses against some imagined criticism, some frightening self-doubt, he too dreams of withdrawing into his work. "How trifling it all is, how boring it all is, he thought, compared with the other thing—work." And for a moment his isolation is such that Mrs. Ramsay—beautiful as she has been, sitting in the window with James or at the table beside him—means nothing to him. He escapes her design and withdraws from her, from family life, from the human race. "Are we attractive as a species? Not so very, he thought. . . . foolish question, vain questions, questions one never asked if one was occupied." But in a moment, when Mrs. Ramsay has turned away and he is left isolated, unsupported, unsolicited, he knows—for all his boast—how fragile- all friendships are. "One drifts apart." And when Mrs. Ramsay turns back to him he forces himself back into her company, into relationship. She, with a rare instinct, finds a way of restoring their intimacy; she speaks with a mocking recognition of their common plight and in a tone that denies this plight with the special idiom of a social manner. It works, for in taking up the language Mr. Bankes joins her conspiracy and returns to her.

It is precisely the artifice of this idiom which Tansley detects as he hears it; he scorns "its insincerity" and seizes upon this new instance of the "nonsense" the Ramsays talk. It will become part of his self-justifying denunciation of the life Ramsay has chosen. But that beautiful moment of self-justification lies too far away, in an uncertain future; Tansley can only feel his immediate discomfort, his need to assert himself, to gain dominance and esteem. Lily Briscoe sees all this "as in an X-ray photograph." She has a deep reluctance to enter once more into that social contract where each helps the other, where men repay by generous protection the helpful dependence shown them by women. As Lily holds back, refusing to join the common enterprise, Mrs. Ramsay reaches out to bring Tansley in: "Are you a good sailor, Mr. Tansley?" He can only reply with vehemence that he has "never

been sick in his life"; but the remark is compact with his sense of class and
defiant pride, his tremendous drive to prove himself and overturn their condescension. And at last Lily yields. For she hears beneath the conversation
Mrs. Ramsay's plea:

> "I am drowning, my dear, in seas of fire. Unless you apply some balm to the
> anguish of this hour and say something nice to that young man there, life will
> run upon the rocks—indeed I hear the grating and growling at this minute.
> My nerves are taut as fiddle strings. Another touch and they will snap"—when
> Mrs. Ramsay said all this, as the glance in her eyes said it, of course . . . Lily
> Briscoe had to renounce the experiment . . . and be nice.

And so she says in a kindly tone that Tansley can recognize, "Will you take
me, Mr. Tansley?" At last "relieved of his egotism," Tansley is free to recount his own adventures at sea and in a lighthouse. Mrs. Ramsay is free to
return to her memories of the Mannings and her talk with William Bankes;
but Lily Briscoe feels, for all Mrs. Ramsay's gratitude, betrayed. Like Tansley she is troubled by insincerity: "She had done the usual trick—been nice.
She would never know him. He would never know her." And she withdraws
once more into her painting, leaving Mrs. Ramsay to feed Tansley the necessary questions. Sincerity seems the refuge particularly of those who are
lonely and without confidence, who distrust social forms because they are
uncomfortable with them and do not depend on the relief they provide from
the constant demands of spontaneity and intensity. Those like Mrs. Ramsay,
who feel more sure of their powers—but almost overwhelmed by the materials (others' feelings) they must evoke, shape, and control—rely upon the
conventions, as the artist must, to give form to their work and to sustain it
in those moments when invention slackens or intensity fails.[19] For the time
being she too withdraws into the past, haunting the Mannings, revisiting
some timeless moment where life seems "sealed up" and lies "like a lake,
placidly between its banks" instead of shooting onward in cascades. But
William Bankes will not join her in the past and seems deliberately to withdraw from intimacy into the general conversation. There is talk going on,
but everyone feels that something is lacking; what they lack is a sense of
involvement. All of them spectators and auditors, detached, withdrawn—
Lily, Bankes, Mrs. Ramsay listen to Tansley, each sure the others feel more
intensely. Bankes senses that Tansley is the new man who will displace his
own generation "and reveal its futility." Mrs. Ramsay finds herself waiting
to hear her husband speak: "It was altogether different when he spoke; one
did not feel then, pray heaven you don't see how little I care, because one
did care."

But just as Mrs. Ramsay feels admiration for her husband and glows with
praise she herself has given him, just then he is exhibiting ludicrous anger

at Mr. Carmichael's asking for a second plate of soup. "He loathed people eating when he had finished." To save their exchange of silent rebukes from becoming too evident, she has the candles lighted. The flames illuminate a dish of fruit, in which Rose has arranged grapes and pears and bananas and a "horny pink-lined shell." This last is a trophy from the sea, brought up from darkness into light, seeming to rise like a small world of hills and valleys where one can climb. Mrs. Ramsay looks at the dish while Augustus Carmichael (who does not like her) looks at it from his own angle and in his own way; and they are united by the objects they both behold. Subject and object and the nature of (shared) reality. As the candlelight rises, the shape of the dish gives way to the larger pattern of order and dry land; they are all composed now into a party. Outside the light and beyond the windows is the sea; the glass gives back a reflection in which "things wavered and vanished, waterily." The effect of the candles is to make everyone at once aware of making "common cause against that fluidity out there."

In what follows we see Mrs. Ramsay exert an irresistible power through her beauty and her urgency: she "put a spell upon them all, by wishing, so simply, so directly." She has the sense of having achieved her work, of their all being held "safe together." "Nothing need be said; nothing could be said. There it was, all round them. It partook, she felt, carefully helping Mr. Bankes to a specially tender piece, of eternity. . . ." The syntax is just ambiguous enough to make one hover over "piece of eternity," as if it were visible, tangible. And when we restore the phrase to its verb "partook," the teasing idea remains. She feels now: "There is a coherence in things, a stability; something, she meant, is immune from change, and shines out . . . in the face of the flowing, the fleeting, the spectral. . . . Of such moments, she thought, the thing is made that endures." Having created the structure and become assured of its stability, its timelessness, she rests upon the "admirable fabric"—the architectural support—of the "masculine intelligence, which ran up and down, crossed this way and that, like iron girders spanning the swaying fabric, upholding the world." Her composition is like Lily Briscoe's painting, color resting upon firm structure; it is also a world like the bowl of fruit, its colors filling out the volumes of curves and shadows. As Mrs. Ramsay's eye plays over the fruit, she senses its formal relations ("putting a yellow against a purple, a curved shape against a round shape") and feels "more and more serene"—until time reenters and a hand takes a pear from the bowl. Everyone at the table seems now to participate in a harmony; even Augustus Carmichael pays Mrs. Ramsay homage: "She looked at the window in which the candle flames burnt brighter now that the panes were black, and looking at that outside the voices came to her very strangely, as if they were voices at a service in a cathedral." And at this moment, as "Luriana, Lurilee" becomes the mysterious hymn that unites them all and evinces for each of them the feeling they share, the work is complete and is "already the past" (I, xvii). It cannot be sustained beyond its completion; but it retains its integrity as a memory they will share. "They would, she thought, going on again, however long they lived, come back to this night; this moon; this word; this house; and to her too." For a short while the "walls of partition" between them had "become so thin that practically . . . it was all one stream" (I, xviii).

Mrs. Ramsay, like Lily Briscoe, creates a work of art, although one composed of materials that do not hold the same relationship so long as the colors on a canvas. But, as Virginia Woolf wrote of Roger Fry, "A picture was to him not merely the finished canvas but the canvas in the making. Every step of that struggle, which ends sometimes in victory, but more often in defeat, was known to him from his own daily battle."[20] There is a related passage in a memoir she wrote as a relief from her sustained labor on the biography of Roger Fry. She is thinking of the painful shocks which used to terrify her until she began to see their use. They have begun to seem more than "a blow from an enemy hidden behind the cotton wool of daily life. They seem, instead, a revelation of some order . . . a token of some real thing behind appearances; and *I make it real by putting it into words.* It is only by putting it into words that I make it whole; this wholeness means that it has lost the power to hurt me; it gives me, perhaps because by doing so I take away the pain, a great delight to put the severed parts together." We have thus far the process of ordering that makes an experience real and whole, giving it a structure that one can contemplate freely, transmuting painful experience into objective form. She goes on:

> Perhaps this is the strongest pleasure known to me. It is the rapture I get when in writing I seem to be discovering what belongs to what; making a scene come right; making a character come together. From this I reach what I might call a philosophy; at any rate it is a constant idea of mine; that behind the cotton wool is hidden a pattern; that we—I mean all human beings—are connected with this; that the whole world is a work of art; that we are parts of the work of art. *Hamlet* or a Beethoven quartet is the truth about this vast mass that we call the world. But there is no Shakespeare, there is no Beethoven; certainly and emphatically there is no God; *we are the words; we are the music; we are the thing itself.* And I see this when I have a shock.[21]

It is an artistry like Mrs. Ramsay's that Virginia Woolf, in the same memoirs, evokes in the image of her mother. As she thinks herself back into childhood she remembers a "great hall," a "great Cathedral space which was childhood" (Mrs. Ramsay thinks of the voices at the table "as if they were voices at a service in a cathedral"; she thinks she is hearing "Latin words of a service in some Roman Catholic cathedral"). "She was keeping . . . the panoply of life—that which we all lived in common—in being." She was "living on such an extended surface" that, except for special need, she could not concentrate upon anyone. Virginia Woolf's memories of her mother are " all of her in company; of her surrounded, of her generalised; dispersed, omnipresent, of her as *the creator of that crowded merry world* which spun so gaily in the centre of my childhood" (italics added).[22] These passages cannot establish the meaning of Mrs. Ramsay's behavior; they only serve to suggest it by their parallels.

What the memoir emphasizes is that sense of the halcyon building its nest in the watery element. Our order and permanence are something we create for ourselves and out of ourselves; they are moments given stability by a structure that simultaneously fuses the experience of many and provides an image in which meanings meet and cohere. There is Mr. Ramsay standing "on a spit of land which the sea is slowly eating away, and there to stand, like a desolate seabird, alone." He sheds "all superfluities," he shrinks down to the barest and sparest of forms, standing "on his little ledge facing the dark of human ignorance, how we know nothing and the sea eats away the ground we stand on" (I, viii). (He recalls Marlow's last view of Jim.) Or there is the moment in which meaning "descends on people, making them symbolical"; then

> The symbolical outline which transcended the real figures sank down again, and they became . . . Mr. and Mrs. Ramsay watching the children throwing catches. But still for a moment. . . . Still, for one moment, there was a sense of things having been blown apart, of space, of irresponsibility as the ball soared high, and they followed it and lost it and saw the one star and the draped branches. In the failing light they all looked sharp-edged and ethereal and divided by great distances. [I, xiii].

Here the image will not quite settle; there remains a sense of solidity dissolved, of a transcendence that commands infinite space. This is most clear when, as we follow the trajectory of the ball, we lose it in the sudden brilliance of the star. Once more the temporal becomes timeless.

It is in such scenes or "moments of being" that Virginia Woolf's novels culminate. As she wrote *Mrs. Dalloway* she brooded over Arnold Bennett's charge that she couldn't create "characters that survive." She knew the tactical reply. "that character is dissipated into shreds now": but she recognizes the less pleasant truth that she hasn't "that 'reality' gift. I insubstantise, wilfully to some extent, distrusting reality—its cheapness. But to get further. Have I the power of conveying the true reality?" And a few lines later, recapturing confidence and enthusiasm, she writes of the novel in progress: "The design is so queer and so masterful. I'm always having to wrench my substance to fit it."[23] As she worked on *To the Lighthouse,* she saw all kinds

of possibilities opened by a single remark or detail: "I think I can spin out
all their entrails this way, but it is hopelessly undramatic." Two months
later, pleased with the way her work has gone, she thinks of other subjects:
"Yet I am now and then haunted by some semimystic very profound life of
a woman, which shall all be told on one occasion; and time shall be wholly
obliterated; future shall somehow blossom out of the past. One incident—
say the fall of a flower—might contain it. My theory being that the actual
event practically does not exist—nor time either." [24] So Bernard reflects in
The Waves: "But if there are no stories, what end can there be, or what
beginning? Life is not susceptible perhaps to the treatment we give it when
we try to tell it." The alternative to such narrative is a "treasury of moments." [25] Those moments become arrests of time, mysterious images or
scenes that are full of suggestion, of implication that cannot be easily artic-
ulated. In her thinking of the past, Virginia Woolf remarks:

> Always a scene has arranged itself: representative; enduring. This confirms me
> in my instinctive notion (it will not bear arguing about; it is irrational) the
> sensation that we are sealed vessels afloat on what it is convenient to call reality;
> and at some moments, the sealing matter cracks; in floods reality; that is, these
> scenes—for why do they survive undamaged year after year unless they are
> made of something comparatively permanent? [26]

This conception tends to create a series of lyrical or symbolical moments
bound by free indirect discourse as characters speculate, ruminate, observe.
The narrative is largely implicit; for the end of the writing is to free the real
from the integument of the commonplace, to reveal the pattern behind the
"cotton wool," to extricate the work of art implicit in our lives and relations.
    "Now . . . cleared of chatter and emotion, it seemed always to have been,
only was shown now and so being shown, struck everything into stability"
(I, xviii). So, too, Lily Briscoe exchanges "the fluidity of life for the concentration of painting" (III, iii). Vriginia Woolf never allows us to forget the
difficult process by which the artist, like the lover, gives to things "a wholeness not theirs in life," and makes "of some scene, or meeting of people (all
now gone and separate), one of those globed compacted things over which
thought lingers, and love plays" (III, xi). But these creations are not the
work solely of painters and novelists, as the instance of Mrs. Ramsay makes
clear; they are the art by which all of us shape our lives.

3

    In contrast to the work of Joyce and Woolf, Thomas Mann's *The Confessions
of Felix Krull, Confidence Man* takes pleasure in both time and appearance,
finding the life of its hero and his art precisely in surface, costume, and

illusion. Mann recognized the "comic kinship" of Krull's story with the Faust theme ("the motif of loneliness, in the one case mystic and tragic, in the other humorous and roguish"). Mann observes, of his use of Serenus Zeitblom in *Doctor Faustus,* that "to make the demonic strain pass through an undemonic meduim, to entrust a harmless and simple soul, well-meaning and timid, with the recital of the story, was in itself a comic idea."[27] In Felix Krull we have a different comic antithesis to Adrian Leverkuhn, and in fact to the romantic artist-hero in general, or at least to the celebration of the artist-hero as a tragic figure. Krull is a criminal with great refinement of manner, much given to euphemism and to elegance of phrase, always writing of his career as if it were a series of performances in which he is both the instrument and the virtuoso. His "comic primness" couples criminal behavior with a sententious, sometimes even sanctimonious, tone; and, while we share the ironic pleasure Krull's tone provides, we know that we must expect him to sustain it with rigor.[28] What we are to make of Krull is never quite clear, for, while he refers teasingly to later misadventures, including a term in prison, he scarcely shows a "later" consciousness with which to disown or even distance the exuberant younger self he presents.

In the novel, Mann resumed a tale he had begun forty years earlier, and he completed only the first volume. It is "a fragment still," Mann remarked of it, "but fragment the strange book will surely remain, even if time and mood might permit me to continue. . . . the most characteristic description which I can make of it is that it will be broken off, stopped, but never finished."[29] It is, like most exercises in the picaresque, a work which celebrates the onward movement of vitality. Felix can hardly be said to undergo an apprenticeship; we see him at the age of eight running a greased bow over a violin, imitating to perfection all the movements of a true musician while the orchestra performs, winning acclaim as a prodigy. "An aged Russian princess, wearing enormous white side curls and dressed from head to toe in violet silk, took my head between her beringed hands and kissed my brow, beaded as it was with perspiration."[30] That sentence makes clear how differently Felix reveals himself from Joyce's or Woolf's characters; he records his experience from the outside as much as from within, with a syntactical elegance that is far from lyrical spontaneity, in an idiom that always exhibits refinement and artifice (often, in fact, parody of a higher style).

There is a distinctive mystery about Krull, for, while he is frank enough about what he feels and does, he is never so deeply involved in any experience that he shows any reluctance in dancing off, a typical picaresque hero, to the next episode. He is a man who loves the night and luxuriates in sleep, and he takes the narcissistic pleasure in himself that a child might show before the acknowledgment had been trained out of him. Krull, like Stephen Dedalus, moves toward myth—the figure of Hermes is his patron and model.

He is a comprehensible enough confidence man, but he is full of fastidious pride in his artistry and benevolent condescension in supplying fantasies which others require but cannot create for themselves. Krull is too brilliant a performer, too arduously trained and dedicated an actor, to be understood merely as a confidence man. To see him as an artist is, of course, to gain remarkable insights into certain aspects of art.

The first of these is quite opposed to Virginia Woolf's emphasis upon the artistry of daily life which Mrs. Ramsay embodies. For Krull is first captivated by the matinée idol of musical comedy, Müller-Rosé. Müller-Rosé, his godfather's old friend, has an elegance that seems "not to belong to this world." His dress is perfect, his countenance debonair, his movements marked with assurance and "fluid grace." He dispenses the "joy of life," allowing his audiences to participate for an evening in a life which is all that they would like their own to be. They watch him with a "precious and painful feeling, compounded of envy, yearning, hope, and love." He confers upon them the bliss of "self-forgetful absorption" in his art. But when Felix is taken backstage by his father, he is shocked to see of what materials such art is made. Müller-Rosé is seated at his dressing table, covered with sweat and greasepaint, his upper body spotted with clogged pores that have turned to pustules. The emphasis falls upon the remarkable transfiguration that Müller-Rosé has made himself undergo, as he has created an art of illusion, fantasy, and wishfulfillment for his middle-class audience (I, 5).

Like Müller-Rosé, but in a body he preserves and cultivates with pride and affection, Felix Krull has a capacity to turn life into play. His joy in the gratuitous is illustrated by the deftness with which he serves as a painter's model, as a liftboy and waiter, and last as a spurious nobleman. Krull is in touch with nocturnal and subconscious powers that he can turn to conscious art; but we never know which needs of Felix's own nature his artistry fulfills, for we see little of his nature but the artistry. While Stephen Dedalus wrests his necessary freedom from family, church, and country, Felix Krull has no such bonds to throw off; nor does he have the high purpose with which Stephen undertakes his vocation. For all Felix's conservatism—an admiration of the splendid forms of power—there is also radical criminality in him, an indifference to conventional rules and limits, the energy of a self that does not live by the laws of the daylight world. His criminality is not the proud defiance of Stephen's *"non serviam";* it is rather the adroitness of the confidence man, conjuror, acrobat—whose ultimate commitments have nothing to do with the beliefs of ordinary men.

Krull's devotion to the transitory is brought to a remarkable amplification late in the book. Professor Kuckuck first startles Krull, when they meet on the train, by referring casually to "this star and its present inhabitants." The words "star" and "present" open up sublime vistas of geological and astronomic time, much greater, as Kuckuck puts it, than that of "short-winded cultural history." Kuckuck summons up an almost unimaginable vision in which Being arises out of Nothingness, only "an interlude between Nothingness and Nothingness." In the brief interval of its duration Being celebrates a "tumultuous festival" whence comes the universe and its countless galactic systems, the Milky Way "one among billions"; and almost at the edge of that galaxy, thirty thousand light-years from its center, is our local solar system. Within the span of Being there emerges the much briefer span called Life. "For," Professor Kuckuck informs Krull, "Life has not always existed and will not always exist. Life is an episode, on the scale of the aeons a very fleeting one." And within that episode is the momentary appearance of Man. The episodic—the discontinuous, inexplicable emergence of a new quality—is in the form of all duration; and the form of the picaresque is thereby rooted in the nature of reality itself. Felix Krull welcomes the vision:

> It was the knowledge of Beginning and End. I had pronounced what was most characteristically human when I had said that the fact of Life's being only an episode predisposed me in its favour. Transitoriness did not destroy value, far from it; it was exactly what lent all existence its worth, dignity, and charm. Only the episodic, only what possessed a beginning and an end, was interesting and worthy of sympathy because transitoriness had given it a soul.   [III, 5]

Mann therefore turns cosmology into comedy, and this becomes more telling when Krull visits the natural history museum in Lisbon. Within the entrance hall stands a triumph of taxidermy, a splendid white stag. Felix sees only the evolutionary process. "If one examines the rump and hindquarters carefully and thinks about a horse—the horse is nervier, although one knows he is descended from the tapir—then the stag strikes one as a crowned cow." As often, Krull is obliviously, unconsciously witty. He feels that, like a visiting prince, he confers upon the display "the added charm of the contrast between my own fineness and elegance and the primitive crudity" of Nature's early works. "All this inspired in me," he writes, "the moving reflection that these first beginnings, however absurd and lacking in dignity and usefulness, were preliminary moves in the direction of me—that is, of Man." And so "with probing eyes and beating heart," Felix sees "what had been striving toward me from the grey reaches of antiquity."

This amiable narcissism, which is only a parody of all anthropomorphic vision, sees a new and weak physical species emerging among the tusks, fangs, and iron jaws that rule the primeval world, a human species that senses, for all its lack of physical force, that it is made "of finer clay." A brilliant study follows of the emergence of consciousness. The primitive man paints in his cave images of game and hunters, or he shapes stones in the image of living forms. Stone pillars are raised as temples, and within the first roofless hall stands "a powerful-looking man . . . with upraised arms presenting a bouquet of flowers to the rising sun!" What makes him remarkable is that he is performing a gratuitous act, not one of utility or appeasement or "crude necessity." The temple and the gift of flowers mark the emergence of a new capacity, for celebration and worship. It is this gratuitousness, this aesthetic pleasure in his own actions, that characterizes Felix Krull from the first (III, 7).

Among the finest passages on the vocation of the artist, more intense and exalted than the account of Müller-Rosé, is the treatment of the Stoudebecker Circus. There brilliant exploits "that lie at the extreme limits of human prowess" are achieved "with bright smiles and lightly thrown kisses"; it is the schooling in grace "at moments of utmost daring" that makes the performance so compelling. The clowns transcend their human limitations:

> Those basically alien beings . . . their handstands, their stumbling and falling over everything, their mindless running to and fro and unserviceable attempts to help, their hideously unsuccessful efforts to imitate their serious colleagues—in tightrope-walking, for instance. . . . With their chalk-white faces and utterly preposterous painted expressions—triangular eyebrows and deep perpendicular grooves in their cheeks under the reddened eyes, impossible noses, mouths twisted up at the corners with insane smiles. . . . [A]re they, I repeat, human beings, men that could conceivably find a place in everyday life? . . . [N]o, they are not, they are exceptions, side-splitting monsters of preposterousness, glittering, world-renouncing monks of unreason, cavorting hybrids, part human and part insane art.

Felix is fascinated by all transposition of human features into the materials of art. The supreme instance is the aerialist, Andromache. Felix watches her with awe: aloof, impassive, infallible. Was she, he wonders, really human?

> To imagine her as a wife and mother was simply stupid. . . . This was Andromache's way of consorting with a man; any other was unthinkable, for one recognizes too well that this disciplined body lavished upon the adventurous accomplishments of her art what others devote to love. She was not a woman; but she was not a man either and therefore not a human being. A solemn angel of daring with parted lips and dilated nostrils, that is what she was, an unapproachable Amazon of the realms of space beneath the canvas, high above the crowd, whose lust for her was transformed into awe.

Felix watches the performance with "passionate attention," with an "element of rebellion" that exerts a "counter-pressure against the overwhelming flood of impressions." He withdraws from the passive crowd, who revel in self-forgetfulness. He is himself "an entertainer and illusionist"; a passive enjoyment cannot satisfy one "who feels himself born to act and to achieve" (III, 1).

Andromache, that "solemn angel of daring," is as inhuman as the girl Stephen sees on the sands, as mythical as the Daedalus with whom Stephen identifies himself; and she is almost as abstract and purified a figure as the structure of volume and color that Lily Briscoe makes of Mrs. Ramsay. This emphasis upon the otherness of art, its necessary difference from the warmth and immediacy of life, finds various forms of statement. The role of artist requires of Stephen cruelty and ruthless self-protection, of Mrs. Ramsay a deep descent beneath personality, of Felix Krull a necessary isolation and loneliness.

While Felix takes pleasure in his skills and disciplines himself to wear each new costume or role with distinction, there is at least one splendid setback that his narcissism must suffer. That is the experience of being incorporated into another's shaping imagination, and a banal one at that. At the end of his train journey to Paris, in the Gare du Nord, Felix sees a wealthy middle-aged lady engaged in an altercation with a customs official; her luggage meanwhile lies unprotected and very close to Felix Krull's. A "very costly small morocco case" slips "unexpectedly" into Felix's bag. "This was an occurrence rather than an action," and Felix walks off with what he euphemistically calls his "accidental acquisition." It is a jewel case whose contents he sells to a fence in Paris. But he sees the former owner again when she arrives as a guest at the hotel where he runs the lift. She arouses not fear but a remarkable kind of gratification: "Without knowing me, without ever having seen me, without being aware of me, she had been carrying me, featureless, in her thoughts ever since the moment . . . when in unpacking her suitcase she had discovered that the jewel case was missing." (It is that sense of impingement which may be felt in a fainter form by the inscriber of graffiti.)

The former owner of the jewels, Mme Houpflé, is the wife of a manufacturer but she is also the author, under the name of Diane Philibert, of dubious novels "full of psychological insight" and volumes of passionate verse. She is a woman, by her own account, *"d'une intelligence extrême."* As she seduces, or thinks she seduces, Felix, she is really seeking someone base to love, as she copiously explains:

> "The intellect longs for the delights of the non-intellect, that which is alive and beautiful *dans sa stupidité,* in love with it to the point of idiocy, to the ultimate self-betrayal and self-denial, in love with the beautiful and the divinely stupid, it kneels before it, it prays to it in an ecstasy of self-abnegation, self-degradation, and finds it intoxicating to be degraded by it."

This flood of egocentric masochism is too much for Felix: "You musn't think me as stupid as all that, even if I haven't read your novels and poems——." But she is delighted when he restores his sense of himself by addressing her as "dear child": "A little naked liftboy lies beside me and calls me 'dear

child,' me, Diane Philibert!" Her transports are only intensified when Felix
reveals that he has never heard of Hermes, the "suave god of thieves." For
someone so narcissistic as Felix and so much the master of the feelings of
others, it is perturbing to be adored as an ultimate debasement by the lyrical
Diane Philibert. When she seeks more brutal treatment, he refuses; but it
occurs to him instead to reveal himself as the thief who took her jewels at
the customs barrier. This provides a response of exquisite but rather patronizing delight: *"Mais ça c'est suprême!* I am lying in bed with a thief! *C'est une
humiliation merveilleuse, tout à fait excitante, un rêve d'humiliation!* Not only a
domestic—a common, ordinary thief!" And she demands that he conduct a
new theft of her remaining jewels in the dark. This done, she dismisses him,
promising him immortality in her writings. Felix is somewhat outraged by
the assumptions that remain unshaken, but he consoles himself with the
experience of having been addressed in alexandrines (II, 7).

In the course of the novel we see Felix Krull as forger, malingerer, model,
pimp, thief, actor. As a waiter he buys himself fine clothes and rents rooms
where he may change into them in order to live out another role as gentleman. This in turn leads to his greatest impersonation. The Marquis de Venosta has no wish to leave the young woman with whom he is happily living
in Paris, and he persuades Felix to adopt his identity and to take a world
tour in his place. This means not only playing the marquis with those who
know his family, but also corresponding regularly with his "parents." Felix
is of course a tremendous success; he pleases his "mother" with his charm
and consideration, and he delights her by his triumphant reception at court
in Portugal. All of these exploits demonstrate a mastery of style. When he
agrees to become the Marquis de Venosta, Felix shivers with joy "at the
thought of the equality of seeming and being which life was granting" him.
And, in fact, he finds a peculiar pleasure in a dual existence, "whose charm
lay in the ambiguity as to which figure was the real I and which the masquerade." For he has "masqueraded in both capacities, and the undisguised
reality behind the two appearances, the real I, could not be identified because
it actually did not exist" (III, 4).

Here the artist has simply become his works. His life is a series of performances, many of them improvisations. Mann has taken the artist to the other
side of art; beyond the austere discipline or the effort to achieve an ordering
vision. Those acts of difficult mastery we see in Joyce's or Woolf's artists—
and in Mann's version of Faustus—are here presented as all but spontaneous;
for while Felix Krull's self-discipline is intense, it is achieved with such a
pleasure in the exercise as to seem to cost very little. The artist as comic hero
creates a world where, himself his own creation, he lives out his inventions,
always eluding—as a masterful dancer seems to defy gravity—the tug toward
a reality he need not acknowledge. There is, of course, something preposter-

ous and wishful about this ease. It catches what Susanne Langer calls a "comic rhythm," and Felix Krull is a superb refinement upon the figure she describes as the "buffoon":

> He is the personified *élan vital;* his chance adventures and misadventures, without much plot, though often with bizarre complications, his absurd expectations and disappointments, in fact his whole improvised existence has the rhythm of primitive, savage, if not animalistic life, coping with a world that is forever taking new uncalculated turns, frustrating, but exciting. He is neither a good man nor a bad one, but is genuinely amoral,—now triumphant, now worsted and rueful, but in his ruefulness and dismay he is funny, because his energy is really unimpaired and each failure prepares the situation for a fantastic new move.[31]

Felix Krull embodies the "heightened vitality" of the comic hero, and he embodies it the better for his inclusiveness. He accepts in himself the regressive and narcissistic, the criminal and deceptive, the transitory and the superficial (at least as they are conventionally understood).

Felix Krull is open to a range of experience more characteristic of Stephen Dedalus than of the characters in *To the Lighthouse.* Felix can celebrate a theft not by its shopworn name but as the "primeval absolute deed." That is a young artist's creation. He does not seek permanence and stability as Virginia Woolf's artists do; nor does he seek some reality deep below the surface. It is the surface of life that is precisely its source of color and charm. Nor does Krull seek to transcend his limited nature in the power of spirit: Felix not only accepts his body; he glories in it. In his first encounter with the prostitute Rozsa, their conversation is "without introduction" and "without polite conventions of any sort; from the very beginning it had the free, exalted irresponsiblity that is usually characteristic only of dreams" (II, 6).

It is in his defense of love against Zouzou, Professor Kuckuck's daughter, that Felix becomes the champion of the surfaces of life. Zouzou is embarrassed by a sexual energy she cannot control, and so she scorns lovemaking as both ugly and ludicrous. She cites the verse she once read in a book of spiritual instruction: "However smooth and fair the skin, / Stench and corruption lie within." Felix combats this bit of ugly asceticism with all the powers of his rhetoric:

> Your spiritual verse is more blasphemous than the most sinful lust of the flesh, for it is a spoilsport, and to spoil the game of life is not only sinful, it is simply and entirely devilish . . . If things went according to that altogether malicious verse, then the only thing really and not just apparently admirable would be, at most the inanimate world, inorganic Being. . . .

A mere "smart aleck," Felix protests, "might say that all Nature is nothing but mildew and corruption on the face of the earth, but that is simply the wisecrack of a smart aleck and never, to the end of time, will it succeed in killing love and joy—the joy in images. . . . Because at all times the earth has been full of fellows who paid not the slightest heed to your spiritual rhyme, but saw truth in form and appearance and surface." Krull is defending the beauty of mortal conditions (III, 10).

The artist in Mann's novel is a counterpart in consciousness of the powers of the human eye as Felix celebrates them:

> What a wonderful phenomenon it is, carefully considered, when the human eye, that jewel of organic structures, concentrates its moist brilliance on another human creature! This precious jelly, made up of just such ordinary elements as the rest of creation, affirming, like a precious stone, that the elements count for nothing, but their imaginative and happy combination accounts for everything—this bit of slime embedded in a bony hole, destined some day to moulder lifeless in the grave, to dissolve back into watery refuse, is able, so long as the spark of life remains alert there, to throw such beautiful, airy bridges across all the chasms of strangeness that lie between man and man!
>
> [II, 4]

It is a macabre emblem but a brilliant one; the eye embodies as well as creates the beauty of mortal conditions. It represents for Krull the "unconditional freedom, secrecy, and profound ruthlessness" that he ascribes to the glance and to its opposite extreme, the embrace. Between them lies the realm of the word, "that cool, prosaic device, that begetter of tame, mediocre morality." In Felix Krull's world morality is an idiom to be cultivated in affectionate, straight-faced parody, what I have called comic primness. It is, for the most part, a delicious joke. Yet at another level we see in Krull a decent forbearance that, as it refuses the bypaths offered by Eleanor Twentyman or Lord Strathbogie, dismisses these suppliants charitably and tactfully. And while he rebukes Zouzou chiefly as a spoilsport in the game of life, he also speaks of her blasphemy. In the circus clowns, those "monks of unreason," Krull sees the asceticism of the artist that may account as well for the solitariness of Krull himself.

In these portraits of the artist—portraits created by writers we associate with modernism—much emphasis is given this solitariness, and not least in Virginia Woolf's characters. Even Mrs. Ramsay's dinner, that triumphant orchestration of feelings at times so ruthlessly elicited, provides only a momentary illusion of stability and unity—in contrast with the moments "when solidity suddenly vanished and . . . vast spaces lay between them" (I, xvii, xiii). The force of Mrs. Ramsay's presence survives in the completion of the trip to the lighthouse and in the simultaneous completion of Lily's painting.

The formal idiom of the painting allows Mrs. Ramsay the kind of survival a scrap of a personal letter might enjoy in a collage, and the reconciliation of her children with their father may belong to their journey more than to their later lives. The fragility of the eye is an emblem of these fusions, and its airy bridges require in turn "the chasms of strangeness between man and man."

Woolf's characters try hard to find a "coherence in things, a stability," a "wholeness not theirs in life." The refrain of William Cowper's castaway runs through the book, parodied by the histrionic self-pity with which Mr. Ramsay delivers it: "We perished each alone." But Mr. Ramsay's tyrannical self-indulgence is the obverse of his anxiety about change and supersession. His ultimate praise of James is perhaps a moral achievement; it relieves for the moment "that loneliness which was," for his children, "the truth about things." But these people are seen less in a moral vision than a metaphysical one. The "waters of annihilation" are as inclusive and as indifferent as are E. M. Forster's India and Conrad's Costaguana; but the eye is able, so long as the spark remains, to span the chasms of strangeness and provide the conditions of life. It is this fragile order, attenuated by the prose of the world, that is the novel's peculiar form and profound opportunity.[32]

Notes

Introduction

1 "Anthony Trollope" (1883), in *Partial Portraits* (London: Macmillan, 1888), p. 106.
2 George Eliot, *Middlemarch,* bk. 8, chap. 80; Jane Austen, *Emma,* vol. 3, chap. 11 (i.e., chap. 47); Charles Dickens, *Great Expectations,* chap. 54.
3 Lionel Trilling, *A Gathering of Fugitives* (New York: Harcourt Brace Jovanovich, 1978 Uniform Edition), p. 41.
4 Henry James, *Letters,* ed. Leon Edel (Cambridge, Mass.: Harvard University Press, 1974–), 3 : 68–69.
5 C. H. Peake, *James Joyce: The Citizen and the Artist* (Stanford: Stanford University Press, 1977), pp. 326–31.
6 Anthony Kenny, *Wittgenstein* (Cambridge, Mass.: Harvard University Press, 1973), p. 163.
7 Ludwig Wittgenstein, *On Certainty,* ed. G. E. M. Anscombe and G. H. von Wright, Trans. Denis Paul and G. E. M. Anscombe (Oxford: Basil Blackwood, 1969), pars. 359, 475, 478.
8 *Pride and Prejudice,* chap. 29.
9 Ludwig Wittgenstein, *Philosophical Investigations,* trans. G. E. M. Anscombe, 3d ed. (New York: Macmillan, 1958), par. 111.
10 Wittgenstein, *On Certainty,* pars. 204, 559; cited in fuller context, p. 179.
11 Mary Warnock, *Imagination* (Berkeley and Los Angeles: University of California Press, 1976), pp. 194–95.
12 Henry James, *Letters,* 2 : 422 (23 June 1883).
13 Bernard Williams, *Morality: An Introduction to Ethics* (New York: Harper and Row, 1972), pp. 85–86.
14 Iris Murdoch, *The Sovereignty of Good* (New York: Schocken, 1971), p. 65.
15 P. F. Strawson, "Social Morality and Individual Ideal," in *Freedom and Resentment and Other Essays* (London: Methuen, 1974), pp. 27–29.

Chapter 1. The Fictional Contract

1 David Hume, "Of the Original Contract" (1748), in *The Social Contract,* ed. Ernest Barker (Oxford: Oxford University Press, 1962), p. 156.
2 Jonathan Culler, *Ferdinand de Saussure* (Harmondsworth: Penguin, 1976), p. 27.

3 John R. Searle, *Expression and Meaning: Studies in the Theory of Speech Acts* (Cambridge: Cambridge University Press, 1979), pp. 59, 67.

4 Arthur C. Danto, *The Transfiguration of the Commonplace: A Philosophy of Art* (Cambridge, Mass.: Harvard University Press, 1981), p. 135.

5 Searle, *Expression and Meaning*, pp. 72—73.

6 John R. Searle, *Speech Acts: An Essay in the Philosophy of Language* (Cambridge: Cambridge University Press, 1969), pp. 50 ff.

7 Richard Wollheim, *Art and Its Objects* (New York: Harper and Row, 1968), sec. 13. Now available from Cambridge University Press in fuller form.

8 On detective stories, see also Frank Kermode, "Novel and Narrative," in *The Theory of the Novel: New Essays,* ed. John Halperin (New York: Oxford University Press, 1974), pp. 155—74; and D. A. Miller, "From *Roman Policier* to *Roman-Police:* Wilkie Collins's *The Moonstone,*" *Novel* 13 (1980) : 153—70.

9 On the last, see Wayne Booth, "Did Sterne Complete *Tristram Shandy?*" *Modern Philology* 58 (1951) : 172—83.

10 Kenneth Clark, *Looking at Pictures* (London: Murray, 1960), p. 197.

11 Roger Caillois, *Man, Play, and Games* (1958), trans. Meyer Barash (London: Thames and Hudson, 1962), pp. 27—29. I have, of course, depended as well on Johan Huizinga, *Homo Ludens: A Study of the Play Element in Culture* (1938), trans. R. F. C. Hull (Boston: Beacon Press, 1950).

12 E. H. Gombrich, *The Sense of Order: A Study in the Psychology of Decorative Art* (Ithaca: Cornell University Press, 1979), esp. introduction, pp. 1—16.

13 Raymond Williams, *Culture and Society 1780—1850* (Harmondsworth: Penguin, 1963), pp. 114—15.

14 Ernst Kris, *Psychoanalytic Explorations in Art* (New York: International Universities Press, 1952), pp. 45—46, 52, 63.

15 Cited by Richard Wollheim, *Freud* (London: Fontana/Collins, 1971), p. 67 from *The Standard Edition of the Complete Psychological Works of Sigmund Freud,* ed. James Strachey, 15 : 129. On the difficulties of the term *identification,* see D. W. Harding, "Psychological Processes in the Reading of Fiction," reprinted in Harold Osborn, ed., *Aesthetics in the Modern World* (London: Thames and Hudson, 1968), pp. 300—17.

16 On the process of "free indirect discourse," *style indirect libre,* or *erlebte Rede,* see Dorrit Cohn, *Transparent Minds: Narrative Modes for Presenting Consciousness in Fiction* (Princeton: Princeton University Press, 1978), esp. chap. 3, "Narrated Monologue," pp. 99—140.

17 Kris, *Pschoanalytic Explorations in Art,* pp. 56, 58—59.

18 For James, see the essay on Flaubert (1902), printed in *Notes on Novelists* (New York: Scribner, 1914), p. 81. For Lawrence, see the "Introduction to *Mastro-don Gesualdo* by Giovanni Verga," *Phoenix II,* ed. Warren Roberts and Harry T. Moore (New York: Viking, 1970), pp. 281—82.

19 Iris Murdoch, *The Sovereignty of Good* (New York: Schocken, 1971), pp. 84—87.

20 Philip Rieff, *The Triumph of the Therapeutic: Uses of Faith after Freud* (New York: Harper and Row, 1968), pp. 30—31.

21 Roy Schafer, "Narration in the Psychoanalytic Dialogue," *Critical Inquiry* 7 (1980) : 29—53, esp. 36, 38. Meredith Anne Skura, *The Literary Use of the Psychoanalytic Process* (New Haven: Yale University Press, 1981), pp. 224, 228.

22 Max Black, *Models and Metaphors: Studies in Language and Philosophy* (Ithaca: Cornell University Press, 1962), pp. 237, 220.

23 W. B. Gallie, *Philosophy and the Historical Understanding,* 2d ed. (New York: Schocken, 1968), pp. 24, 28, 40.

24 Louis O. Mink, "History and Fiction as Modes of Comprehension," *New Literary History* 1 (1969–70) : 547, 554–55.

25 Frank Kermode, *The Sense of an Ending: Studies in the Theory of Fiction* (Oxford: Oxford University Press, 1967). See also his "Novel, History and Type," *Novel* 2 (1968) : 231–38.

26 Iris Murdoch, *The Fire and the Sun: Why Plato Banished the Artists* (Oxford: Oxford University Press, 1977), p. 85.

Chapter 2. Relevance and the Emergence of Form

1 "The Art of Fiction" (1884), reprinted in F. O. Matthiessen, *The James Family* (New York: Alfred A. Knopf, 1947), p. 360.

2 There is an entertaining account of literary treatment of teeth as signs of potency and beauty in Theodore Ziolkowski, "The Telltale Teeth: Psychodontia to Sociodontia," *PMLA* 91 (1976) : 9–22.

3 E. H. Gombrich, *Meditations on a Hobby Horse and Other Essays on the Theory of Art* (London: Phaidon, 1963), p. 5.

4 Cf. Darrel Mansell, Jr., "Ruskin and George Eliot's 'Realism,' " *Criticism* 7 (1965) : 203–16. See also Peter Demetz, "Defenses of Dutch Painting and the Theory of Realism," *Comparative Literature* 15 (1963) : 97–115.

5 *Anna Karenina* (1878), pt. V, chap. 10; trans. David Magarshack (New York: Signet, 1961), pp. 472–73.

6 "Mr Bennett and Mrs Brown" (1924), in *Collected Essays* (London: Hogarth Press, 1966), 1 : 333, 336–37. But see n. 23, pp. 362–63.

7 *Madame Bovary,* I, ii ("en robe de mérinos blue garnie de trois volants").

8 Letter to N. N. Strakhov, 23 and 26 April 1876, cited by David Magarshack in the foreword to his translation of *Anna Karenina* (see n. 5). For another version, see *Tolstoy's Letters,* ed. and trans. R. F. Christian (New York: Scribner, 1978), 1 : 296.

9 On figure and ground, see Rudolf Arnheim, *Art and Visual Perception* (Berkeley and Los Angeles: University of California Press, 1954), pp. 177–85, 198–203. The analogy introduces spatial terms that may be misleading, but it catches better than any other I know the shifting structure of the field of our attention, and, by implication, the shifting function of elements of the novel. See also Joseph Frank, "Spatial Form in Modern Literature" in *The Widening Gyre: Crisis and Mastery in Modern Literature* (Bloomington: Indiana University Press, 1963), and two more recent essays: "Spatial Form: An Answer to Critics," *Critical Inquiry* 4 (1977) : 231–52; "Spatial Form: Some Further Reflections," *Critical Inquiry* 5 (1978) : 275–90.

10 Roger Fry, "The Artist's Vision" (1919), in *Vision and Design* (London: Chatto and Windus, 1920), pp. 32–33.

11 "L'effet du réel," *Communications* 11 (1969) : 84–89. Barthes cites as one illustration the description of Mme Aubain's household in *Un coeur simple:* "un vieux piano supportait, sous un baromètre, un tas pyramidal de boîtes et de cartons." The piano, he suggests, may imply middle-class standing, the heap of boxes the disorder of the household. But the barometer has no such function, however indirect, to account for it. As Jonathan Culler restates the argument, items in a description "which are not picked up and integrated by symbolic or thematic codes . . . and which do not have a function in the plot produce what Barthes calls a 'reality effect' . . . : deprived of any other function, they become integrated units by signifying 'we are the real' " (*Structuralist Poetics* [Ithaca: Cornell University Press, 1975], p. 193).

12 "An Introduction to the Structural Analysis of Narrative" (1966), trans. Lionel Duisit, *New Literary History* 6 (1975) : 224–45.

Chapter 3. The Other Self: Problems of Character

1 Kenneth Clark, *The Nude: A Study in Ideal Form* (New York: Pantheon, 1956), pp. 4–7.
2 Maurice Merleau-Ponty, *The Primacy of Perception,* ed. James M. Edie (Evanston: Northwestern University Press, 1964), pp. 3, 5. This passage occurs in a prospectus of his work translated by Arleen B. Dallery.
3 E. H. Gombrich, *Art and Illusion,* 2nd ed. (London: Phaidon, 1962), esp. chap. 4, "Reflections on the Greek Revolution."
4 Orville E. Brim, Jr., "Personality Development as Role-Learning," in *Personality Development in Children,* ed. Ira Iscoe and H. W. Stevenson (Austin: University of Texas Press, 1960), p. 141; cited in John Milton Yinger, *Toward a Field Theory of Behavior: Personality and Social Structure* (New York: McGraw-Hill, 1965), p. 145, with Yinger's demurrer.
5 Yinger, *Toward a Field Theory of Behavior,* p. 108. See also Michael Banton, *Roles: An Introduction to the Study of Social Relations* (New York: Basic Books, 1965), esp. pp. 127–50; and Anne Marie Rocheblave-Spenlé, *La notion de role en psychologie sociale; étude historico-critique* (Paris: Presses Universitaires de France, 1962), esp. pp. 213–73.
6 *George Herbert Mead on Social Psychology: Selected Papers,* ed. Anselm Strauss (Chicago: University of Chicago Press, 1964), pp. 226, 222. For a fuller text, see G. H. Mead, *Mind, Self, and Society,* ed. Charles W. Morris (Chicago: University of Chicago Press, 1934), pp. 135–63. For the protest, see Edward A. Tiryakian, *Sociologism and Existentialism* (Englewood Cliffs, N.J.: Prentice-Hall, 1962), pp. 104 ff.
7 D. H. Lawrence, "A Study of Thomas Hardy," chap. 4, in *Phoenix: The Posthumous Papers of D. H. Lawrence,* ed. Edward McDonald (London: Heinemann, 1936), p. 423; *The Rainbow,* chap. 13.
8 Virginia Woolf, *Moments of Being: Unpublished Autobiographical Writings,* ed. Jeanne Schulkind (New York: Harcourt Brace Jovanovich, 1976), p. 70; *A Writer's Diary,* ed. Leonard Woolf (New York: Harcourt Brace Jovanovich, 1954), p. 97.
9 James, *Notes on Novelists,* pp. 112–13, 150–51, 159. The extracts are from two essays on Balzac, written respectively in 1902 and 1913.
10 See Robert Langbaum, *The Poetry of Experience: The Dramatic Monologue in Modern Literary Tradition* (New York: Random House, 1957), esp. pp. 160–81.
11 *To the Lighthouse,* "The Window," sec. 17 (New York: Harcourt, Brace, 1927), p. 138.
12 Nathalie Sarraute, *The Planetarium,* trans. Maria Jolas (New York: George Braziller, 1960), p. 116.
13 Foreword, *Tropisms* (1939), trans. Maria Jolas (New York: George Braziller, 1963), pp. vi–vii.
14 Stephen Heath, *The Nouveau Roman: A Study in the Practice of Writing* (Philadelphia: Temple University Press, 1972), p. 55.
15 Gombrich, *Art and Illusion,* pp. 238–40; Edward Fry, *Cubism* (New York: McGraw-Hill, 1966), p. 20. See also Wylie Sypher, *Rococo to Cubism in Art and Literature* (New York: Random House, 1960), pt. 4, "The Cubist Perspective."
16 Edgar Wind, *Art and Anarchy* (New York: Vintage, 1969), pp. 24–25.
17 Leo Bersani, *A Future for Astyanax: Character and Desire in Literature* (Boston: Little, Brown and Co., 1976), pp. 56, 314–15.
18 Skura, *The Literary Use of the Psychoanalytic Process,* pp. 240, 237–38.
19 Paul Ricoeur, *Freud and Philosophy: An Essay on Interpretation,* trans. Denis Savage (New Haven: Yale University Press, 1970), pp. 32, 24.

20 Alfred MacAdam, "Pynchon as Satirist: To Write, to Mean," *Yale Review* 67 (1977–78) : 555.

21 René Girard, "Myth and Ritual in Shakespeare: *A Midsummer Night's Dream,*" in *Textual Strategies,* ed. Josué V. Harari (Ithaca: Cornell University Press, 1979), pp. 203–4.

22 W. J. Harvey, *Character and the Novel* (London: Chatto and Windus, 1965), pp. 191, 203.

23 Richard Rorty, "Freud, Morality, and Hermeneutics," *New Literary History* 12 (1980–81) : 179–80.

24 Herbert Morris, *On Guilt and Innocence: Essays in Legal Philosophy and Moral Psychology* (Berkeley and Los Angeles: University of California Press, 1976), pp. 32, 42, 43.

25 H. L. A. Hart, *Punishment and Responsibility: Essays in the Philosophy of Law* (Oxford: Oxford University Press, 1968), pp. 182–83.

26 Mackie sees an "established concept of personal identity through time . . . functioning analogously to an institution like promising, introducing a requirement for attention to the future well-being of what will be the same human being as the agent in question." *Ethics: Inventing Right and Wrong* (Harmondsworth: Penguin, 1977), p. 78.

27 Richard Wollheim, "On Persons and Their Lives," in *Explaining Emotions,* ed. Amélie Oksenberg Rorty (Berkeley and Los Angeles: University of California Press, 1980), pp. 299–321, esp. 302, 305, 315, 320.

28 Gombrich, *Art and Illusion,* p. 110.

29 Frank Kermode, *The Genesis of Secrecy: On the Interpretation of Narrative* (Cambridge, Mass.: Harvard University Press, 1979), pp. 91, 97.

30 Bersani, *A Future for Astyanax,* pp. 310, 272, 313.

31 Richard Wollheim, "Freud and the Understanding of Art," in *On Art and the Mind* (Cambridge, Mass.: Harvard University Press, 1974), pp. 209, 213. On "self-mastery," see also Philip Rieff, *Freud: The Mind of the Moralist* (New York: Anchor, 1961), chap. 10, sec. 3, pp. 379 ff.

32 Danto, *The Transfiguration of the Commonplace,* p. 159.

33 Margaret Macdonald, "The Language of Fiction," from *Proceedings of the Aristotelean Society* (1954), reprinted in *Perspectives on Fiction,* ed. James L. Calderwood and Harold E. Toliver (New York: Oxford University Press, 1968), pp. 66–67.

34 William H. Gass, *Fiction and the Figures of Life* (New York: Alfred A. Knopf, 1970), p. 27.

35 A. D. Nuttall, "The Argument about Shakespeare's Characters," *Critical Quarterly* 7 (1966) : 113.

36 Harvey, *Character and the Novel,* pp. 204–05.

37 Ludwig Feuerbach, *The Essence of Christianity,* trans. George Eliot (New York: Harper and Row, 1957), pp. 14, 274.

38 George Lichtheim, *Marxism: An Historical and Critical Study* (New York: Praeger, 1961), p. 36.

39 Karl Marx, *The German Ideology* (1845–46), pt 1, in *The Marx–Engels Reader,* 2d ed., ed. Robert C. Tucker (New York: Norton, 1978), pp. 154–55.

40 Lichtheim, *Marxism,* pp. 44, 197.

41 Raymond Williams, *Marxism and Literature* (Oxford: Oxford University Press, 1977), pp. 61, 65–66, citing Marx and Engels.

42 Eugene Kamenka has written of the "enthusiasm with which communist legal theorists now elevate the social function of law in socialist societies." They believe there are "legal precepts and legal techniques which (and this is true even of past societies) serve the interests of all, reflect objective social and human requirements and are heritable from one social system to another." As Kamenka sees it, these theorists "understand what most

Western Marxists do not—that a legal system may be a social product, used by many interests, and yet have a conception of itself as a form of public rationality and seek to extend that rationality through specifically legal conceptions, principles and institutions which both guide and take into account wider social sentiments." "Demythologizing the law," *TLS,* no. 4,074 (May 1981) : 475–76.

43 Michael Podro, "Cubism and Its Worried Interpreters," *The Listener,* 20 August 1970, pp. 238–40.

44 For Degas, Elizabeth Gilmore Holt, ed., *From the Classicists to the Impressionists: Art and Architecture in the Nineteenth Century,* A Documentary History of Art, 3 vols. (New York: Anchor, 1966), 3 : 401–02. On Cézanne, John Rewald, *Paul Cézanne: A Biography,* trans. Margaret H. Liebman (New York: Schocken, 1968), pp. 135, 196.

45 Jack D. Flam, ed., *Henri Matisse on Art* (New York: Dutton, 1978), pp. 94–95, 121.

Chapter 4. Austen: Manners and Morals

1 Ludwig Wittgenstein, *Zettel,* ed. G. E. M. Anscombe and G. H. von Wright (Berkeley and Los Angeles: University of California Press, 1970), pars. 241–42.

2 The phrase is from David Lodge, *Language of Fiction* (New York: Columbia University Press, 1966), p. 99. See also Norman Page, *The Language of Jane Austen* (Oxford: Blackwell, 1972).

3 *Sense and Sensibility,* chap. 28. All citations within the text are by chapters numbered continuously throughout the novel.

4 "The 'Irresponsibility' of Jane Austen," in *Critical Essays on Jane Austen,* ed. B. C. Southam (London: Routledge and Kegan Paul, 1968), p. 16.

5 *Boswell's Life of Johnson,* ed. G. B. Hill, rev. L. F. Powell, 6 vols. (Oxford: Clarendon Press, 1934–50), 4 : 50; 2 : 359. Cf. *Northanger Abbey:* "though in all probability not an observation was made, nor an expression used by either which had not been made and used some thousands of times before, under that roof, in every Bath season, yet the merit of their being spoken with simplicity and truth, and without personal conceit, might be something uncommon" (10).

6 Lodge, *Language of Fiction,* pp. 101–04.

7 *Sincerity and Authenticity* (Cambridge, Mass.: Harvard University Press, 1972), p. 79.

8 Wordsworth to Sara Hutchinson, 14 June 1802, *The Early Letters of William and Dorothy Wordsworth,* ed. Ernest de Selincourt (New York: Oxford University Press, 1935), p. 306.

9 "Jane Austen's Comedy and the Nineteenth Century," in *Critical Essays on Jane Austen,* ed. B. C. Southam, pp. 173–74.

10 On Jane Austen and Shaftesbury, see Gilbert Ryle, "Jane Austen and the Moralists," in *Critical Essays on Jane Austen,* ed. B. C. Southam, pp. 106–22. I have dealt with aesthetic and moral taste in Shaftesbury in *To the Palace of Wisdom* (New York: Doubleday, 1964), chap. 3.

11 "On the Artificial Comedy of the Last Century," *The Works of Charles and Mary Lamb,* ed. E. V. Lucas (London: Methuen, 1903), 2 : 142.

12 Lionel Trilling, "Manners, Morals, and the Novel," in *The Liberal Imagination: Essays on Literature and Society* (New York: Viking, 1950), pp. 219–22; and see also the essay in that volume on Henry James's *The Princess Casamassima,* pp. 58–92.

13 Alexander Pope, *An Essay on Criticism* (1711), ll. 82–83, 301–04. For the discarded lines, see the Twickenham Edition, vol. 1, ed. E. Audra and Aubrey Williams (New Haven: Yale University Press, 1961), p. 258.

14 Stuart M. Tave, *Some Words of Jane Austen* (Chicago: University of Chicago Press, 1973), chap. 3.

15 From his unsigned review of *Emma*, *Quarterly Review* 14 (1815); reprinted in *Jane Austen: The Critical Heritage*, ed. B. C. Southam (London: Routledge and Kegan Paul, 1968), p. 68.

16 Trilling, *Sincerity and Authenticity*, pp. 76—77.

17 David Miller has treated with great astuteness the process of Elinor's relaying to her sister and mother the import of Willoughby's final visit. This process "offers us in almost diagrammatic form the mechanics of closure. Willoughby's narrative, dangerously open, gives way to Elinor's retailing, modifying it in order to close it up. Willoughby's account does not inherently resolve itself; only when reconstructed and reduced by Elinor's account does it acquire a meaning of closure." D. A. Miller, *Narrative and Its Discontents: Problems of Closure in the Traditional Novel* (Princeton: Princeton University Press, 1981), p. 75.

18 This is discussed by Kenneth L. Moler in "The Two Voices of Fanny Price," in *Jane Austen: Bicentenary Essays*, ed. John Halperin (Cambridge: Cambridge University Press, 1975), pp. 172—79, and in his *Jane Austen's Art of Allusion* (Lincoln: University of Nebraska Press, 1968), chap. 4.

19 Trilling, *Sincerity and Authenticity*, pp. 77—79.

20 Here as elsewhere in this chapter I draw upon Valerie Shaw's essay, "Jane Austen's Subdued Heroines," *Nineteenth-Century Fiction* 30 (1975) : 281—304. While she writes of tragic aspects and I of comic, we are responding to the same elements, and I share her view that in the "muted novels" (she cites *Mansfield Park* and *Persuasion*) "irony is enlarged rather than renounced" (p. 282).

Chapter 5. Stendhal: Irony and Freedom

1 The text of the novels will be cited in the translation of C. K. Scott-Moncrieff and will be given by volume and chapter number, as here (I, 6), or simply by chapter number where that is unambiguous.

2 *Selected Journalism from the English Reviews by Stendhal, with Translations of Other Critical Writings*, trans. Geoffrey Strickland (London: J. Calder, 1959), pp. 187, 170, 172.

3 *The Private Diaries of Stendhal*, ed. and trans. Robert Sage (Garden City, N. Y.: Doubleday, 1954), p. 82.

4 *Love (De l'amour)*, trans. Gilbert and Suzanne Sale (Harmondsworth: Penguin, 1975), bk. 2, "Various Fragments," no. 39, p. 224, n. 1.

5 *The Life of Henry Brulard*, trans. Jean Stewart and B. C. J. G. Knight (New York: Minerva Press, 1968), chap. 41, p. 307.

6 *Life of Rossini*, trans. Richard N. Coe (New York: Orion Press, 1970), chap. 46, pp. 463—64.

7 Byron in his Letter to [Murray] on W. L. Bowles's Strictures on Pope, March 1821, *Letters and Journals*, ed. Rowland E. Prothero (London: Murray, 1901), 5 : 542.

8 *Selected Journalism*, ed. Geoffrey Strickland, pp. 306, 297, 298.

9 *Love*, bk. 2, "Various Fragments," no. 100, p. 244.

10 There are fine treatments of Stendhal's narrative methods in Victor Brombert, *Stendhal et la voie oblique; l'auteur devant son monde romanesque* (New Haven: Yale University Press; Paris: Presses Universitaires de France, 1954); and Georges Blin, *Stendhal et les problèmes du roman* (Paris: Libraire José Corti, 1953), esp. pt. 3, "Les intrusions d'auteur."

11 The most extensive discussion of this problem is in René Girard, *Deceit, Desire, and the Novel: Self and Other in Literary Structure*, trans. Yvonne Freccero (Baltimore: Johns Hopkins University Press, 1965).

12 *Romans et nouvelles,* ed. H. Martineau (Paris: Gallimard, Bibliothèque de la Pléiade, 1952), 4 : 712–13.

13 Geoffrey Strickland, *Stendhal: The Education of a Novelist* (Cambridge: Cambridge University Press, 1974), p. 141.

14 Eugene Goodheart suggests that "the ascetic impulse would not have asserted itself if the world had provided occasions for spiritual fulfillment." *The Failure of Criticism* (Cambridge, Mass.: Harvard University Press, 1978), p. 131.

15 *Love,* bk. 1, chap. 31, "Extract from Salviati's Diary," pp. 101–02.

16 *The Life of Henry Brulard,* chap. 9, pp. 68–69; chap. 25, p. 182.

17 *The Life of Henry Brulard,* chap. 44, p. 328. On Stendhal's use of the "motif of height," see Stephen Gilman, *The Tower as Emblem: Chapters VIII, IX, XIX, and XX of the Chartreuse de Parme, Analecta Romanica,* Heft 22 (1967), Frankfurt am Main.

18 Irving Howe, *Politics and the Novel* (New York: Meridian, 1957), pp. 47–48. On Gina's recklessness, see Michael Wood, *Stendhal* (London: Elek, 1971), p. 184: "Gina has the prince assassinated out of hatred, worse, out of the festering memory of her helplessness on the day Fabrice was put in gaol. It is a crime of the head, a work of slighted disregard; it is a harsh act without dignity."

19 The relevant texts are cited by Strickland, *Stendhal: The Education of a Novelist,* p. 227.

20 Henry James, *Literary Reviews and Essays,* ed. Albert Mordell (New Haven: College and University Press, 1957), pp. 156–57 (reprinted from *The Nation* for 17 September 1874).

21 *Don Juan,* canto 4, stanza 27.

Chapter 6. Dickens: Selves and Systems

1 Thus in *Little Dorrit* the inhabitants of Bleeding Heart Yard, low in social status, marginal in economic, find a genuine (and sincere enough) pleasure in teaching an Italian immigrant English: "They spoke to him in very loud voices as if he were stone deaf. They constructed sentences, by way of teaching him the language in its purity, such as were addressed by the savages to Captain Cook, or by Friday to Robinson Crusoe." Mrs. Plornish's triumph is "Me ope you leg well soon," regarded by her neighbors as "a very short remove indeed from speaking Italian" (I, 25).

2 Northrop Frye has written splendidly on "Dickens and the Comedy of Humours," in *The Stubborn Structure: Essays on Criticism and Society* (Ithaca: Cornell University Press, 1970), pp. 218–40.

3 On such matters see H. M. Daleski, *Dickens and the Art of Analogy* (New York: Schocken, 1970).

4 Robert Caserio, *Plot, Story, and the Novel: From Dickens and Poe to the Modern Period* (Princeton: Princeton University Press, 1979), pp. 113–17. On plot and counterplot in Dickens, and especially the external as a figurative presentation of the internal, see Peter Garrett, *The Victorian Multiplot Novel: Studies in Dialogical Form* (New Haven and London: Yale University Press, 1980), chap. 2. On the attractions and difficulties of a "deconstructive" reading of the novel, see Alistair M. Duckworth, *"Little Dorrit* and the Question of Closure," *Nineteenth-Century Fiction* 33 (1978): 110–30, and the remarks upon it in the same issue by Frank Kermode, "Sensing Endings," pp. 150–52.

5 *Collected Essays* (Oxford: Clarendon Press, 1935), 1: 137.

6 Julian Moynahan, "The Hero's Guilt: The Case of *Great Expectations,"* *Essays in Criticism* 10 (1960): 60–79.

7 Letters to W. W. F. de Cerjat (3 January 1855), Austen Henry Layard (10 April 1855), John Forster (30 September 1855); in Nonesuch Edition of Letters, ed. W. Dexter (London, 1937–38), 2 : 615, 652, 693. See John Butt and Kathleen Tillotson, *Dickens at Work* (London: Methuen, 1957).

8 Letter to W. W. F. de Cerjat (25 October 1864), Nonesuch Letters, 3: 402.

9 John Forster, *The Life of Charles Dickens*, ed. A. J. Hoppé (London: Everyman, 1966), 2 : 422. See his letter to his son Henry Fielding Dickens (15 October 1868) where he recommends the "priceless value" of the New Testament for the "character of our Saviour, as separated from the vain constructions and interventions of men" (Nonesuch Letters, 3 : 673–74).

10 Letter to W. C. Macready, the actor (4 October 1855), Nonesuch Letters, 2 : 695.

11 Forster, *The Life of Charles Dickens*, 2 : 183 (bk. 8, chap. 1).

12 Lionel Trilling, *"Little Dorrit,"* in *The Opposing Self* (New York: Viking, 1955), p. 65. Alexander Welsh, *The City of Dickens* (Oxford: Clarendon Press, 1971), esp. pt. 3.

13 Mary McCarthy, "Characters in Fiction," *On the Contrary* (New York: Farrar, Strauss, 1964). Her instance is, in fact, Micawber.

14 We can see in Wackford Squeers the emergence of what Pecksniff will become: "Squeers covered his rascality, even at home, with a spice of his habitual deceit, as if he really had a notion of some day or other being able to take himself in, and persuade his own mind that he was a very good fellow" (*Nicholas Nickleby*, chap. 8).

15 Barbara Hardy, *The Moral Art of Dickens* (New York: Oxford University Press, 1970), pp. 58–69. For an instance of the denial, see F. R. Leavis and Q. D. Leavis, *Dickens the Novelist* (New York: Pantheon, 1970), pp. 23–24.

Chapter 7. Eliot: The Nature of Decision

1 "The Natural History of German Life" (1856), *Essays of George Eliot*, ed. Thomas Pinney (New York: Columbia University Press, 1963), pp. 269–70.

2 "The Morality of Wilhelm Meister" (1855), *Essays*, pp. 146–47. *The George Eliot Letters*, 7 vols., ed. Gordon Haight (New Haven: Yale University Press, 1954–55), 6 : 112.

3 *Middlemarch*, chap. 31. "It is the habit of my imagination to strive after as full a vision of the medium in which a character moves as the character itself," *The George Eliot Letters*, 4: 97.

4 *Essays*, p. 135.

5 From the selection on "Moral Freedom" in "More Leaves from George Eliot's Notebook," ed. Thomas Pinney, *Huntington Library Quarterly* 29 (1966): 365.

6 P. F. Strawson, *Freedom and Resentment and Other Essays* (London: Methuen, 1974), pp. 1–26, esp. pp. 9–10, 13n. For a more general discussion of the contrast between internal (participant) and external (objective) views, see H. L. A. Hart, *The Concept of Law* (Oxford and New York: Oxford University Press, 1961), pp. 79 ff., discussed further in the following chapter. See also Richard Rorty, *Philosophy and the Mirror of Nature* (Princeton: Princeton University Press, 1979), p. 190n.: "We *are* tempted, when we are particularly good at predicting something's behavior on the basis of its internal structure, to be 'objective' about it—that is, to treat it as an *en-soi* rather than a *pour-soi* and 'one of us.' "

7 Jerome B. Schneewind, "Moral Problems and Moral Philosophy in the Victorian Period" (1965), reprinted in *English Literature and British Philosophy*, ed. S. P. Rosenbaum (Chicago: University of Chicago Press, 1971), pp. 185–207, esp. pp. 192, 204, 206.

8 Pinney, *More Leaves*, p. 365.

9 Ibid., p. 364. Judgments of taste must also be seen as "decisions of the organism," "resulting from dispositions, habits, or character as a whole," or having "congruity with the fullest knowledge directing sympathetic feeling" (p. 366).

10 Ibid., p. 366.

11 Ibid., p. 364. "We could never have loved the earth so well if we had had no childhood in it," *The Mill on the Floss*, chap. 5.

12 Stuart Hampshire, "Spinoza and the Idea of Freedom" (1960), in *Freedom of Mind and*

Other Essays (Oxford: Clarendon Press, 1972), pp. 198–99. For an example of the man who is, in Spinoza's terms, not free, see *The Mill on the Floss,* chap. 35: "It is the moment when our resolution seems about to become irrevocable—when the fatal iron gates are about to close upon us—that tests our strength. Then, after hours of clear reasoning and firm conviction, we snatch at any sophistry that will nullify our long struggles, and bring us the defeat that we love better than victory."

13 Iris Murdoch, *The Sovereignty of Good* (New York: Schocken, 1971), pp. 41, 84–85. The final sentence is quoted from Ludwig Wittgenstein, *Tractatus Logico-Philosophicus,* 6.44.

14 "To speak within an institution is to use its characteristic concepts, to assert or appeal to or implicitly invoke its rules and principles." An institution "does not need to be instituted"; it may "grow very naturally out of the ordinary conditions of human life. But that does not alter its logical status, or the logical status of conclusions that can be established only within and by invoking that institution." Mackie, *Ethics: Inventing Right and Wrong,* p. 81.

15 Murdoch, *The Sovereignty of Good,* pp. 37–38, 40, 67.

16 Iris Murdoch, *The Fire and the Sun: Why Plato Banished the Artists* (Oxford: Oxford University Press, 1977), p. 81. Hilary Putnam, *Meaning and the Moral Sciences* (Boston and London: Routledge and Kegan Paul, 1978), p. 87.

17 Alisdair MacIntyre, *After Virtue: A Study in Moral Theory* (Notre Dame, Ind.: University of Notre Dame Press, 1981), pp. 104, 135, 121, 118, 192, 199–203.

18 Pinney, *More Leaves,* p. 364. In *Romola,* chap. 11, Eliot writes of "obligations which can never be proved to have any sanctity in the absence of feeling." Eliot condemned pantheism because it "is an attempt to look at the universe from the outside of our relation to it (that universe) as human beings. As healthy, sane human beings we must love and hate—love what is good for mankind, hate what is evil for mankind," *The George Eliot Letters,* 5 : 31. "No man can know his brother simply as a spectator," *The Impressions of Theophrastus Such,* chap. 1.

19 Gordon Haight, *George Eliot: A Biography* (New York and Oxford: Oxford University Press, 1968), p. 465.

20 *Adam Bede,* chap. 54. She asserts, in a letter to the Hon. Mrs. Frederick Ponsonby, 10 December 1874, that all her books "have for their main bearing" the conclusion that "the fellowship between man and man, which has been the principle of development, social and moral, is not dependent on conceptions of what is not man; and that the idea of God, so far as it has been a high spiritual influence, is the ideal of a goodness entirely human." *The George Eliot Letters,* 6 : 98.

21 *Middlemarch,* chap. 42. While I would deny Mrs. Transome tragic stature, I have no doubt that she was conceived in the light of tragedy. See Fred C. Thomson, *"Felix Holt as Classic Tragedy," Nineteenth-Century Fiction* 16 (1961–62) : 47–48.

22 S. L. Goldberg, "Morality and Literature; with Some Reflections on Daniel Deronda," *The Critical Review* (Melbourne), no. 22 (1980): 3–20.

23 *Scenes of Clerical Life* (1858), "Janet's Repentance," chap. 10.

24 *Middlemarch,* chap. 76. Eliot sometimes uses the term "moral stupidity" for "that state of insensibility in which we are not alive to high and generous emotions." We make a mistake in "supposing that stupidity is only intellectual, not a thing of character." *The George Eliot Letters,* 6 : 287 (a report of her words by Emily Davies).

25 The words of Constantius in *"Daniel Deronda: A Conversation," Partial Portraits* (1888), reprinted (Ann Arbor: University of Michigan Press, 1970), p. 89. Theodora has just remarked: "It is the tragedy that makes her conscience, which then reacts upon it; and I can think of nothing more powerful than the way in which the growth of her conscience is traced, nothing more touching than the picture of its helpless maturity."

26 *The George Eliot Letters,* 7 : 56.

27 "Three Months in Weimar" (1855), *Essays,* p. 88. Eliot later revised the last part to read, "he has spread over those coarsely cut features the irradiation of genius."

Chapter 8. Tolstoy and the Forms of Life

1 Isaiah Berlin, *The Hedgehog and the Fox,* vi, now in *Russian Thinkers,* ed. Henry Hardy and Aileen Kelly (London: Hogarth Press, 1978), pp. 71, 74.

2 *War and Peace,* trans. Louise and Aylmer Maude, ed. George Gibian (New York: Norton, 1966), XII, 3. Hereafter *WP.*

3 *Anna Karenina,* trans. David Magarshack (New York: Signet, 1961), VIII, 10. Hereafter *AK.*

4 Ludwig Wittgenstein, *On Certainty* (1969), ed. G. E. M. Anscombe and G. H. von Wright, trans. Denis Paul and G. E. M. Anscombe (New York: Harper and Row, 1972), pars. 519, 625, 152.

5 Norman Malcolm, *Ludwig Wittgenstein: A Memoir* (Oxford: Oxford University Press, 1958), pp. 41–42 on Tolstoy, p. 44 on Johnson, p. 80 on Moore. On his praise of Tolstoy's *Twenty-Three Tales,* see p. 52 and cf. James Joyce to his daughter Lucia (27 April 1935) : "In my opinion *How Much Land Does a Man Need* is the greatest story that the literature of the world knows."

6 Ludwig Wittgenstein, *Zettel,* ed. G. E. M. Anscombe and G. H. von Wright, trans. G. E. M. Anscombe (Berkeley and Los Angeles: University of California Press, 1970), par. 173.

7 Ludwig Wittgenstein, *Philosophical Investigations,* trans. G. E. M. Anscombe, 3d ed. (New York: Macmillan, 1958), p. 224. Hereafter, *PI.*

8 Antony Flew, "Tolstoy and the Meaning of Life," *Ethics* 73 (1962–63) : 110–18, esp. 116–18. Tolstoy, *A Confession,* chap. 5; Wittgenstein, *Tractatus Logico-Philosophicus,* trans. D. F. Pears and B. F. McGuinness (New York: Humanities Press, 1974), 6.52, 6.521, 6.522.

9 Bertrand Russell, Letter of 20 December 1919 to Lady Ottoline Morrell, quoted in Ludwig Wittgenstein, *Letters to Russell, Keynes and Moore,* ed. G. H. von Wright (Ithaca: Cornell University Press, 1974), p. 82*n.*

10 Wittgenstein, *Zettel,* par. 233.

11 H. L. A. Hart, *The Concept of Law* (New York and London: Oxford University Press, 1961), pp. 87–88.

12 Gustave Flaubert, *Madame Bovary; moeurs de province,* pt. II, chap. 15; the translation is that of Paul de Man in the Norton Critical Edition (New York: Norton, 1965), pp. 161–62.

13 *Marcel Proust on Art and Literature 1896–1916 (Contre Sainte-Beuve),* trans. Sylvia Townsend Warner (New York: Meridian, 1958), pp. 378–79. See also Walter A. Strauss, *Proust and Literature: The Novelist as Critic* (Cambridge, Mass.: Harvard University Press, 1959), pp. 168–71.

14 The phrase is from Raymond Williams, *Modern Tragedy* (Stanford: Stanford University Press, 1966), p. 129.

15 Ludwig Wittgenstein, *Notebooks, 1914–1916,* trans. G. E. M. Anscombe (New York: Harper and Row, 1969), p. 73.

16 Warner, *Proust on Art and Literature,* p. 376.

17 "Notes on Form in Art," *Essays of George Eliot,* p. 433.

18 For a brief discussion of this scene in terms of "will," see Leslie H. Farber, *The Ways of*

the Will: Essays toward a Psychopathology of Will (New York: Harper and Row, 1966), pp. 12–15.

19 *Philosophical Investigations,* par. 129; *On Certainty,* par. 559; *Philosophical Investigations,* p. 226. In a letter to V. G. Chertkov, December 1889, Tolstoy wrote: "the only thing one needs to know is—how should I live? It's not necessary to know whether I have free will or not, but only to use the force which I'm conscious of as free will. . . . It's not given us to know what the world is or ourselves in it, even if we devote half our life to the study of everything written about; but we always know what we need to know, as soon as we want to know." *Tolstoy's Letters,* 2 : 449.

Chapter 9. James: The Logic of Intensity

1 In this chapter I have used the following editions of James's novels: *The Wings of the Dove,* 1st ed. of 1902; *The Awkward Age,* New York Edition of 1907–09; *The Ambassadors,* 1st ed. of 1903; and *The Golden Bowl,* 1st ed. of 1904. All references are by chapter, except in the case of *The Ambassadors,* where book and chapter numbers are given.

2 *The Art of the Novel: Critical Prefaces by Henry James,* ed. R. P. Blackmur (New York: Scribner, 1934), preface to *The Princess Casamassima,* pp. 63, 64, 65–66, 67, 71; preface to *Roderick Hudson,* p. 16.

3 *The Letters of Henry James,* 2 vols., ed. Percy Lubbock (New York: Scribner, 1920), 1 : 341–42 (To Henrietta Reubell, 12 November 1899).

4 Matthew Arnold, "To a Friend" (1849) contains the tribute to Sophocles: "Who saw life steadily, and saw it whole."

5 Robert L. Caserio, *Plot, Story, and the Novel: From Dickens and Poe to the Modern Period* (Princeton: Princeton University Press, 1979), pp. 208–09.

6 For the preface, see Blackmur, *The Art of the Novel,* pp. 129–30. Joseph Conrad, "Henry James: An Appreciation," reprinted in Walter F. Wright, *Joseph Conrad on Fiction* (Lincoln: University of Nebraska Press, 1964), p. 86.

7 Blackmur, *The Art of the Novel,* p. 45. "The Art of Fiction" can be found in Henry James, *The Future of the Novel: Essays on the Art of Fiction,* ed. Leon Edel (New York: Vintage, 1956).

8 For the letter to W. D. Howells, see Henry James, *Letters,* ed. Leon Edel (Cambridge, Mass.: Harvard University Press, 1974–), 3 : 28. James regards Howells as the "great American naturalist" but feels he does not go far enough. On Balzac and Thackeray, "The Lesson of Balzac" (1905), in *The Future of the Novel,* pp. 116–17.

9 Henry James, "Baudelaire" (1876), in *French Poets and Novelists* (London: Macmillan, 1878), pp. 64–65.

10 *Letters,* ed. Leon Edel, 1 : 46 (To Thomas Sargent Perry, 1 November 1863).

11 *The Letters of Henry James,* ed. Percy Lubbock, 2 : 490 (10 July 1915).

12 *The Notebooks of Henry James,* ed. F. O. Matthiessen and Kenneth B. Murdock (New York: Oxford University Press, 1947), p. 415. For the thoughts of five years earlier, see p. 228: "It is too late, too late *now,* for HIM to live—but what stirs in him with a dumb passion of desire, of I don't know what, is the sense that he may have a little supersensual hour in the vicarious freedom of another." See also the letter to Hugh Walpole, *The Letters of Henry James,* ed. Percy Lubbock, 2 : 244–46 (14 August 1912).

13 Stuart Hampshire, "Figures in the Carpet" (a review of the final volume of Leon Edel's biography of James), *New Statesman* 84 (4 August 1972) : 162–63. I am indebted throughout this chapter, however I use their insights, to Laurence Holland, *The Expense of Vision: Essays on the Craft of Henry James* (Princeton: Princeton University Press, 1964),

and to Dorothea Krook, *The Ordeal of Consciousness in Henry James* (Cambridge: Cambridge University Press, 1962).

14 Ruth Bernard Yeazell, *Language and Knowledge in the Late Novels of Henry James* (Chicago: University of Chicago Press, 1976), p. 117.

Chapter 10. Conrad: The Limits of Irony

1 Dr. Johnson's comments are of value: Mandeville "reckons among vices everything that gives pleasure. He takes the narrowest system of morality, monastick morality, which holds pleasure itself to be a vice . . . and he reckons wealth as a publick benefit, which is by no means always true." *Boswell's Life of Johnson,* ed. R. W. Chapman (Oxford: Oxford University Press, 1953), p. 948 (15 April 1778).

2 *Lord Jim* (1900), chap. 22; "Well Done!" (1918), collected in *Notes on Life and Letters* (New York: Doubleday, 1921).

3 *Letters from Joseph Conrad 1895–1924,* ed. Edward Garnett (Indianapolis: Bobbs-Merrill, 1928), pp. 135–36 (29 March 1898). These passages also appear in Gérard Jean-Aubry, *Joseph Conrad: Life and Letters* (London: William Heinemann, 1927), 1 : 232. The third passage is from a letter to Mrs. E. L. Sanderson, 31 August 1898, in Jean-Aubry, *Life and Letters,* 1 : 247.

4 *The Secret Agent* (1907), chap. 6 (italics added).

5 Jean-Aubry, *Life and Letters,* 1 : 247 (italics added).

6 *Joseph Conrad's Letters to R. B. Cunninghame Graham,* ed. C. T. Watts (Cambridge: Cambridge University Press, 1969), p. 53 (14 December 1897).

7 *Typhoon* (1902), chaps. 1, 5.

8 Watts, *Letters to Cunninghame Graham,* p. 55n.

9 Ibid., p. 50 (6 December 1897).

10 *A Personal Record* (New York: Doubleday, Page, 1912), chap. 2, p. 37.

11 *Letters of Joseph Conrad to Marguerite Poradowska 1890–1920,* trans. and ed. John A. Gee and Paul J. Sturm (New Haven: Yale University Press, 1940), p. 65 (20 July 1894).

12 Watts, *Letters to Cunninghame Graham,* p. 68 (23 January 1898).

13 Jean-Aubry, *Life and Letters,* 2 : 83–84 (29 August 1908).

14 "Anatole France" (1904), reprinted in *Joseph Conrad on Fiction,* ed. Walter F. Wright (Lincoln: University of Nebraska Press, 1964), p. 63. Wright's fine collection includes many extracts from letters as well as essays and prefaces. For the letter to Colvin, 18 March 1917, see Jean-Aubry, *Life and Letters,* 2 : 184–85.

15 "Henry James: An Appreciation" (1905), in Wright, *Joseph Conrad on Fiction,* p. 88.

16 "Anatole France," in Wright, *Joseph Conrad on Fiction,* pp. 66–67, 63; *Nostromo* (1904), pt. I, chap. 6; on Tolstoy and Christianity, *Letters from Conrad,* ed. Garnett, p. 245 (23 February 1914).

17 "Alphonse Daudet" (1898), in Wright, *Joseph Conrad on Fiction,* pp. 54, 55, 56.

18 "Books" (1905), in Wright, *Joseph Conrad on Fiction,* p. 81.

19 "Well Done!" in *Notes on Life and Letters.* "Books," in Wright, *Joseph Conrad on Fiction,* p. 81.

20 *A Personal Record* (1912), chap. 5, pp. 92–94. Those, like George Eliot, who can accept the death or disappearance of God without a sense of vertigo or outrage inevitably win Nietzsche's scorn. "They are rid of the Christian God and now believe all the more firmly that they must cling to Christian morality. That is an English consistency; we do not wish to hold it against little moralistic females à la Eliot. . . . When the English actually believe that they know 'intuitively' what is good and evil, when they therefore suppose

that they no longer require Christianity as the guarantee of morality, we merely witness the *effects* of the dominion of the Christian value judgment and an expression of the strength and depth of this dominion. . . . For the English, morality is not yet a problem." Friedrich Nietzsche, *Twilight of the Idols,* "Skirmishes of an Untimely Man," para. 5, in *The Portable Nietzsche,* trans. and ed. Walter Kaufmann (New York: Viking Press, 1954), pp. 515–16.

21 Preface to *The Nigger of the Narcissus* (1897). But cf. Eliot's view of pantheism, p. 354, n. 18.

22 Bertrand Russell, *Portraits from Memory and Other Essays* (London: Allen and Unwin, 1956), p. 82. Russell speaks of Conrad's awareness of "the various forms of passionate madness to which men are prone" and of his "profound belief in the importance of discipline." What interested Conrad more than politics was "the individual soul faced with the indifference of nature, and often with the hostility of man, and subject to inner struggles with passions both good and bad that led towards destruction" (83).

23 Preface to *Within the Tides* (1920); this passage is cited by Ian Watt, *Conrad in the Nineteenth Century* (Berkeley and Los Angeles: University of California Press, 1979), chap. 5, iv, b (p. 322), in his discussion of Stein's role in *Lord Jim.*

24 On the motif of the practical joke, see Alexander Welsh, *Reflections on the Hero as Quixote* (Princeton: Princeton University Press, 1981), esp. chaps. 5 and 6.

25 Peter Ure, "Character and Imagination in Conrad," in *Yeats and Anglo-Irish Literature: Critical Essays,* ed. C. J. Rawson (New York: Barnes and Noble, 1974), p. 236.

26 *Letters from Joseph Conrad,* ed. Garnett, p. 164 (20 January 1900).

27 There is an interesting resemblance between Dr. Monygham's view of politics and that of Pascal. Erich Auerbach has discussed the case of Pascal (based on Fragment 298 of the *Pensées,* e.g., "being unable to make what is just strong, we have made what is strong just"). Pascal combined an Augustinian view of a fallen world with a Machiavellian *raison d'état.* Power is justice in the fallen world: "our world is evil, but it is just that this should be so." Thus Pascal arrived at the "paradox of might as a pure evil, which one must obey unquestioningly." For Dr. Monygham the very methods he despises are just when they are used in Mrs. Gould's cause; but they are also evil, and only he is debased enough to adopt such methods gratefully. For Auerbach on Pascal's politics, see his *Scenes from the Drama of European Literature: Six Essays* (New York: Meridian Books, 1959), pp. 101–29.

28 H. M. Daleski, *Joseph Conrad: The Way of Dispossession* (New York: Holmes and Meier, 1977), pp. 117–18.

29 To D. S. Meldrum, 10 August 1898, in *Joseph Conrad: Letters to William Blackwood and David S. Meldrum,* ed. William Blackburn (Durham: Duke University Press, 1958), p. 27.

30 "To put matters bluntly: Conrad may be condemning Decoud for a withdrawal and skepticism more radical than Decoud ever shows; which are, in fact, Conrad's own." Albert J. Guerard, *Conrad the Novelist* (New York: Atheneum, 1967), p. 199. Guerard goes on to show that there are "two Decouds, . . . two very different men, two different 'potential selves' " (p. 202). I would cite as examples of overindulgence the degradation of Giorgio Viola as he is made the inadvertent murderer of Nostromo or (a comparable instance) Winnie Verloc's degradation in her desperate appeal to Ossipon near the close of *The Secret Agent.* Another instance is the cry of love and pain with which the betrayed Linda Viola asserts her fidelity to Nostromo. It in turn is heard by Dr. Monygham as "the greatest, the most enviable, the most sinister" of Nostromo's triumphs, the more bitter for Monygham's conviction that he himself can never be loved. There is a comparable note of unyielding devotion or necessary illusion at the close of *Under Western Eyes,* where Sophia Antonovna declares "in a firm voice," "Peter Ivanovitch is an inspired man."

Sophia Antonovna is a stronger figure than Winnie Verloc and a more capable person than Linda Viola; she can sustain the irony without becoming its abject victim.

Chapter 11. Lawrence: Levels of Consciousness

1 *Women in Love,* chap. 23. The texts of the novels are cited from the former Viking Compass Edition, now superseded by the Penguin Books edition of 1976.
2 Montaigne, "Of Experience," *Essays,* vol. 3, trans. Donald M. Frame (Stanford: Stanford University Press, 1958), p. 837.
3 Lawrence, *The Crown,* in *Phoenix II: Uncollected, Unpublished, and Other Prose Works,* ed. Warren Roberts and Harry T. Moore (New York: Viking Press, 1959), pp. 373, 412, 413.
4 Lawrence, "Prefaces and Introductions to Books," in *Phoenix: The Posthumous Papers of D. H. Lawrence,* ed. Edward D. McDonald (London: William Heinemann, 1936), p. 219.
5 *Phoenix,* p. 220.
6 *Phoenix II,* pp. 413–14.
7 "Return to Bestwood," *Phoenix II,* p. 265.
8 "Prefaces and Introductions to Books," *Phoenix,* p. 216; "Democracy," *Phoenix,* p. 713.
9 "Democracy," *Phoenix,* p. 708.
10 "The Reality of Peace," *Phoenix,* pp. 672–73.
11 "Benjamin Franklin," *Studies in Classic American Literature* (New York: Thomas Seltzer, 1923), p. 30.
12 "Study of Thomas Hardy," *Phoenix,* p. 425.
13 "Study of Thomas Hardy," *Phoenix,* p. 431; "Democracy," *Phoenix,* pp. 710, 711, 712.
14 "Moral Clothing," *The Collected Poems of D. H. Lawrence,* eds. Vivian de Sola Pinto and Warren Roberts (New York: Viking Press, 1971), p. 607.
15 "Life," *Phoenix,* pp. 696–97.
16 "The Work of Creation," *Collected Poems,* p. 690.
17 *The Collected Letters of D. H. Lawrence,* 2 vols., ed. Harry T. Moore (New York: Viking Press, 1962), 1 : 273 (22 April 1914); 1 : 282 (5 June 1914).
18 Mark Schorer, "*Women in Love* and Death," *The Hudson Review* 6 (1953) : 34–47; reprinted in *D. H. Lawrence: A Collection of Critical Essays,* ed. Mark Spilka (Englewood Cliffs, N.J.: Prentice-Hall, 1963), pp. 50–60.
19 "Study of Thomas Hardy," *Phoenix,* p. 479.
20 "Morality and the Novel," *Phoenix,* p. 527. Remaining page references to this essay in parentheses.
21 "Introduction to These Paintings," *Phoenix,* p. 570. Remaining page references to this essay in parentheses.
22 "The Novel," *Phoenix II,* p. 416. Remaining page references to this essay in parentheses.
23 "The Novel and the Feelings," *Phoenix,* pp. 759–60.
24 "Foreword to *Women in Love,*" *Phoenix II,* p. 276. For the relation of metaphysics to narrative, see Frank Kermode, *Lawrence* (London: Fontana/Collins, 1973); and Stephen J. Miko, *Toward Women in Love: The Emergence of a Lawrentian Aesthetic* (New Haven and London: Yale University Press, 1971).
25 "Review of Books," *Phoenix,* p. 369.
26 *Collected Letters,* 1 : 468.
27 *Collected Letters,* 1 : 493 (20 December 1916).
28 Cited in David Gordon, *D. H. Lawrence as a Literary Critic* (New Haven and London: Yale University Press, 1966), p. 116.

29 *Phoenix II,* p. 100. Remaining page references in parentheses.

30 Colin Clarke, *River of Dissolution: D. H. Lawrence and English Romanticism* (London: Routledge, 1969).

31 "The moon that had been sinister and deadly in self-sufficiency grows into a radiant rose" and we come to see "why we should welcome both the disintegration and the tenacity of the coming together of the rose-in-darkness, 'to get over the disfigurement and the agitation, to be whole and composed, in peace.' " Mark Kinkead-Weekes, "The Marble and the Statue: The Exploratory Imagination of D. H. Lawrence," in *Imagined Worlds: Essays in Some English Novels and Novelists in Honour of John Butt,* ed. Maynard Mack and Ian Gregor (London: Methuen, 1965), pp. 411–12.

32 On this passage and related matters, see Mark Spilka, *The Love Ethic of D. H. Lawrence* (Bloomington: Indiana University Press, 1955), pp. 91–173, esp. pp. 121–47.

Chapter 12. Forster: Inclusion and Exclusion

1 E. M. Forster, *A Room with a View* (1908), chap. 1.

2 *Aspects of the Novel* (1927), chap. 4.

3 Peter L. Berger, *Invitation to Sociology: A Humanistic Perspective* (Garden City, N.Y.: Anchor, 1963), pp. 148–49.

4 "E. M. Forster," an interview by P. N. Furbank and F. J. H. Haskell, in *Writers at Work: The Paris Review Interviews,* ed. Malcolm Cowley (New York: Viking, 1958), pp. 24–35, esp. p. 29. Hereafter by page number, as WW 15.

5 E. M. Forster, *Arctic Summer and Other Fiction,* Abinger Edition, vol. 9, ed. Elizabeth Heine (London: Edward Arnold, 1980), p. 161.

6 E. M. Forster, "Anonymity: An Enquiry," in *Two Cheers for Democracy* (London: Edward Arnold, 1951).

7 P. N. Furbank, *E. M. Forster: A Life* (New York: Harcourt Brace Jovanovich, 1978), 2 : 107 (Letter to G. H. Ludolf, 13 June 1922).

8 D. J. Enright, "To the Lighthouse or to India?" in *The Apothecary's Shop: Essays on Literature* (London: Secker and Warburg, 1957), pp. 168–86, esp. pp. 183–84.

9 E. M. Forster, "Adrift in India: 5. Pan," in *Abinger Harvest* (New York: Harcourt Brace, 1936).

10 E. M. Forster, *A Passage to India* (New York: Harcourt Brace, 1924), chap. 29.

11 Compare Dickinson's letter to Forster on his move from India to China (8 June 1913): "China is a land of human beings. India, as it glimmers in a remote past, is supernatural, uncanny, terrifying, sublime, horrible, monotonous, full of mountains and abysses, all heights and depths and for ever incomprehensible. But China! So gay, friendly, beautiful, sane, hellenic, choice, human. . . . No reaches into the infinite; but a clear, non-restricted perception of the beautiful and the exquisite in the Real. . . . Round Peking, it's Italy. You go out to the hills, and wander from monastery to monastery, each more exquisitely placed than the last." In E. M. Forster, *Goldsworthy Lowes Dickinson and Related Writings,* ed. Oliver Stallybrass, Abinger Edition, vol. 13 (London: Edward Arnold, 1973), pp. 122–23.

12 Compare the letter from Forster to R. C. Trevelyan (28 October 1905) on the scene in *Where Angels Fear to Tread* in which Philip Herriton is beaten by Gino. Philip "is a person who has scarcely ever felt the physical forces that are banging about in the world, and he couldn't get good and understand by spiritual suffering alone. Bodily punishment, however unjust superficially, was necessary too: in fact the scene—to use a heavy word, and one I have only just thought of—was sacramental." In the Abinger Edition of *Where Angels Fear to Tread,* ed. Oliver Stallybrass (London: Edward Arnold, 1975), p. 150.

13 *Arctic Summer,* p. 129. Compare Roger Fry, pp. 321—22.

14 "We are all parts of God, even the stones, though we cannot realise it; and man's goal is to become actually, as he is potentially, divine. . . . The Christian promise is that man shall see God, the Neo-Platonic—like the Indian—that he shall be God." E. M. Forster, *Alexandria: A History and a Guide,* new ed. (Garden City, N.Y.: Doubleday Anchor, 1961), pp. 71—72.

15 "The Gods of India," reprinted in *Albergo Empedocle and Other Writings by E. M. Forster,* ed. George H. Thomson (New York: Liveright, 1971), pp. 220—21. Of relevance to the festival is this passage, p. 223: "Nothing is more remarkable than the way in which Hinduism will suddenly dethrone its highest conceptions, nor is anything more natural, because it is athirst for the inconceivable."

16 "He noticed and commented on our inattention to detail, our idleness and incompetence. . . . We took it from him (even Godbole's highbrow incoherence) for two reasons. First, because he was harder on his own people. . . . Second, because he seems to have taken to heart the words of Tagore: 'Come inside India, accept all her good and evil: if there be deformity then try and cure it from within, but see it with your own eyes, understand it, think over it, turn your face towards it, become one with it.' " K. Natwar Singh, "Only Connect . . . : Forster and India," in *Aspects of E. M. Forster,* ed. Oliver Stallybrass (New York: Harcourt Brace Jovanovich, 1969), p. 44; also in H. H. Anniah Gowda, ed., *A Garland for E. M. Forster* (Mysore: Literary Half-Yearly, 1969), p. 110.

Chapter 13. Joyce, Woolf, Mann

1 "A Portrait of the Artist" (1904), in *The Workshop of Daedalus,* ed. Robert Scholes and Richard M. Kain (Evanston: Northwestern University Press, 1965), and in Chester G. Anderson, ed., *A Portrait of the Artist as a Young Man: Text, Criticism, and Notes* (New York: Viking Press, 1968), pp. 257—66. References to the novel are by chapter number.

2 Meyer Schapiro, *Cézanne* (New York: Abrams, 1962), pp. 19, 17. Murdoch, *The Sovereignty of Good,* pp. 96, 86.

3 "Drama and Life" (1900), in *The Critical Writings of James Joyce,* ed. Ellsworth Mason and Richard Ellmann (New York: Viking Press, 1959), pp. 38—46.

4 The letter appears in Richard Ellmann, *James Joyce* (New York: Oxford University Press, 1959), pp. 175—76; the phrase "gestation of a soul" appears on p. 307.

5 The fullest examination of the villanelle I know is by Robert Scholes in "Stephen Dedalus, Poet or Esthete?" *PMLA* 89 (1964): 484—89; reprinted in Anderson's edition cited above, pp. 468—80. Scholes would claim more for the poem than I do. What I have called a "fantasy of erotic fulfillment" he sees as Stephen's "spiritual copulation" with a muse, a "moment of inspiration when 'in the virgin womb of the imagination the word was made flesh.' "

6 Virginia Woolf, *To the Lighthouse* (New York: Harcourt Brace, 1927), pt. I ("The Window"), sec. vi, p. 56. Hereafter cited in the text as I, vi.

7 Quentin Bell, *Virginia Woolf: A Biography* (New York: Harcourt Brace Jovanovich, 1972), 2: 97—98.

8 Bell, *Virginia Woolf,* 2 : 123 (September 1926).

9 Virginia Woolf, "Roger Fry" (1935), *Collected Essays,* 4 vols., ed. Leonard Woolf (London: Hogarth Press, 1966—67), 4 : 90. I am indebted to the admirable discussion of Woolf and Fry in Allen Mc Laurin, *Virginia Woolf: The Echoes Enslaved* (Cambridge: Cambridge University Press, 1973). Mc Laurin reprints, as appendix A, part of an article of 1919 in which Fry likens methods of cubist and futurist painting to Virginia Woolf's method in prose description.

10 Roger Fry, in a letter to Robert Bridges (22 January 1924), cited in Virginia Woolf, *Roger Fry: A Biography* (New York: Harcourt Brace, 1940), p. 230.

11 Roger Fry, *Vision and Design* (London: Chatto and Windus, 1920), pp. 18, 52.

12 Roger Fry, *The Artist and Psychoanalysis* (London: Hogarth Press, 1924), pp. 16, 12, 19–20.

13 Phyllis Rose, *Woman of Letters: A Life of Virginia Woolf* (New York: Oxford University Press, 1978), p. 152. On the "insane instinct for life" in Ottoline Morrell and others, see Virginia Woolf, *A Writer's Diary*, ed. Leonard Woolf (New York: Harcourt Brace Jovanovich, 1954), entry for 4 June 1923, p. 54.

14 Charles Mauron, "The Nature of Beauty in Art and Literature," Hogarth Essays, 1926. For Virginia Woolf's attack, see "Mr. Bennett and Mrs. Brown" (1924), *The Captain's Death Bed and Other Essays* (London: Hogarth Press, 1950), pp. 90–111. Also in *Collected Essays*, 1 : 319–37.

15 *The Letters of Virginia Woolf*, ed. Nigel Nicolson and Joanne Trautmann (New York: Harcourt Brace Jovanovich, 1976–), 2 : 598–99.

16 *Recent Paintings by Vanessa Bell*, with a foreword by Virginia Woolf, The London Artists' Association, 1930. The foreword closes thus: "One feels that if a canvas of hers hung on the wall it would never lose its lustre. It would never mix itself up with the loquacities and trivialities of daily life. It would go on saying something of its own imperturbably. And perhaps by degrees—who knows?—one would become an inmate of this strange painters' world, in which mortality does not enter and psychology is held at bay, and there are no words. But is morality to be found there? That was the very question I was asking myself as I came in."

17 Roger Fry, "Art-History as an Academic Study," in *Last Lectures*, ed. Kenneth Clark (Cambridge: Cambridge University Press, 1929), pp. 12, 13. In a lecture on De Quincey (*Collected Essays*, 4: 6) Woolf contrasts "two levels of existence"—"the rapid passage of events and actions" and "the slow opening up of single and solemn moments of concentrated emotion."

18 *The Letters of Virginia Woolf*, 3 : 385. She goes on: "I saw that all sorts of feelings would accrue to this, but I refused to think them out, and trusted that people would make it the deposit for their own emotions—which they have done, one thinking it means one thing another another."

19 "We both [i.e., Vanessa and Virginia Stephen] learned the Victorian game of manners so thoroughly that we have never forgotten them. We shall play the game. It is useful; it has beauty, for it is founded upon restraint, sympathy, unselfishness—all civilised qualities. It is helpful in making something seemly and human out of raw odds and ends." "A Sketch of the Past," in *Moments of Being: Unpublished Autobiographical Writings*, ed. Jeanne Schulkind (New York: Harcourt Brace Jovanovich, 1978), p. 129.

20 "Roger Fry," *Collected Essays*, 4 : 91.

21 Woolf, *Moments of Being*, p. 72.

22 Woolf, *Moments of Being*, pp. 81, 83, 84. Whatever Lily Briscoe's need to present Mrs. Ramsay as a formal element of shape and color, Woolf regarded this novel as "subtler and more human" than its predecessors, and she records her sister's tribute: "She says it is an amazing portrait of mother; a supreme portrait painter; has lived in it; found the rising of the dead almost painful." *A Writer's Diary*, pp. 98, 106. For Vanessa Bell's letter, see *The Letters of Virginia Woolf*, 3: 572–73. For a view of the transfiguration of the author's experience in the novel, see Rose, *Woman of Letters*, chap. 8.

23 Woolf, *A Writer's Diary*, pp. 56–57. In the early version of "Mr. Bennett and Mrs. Brown" (*Nation and Athenaeum*, 1 December 1923) she writes: "After reading *Crime and Punishment* and *The Idiot*, how could any young novelist believe in 'characters' as the

Victorians had painted them?" In a letter to Vita Sackville-West (8 January 1929), she refers to the greatness of Balzac and Tolstoy: *"That* is the origin of all our discontent. After that of course we had to break away. It wasn't Wells, or Galsworthy or any of the mediocre wishy washy realists: it was Tolstoy." *The Letters of Virginia Woolf,* 4 : 4.

24 Woolf, *A Writer's Diary,* pp. 98, 101.

25 *Jacob's Room* and *The Waves* (New York: Harcourt Brace, n.d.), pp. 362, 276.

26 Woolf, *Moments of Being,* p. 122.

27 Thomas Mann, *The Story of a Novel: The Genesis of Doctor Faustus,* trans. Richard and Clara Winston (New York: Alfred A. Knopf, 1961), pp. 23, 28—29.

28 I have borrowed the term *comic primness* from William Empson's discussion of the Peachums in John Gay's *The Beggar's Opera, Some Versions of Pastoral* (London: Chatto and Windus, 1935), chap. 6.

29 *Thomas Mann: A Chronicle of His Life,* ed. Hans Burgin and Hans-Otto Mayer, trans. Eugene Dobson (University: University of Alabama Press, 1969), p. 251.

30 Thomas Mann, *Confessions of Felix Krull, Confidence Man,* trans. Denver Lindley (New York: Alfred A. Knopf, 1955), bk. I, chap. 3 (hereafter I, 3). An important discussion of the book is Robert B. Heilman, "Variations on Picaresque *(Felix Krull),*" *Sewanee Review* 66 (1958) : 547—77. For a recent treatment from a point of view different from mine, see Walter L. Reed, *An Exemplary History of the Novel: The Quixotic vs. the Picturesque* (Chicago: University of Chicago Press, 1981), pp. 232—46.

31 Susanne K. Langer, *Feeling and Form: A Theory of Art* (New York: Charles Scribner's Sons, 1953), pp. 133—34.

32 "Let us not deceive ourselves—to comprehend unconditioned spirit is not so very hard, but there is no knowledge rarer than the understanding of spirit as it exists in the inescapable conditions which the actual and the trivial make for it." Lionel Trilling, "Anna Karenina," *The Opposing Self* (New York: Viking Press, 1955), p. 75.

Index